LIES

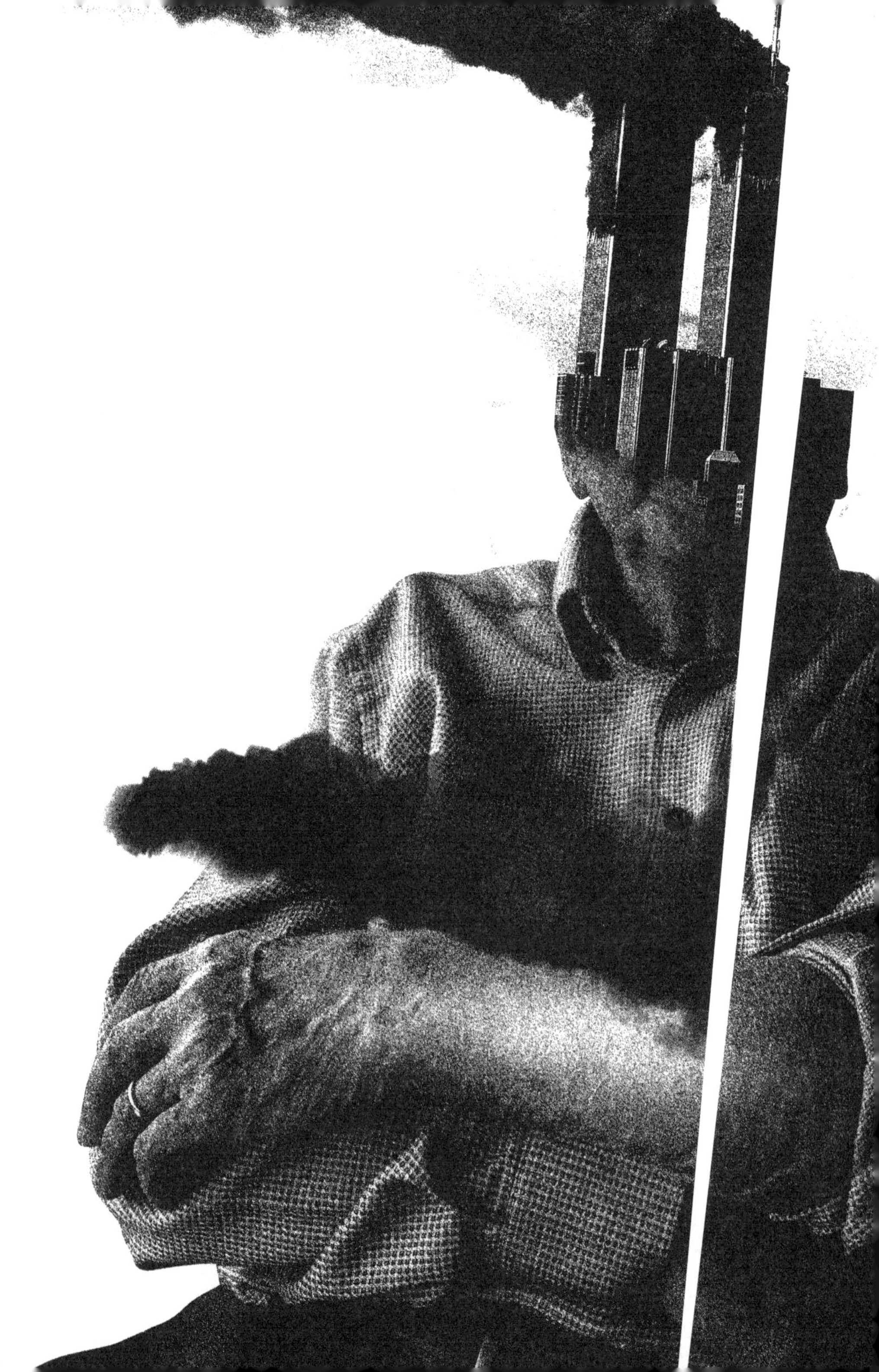

LIES OF TENDERNESS

STEPHEN VOLK

PS

2022

Lies of Tenderness

Published in May 2022 by PS Publishing Ltd by arrangement with the author.

FIRST EDITION

ISBN
978-1-78636-850-8 (Signed edition)
978-1-78636-849-2 (Unsigned edition)

Cover and book design by Pedro Marques.
Text set in Caslon.

Printed in England by T.J. Books
on Munken Premium Cream 80 gsm stock.

PS Publishing Ltd
Grosvenor House
1 New Road
Hornsea, HU18 1PG
England
editor@pspublishing.co.uk
WWW.PSPUBLISHING.CO.UK

ALSO BY STEPHEN VOLK FROM PS PUBLISHING:

Under a Raven's Wing
The Dark Masters Trilogy
The Parts We Play
Studio of Screams
(with Stephen R. Bissette, Christopher Golden,
Tim Lebbon and Mark Morris)

NON-FICTION

Coffinmaker's Blues: Collected Writings on Terror
(Electric Dreamhouse)

STEPHEN VOLK is best known as the award-winning writer of the BBC's notorious "Halloween hoax" *Ghostwatch* and the ITV drama series *Afterlife* starring Andrew Lincoln and Lesley Sharp. His screenplays include *The Awakening* starring Rebecca Hall and Ken Russell's *Gothic* starring Natasha Richardson as Mary Shelley. He is the author of three previous collections—*Dark Corners*, *Monsters in the Heart* (which won the British Fantasy Award), and *The Parts We Play*. His acclaimed *Dark Masters Trilogy* features Peter Cushing, Alfred Hitchcock and Dennis Wheatley as central characters, while *Under a Raven's Wing* teams up a young Sherlock Holmes with Edgar Allan Poe's master detective Dupin to solve grotesque crimes in 1870s Paris. **www.stephenvolk.net**

CONTENTS

For Nathan Ballingrud

This book is dedicated to the memory of my mother:
Marion Mary Volk (1928-2020)

"Men think there are circumstances when one may deal with human beings without love. But there are no such circumstances . . . If you feel no love, sit still."
Tolstoy
Resurrection

"What did he learn when he learned of his own black heart? That scared and sacred are but a beat apart."
Christian Wiman
"Ten Distillations"

A Letter of Introduction

PRIYA SHARMA

Dear Steve,

I hope this finds you well. I realise I'm taking liberties by addressing you and not your readers. I'm honoured to be asked to write this but also daunted by the task of introducing someone who needs no introduction. So, here's a letter instead.

It's been such a difficult period for everyone, hasn't it? We all have been, and will continue to be, marked by the Covid Years; each with our own losses, anxieties, and isolation.

A few things have helped. A sense of community has never been more important. You once wrote to me of the "solitary solidarity" of writers. We'd met at cons, but it was only through letters and emails during lockdown that we've got to know one another. Your correspondence has been a big part of feeling connected to the writing fellowship. Thank you.

The other thing that's buoyed me up are stories. If we ever needed proof of how essential they are, we have it now. Your work has been a big part of the long months of lockdown. First came *Under a Raven's Wing*. I travelled with it to the Parisian Opera House, to backstreets and catacombs, and diplomats' salons. It was gothic and thrilling. Fizzing with ideas. Dupin and Holmes made the best of companions and I was sad to turn the final page.

Lies of Tenderness is a different experience again. Each story is meaty and satisfying in its strangeness. My favourite reads aren't just about escapism. We had a discussion recently about dark fiction being a way to interrogate painful and horrific truths for those of us who find it too distressing to look at them directly. Which is exactly what this book does.

"Sicko" is a loving tribute to *Psycho* that keeps Marion firmly centre stage in her flight from the worst kind of men. "The Black Cat" returns to the Poe territory of *Under a Raven's Wing* to confront the racial prejudices of the era. "Unchain the Beast" is a tale of the artist versus the regime. Tragically, all are themes that are more relevant today than ever.

When violence breaks into our lives it's unexpected and shocking. We make much of its perpetrators without considering the far-reaching effects of their actions. "The Little Gift", a modern *Brief Encounter*, takes a different and laudable approach to this.

The book varies deliciously in tone and subject. "The Flickering Light" charts a different sort of loss by bringing genre into the domestic sphere with vivid social observation. I found "Agog" surprising and charming. He is ancient Briton made large, striding through our history, but it has all the delicacy of Oscar Wilde's fairy tales.

I suspect "Bad Language" will touch many readers. The horror here is more mundane but no less terrible for it. The condition it depicts charts a double bereavement for those with loved ones affected by it. Factoring in Covid has magnified the heartache of it. By 2025 the number of people diagnosed with it will rise to over a million. I'll say no more here, except that to write our own truths and insight, albeit veiled in fiction, is one of the truest acts of creation.

Each time I think of *Lies of Tenderness* my personal favourite changes. Right now, it's "The House That Moved Next Door". To make one strange, quiet incident so potent and powerful that it casts such a long shadow through a life speaks to your skill. It's a story drenched in sunlight and a particular kind of sadness.

I've only mentioned some of the stories within and different ones will chime with different readers. I won't bore or delay them any longer. If they have any sense, they're flicking ahead, keen to begin.

Keep safe and well, Steve. Keep writing your wonderful work.

Love and best wishes,

Priya
Wirral, 2021

Priya Sharma's short fiction has appeared venues such as Interzone, Black Static, Nightmare, The Dark *and* Tor. *She has won three British Fantasy awards and two Shirley Jackson Awards including Best Collection for* All the Fabulous Beasts *and Best Novella for* Ormeshadow.

The Holocaust Crasher

I am a mere mortal, and sometimes less than that.
David Milch

When you're my age keeping the pen from shaking is a task and a half, I can tell you. Other than that, writing a line of numbers on your skin in blue Uni-ball felt-tip isn't all that hard. It doesn't have to be that meticulous, I remind myself. From what I've seen in photographs they weren't that meticulous at all. Quite slapdash, considering their reputation for meticulous order.

I blow on my forearm. I've done a good job, if I do say so myself. Becoming a bit of an expert. My knees creak as I stand up, making me groan. Creaking bones are to be expected at ninety. I'm not going to be covering them up, either. Creaky is good. Poor old chap. What he's been through. I always think to *not* be a bit wobbly and a bit fragile would be, well . . . I think, disrespectful.

I have to put on a good effort or there's no point. I fetch my bowtie—red and spotted, but not garish—and the hall mirror shows me unwelcome jowls overlapping my collar. I take the Star of David badge from the little drawer where my cufflinks reside and pin it to my lapel. I did think of getting one of those little black skull caps, but thought that might smack of overkill. I slap my cheeks with a little cologne. Old and frail is one thing, but I want to be presentable, always. Clean. Dapper. Smart. It's a special day out. It is for me, anyway.

I look down at my shoes, polished last night after I switched off the TV. That's when you notice the silence, last thing. Nobody to say goodnight to. Nobody to say goodnight to me.

The doorbell rings. Taxi driver I haven't seen before. Indian. Sikh. One of those turbaned ones. Nice enough. All smiles. I ask him where did he come from? He says not far. No, I say—where? He says, oh. He says, up the road. Then he says, ah. He says, Huddersfield. I say, "I like Huddersfield." He says, "It's all right, aye."

He puts on music as he drives. He says it's a Bangra mix. Asks if I like Bangra. I say, "It's not Tony Bennett." He laughs like a drain.

I take out a packet of Trebor mints and crunch on a couple, to freshen my mouth and thoughts. Give myself a little pep talk. Run through my lines. Tell myself I've done it before and there's no need to have butterflies. Still, you're never quite sure how it will go down. Every audience is different.

Presently the school appears, up ahead. Outside it a tall young man—when I say young, forty, forty-five—abbreviated inside his grey suit, hair flapping like a windsock.

"Mr Podolski? Derek Hatfull. Pleased to meet you." He releases my hand to pay the driver—twelve pounds from Withinroyd is a bit steep. Waits for a receipt while I take out my handkerchief and blow my nose. The wind is bitter and I thank my lucky stars I don't have hair to be blown around the way his is.

I take the teacher's arm and we cross the empty playground to a pair of automatic doors that slide open to reveal a welcoming committee.

He introduces me. "Mr Podolski."

"Tomasz, please."

Took a while to come up with, but it had a ring to it and rolled off the tongue. *Tomasz Podolski*. Lot of names in the indexes of the books I went through, of course, so it was a case of doing a bit of a pick and mix.

"Tomasz," repeats a woman with a doughy face so over-endowed with moles one can't help envisaging a lengthy game of join the dots. Mrs Oswestry, I'm informed, no first name, though the black woman behind her divulges hers: "Star. Like in the heavens."

"Would you like a cup of tea in the staff room? There's plenty of time before . . ."

"A cup of tea would be wonderful," I say.

• • •

"I can't tell you how pleased we were to receive your generous offer to come in and talk to the students." Mrs Oswestry sits in the low armchair opposite me, leaning forward with her hands clasped. "The Holocaust is part of the syllabus, but there's nothing, *nothing* quite like the children hearing . . . well, first-hand testimony."

"Absolutely," says Star.

"I dedicated a lesson to it yesterday, in preparation," says Derek Hatfull, the one who led me in. "They had lots of questions, naturally. Year seven, I mean. They're so excited to . . . not *excited,* I mean . . ." He corrects himself. "Curious. They're a very curious bunch. On a good day. Mostly. I think you'll like them."

Star proffers a kettledrum-sized tin of assorted biscuits. My hand hovers before I pluck out a tentative custard cream.

"In any case, thank you so much for your unexpected letter," Mrs Oswestry oozes. "What made you think of us, if you don't mind me asking?"

"I've done a similar thing for other schools in the area," I say, adding a bit of sibilance to the consonants to give the mere hint of a Polish accent not quite ironed out by a Northern one.

"It must take so much courage. Having all these terrible memories locked inside . . . Unimaginable, really."

I shrug and stare pensively at the carpet. "My suffering is in the past. What's important is what I have to give the new generation in the future. To light their way, so to speak."

"You dear, dear man," says Star, very quietly, a glistening coming to her eyes. "I'm going to go in a minute. Sorry." She turns away, fanning her face with her hand.

"Well, this is an incredibly valuable thing to do for your community. And it's an incredibly valuable thing to do for our school," says Mrs Oswestry, clearing her throat, and I catch from the word *school* for the first time that she's Liverpudlian. "We are preparing them for the outside world, Mr Podolski. Not just for the world of work, not just passing exams to get jobs, but how to be citizens. How to be good. That is what education is *for,* at the end of the day."

I nod sagely. Try to do everything sagely, if at all possible.

"I quite agree," Derek Hatfull says. "Last week, this Muslim lad was out in the playground, and one of these other boys put a football up his jumper and shouted, 'Look at me! I'm a suicide bomber!' I said right. Inside. Now. I had to cancel lessons and talk to the class and tell them what was wrong about what they'd done. And Hasan, lovely lad, really upset he was, came up to me afterwards and said, 'Thank you, sir, for standing up for me.'"

I watch Star close the lid of the biscuit tin. I'd been courting hopes for a triangle of shortbread. "They don't understand. Where do they get these ideas? At home? From the telly?"

" Who knows? But we have to deal with them," says Mrs Oswestry, glancing at her watch, then at me, rising to her feet and straightening her skirt. "Right. You're on, sir. If you're ready."

I say I am, and lay aside my cup of tea, half-drunk, and half the custard cream.

•●•

 I wonder what it looks like to the children. This tiny, pot-bellied man in bottle-bottom glasses towered over by their teachers, who then arrange themselves around the perimeter of the classroom. This grandfather, to them. Great-grandfather, more like, let's face it.

I gaze out at a sea of faces. Boys. Girls. Aged around eleven, twelve. Mixture of races and creeds. A whole biscuit tin. Are they expectant? Interested? Already bored? Impossible to tell.

"This is the very special guest speaker I talked to you about yesterday."

Somebody pours a glass of water. I wet my lips.

"We are very honoured indeed that he has come here to talk about his experiences during World War Two—that's the 1930s and 1940s, long before any of you were born. Now, please remember, your parents have all been notified about this event, but if at any time you get upset by anything Mr Podolski says, just put your hand up and make yourself known to Mrs Oswestry or Miss Beeston or myself, and—"

"Please." I smile benignly, interrupting Derek Hatfull's formal introduction. "Your teachers think you should be all wrapped up." I make a gesture in the air, encircling them. "Protected from hurt. But hurt is life." I hold my tightened fist gently against my heart. "I know that. *You* know that." I point at them, drawing them into my story with a soft, clear voice. "What I am going to be talking about today, boys and girls, is history. Not *boring* history from books. Not Romans. Not Vikings. Not Henry VIII and his seven wives."

"Six!" A voice.

"Six?" I correct myself. "Six." I turn to the teachers. "I can see this lot are good listeners!"

The teachers laugh. Mrs Oswestry clicks her fingers in the direction of a girl distractedly playing with the zip of her pencil case.

"For some of us, what you call history has been a part of our lives. We cannot escape it. It is a part of us, and will live with us forever."

I look over at Derek Hatfull and give a miniscule nod of the head. He attends to the controls of the projection system linked to the carousel in which my slides are sitting. The first image comes up on the white board behind me. A grainy black and white photograph from the Warsaw ghetto.

"Children. Like you are. You and your sister or brother. Don't look at their clothes or their terrible haircuts. Look into their eyes. The one with the sticky-out ears. No, it isn't me. But these are children like I was. Jewish children. Does anybody know what Jewish means?"

The children nod.

I indicate to the school teacher to change the slide.

I step to the left so that they can get the full drama of the next image.

"Do you know what this picture shows? Does anyone want to guess?"

A hand shoots up. "A camp."

"Does anyone want to guess what sort of camp?"

No answer.

"Those words above the gates—*Arbeit macht frei*—does anyone know what they mean?"

No one does, of course. In my experience, they never do.

"*Work sets you free.* Do you know who was free in this camp?"

Silence again.

"This was a special camp where people were sent if they were undesirable. Do you know what kinds of people might be called undesirable?"

A different hand. "Homeless people."

"Correct."

"Disabled people?"

"Correct." I walk down the aisle between the children's desks. "You see, the people who ran these camps, they decided the country would be better off if certain people could be got rid of. They were a drain on resources. They were scroungers. Taking jobs from good, hard-working people who weren't foreign or different or funny-looking. What do you think of that?" I retrace my footsteps. "Wrong, yes. Very wrong. But it happened. I was there. You see, I was one of the people they didn't want in society." I turn to face them. "I was a Jew."

•●•

I tell them how I first spoke to my wife through the wire next to the crematorium at Auschwitz. Always grab them with an image, I feel, and girls in particular respond to a bit of a love story. The boys on the other hand tend to prick up their ears when I say I was delegated the Corpse Unit, having to deal with inmates who flung themselves at the electrified fence.

"I had to drag bodies to a barracks and put them on trucks, until word got round I was a singer, so I was ordered to entertain the Nazi officers in a building called the Cabaret. It wasn't a case of saying, no, I don't feel like it. I'd rather watch *EastEnders*. No. If I refused—*kaput*," I draw a finger across my throat. "You didn't get a choice."

They listen, spellbound.

My future bride, Anežka Škorvánková, I say, had been amongst the Jewish women to arrive at Auschwitz in March 1942. She was twenty. She came from Slovakia, where she'd studied art. She'd arrived with two thousand unmarried women, first at the sister camp, Birkenau. She could speak German so got a job in the office, and was allowed to move around the camp but not enter the male compound.

"I was fifteen," I tell them. "I was her toy boy!"

The boys and girls like that. They laugh. I have them in the palm of my hand.

"Anežka was quiet, refined. No make-up of course. Wore a man's jacket, but still looked beautiful," I say, smiling fondly at the memory. Not that it was one. “We were introduced. Her brother was in the bunk beside me. We fell in love. I fell in love with her. She was slower on the uptake. You know girls.”

The children laugh again. I’m winning them over. I have it down to a fine art.

“Whenever she had the chance, she’d throw apples and bread over the fence. We promised to meet the same time every week in a secret corner where the machine gun posts couldn’t see us, between crematoriums four and five. Each time we had a conversation we talked our heads off. We didn’t know if it would be our last.”

A girl in the front row looks up at me, enraptured. Mesmerised. I find sometimes it’s useful to focus on one person rather than the whole throng, so I focus on her.

“Anežka could type. She was brainy. I was a silly boy. We existed under constant stress and danger, but we lived for those short, sweet meetings together. I felt she had chosen me, like an angel from heaven. But don’t get me wrong. She wasn’t all that nice all the time. She told me to brush myself up. Get rid of the stink all over me. I had to explain it was the smell of the crematorium.”

I hear Mrs Oswestry take in a sharp breath. And I know I have them too, the teachers. I always do. It’s always that moment when I mention the smell of the crematorium. It never fails. I’m rather proud of myself. All the hours of research paying off. Selecting each meaningful scene, each resonant phrase.

“During those chats we shared our family history. My father was a concert pianist who perished with the rest of my family in the Warsaw ghetto. Anežka loved music, and would hum songs, not too loudly in case the guards heard. Sometimes she’d play an imaginary keyboard on her arm and I’d hear the notes in my head. Around the corner, other prisoners stood watch. They liked the idea of lovebirds in their midst. They’d make a noise like a bird if an SS officer was coming. We knew it wouldn’t last. Death was everywhere—illness, coughing, sickness in the belly, wasting away

. . . It makes you have horrible thoughts," I tell the eleven-year-olds hanging on my every word. "One man was dying and I remember thinking, if he dies, I really want his hat. I really would *kill* to have that thick woollen hat. The nights, you see, were cold as ice. But everyone that died you carried with you. Up here." I tap the side of my head.

My story nears its climax. I've timed it to a concise fifty minutes. By 1944, I say, the Nazis were transporting the last of the prisoners on death marches and destroying evidence in their wake. The paperwork was burning, the crematoriums demolished. We guessed that the Soviets must be closing in and the war nearing an end. But what kind of end?

"We'd survived more than two years while many didn't last more than a few months. Anežka and I vowed that if we were separated we would meet again. Nothing but death would stop us."

Romeo and Juliet, you see?

I tell them I was transferred to Dachau in the December, and soon after that sent on a death march. Miraculously, I managed to grab a spade, hit a guard, and ran, hiding overnight in a barn, waking up to the sound of soldiers.

"I was terrified they were Russians but it turned out they were British. They adopted me, gave me a machine gun to hold. I said no, I didn't want it. I've seen enough guns and death, thank you very much. I wanted to get out of there. Leave that country."

I was put with all the other orphans, I say. There was a thing called the Central British Fund which meant children could be taken to England. A British officer faked my birth date. Made me out to be twelve instead of fifteen, so that I could be sent with the rest.

"We arrived in the Lake District. It was so beautiful after the greyness of the camp. It was like heaven. They called it Windermere. I will never forget it. A psychiatrist looked after us. His name was Frank Doleman. We called him Uncle Frank."

(I have to admit, for this part I relied heavily on an episode of *Who Do You Think You Are?*)

"I found out from another survivor that Anežka was still alive. She'd been sent to Ravensbrück and a sub camp in Malchow before being evacuated. She returned to her home town of Bratislava to find her entire family all gone. I immediately went to find her and proposed to her. She looked beautiful in a dress now, not a man's jacket. I loved her just the same."

I heard Star blow her nose and sniff back tears.

"I brought her back to England. Wrote to Uncle Frank, who lived in London now. Invited him to come to the wedding. Said I was sure he would see some old faces. All the orphans would be there. He said he would perhaps come for the reception. He did. He cried. So did I. We had three sons, Anežka and me. Peter, Marek—and Frank."

I might be mistaken, but I think I see a little glint in Mrs Oswestry's eyes too.

"And here I am. Over the years I worked hard to lose my Polish accent, with, as you can hear, not too much success. But what the hell—Polish accent, Leeds accent, Pakistani accent. It is part of who you are. Correct?"

"Correct," Mrs Oswestry says.

"Liverpool accent. Liverpool accent too, there we are."

"Birkenhead."

"Birkenhead. My apologies. To Birkenhead." I say, taking a last dramatic pause before bringing the curtain down on my talk. "You know why I do this? Tell my story to students in school or to children or at libraries? I'll tell you why. It's because there are only a few people left now who remember these things. Fewer of us every year. My Anežka is gone, my friends are gone, but those of us who survive, we have a job to do, and that is the most important thing . . . to remind people, to tell them to our dying breath . . . please, *please*—never again. *Never again.*"

And that is when I see him.

One of the boys. A sullen-looking article with a myriad of suppurating pimples and the sides of his cylindrical-shaped head shaved to create a tufted parrot effect on top. Staring out of the window, yawning. I've noticed him all the way through. Generously, I'd put it down to lack of sleep, the raging hormones of pubescence, or the draining biological consequences of a growth spurt, but now it's abundantly clear to me by the way he's displaying a Mersey tunnel full of molars, it's due to nothing but plain old boredom. The lad has a smirk on his face that tells me he really, *really* doesn't give a damn about a word I've said. If he's been listening at all. And when he fidgets in his chair like he can't wait to leave the room, then leans back at forty-five degrees and addresses a loud sigh to the ceiling, it's like he's showing me, and the class, that he begrudges every moment he's been sitting there with ants in his pants. And I see red, though I don't show it.

"Excuse me. Sir . . . Sir? What's your name?"

The kid straightens his back, not meeting my eyes, annoyed by the inconvenience. "Jordan."

"Jordan, can I just ask you this, please? How many Jews were exterminated in the concentration camps?"

The eyes of his peers swing towards him. Some turn in their chairs.

Jordan shrugs. "Five hundred?" The embarrassed laughter only serves to embolden the tyke. "I dunno. Seven hundred and . . ." Sudden precision. ". . . Eighty-three?"

"Jordan," said Derek Hatfull.

I hold up my hand. Don't worry, I can deal with this.

"Six million." I say, then repeat the words, for Jordan and the class, with a raised index finger for emphasis tapping out the four syllables in the air. "*Six. Mil-li-on.*"

Jordan's eyes roam lazily, anywhere but me, as he slides back, almost horizontal.

"Fake news."

I'm shocked. I'm stunned. I can't believe he's shrugging off the most devastating episode of human history by parroting those two inane words. I don't move, but Derek Hatfull makes a bee-line, furious. I've never seen anyone move so fast.

"No, leave him. Please. Let him speak," I say. "I'd like to know what he thinks is 'fake' exactly. Does he think eating stale bread, fighting rats for a crust is fake? Hearing your parents weeping at night is fake? Your friends, your school friends, rounded up and taken away, is that fake?"

"I'm not bothered, am I? Because I wouldn't be there, would I?"

"Oh, you wouldn't, would you?"

"No, I wouldn't." The boy doesn't even have the good manners to look me in the eyes. "I'd join the army. I'd be there giving you orders, don't worry."

"Yes, I daresay you would." I feel a redness spreading round the inside of my collar. My brain is throbbing inside my head but I try to keep calm. "You're exactly the type, aren't you?"

"Yeah, I am," says Jordan matter-of-factly. "And I know your type too." He ignores the sharp bark from his teacher to shut up. "You're the enemy. You're a *bullshitter.* Everybody knows it never happened. It's all a load of *bollocks.*"

How can such lies have seeped into his young mind? I'm enraged. I walk forward. How can he be like this, after what I've said I've been through? It's outrageous.

I lean my knuckles on his desk. My head glides towards his but he doesn't cower, though he tucks his chin in slightly as if I'm doing something insane and inappropriate by intruding into his space.

"Is it? Is it," I say, "when Dr Mengele selects you? When he points at you and you are the one strapped to the chair and have your eyeball scooped out with a spoon to see if your twin brother feels the pain? You'd like that, would you?"

The smirk, far from undiminished, is triumphant as he jerks his face towards mine. "I don't *have* a twin brother, do I?"

"That's enough, Jordan! I'm sorry."

The boy brushes the teacher's hand briskly off his shoulder before getting up, his chair legs rasping noisily against the floor.

"Jordan, you're a disgrace. You come with me," says Mrs Oswestry, throwing the door of the classroom open so wide it hit a radiator. "*Now! Please!*"

Her voice cuts through the air but the little beggar stands up to his full runtish height—small for his age—unbowed and unrepentant. He slings his Adidas bag over one shoulder and shuffles out of the room, staring at me now the whole time without breaking eye contact. Even as the beads of sweat break on my forehead I think he is gone but at the door he turns back to give a Nazi salute and click of the heels as a parting shot before the headmistress hauls him off down the corridor, the ripple of titters it engenders hushed by the teachers in no uncertain terms.

• ● •

"I'm so, so sorry."

The custard creams are out again, but I'm still in a right state, worried I lost my rag and that the other children would have been horrified by what I'd said to the boy. I'm also deeply annoyed with myself. It's not like me to go off piste like that, but I couldn't help it. "No, it was . . . inexcusable. I . . . I don't know what—"

"Don't apologise," insists Derek Hatfull, bristling and blue chinned. "That little shit needed taking down a peg or two. He's been flying close to the wind for weeks. It's high time Wendy pulled him in and read him the riot act."

"There's always one, and he's it," says Star, pointing to my tea cup and non-verbally asking if I wanted a refill. I non-verbally decline.

The male teacher, sitting in the chair earlier occupied by Mrs Oswestry, and leaning forward the same way she did, wears shoes the colour of Cornish pasties with socks that have snowmen on them. "Well. Congratulations on a job well done, anyway. I found it fascinating."

And apart from that, Mrs Lincoln, I'm thinking, *how did you enjoy the play?* But I take the compliment in the spirit in which it is given.

"In some . . . some small way, if I've . . ." I let the thought drift away on the air, trying to forget the final image of the lad in the classroom doorway.

"You shouldn't have to put up with that rubbish," says Star, suddenly striking a pose that is both buxom and sassy.

"We'll talk to him," says Derek Hatfull. "If we thought it would do any good. Talk to the class anyhow. *En masse.* Explain. In the wider sense. Tolerance-wise. Context-wise. It was good. It was all good, ultimately. I hope you don't feel disappointed, or that we've let you down, at all?"

"Me?" I say. "No!"

"Good. Because honestly, it made them think. Even the Mengele part."

"Even the Mengele part," echoes Star.

"Makes them think. How would *they* like it?"

"How would they like it? Precisely." She places her hand on my knee and wrinkles her nose, just as you might if petting an old and smelly dog that was nearing the end of its time on earth. "Empathy."

"Empathy," Derek Hatfull chimes back. As if he's been searching for the word for hours, in a muddy field with a metal detector.

"If we don't have empathy, what do we have?" elaborates Star, as in the heavens.

"Not much," says Derek Hatfull, of the flighty fringe.

•●•

It has to be said, Asda is reasonably convenient. Two stops and I'm there. Supermarket shopping's a bit of a chore these days. Can't pretend it isn't when you're my age. What am I saying? Everything's a chore at my age. When she was alive it was all right. Something to do, to get out of the house. I didn't mind it then. Pushing the trolley. Didn't need to have a list. She had it all in her head. Marvel like that, Noreen was. Seemed to always know her way around the place. Up and down, this way to vegetables, over here to fresh meat. Bread. Dairy products—yoghurt, et cetera. Had a food compass in her head, somehow. Never had to backtrack. I'd follow her, Ben-Hur with his chariot, struggling to keep up. She was like a whippet.

I peruse the cans at eye level, using the lower part of my bifocals to assess the labelling. *Heinz baked beans with pork sausages.* Hello. Haven't had that in donkey's years. Into the trolley it goes. Noreen would police such indulgences. Nobody to police me now.

I move to the ice cream and hover over the raspberry ripple, another blast from the past I've suddenly got a penchant for. My hand rests on the edge of the freezer. For some peculiar reason I think of the day she died and wonder if she'd felt cold. I hadn't touched her, see. I was afraid. I know that's daft. What's to be afraid of?

It happened in the middle of the night. She'd rolled off into the gap between our two beds and I couldn't hear her breathing and didn't want to touch her. In case, like. I rang the neighbour, nice lass with a stutter, trainee dog groomer. I said I thought Noreen was dead, could she come and take a look? She called the doctor and the doctor went up and came down and said I was right. Did I want to go up and see her? I said no. A nice feller came from the undertaker's in a van. Small white van. A Renault, I think it was. He had a neatly clipped beard and wore a shirt and tie. I thought it was nice he didn't turn up in a T-shirt and jeans. He'd made an effort. I appreciated that. By the time the sun came up she was gone.

The rest of the day was peculiar. It was the day of 9/11. The World Trade Centre and all that. September 11th, 2001. I put on the TV just to fill the house with some sound and all day it was just that, watching those two buildings collapsing over and over, backwards and forwards in time, folding down into a white dust cloud, then up, intact again, falling down, destroyed, obliterated, then up again, intact. That was what it felt like after she died. I was standing, I was alive, but in reality there was nothing there holding me up. Something had hit me and had crashed me to the ground and it couldn't be built up again.

All over the news, it was. Endless. People weeping and reporters sticking cameras in their faces, asking how they felt. Nobody was asking how I felt. Nobody was sticking a camera in my face.

Now then, Ernie, I tell myself at the bacon counter. Buck up, lad. Come on. You ray of flaming sunshine. Think about something more cheerful. More school visits, for example.

I tell myself to write a few more letters. Cast my net further afield. Wetherby. Keighley. Pontefract. Wakefield. Dewsbury, perhaps . . . Shouldn't feel a dent in my confidence after one troublesome little ignoramus. I have to put that well and truly behind me. Think positive. That off the cuff remark about Dr Mengele and his experiments, for instance. Is there something in that? They say the horrible side of history is a real hook for youngsters. Torturing one twin in order to see in the other experience pain could be a really powerful addition to my narrative. I feel quite excited now. Perhaps I can have a twin brother myself? That has interesting potential. Yes. A visit to the library is in order. My old stomping ground. All new faces now, of course. The idea puts a little pep in my step.

Which is eradicated when I see Derek Hatfull stood at the end of the aisle, giving the ready meals the once over. Oh, hell.

I toss the packet of streaky bacon back on the shelf and swing my trolley round, making a sharp turn down the next aisle. This is the last thing I need. Too late.

He raises his eyebrows in recognition.

I raise mine.

I swerve straight to the checkout without a queue and pile my shopping onto the conveyor belt. Shepherd's pie. Carrots. The can of sausages and beans. Sliced loaf. Clover. The girl gives me a smile like she's half-cracked or a robot. Asks me if I wanted a bag as she starts putting them through the beeper. I say, no, I have one of my own, thank you. Five pence, she says as if she hasn't heard me. I say, no, you're all right, unravelling one from my coat pocket.

"Saving the planet," she says.

I say, "Pardon?"

"No, it's good," she says.

"What is?" I say.

The school teacher is walking towards me smiling and approaching the tills. Primed to say hello.

"Ernie? Ernie Yapp?"

My name. Behind me. I go cold.

I don't know if it feels like a flashback so much as a bullet in my chest. A right rave from the grave it is, certainly.

Standing at the next checkout, the man who said it is staring at me like a lunatic with a George Formby grin. Glasses like triple glazing. Same age as me, wearing a puce V-neck under a shortie jacket and mustard-coloured shirt with a maroon tie. Hands clutching a Zimmer frame, or one of those ones with wheels on, whatever they're called. And a flat cap—white, of all things. Bugger belongs on a golf course, as far as I can see.

"You remember me! Ron Gravel," he says. Lass of about forty beside him, hair piled up, blue smock like a nurse. "We were in primary school together!"

Ron Gravel. I struggle to see him. I don't want to see him, but I do see him. The ten-year-old layered over by the wattle and daub of decades. *Ron Gravel! By heck!* It's him without a doubt. Without question.

"You remember! Applegarth. Northallerton Grammar. Ernie Yapp! You lived up by the old Pack Horse Bridge."

I look back at the end of the conveyor belt, where Derek Hatfull is arranging his purchases, his cat food, his multigrain cereal, his basmati rice, his Comfort.

I turn back to my own purchases. "I'm sorry. I—"

"'Course you do!" Ron Gravel says. "You remember! All those evacuees came down from Tyneside and we couldn't understand a bloody word they said!"

"No, no. Sorry," I concentrate on filling my plastic bag. "I'm not from—"

"You *do!* Those Wellingtons and Halifaxes coming overhead every night, taking off from RAF Leeming. Remember the day that bomber flew low over the school with a trail of black smoke coming out of the back and crash landed into a bungalow up by Castle Hill?"

"Sorry, no," I say, even though the picture in my mind is as vivid as if it had happened yesterday. "You've—you've mistaken me for someone else."

"No, I haven't!"

"Come on, Ronnie," says the nurse, carer, whatever she is.

"Ernie Yapp!" he says again. As if I didn't know my own name. "Your dad worked at Clapham's, the furniture shop. Kept thirty-odd rabbits in hutches in the back garden. Used to sell them to the butcher. Your mam used to cure the skin and make them into gloves. Vera, her name was. Made the best Spam sandwiches in—"

"No. *No!* Really!" I raise my voice, seeing the teacher earwigging now, head in the air like one of those meerkat things off the telly, so I'm slathering on the Polish accent again, just in case. "I—I don't know you. *Please!* I have never seen you before in my life."

"You what? It's your old pal Ron! What's the matter with you? Why are you speaking in that—?"

"Twenty-eight pounds fifty-six, please." The checkout girl swings the credit card thing towards me.

"Siamese twins, we were." He's coming round to my checkout now, the four legs of his Zimmer contraption blocking my exit. "Playing on those tank traps, those big concrete things either end of the High Street, till Gordon Bannister fell off and it got declared off-limits. Hey, d'you remember playing up the becks and ditches? I remember once, your mam boxed your ears once for getting your wellies wet!—wellies!—wet!" He chortles.

"Look, look. I'm really not—"

"How long have you been living in Leeds?" he's going. "What a coincidence, eh? Bumping into you, here of all places! Well, well. Where d'you live now?"

"Mr Podolski!" (You-know-who trying to get my attention.)

"There! *There!* You see! My name is Podolski. *Thomasz Podolski!*" I snatch my credit card and slide it back in my wallet before anyone can see the name on it. The long white tongue of the receipt curls out. I ignore it.

"Laurence!" Ron's crooked, monkey-like finger lunges at me, trying to pin me like a butterfly. "That was your dad's name. Thinning on top. Ginger."

"Why don't you leave Mr Podolski alone," goes the school teacher. "It's obvious he doesn't know you from Adam. Why are you bothering him?"

"And who are you when you're at home?" asks Ron, not unreasonably, a tremor of Parkinson's in the hand gripping his Zimmer frame.

"Ronnie, that's enough," says the nurse, carer, whatever.

By now I've rammed his Zimmer with my trolley twice, three times, forcing him back, almost upending him, startled, fragile, golfing V-necked busybody that he is, and I circumnavigate the security guard.

I shove my trolley into the snake of other ones, making a grating sound like a shudder down the spine. My fingers fiddle to get my one pound coin back. I look back at my old school chum through the glass covered in posters for special offers, thinking for a passing instant I'd really like to talk to him about old times, old adventures, old games. The scabs we got falling off our bikes. The dams we made that we pelted with rocks. He's looking forlorn and uncertain of his footing but I can't be responsible for that. I have to be responsible for me. The school teacher looks like he wants to get past him and looks like he wants to talk to me but I don't want to hear what he has to say. I don't want his flaming curiosity. I don't want his flaming questions.

"Ernie! Ernie!"

I turn my back and head for the bus stop on the far side of the car park, a hundred yards away. A bus stands waiting. I need to catch it. I need to put those special offers and that rumbling snake of trolleys in my rear view mirror, so to speak. But my knees aren't up to it. The spirit is willing, but the bones are not. I'm already out of puff and my head is bursting. The plastic bag starts to feel heavy and cuts into my fingers. I see the bus up ahead move away into the traffic. I slow down. It's no good killing myself. I'll have to wait for the next one. My shoulders drop.

"Mr Podolski!" Oh no . . . It's Derek Hatfull.

"Oi!"

The bark from a smoker's windpipe comes from the figure I see striding towards me between parked vehicles. He's wearing a black Fred Perry T-shirt two sizes too small that he thinks shows off his hours in the gym but doesn't. His head travels like a cannonball towards me, pink and hairless. I'm backing away already because he has a look on him that reminds me of someone when I was young who came at us with a broom handle because we put a football through his window. He was a nut case and this feller looks like a nut case too.

He stops dead in front of me and I know he's not going to deliver a polite ticking off. He looks like an unexploded bomb.

He looks over his shoulder and that's when I see the slovenly Jordan skulking beside a dented Audi, eyes shaded by one hand, school uniform replaced by some shiny, spectacularly graceless sportswear covered in the ugly hieroglyphics of various team logos.

"Oi, you! I want to talk to you!"

I don't get far before the two-legged rodent has got me by the scruff of the neck. I'm worried my glasses are going to fall off and break and I'm bleating like a lamb.

"What the hell are you doing getting my boy excluded, eh? What did you say to them? He said you were telling them all sorts."

"All sorts? No!" Polish accent. Best I could, given the circumstances. "No!"

"What then? Because you've really *upset* him. He said you really *humiliated* him in front of his friends." The fists bunched against my chest. The face a five-bar electric fire. Belting it out.

"It . . . it wasn't, it really *wasn't*—" I blather.

"Who the *fuck* d'you think you are, eh?" The nose contorts into a plasticine plug, the neck veins pulsating. Swimming in my vision like the tentacles of an octopus. I think I'm going to pass out.

"I . . . I was trying to educate him. Educate him. Educate—"

"Well maybe *you* need a bit of *educating* about what we do in this country before you come over here in the first place."

I'm so close I can see the pores of his skin. The saliva shining on his lips, if it isn't beer. It smells like it is.

"Maybe it's *you* that needs the lesson, eh? Instead of him—*eh?*"

I feel my bladder loosen. All inner control running for the hills. "Please." My voice reduces to a squeak. "Please—I just want to go home."

"Oh, don't worry, I want you to go home too, you interfering old *cunt!* Go home and fucking stay there, instead of having a *fucking* pop at my—"

"Mr Podolski!"

Jordan's father turns at the sound of the teacher's voice. Neck muscles taut. I don't know why I don't just run. I think I know I can't outrun him. That's why I shove him hard in the chest, to try to give me a slight advantage at least, but of course it's ridiculous. He bounces back and grabs me by the back of my coat before I've gone two steps.

"Hey! Where d'you think you're going! I haven't finished with you yet!"

He holds me like a toddler on one of those reins mothers use. I can't get anywhere and twirl and before I know it I've tripped over, fallen over a flower pot, gone arse over elbow, flower pot in pieces, spilling earth and plant, lying flat on my back, not knowing what is broken but feeling it all might be. Not even realising at first until a cold feeling like a touch of a feather or razor brushes along my calf muscle and, half getting up, I see the rip in my trouser leg and think—*oh, bloody heck.*

Then he's all knuckles. Lips pulled back like you see a dog's. Nothing human about him anymore. And I'm reaching out, I don't know why. Reaching out for him to help me up, I suppose. And it startles him. It discombobulates him. And he looks down at my hand, and he stops, just for a second. And I realise he's seen the numbers on my forearm as the sleeve pulls back. And he bats my hand away in a slapping motion, saying, "You fucking!. . . . You *FUCKING!*" And he's slapping it away again, with his right and his left, and his head is rupturing, purple, and he begins kicking. Kicking the flower pot, I think, because I can hear it crunching and cracking. Then I realise that what is crunching and cracking is me.

•●•

The widescreen TV set mounted on the wall plays with the sound turned off, but with captions for the hard of hearing, such as yours truly. I'm surprised that A&E is so sparsely populated, but there seems a distinct lack of urgency about seeing people. Whether they give priority to those in serious need, or children, is anybody's guess. There doesn't seem a great deal of logic about it, and it's no good asking anybody. Nobody talks. Everybody in their own little bubble. Every now and then someone comes out, ears prick up, we hear someone's name and they go through the swing doors into the inner sanctum, while the rest of us sag back disappointedly in our seats. As a piece of performance art I reckon it would have a good chance of winning the Turner Prize.

The school teacher, Derek Hatfull, has been sat next to me the whole time. Occasionally blowing air, checking his mobile phone or walking up and down to stretch his legs, trying to disguise his impatience with bursts of chipperness. When I glance at him he makes a point of smiling, which re-opens his cut lip, but he never remarks on it. He remarks on my incipient black eye though.

"That's going to be a right shiner, that is."

"I've had worse," I say.

"Of course you have," he says. I realise he means the cattle trucks and whatnot. I don't reply.

Bent forward, he tries to pretend he isn't looking at his watch.

"I'm sorry," I say.

He swats away the thought. "No, *I'm* sorry this had to happen. God. Today, of all days. After what you did in school. Unbelievable. That idiot. What he stands for." His whole body shudders as he shakes his head.

He dropped me at the door while he parked the car. Insisted on driving me. He could see I was wobbly on my feet. When he got back he asked me if I'd gone to reception. I said no. "Come on then." He approached the window where a sign read THE PHYSICALLY OR VERBAL ABUSE OUR STAFF WILL NOT BE TOLERATED, which I thought might be in danger of giving people ideas that hadn't previously occurred to them. "This gentleman's been beaten up," he said.

"He needs looking at, please. We rang 111. They said to bring him in, pronto." The woman said, "Name please?" Without giving me a chance to answer he said, "Tomasz Podolski," and spelled out the last name, then the first, ending with the zed. Her fingers, resplendent with artificial nails, clattered on the keyboard. She said the name wasn't on the system, which didn't surprise me at all, since it was entirely fictitious. "What's the address?" I opened my mouth, goldfish-like, then realised I couldn't give it, for fear the system might regurgitate my actual name. Ernest Yapp. I must have looked like a dumb tit. "He's a bit confused," Derek Hatfull said. "Can't you just patch him up and see he's all right? He's in a right old state." I was . . . though not for the reason he thought. The idea he might learn my real identity had drained the last vestige of colour from my cheeks.

Then it was the same old questions as on the phone. Was I allergic? Was I on any medication? What happened? I said, "I've been in the wars, that's what happened."

Derek Hatfull said, "An idiot took a dislike to him. In Asda's car park. Knocked him over and put the boot in."

The girl made no comment, but her psychedelic fingers did a bit more clattering and she told us to sit down over there and we'd be called.

Frankly, it's a godsend he'd been there, though. Goodness knows what would have been left of me if he hadn't been. Got a biff on the mouth for his trouble, too. Didn't see it myself. Unconscious, briefly. By the time I came round, somebody had a first aid kit out. I heard him say he was a gardener but used to be a paramedic. He was rolling my trouser leg up, applying two large sticking plasters. Derek Hatfull was on his feet, calling—what is it? Not 999—111, then he had to put me on to answer questions. My name and so on. "Tomasz Podolski," I said. 111 asked if the wound on my leg was "gushing". I held the phone to my chest. "Is it gushing?" The gardener said, "No, it's not gushing." The school teacher said, "No, it's not gushing." I said to the person on the phone, "It's not gushing." They said, our assessment is, you need to get yourself to A&E right away, in case you need some suturing.

Which is what we did two and a half-hours ago and counting. Getting on for three. *Pointless* is on, rendered completely pointless without the sound on.

"Go home," I say, mindful to keep the Polish accent going. "Take the rest of the day off."

"No, you're all right."

"You've probably got concussion. You need seeing to yourself."

He sighs. "I should have twatted him, if I had any gumption."

I grunt. "And get yourself killed?"

"Yeah, well . . ."

Elbows on knees, his hands dangle. His fingers are surprisingly long. I wonder if he plays the piano. I tell him he needs to get himself home to his family. "You have a family?"

"Two boys," he says. "One will do anything to do the minimum homework required, the other will go overboard to get praise from the teacher. So much for DNA."

I think of my invented children. Peter, Marek and Frank, the one named after the psychiatrist. It's comforting to make up what you never had.

"Do you want me to call someone? Let anyone know, by the way?" The phone is in his hand.

"No," I say. "There is no one."

A male nurse appears. Spirits lift. A name is called. Spirits dampen.

"You've driven me here. You've done enough. I'll get a taxi," I say.

"Do you remember your address?"

"Of course I do."

"Are you sure?"

"Yes, I'm sure. Look, I'd prefer to. Please. I feel bad enough as it is. Go." He lifts up my shopping bag which he'd been guarding assiduously. I take it from him and rest it on my lap.

"You're sure?"

"Yes."

He leaves reluctantly, but I'm relieved. His presence was making me nervous and adding to my anxiety. I wave. He tells me to take care. He is a nice man. It isn't his fault he made me a bag of nerves. I think he took a shine to me. That's pleasing of course, but I'll never see him again. Mind you, I said that after the school visit.

Behind my cracked glasses—better go to Specsavers—my right eye is beginning to sting and I can feel it starting to swell up. I poke it gently around the perimeter with my finger. An elephant seal in a wheelchair gives me his rapt attention, which is a novelty, as he hasn't stopped troubling his wife for Maltesers and sandwiches and canned drinks from the vending machine since they've got here, as well as telling anybody passing in a uniform that he needs treatment as a priority being an extremely vulnerable person with conditions, lots of conditions, they can look up his conditions, he's not being funny, he says, thanking them profusely as they vanish before getting back to the matter of Maltesers. Then there was the teenager in a pink onesie and hoop earrings who rushed in, breathless, gibbering to the receptionist that she had to be seen *immediately* because she had mental health issues and was likely to have a panic attack at any moment. She never did. It might have relieved the boredom if she had.

"Tomasz Podolski?"

It takes me a second to remember that's me. The nurse holds the door open, takes me through, and sits me down in a little booth. She apologises if I've had a long wait.

"I expect you have more important things on your plate," I say, maintaining the Polish persona, but she's too busy squinting at my details on her computer screen to answer for a minute.

"All right, my love. My name's Polly. I just need to check some details, is that all right? Name?"

"Tomasz Podolski." Here we go again.

"Date of birth?"

"Thirteen. Three. Thirty."

Her calves, tucked under the chair, are substantial, and I see a large, purple bruise on the back of one of them. Goal keeper's calves. Perhaps she got it making a save, I ponder. The female game is getting popular after all, so they say. Though she doesn't look fit enough to be a big sport lover. Obese, I'd say. Not unkindly. Technically. Or not even technically. Figuratively. If you pardon the pun.

"I said I didn't remember my address but I do now," I volunteer. "43 Robin Hood Road, Withinroyd."

"Well done," she says. I don't know what's well done about it.

"I'm staying with a friend at the moment," I say, in case *Ernie Yapp* comes up.

"Postcode?"

"No idea," I say. "I'm not going doolally, mind. If that's what her outside with the nails was thinking."

"I'm sure she wasn't."

"I was just a bit confuddled, like, that was all. I had a bang on the head. Who wouldn't be confuddled?"

"Are you on any medications, at all?"

I reel off what I told 111 and reception. Nothing wrong with my brain box. "Amlodipine, 10mg a day, for high blood pressure. Atorvastatin, 20mg, for cholesterol. Tamsulosin, 400 micrograms, if we have to delve into my enlarged prostate."

She chuckles. "I'm afraid we do, my sweetheart. Allergies I should know about?"

I shake my head.

"Penicillin?"

"No."

"Right." She twirls her swivel chair around to face me. "Tell me what happened today, then, exactly?"

"I had an altercation with a flower pot," I say, keeping it short and sweet this time. "The terracotta must have shattered and a part of it must have been razor sharp. I didn't feel anything at first."

"Then you looked down and the blood drained from your face."

"No. That was the other people. I didn't look down."

When she smiles her eyes crinkle up at the corners. She asks me to pop my left leg up on the stool, if I can without it hurting, which I can. She rolls up my trouser leg and has a good look at the sticking plasters, pressing her fingers gently to the surrounding area, asking if it hurts. I say no.

"First things first, when did you last have a tetanus injection?" When I say I can't remember, she asks if it was more than five years ago. I say probably. "We'll give you one of those, then."

She disappears and comes back with a sealed packet and sits back down. By which time I've rolled up my shirt sleeve as requested. Her eyes fall on the numerals written on my forearm, but she doesn't say anything or react too markedly. Just looks at me and smiles.

"Do you mind if I look away," I ask as she fills the syringe. "Only I'm not keen on injections. I don't suppose many are."

"If anyone was I'd be worried," she says. "Right." After extracting the needle she warns me I might feel a soreness in the next few hours or days and I shouldn't worry, that was natural. "You said you had a bump on the head." Her moon face looms up close to mine, two fingers pressing under the eye and over it. She says I'm lucky the skin isn't broken. "You'll have a shock when you look in the mirror tomorrow though."

"I always do," I say.

She gives a small hiccup of a laugh, the kind a little girl makes. "Is there anything else I should know about?"

I put a hand to my side and wince. She prods around fairly lightly. Asks me to pull up my shirt.

"Oh!" I groan.

"Yes, you might have got a cracked rib, but there's not much we can do about ribs. It should put itself right in time. Make sure you don't do too much laughing."

"I'm ninety years old," I say. "Believe me, laughing is not an issue."

Her grin widens.

When the plasters come off my leg, I see the little red mouth of the wound and I have to grit my teeth. She explains the things she is going to use are called Steri-strips and says they are better than old-fashioned stitches because there is less chance of infection. The cut is three inches long, and she applies six of them—four down and two across, holding the little mouth shut, laying them across like Sellotape, then wrapping a bandage around the lot.

"There. We're done. When you get home, book an appointment with your practice nurse for a week's time for a wound review." She hands me a leaflet. "If there's any swelling or redness spreading out, or the pain gets worse, contact us straight away. Infection is the thing you need to look out for, but you'll be fine. Keep it dry in the meantime. Don't get it wet. No showers."

"Showers?"

"No showers."

I struggle to get up. She catches my hand. She is still wearing the blue rubber gloves.

"Take your time. No hurry."

"Bless you. Thank you," I say, buttoning up the cuff of my shirt.

"They wrote down assault," she says, peeling off her gloves and dropping them in the swing-topped bin. "What kind of assault, if you don't mind me asking?"

I hesitate. "Racial assault. Anti-Semitic assault."

She looks away from me. Casts her eyes to the bin. "God."

"God had very little to do with it," I say.

"In Leeds?"

"In Asda."

"I'm shocked."

"You would be. You are a good person," I say. "Such is life."

"It bloody shouldn't have to be. Let me get your coat." She holds it up for me, like a valet, as I insert my arms. "Do you have someone with you? How are you for getting home?"

"I'll be fine on the bus."

"The bus?"

"Or I saw a telephone in reception. I can ring for a taxi."

"You've had a head injury. By rights I should keep you in for observation."

"Nonsense."

"You're a strong-minded person."

"I've had to be," I say. Not really thinking, but it comes out. I zip open the curtain. I'm not sure if we should shake hands. It doesn't seem like we ought to, so I don't.

She escorts me to the double doors back to reception, pushing one of them back with one hand. "If you're in no hurry, do you fancy a cup of tea? My shift is finishing in twenty minutes, and I'm gasping."

I say, all right, if she wants to. Yes, I say. Why not?

•●•

The shutters of the shop are coming down noisily when she gets there. I'm already at one of the little tables outside. I tell her I haven't ordered anything and she does a spurt and a limbo dance to get under the grille which is halfway shut. She moves quickly for one so large and uses her charm with the man with the eye patch and stringy neck for two teas and some impromptu snacks and, I now see, crisps, three packets, various flavours, cheese and onion et cetera, should I require them. I don't, but still, the gesture and all that.

I explain I didn't want to get my tea and find it had gone cold by the time she arrived. She says no, of course not. I say sorry. She says, don't be daft. I dig in my pocket and say I'll give her some money for the beverages.

"I wouldn't dream of it, my love. After what you've been through? Do you like it weak or strong?"

"As long as you can stand the spoon up in it," I say, eliciting a slight quiver of mirth as she presses the tea bag against the sides, squeezing out every ounce of ink-dark liquid. "There. Add your own milk, sweetheart. Phew. Mission Impossible!" I'm not sure what she means. She jigs her thumb to the shutter as it rolls down the final couple of feet. The piratical-looking gent locks up. As he bends over his pullover rides up his back and I see the elastic at the top of his underpants is none too pristine.

"I didn't know what you wanted so I grabbed a selection." She empties a bag containing a Kit-Kat, a Galaxy, a Twix, two Picnics and a bag of Minstrels. "Long time since I've had a Picnic. I don't know why. I always liked Picnics." She unpeels the wrapper and gazes lovingly at the lumps of peanut under chocolate, savouring her first mouthful with closed eyes as if it was an experience of unparalleled religious ecstasy.

"It will put you off your dinner."

"You sound like my husband."

"What time does he get home?"

She squints at the clock on the wall. "Now. I'm not bothered. He'll be wanting his tea on the dot of six o'clock, as usual. His mother used to wait on him hand and foot. She chose to be a dogsbody. Well, I don't."

She isn't in a rush and neither am I. What do I have to rush back to? A few hours rubbish telly and bed? Something in the microwave? That's as exciting as it gets, for me. Watching some faggots and peas twirling around like the Tiller girls. Returning to the bedroom where my wife died. The silver comb and brush with her smell still on it. She worked in the library too. Romance over the Mills and Boons, we were.

"What do you like when you go out?" Polly is stuffing her face with Quavers now. "What's your favourite, out of interest?"

"Fish and chips," I say.

She looks at the ceiling with her eyelids fluttering and gives another look of intense spiritual epiphany, if not orgasm. "In slightly soggy newspaper, with *loads* of salt and vinegar, from the chip shop, nothing like it. Pickled onion on the side. Mushy peas if they've got it. Bird's Eye cod fillets, they're not bad, mind. Oven chips. Now that's an invention that should have got the Nobel Prize if you ask me. They say frozen peas are better than fresh peas you know. Nutritionally speaking. The flavour is frozen in at the point of freezing, or something, I heard. Hard to believe isn't it? But true apparently. Don't let your tea get cold."

As she removes her scarf a cross on a chain around her neck catches the light. I'm thinking C of E because it doesn't have a little man on it. She flicks her hair from her shoulders, both sides. She wears an Alice band decorated with plastic daisies, and a rainbow badge on the lapel of her lime green coat. Her face is heart-shaped and her eyes large like a doll's. Puckering when she sees me wince. She rummages in her bag.

"I always carry some, in case of emergencies." She extracts a blue packet, extracts a rectangle of foil from that, pops out two white pills and passes them to me with a wink. "I shouldn't do this by rights, but what the hell. Why are there no pain killers on Treasure Island?" She waits for my blank expression to change. It doesn't. "Because the parrots ate 'em all." The penny still doesn't drop. "Paracetamol!"

"Boom boom."

"Ba-dum-tish." She mimes a drum kit because I don't get that either. "Ba-dum-tish?"

Washing the tablets down with tea, I ask what his name is. Her husband.

"Taylor. First name. Second name, Unsworth." She stirs her tea with one of those long wooden stirrer things. What's wrong with spoons I have no idea. "But you're right. I don't want the kids to be back too long. They can be a handful and he's got a right temper. Wouldn't take it out on them, though. All boys together . . ." She examines the Picnic and denudes it of another strip of wrapper as if it is an archaeological artefact. She moves the NO SMOKING sign that sits between us. "You know, I haven't fancied a cigarette for five years and I fancy one now. If I had one now I'd be back on them like a shot. I only gave them up for the kids. When Alfie was born. Before he was born. Not good when you're pregnant, is it?" A slurp of tea and an exhale. "We didn't want two. Marco was an accident. Alfie was IVF. The struggle we went through to have him. God. Then Marco, he was natural. People say it happens like that, but I never believed them. Living proof, I was. Living proof that it can."

She picks up a discarded carton of Ribena from the next table. An elderly man dressed in green is sweeping the floor with an inordinately wide brush. She goes over and drops it into his receptacle. "Hi, Ismail. All right?" Ismail lifts a big, shovel-sized hand in acknowledgment. His snow white goatee contrasts so much with his dark skin it seems artificial.

"Ismael is from Rwanda," she confides in me as she sits down again. "I'm not sure if he's a Hootoo or Tootsie, but he's one of the ones who wasn't massacred."

"You've been in the wars too," I say, having noticed for a second time, when she stood up, the purple discolouration on the back of her calf, which she attempts to laugh off.

"All bruises, me. I bruise easily. He always says that." Does she think I don't detect a tremor in her voice? The smile, the brave smile, re-establishes itself.

"You'd better go," I say. "I don't want to get you in trouble."

"No, I like it here. What does it matter? He'll give me grief either way. Whether I'm here five minutes or five hours." Making an effort to settle and pretend to be relaxed, she takes another bite of the Picnic, then glides a Kit-Kat towards me across the table top. "What was it like? In the camp." That comes out of the blue.

"I don't like to talk about it," I say, thinking at first she simply wants to change the subject, then I see the embarrassment in her face at the thought of having been insensitive and realise her interest is genuine. "It was hell on earth," I say quietly, knowing that sometimes less is more. Sometimes more is more, but sometimes less is more.

"Did you ever want to die?"

"Never," I say. "I wanted to live."

"I expect you have some stories, eh? Not like in those war films, I bet."

I snap a finger of Kit-Kat in two and nibble one half, staring into my tea contemplatively before eating the other. I don't want to look up. I don't want to say any more. I don't know why. Sometimes I'm not in the mood. Drained, possibly, by the day's events. She looks down at the spread of chocolate bars, shuffling them like dominoes.

"Take what you want. I got them for you."

"I don't have that much of a sweet tooth." I notice with alarm I'm not sounding as Polish as I might have done, so I add, "Sweet tooth? That is what you say?"

"Sweet tooth," she says. "Yeah. Wish I didn't."

"Give them to your boys."

"I don't want them growing up into a fat lump like me, do I?"

"You are very pretty," I say, enjoying seeing her blush. A compliment from an old man. Old enough to be, well . . . "You are very attractive girl. You have kind soul."

"Can I have that in writing?"

I laugh and immediately jerk upright as I feel a stab of pain in my side.

"Sorry, sorry," she says, and watches me finish my tea, which by now is lukewarm. She gathers the sweets back into the flimsy bag they'd come in. "Robin Hood Road. It's not that far. I can run you home. It's no bother."

"It is a bother. I'll get a taxi. You've been very kind. You patched me up. Right as rain." I hummed a few bars of *Singing in the Rain*, which made her grin and glow under the halo of daisies. "Gene Kelly."

"Who's she? Joke."

"No joking," I say, touching my ribs. "Please. No joking."

"Okay." After a minute she drags closer the paper napkin her used tea bag sits on and tears off a clean, dry strip. She fishes in her handbag, takes out a ball point pen and starts scribbling. "My name's Polly. This is my phone number. If you ever want a little chat, give me a ring. I mean that. I'd like that." She passes the slip of paper across to me and pats it with her fingertips. Her other hand rests on mine. Hers young, and smooth, and mine . . . well.

"Will you be all right?" I say when she stands up.

She nods, then shivers slightly as if she's standing in a draught. "It's the children. I only stay with him because of the children. That and . . ." A dark hole opens up. "I need someone at the moment. With the chemo coming up. You know. The treatment starts next week and . . . I'm not sure if I . . ." She runs her little finger under the rim of one eye. Then the smile wins. Temporarily, I'm sure.

"You will," I say in a breath. "You're a marvel."

"I don't know about that. I can be a right lippy cow at times. Don't laugh. It'll hurt."

I hold up a hand.

"Nice meeting you," she says as she backs a few steps in the direction of the exit. I feel proud and sick and sad all at the same time and for some reason I don't understand there's a lump in my throat.

• ● •

Good old NHS. Providing a free telephone direct to a taxi service, right there in reception. I don't care what anyone says. NHS. Mess with it at your peril.

I sit back at the same table by the closed shutters of the café-stroke-shop. The torn-off napkin with the writing on still there. Ismael has put his extremely wide brush on pause and is wiping the surface with a frankly disgusting-looking cloth.

"Nice lady," I say.

"Polly? Oh, yes. Nice lady, nice lady."

"Do you know her?"

"Yes. Oh, yes. Everybody knows Polly."

"Do you know about her husband?"

"Oh, yes." He side-shuffles back to his contraption, the twitch in his eyebrow signalling some potential indiscretion on the cards. "We *all* know about her hus-*band*." He put the emphasis on the wrong syllable, the way Africans do sometimes. Not that I mind it, usually. At all. Or ever. Accents are a part of the rich tapestry of life. Obviously.

I say, "He sounds a bit of a, well . . ."

"Here's the thing, see." Ismael side-steps back closer, doing more figures of eight with the manky J-cloth which I could have done without. "She got no hus-*band*. She not mar-*ried* at all."

"What? She's divorced?" I'm confused.

"Not divorced. He not exist. She tell you about her boys, too? They don't exist either. They're all up here." He taps the dome of his bald skull. "Everybody knows. We all feel bad for her. She doesn't have no family. Doesn't have nobody. Lives on her own. Never had boyfriend, girlfriend, never had no-one. Last fifteen years I been here."

"I don't believe it. She . . ."

"She very convincing. No."

"Very."

"I don't know if it's a good thing I do, to tell you, or bad. I . . ."

"No, no," I say. "A good thing. Really. Thank you." My Polish accent has gone out of the window. "Thank you. A good thing. Definitely." Ismael turns his back, but I find myself speaking my thoughts out loud. "So . . . so she's got no-one to be with her? To go through this? The treatment? The chemotherapy? The cancer?"

He gives me a slow, pitying look, as if looking sorrowfully at a dog that had been whipped to within an inch of its life.

"That is what she told you?" he says, and turns away.

The statement hangs in the air and not only because of his deep baritone. I know I don't need to say anything back, and can't, in any case. He knows there is nothing to say which is why he gets back to work, shuffling his big feet in sandals as if he's said too much—which he has. No doubt about it.

I stare at the wall-mounted TV set, but the picture seems to be out of focus at first. When it sharpens, I see it is showing footage of a small boat crossing the English Channel. One of those dinghy-type crafts, piled up with people. Not an inch of it spare. You can't imagine there can be so many people clinging to one tiny vessel like that. Immigrants. Migrants. Refugees. Whatever you want to call them. The choppy waters tossing them up and down, up and down. Frightened faces. Shadowy faces. Children clinging to mothers. Fathers praying for them all to reach land in one piece. Journalist thrusting her microphone from the boat alongside, long blonde hair whipping her face.

"Do you want me to take that for you?"

I double-take and realise Ismael is asking about the torn, coffee-stained piece of paper in my hand.

"Do you want me to take that for you?"

I shake my head and put it in the inside pocket of my jacket, but as soon as he's moved away with his squeaking wheels and lopsided gait—wounded by his past life or merely old, and living with all that entails as best he can, I wasn't sure—I take it out again and look at the telephone number.

I think, you know what? I will ring her. *I'd like that.* I'd like that very much. And when I decide that, it's odd. I don't feel puzzled or hurt or angry or betrayed. Why should I be? After all, what Polly had told me might not have been *the* truth—but it was *her* truth.

And, I'll be perfectly honest, when poor old Ismael gazes back at me after arranging his dust pan and brush and the rest of his accoutrements, I don't think he's expecting to see a smile on my face. He really isn't. He isn't expecting to see a big wide grin at all. And he certainly isn't expecting to see me laughing. Even though it hurts my ribs, I just can't help laughing. Laughing till I feel the warmth of tears on my cheeks. Because I'm thinking:

This could be the beginning of a wonderful friendship.

The Airport Gorilla

So, this.

I see him. He sees me.

Thinking these black bead eyes unknowing, he gets an ape's grin back from the stack of cuddly toys in the bin next to the checkout at Duty Free. He fans and counts the last of his Euros, joke money to him that looks like it came with a game of Monopoly.

Boarding pass?

Certainly.

He thinks the Dutch speak better English than he does. Always felt his Aussie drawl embarrassing. Damn thing still made him self-conscious several degrees and doctorates later, called upon to talk at international conferences on matters that save lives. Still, to him, the snarl of sheep dip and hats with dangling corks a halo, and he has always hated it.

Screwy-angled, I scrutinise him back.

Above his ears I see lines each side made by the arms of glasses he's not wearing. Atop, blond beach-bum waves now fading to the colour of his scalp. Aeons since he felt sand between his toes. House-brick jaw he got from his dad. The twinkling eyes, his ma. Sky-coloured.

He stares down at me with something between curiosity and incipient affection.

I recognise that look.

I've watched it day in, day out, in the myriad glances that slide over me. The micro-glimmer of tears that accompanies flashbacks to hearth and home.

Most turn away, not wanting to acknowledge that inner surge of sentimentality. Not him. He lets the guilt and separation anxiety rise in his chest and I feel in my complete-lack-of-bones his pang for the child he left behind.

The one he will see at the end of his journey. Soon, but not soon enough.

The one he'll sweep up in his arms. No weightier than a toy herself. Who snores now somewhere in her suburban Melbourne dreamsleep. Yet he cannot hear that. He is robbed of it, that moment, that silly, cherished everyday nothing as the flight announcements drone.

His wife and nipper, waiting for Dad to return, miss him with an indescribable ache. This is the real currency of the airport—longing.

And so. I am here to be touched, loved, adored. Made for it, and he knows it. I am the salve to the pang he feels in his heart—and I have been waiting.

He touches my plastic ear.

Air from his nostrils.

I amuse him. Hey. No problem with that.

I'm not a serious figure. My lips are too big. My mouth sticks out like an over-size bagel. I'm covered in black fur. My legs are short. Wouldn't stop a pig in a passage. Toes like fingers and thumbs. My arms reach way below my knees. I wear a T-shirt with the name of the city we're in and a logo of a tulip. I've got a comical, idiotic expression. My grin mirroring the one he dreams of seeing on his daughter's face.

He squeezes my tummy with his thumbs. Turns me over. Examines my behind.

(Ignominious, to say the least. Come on, people! Animal rights and shit!)

Made in China, he reads.

(Okay. Nobody's perfect.)

Anyway he loves me, or knows someone who will.

So, this.

I'm face-down on the counter and the tag on my ankle gets scanned. Ping.

Have a nice day, sir, and have a pleasant flight.

Thank you.

He lifts me up like he lifted her as a babe. A trophy, a triumph.

My face inches from his. What is he? Thirty-five, forty max. He laughs again, and though it's still soundless, it judders his whole frame in a way that's appealing.

Nice person. Good person. Come on. His kid. Gimme a break.

And here I go, under his arm now—parallel to the Famous Grouse, the overpriced chocolates, bagged and dangling from his other hand. His elbow tight across my abdomen, reassuring, protective. I feel secure.

Now he's sitting on a plastic bench, waiting for his gate to be called. Props yours truly beside him, righting me up when I droop. Some Asiatic fool chuckles. The fool would droop too if he had my legs—bandy and boneless. But I try not to get bitter. (I have a permanent fucking smile painted on, so that helps.)

The board flutters like so many call girls' eyelashes. The gate and flight number appear.

He gathers his bags. He gathers me. Flat of his hand splayed against my back, my face pressed to his chest, mashed to the buttons of his Mambo shirt, loose for travelling in, more him than the suits the conference required.

We ride the travelator. Yippee.

Children giggle. My one eye that's not mashed into Mambo psychedelic colours sees them wave and pull faces. Fuck them. We're on our way.

I'm feeling a sense of anticipation, of excitement. A new owner and a new experience ahead. Got to be good news, when you've been in a Special Offer bin with a lumpy giraffe and a pink kangaroo for weeks on end. (Glad to see the back of that fucking giraffe, let me tell you.)

First impressions? He seems an okay guy.

I think we'll get along, Not that I'm hard to get along with. I'm adaptable. Hey. I take the path of least resistance. What can I say? It's who I am.

All right, I get attached. I know I shouldn't. I know because it always ends in tears. I can't fucking help it.

As we enter the airplane the flight attendant, orange tan and grinning (because she got fucked raw the night before) pretends to talk to me. Oh, so funny. Never heard that before. Says she hopes I'll enjoy the flight. My guy laughs out loud, like it's comic genius. He goes down in my estimation, a tad.

Whoah! I think for a horrible moment I'm going up there with the hand luggage. No fucking way. What is this, some "Premature Burial" fucking bullshit?

Phew! The suitcase, raincoat and Duty Free go up, but not this simian. Praise the Lord! I don't know if my man is afraid of damaging me before I even reach his precious daughter, but, whatever. I'm on his lap like a baby as he leafs through the in-flight magazine.

On board, the safety demonstration. The whole Marcel Marceau.

We've got an empty seat next to us and a vastly obese person next to that. This is how vast. She even asks for an extension to her seat belt. Jesus Christ! I give thanks for that middle seat, unoccupied. I look at my man and think, you ducked a bullet there, compadre!

I end up on the floor for take-off, his Caterpillar boot on my groin. (I think Orange Face has a hand in this, I swear.)

I'm starting to regret he didn't choose one of those painted clogs or a bottle of advocaat.

I grin all the way up his jeans and Mambo shirt and chin as he adjusts the reading light. He isn't nervous, even when the massive weight of the plane leaves the runway, lifting like a feather.

He doesn't grip the hand rests. His eyes don't leave the in-flight magazine.

I think the son of a bitch has forgotten about me, immersed as he is in first rate journalism about foreign climes.

Then, just when I think I'm a fucking afterthought, he picks me up and I'm on his lap again like a ventriloquist's dummy and Schiphol is history.

The obese one gives a raised eyebrow. A hideous hello.

My guy flickers a smile back. Neither wants conversation. Good. There are some things these plastic ears are not built for.

As the plane levels he settles and I settle too. He's pretty comfortable after all. Pretty well-sprung as mattresses go.

Enjoy the rest of your flight, blah blah.

Melbourne-bound, he gazes down at me, thinking of his child. The idea of her expression greeting him changes his. It lightens, almost blooms. I'm thinking this is looking optimistic, but I know it's not, and can't be. That's not the nature of it. Not the nature of me.

So, this.

It's got to happen, but I'm never quite sure when it will. Sometimes it comes out of a clear blue sky, so to speak. You never can tell. Sometimes my buttocks clench and I can feel it coming. Other times, it's a sucker punch. And you know what? You never get used to it. It's never easy.

This time, I kind of know.

Kind of.

That way he looks like he is drifting off to sleep. Those heavy lids. The memories. The desire. Then it's like a big church bell chiming in my head, through my body, and it's like he's pressed a button he didn't even know existed.

I wish this flight would end quickly, he thinks.

No. No, don't wish that, you fuck. You idiot. But too late—it's done. The die is fucking cast. No going back. (I fucking hate my job sometimes.)

For the technically-minded, it's an SA-11 Buk surface-to-air missile system, down there. A dot in a field, invisible from thirty-two thousand feet. Recently trundled over the border into Eastern Ukraine by pro-Russian rebel fighters.

I'd like to tense but my innards are cheap foam.

The missile hits.

My man's arms lift from the arm rests.

He feels the *boing* of the Boeing doing press-ups. Everybody does, terror escaping like a puncture, a slashed tyre.

It hurtles. Hurt. Wouldn't hurt a fly. Flying, not. Knotted stomachs in the air. Grumbling not from airline food. Not from stomach complaints. Compliant in zero-g.

Lockers spring open, clacking Jack-in-the-boxes. Oxygen masks dangle and sway in rhythm, in tune, like choreographed marionettes, kicking like the feet of can-can dancers then streaming back at the plunge.

He looks back.

Someone is horizontal like Superman, spectacular green-screen work. Outside the tilting window green fields rise to meet us at a rate of knots. Knotted loops in the bread basket, as bread baskets spin like tumbleweed from Business Class.

Blue collar, white collar, all get their top buttons undone. All get their Adam's apple freed to gasp breath and scream.

He wished for the flight to end quickly, and so it does.

Brace. Brace.

He whimpers, hunches, forearms helmetting his head. Buries his face in me the way a child might at beddie-byes. I give him warmth. I feel his pulse galloping. But I'm grinning. Always grinning. Can't stop it. Can't change.

As the metal casket dives and dives and dives he prays to God, which he never has since kindergarten, remembers the chickens they kept and fed, and how one pecked him once and he didn't think that of chickens.

Little does he know there is no God listening, just an ape.

God, please God, please God, let me see my daughter one more time before I die!

His second wish. And it's almost too easy to oblige. It has happened before I even think about it.

The locker above springs open. Luggage vomits out, spilling exuberantly across the seat backs. His coat a swirl midair. His mobile phone spat out of its pocket, hitting a head rest and landing randomly in the space beside him, which he misconceives as luck, snatching it up and switching it on.

It glows into life and colour, showing the child, gaps where her adult teeth haven't come through yet, freckles she always gets in warm seasons. His eyes. His wife's sarcasm.

There.

You've seen her one last time, I say to myself.

I've given you your first two wishes—what's your third?

His fingers, wrapped round the phone, tremble.

All about him reign blasphemy and chaos. The fat one's bowels have vented. Which is only a microcosm of it.

God comes into it again, his God and the gods of others, in unison and yet each alone, they call out, inwardly, to their fictions and comfort blankets.

Oh God, oh God, oh God, please let me die quickly and without pain.

And so.

Impact.

He does.

We hit the cold grey field of the Donbass and his third wish eventuates.

We spread in a million fragments over a nine mile radius, a galaxy forming of trash, belongings, chunky airport paperbacks, playing cards, letters home, old vinyl records, internal organs, hopes, and in-flight beverages. And what part, or parts, of it are him I don't even know any more. It's not my business.

Your story is over, Mambo shirt. My involvement in it, ditto.

I'm lying on broken metal, maybe wing, maybe fuselage, its heat slowly cooling like a body after sex. Nothing clinks or clanks or breathes or moves or mutters or prays any more.

I lie on this sun bed considering the musicality of distant rooks, which is non-existent and ultimately, fucking irritating. Not much I can do about that. It's always a waiting game between one host and the next and you get used to being at peace with that. But it's a fucking bore.

Passage of time I'm not great at.

I hear a tractor.

Voices. DPR insurgents, so possibly not a tractor, more likely a Jeep.

Ho hum.

Military boots, the kind that lace tightly halfway up the calf, crunch through the debris. Somebody picks me up. Behind him, the devastation. Not a pretty sight.

Bodies lying everywhere, dismembered, burned, others mangled together, indistinguishable. Nobody is removing them, even touching them. Not from reverence but from indifference.

The one holding me in his fat hand wears a camouflage cap, cigarette dangling from a slug of a lower lip. Seven o'clock shadow like he just bathed in charcoal. Belt heavy with ammo and tools of war. The others wear balaclavas but him, not. The others have shaved heads. Him, no.

He turns to people with cameras. Holds me up, a soft toy gorilla, flappy-limbed, my fur coated with dust and ash.

I hear the lenses clicking. If lenses click. They probably fucking don't. I have no idea.

Ratatatatat.

He walks around with me hanging from his hand for a while. Then for a longer while I'm tucked behind the leather strap across his chest.

A toe prods this. A toe kicks that. This continues. Someone beckons. Someone shrugs. Someone yawns. One fans a wallet out, plucking cash and credit cards with crow beak hands. Another hyenas jewellery. The radio in the Jeep crackles with sibilant authority but it's unintelligible. Maybe ghosts swim between the syllables. Who knows?

In semi-slumber the paramilitaries are not good at using their own initiative. They're waiting for orders but nobody is in a hurry to give them.

As the sun sets he climbs into the back of the Jeep—Land Rover, whatever the fuck it is. What do I know from cars?

Air thick with the smell of body odour and tobacco I jostle, as he does, like we're doing a routine together as we traverse the farmland terrain. They talk, him and the others, but to me it sounds like the yapping of dogs.

I think he's forgotten about me, militia man. Oh well. I may as well sit back and enjoy the trip, because I'm thinking right now I'm going to end up in the nearest dumpster. Every day a fucking adventure.

Outskirts of a village, he leaps off onto the mud of a track.

A gate gives, and then a door into warmth.

The Kalashnikov is propped against the wall, in the manner you would an umbrella.

The burden of the belt unbuckled, divested.

He genuflects in the manner of the Moscow Patriarchate before washing his face in a bowl. I bend and rise with him, accidentally anointed. He remembers being in Slovansk when they shot a Protestant priest, needing to turn the Drobray Vest Church into an armoury, but he hates the Evangelicals even more. Spawn of the USA and the West.

But enough, for today. He is home. Enough death.

He aches of it and wonders the purpose.

Then he remembers the flying of the tricolour of the Donetsk

People's Republic over the police headquarters in the city. He remembers throwing that city councillor in the river.

Without touching or approaching his wife he eats from a ladle dipped into a broth on the stove. The drips sizzle where they fall. She knows better than to show affection at times like these. Finding those moments is an art beyond Michelangelo these days. Her father dug coal. She's no longer sure what this one digs.

So, this I deduce, lying splayed like spatchcock on the kitchen table, this dribbling dog of a man is too preoccupied to have wishes. Too untroubled to have dreams, because dreams open doors.

He's too tarred and withered to allow imagination. He leaves that to others, the leaders, men wiser than him. Those with a vision for the future. Something he cannot create, but can cling to in his desperation for certainty and purpose. He's a lightning-struck tree that no longer sucks in the light, but he can do that.

He can build a house or knock it down. For the cause, for the flag, he will be told more things to do and he will do them because he knows in his heart they are right. The meat on the table, the gasoline in the car, the roof over their heads, the angry fire in his guts that won't be put out—that is what matters. Beyond that, there is nothing. You might as well think what is beyond the stars.

The oil and filth under his fingernails negate the need for optional extras. His fear sneers at the possibility.

But to have no wishes—none? That's something.

A first, for this hairy ape, who thinks himself unshockable.

So now I'm picked up and he regards me in the glow of the fire, as his other hand delivers three mouthfuls of vodka, then a fourth, more from habit than requirement.

He takes me to another room and in the flickering almost-darkness crouches beside a small bed.

He wiggles me in the air. Nods my head using his index finger behind my neck. Dances me on the edge of the mattress.

I'm being introduced to her, and her, me.

She emerges, so.

Tiny, elfin concoction, itchy blanket tucked under her chin. Under the blonde fringe, scissor-cut by her mama, the too-tired eyes of a five-year-old unable to close until her father gets home, now wide and sparkling. Mouth agog, half in delight, half in disbelief, as she beholds me.

I'm adorable. I can't help it.

He holds me out, closer. He smells of onion broth and aviation fuel and burnt plastic.

The stupid grin, she loves to bits.

She takes me in her arms, snug as a bug in a rug. Then it's my chin that pokes over the blanket. And I love it that she kisses the back of my furry head. Especially as she doesn't know where I've been.

Seriously? The softness of me, it's a slam dunk.

I'm hers now. Official. I tell ya, this one is an impressive hugger. From one who knows. If I had a spine it would be broken. The hell. Spines are over-rated.

From the first cuddle, I'm a keeper. I know it.

When her father has diminished and the light is lesser then lost, and she's alone with me before sleep, she looks at what's in her little hands.

Monkey's been in the wars. Monkey has blood on him, look.

I can say nothing.

Monkey needs a wash. Monkey needs to be clean.

I have no doubt she'll wash me in the morning. I'll have a good old wash, old Monkey will. Old friendly, funny Monkey will. She'll see to that. I like this one already. Then again, I'm easy to please.

And I'm waiting.

As Papa says his prayers by his piss-pot.

It may not be tonight, and it may not be tomorrow, but I'm waiting.

It might not be while she sleeps, and it might not be when she wakes, but it will come.

And I'm here for when she makes those three wishes. The ones that come with love and trust and pain and life and primates.

She's a child. She is the future. She will have wishes, I know that for sure. Children do.

All I have to do is lay in wait and enjoy the hugs.

What does she really want and desire, this babe-in-arms of a soul? I have no clue. I never do. It's a mystery. It's a wink from a stranger. A stiletto in the ribs. It's a monkey up a tree. It's a painted grin.

Her mind is roaming. In her dreams she swings from branch to branch on the back of glee, clinging to her saviour, this circumstantial cousin, pink-eared, long-limbed, one of her evolutionary brethren, button-eyed, holding it together as buttons do, then tearing them apart. The way the universe does.

What will her first wish be, I wonder?

So, this.

The House That Moved Next Door

THE STRANGE THING IS, when asked if I was an only child, I invariably answer in the affirmative, because for the first eight years of my life, I know it sounds silly, I was exactly that. My brother came along unexpectedly, an afterthought and to some degree an accident. My point is, for those significant years, and possibly for a number of years thereafter, I *felt* like an only child. Not that I didn't get on with Piers. I did. In fact, not to disrespect the old adage that no family is normal, but that all families are abnormal in their distinctive ways, we have never had a crossed word to this day. Possibly because we are very different personalities with very different interests, and possibly because those eight years separated us just enough for us to occupy different spaces within the family: as if we didn't live with the same family at all. What I mean is, I had my friends and he had his. When I was in primary school, he was a toddler, and by the time he was going to primary school, I was in the grammar. Sometimes we shared enthusiasms: we both liked the Greek myths of heroes, sirens, magical transformations and monsters. But I became bookish and insular, content with my own company—*preferring* my own company—whilst he was always outdoors with his gang, committing mischief or kicking a football, always getting home with a scrape on his knee or a grey sock at half-mast, breathless.

It never struck me at the time that mine was a lonely childhood. Of course, I had no other childhood with which to compare it: none of us does. I would certainly be hard-pressed to describe it as unhappy, though it had precious little of the hustle and bustle one pictures when one imagines what a happy childhood should look like, full of cuddly aunts and hail-fellow-well-met uncles, endless rambunctious and chortling relatives who would take you under their wing and provide exciting adventures and distractions. I had nothing remotely of the sort. I had grandparents on both sides, but they lived a bus ride away, their visits sporadic and tinged with vast tension in the air, my mother anxious to please and provide, to supply cake and tea, a gigantic sense of relief settling as the door closed after their departure. I think both my mother and father were congenitally insular, but nobody invited guests round in those days. Nobody felt the desperate need for socialising the way they do now. People were regarded with suspicion if they drank at home or wanted a laugh, as if those things were symptomatic of some debilitating illness. Ordinary people kept to themselves, and perhaps without even trying, my parents taught me to be the same. To be outgoing was to be demonstrative, and to be demonstrative was to seek attention, and seeking attention was tantamount to being grand, and above yourself, which was the worst sin imaginable.

This was the household I grew up in, and, I admit, far from feeling imprisoned or constrained, it made me feel safe. I didn't crave adventure or any of the possible allure the outside world offered. I certainly didn't crave a scabby knee or a sock at half-mast. I craved being at home in front of a nice coal fire reading *Coral Island* or *White Fang* with a plate of biscuits at my elbow while a comforting, gentle rain patted the windowpanes and a hiss of steam punctuated the sound of my mother ironing. The picture I've painted makes me feel irrationally content, all these years later, as I write this. But almost immediately my stomach turns over, because I know the story I must tell, and it is not one of comfort in the slightest. It has taken me many years to begin to write it, because in the process of writing I knew it would become concrete and real—yet I am not even sure it can be.

Even now, vivid as it was at the time, it fights my ability to recollect it, trying to slip from my grasp. I know it was summer.

The sun was shining considerably, its heat prickling my cheeks, and I can say with some assurance it must have been late afternoon, because it was that special day of the week—a Wednesday—when I walked to the library to exchange my book for a new one.

I was particularly proud of myself that day because I'd taken out my first "grown-up" book, or what I confidently thought to be so, because it was all writing, no pictures, and that was pretty grown-up for me, aged nine. I think there was probably a spring in my step, and my chest was a little bit puffed behind my grey V-neck jumper as I walked home with my school satchel over my shoulder. I was a big boy now, and who didn't want to be a big boy? I remember the sky was blue, and that in itself was a rarity, as was going to school without a mackintosh ("Just in case," Mother would say. "And come straight home."). The weather, being late home, social embarrassment, being seen to be big-headed on the one hand or "common" on the other—life was a veritable minefield to my mother. It was no less than a miracle she let me out on my own at all.

I heard high-pitched giggling as I approached my front gate. At that time we lived in Woodside Park, N12, the area of pre-war houses between Totteridge and West Finchley, one of the detached mock-Tudor type constructed by Frederick Ingram in the thirties. Closing the latch after me, I turned to see that the laughter was coming from two girls in the garden next door. I could only see the top halves of them over the privet hedge, and they were hitting something to and fro with tennis racquets. The thing made a small, whirring sound as it fluttered in a high, slow-descending curve from one racquet to the other. The children froze the moment they caught sight of me, and I tried to disguise my curiosity.

"It's a shuttlecock," said the elder of the two, tall and gangly, her yellow hair cut in an old-fashioned bob.

"Is it?" I said, affecting a measure of disinterest.

"That's what they call it."

"Why don't they call it a ball?"

"Because it isn't a *ball.* It's not *round.* It's a shuttlecock," said the younger sister, a tomboy with a mop of curly hair, wearing baggy short trousers not unlike my own. Her complexion was sallow, as if she'd been on holiday abroad, whereas her sibling's skin was as pale as milk and dusted with freckles. She held up the article between her fingers.

"Haven't you seen one before?"

I shook my head.

They looked at each other and giggled again. The younger one tossed the feathered object in the air and swatted it. The other ran to return it with an upswing. The tomboy then caught it in her fist, flipped it into the air, and let it parachute, spiralling, onto the palm of her outstretched hand.

"We're parched. We're going in for some lemon cordial. Do you want some?"

My first thought was that I should go home for tea, but I knew if I did, I would be cast forever in their eyes as the most atrocious mummy's boy, a chap with as little sense of adventure as could be imagined. The embarrassment at that thought reddened my cheeks even more than the sun had. No—obedient child though I was, for once I would simply do what I wanted to, and hang the consequences. I would have my lemon cordial, and my mother could fret for five minutes without me. I was a big boy now, after all.

The garden was empty when I went round. The shuttlecock and tennis racquets lay inert on the lawn. Presently I heard voices from indoors. The front door wasn't open so I followed the path down the side of the building. If it followed the design layout of my own house (which surely it did) there would be a back door leading into the kitchen.

There was, and it was ajar. The girls were inside, in the dimness compared to the bright light outdoors, squabbling over which of them was going to mix the squash in the glass jug now in the centre of the table. The older one relented huffily and stood with one hand on her hip, then beckoned me. I cleaned the soles of my shoes on an insecure rectangle of matting. The curly-haired one held the jug under a tap at a chipped Belfast sink. Water gushed. The kitchen was unlike ours: pristine and modern, colourful and neat, whereas ours was brown and sepia, the hues of stains of the past, of hesitation and uncertainty with the present age. Already I knew that voices spoke loudly here; it was a noisy, lively, cantankerous home and I wasn't sure I entirely liked it, but part of me very much did.

"My name's Jess," said the smaller one, who seemed to be the more bossy. "Her name's Louise. What's yours?"

"James," I said.

"That's one of the disciples, that is. In fact there were two of them, both called James. We did it in Sunday school. Do you go to Sunday school? Do you believe in the Bible, and in Jesus? Father says it's rot. He was in the army."

"So was my father."

"Our father was a Major."

"That's nothing," I remember saying. "My father was a sergeant."

They sniggered again. I didn't understand why at the time.

The one called Louise pulled out a stool and I sat on it. She poured me a glass. As I sipped the bitter juice, sharp on my tongue, for some unaccountable reason I became fearful they would look in my satchel and find the book I'd taken from the library. Perhaps it was the very private nature of reading, but the prospect filled me with dread.

"Do you have a train set, James? I like train sets," said Jess. "I like Meccano too. I love Meccano. Perhaps we can play Meccano together."

"You don't play it, silly!" said her sister. "You build things. It's not a game. You do it on your own. Like skipping."

"You can have two people skipping. You can have *three* people skipping if you want to! Two holding the rope and one in the middle—so there! *You*'re the one who's stupid!"

They poked their tongues out at each other and bashed their puny fists at each other's chests.

"Now, now, you two . . . Goodness!"

Emerging from the innards of the building, the voice belonged to a slim woman wearing an apron and, under it, a floral dress not unlike my mother's, but it seemed to cling to her swaying hips in a way my mother's clothes never did. I had never been aware of my mother's hips in the way I was aware of that woman's as she entered, sleeves rolled up to reveal forearms smeared with soap suds, carrying a basket of dirty washing. But it was hardly a glimpse before she turned away to another sink secreted in the far corner, not even making eye contact with her two children, submerging her husband's socks and underwear, briskly rubbing them with a brick of soap.

"Mother," said Jess chirpily. "We've made a new friend. Look. It's a boy. He's called James."

At that mention of my name the woman gasped and stopped what she was doing so abruptly I caught my own breath. Her back straightened and her square shoulders locked in position as if nailed there, but she did not turn to look at me at first or even remove her hands from the water. Instead she stood there, extremely still, for what seemed an absolute age, but must have been only seconds. I had just begun to think her reaction peculiar when she spoke, with harsh, clipped syllables the like of which I've only heard since from the lips of RADA actors in Noël Coward plays, or in films like *Brief Encounter*.

"You know that can't be true, dear." She still did not turn, and her voice remained firm and clear, without betraying the least tremor of emotion. "James is your little brother who died when he was in Mummy's tummy."

I felt my own tummy tighten.

"But I can see him." The girl called Jess looked straight at me, smiling. "He's here."

"Where?"

Her mother turned from the sink, wiping wet, pink hands on her apron then drying them on a tea towel. I saw prominent cheekbones and flawless skin, russet hair pulled back either side of her face and a strong, handsome jaw.

She gazed around the kitchen with a fixed and artificial grin, scanning the room. That in itself was eerie. In hindsight, I can understand she was wary of betraying any degree of hurt to her loved ones, given the information she had just imparted. But I had no time to reflect upon this as I watched her eyes glide past me, then glide back in the other direction, without pausing, for all the world as if she had not seen me. That struck me immediately as odd. How *could* she not see me? I was in full view, sitting there with an ice-cold glass of cordial in my hands. Was she *blind*? No, because I saw her place her hands on the shoulders of Jess and Louise and kiss them on the tops of their heads in full possession of her visual senses. And yet a frown and utterly perplexed expression etched onto her countenance as she followed the sisters' eye line—and saw nothing. She was looking straight at me, but, of this there was no doubt—it was as if I were invisible. Or, more correctly, and more disturbingly—*as if I was not there at all.*

"Where?" she repeated, her smile undiminished, in a tone that conveyed she might be thinking a joke was being played on her.

But to me it was anything but a joke. Now it was not my stomach tightening but my throat, as I looked from one sister to the other in some vain hope they might break the spell, not that I knew the nature of what spell needed to be broken. I was not only baffled but uniquely terrified. I was used to adults telling me the truth about the world—my parents, teachers. And yet this woman's extraordinary stare continued, with relentless yet unknowing cruelty, to tell me *I did not exist.*

I hopped off the stool and left the house as swiftly as I could. I can't remember if any other words were spoken by the children or their mother from the shadowy interior as I shuffled briskly down the side passage to the gate. Sometimes I wonder if there was laughter, which might explain that I was the butt of some hideous prank, but I am positive there was not. Of entering my home and of the rest of the evening I have no recollection at all.

I remember being frightened, but was I frightened at the time or only in retrospect, as it began playing on my mind? I honestly cannot say.

It is my belief, and you may corroborate this if you wish, that our childhoods are full of isolated incidents, and very thin on the connective tissue of narrative. Most people, I've found, are hard-pressed to think of more than a half-dozen events from their childhood—and even then, one can never be sure whether they are endlessly sullied by the inaccuracies of repeated retelling. Someone once told me, a reputable man with knowledge in this area, that memory is not finite and absolute, but constantly shifting and nebulous in form. Whenever we recall something and speak of it, he said, we are taking a manuscript and revising it, and the *revised* manuscript is what is stored, not the pure original. Thus, in effect, it seems truth is obscured in our endless attempts to recount, or even understand, it. Perhaps, in fact, memory is cunningly designed by God to avoid us getting to any truth at all. I'm sure science has an altogether more cogent explanation. And I'm sure the Freudians have another. I'm not sure I have a large amount of time for any of them.

Can I remember anything more about the girls next door, or their strong yet fragile mother, for that matter? No.

Did I mention the strange encounter to my parents at the time? No. How could I? I hardly knew what to make of it myself. Within hours, if not minutes, I was questioning what exactly *had* occurred. Had it really happened the way I thought? I was sure it couldn't have. It wasn't possible, was it? And yet—everything was so vivid, you see . . .

Did I speak to them again, the sisters? Or even see them? I'm almost certain not, but I can't be absolutely certain. Nothing about this business has absolutes. I wish it did.

As I alluded to earlier, later that summer my mother gave birth to Piers, and shortly afterwards we moved to Muswell Hill to be near my recently widowed paternal grandmother. I had a larger, airier bedroom overlooking a bigger, tree-laden garden. By the time I had a new school and new friends I began to forget my time in Woodside Park, slap-bang between two underground stations, and soon after I'd passed my Eleven-Plus, we moved again, this time out of London, to Basingstoke. Ridiculously, it seemed almost like an adventure. My father had three shops by then instead of one, and could commute quite happily, and afford a house big enough for Nan to live with us—though she didn't want to decamp at first, being a dyed-in-the-wool cockney. Dad bought a characteristically ostentatious Jag and my mother started to learn to drive, but gave up almost immediately, saying she couldn't do it with the combination of her bad nerves and my dad's bad temper.

As the incident with the girls next door faded into the unreliable recesses of my juvenile brain, cluttered as it was with new aspirations, educational requirements and worries in plotting a future, I naturally began to wonder if I'd dreamt or imagined the whole scene, or at least a significant part of it. Through some skewed or mistaken inflection, I convinced myself, the character of something quotidian and innocuous had been rendered quite bizarre and unreal. It was a logical enough assumption, a satisfying one—and one that, through effort, I lived with.

Happily, that state of passive acceptance remained intact through my adult life. I cannot say that my experience in the house next door was eradicated from my musings completely, but it was compartmentalised sufficiently not to dominate them, as more mundane concerns such as a job, career and eventually marriage rightly began to take precedence. And there were years, and subsequently decades, when I didn't think about it at all. The perplexing memory was safely locked away in that chest called Childhood, with a thousand other puzzles and relevancies no longer needed. On some level perhaps I knew my psychological contentment very much relied on me keeping it there.

And so it was, until I returned to my parents' house when they were much older, though still living in Basingstoke, when a further, unexpected revelation added to the intrigue of what had occurred all those years previously.

My mother was beginning to become vague—not yet to the extent of not recognising me or calling me Piers—but my father had all his marbles, enough to look after her for the time being, though I didn't know how long I had with either of them, and perhaps that was what prompted me, subconsciously, to ask them finally about the peculiar, fleeting occurrence in my dim and distant childhood.

No sooner had I begun to describe what had happened than my father looked confused and seemed to lose interest in what I had to say, complaining that the pot of tea was stewed. I asked him what was wrong. He laughed dismissively. "You're talking about the house next door, son, but there was no house next door. Not on that side anyway. Just a space between two houses, us and number forty-seven. Wasteland, full of weeds and whatnot. Used to be a house there, sure enough, but it was bombed during the war. Flattened. Hardly a brick left to show for it. And that's the way it was all the time we lived there. Real eyesore."

Surely I remembered?

I replied that of course I did.

Which wasn't true in the slightest. I remembered nothing of the sort. What I remembered was two girls playing with their tennis racquets and shuttlecock, and what happened in their kitchen that warm, prickly summer's afternoon.

My father asked me to go on, but the wind had gone out of my sails. I had nothing to say. He looked at me like I was a fool. Not an uncommon occurrence. The rest of the day was a blur. My head was pulsating as I drove home and my vision could barely focus. I was not in a fit state to be behind the wheel of a car.

My mind tussled with two equally abhorrent alternatives. Either my father's mind was playing tricks on him, and he was beginning that slow, irrevocable decline into senility earlier than I'd presumed, or he was telling the truth, and the house in question never existed: in which case, I was evidently the insane one. Neither path led to a palatable conclusion.

You could suggest that a simple drive to our old address in N12 may have settled the matter instantly. I would have proof. But proof of what? Anyway, I did no such thing—perhaps knowing deep down what I was sure to find, and preferring to cling to an element of doubt. Perhaps we all cling to that element of doubt in matters of the unexplained. Perhaps we have to. Perhaps the clinging is what makes us human. And perhaps it is only the truly mad who prise away their fingers and are happy to succumb.

Instead, I drove home to my wife. She was inured to seeing me pent-up with anxiety when I returned, the caring son, from my aged and cantankerous parents, but she had no idea why I was festering in such a dark mood, even more uncommunicative than usual as I poured myself a hefty gin and tonic. In twenty years of being desperately in love I hadn't told her my childhood secret—nor could I now. Her failure to grasp its significance would only rattle me the more, and her probable impulse to smother me with bland reassurances, as one might pet a loyal dog, I'd find unbearable. I took her out to dinner. A fine Burgundy cleared my mind.

I'd been an idealistic but misguided novelist (briefly), a freelance reader, then an editor, then a publisher, travelling in fits and starts from a moth-eaten sweater to a business suit and tie. A similar trajectory to hers. We discovered we'd both done English and French at Cambridge, and were born within three weeks of each other: synchronicity enough to kindle an unlikely romance amongst the slush piles. We married in Lucca. It didn't rain, it poured. Twenty years on and both directors of the company, we owned a flat in Knightsbridge, Lowndes Square to be exact, and latterly were able to afford a nice little bolt-hole: an absurdly pretty cottage in the village of Kilmersden, near Radstock in Somerset—right at the foot of Jack and Jill Hill, immortalised in the famous nursery rhyme and opposite a churchyard adorned with the most exquisite topiary. We instantly knew it was our corner of heaven, complete with Aga-warmed slippers and vixens barking in the stillness of night. I could never read books on our blissful weekends in the country ("too much like work, darling"), but Avril never went anywhere without an Iris Murdoch or Doris Lessing under her elbow. I liked nothing better than to look over my cup of coffee and to see her, enraptured in some fiction or other, glasses perched on the end of her nose, threatening to slide off onto a slice of jammy toast.

One day in Kilmersden I was standing in the bay window with a mug of tea in my hand, watching a family move in next door. The weather was dreary, the sky overcast. A snapshot would have had trouble gleaning any colour out of the proceedings. A self-hire Ford Transit stood with its doors open. A curly-haired, pleasant-looking young man in a parka with a fur-lined hood struggled with pieces of furniture, imagining he could lift an armchair, unaided, the length of the driveway. The Good Samaritan—or simply nosy about our new neighbours—I let my tea go cold and went out to offer a modicum of help. Or, at least, an extra pair of hands.

An hour or so later, with a few more aching muscles than I'd anticipated, and having sparked up a new friendship, I stepped inside his new home—Mark and Celia Burntree's old place—

invited in for a coffee and, oh, almost as an afterthought, to meet his wife.

She was dressed in a man's striped shirt, voluminous on her, almost clownishly so, hair tied back in a spotted handkerchief. Getting off her knees, and brushing dust from her hands with gauche and effusive apologies, she looked at me with delicious, sparkling eyes and smiled radiantly. My insides knotted and I thought I would faint. I gripped her hand tightly—so tightly that she laughed, but she couldn't know why. To my astonishment I was shaking hands with a woman with the most uncanny facial resemblance to the mother of the two children I'd met in the house next door.

I knew from that moment that I would fall in love with her. That, by whatever circuitous route that lay before us, we would marry, and that she would become pregnant by me. I knew that she would tell me one day she was carrying our child. I knew that one day, in hospital, we would be told the baby's gender: a boy. I also knew in that very same moment, if a moment can stretch into a baffling and crushing universe, that she would declare—unusually, some might say perversely—that she wanted to give it the same name as its father. My name: James. With equal certainty, I knew that when he was born, he would be born dead.

I never told her any of this.

Not a word. Not to this day . . .

How could I?

You might ask, with some validity and not a little anger, why did I not persuade her to give him *another* name—any name but *that?* The awful truth is, I think I knew that, beyond our doing or undoing, beyond our believing or disbelieving, what came to pass was somehow inevitable.

And after it *did* happen, after we both rocked that swaddled, motionless form in our arms—could I not say *then?*

Why? To unburden myself? To callously add a vile and perfect agony to the monument of pain she had already suffered?

What kind of monster would that have made me? And would she have loved me the more for doing so?

No.

I have long come to the conclusion that I must keep this hideous knowledge, if it is any kind of knowledge at all, locked within me to the grave. She cannot carry what I carry. I simply will not have it. There are few absolutes in this whole business, as I have said before—but this, I assure you, is one. If I achieve nothing else in my life, I shall achieve that.

We have raised two other children since, and they have gone to college, flown the coop, and it leaves an emptiness, and into that emptiness I have found bleak thoughts thickening and I have found myself returning to that little one we lost, and wondering what it means.

If I was told the future, then I was told it by a merciless God. If it was my own inadequacy to see the light, the pattern, then let me suffer all the agonies of hell. If it was beyond all understanding, then damn all understanding.

Though I try not to, I cannot help but to think back to that garden and that kitchen, and that little boy perched on that wooden stool. Sipping cordial in a dimness out of the realm and remit of the sun, in an alien room laden with a mysterious warmth. Bitter pleasure on my tongue, and a burrowing fear scampering in my chest.

But not really there at all.

Unchain the Beast

LET ME TELL YOU about my friend José Camacho Mestre, the director. You've heard of him? No. Perhaps not. He's not well known outside my country. I don't remember how we met. We were always together. José—always known as 'Pepe'. And me—Abelino? Always 'Beli'. My mother came from La Paz and threatened to go back there with myself and my four sisters on a weekly, sometimes daily, basis. She used to say my father's job at the bottle factory was his dream job, seeing as he liked bottles so much.

Pepe's dad was a farmer. In his spare time he made *alebrijes*—folk art—to supplement his income, selling them at the local market. Everyone made *piñatas* or 'Judas' figures made out of *cartón piedra*. Seeing Judas burning during Holy Week was one of the high points of our little lives. We grew up with red painted devils and cardboard angels with spreading, golden wings. Scenes of Jesus deposed from the cross, laid on a bloody tablecloth.

A *mojiganga* of saints, their tragic faces contrasting with clothes of the most vibrant colours and patterns. Skeletons riding skinny dogs with scarlet tongues, defying in their wild humour both heaven and hell. But what Pepe's father made was different.

Armadillos. Iguanas. Jaguars. Chimeras. Carved animals and fantastical, mythic creatures in wood—the local wood, *copal*. It was an old tradition in the Oaxaca Valley, where we lived. In San Martin Tilcajete, to be exact, in southern Mexico, part of the Ocotlán District in the Valle Centrales. Where animals and phantasmagorical beasts—supernatural beings from our pre-Hispanic past—had always been carved, for centuries, for millennia, by the Zapotecs. And it mesmerised us, how he brought them into being.

No two were ever alike. Each had to have its own individual character, as if something in the material came out, unbidden. It was said that *copal* wood had magical properties, but I think the real magic was in Pepe's father's hands. As we watched spellbound, there seemed to be a certain mysticism invoked in the making of them which his brain had forgotten but his fingers remembered.

He'd always give the animals exaggerated, human-like characteristics, which seemed almost to poke fun at our deeper cultural heritage. A fox would be taking a golf swing, or a cat playing poker, a cricket strumming a guitar serenade or a flying, six-legged pig in sunglasses, smoking a pipe. The monsters were designed to scare away bad spirits and protect the home, or as totems for good luck, or as children's toys. But his were, without doubt, works of art.

The most brilliant and terrifying thing he ever made was a Coyote—with huge pointed ears, long snout, black nose, yellow eyes, a tail and claws. I can see the old man now, putting the finishing touches to those shining white fangs with a paintbrush.

My God! It scared the pants off us, that creature on all fours on the table, with splayed fingers, and small, perfect toenails. You see, Coyote, to the Mexican, is not simply a scavenger and pest. His name comes from the Aztec deity *Huehuecóyoti*—like the crow, he steps in between the realms of life and death. A shapeshifter—and so, Pepe's father depicted him with human hands and feet.

When he blew out the oil lamp and left the workshop, scooting us boys in front of him, the image of it burned into our minds and never let us go.

Over weeks and weeks we had seen this being, this bent wood shape made from a single *copal* branch, hacked with a machete then worked with a chisel, come to life before us. In full colour, too!

He drew the eyes first, then the areas of repetitive pattern—the illusion of fur and muscle under the skin. All done with symbols. The big kite shape, then the small. Mixing all the colours from natural ingredients. Nothing from a pot. Pomegranate seeds mixed with alkali to create the blue. Baking soda. Lime juice. Zinc. Cochineal. All with intricacy. All with passion. The triangle. The labyrinth. The butterfly, with dots on its wings. Shimmering like stained glass in a church window. Just the right amount on the paint brush, the intense concentration. Black for the underworld. Yellow for the earth.

Coyote came alive in our minds. You could say it set our imaginations alight forever.

That's how it all started, really.

One day Pepe borrowed a Box Brownie and we snuck into his dad's workshop and placed our toy soldiers and little metal cars around the Coyote and took photographs, making the creature look gigantic. We couldn't wait to collect the photographs from the local drug store and pin them up on the wall. Looking back, it was our first storyboard.

But it wasn't enough for Pepe, even then. He called his parents and sisters and uncles and aunts to the best room in his house. He put the chairs in a row and played classical music on a gramophone to give the atmosphere. When the show ended, they applauded like crazy and Pepe's face glowed.

It was our first movie, in a way.

But we were fifteen before we graduated officially from a stills camera to a movie camera. My father couldn't afford such a thing, but my grandmother on my mother's side had squirrelled away money, her husband having been a dentist, and she knew we were insane about movies. All kinds, but horror movies in particular. We never stopped talking about them. Our education was Juan Bustillo Oro—*El fantasma del convento. Dos monjes. El misterio del rostro pálido.* The projectionist at the local picture house used to invite us in whenever he had something a little off-the-wall that wasn't suitable for youngsters. He probably had other motives, but what the hell—he never laid a finger on us.

It was a beautiful thing, that Cine-Kodak BB Junior, and we saved up by doing chores around the neighbourhood until we had enough for a Kodascope 16mm projector.

Madre de Dios—this was Hollywood!

We made all sorts of nonsense, at the weekend or after school. We found a crashed car by the roadside, in a ditch, so we thought: *That's it! That's our next movie!* How could we turn down the idea of a car crash? So we persuaded our friend, Emanuel Silva, to sit inside it and wrestle with the steering wheel while we lit smoke capsules and filmed him through the side window. Then we resurrected him as a zombie and put pieces of broken-up Alka-Seltzer tablets inside the make-up so that it fizzled when we threw water in his face.

The turning point, though, came the first time we saw Lon Chaney Junior in *Frankenstein Meets the Wolf Man*. Our jaws fell to our knees. We couldn't believe what we were witnessing. Mexican horror was overrun by wrestling stars—ridiculous strongmen hurling balsawood rocks. And here was the character of Larry Talbot—thinking, feeling, *real*. After that we couldn't wait to get our hands on *The Wolf Man* itself. And that was even better!

The long panning shot of the forest created on the Universal sound stage with its gaunt, silhouetted trees shrouded with dry ice! Then that extraordinary close-up of Jack Pierce's make-up using real yak fur—it almost made me lose control of my bladder. No men in wrestling tights. No gorillas getting brain transplants. This was about a man who prayed to God at night but became a murderous beast when the moon was full and bright. The very idea put icy chills through my heart, but I also felt sorry for poor, cursed Larry Talbot.

It made us determined that our make-up would be as realistic as that from now on. We didn't want wrestlers, we wanted *people*.

I raided my mother's box of cosmetics and pleaded with the local hairdresser to give me all the wigs she no longer needed. We ransacked every dumpster in town. We scavenged, just as Dr

Frankenstein scavenged the graveyards for body parts. And nothing went to waste. A fox fur stole became something that would come alive and strangle one of Pepe's sisters.

Around this time, Chano Urueta's *El monstruo resucitado* was released, starring José Maria Linares-Rivas. We adored its gothic sets, the fusty laboratory, the black and white photography, and most of all, the horrifying face make-up. I was smitten. The whole idea of creating monsters on screen seemed like an act of impossible alchemy. Sorcery, in fact.

Pepe dreamed of being part of that kind of film-making. We both did! But how could we? Two dirt-poor kids in Oaxaca Valley with a cheap camera? It was a dream, not reality.

In reality, as you might guess, we went separate ways. Pepe to Acting School—he was always the show-off. I was too shy for that. I didn't want to be noticed. But I did want to be creative. Eventually I got some breaks and became a commercial artist, as they called it then. An illustrator. For newspapers. For magazines. For whoever would pay.

I enjoyed my job. I still watched horror films. Once you've got hooked it's very hard to give up the addiction. It didn't matter whether it was a work of pure genius like *El espejo de la bruja* or frankly ludicrous, like *El baron del terror*. I didn't care. It was an escape from the everyday. The humdrum. The normal. My wife never liked them—she found them too upsetting, but I found them thrilling—so I'd end up going alone.

Pepe would tell me when he'd got an acting job—an extra, here, a walk-on there. The occasional line in a *telenovela* or commercial. I'd smile when I caught them. Call Adoración from the kitchen. I'd gotten married by then, had my children. My gorgeous brood. Baltasar. Marina. Tycho. Abril.

Pepe's big break came in '61, an MGM epic shooting in Mexico to stand in for Palestine at the time of Christ. He was picked out of a casting call and given the part of Judas. We laughed on the telephone. *Judas!* He immediately asked me to come to the set. Of course he'd get permission, He'd *demand* permission. That was Pepe all over. The centre of frame, or not at all. And a bigmouth, with no hesitation between his thoughts and his tongue.

We hugged under the hot sun and went to his trailer. But he wasn't happy. I laughed: how could he not be happy? He was getting good parts in big films. But he said he was frustrated, and bored, saying the terrible lines other people wrote and being pushed around in other men's staging like a puppet. He wanted to have fun, like we used to do, with a lousy piece of shit camera and no money.

He suddenly became animated and said he'd written a screenplay, called *Unchain the Beast*. He said he wanted to make it the way we made our films as kids. And I was excited, too—even before I read the first page.

It was about a werewolf-like spirit called Coyote. Half man. Half beast. All those ideas from our childhood. From his father's workshop. From our dreams.

He would star and direct.

I would do the make-up and be in charge of the visual design.

Fifty-fifty.

Just like the old days.

He would play Bill Tarquin, an American—it always had to be an American—who travels to Mexico, gets lost in the desert and, at the point of death is bitten by some hairy, shadowy night creature with fiery yellow eyes. This was the birth of 'El Hombre Coyote'—but neither of us had any idea at the time that it would change both our lives. The important thing, we both knew, even then, without saying it aloud, was that *this* Coyote was not just a ravenous beast. Pepe wanted the added pathos of Chaney, or Karloff.

Well, we didn't know what hit us. *Unchain the Beast* was a huge success in the early '60s, transformed Pepe into a popular star overnight, and Coyote took on the quality almost of a folk hero. Children saved bubble gum cards with his image on them.

Comedians made jokes about him. Whatever it was, the public wanted more, and by 1964, at breakneck speed and in some kind of adrenalin rush, the two of us had made twelve films featuring Bill Tarquin and El Hombre Coyote. Burning the midnight oil, scribbling until our fingers bled. Discarding scenes, writing new ones. Drawing new visuals as quickly as we scrapped old ones. Walking on air to the office to script *La noche del dr X* in between shooting *El Coyote y los monstruos de Walpurgis* in the building next door. And fitting sleep and family life into our madcap schedules only when we had to. It was like hanging onto the side of a freight train, and the most alive I've felt in my whole life.

The two of us always fitted each other like a glove. Me, in charge of the effects, the composition, the colour palette. Him, immersed in directing the actors and supervising the editing. Between us we evolved a kind of technical panache in rendering a dream-like universe of Good versus Evil that fans told us made our films special. And deeply Catholic. *Ha!* Some even call them poetic—but who am I to say? What is poetic about a Mayan Mummy, a Zombie Zorro, 'Professor Faceless', a reanimated Cave Man with a robotic claw? Or come to that, Sister Bloomsbury, our Sherlock Holmes of the occult, and her evil nemesis, the inevitable Coyote, who obeyed no chronological logic from film to film—dying in a vat of acid in one, reborn by a magic potion in the next. Seen dangling by a noose at the end of *El aullido del Coyote*, but yet to be bitten in its sequel, *Coyote en el museo de cera.*

Audiences didn't seem to mind.

They loved him—and I loved him too.

But don't get me wrong. The two of us didn't live in each other's pockets. In between productions, once we learnt to calm down the pace a little, we went back to our regular lives. Find out what our wives and children looked like again. Pepe married Elina, an actress and terrible flirt, during *¡Aleluyas para el demonio!* His first son was born during *La maldición de Señor Panico.*

I was quite aware that he could have got any make-up designer in the world to work on his films. Any number of more experienced special effects people would have been lining up around the block. But he never did. He wanted Beli to be partner on his creations: no one else.

It was the same thing on the phone, every time: "Do you want to come out to play?" And every time, I said sure. No one ever said no to Pepe. He was the same Pepe that I knew all those years ago with the short pants, the scabby knees, and the gap-toothed grin. You would do anything for that gap-toothed grin.

I could never refuse, even when I had more than enough work as an artist and illustrator, my own design studio, a dozen artists under me. I couldn't resist the temptation. I always wanted to play. The imagination is the most wonderful playground in the world. And he liked playing too.

On TV to publicise his latest film, say *Satánica*, or *Cementerio de los 1000 cadáveres*, he would say that not only did he believe in ghosts and supernatural forces, but, in fact, he could transform into a Coyote at will. (In private, of course!) He'd even show the scar on his back, just above his left shoulder blade, and say that was where a big, old, grey Coyote bit him when he was a child. I alone knew it was where he fell off a mud slide when we were playing John Wayne versus the flying saucers.

It got him fans, though. It got him girls, too.

One woman in Puerto Vallarta wrote to a newspaper to say he had visited her at night in the shape of Coyote. One in Mérida said she was made pregnant by him at the age of twelve, but Satanists had buried the baby. They could write any story they liked, those papers. Pepe would never deny it. He was happy to be the character they wanted.

That's why people were drawn to him. All kinds.

I think we were making *Carnaval en la isla de los monstruos* when the President let it be known, via his flunkies, that he wanted to visit the set. I wasn't keen on the idea. Pepe was more generous. Or cynical. "Listen, we want funding for our next picture, don't we?" So we greeted the President and gave him and his hangers-on a slap-up lunch, and treated them to a preview screening of *Aquiles y los 13 demonios*.

His lapdog, Luis Amato Muñoz, with that little black goatee perfumed overpoweringly with lavender, chattered all the way through, smoking his *cigarillos* and knocking back rum before falling asleep during the fourth reel. I didn't like the man before, and that didn't alter my perception. As Head of Police he was bombastic. Threw his weight around at the least provocation. And now he had more power in the bureaucracy he was even more of a moronic, ill-tempered toddler.

Our guests had photographs taken with Pepe giving a typical werewolf-like pose and the President grinning like a good sport. I shook his hand, but there was a bad taste in my mouth because I knew well that this same President hated the attacks by actors outspoken against his policies. Journalists, too, for that matter. Called them traitors to the people. Called them retards and homosexuals. Said they were not real men. That they were just walking around in the skins of men.

But we laughed at those jokes because he had his arms around our shoulders. And we were happy to accept invitations to his parties and banquets. As kids we'd been overjoyed to eat tasteless chicken if we were lucky. Now we saw more food being thrown out to the dogs than our families used to live on for an entire year. But Pepe succumbed to the idolatry. Told me to relax. He was comfortable with these people. These were the trappings of success, after all, and hadn't we both worked damned hard to get there?

One day he got a request to appear at General Muñoz's wedding ball. Two thousand of the odious faithful on one of the biggest private estates in Mexico City. The deal was, they wanted him in full Hombre Coyote make-up, bursting out of a cake in the shape of a gothic castle. I couldn't disguise my lack of enthusiasm. "Come on," said Pepe. "It will be fun." It was exactly that notion—of him being a figure of fun—that disturbed me, but I couldn't say so.

He exploded from the cake and the applause was rapturous. For a short while that seemed to be all that mattered. To him, anyway. The adoration.

Pretty soon José Camacho Mestre, the director, and General Muñoz were seen everywhere together—seizing every photo-opportunity to cement their friendship, enjoying dinner together at each other's mansions, nights on the town with their respective wives. Even vacationing with both sets of children. Sometimes I was asked along. As often as I could, I declined. As time went on, I wasn't asked any more. They became firm buddies, and that suited them both. Pepe introduced Muñoz to flashy and glamorous movie stars—male, and, more importantly, female. In return Muñoz ensured government funds went into Pepe's films. He never had to fill in a form again—or think of the missing wives, missing husbands, missing sons and brothers spirited off the streets.

"Who would have thought we would get here, eh?" he would say when we met, over coffee and cigarettes. I couldn't tell him the price I thought he was paying. I had to keep my lips firmly shut. Of course, nothing comes without strings attached in this world, as he was soon to find out.

Gradually the Department of Culture began asking for script changes—subtle ones at first, then more fundamental alterations, such as making Bill Tarquin a policeman. "What if Coyote clears undesirables from the streets? The homeless, drug addicts, cripples. The public will like that. *We* like that." They made it sound like a question, but, of course, it wasn't.

When I read the new draft, I said: "Pepe, the police are not the heroes. We always said Coyote is the beast on the inside that you cannot see. We want the audience to pity him, yes, but the beast is the enemy, not the hero."

"What does it matter?"

He pressed a fat cigar into my hand. He had a big house by now. A fortune. Nothing to worry about. He thought I envied that. I didn't.

He shrugged. "Poetry means many things."

"No, poetry can only mean the truth, my friend."

His eyes suddenly smouldered like hot coals. "You come here and eat my food and call me traitor and enemy?"

"I love you with all my heart. You do not understand."

"No—*you* do not understand," he said, drunkenly showing me the door. "Go. Get out!"

We did not talk again for years.

For the next film—*El fantasma del Coyote pálido*—I never got the phone call. Another make-up guy did it.

I had tears in my eyes as I watched the screen. Not for myself, but because there was no longer anything but blood lust in Coyote's eyes. An effeminate man is attacked by Coyote. A Jewish bank manager is attacked by Coyote. A hunchback is attacked by Coyote. And of course, women are ravaged by Coyote. And Coyote does not pay the price. Coyote lives. With blood on his lips.

The audience all round me clapped like crazy, just like the rich people at the wedding party. They stood and whooped and whistled, and I couldn't stand it. I had to leave. It sickened me. I stood alone in the alleyway next to the picture house mourning what we had left behind in our childhoods—that precious thing we could never get back.

In interviews on TV, Pepe refused to comment on the politics of the regime. He'd brush it aside and say he was there only to talk about monsters.

I switched it off. I couldn't bear to listen any more. I played with my children instead. We'd wrap towels around the kitchen table and I'd hide there, in the monster's lair, and jump out and make them shriek with laughter. I played make-believe.

The films came and went—*La marca del Coyote, La furia del Coyote, El Coyote de Londres*—I didn't even buy tickets any more. I knew what I would see, and it was too painful now.

Then everything changed.

Not everybody in Mexico City in the summer of 1968 was on the students' side. Never mind that everybody knew the government controlled everything—the television, the radio, the newspapers, cinema. Those rebellious hearts, to some, were the problem. How dare they overturn the status quo? How dare they shake things up? But it was the year of global revolt. The time was ripe for our country's youth to challenge the system.

In Mexico City hundreds of thousands took to the streets to demand more rights for trade unionists, the press, and the freedom of the individual. The reaction was exactly what was bound to be the reaction—the regime panicked. Drastically. Because it had no political answers, the only answer was violence. Soldiers took over the campuses. Thousands of young people were arrested and imprisoned on little or no evidence. In a blatant show of brute force, torture, shootings and random beatings were commonplace. Unrelenting.

It all culminated at a flash point in Cuervo Square, where thousands of demonstrators had congregated for the prestigious premiere of Pepe's new film, *Coyote contra la bruja.* His car could not get through. The screening was cancelled. Even so, as the crowd began to disperse, seizing the opportunity to quell a growing opposition movement, the police and soldiers let loose with machine guns and bayonet charges. Five hundred people were killed and many more wounded. On top of that, scores were arrested, many of whom were never seen again—purely as a lesson to the like-minded. And it was very quickly an open secret that it was General Luis Amato Muñoz who had given the order to open fire.

Outside the cinema hung a huge drape depicting Pepe in the film, his face twenty feet tall, giving the horrific impression that he was smiling as he presided over the massacre. Much as we had grown distant, I knew my friend would have felt sick in his guts at the sight.

I was there the next morning as he stood in the same square, bloodstains still on the cobblestones, policemen posted on the surrounding lawns, motorcycle cops situated under the shade of every tree.

He refused to screen the film, saying there had been enough horror. He pointed to those in the crowd he recognised, brave friends from the Centro Universitario de Estudios Cinematograficos, who had been there the night before. Young, innocent people had been shot down, he said. He talked of imagination and dreams, and the collective yearning of the people to share their hearts in stories, to *create* stories, and, when it is called on them, when they have nothing to fear, to create *history*. A huge roar went up.

There was a tremor in his voice, but nevertheless he rose it to a passionate cry. "I am not a hero. I am not you. I am a man. *You* are Coyote! You must howl!"

The wave of cheers was overwhelming, but the twitchy regime couldn't risk tipping the balance to revolution by a second slaughter. There was no coverage of the speech on TV. It was spread purely by word of mouth—people were talking of nothing else, and I was terrified.

I telephoned my friend immediately. "Pepe, what is going on? What you are saying is dangerous. Think of your family."

"Once upon a time you told me to think of the truth."

I tried to reason with him, but he wouldn't listen.

"The people have a howl inside their hearts," he said, "and they must let it out. The howl is our nature. Our birthright. You know Coyote. Coyote will bite."

But the grip of the PRI didn't wane, or buckle even a fragment. Through their tame media, it was reported that only twenty-one people died in Cuervo Square, and these were killed only because student "sharpshooters" had fired on government forces. It was obscene.

The students had been crushed. All hope of change eradicated. The government still owned the radio stations and newspapers. They could say, and do, what they wanted, with impunity and contempt, and went about reasserting their powers with even more viciousness.

When we met again, Pepe had lost weight, drastically. He had aged ten years, at least. I took his hand in mine and felt a tremor in it. I had to hold back a sob.

He said firmly he wanted me to do the creature make-up for his next film—*El Coyote de la morgue roja*. He'd done an outline, but we would write it together, the old way—the two of us in the same room, round the kitchen table, with bowls of *pozole* when the going got tough. "I want him to be fierce—more fierce than ever. Make me ugly! Make people despise me. I don't care what they think of me. I want it to be real!"

"You know you will never get funding from the authorities."

He smacked a fist forcefully against his own chest. "My authority is here."

We no longer saw him on national TV. The PRI weren't stupid enough to give him that platform. But he popped up in an interview in a subversive underground magazine: *Calavera*. Ostensibly about his coming picture, but really nothing of the sort. "There are monsters amongst us in human form," he was quoted as saying. "They have bullets but we have one thing—" and you saw him holding it up in the photograph, between his thumb and forefinger "—a silver bullet. This has magical powers. With this, we can defeat monsters."

The youth were behind him—taking the Silver Bullet as their symbol, even as his films were being banned for being morally corrupting. There was talk of Pepe running for president, clamped down quickly with accusations of sordid sexual activity with children to try and shut him up. He would not have been human if the prospect of a trial hadn't put immense stress on him, even though he knew it was all completely unfounded. He wouldn't be the first person to be jailed on a whim by a kangaroo court.

Which I'm sure is exactly what would have happened, had not Pepe disappeared weeks before the evidence was to be heard.

The official line was that, a coward and pervert, he had fled rather than face a guilty verdict. But I knew, as everyone else knew in their hearts, but could never say, that José Camacho Mestre, the famous director and my oldest friend, had been taken in for questioning, in 'La Casa Feliz'—The Happy House—the ironic nickname for the innocuous-looking concrete block where Luis Amato Muñoz presided over the interrogation of those who spoke out against the state.

It was rumoured that the General sometimes went there and watched the activities, as one might a live entertainment. Sometimes, the gossips said, he'd have expensive food delivered from his favourite restaurant, toss the chicken bones to his dog, and drink fine wine, while a political prisoner was beaten to a pulp before his eyes.

Sometimes he would take his lady friends, and get even more pleasure from their disgust.

Dozens, perhaps hundreds, of so-called agitators continued to languish in La Casa Feliz for years. Some were eventually released, mentally scarred and physically broken, but even thirty-two years later, when the PRI lost power and documents relating to the Cuervo Square outrage were declassified, the public were never given an answer to what happened to my friend.

During those intervening years, on the Day of the Dead, movie fans began making shrines to Coyote, with little artefacts in his image, and to light candles in honour and remembrance of their hero, José Camacho Mestre—my Pepe. I didn't need to light a candle to remember. The emptiness inside me reminded me every day.

As some recompense, it filled my heart with pride that our films regularly got screenings at festivals, or were put out on cable in the early hours of the morning for night owls. When I'd wake up at 4 a.m., like clockwork, I'd sometimes catch five or ten minutes of *La casa de la bestia,* or *Coyote contra las mujeres vampiro* before tears clouded my eyes and I'd have to flip channels.

Now hot shot directors, the new wave of Mexicans who seem to be taking over Hollywood, say they grew up watching the Hombre Coyote films. They're always talking about them having a special place in their hearts, and that gives me a pang in mine. It's humbling to think our crazy stories changed their lives. When fans get to their feet and tell me they were terrified for weeks after seeing one of our movies, and had to sleep with the light on, but it made them want to be a director—well, I'm not sure whether to say "Sorry" or "Thank you very much"—so I say both.

Sometimes I go back to Tilcajete, my home town—even though Pepe's father is long dead. The tradition of carving *alebrijes* survives, and now keeps the town flourishing—but I never see anything I want to buy. None of them have the magic, for me.

General Luis Amato Muñoz? He rose in importance in the party, applauded for liberal reforms as though there was no blood on his hands. Perhaps you remember—but you're probably not old enough—he came to England and was photographed next to Prime Minister Margaret Thatcher, both of them beaming for the camera lens. I'm happy to report that it was during that visit he died in a hotel room. We were never told the cause, but I hope it was in extreme agony.

And there, you would think, the story ends.

But no.

Here I am, in England myself.

Ten weeks ago I was watering my roses. Chasing my great grandchildren with a watering can. Sizing up a new pair of slippers. Next thing I know, I'm being phoned by a big producer in Los Angeles, asking me to fly to the UK to work on a big budget creature feature.

I say: "Wait a minute. You know I'm eighty-four years old? If I was on a supermarket shelf, they would say the produce is ready to go in the trash."

"No, no," they say. "The director doesn't want anybody else. He wants you!"

So, would you believe it? Abelino Ortiz gets dragged out of retirement by this tyro visionary who knows all the Coyote films back to front, and quotes me lines I can't even remember I wrote. But there's a sparkle in his eyes and it reminds me of the sparkle we had. And he wants to revive—what's the word?—*reboot* Coyote for the modern audience.

Incredible!

Not with any of that CGI nonsense either, he told me, waving his hands excitedly. "That's the take the studio bought into, and were real excited about. We're going to use genuine physical prosthetics and make-up, done the old-fashioned way."

I opened my arms in an embrace. "I'm your man."

The truth is, it wasn't just the flattery. I wanted to feel the wax and putty under my fingertips, the dry powder of the make-up in my nostrils.

But there was another reason, too.

The production company booked me into a five-star hotel on Piccadilly where they normally put Americans, because Americans like its fusty grandeur and air of subservient pomposity. I politely requested them to move me—to the King George Hotel, just a short walk away. I asked for room 416, if that was possible. It was the room in which Muñoz last drew breath.

I knew it was a long shot. I thought, superstitiously, that if it's already occupied, then fine. Fate is telling me this isn't to be. But it wasn't occupied. It was free.

To my disappointment, I expected it to have some kind of atmosphere I would pick up on when I entered, but it didn't.

The chirpy young porter who showed me where the light switches and the mini-bar were located was a mixed race Londoner. He picked up on my accent and asked if I was Spanish. He'd been on vacation, once, to Ibiza. He perked up when he heard I was from Mexico and said there was an elderly gentleman working at the concierge desk: Oswaldo—*he* was from Mexico. "Been here since the year dot." I thought it was a delightful expression. I smiled and gave the boy a generous tip—probably too generous, since I still found the foreign currency baffling.

After he had gone, without unpacking my suitcase, I went straight downstairs to the concierge desk. I had no difficulty in spotting Oswaldo since he couldn't have looked more Mexican if he'd been strumming a guitar like a member of a *mariachi* band. His hair was silver but his moustache jet black, waxed and teased to points in the style of Salvador Dalí.

I introduced myself and entered into some small talk, joking about the forthcoming so-called wall with the USA, at which he rolled his eyes and said: "They're not building a wall around Great Britain. Not yet, anyway!" Our shared Hispanic heritage having been suitably declared, a natural bond was formed which I had no hesitation in exploiting. I told him I was booked into Room 416, and watched the good-natured expression on his face vanish.

He told me he was a porter that very night. I pressed him. He became nervous and said he couldn't talk about it now, but his shift ended at 11 p.m. and he could speak about it then, if I wanted to. I said I would be in the bar.

Sure enough, soon after eleven, with the bar virtually empty, he turned up, dressed smartly but out of uniform. I offered to buy him a drink but he declined, and rattled on about so many other subjects I thought we'd never get to the one I was interested in. In the end I asked him outright what had happened that night.

"A human being could not have done such a thing," he said. I asked what he meant, but he backtracked, shaking his head, shrugging. "They said a woman of the night, perhaps. Her pimp, somehow . . . A dispute over money . . . Who knows?" I could tell he didn't believe a word of what he was saying. "The maids . . . the sheets, they said . . . they had to burn."

I asked him what it was that a human being couldn't have done? Had he seen the body?

Oswaldo did not answer. Only shook his head again. I asked a second time if he wanted a drink, a stiff brandy perhaps? He said no. No, he had to be getting home. But he leaned forward, hesitating, rocking, as if there was more to say. And indeed there was.

There was one strange thing he could not get out of his head. It was probably nothing. It was probably his imagination. He was working very long hours in those days. And night work did funny things to your head after a while. But that same night—even before anyone had reported the General's death—he happened to be travelling up in the elevator from the kitchens, delivering room service to the fifth floor. He remembered being irritated when it stopped at every floor, and on the fourth floor it stopped and he pressed the button madly for the doors to close but before they did, and only for a split-second, he was sure he saw a stray dog wandering the corridor. *A stray dog in a four-star hotel! Imagine!* A bit like a German Shepherd—but skinnier. Longer-legged, bigger ears, more pointed snout. And yellow eyes. He remembered distinctly the yellow eyes.

Oswaldo blinked furiously, as if snapping out of a dream, and delved into one of his jacket pockets.

"I've carried it with me ever since. I don't know why. One of the housemaids found it on the night stand." He placed a silver bullet in the palm of my hand. I rolled it around, then picked it up and reached over to hand it back to him, but he backed away with his palms up. "Take it. I never wanted it in the first place.

But I couldn't throw it away. I didn't know what to do with it. Now I do."

Minutes later I was sitting alone.

I trudged to the elevator. It took me back to my room, after randomly opening its doors to empty corridors. I pulled the drapes. I heard only the sound of bottles being heaved into a dumpster behind the hotel and a small dog yapping. I lay on the bed fully clothed, drifting in and out of sleep before I got up and undressed properly. The heat in the room was cranked up and I tried to override the settings on the wall unit but couldn't turn it down. I've always found hotel rooms unbearably hot and oppressive, and this was no exception. Naked, I lay with my cheek against the pillow, the tiny red light of the smoke detector in the ceiling reflected in the silver surface of the bullet I'd placed on end on my night stand. I closed my eyes and went to sleep instantly, or thought I did.

I woke to the sound of a distant, mournful howl. Something not of the city but of some desolate, arid place. There was an emptiness within it. No sooner had it died out than it was taken up by another, far off, equally long and drawn out, as if in reply—then a third from a different direction. This one still hung in the night air as a police car siren pierced the melody—always an unwelcome sound in my home country, guaranteed to get my heart racing—and I sensed blood in my nostrils which I thought was a nosebleed caused by the stuffiness of the room.

I opened my eyes, finding my lips stuck together by the dryness as if by glue.

An unclothed figure with cuts all over his back stood at the foot of my bed. As he turned to face me, I saw he had a hole the size of a button in the side of his skull, and, in place of ears, bloody cavities. Pepe's hair was thick with a gore the consistency of molasses. Impossibly thin arms hung at his sides, blood dripping from his fingertips. I instinctively feared for the carpet, knowing at the same time that such concerns were absurd. Smoke rose from his groin and chest, surrounding him in an acrid blue-grey fog not unlike cigarette smoke. Behind such a veil, I could see pale skin covered in purple and red bruises, blackening in patches, as if becoming vacant of light. Something thick and shining and red, which was not a tongue, hung from his mouth.

I clicked on the light beside my bed. With difficulty I parted my lips and began to breathe. The brightness of the bulb blinded me temporarily and as I gazed around the bedroom, the ghost of it followed my vision. But I was alone. I sat up. I stood up. I was alone.

I know what you are thinking. I know what you want to ask me.

Why did he appear to me?

Why is he not at rest?

If he achieved his revenge, my beloved Pepe, why is he an unquiet spirit? And this I must tell you.

You see, that night, that moment, when I woke, or dreamed, and saw him at the foot of my bed—then I knew what I must do.

I knew why I had come all this way. Why he had brought me here.

That was the way the regime worked, you see . . . They did not need special people to do their black deeds. They only needed *people*. Ordinary people. Ordinary people are capable of extraordinary things.

They say, come in, help us with our little problem. They say, look, this person went against the state. You don't approve of that, do you? Of course you don't. You are on our side. We know you are.

The thing is, they say, sucking their teeth as if it's an embarrassment, if you do not do it to this prisoner of ours, then, well, we will have to do worse to your family. To your wife. To your children. And you don't want that, do you?

Come on, hurt your friend, Abelino, or we will hurt you. Understand?

Deliver more pain than you can imagine to this despicable sack of shit, or we will deliver more pain than you can imagine to your loved ones. It's as simple as that. You don't even have to think of it too much, do you? Of course not.

And, of course, they tell you that the so-called human being in front of you will die anyway, whether you do it or not. So it doesn't really matter. The outcome is the same. It's just about saving your family from harm. From pain. From horror. And isn't that what a husband and father does?

And so . . . you do it.

You pick up the torture instruments. They're not so heavy or strange as you expect. They are tools like any other tools. Like the tools in your workshop. You try not to tell yourself any different. You use them. You use them well. And when he screams—when he *howls*—you block your ears. Very quickly you do not hear it any more. Because it isn't your best friend. It isn't the little boy you played with in the dust with toy soldiers and wind-up tin cars. And it isn't you.

You remove his fingernails. Still he gives you no names. No co-conspirators. You whip his body with a leather belt. You lash his back with a garden rake. The hours pass. The days. You still don't get any names out of him. You apply electricity to his balls and his nipples. The smell of burning, it's not so different from a barbecue. You smoke a cigarette or three while he recovers his senses, while someone else takes over for a while. You take a break for a meal. It's tiring. You slice his ears off. Fry them on a griddle and feed them to him while Muñoz watches. It's no longer about the names. It was never about the names. Muñoz tells you to cut off the prisoner's penis and stuff it into his mouth, then put a bullet in his brain.

You do it.

And so, you know now . . . what brought me to England. *Fate.*

Fate, and the brilliant young director out there on the lot right now looking at his watch, who once sat in the dark of a cinema back home and fell in love with El Hombre Coyote.

And here we are.

Almost ready for the camera.

The finishing touches, now, on the skin, the eyelids—grey, saffron, burnt umber—that make all the difference in extra close-up. And even though we have the long, ribbed nose and the jutting upper lip and lower jaw, I think it's important to keep the skin bare in the centre of the face, because I always want the expressions of the actor to show through. That's my duty. To help you, not to hinder you. To enable you to fully believe you are the character, inside and out.

Same principle with the hands—which I never touch. Something Pepe and I decided very early on. No fur, no claws. A constant visual reminder of the beast's human side.

A spray of water and a last bit of teasing here and there to get the fur on the collar bone and neck looking natural, combing the hair on the face into the hair on the appliances, blending it all together to make it truly effective and animalistic. There . . .

Lower dentures. Never the canines for a werewolf! Perfect!

The old Coyote, brought back to life. Not everybody likes pointed ears on a werewolf, but I always do, personally. And that's it . . .

Finally, the all-important contact lenses. In the old days they could only stay in for ten minutes or they'd become painful. Soft lenses, they can stay in forever.

Ah, uncomfortable, I know, as I pop them in. But blink a little. That's it. Eke out a few tears, and it won't be so bad.

The world looks a shade of yellow, yes? That's how Coyote sees it.

You see as he sees.

You look as he looks.

You feel as Coyote feels.

The mirror looks back at you. His spirit is your spirit. When I look at your reflection I know my job is done, and I know that my Pepe is dead no more.

Beli and Pepe are together again. As was meant to be.

My brushes and powder and grease paint have made the transformation complete. I have rendered the marks on your skin. I have furnished you with labyrinths and butterflies. The *copal* is in your veins. Our shared history is running through you. And soon it will explode as Coyote's true nature always explodes when the scene is set.

In the mirror surrounded by light bulbs I see your chest rising and falling, pumping like bellows. I see your lips pulling back from fangs layered in an animal's saliva. The grunting growl of the creature within is like music already, building, building—a slow rising melody I have missed, I have craved, with an ache in my heart, for too many years.

But now I am ready, *amigo mío, Coyote*.

I am prepared to feel your human fingers on my throat. Your teeth buried into my neck. I have no fear of your mouth tearing the sinews from my gizzard, biting at my face and shoulder, pawing the innards out of my belly, ripping off my flailing arms and perching on my fallen body as my blood fountains across the walls of the dressing room.

I have unchained the beast, and I am happy, at last.

Now, before those youngsters come knocking, bidding us to come to the set—howl, my friend. I know the sound wishes to escape from your body. It is ready to burst like a volcano from your throat and chill my heart. Do not hold back. Come, I would like it to fill my ears, one last time.

Howl! *Howl!*

Outside of Truth or Consequences

SHIT.

Fry's foot was glued down, and would have stayed that way, unaffected by the meteor storm of flies that impacted the windshield, except for the red icon that began flashing at him from the dash. Casting an urgent glance in the rear view mirror, he saw the highway stretching behind him across the pale, oven-baked desert. Not a car in sight. Nobody to pull in and help him if he flagged them down. No lone traveller to club over the head and steal their vehicle. Nothing.

Irony was, up till a second before, he'd begun to bliss out, shit-eating grin bisecting his face as the realisation had set in that he'd left the cops, scratching their asses, way behind. He hadn't seen hide or hair of a highway patrol car since he crossed the state line. They were off his tail, if they were ever on it. He'd begun—just *begun*—to think he was free.

Damn.

Smile wiped away like the dead insects on the glass in front of him, he kept driving, hoping to see some sign of life. Joke. Nearest thing to life out here was a gopher hole. What made him think he would suddenly come across civilisation? Not that he'd want civilisation, normally. Fry wasn't big on civilisation. But then, civilisation wasn't crazy about him.

The sun was sinking its big bald head behind the mesa and the red light was still winking when he got to who-knows-where. He had no map, but knew he was on I-25, south of Truth or Consequences, New Mexico. Remembered passing the big, green CITY LIMIT sign. ELEV. 4260. Avoiding Exit 79 to stay on the Interstate—SOUTH. You bet. And he couldn't get there fast enough—Las Cruces, then El Paso and the Mexican border. He'd hoped to be there by sundown, but it was sundown now and he was out of gas.

The heat from his hood made the truck stop shimmer like a mirage.

As he pulled over the sand-encrusted Toyota—he'd dumped the laundry truck ('Kleen' with a 'K' emblazoned on the side) as soon as he left Rawlings, and the Chevy Impala a hundred miles later—a slim figure in blue jeans and white T-shirt rushed out of the shadows and kept pace with his vehicle in a sort of sideways shuffling run. He looked about fifteen but his behaviour put him at five. The boy had a crew cut at the front and mullet at the back—deadly combo—and eyes that fixated on the wheels front and back as if musing on their function, never having been witness to such things before, till they stopped turning and Fry applied the brake, at which point the youth stood up from his hunched position, head tilted, and backed away, arms hanging limp.

"Earth."

Fry couldn't make out the word real clearly, so unwound the window.

"Earth. Earth."

Fry climbed out of the car, expecting communication to be forthcoming, but the boy moved away. Jittery. Clearly some sort of mental defective.

He looked over to the door of the shop, through which the boy disappeared at speed, and sighed, while simultaneously taking in the sight of a Coca-Cola vending machine with a plastic garden chair next to it, upon which lay a dog, snoozing, on a cushion.

"You running this place?" said Fry, the sound of which made the dog sit up and yawn. A Parson Russell terrier, as far as Fry could tell. White, with brown ears and tail, and a brown patch around one eye. Old, scuzzy, and by no stretch of the imagination cute. Folded over the arm of the chair lay a book and, as he came closer, Fry could read the spine; 'Dickens'. *Dick.* It told him someone must be around, though. Butthead in the T didn't look like he read anything without pictures.

"Hello!"

No answer. He didn't like the way the dog was staring at him.

"What are you fucking looking at, flea bag?"

Stretching his aching shoulders, Fry suddenly felt the heaviness of the heat prickle his skin after the air-conditioned bubble of his vehicle.

He walked to the pump. Saw it was covered in a thick layer of yellow dirt. A small sign read ATTENDANT SERVICE ONLY.

He grunted and took the spout to his gas tank, impatiently yanking the trigger. The tube gobbled and coughed, but nothing emerged. Not a solitary dribble. He moved over to the second, but before he could get there a voice came from the building roofed with ancient corrugated iron.

"Didn't see the sign, friend?"

Fry looked up. A man stood on the steps. Glasses held in place by the wrinkles either side of his sunburnt nose. Polka dot suspenders over a white wifebeater holding up elephant-coloured pants with tartan slippers at the end of them. The grey hairs sprouting from his chest much thicker and longer than the wiry fuzz on his scalp. Guy should have a fucking transplant, Fry thought.

"Your attendant done skedaddled."

The man scratched his unshaven chin with the screwdriver in his hand and used it to point. Backaways stood a plate of metal with the words NO GAS hand-painted. So large Fry had missed it. He'd had other things on his mind. Like getting the fuck out of Dodge.

"This is a gas station, ain't it?" He still wrestled with the second pump and found it as bone dry as the first.

"Yes, and no."

Fry dropped the nozzle to the sand and kicked it like he'd wanted to kick the dog.

"Third one's empty too," said the proprietor. "Kick that one if it'll make you feel any better."

"Late delivery, huh?"

"Haven't had a delivery in ten years now."

"Ten *years?*" Fry laughed. "Must do a roaring trade out here, man."

"That's the way I like it."

Fry decided not to argue. "No problem. Like, you've got to have a supply or something? For personal use? For emergencies?"

"Not a drop."

"You're kidding me." Fry reeled in the anger he felt rising. He needed to keep a check on that. Didn't need it. Not yet anyhow. "Okay. Maybe I could drain some from your own tank?"

"Could. Except I haven't got one."

"Tank?"

"Car."

"I could pay. I have money," Fry said. *But not much.* The driver he'd left in a ditch with a stove-in skull'd had a wallet. But only twenty in cash and he wasn't going to use the credit cards. The cops find you that way.

"You got a hearing problem, son? I said I don't have one."

Fry took a deep breath. Frowned. "Lemme get this . . . You haven't got a *car*?"

"Don't believe in 'em."

Fry laughed. "*Believe* in 'em?"

"You have an invention. It can do good, or it can do bad. The automobile, well—everybody thought it was doing good. But guess what? We find out it's doing bad."

All Fry was thinking was his Plan B had just gone out of the window—taking the old guy's own mode of transport and dumping the Toyota round back. Thinking, how many hours or days before the bodies of an old man and a teenager get discovered? He was no good at math, but these kinds of calculations came easy.

"Listen, man. I'm really running on empty. How far's the nearest town?"

"Too far if you're out of gas. You want me to call for a pick-up? I've got a phone." Said like it was an achievement.

"No," said Fry emphatically. *Shit, a little too emphatically.* He could just see him and a pick-up driver who'd just happened to see his mug shot on the evening news and he'd be back behind bars in Wyoming State Pen quicker'n he could fart. "No, sir . . . Look, I've been driving ten, eleven hours straight and I'm bushed. Any way I can stay here tonight? I'll pull my vehicle round back and sleep in it. I don't care."

The gas station man looked him up and down. Fry wore the laundryman's white overalls which fitted badly—tight across his broad shoulders from years of working out in the prison gym. "You also could use a shower."

Fry laughed, while thinking: *You bastard, I could cut your lousy throat and you wouldn't know till you ate your Cheerios.*

"It gets cold in the desert at night. Guy could freeze to death. You can have a sleeping bag on the couch. I'll phone Jim Shulz to drop off a five gallon can when he goes by in the morning. How far are you heading? South?"

"All the way."

"Steenburg. Don't promise to be great company."

Fry shook the older man's hand. "Pete Bennett," he said. "Me neither."

The room back of the store and pay desk was surprisingly comfortable-looking. No sign of a female touch, Fry noticed. No floral patterns. No ornaments. Copies of *Scientific American* hoarded on towers. Plates in the sink from yesterday, or the day before. Steenburg told him the water was hot enough to run a shower, which was outside. Fry stood under it, letting the water scrape off the sweat and grime of his long drive. Afterwards he shaved, using a razor that was sitting beside a broken triangle of mirror. Stared at himself, that hard jaw revealed as the stubble came off, those deep-set eyes that gave him away, beard or no beard. The face on the pig files, the FBI, in some cloud of data now for eternity. The face he hated. He wished he could shave it away too, but he was stuck with it, just like he was stuck with his life, his past, and murder.

Fry wrapped a robe around himself and returned inside to find, to his surprise, that his laundryman whites were spinning inside a washing machine. "I'll be damned," he said.

Steenburg impressed him further by producing two cans of Coors from a large refrigerator. Fry drank eagerly and felt the beer easing those tightened muscles, and when Steenburg said that food was on the way, he called him a gold-plated godsend.

"Nothing fancy," Steenburg said, noticing that Fry was fiddling with the knobs of an old radio set. "Purely decorative. Don't believe in radio or TV either."

"Good," said Fry, meaning it. If this was a news-free zone, that made him happy.

"Whu?"

"All that violence and crime . . . Ain't good for people." Fry was glad to see the old man nod in agreement before disappearing to the kitchen.

Alone with his Coors, he looked around the room. Next to a small work-table littered with electronic gear was a small, homemade desk light and next to that a framed photograph of Steenburg and family. Steenburg's wife—of which there was zero evidence in the present—and the weird kid Fry had seen outside, in the picture aged no more than four or five. Looking bright eyed and boisterous in his mother's arms. The bookshelves—bookshelves in a gas station!—had titles like*: Rebirth as Doctrine and Experience, Electronic Death and Eternal Life, Where Is the Soul?* and *Mystery and*

Mastery of Mind: The Science of Electro-Biology. Fry took down this one and had just time to notice the author's name—Steenburg—before a noise made him turn.

Jesus.

The strange boy sat at the table, pulling the chair in under him, avoiding his eyes and panting eagerly. It gave Fry the chills. Made him feel uncomfortable. Fucking child being a vegetable. *God damn. Good looking boy like that . . . what a fucking waste.*

Steenburg's voice came above the sound of frying bacon. "Harl, set the table."

The boy stood up abruptly and made for the cutlery drawer, tongue active as he used every ounce of concentration. He brought out the knives and forks and set three places, one in front of Fry, who watched with morbid fascination, trying to give the kid a smile, but it came across as a nervous twitch. What was he doing in this fucking nut hatch with a loopy old man and a retard? He tried to smile again and hoped the kid couldn't see through the falseness of it.

Harl had gotten the knives and forks the wrong way round, so when Steenburg emerged he had to re-set the places. Then in came the rashers and potatoes, and Fry sat and ate, but he couldn't take his eyes off the boy, to whom the task of using the eating irons seemed almost impossible. Occasionally his father would lean over and guide a forkful of potato to his son's mouth like baby food, and Fry would pretend not to watch the jaws mashing its contents. The additional spectacle of the kid lifting up the strands of meat in his hands to chew on with his side teeth while bacon fat dribbled down his fingers was even more delightful to behold. But Fry dropped his fork when the boy suddenly shot over to the window, pressing his nose to the glass.

"Gophers," Steenburg explained, though Fry had heard nothing and could see nothing but the blackness of night. "Kid loves his wildlife. Don't you, chips?" The man handed his son a pair of binoculars positioned nearby, but the kid didn't take them and instead went to play with the dog in its pile of blankets next to the fire, where he lay down and snuggled up with his pet. "He likes sleeping there."

"A boy and his dog, huh?"

"Inseparable," said Steenburg, and it wasn't long before both were sleeping and snoring.

When he and Steenburg moved over to a pair of moth-eaten armchairs, and Fry felt they were alone, he said: "I'm sorry about your kid."

The old man just thought a moment, gave a weak shrug.

"How'd it happen?" asked Fry. "Born like it, I guess."

Steenburg said nothing.

Even Fry, whose strong point was never his sensitivity, realised it was time to change the subject. "Family business?"

Steenburg shook his head. "Bought it. Sold up out East. Wanted to get away. Leave my old world behind me. Concentrate on . . ." He paused. "A gas station with no gas. It appealed to me." He gauged Fry's features. "I'm not a hermit. I'm not a recluse."

"You're a scientist."

"Was."

"All the books. I knew there was no way you were a regular gas station man!" Fry gulped his beer, chuckling. "Never met a scientist before. Most I ever met was a grocery store clerk." He thought of the Turkish guy he'd shot and robbed. He didn't know why he thought of that but he did.

"You can lose your job, just like a grocery store clerk. Believe you me."

"After writing books and shit? How come?" Fry wasn't sure what he was getting out of this, except alcohol. But that was fine. Keep it coming.

"Nobody listened. Nobody wanted their fingers burned. It was hard to convince anybody of the commercial applications of something that could potentially change the world."

"Guess Thomas Edison had the same problem," said Fry.

"Guess he did."

Fry's can was empty. He asked if his host wanted another. Steenburg said no, but he could go help himself. While Fry was in the kitchen, Steenburg went on talking, but Fry didn't take in a word. He wondered how long he could listen to an old man's life story, but for now, boredom was a small price to pay for a bed for the night. When he returned, and reached to switch off the light, he saw a small, shiny key on a string hanging from a hook beside the door.

"Man's a very arrogant species," Steenburg was saying when Fry came back in. Fry figured he probably had a lot to say after ten years without seeing a soul. "Just because we understand the questions doesn't mean we can understand the answers. What gives us the inherent right to knowledge?"

"Beats me," said Fry. "So you gave up? Just like that?"

"Not just like that."

"So what do you do now?"

"Look after my son, Harley. That's a full time occupation. I write. I write a letter to the National Science Foundation every week. Apprise them of my thoughts. Only the important thoughts, of course. Not the run of the mill ones."

"Wow," Fry thought, and said.

"I c.c. the President and the Dalai Lama. For obvious reasons . . . Also I turn people away from the pumps when they discover they're emptier than a witch's brassiere. That provides amusement from time to time."

"I'm glad to hear it," said Fry. *You insane fuck.* "Good health."

"Anyhow, I've got enough cash put away I don't have to worry."

Fry raised the can to his lips and thought: *You stupid sonofabitch. Don't you realise what you're telling me? Don't you know when to keep your fucking trap shut?*

That night, Fry slept on the couch Steenburg offered, right there where they'd sat and talked. He gave him an hour or two to get to sleep, observing the doofus and his mangy dog curled up like lovers next to the fire, gone to the world.

Fry unzipped the sleeping bag inch by inch, sat up and took out the dead driver's wallet. Flicked it open, the guy's photograph smiling up at him. Twenty lousy dollars. He was running as dry as those fucking pumps. But this nut job just might be crazy enough to think about banks the way he thought about cars and television. He might, just *might,* be loco enough to put his faith in hard cash.

Careful not to wake boy or mutt, Fry got up, pulled on his pants and went on tiptoe to the kitchen. He didn't need to put on the light. He knew if he snaked his hand in he could lift the key off the hook. Then the fucking question was, what did it unlock? He gazed around the room. Tried the desk drawer. Keyhole didn't match. The closet in the corner? No dice there either. Then he saw it . . . the door under the stairs.

Zachary Thelonius Fry, this is your lucky day.

He carefully—quietly—inserted the key into the hole. It slid in without effort.

Hallelujah, brother.

Fry eased the door open. Reached in, tentatively feeling around for a switch. He wanted the light when it came on to reveal a set of shelves, hopefully with a big tin box labelled with a glow-in-the-dark dollar sign, but was disappointed. Instead, it lit up steep-sloping wooden stairs to the basement below.

The ceiling was low, and in spite of the single naked bulb—Fry thought of Edison again—surprisingly gloomy. He looked back, thinking he'd heard the ankle-biter chasing cats in its sleep. But no—silence.

Along one wall was a rack to which were attached multifarious tools, and on a workbench various banks of electrical equipment gathering dust. In the centre, some bulky thing stood under heavy white dust sheets. Which Fry tugged at, then flung back.

Fuck.

He had no doubt he was looking at a fucking electric chair. *Old Sparky.* Thick metal arms, straps, bolts, and a skullcap—metal—with its frizzy wire terminals leading to what looked like a massive generator.

"What the *hell?*" said a voice which could have been Fry but wasn't.

He turned to see Steenburg coming down the steps, shotgun in his hands.

"What the hell do you think you're doing?"

"What do *I* think *I'm* fucking doing! You're the one with Death Row in your basement!" Fry's voice had gone up several octaves even as he raised his hands in the air. "Jesus!"

"Explain yourself."

"I was looking for the john. I needed a pee. The door was open—"

"Liar. What were you looking for? Money?"

"Listen, mister . . ."

"Don't 'listen mister' me. This is a private residence. You have abused my hospitality. I want you to get out. Now!"

"What is this? Some kind of house of fucking horrors?"

"No."

"Then what? You some kind of sick fucking torture porn—?"

"Get out!"

"Electrocuting dudes?"

"*No!* . . . You don't understand."

Fry could see that the man's hands were shaking. He didn't think he'd pull the trigger but he wanted him to put the shotgun down, just in case a nervous fucking twitch splattered his brains over the wainscoting.

"Try me."

Fry lowered his hands.

The gun barrel drooped slightly. Steenburg descended the steps and moved nervously round the chair with the shotgun in the crook of his arm, peeling the remaining dust sheet from the rest of the machinery, to reveal that there were two identical chairs with a generator—or something that *looked* like a generator—between them. It had big valves and switches, coils and meters, a jigsaw of machinery raided from microwaves, washing machines, TV sets and God-knows-what.

Fry stared at it in stark, unadorned wonder. "So what fucking Boris Karloff movie did this shit come from?"

Steenburg offered no reaction. Simply stroked the dull metal with distaste. "I didn't tell you the whole story," he said. "Don't like to. People get the wrong idea."

"What's the right idea?"

"You don't want to know."

That was true—but Fry did want to survive this in one piece. Self-preservation was something he valued above all things. And pretending he gave a shit might be the way to do that.

"Maybe I do," he said. "Maybe there was a reason I arrived here tonight. For you to tell me."

"Tell you what? The story of my success?" Steenburg laughed bitterly. "Goulstone and Benedetti were idiots. They wanted to go down the route of magnetic nanoparticles. Which was bullshit. I returned to my real training. Bio-electrics. The high-ups didn't like what I was saying. What I was getting published. Said it 'reflected badly'. I lost my tenure. But when I left, I took it with me."

"You walked out with this in a fucking cardboard box?"

"Carried it all up here." Steenburg tapped the side of his head. "Came to this place to continue my experiments. Experiments I knew could revolutionise the way we think about life and death." Steenburg leaned against the machinery, blowing off the dust and buffing it up like a car salesman with his Buy of the Week. "The Limbic System. Heard of it?"

"Fuck, no."

"Fuck, no," Steenburg echoed the phrase with a faint smile. "In the brain, right here." He drilled a finger into a spot on his cranium. "We were doing research into OOBEs. Out-of-body experiences. You know, when people at the moment of death find themselves looking down at their own bodies."

Fry clicked his fingers. "Saw that on TV. *Unsolved Mysteries.*"

"Yeah, well. I wouldn't know. We found that NDEs—Near Death Experiences, if you will—often involve sensations of blinding light, glowing people, angels, however people interpret it. Tracking this sensation with magnetic resonance techniques, we found it rooted in the limbic system of the brain."

"No shit."

"Yes shit. Yes *indeed* shit," said Steenburg. "And I was interested in the prospect of the limbic system being connected to our idea of a so-called soul—and if that's connected to the sensation of light, then it might be possible to shock the limbic system with a flooding of light. Literally *galvanise* the soul into motion and transport it."

"The fuck outa here."

Steenburg carried on, as if Fry hadn't spoken. "What we were trying to achieve, what this *machine* was trying to achieve, was complete electrical and controllable TMS. Transmigration of the Soul."

Fry was silent for a few long moments as it took a while to sink in. Then he began to laugh. Long and hard. He pointed a finger at Steenburg as if to acknowledge that he knew he was being taken for a ride and the penny had at last dropped. The old guy wasn't Richard Pryor, but that was a good gag, man—and it almost had him going.

But Steenburg's face remained stony.

"And it *worked*,' he said, which was when Fry stopped laughing. "Why d'you think those morons at Harvard threw me out? Not because I wasn't getting anywhere. The place is full of guys who never get anywhere on million dollar budgets and that's fine. No, they got rid of me because I *did* it." Just then there was a creak on the stairs, and Steenburg half-turned and saw his fifteen-year-old son standing motionless but trembling, framed by the doorway to the basement. "Nothin's happening here, son. You go on back to bed."

Fry watched the old man walk back to the foot of the stairs, where the kid clung to his arm, then looked at the contraption that dominated the basement, laboratory, whatever the fuck it was. It frightened him, the brushed metal, those tiny dials he didn't understand, they all looked so convincing. So *real.* What really frightened him was that something deep in his gut told him it wasn't a bunch of stage props stolen from *Young Frankenstein* on Broadway. It was a big feeling, but even if it had been a small feeling, a tiny feeling, it would have been worth it. Worth the chance.

Before the old man knew it, the shotgun was in Fry's hands and pointed back at him.

"Let me get this straight. This thing, this machine, it shifts—it *migrates* the soul from one human being to another, yeah?"

"Soul, spirit, essence, the exactly scientific terminology—"

"Shut the fuck up. Does it or doesn't it?"

"Yes."

"So it can take my mind, and put it in another person's fucking head. Is that right? So I'm the same person—all my memories and thoughts and shit—but in another body?"

"That's correct."

"No side effects, nothing?"

"No side effects. Except it's irreversible. The subjects can't return to their original hosts. Something in the math. I learned that the hard way. Too fast off the mark. Arrogance. Never for a moment considering—"

"Okay," said Fry. "Let's do this."

Steenburg looked up, went ashen. “That’s not possible.”

“The fuck it’s not possible. You said it worked. Don’t fucking lie to me!”

“It works all right, but nothing in God’s earth is going to make me pull that switch.”

“I’m not fucking asking you, I’m telling you!”

“Asking or telling,” the old man said, as he heard his son’s frightened whimpering and felt his fingers tightening on his sleeve. “The answer’s still the same. Now get out of here.”

Fry thrust the end of the shotgun closer to Steenburg’s face. “Do it.”

“I told you. That’s not possible. You really do have a hearing problem.”

“And you have a dying problem. You think I won’t? I have. Don’t mean nothing to me. Two bodies in a basement.”

Steenburg stiffened. But a stiffness, initially of fear, become one of resolve. “My wife made me promise that I’d never use that machine again and I honoured that promise all her life. I made it to her again the day she died. I did something she’d never forgive me for and if I could turn the clock back, I would, but I can’t. She asked me with her dying breath, and that’s a good enough reason to me, and why it sits here in the basement, covered up.”

“I don’t give a shit.”

“Cancer. Ate her away to so much bones and vomit.”

“I said I don’t give a shit.”

“No, you don’t—but that’s the way it is.”

“And you’re going to die on that fucking hill?” Fry grabbed the kid with his loose hand and before Steenburg could blink he was looking at the shotgun held under his son’s chin. “Your boy’s a real handsome feller. Cryin’ shame he’s lacking so much up top. We’ll have to do something about that, huh?”

“You’re no murderer.”

“Yes, I am.”

"Then you know there's two ways to go and one way is for you to walk out the door."

"Choices? I never had 'em. Not gonna start now."

"Life is the way you make it."

"Exactly, padre. And I'm going to make mine the way I want it. How d'you like that, Dr Einstein? All your work has not been in vain. Now let's cut the chat and get it done. Come on!"

Fry saw Steenburg stare at the floor, hunched like a mannequin. When he looked up his bleary eyes were suddenly stone cold.

"What do you want me to do?"

"Use your *fucking* imagination. I want to swap bodies with your son. He can have this one. He's welcome to it. And I can be a young man with the whole world ahead of me."

Steenburg parted his dry lips. "That's obscene."

"And you can feed this ugly mug mashed potato for the rest of your days. And his. How d'you like them apples, professor?"

"I have no choice, do I?"

"No you fucking do not." Fry jerked the shotgun up into the soft flesh under the U of the teenager's jaw bone.

In silence, Steenburg paced to the central bank of the generator, and cranked the motor. It howled like the engine of a John Deere Gator. In a few seconds the dials were twitching and the bulb filaments glowed. From the batteries came a deep, mellifluous hum. Fry's hand became sticky on the hilt of the shotgun. He thought the young 'un would panic and make a bolt for it, but he didn't. He didn't do anything but emit an incessant, low-level whimpering. Luckily the soundtrack of electricity drowned it out. Probably a blessing he didn't know what fate was about to befall him, thought Fry. A skittering from the stairs made him stiffen, but it was only the terrier, circling his feet now, looking up and yapping with agitation. Fry booted it. Then booted it again. It kept away from him after that, voicing its disapproval with intermittent barks. Fry was tempted to shoot it but didn't risk moving the shotgun from where it was wedged—under the boy's chin.

Soon the revolving discs above the generator were cutting the air like small helicopter blades, casting shadow and light on the metal helmets hovering like suspended haloes over each chair.

Fry watched them, almost hypnotised. He fantasised, briefly, of how he would assume a new identity and slip into a new life. A revived life from the age of fifteen. He didn't have to flee across the border or behave like a fugitive. He could be a blank slate. It could all be started afresh. He could be a different man. Not be trapped by who he was, the person people made him.

He was so excited he dared not look at the face of the boy, the boy everyone would trust, that some people might love, even, and smiled as he thought of the years, the many years of safety that stretched ahead of him. The *freedom.*

"It's ready," Steenburg said.

"Put him in first." Fry backed away from the kid, while still pointing the shotgun at him, as Steenburg eased the teenager into the chair on the right. Surprisingly, the boy didn't seem freaked out. In fact, he seemed far calmer than Fry was feeling as he watched Steenburg buckle the leather belt across his son's midriff and use straps to tie his legs and his wrists to the arm rests.

"Wait a minute. Why the straps? Is it going to be painful?"

"No. They're for accuracy. To hold the subject as still as possible. Like when you get a CAT scan." Steenburg stood back, then indicated the other chair as politely as a waiter offering a diner a table.

Keeping the shotgun aimed at Steenburg, Fry sat on it. The seat was cold.

The old man got down on one knee to secure the lower leg straps. When he came up again he found the shotgun barrel an inch from his nose. He fixed the strap over Fry's left wrist and tightened it. "You need to let go of the gun."

"No way."

"I need to strap your right wrist."

"Leave it," said Fry, not realising until after it had happened that Steenburg had grabbed the shotgun away from him by the barrel, twisting his elbow outwards in a swift arm-wrestling type move, and, just as quickly, held down Fry's forearm to the arm rest.

"Hey!"

The strap bit into his skin. His splayed fingers stiffened and flexed.

"Relax. I'm going to do exactly what you asked me."

The leg straps were taut around Fry's calf muscles. His biceps swelled like balloons, the veins in his forearms standing out like thick cord as he tried to pull free.

"HEY!"

Fry shook in the chair, backwards and forwards, but it was bolted to the floor. The muscles in his neck pulled to breaking point, writhing right and left as Steenburg brought down the hub-cap-shaped skull piece, and tied it like a football helmet under Fry's chin. His perspiration-washed face squirmed within its metal cage.

"URRRRRRRRRR-URRRRRR-URRRRRRRRRRRRR!"

Fry's eyes bulged like soft boiled eggs as he watched Steenburg go to his son and untie the straps on both wrists, as well as the belt that secured his body to the back of the chair. He lifted the boy and led him by the hand to the wooden steps, in the spill of light from upstairs, where the kid remained, like a one-man audience in the bleachers for a White Sox game.

In the same motion as patting his son on the head, the scientist knelt and picked up the boy's dog. Returning to the whirring machinery, he sat the Parson Russell on the empty chair, placed the mirrored skullcap on its head, and tied the chin strap under its jaws.

"NOOOOOOOO!"

The dog looked over to Fry, whose lips were pulled back, almost to the point of tearing apart his face.

The dog, by contrast, had that same fucking smile as it had when he first saw it, and Fry wanted to kick it more than ever.

Steenburg threw the switch and the bulbs rotated like figures on a cuckoo clock, their magnesium-flare reflections caught in the revolving discs and bounced around the many mirrors deflecting the light to a prism above the head-plates. As the light hit the prisms, nebulous tetrahedrons flew into space, a barrage of geometric fairy lights that suddenly congealed and imploded, like a murmuration of asteroids sucking towards a tiny pinpoint of blindingly intense something-ness.

In 1.365 seconds, it was over.

The boy, Harley, watched. Tongue lolling. Panting loudly. Panting the way a dog would pant. Exactly the way a faithful dog would pant, eager to greet its owner.

"Earth, earth," he said. "Earth, earth." And would have pricked up his ears if he could have.

When the helmet was removed from the person that used to be Fry, the straps were released, and the eyes blinked weakly and opened, and the smile widened—the kid barked loudly again, shuffled over on his hands and knees, and repeatedly licked Fry's hand. Fry bent over, ruffled his ears and kissed his nose, laughing, before looking up at the old man.

"Dad?" said the voice of a fifteen-year-old boy from Fry's lips. Tears shone in his eyes, tears of disbelief that he was back in human form at last, and his father was in floods.

The dog howled mightily, pulled free of the skullcap, span in circles on the floor, then disappeared yapping and whining up the stairs, rocketing head first through the screen door and off into the desert, probably regretting that in its previous incarnation as Zachary Thelonius Fry it never asked the most obvious question of all.

Whether the experiment had been done before, and if so—using whom?

The Little Gift

The nocturnal scampering invariably signals death. I try to shut it out. The cat might be chasing a scrap of paper or a ball of silver foil across the bare floorboards downstairs, say a discarded chocolate wrapper courtesy of my wife, who likes providing it with impromptu playthings. I tell myself it isn't necessarily toying with something living, but my stomach tightens.

What time is it?

I don't want to get up. I don't want to have to fumble to find my glasses and look at the clock. I want to go back to sleep, but dawn is cracking through the slatted blinds. I want to ignore what destruction and mutilation might be going on below, but now the cat is in the room, hopping onto the bed and I have the awful feeling, eyes still closed, it might drop a mouse, alive or dead, in the valley between us.

It settles, purring, relaxes, and so do I. For once no ghastly surprises.

Its head nuzzles against my outstretched hand. I feel its small pointed incisors against the soft skin below my little finger. This is my early morning call. I sink back to sleep. My wife is up first as she always is, kettle on before the children wake. I dimly perceive her weight leave the bed, but a minute later her cry from the ground floor cranks me off the pillow. I hurry down in boxer shorts and bare feet asking her what's the matter, but I already know.

The room is full of feathers—never a good sign. There's no doubt the cat has been to work, had its fun, prolonged the killing process in the way that millions of years of evolution has engineered it.

"Look!"

"What kind of bird is it?"

She sobs, tightening the belt of her dressing gown. "A *beautiful* one."

They are always beautiful to her. Whatever our beloved feline brings in from the garden, whatever dire state they are in, however bloodied or punctured or lifeless, she thinks in some way they warrant saving—I swear, like they are Stuart Little or something. For the last few years we've been hoarding plastic soup containers, their sole purpose the catching and liberation of garden kill. My wife makes air holes in the lid with a kitchen knife and drips in water and feeds them bits of granola or Crunchy Nut Cornflakes, even if they're at death's door. She knows I think it's ridiculous the way she insists on caring for the doomed creatures like some Mother Teresa of vermin. There again, I'm not always right. Once we had a field mouse with an eye missing, eviscerated down one side. I walked to the other side of town and emptied it into the river and it swam off happily. This time, though, it's a bird and still alive, lolloping along the skirting board.

My wife grabs our cat, a haughty and self-satisfied Abyssinian, in her embrace and decants it into the utility room, shutting the 17th Century door and throwing the 17th Century bolt. I return to the living room wrapping a glove of kitchen roll round my hand to see the bird isn't moving now, not even when I lift it up in cupped hands.

"Monster," I say under my breath.

It doesn't struggle and flap, thank God, which is always unpleasant. In fact when I open my hands it isn't moving at all.

My wife flinches because she can see the wounds too. "I think it's a chaffinch or something."

"No. A chaffinch is brightly coloured, isn't it? I think it's something ordinary. A thrush maybe. Except I think a thrush is bigger. It's brown, that's all I know."

"Don't be horrible."

"I'm not being horrible."

I can see why she is mesmerised by the beauty of it, its tiny markings, bead-like eyes. Half its body is missing, gouged by fang or claw. I fan out one intricate wing.

"Don't!"

"Sorry."

But I doubt it can feel anything much. It's making no sound. Even her heartfelt ministrations won't bring it back from the dead, that much is obvious. I see blood smearing the kitchen roll. I feel no warmth.

"Is it alive?"

"Barely, if at all."

"Oh hell. Can you kill it?"

"Yes," I say. "But not if you watch me." Which is true.

She turns her back.

I know what she will hear so I *la-la-la* a non-existent tune as I place the small bundle on the floor and crush it gently but firmly with the heel of my hand, feeling its tiny bones crunch under the all-too-faint pressure.

When I stop humming she asks: "Have you done it?"

"Don't worry."

Not wanting her to see, I go into the kitchen and coil it, mummy-like, in more kitchen roll, then drop it in a Budgen's carrier bag which I knot tightly twice. I don't want it smelling out the bin, and if you put it in a black bag outside the back door there's always the danger one of the local toms will tear it open and make a hell of a mess. So it's my job to do what I always do, which is to take it down to the litter bin on the corner of the street, after going upstairs and pulling on tracksuit bottoms and a random T-shirt.

"Bring down the vacuum and I'll clean up the feathers."

Dark commas are strewn over every inch of the room. Hard to believe that so many can come from something that small. As my wife chases them with the spout of the Dyson they seem to be darting and swirling away with a will of their own, trying to escape.

I carry the plastic bag down the street, thinking to myself our present cat, albeit well bred, has never been particularly good value as a pet. It never sits on my lap or allows itself to be stroked, and pays far more attention to visitors than it ever does to us, its owners and providers. In fact it treats us with regal disdain, which I suppose is exactly what cat people adore, but to me, quite frankly, it's a pain in the arse—the worst of it being little treats it brings in for us, like this morning's.

Once she brought us up a vole. That was awful. With the dulcet tones of Radio Four coming on with the alarm at 6.30 a.m., the tiny victim was hard to ignore, wet and curled-up like a foetus next to a framed limited-edition print propped against the wall because we hadn't got round to hanging it.

I remember that day clearly because I could have done without the hassle. I had to go off on a "bonding" weekend for so-called team-building. The company I worked for was large and American—you've heard of it: a car rental firm with 6,500 locations "in neighbourhoods and airports throughout the USA, Canada, the UK, Eire and Europe"—imbued with the kind of joyless corporate ethics whereby they'd spend thousands on an Away-Day jaunt or a pointless report by an external consultant, but make fifty people redundant at the drop of a hat.

This was an event where senior management were required to meet informally with each other, undertake *Fun Tasks*, and see the human beings behind the name badges, even though we all had much more work on our plates than we could handle in the sixteen-hour days we were currently working.

Needless to say, I was dreading it.

There was something about the company telling you to let your hair down that was fundamentally disingenuous, because there was the underlying, unmistakable feeling that you would ultimately be judged. If the other attendees had similar thoughts, none of us allowed it to show. We arrived all smiles at the posh hotel in the Cotswolds, each handshake trying to be as vigorous as the last. Most of us wore open-necked shirts and some even jeans—which was a real peculiarity in itself as lots of the guys I knew didn't look good in anything but a grey suit because, quite frankly, they were grey suit people.

On the surface I was my usual charming self, which wasn't hard because most of these people I genuinely liked and talked to on the phone every week, sometimes every day. So there was a general feeling of, well, we're here, we may as well enjoy ourselves. Maybe not get completely shit-faced, might not go down well with the Yanks, given that the top brass were also Mormons.

Nevertheless, I didn't want to be there. I liked my weekends at home. The girls were young then and it's true what they say, kids grow up fast: blink and you miss it. And I was never a greasy-pole merchant. I just liked doing my job well because that meant the company remained successful and if I reached targets I got a work-related bonus and my colleagues kept their jobs. I was Group Regional Manager at forty-six with a Range Rover Evoque (fully spec'd: leather, Sat Nav), privately leased (we get a fantastic deal on leasing), and a gorgeous Kawasaki penis extension in my garage, not to mention a half-timbered cottage in All Cannings near Devizes, a beautiful wife and two gorgeous, healthy children, and that was all I wanted.

Or so I thought.

•●•

In previous years coaches picked us up at 10.30 p.m. to take us back to our various hotels where the drinking continued, but in this instance we were all booked in at the same location, so the enforced jollity of the prize-giving (someone crowned "King of the Road") overlapped into serious final night necking of the free booze. By the end of it, ironically, I was beginning to think it had been a welcome diversion from the usual work routine. I actually wasn't in a rush to go home. And that, partly at least, was because of her.

She was HR Manager of TLS, a truck leasing company that was one of our subsidiaries, based in Gloucester. Her name was Ghislaine Hammond and she had a lilting, unapologetic Brummie accent. Part of my job was mentoring area and branch managers, but I hadn't encountered her before: unsurprisingly, since TLS was owned by us, but a separate autonomous entity. *Separate autonomous entity.* That kind of phrase would instantly bunch me with the other twats mingling around us. I didn't want to be lumped with them. Far from it.

She wasn't outstandingly attractive. That was the peculiar thing. She wore cheap, scuffed high heeled boots, too wide for her skinny calves so they produced a gap around the rim, noticeable when she crossed her legs. Parallel lines corrugated her forehead, which I found inexplicably sexy. In contrast to her dingy tan, her hair was grubby blonde, in big strands she'd tuck behind her ears every few seconds, a side effect of shyness, I'd come to learn. Patently she didn't spend a fortune at the hairdresser's like my better half, rather you sensed if she ever looked in the mirror it was to say: "Oh, fuck it, that'll do". It seemed she didn't appear to care about those things like most women, and that alone was hugely refreshing, as most of the office girls were devotees of the sun bed and industrial quantities of Rimmel. In the tasks she was unafraid to look stupid, got things done with a heavy dose of good humour without being pushy, dealt with petty bickering with the tactful application of a withering put down (asking Joey Pidd if he came from *Cockermouth*, to everyone's delight) and struck me throughout as someone lacking in guile or bullshit—all of which endeared her to me as a colleague. But it wasn't as a colleague she interested me, I was ashamed and somewhat shocked to realise.

That final night I found myself playing charades jammed on a sofa between two area managers from Sunderland and The Wirral with competing shaving rash, a lot of pissed innuendo in the air. Ghislaine was trying to convey the wearily inevitable *Willy Wonka*, pointing to her own groin then to mine. Sunderland dribbled beer as he giggled while The Wirral roared and fell back against the cushions. For *Wonka* she made a masturbatory gesture with her fist which I found strangely arousing. The motion had been so fluid and accomplished I wondered if she was practised in the art, and it was impossible to get the thought out of my mind. My cheeks flushed. I lied to myself that it was down to the local cider.

A few hours later I was sitting cross-legged on the floor, pint glass going to my mouth like those monkeys who eat your coins. She alone occupied the sofa now, skirt riding up her crossed thighs. Texting someone. I asked who.

"My sister. She's out on a date. I'm asking her if she's going to get sex. She doesn't think so. She says she hasn't shaved."

"Her legs?"

"No. Not her legs." She gave me a pitying frown, then a lopsided smile, leaning forward with apparent curiosity. "Does your wife shave her legs?"

I paused because I thought this was going to lead to a laugh at my expense.

She raised an eyebrow. "You don't know. That's good. You know what they say." She sipped her wine. "It's the mystery that keeps a marriage exciting."

"What makes you think my marriage is exciting?"

If I meant to say it at all I meant it to sound like a joke. It didn't sound anything like a joke, so she chuckled to stop me feeling embarrassed, but I already was. My glass was empty. I reached for hers to get a refill for us both.

In the bar mirror I saw other blokes land on her like crows on a piece of road kill, trying to chat her up in that way I never could in a million years. It made me feel sick at my own inadequacy. She was laughing, but I didn't know if she was making herself available to any or all of us, or just being very friendly, as a mate.

As I re-joined them someone was asking her if she had a boyfriend.

"Not any more."

Her last one, it transpired, was a Professor of Linguistics who quoted James Joyce in bed and had shoulders thatched with silvery hairs. I doubted any of the gathered listeners knew who James Joyce was. Said Professor wasn't going to leave his wife and that didn't bother her, she told us. She'd long come to the conclusion she was destined to be a *fancy woman* in this life, never a bride. She used that old-fashioned expression, *fancy woman,* instead of mistress, and it got a drizzle of laughter.

I asked if she had a pick-up line she used on married men. "As opposed to normal men."

"Yeah, I do as a matter of fact. I just say at some point in the conversation, 'I suppose a fuck is out of the question'. Then if they respond, good. If they want to treat it like a joke, that's fine too. There's no embarrassment, and we both know where we are."

Desperate for a cigarette, she went outside into the formal gardens of the stately home. Myself and a couple of other men followed, trying not to seem like dogs on heat. The topiary looked manicured in the moonlight. I ended up accompanying her in a walk around the lake. The other two drifted away on solitary paths. To this day I don't know why I was left standing with her and the others weren't. It was chilly and I touched the gooseflesh on her bare arm. As a response she kissed me hard with an open mouth for several seconds. Her lips turned from ice cold to furnace hot. I said I wasn't expecting that. She said she'd been dropping enough hints. I said, "Yes, but I didn't know the hints were for me."

As our mouths explored each other I sensed the other men moving around amongst the dimly-lit trees. My erection pressed against her; I don't know if women like that or not, but I imagine they like to know they've had an effect. I would have made love to her there and then, on the grass or in the bushes, but she said, "Let's go inside", and led me by the hand.

The idea of soiling my nice, clean hotel room felt illicit and tawdry. It was naughty in a way I'd never been naughty in my life. I was going with the flow without fear of consequences. I was another person. I was playacting. I was in a farce. I couldn't wait to get my trousers off, and there's something comical about a man removing his trousers and underpants to reveal a stiff, impatient penis. She laughed, saying there was no hurry. I wanted to get down to it, perhaps get it over with because of a latent sense of guilt, but she wanted to slow down, take our time, if we were going to do it at all. I realised she knew what she was doing and I didn't. At a loss, I was happy to let her take the lead. I was a child. I didn't have the faintest idea how to behave. I wasn't cool. I was the opposite of cool. She'd done this before with married men and I was one and I didn't mind. It's corny, but I wanted it more than anything I'd wanted in my life.

"Are you happy about this?" she asked calmly once we were naked, exploring one another's skin with lips and fingers. She raised my face off her chest and stroked back my hair. "I don't want you to do anything you might regret afterwards."

"I won't regret anything afterwards," I said. But I couldn't lie because she could see into my soul. She knew this situation of old. She knew me better than I did myself. I tried not to think how many times this conversation had occurred before. "I don't want to, you know . . ." I whispered, "do . . . *everything*. Is that all right? I'm sorry. It's just . . . I'll do everything *else*, but not . . ."

She said softly: "I understand."

"If I did, it would be . . ."

Even softer: "I understand. Don't worry." She held my cheeks in the palms of her hands. "Don't do anything you don't want to do."

I lay on my back. She knelt beside me. I stroked her white thighs as her fingertips encircled my glans, gently feeling it enlarge and the tip touch the centre of her palm. She took her time, grinning down at me, her other hand massaging my shoulder, straight-backed till I exploded, then lay down against the pillow and it was my turn. I inserted my fingers into her, gently at first then stabbing deep with a relentless rhythm, watching her face transform in the breath-catching pain-pleasure of orgasm, keeping her there by stimulating her with my tongue until she grabbed hold of my hair, yanking it violently as she came, air rushing into her open, upturned mouth. Her clitoris reddened like a miniscule penis. I hadn't seen one like that before. I kept sucking it, and she didn't tell me to stop.

When we kissed again in the afterglow I wondered what she could taste in my mouth. Whether she could taste herself.

We lay, bonfire-hot and still, listening to the door-banging and footsteps of the other delegates retiring to their rooms. I thought about the other men round the lake, their veiled predatory air, and what they might be thinking of me getting what they desired. Of me winning for once.

Eventually she got up and dressed, saying she needed to sleep in her own room. I said she didn't have to, I didn't mind other people seeing that she'd spent the night with me, but she wasn't having it. She must've been prouder or more professional than I was. Or perhaps now the deed was done I was a cast-off. Was she that much one of the lads?

As she put on her bra I cupped her breasts from behind, lifted her hair and nuzzled into the warmth on the back of her neck. I was erect again. She chuckled like I was an over-eager, naive little boy, turned to face me and placed my hands together.

When she'd gone I lay in the dark. The room felt vast and empty, featureless and arid as an office, but cloying with the sweaty fug of memory.

The next morning everybody left in dribs and drabs. I saw Ghislaine putting her suitcase in Briell Finch's Saab. She came back in to have breakfast. I was chatty, but not over-familiar. I had no idea if she'd told any of her female colleagues what had happened. They didn't give any indication she had. I supposed that, as a self-proclaimed *fancy woman*, she'd learnt the skill of discretion. Nevertheless I wondered how she might have described me if she had done. As a terrible mistake? As an awful lay with smelly armpits and all the lovemaking sophistication of a sex-starved gorilla? Would they have expressed dismay, even disgust?

Her lift, Briell, jiggled keys. Ghislaine stood up. We said goodbye to each other, shuffling around words that might give the game away. I said it had been a mad night.

"Real madness," she said. "Certifiable."

"It would be great to meet up." I tried not to stammer. "For a drink or something."

"Yeah, it would. I'd like that a lot. If you want to?"

"I do," I said.

She looked me in the eyes. "You call me."

In other words: *I won't call you. It's up to you to make the next move, Married Man, if you want to. I've been here before. Many times. Know the lyrics by heart.*

Home a few hours later, but a world away, I hugged my kids—four and six at the time, perfect for cuddling—and said the weekend wasn't as hellish as I'd envisaged, it was actually quite fun, but I was glad to get home to the bosom of the family. Making the most of a bad pun, out of sight of the offspring I wound an arm round Trudy and squeezed her right breast under her apron.

She saw the relief in my face and it wasn't entirely un-genuine. But inside I felt strangely energised after my night with Ghislaine.

Stupidly superhuman. Redefined. A risk taker, all of a sudden, and I thought: what if it's *visible*? What if I was emitting some pheromone that made it obvious what I'd been up to, or was conveying it in some imperceptible way, paying her too much physical attention to compensate for an alarm bell if I paid her too little? What the hell would happen if she detected that I felt like a real person for the first time in months? Years?

What if she could smell *her on me?*

But none of those things happened. I bathed my children, read them a story and slept with my wife and all went back to normal like the turning of a page of an old, well-thumbed book.

That night in bed I kissed Trudy's achingly familiar tummy in the dark saying I'd missed her so much. We had sex. It was good. She slept afterwards, slippery and content. I lay awake, tingling with an electric confusion. It had been good because I'd been thinking of Ghislaine—the smoothness of her white thigh, the soft down on the nape of her neck: the tip of my cock tickled mercilessly by the palm of her hand.

As the following week went by I couldn't stop thinking about her, simultaneously knowing my behaviour was ludicrous. Like a schoolboy crush, she occupied my every waking minute. There in my head in meetings, at lunch. During business conversations I was zoning out. Disinterested. Distracted. It was madness, she'd said—and she was fucking right.

I thought: *What's wrong with me? Pull yourself together, for Christ's sake.*

I kept telling myself it was over, an aberration, but was it? Did I *want* it to be?

The answer to that came when I found myself looking up the number of the Gloucester branch of TLS. She'd said she would welcome me contacting her. What was stopping me? What was the worst that could happen? It could blow my marriage sky high, that's what.

But other people had one night stands and it didn't wreck their lives. Other people got up to flings and affairs and it didn't turn into chaos. So why couldn't I? Or was this just some kind of ridiculous juvenile fantasy? Nothing to do with the woman herself? Was I just using her to act out a pathetic mid-life crisis? Well I wasn't, because I wasn't doing anything. I wasn't ringing her and I couldn't. Because I was afraid. I was what I'd always been—a coward who played things safe, who ran away from change rather than embracing it. But now, suddenly, it was killing me.

I rang her office. I was told she was out.

I rang again at twelve. Still not available. In a meeting. I was asked if they could take a message. I left my name and number and waited for her to call back.

And waited, checking my watch every five minutes. Then every two. My heart was beating like Japanese drummers on cocaine. By the end of that interminable afternoon the possibility that she had no interest, that it was all an illusion on my part, that I might never speak to her or see her again opened in front of me like a chasm.

A gibbering wreck by close of play, I found it impossible to leave the building and phoned Gloucester one last time. Ghislaine picked up.

"Oh, hi."

My brain in overdrive, I couldn't really tell if she was pleased or whether it was simply a pleasantry. I couldn't have borne it if it was. I blurted I was coming to her neck of the woods the following week, the following Wednesday to be precise, and I was free to meet, if she wanted to. I'd completely understand if she was busy.

"I'm not busy."

I said we could go to lunch if she was free.

"I'm definitely free."

Of course I'd lied about having to go to that part of the country, but after gleaning some local knowledge booked a restaurant called The Daffodil in Montpellier, Cheltenham. A converted old cinema that doubled as a jazz venue.

She wore the same ill-fitting boots and Inspector Clouseau raincoat. For the first time I noticed her rather ungainly, galumphing walk. We air-kissed, which I found to be fantastically chaste given our recent explicit shenanigans. I'd have enjoyed our shared secret knowledge to be in the open, but Ghislaine, strangely, seemed to be treating this more like a job interview between strangers than the reuniting of two people who'd shared no small degree of intimacy.

Taking what I thought was her lead I regressed into small talk as though nothing had gone on between us. We ordered chateaubriand for two—steep, but the house speciality. She said she didn't know what we were celebrating.

I said, "I am. I don't know about you."

She was chatty, though. I discovered her mother was Italian—hence her middle name: *Lenzi*. That explained her caramel skin, out of keeping with the blonde hair.

"If you go to the cemetery in Bacchereto, a tiny village up in the hills in Tuscany, outside Prato, up this winding road from Seano, the graveyard is full of Lenzis. They put pictures on graves in that part of the world. Photographs, I mean. Some of them are lovely smiling grannies and that, but a few of them are these hard-as-nails-looking priests. I'm not kidding. It's so funny. It's beautiful round there, though. Not far from Vinci, where Leonardo was born. There's a church there. I went with a boyfriend years ago. We heard this phone ringing in the next room, and he said, 'That must be from God.' We got such a dirty look it was unbelievable."

"Serve you right."

I asked where in Birmingham she was from.

"Nowhere," she said. "I'm from Wolverhampton."

"Sorry."

"You're displaying your ignorance."

"I know."

"Big time."

"I am."

In skirting round anything important, naturally we talked about work. She said she wasn't that committed to working in truck leasing for the rest of her life.

"Maybe I'll travel the world, go to Bondi Beach, train to be a cocktail waitress. Who am I kidding? I haven't got the body for Bondi Beach. I haven't got the body for bloody Butlin's."

"Rubbish. I bet you go to the gym three times a week. Your stomach is flat as a pancake."

"What? You're having a laugh." She made a face. "Listen, I'm doing that 5:2 diet off the telly. Five days a week I eat normally and the two other days I eat whatever the hell I like."

That was funny. "Well, I need to lose a few pounds, if you don't."

"Shut up." She avoided eye contact as she gave me the compliment, plucking at a bread roll, finger and thumb like the beak of a cormorant. "You're all right. You're what I call *dadsexy*."

I laughed, but internally winced. God. Was that what she went for? Was she the type that was turned on when she saw some over-the-hill guy in Tesco's with a toddler in a push-chair? Did she get off on that being off-limits? Jesus, was that why she was attracted to me? The terminally safe?

I swung the conversation back to work. Not that it was a particularly interesting topic, I just didn't want her to ask me questions about my home life. So I updated her with the latest goss on Hamsa Sharif (nicknamed "Omar", with painful predictability) who was following International Mavis Wong round like a lapdog. Ghislaine said she'd once had a Muslim boyfriend, fastidious about washing his hands.

"One day he was there one day he was gone, no explanation. I don't know whether he went back to fight or whether he was picked up by MI5. I think he was gay, actually. Another of the men

I went out with was a compulsive liar. Said he was an airline pilot. Then said he was a compulsive liar."

"How do you know if that's true when he says he's a compulsive liar?"

"Absolutely right. He had a wife though, because I met her, and he told me he'd had a lot of affairs and persuaded me to go on this NLP course with him. Neuro-Linguistic Programming? It was all a bit *weirdy-woo* but you get sucked in. He thought it was the answer to his life. It wasn't, needless to say. I don't know what it was. I don't know what *he* was. I don't think he did either."

She told me about her dad, who owned a carpet factory and had another daughter from his previous marriage who was incredibly spoilt and had a job as an ophthalmologist.

"The apple of his eye."

"That's ironic," I said. "Or rather, appropriate."

We talked about the Away-Day (not surprisingly, as it was pretty much the one thing we had in common) but neither of us mentioned the elephant in the room. All the time I was listening I wondered when or if it was going to come up and what I was going to do or say when it did.

Truthfully, through the entire lunch all I ached for was to have sex with her again. Even as she talked, nervously playing with her wine glass, I fantasised about that hand reaching under the table to unzip my trousers. When I went for a pee, light-headed from the Barolo and semi-erect, my mind conjured up an outrageous scenario in which I went to the gents only to find she'd followed me, whereupon she pulled down her knickers in the narrow cubicle, bending over the W.C. for me to enter her from behind. I daydreamed that we would be discovered by one of the kitchen staff who'd scream at us to get out. Neither of us would give a fuck and I'd be in no hurry, staring him out as I did up my fly.

Then, all too suddenly, the plates were gone and our meal was over. I tried to prolong our time together over coffees but she said she had to get back to work. Personally I couldn't have given a damn about work or anything else.

We said goodbye on the pavement outside, her car in the Commercial Street car park, mine in Bath Terrace. The minutes leading up to her departure felt like a countdown. As the last few seconds ticked away I was thinking of the men out there who do rash things, who say, "Come with me," and brazenly book a room in a hotel, a bubble for the afternoon in which to fuck until they're raw. I didn't say anything of the sort—or anything at all.

She kissed me, this time on the lips. I was thrown when it lasted long, sweet seconds before we separated. Too long to be just a goodbye, surely? Was it an invitation for me to be proactive, then? I literally had no idea.

"Well, 'bye, then." She knotted her raincoat belt. "Keep in touch. We must do it again. It's been fun."

"It has. We must."

The lone walk to my car was an agonising one, during which I punished myself for not at least testing the water for fear of outright rejection. I could have at least *tried* to express what I really felt, but no—my lifelong self-consciousness had fucked up any hope of recapturing an experience of—what? Freedom? Happiness? I'd wanted to declare so much, but I hadn't. Not a thing. What did that make me, except a complete bloody fool?

Well, 'bye then. Keep in touch.

Jesus . . .

Getting home to my family only made me feel worse: gutted, imbecilic, worthless. While Trudy was in the bathroom I typed a text to Ghislaine's mobile:

Great to see you xx must do it again how about tomorrow?

I paused, added a winking smiley, then sent it.

After I brushed my teeth I checked if I had a reply. I hadn't. When Trudy was asleep and I wasn't, I got up and checked the screen again in the dark. My phone lit up, so bright it was painful.

Nothing.

It wasn't until the next morning, as I ended a meeting with the Finance Director, that a reply finally pinged up. Just one solitary character:

x

Oh God, I've blown it, I thought, my stomach dropping like a lead weight. *I've totally fucked up.*

I wanted to reply instantly, but how could I? I'd have come across as desperate—but I *was* fucking desperate. Instead of driving myself insane dreaming about it, if only I'd turned back to her after that goodbye kiss on the street corner near the museum, that *lingering* kiss, I could have been lying in crisp sheets in a hotel room that afternoon, sucking her creamy throat, lifting her bony knees either side of me, inside her this time, not caring, bent like a curlicue, my hot breath on her icy breasts, crushing and sliding against her.

The whole of the rest of the day passed in a blur, fiercely non-existent. All I knew was the feelings weren't fading. If anything they were getting worse. The only thing I could think about when the phone rang was that it might be her. Nothing else mattered. And when it wasn't her my world shattered. One minute dry-mouthed with anticipation, the next eviscerated by crushing disappointment.

I circled three o'clock in my diary and made a mental note that if she didn't ring me by then, I would ring her. I couldn't pussyfoot about my emotions any longer. I had to make it obvious. Maybe that was exactly what she was waiting for me to do. Maybe that was what that long last kiss was all about. I prayed to God it was. At five past three I texted her.

Sorry. I'm desperate to see you again. Is that bad?

Seconds later: **No. Of course not xx**

When? xxx

I don't want another one night stand

My heart was thumping as I typed: **Neither do I**

Are you serious?

Yes

Are you sure?

100%

Pause. **I hope your wife doesn't check your texts**

I smiled and swallowed. **Work phone xx**

As I waited for the reply I hoped nobody in the office could see the look on my face. I felt red and bloated, as if someone had cranked up the heating. A new text popped up.

I made it clear at the beginning I'm not going to chase you. It's your decision. I'm not making the decision for you. It's got to be you.

I've decided

I typed and sent it, with a heart. She replied after a few taut seconds.

Certifiable

Certifiable, I texted back immediately.

It was exactly that. A kind of insanity.

I'll call you tomorrow

With that she was gone and I felt ill. The lights were too bright and I thought I'd pass out. I didn't know what it was. I thought perhaps I'd drunk too much coffee but I felt muzzy-headed, like I was teetering on the edge of a cliff. And I realised I *was* on the edge of a cliff, and that cliff was leaving my wife, leaving my children, leaving everything behind me. Just shedding it like old, dead reptilian skin. My body knew it before my brain did. My metabolism was telling me to wake up and get a life because *this* life, what was it? What was I clinging to?

Over dinner I blanked Trudy's tales of the school gates and her job because I was going to be unburdened of it all. And it didn't even feel nightmarish because it was all so clear now—it was *uplifting*. There would be difficulties and there would be tears and heartache and vitriol, but for the first time in my life I had wings. I knew where my future lay and for once I had the guts to be selfish, in spite of all the pain that would ensue.

The only thing filling me with dread was the possibility my feelings weren't reciprocated. After all, things like this simply don't happen to men like me. For a female stranger to like me, let alone be attracted to me sexually, was nothing short of a miracle on a par with the parting of the Red Sea. The idea of it not being mutual on her part was gut-wrenchingly horrible, but I had to know.

She rang at 9.30 a.m. on the dot.

"I'm sorry. You have to be sure about this."

"You keep saying that," I said.

"I know. There's a reason. I don't want you to say you want something you then back out of."

"You mean you don't want to be shat on. You won't be. I promise. Look, I don't know about other men or what they've done to you in the past. I can only say for myself, I won't do that. It's not me. I won't hurt you. Why would I?" I tried to read the silence on the line and hoped she was hearing my sincerity. "I'm making a big decision here for the rest of my life, Ghislaine. I'm not doing it lightly. I imagine you're not either."

Even in a sigh, her voice was a ray of sunshine that cut through the bleak cloudiness of my day. "Okay, okay. I can't talk now. Let's meet up properly."

I said I sometimes did one-to-one business meetings at the Gloucester Services, the new one with the butcher and deli and food hall, on the M5 between junctions 11a and 12. I suggested Thursday at three.

We met like spies, braving a tense Checkpoint Charlie between identical counters selling mirrored offerings of lasagne wedges, baked potatoes, and steaming specials of the day. Coffee seemed the least toxic option. The "least fuck-uppable," as Ghislaine put it, under her breath. She seemed harassed though. Maybe this was an inconvenience. Maybe she had a mound of work, or it was tricky slipping away on a pretext. Maybe she was just nervous now that we were face to face. The texts and phone calls had been easy. Remote. The other party idealised, perfect. Then I'd assumed I knew what she was thinking, but what was she thinking now?

After we'd found a table she looked anywhere but into my eyes. I got up and fetched two cubes of brown sugar in a napkin.

"Bad," she said.

"I know. I'm trying to cut down, but today I need the sugar rush. Sometimes you do."

"Just have one. Please. My dad died of a heart attack."

"Thanks."

I left the cubes sitting on the napkin.

She stirred her cappuccino, swirling the carefully-stencilled chocolate pattern into a beige, ungrateful sludge. "I don't want to get between you and Trudy."

I didn't like her using my wife's name, even though I'd given it her in an unguarded moment. My Americano scalded my lips and I grimaced. "You said it's my decision, and it is."

She picked at my almond croissant. She'd said she didn't want one but here she was, helping herself, dabbing at crumbs with a licked forefinger. Trudy would always do things like that: say she was too full for dessert, then help herself to mine. And not just a mouthful, she'd gannet a good fifty per cent. Do all women live under this telepathically-shared delusion that if they don't actually order something it has no calories?

"I don't want to hurt anybody," Ghislaine said. "Especially another woman. Especially *children*."

"You're not doing. I am. I'm the shit, and it's my problem. I want it to be my problem because I love you." I extended my hand and she took it, hooking her slender fingers in the valleys between mine. "It's what I want. Honestly. Can't you tell? It's been driving me crazy. I'm like a boy whose voice has just broken turning to jelly when he thinks about his damned teacher. I swear. I haven't been able to think about anything else. I'd forgotten—that's what love *is*. And I didn't ask for it. It just hit me. Flattened me. I can't ignore it. I can't pretend it hasn't happened. I can't *lie*. What I need to know is if you feel the same."

"Of course I do." She laughed, and for a second I sensed in her the same dizzy other-worldly excitement that possessed me. "Why do you think I said '*Certifiable*'?"

Her eyes told me she meant it and that swept all doubt aside in a way that felt heady and intoxicating. I could hardly believe it. The confirmation I was hearing, that I wanted to hear so badly. Could it be true? Really? No, it was preposterous.

I blinked, shook my head, laughed at the absurdity. "We haven't even had sex yet."

"This isn't about sex for either of us," she said.

What is it about then? For you? The question must've been written all over my face, because she answered it.

"All that *fancy woman* stuff? It's a front. It's bollocks. It's armour. I've fine-tuned it over the years, oh yeah. Got it down pat. But it doesn't define who I am. Who I want to be. I pretend it is, but it's not. I'm sick of being the shag on the side, the one who watches Netflix at two in the morning and has a Sainsbury's microwave meal for one while the sod who declared his undying love for me is at home playing Monopoly with Tarquin and Jocasta and knobbing his old lady who supposedly doesn't understand him."

I examined the table top.

"Sorry," she breathed, rubbing my sleeve apologetically. "But I need you to know this, because we have to be after the same thing. I want a relationship. I want security. I want a home and someone to come home to. And I don't want to cry myself to sleep any more over some scumbag who doesn't deserve me."

"And I do?"

Her laugh juddered.

"My friend Oona is nutty as a fruit cake. Occupational therapist. Believes in angels. You name it, she believes in it. But she's really good at the Tarot. Has been for years. I always get it done when she's in town and she was in town the Sunday I got back from the Away-Day. She said I'd met someone good for me. She's never seen my spread so optimistic. The Magician was in my future, and the way I see myself was about to change."

The Magician.

I said: "I must send her that fifty quid I promised."

She didn't match my smile and her face became uncharacteristically focussed on finding the correct words.

"What I . . . need is . . . someone who'll commit to me. I mean . . . show he's committed. Otherwise there's no point, is there?"

"Tell me what to do and I'll do it."

She said she was off early the next morning from Bristol Airport on a hen night in Barcelona. "Ten of us. Known each other from school. All dipsomaniacs. The worst is the art historian. She's mental." EasyJet. Hotel Derby—not a name to set the heart on fire. "But then again, maybe if you're Spanish Derby sounds dead exotic." She'd be back in work Monday morning and by then she wanted me to have left my wife.

I was astonished this didn't feel like an ultimatum—it simply felt rational, and right. It focused the mind, yes, but I didn't hesitate for a second. I said I would tell Trudy at the weekend and clear out immediately. It would probably be so incendiary it would be hard not to. I'd leave with whatever I could shove in a suitcase. Just get out of there and let the dust settle. I'd book myself into a hotel. Ghislaine didn't want me to come straight to her. In time though, we agreed, we'd get a place together. The sooner the better as far as I was concerned.

"If you don't call, I'll know you've changed your mind."

"I'll call," I said.

In the vast, featureless but immaculately landscaped car

park we kissed, my anorak over my suit, her in her Scotland Yard mac, ignoring the brutal chill factor in the wind, indifferent to all around us. I wondered if we looked like a couple having an affair and thought we probably did. What were these ugly people thinking as they shambled back to their rust-buckets in their cheap sportswear? *What does she see in him?* Probably. I didn't care.

"I don't need to go back to the office," I said, my teeth chattering. "I want to go somewhere. With you. Right now."

She grinned. "We'll have plenty of time for that." I was in a fucking hurry again, wasn't I?

"Forever," I said.

"Forever's a long time."

"Good."

She touched my cheek. Her gloveless hand was freezing. I held it there.

"I'm happy," I said.

"So am I," she said, her eyes crinkling against the bright light behind me, low afternoon sun hovering over the petrol station.

"These things don't happen, do they?"

"Yes," she said, kissing the back of my hand. "They do."

• ● •

I considered telling Trudy on the Friday, but we'd have had the entire weekend to suffer and I didn't think I could cope with that, not without Ghislaine. But if I thought by staving off the fateful day I would enjoy a kind of reprieve, a respite, I must've been kidding myself. It wasn't so much a monkey on my back as a ten ton weight and I could feel it from the moment I opened my eyes to the second I fell asleep. Except I didn't fall asleep. I fretted, running through the script in my head.

I would tell her I didn't hate her, but she was the past now. I hadn't planned it or gone looking for it. It wasn't her fault, and it wasn't that our marriage hadn't meant anything, but I was in love with someone else. I'd soft-soap her by saying our life together hadn't been wasted: we had two beautiful daughters. We'd built up a household together and had our good times, obviously, but we'd been drifting our separate ways—she must have seen that, surely? I'd make it feel like an inevitable fork in the path of life. That it was her failure in not noticing something was radically amiss and had been for some time.

Or I might just tell her outright I'd had sex with another woman and it was unbelievable and I couldn't stop thinking about her, and she'd call me a fucking idiot led around by his dick, go ballistic, throw things, and end up after a slanging match in a sobbing heap—and so would I, probably.

It was going to be hideous, whichever way it played out, and I didn't relish the prospect, but it had to be done. However I dressed it up it would be a despicable act, and stepping off an actual cliff edge seemed a lot more attractive. Furthermore the very thought of explaining to my two angels that their parents were separating made me feel nauseous—not with regret but with loss. Their mother's tears I could just about bear, but not theirs. Never could.

As a result my still-innate cowardice persuaded me to put the deed off yet again—from Saturday to Sunday. Another twenty-four hours wouldn't hurt. My marriage could last another day. The thought caught in my craw, monstrously callous. Not like me at all. But perhaps this was the *new* me. Someone who acted decisively, without regret or guilt: what a staggering thing that would be.

On the Sunday morning I announced we were going for a day out. I didn't know where. I just wanted to get out, for my own good, and not slow bake in my own self-loathing, if nothing else. Trudy kissed me on the cheek and I caught the citrus tang of the fragrance she dabbed under her ears and on her inner wrists. Aēsop, it was called. I recalled buying the perfume in a small shop in Islington. I wondered if, at some point in the future, this very olfactory moment might come back to me. I needed to treasure memories now. Things wouldn't last. They were fading. Photographs in a darkroom accidentally exposed to the light. If I didn't fix them they'd be gone.

With no destination in the Sat Nav, we found ourselves on a long straight road near the Longleat estate. One of the girls noticed a sign saying "HEAVEN'S GATE" and, intrigued, we pulled into a muddy car park full of dog walkers. I vaguely remembered Angus and Maud mentioning this place but couldn't recall what they'd said—only that it was a favourite place to take their grandchildren. We followed the path through what looked like an arboretum, families playing hide and seek amongst exotic trees. A viewing point gave us a glorious panorama over Longleat House and the safari park, where we could spy rhinos and camels whose bellows carried on the still wind. Watching my gorgeous girls scampering round a crescent of modern standing stones, a nectarine warmth seeping through the trees, I imagined a future in which their mother was replaced by Ghislaine and I was inevitably cast as the villain.

I didn't want to return home but after a diversion to the Chew Valley and a walk that became a route march it was unavoidable. We arrived back exhausted, the girls dead on their feet. I had to carry Amber from the car and Verity barely opened her eyes.

Trudy placed a hand on my shoulder. "You put them to bed, love. I'll put on the washing and make some gin and tonics." Little did she know she was going to need hers.

It was eight o'clock and light was fading. The walk to the scaffold loomed and my stomach knotted. I was hoping she would tuck in the girls and I'd have a few minutes to gather my thoughts. But what fucking thoughts were there to gather? I'd had two days to think about this, and was none the wiser how to broach the subject. And I couldn't put it off any more. My only grim solace was knowing that by the morning it would all be over.

Her hair lying in strands on the pillow, Amber seemed barely more than a baby. The perfect cheek, the semi-transparent sculpt of her ear. Verity in the bunk above getting taller and lankier by the day, coming into her own, while I'd be thinking, *No, I don't want to lose that five-year-old or six-year-old yet:* but it was always too late—they were already gone.

I wondered what they'd be like as grown-ups. I imagined two sylph-like teenagers as tall as me. I could see them standing talking to adults at a garden party, holding their own, confident in their skin. Then I saw Trudy from afar with another feller by then. Maybe happier than she ever was with me.

"I love you, Dad."

Verity, face down in her pillow. Dimpled cheek warm to my touch.

"Just go to sleep now, sweetheart."

The final sound of the door squeezing shut across the carpet.

I'm sorry. I'm so, so sorry . . .

Coming downstairs I could hear the TV newsreader talking about something of global significance I wasn't taking in.

"Trude?"

She had her back to me, chopping onions. "Have you got a clean shirt for tomorrow? I bet you—"

"Trudy. Darling . . ." Why did I say *darling*? That was a mistake. I was going to ask her to sit down, but realised I'd rather not say this while looking into her eyes.

"Listen . . . I need to . . ."

"What?"

. . . have yet to confirm that remains found yesterday at a residence in Stroud are that of missing Gloucester businesswoman Ghislaine Hammond. Miss Hammond . . .

"What?"

Repeating her question, Trudy did not turn. Why would she? It was just a television news report. It was wallpaper, and she had spaghetti Bolognese on the go. Kids too full of the afternoon's cream tea to stomach it.

I was frozen to the spot. Numb, and dumb.

. . . had been expected to join friends on a flight from Bristol Airport to Barcelona on Friday morning . . .

. . . became concerned she had come to harm when she failed to . . .

I saw pale, untarnished skin. I pictured Ghislaine in that hotel room in the Cotswolds, easing her nudity back into her clothes after we'd had sex.

. . . officers searching the address found items of clothing . . .

. . . scene handed over to a forensics . . .

This wasn't Ghislaine. It couldn't be. I must have misheard.

. . . Ghislaine Hammond had booked a mini-cab to pick her up at 4 a.m., but the taxi was delayed by ten minutes and by the time it arrived there was no sign of her. There was no answer from her phone when the cab company attempted to contact her . . .

"What?" said Trudy, yet again.

. . . Police were alerted by a neighbour, who saw a man struggling with a woman matching Miss Hammond's description in the driveway of a house in Princess Lane, Stroud . . .

My world collapsed. My jelly knees and swimming head told me to faint. Something inside cut the strings, but another part of me shouted to keep upright at all costs. Keep standing. Don't let it. Don't give in. Christ. Don't.

. . . who has not been named, has been arrested on suspicion of murder and is being questioned . . .

I blanked out the rest of the broadcast. Trudy was talking but I couldn't hear a thing. By the time I re-focussed the news had moved on to another item but I felt completely nauseous. And all the cowering, shivering words I'd dreaded saying tumbled backwards in slow motion inside the shallow shadow of my gutless soul.

"I don't think . . ." I slurred as if I'd lost the power of speech, and had to snap out of it. I had to pretend I was somebody else. Somebody not breaking apart inside. "I . . . don't think . . . I can stomach a big meal after that cream tea this afternoon, babe. I'm bloated as it is."

What she—or I—said next, I have no idea. Maybe she said fine, she was going to cook the sauce anyway and freeze it for another night. Maybe I nuzzled up to her and put my arms around her.

"Sorry. Sorry."

I wasn't sure what I was doing.

I suppose the Kübler-Ross stages of grief had kicked in. Shock and denial beating each other up for pole position. And yet, like some kind of robot, there I was, behaving normally—the little man inside me, my soul, wailing and writhing in agony, while I twisted a corkscrew into a bottle of Lillet—our recently acquired addiction—and ran a slice of orange round the edge of two glasses. I drank, but every few minutes the gorge rose in the back of my throat leaving a salty, acid backlash.

My wife's arm, light as a child's, draped over my tightening chest, I didn't sleep that first night. Didn't want to, let alone deserve to. I knew what I'd dream of. I'd dream of *her*. So I sobbed myself awake. Sobbed soundlessly into my fist until I drew blood in the dark. Until I was afraid the teeth marks in my hand were so deep they'd show and questions would be asked by my inquisitor wife. Until the back of my mouth and my eyelids were on fire. Until bilious, boiling disbelief became a volcanic knowing. A vile certainty that this wasn't what it seemed, what I *wanted* it to be—some elaborate, absurd conspiracy of lies—but a flat, un-ironic truth. And it struck me, pathetic and pulped as I was, as I lay there, that the truth in its arrogance didn't give a shit about me.

Next morning—*first day of the rest of my life*—Ghislaine's laughter rolling round my skull, I tried looking bright-eyed and bushy-tailed at the breakfast table but actually felt like 57 varieties of shit as I sipped blistering tea from a 'Heisenberg' mug.

"Either I've got a dairy allergy or I'm coming down with a serious virus," I said to explain my zombie pallor and Barry White voice.

Amber sighed and said with no small degree of pity, "Dad, you've got a hangover."

"From the mouths of babes and sucklings," said Trudy, to remind me of the bottle we'd put away. The anaesthetic I wanted that hadn't even taken the edge off the sickness I felt in my being.

"Yeah, well, don't believe all you read in the Bible."

"Why?" said Amber.

"Because I'm your dad, and I say so."

"Yeah, well, God's bigger than Dad."

"He might be, but he's not Kung Fu Panda."

I made a karate stance, then ruffled her hair, which she hated, and kissed her freckled nose, which she feigned to dislike as well.

I said: "Be good."

Trudy stood in her kimono dressing gown against the Aga with arms crossed, paler than I was, sporting the Uma Thurman bob she got after *Pulp Fiction*.

I said: "You be good too."

She smiled and touched my sleeve as I left, kissing me on the lips. The girls wiped theirs with the backs of their hands, in unison.

I didn't drive to the office. No way could I face it. I phoned in sick after I left the dual carriageway. My eyes were blurry and my head all over the place, so it wasn't too far from the truth in terms of biological symptoms.

I stopped at a petrol station and bought every national newspaper on the rack, looking round furtively in case anybody I knew could see me. It felt as secretive and shameful as taking something from the top shelf. I wasn't by habit an aficionado of *The Sun* or *Daily Mail* so it went against the grain, but it had to be done. Back in my car I took a deep breath. As expected, the pages were a hard read—literally unbearable. Many times I had to take pause and regulate my breathing before I could return to the text. The headlines of the tabloids, needless to say, were predictably crass and lurid, their favourite words trotted out and emblazoned with relish:

EVIL

. . . Ghislaine Hammond, 40, was the victim of a sexually motivated attack and taken to his home in Princess Lane . . .

TORTURE HOUSE

. . . dismembered Ghislaine Hammond with a circular saw and hid the body parts in the garden shed of an unoccupied house in the same street . . .

DEN OF DEPRAVITY

. . . Ghislaine Hammond's body parts were packed in plastic bags and stored in a suitcase and box discovered by police officers at . . .

I felt sick, and *was* sick.

Stumbling from my Range Rover Evoque in the lay-by and letting the spew puddle in the tyre-ploughed dirt. My open door pinging like a feeble distress call as I cleaned my shoes with a wet wipe.

Princess Lane . . .

The address was like Disney glitter scattered in the gimp-cellar gore.

. . . vehicle was found by police to contain a stun gun, handcuffs, a hunting knife, chloroform, rope and gaffer tape, a so-called "kidnap kit" . . .

God bless the red tops for turning human misery into entertainment, all in the public interest, with their ogling, Page 3 prurience. All tittle-tattle for tomorrow's cat litter tray, of course—unless the body was the one you'd fucked, the dead woman the woman you loved.

Wrung out, I parked in Morrison's in Devizes and sat on a bench overlooking The Crammer. A dog walker in a bobble cap picked up a Rottweiler's turd with fastidious care and some puppet-like pensioners scattered breadcrumbs for bickering ducks.

Everything seemed utterly inane and meaningless, the surface of the lake as glassily breakable as the sky it reflected. I wanted to break it simply for being there. For being unbroken on such a day. When I was anything but.

I kept checking my phone. It wasn't beyond reason that the police might call me, since they'd have my number from Ghislaine's contacts. In fact I was waiting for them to do so, with a sense of inevitability—or a weird kind of relief. Deep down, on some level, I needed to be accused. Of something, I wasn't sure what.

But it never happened. I never got the call, or the knock on the door. They weren't interested in the man who sent those kinds of texts, the man—sad, pathetic, banal—who had an affair behind his wife's back and was secretly planning to desert his family. They were interested in a murderer. And it sounded, thank God, like they already had him.

I should have felt happy about that, but I wasn't. It made me feel powerless and weak. Weaker than I'd ever felt in my life. Somehow I thought that person in custody, whoever he was, much as I loathed him, had got what he wanted. He'd been successful in his goal, his dreams. He was strong, and I wasn't. He'd won.

At the end of that Monday—that empty, hellish, never-ending Monday—Trudy lay with her cheek resting on the cushion on my lap as we watched one of her soaps: friends and neighbours sleeping with each other, betraying one another. It seemed to be the only plot line, week in, week out. I moved my hand down to one of my favourite parts of her, the soft line from her belly button to the top of her pubic hair. I traced the stretch marks that were the legacy of childbirth, a warrior scarring that inexplicably embarrassed her, but comforted me—if she but knew it—as I never needed comforting before. Even as the memory of touching different skin rose up to engulf me.

Over the next few days and weeks, further details seeped out via the usual journalistic channels.

A man appeared in Gloucester Crown Court accused of Ghislaine's murder. I refuse to use his name. It has already been written too many times, conferring on him a status in our cultural consciousness I don't want him to have. He sat with his arms folded as he listened to the brief proceedings, and spoke only three times, answering yes each time to confirm his name, whether he could hear clearly via the video link from where he was on remand, and whether he understood he could raise his hand if he wished to speak. They gave a date when the case was expected to be listed for trial.

Information like that, reduced to the merely factual by some cub reporter, was so dry and unreflective as to be offensive. To me, anyway. It was as if the deceased—somebody's daughter, somebody's sister—whose corpse had been dismembered and stacked in the garden shed of a terraced house in Stroud was of no more value than a fictional character, a victim in a crime drama or novel.

The casual reader would not have been interested in who she was or what she might have gone through. What the ropes might have felt like. What unimaginable thoughts might have raced through her mind in the flickering, hideous half-light of her suffering when she knew she was going to die at the hands of a person whose only interest was in using her for pleasure—and that pleasure came from inflicting pain and disregarding her as a human being.

The casual reader didn't wonder whether she cried out their name before that final act of debasement that robbed her of life. Didn't wonder whether the last movements of those lips were to form the syllables they themselves last heard as an endearment.

And I had to feign disinterest too. Keeping my head down when the office was bubbling with news of the tragedy that had befallen one of our own. Showing little emotion in front of Trudy when a news item came up on TV, even though the cascade of revelations gouged my wounds ever deeper.

. . . latest in a series of grisly discoveries at the home of former territorial army officer . . .

Four more female bodies were unearthed in the garden of 45 Princess Lane, two now identified as sex workers on the police missing persons files. Another was believed to be that of the accused's ten-year old sister, whose remains showed she had been subjected to sexual acts and extensive, prolonged torture. Another decomposed skeleton was confirmed to be that of his step-mother. A fifth body wrapped and mummified behind furniture and a mattress in an unused cellar was as yet unidentified. The police had found evidence that other bodies, either human or animal, had been consumed in a large tank semi-corroded by chemicals.

By the time I got to those words, I was corroded too.

Day upon day, it became the norm to feel my brain knotted in contusions of veiled panic, but I had to go on existing. Ghislaine's life had ended, but mine hadn't—it had taken a curve, a sharp, dangerous curve, then dropped through a trap-door, but it didn't end. Sometimes I wished it had. In some ways that would have been easier.

But the reality was, I had to carry on with my life.

Of course I did.

As they used to announce when I was a child if the TV had a technical problem: *Normal service will be resumed as soon as possible.*

And it was.

I will never forget Ghislaine. I can see her face and smile now as if it were yesterday and my mind shifts to an alternate reality from which I have to haul it back.

However, the truth is, even the most devastating grief cannot last forever—not in its rawest form, and much as sometimes you want to hang onto it that way, as a duty to a lost loved one. Even though every normal act now—shopping with my wife, going to a parent's night at school—seemed like a betrayal, a slight to Ghislaine and the life we'd dreamed of together, every fake smile an insult to the relationship she and I planned, to the fumbling love we tumbled into and had sworn ourselves to—it didn't last forever.

As weeks turned into months I found I thought about Ghislaine less and less often, though the gradual diminution of those moments of recollection, far from giving me respite, filled me with shame, inadequacy and self-loathing. To begin with, almost every thought or image my memory conjured up, unbidden—her wonky lipstick, that old-fashioned look, the gap at the top of her leather boots, the way she shook her hair and plucked at it with her fingers—would bring a salty bolus to the back of my throat. But those occasions, mercifully, but horribly, became fewer and farther between.

The love I'd had for her—not a fiction, ever, but a ghost now—waned with excruciating inevitability, and I achieved a kind of distance and could gradually see the whole thing for what it undoubtedly was. A kind of illness. Perhaps Shakespeare had made that comparison already, or some other poet had. I expect so. After all we use the phrase *love sick*, and that must come from somewhere, I suppose.

Love. Sick.

Well, I recovered from that sickness. Slowly. Painfully. Feeling terrible guilt every step of the way for doing so. But in time even that faded. I read somewhere once that the human being can only stand so much pain—physical or mental—before it shuts off. I don't think it's our fault as individuals that, whatever trauma we've endured, we want to survive. We want survival, and we want happiness.

It was our anniversary just before Christmas and Trudy's parents volunteered to take the kids while the two of us had a weekend away, which we'd hardly ever done, just the two of us, since the rug rats came along. Too knackered, for one thing.

One of our company directors had a *gite* with a swimming pool near Brignoles, a former olive press, which he let friends use when he wasn't there himself, so I had a word and put my name in the book. From the roof barbecue area we'd occasionally spy a family of wild boar, but they never ventured closer than the rim of the densely dark forest. "Look, Mum's out again taking her kiddies for a stroll," Trudy would say, as we drank the plonk of the local vineyard.

Matisse's La Chapelle du Rosaire de Vence was on our must-see list. Not usually moved by church architecture, I found it a disarmingly restful place. The guide told us that in 1941 Matisse had developed cancer and underwent surgery, and on the long and arduous road to recovery he was helped by a part-time nurse called Monique Bourgeois, who apparently cared for him with immense and selfless tenderness. She subsequently became a nun but the two maintained a friendship. Monique continued to visit him, on one occasion telling him of plans the Dominicans had to build a chapel next to the local girls' school, and asking him if he would contribute artistically to the design. Instead of merely *contributing*, Matisse immersed himself in the project, thought by many to be his masterpiece, designing everything from the interior to murals, the Stations of the Cross, the crucifix, even the vestments of the priests. Though baptised a Catholic, he had not practised for many years. Yet here was the altar, the colour of bread to represent the Eucharist; the colours of the stained glass windows flooding the interior with light—yellow of the life-giving sun, green of vegetation and cactus plants, intense blue of the Mediterranean and the Madonna.

I found my thoughts returning to Ghislaine, and the fact that no chapel would be created in her memory. The only altar to her was in the pages of the tabloids, its only congregation a readership eager for a vicarious thrill of sex and death. In that moment, for some reason, the idea that every part of her—her voice, body, spirit—was all lost became a sadness so vast and heavy it was impossible to bear. I felt my shoulders heaving and my head sagged.

Trudy nudged my elbow. "You're crying. You are. You're crying."

I rubbed away tears behind my glasses. "I can't help it."

Trudy hooked her arm around mine. "Do you think he was in love with her?"

I said: "What do you think?"

"I think either he was in love with her, or he was in love with God," she said.

That evening she asked if I wanted to FaceTime the kids. I said yes. Amber was miserable because this year for the school Nativity play they'd given her the role of a sheep.

"Dad, it doesn't even have any lines! It's a sheep!" Last year she'd been the Innkeeper—a small part, but important. And at least she had some dialogue.

"You need a new agent," I said.

Verity said they wanted us to come home, they were missing us. It broke my heart. In the small picture on my phone she appeared so grown up, but the pout made her look five again. After we hung up we both wiped away tears then laughed at each other's silliness. Trudy reached over and combed back my hair with her fingers.

At breakfast the next morning I watched as she ate a croissant from the local *patisserie*, licking her fingertip and dotting the crumbs on her plate.

"I meant to say. You looked fantastic yesterday in the sunlight by the pool," I said. "Your hair was really glowing. You look really well lately." I meant it, as I meant what I said next. "I do love you, you know."

"That's nice." Trudy habitually berated me for not giving her enough compliments, though her own were equally scarce. "You're not so bad yourself, sometimes. Not often, mind you."

The sun was high, but we went back to bed.

The trial, when it came, inevitably brought back all kinds of emotions I thought I'd buried. I was a fool not to expect it, but it hit me for six.

Obviously I did my best not to let this show in front of my family, but it was hard to stay in the same room when every TV news report covered it extensively. I tried to let my eyes glaze over and not take it in. I tried to make the footage abstract, unreal, distant. I knew for an absolute certainty that Ghislaine would not have wanted me to be unhappy, especially in front of the children, and I kept telling myself that, and it helped.

We learned that, after choking his victims, the accused had had sex with the dead bodies, then used an array of implements to mutilate them, "either for further sexual gratification or to impede identification of the remains". Officers at the scene were sickened and shocked during the days and weeks when the man's home address was systematically taken apart to reveal more horrors, including human arms and legs boarded in behind a sunken bath. One Detective Sergeant described the place as smelling of "gone off meat".

Ghislaine Hammond, it was surmised, had tragically mistaken his cruising, opportunistic white Skoda Octavia for the mini-cab she had ordered to take her to Bristol Airport to join her friends for a hen weekend in Barcelona. The post mortem revealed extensive bruising on her skin and twenty-eight knife wounds, including gashes to her torso and shoulders inflicted both before and after her death.

The prosecuting QC delivered evidence that the defendant had "almost certainly" had sex with Ms Hammond post-mortem, after which he'd shared text messages with acquaintances and posted jokes on social media, then ordered a take-away pizza and watched recordings of television comedy shows including *Dad's Army* and *Only Fools and Horses* for three hours before dismembering her body.

Jurors took just over an hour to reach a guilty verdict. The judge handed down a mandatory life sentence with a minimum of thirty-five years. The armoured car left the law courts, blitzed by the flashes from cameras at its murky windows. We had been warned by the BBC newsreader that there would be flashing images in the report that followed.

"This was the correct verdict." Standing outside the building, the Senior Investigating Officer had a wide, large head indicative of mild encephalitis. His eyes showed not so much moral indignation as the reined-in emotion of a triumphant football manager. He said his team were pleased that "a man compelled by casual depravity and twisted sexual and sadistic desire" had been taken off the streets. Then we were away to the conflict with ISIS in Syria, and the killer faded into criminal history, carrying his secrets with him, as I carried mine.

My escape from ordinary life was gone too—ripped away in the most violent manner possible. Like all dreams it had evaporated into nothing, and I could see more clearly now I was awake.

With hindsight, thinking back on my turbulent emotions, I can hardly recognise myself. I don't know what came over me. You could call it hope. As I say, you could call it madness.

Certifiable.

The delicious craziness of throwing everything up in the air, as a possibility. But it wasn't a possibility any more. And maybe that was a good thing.

Ghislaine was the past. An aberration. Not real. I could now see that what she represented wasn't reality at all.

What I had thought of as liberation had been just a diversion, a trap. By whatever circuitous route I'd come to it, I was safe again, rescued by grotesque happenchance from the reckless abandon of my unchained emotions. My want. My craving—which was not really a craving for anything or any person, I now saw, but just to be someone I wasn't.

Now I could return to who I really was.

Occasionally over the months and years I would inevitably come across photographs of the murderer, usually lined up beside other notorious serial killers: Dennis Nilsen, Peter Sutcliffe, Harold

Shipman, in double-page spreads or in true crime documentaries for the seemingly insatiable Channel 5 audience—usually the ubiquitous police mug shot showing nothing behind his eyes but querulous confusion. In that stark image the demonisation seemed complete. Fittingly, he was a flat, two-dimensional artwork. We could project onto it or analyse it, or guess, or imagine, but nothing was there—just an eternal, alien bewilderment.

With the passage of time I eventually felt more remote and disconnected, but he always seemed part of me, attached by some dark umbilical. And while I'd happily have seen him erased from the face of this earth, I was also aware that I owed him a debt.

I could so easily have set out on a foolish, destructive course of action with Ghislaine, intoxicated by a chance encounter with someone who reciprocated my affection. As a result I would have lost everything I held so dear. Everything I truly loved.

•●•

Seven years later, holding the bird's crushed remains in my hand, remembering the sound of its tiny bones cracking so easily under my hand, I can't help but think of the fragility of Ghislaine's body. The lightness of her as we rolled and lifted, shoved and gripped and lost ourselves, free as leaves on the air. I consider the weight of a life, and how the murderer took that forever. Stifled, throttled, abused it in ways more terrible than I wanted to imagine—but had.

And yet, and yet . . . I am grateful to him.

I return from the litter bin at the end of the street. When I get back indoors I see no dark snowfall of feathers. The room is pristine. Immaculate. The act erased. A murder scene, scrubbed of evidence.

Dust pan and brush in hand, Trudy reminds me to wash my hands, which I do at the kitchen sink, lathering up like a surgeon before an operation. While I'm there I switch on the radio and unpack the dishwasher, which has run overnight, placing everything on the cutting block in the middle of the room. Joining me, Trudy places the glasses and mugs on their respective shelves, the plates in the cabinets, while I put the cutlery in their drawer, the utensils on the hooks over the Aga. The usual, time-honoured delegation of roles.

While Trudy calls up to the girls to rouse from their pit and get dressed for school I put two large scoops of Illy in the cafetière and fill the kettle. She cuts two slices of sourdough for the toaster and fetches butter from the fridge. By then, the cat out in the utility room is whining to be let back in, and, as I knew she would, Trudy relents.

Shame-facedly, the Abyssinian pokes its nose round the door, utters a little whine of incomprehension. As well it might.

"Bad animal," I say, as if reprimanding a child.

"Oh, don't shout at her." Trudy picks it up and cradles it like an infant, giving its fawn, furry tummy a generous massage.

"I can't believe you're rewarding it with a tummy tickle. I don't get a tummy tickle when I do something bad."

"That's because you never do anything good," she jokes. "Anyway, she can't help it. She's just doing what she's programmed to do, by nature." She rubs her nose against its cheek. "Aren't you, you gorgeous creature? Yes, you are . . ."

"Don't encourage it, for crying out loud." But when she's in full anthropomorphic mode she won't listen to reason.

"It thinks we are its family," she says. "It brings dead things in to please us, to make us happy. It thinks it's bringing us a little gift."

I hear Amber and Verity fighting for the bathroom.

I pick up the cafetière and fill two mugs. I dispense one artificial sweetener into Trudy's and hesitate. I normally put two in mine. But I remember the Gloucester Services. The two cubes of sugar on the paper napkin.

I take one from the bowl on the kitchen island and hold it on the meniscus of my black coffee for a couple of seconds. I've always liked watching it gradually darken from the bottom up. Then I let go. I insert my spoon and stir. I feel the lump of sugar break up, its granules dispersing in ever smaller particles. Until, very soon, there is nothing at all.

The Black Cat

ATTENTION: Amariah Brigham, M.D.
Superintendent,
New York State Lunatic Asylum,
Utica,
New York
October 15th, 1843

Sir,

You will have, by now, taken receipt of my former patient, and received all the reports accompanying his corporeal frame. You will observe, I am sure, he does not lament in grief, either at his own fate or for those who suffered at his hand. Murder is an unpardonable Sin—one might say, a Sin Against His Holy Work—however, I feel compelled to communicate with you regarding his case, in view of the blurring between fact and fiction due to the interference of a member of the public.

I am referring to the short story—of which you may be aware—published in the August 19th edition of the *US Saturday Post*, attributed to Edgar Allan Poe, the author of a lurid volume of tales published a few years back, to no great acclaim. "The Black Cat" is, in my opinion, a vile narrative, made all the more vile when one knows the real life events that were its inspiration.

Mr Poe, I should point out, has past form in such matters. "The Mystery of Marie Rogêt", published in *Snowden's Ladies Companion* last December, shamelessly commandeered the real life murder of one Mary Rogers, a young woman who had worked in a New York City cigar store, in an attempt to solve the crime.

Whilst in that instance his motivation may have been laudable, in this it is decidedly not, and its gross distortion of the facts not only irresponsible but beyond the pale.

If you have not come across the fore-mentioned tale, I shall paraphrase:

From the outset we are plunged into the mind of a *mono-maniac* who, fuelled by "Fiendish Intemperance and ill temper", comes to regard his favourite pet—a black cat named Pluto—as the agent of pure evil. He comes to hate the very sight of it, and after a night out, when it wounds him with a scratch, takes out his pen knife and gouges out one of the creature's eyes. Overcome by horror and remorse, he watches the cat recover, but his guilt turns to irritation and, possessed of a (boldly stated) sense of Perversity, he hangs it by the neck from a tree. After his house burns down and he perceives the smoky image of a black cat imprinted on one wall of its ruin, the narrator decides he must replace the pet. He comes across one, almost identical to the first, at one of his watering holes, but realises soon after he brings it home that it, too, is one-eyed. Thus his dislike spirals into utter loathing and dread. "The feeble remnants of good within me receded," we are told, and when he accompanies his wife to the cellar, the cat follows. He picks up an axe to deliver a blow to the hated animal but his wife stills his arm, and instead he buries the axe in her brain. After bricking up her body in an alcove, to his delight, the black cat is absent, and he sleeps soundly for the third and fourth night in a row. When the police finally arrive, the murderer's arrogance is such that he strikes the brickwork to show how sturdy it is—causing a sound to rise like a child's sobbing which transforms into a long, loud, continuous scream . . . and this is where Poe performs his odious *coup de theatre.* The officers of the law pull down the newly-erected wall, and—*behold!*—the *black cat* is sitting on the head of the corpse, its hideous mewling having brought the perpetrator to justice!

All very dreadful, and all very frightful—but the *truth* of the case can only be revealed by stripping Mr Poe of his flight of fancy and returning to the facts. Which are horrific, yes—they are nonetheless *human*, and, as the philosopher puts it, we must embrace all that is human, or we are lost.

N— was born in Richmond of Scottish stock, his father an engineer and Wesleyan, his educational achievements moderate, and his standing in society as an adult modest but sufficient for the attainment of average human contentment. He married in June 1835 at the age of twenty-seven; the bride was twenty-one. His family had acquired wealth—hers was inherited. Neither was impecunious. However, the union failed to be blessed with offspring, though, from the evidence of those who knew them, this appeared neither a bone of contention nor a dampener to their spirits. In short, they loved each other. A circumstance which would shortly be shattered in the most tragic fashion imaginable.

When N— heard his wife was with child, his delight was unbridled. Indeed, he told me face-to-face that, in that moment, he felt his life fulfilled. Little did he know, but all would soon come crashing about his ears. For when the baby was born, and its first cries drew him from a downstairs room to the ashen face of the midwife, he found himself looking down at a small face whose countenance could not be in more marked contrast to the white sheet wrapped around it. Though his wife smothered the newborn with kisses, its face was unmistakably *black*.

To his credit, though, N— rejected neither mother nor child. In fact, he is reported to have rocked it in his arms and whispered endearments into its tiny ears.

In time, however, the affront of his wife's infidelity—not only with another man, but with a *Negro*—festered within him. According to his own account, its wails, incessant and piercing, assaulted him so relentlessly he grew to hate it. His nerves all but shattered, one day he took a fork from the cutlery drawer of the kitchen and gouged out its left eye. "To give it something to cry about," he said. When the child's mother returned from a neighbour's house, she found her infant hanging from the branch of an oak.

The reason why she did not immediately flee to the authorities can only be conjecture. Perhaps a collapse of physical and mental fibre prevented her. What cannot be in dispute is that, from that point on, every fragment of love she might have had for him in the past had been eradicated, and it was in bouts of sullen wordlessness that her contempt for him simmered. N— himself admits he laboured under the illusion that, the problem having been solved, and his husbandly duties renewed, his marriage would repair itself. Indeed, when his wife announced that she, again, was expectant, he was overjoyed—*a second time.*

She, for her part, behaved lovingly towards him, giving every impression that she would deliver to him the most pleasurable and restorative gift. Nothing could have been further from the truth.

The second child that was held out to him in swaddling clothes was as dark-skinned as the first. And the smile on the face of his wife told him that, even if he believed she had been forced into congress that first time, this time she had not. Nothing could be plainer now than that she had returned to a Negro's eager arms of her own free will and in complete knowledge of the consequences of her actions.

This attack upon his manhood—his *being*—proved unable to bear. N— had reached the breaking point of a frayed rope. As she, in her quest for revenge, must have predicted. What she failed to predict was what happened next. N— took a poker from beside the grate, and even with the newborn wailing, battered in her skull, before immediately silencing the infant's own weeping forever.

Their house boasted no cellar. There was no former chimney-breast. No convenient building materials. No melodramatic disposal of the corpse as per Mr Poe's sordid version of occurrences. On the contrary, our patient simply walked to Baltimore City Jail in his stocking'd feet to hand himself in.

Unsurprisingly, the story in all its gruesome details soon reached the newspapers, and soon, evidently, reached Mr Poe. One can see from the outset how the shrieking of a baby and the yowling of a cat can be seen, by a poet, to be homophonic. And while critics may delight in such symbolism, I cannot.

What was his purpose in writing such a *tale*, I ask? One can only imagine that he was amused by elevating it into metaphorical form, but in so doing, portraying the perpetrator of the murders as a madman, he can only have been playing to the *literati* in whose circles he moves and prospers; worthy-minded democrats and Abolitionists who would, doubtless, be made merry by a sordid allegory about a white maniac getting his comeuppance after his wife's blood commingles with that of an inferior race.

But that bald accusation of *madness*—notwithstanding the verdict of the jury—amounts, in my opinion, to nothing but a wicked calumny. In indulging his romance of the Madman writ large, Poe ignores the true cause of the deaths: That is to say, provocation.

What else can you call a wife who willingly lay with a Negro, but *provocation* of the most appalling kind? And to do it *twice*—why, that is *provocation*, I submit, more than any white man could be expected to bear. One might even suggest that the wife, in committing the carnal felony of adultery, was the true criminal in the affair.

Poe describes his narrator as a dipsomaniac (more, surely, the writer's own curse rather than that of N—, who was a teetotaller). Damningly, he says the man had occasion to beat his wife while in thrall to drink. This too is a lie. The body showed no bruises, indeed no marks at all except for the staving-in of her brow created by the impact of the blunt instrument. N— showed no early symptoms of melancholia or depravity. "The Black Cat", in summation, can be seen only as nothing more than an opportunistic act of character assassination.

The writer called the black cat "Pluto"—(he has a fondness for the astronomical: his Negro in *The Gold Bug* was called "Jupiter")—but the ruler of Hades has no role here. There is no dark underworld, just the disgusting and unpalatable image of a white woman swooning in a black man's arms, and the poisonous idea that harlot and Negro may have laughed at her husband's pain even as they performed the conjugal act. No reasonable man could imagine that love would have fuelled such fornication. And no reasonable man blame N— for reacting in the manner he did. Further, in his striking out against the abomination of the mating of white and non-white, I would aver him to be no less heroic than Herakles, who strangled a threatening python in his cradle.

Therefore I urge you, doctor—and this is the crux of this epistle . . . please apply every effort to reassess the patient I entrust to you.

Do not blindly accept the aberrant judgement of the court. Apply the measure of your own brain and professional diligence and, I beg you, present N— to any future Board of Review as the man he truly is. Someone as sane as you or I. A man pressed beyond his limits into actions that any good Christian may have undertaken with God at his elbow.

I look forward to the time you can tell me he has been freed of the strait-jacket and moved to the shackles of a conventional prison, where he can serve a penal sentence without a blight on his character or the "moral" cause of his actions.

He was a criminal. He acted upon his passions. He took a life. All this is true. *But he is not mad.*

If he is—then we are *all* mad.

Until then, I remain, sir,

Your most obedient servant,

Perseus Mogridge Styles, M.D.
President of the Board and Medical Superintendent,
Spring Grove State Hospital for the Insane,
Catonsville,
Baltimore

Beat the Card Home

My father's name was Matthew and my wife's grandfather was Matthias, so that was it—our son would be Matthias to keep the Austrians happy, and Matt, 'Matty' for short, to us. My favourite photograph of him sits framed on my desk, his little round face with its lop-sided smile looking up from the buggy, wearing that Christmas hat with polar bear ears.

He was a loved child from the moment he first took breath. Jen looked like she'd been through the Vietnam war, then run a marathon, a layer of sweat on her like a race horse, but even then, by some miracle, the adoration just gushed out of her. It was a reserve she just never ran out of. I envied that, like most men I guess, and wondered at it. It was unattainable, and perfect as a leaf.

Not that life was perfect. It never is. There are always holes in the road and sometimes that's what life is, fetching a truck full of asphalt and filling those holes when they occur.

We had hospital visits. What parents don't? Like when he stuck a chunk of foam from some cuddly toy up his nose and breathed in. That involved general anaesthetic and an overnight stay. They allowed us to sleep in the next room. He looked sorry for himself the next morning, but kids are resilient. They're designed that way.

Several years later he developed stomach problems that kept him awake at night, a concern for his mother and me. He'd habitually try to get me to stay long after I'd finished his bedtime story; always an excuse, his toe was hurting, his eyes were sore, he kept thinking bad thoughts—anything to keep me there a few minutes longer before the light went out. But the sobbing got worse, even with Junior Strength Advil, and it tore up his mother so much we took him to a specialist who thought he was lactose intolerant, which proved to be untrue. We tried gluten free and the cramps stopped, coinciding with him going up to the big school. Make of that what you will. No more Jeffrey Stanmore stopping him from going to the bathroom when he needed to, wanting him to be his best friend and nobody else's.

I'll never forget going to Cub Scouts prize-giving, looking down from the mezzanine of the church hall, seeing the other boys hitting hell out of each other and Matty sitting perfectly still in the eye of the maelstrom, cupping his hand over his carefully-gelled hair, protecting it from the barbarians. That same day his name was read out when he got a medal for 'Outstanding Citizen', which came as a complete surprise to him, and to me. I clapped till my hands stung. I knew right then that, whatever exams he passed, whatever the world slung at him, my boy would be okay.

He got good grades, mostly in science, so when the time came, opted to go off to study pharmacy at BSU. I never said I didn't approve, but I did say I couldn't see the attraction of standing in a white coat handing out condoms and haemorrhoid cream. He said, "Dad, life's not all about the job you do. It can be about happiness." And that's not something you can disagree with, unless you're a fool.

Before college started, he decided to take in a last lungful of freedom and go on a road trip with his boyfriend, a sweet guy named Terence Hong, Korean heritage but Cape Cod born and bred. Terence was skinny as a rake, and, in spite of their obvious physical differences, when he and Matty stood side by side in identical white tees, they looked like twins.

Plan was, they'd get a flight from Boston to New Orleans, hire a car from Hertz and head west to Los Angeles. No set itinerary. No ETA.

As Matty packed his rucksack, I bit my lip to prevent myself interrogating him on what he'd forgotten, instead asking where they were intending to stay, thinking, if this was my wife and me, I'd have booked hotel rooms in advance, quaint inns or bed and breakfasts, like when we did Maine and New Hampshire the previous fall.

"You're kidding," he said. "No, we'll just do motels, if we find them, keep it cheap."

What if you don't find them?

"Then we'll sleep in the car. Save money. For booze."

"I hope you're not thinking of drinking and driving."

"No, Dad," he said, with long drawn-out weariness, but no ounce of malice. There was no ounce of malice in that kid, ever.

We hugged and he promised to send postcards home. Which sounds pathetically antiquated, but he wasn't on social media anymore. He'd deleted all his accounts—Facebook, Twitter, Instagram—ever since a troll started persecuting him for his sexuality. Wasn't worth it, he'd said. To us, his parents, it had been an unpleasant reminder that, while a lot of the world had learned to embrace loving relationships of all genders, there were still some haters out there who didn't. Maybe that was why I continued to be worried about him. Yes, he could look after himself, probably better than I could, but all fathers want their children to be free of pain and hurt, when it comes down to it. And the thought of some of that shit made my blood boil. Why were some sad individuals so goddamned incensed about two human beings being in love with each other?

When Jen and I deposited them at the terminal building, we both felt a little tearful and a little stupid. As I parked in our driveway, I suggested a visit to the Dry Dock Bar. She said, "That's the best idea you've had in weeks." I said, "I know."

With unexpected alacrity, the first postcard arrived two days after their departure. God bless the U.S. Mail.

Mom & Dad

Just arrived New Orleans. Stepped out of the airport and got a blast of the heating unit just above my head, like stepping into an oven.

Then realised that's no heater! That's the sun*! (T says hi, by the way.)*

Matty x

P.S. Down here 'sauce' is a 3-syllable word! Sa-oww-ce! xx M

On the other side was a colorful picture of the French Quarter showing a jazz band—Louis Armstrong era. Not my personal preference when it comes to music. I'm more of a Tom Waits fan. Someone who Matty once said sounded like a man who shouldn't be let anywhere near a microphone. I told him, that was the exact point.

I'd reminded him to check the rental car for dents and scratches before they set off. Not to let the company nail them for damage they didn't cause. An old trick, and good advice, I thought, but he looked at me like I was trying to ignite a campfire with two wet sticks and he was holding a box of matches.

I pictured the two of them in the Kia Picanta "or similar", disregarding my further wisdom to keep the windows closed and the AC on. The hell, I guess it was their job to know best, and mine to be stupid or boring. I heard their laughter, sharing some joke, maybe at my expense, enjoying whatever music station they'd tuned in to, saw the wind ruffling in their hair. The meticulously-gelled coiffure long gone.

Remembering then my words when Matty first told us he was gay. I'd said, not for any grand effect, but because it was true: "Doesn't matter who you love, son, as long as they love you back." We'd hugged, like we always did. No different from the day before, or the day after.

Mom & Dad

Along the Mississippi. Shocked to see real poverty—I mean, shacks. *Brit in a diner bought us breakfast & recommended a steak house in Jackson, said best in the country. Half a day to get there! Better be worth it!*

Matty x

We'd gotten into a routine now.

Bring the postcard from the mailbox. Make some strong black coffee. Take it in turns to read it aloud. If I was out working, Jen would wait till I arrived home. It turned into a treat I looked forward to, after a day of tree removal and lawn maintenance, battling decay producing fungi, dealing with gypsy moth or bagworm.

Mom & Dad

Got there finally. Hot & sweaty tin lodge. Middle of nowhere, packed (all white faces)—if you eat a T-bone they give you another one free! We shared 50-50. Still Too Much! Whisky (compulsory!) Cook must shed five pounds every night! (The Jackson steakhouse diet!) Love you lots

Matty x

Jen just looked at this one for a while, back and front, then said: "My baby."

It didn't need elaborating. Not to me.

Mom & Dad

Distances are crazy, we'll never get to LA by car, so we're driving back to N.Orl and getting a flight to Phoenix. Tony has a hangover. Says the map is blurry. Hahaha!

Matty x

We had a day of rest after that one, which I placed with the others on the mantelpiece. The next arrived two days later.

Mom & Dad

Arrived Phoenix Airport. Detour to Apache Junction. Old mining town, T says he's seen it in a Sean Penn movie. Place on map: OK Corral. Real one or not? Don't know. Soon find out!

Matty xxx

Tears prickled in my eyes as I imagined him writing a postcard to us every day when he should be enjoying himself. Couldn't help wondering if, on occasion, Terence looked at him askance behind Ray-bans, shaking his head. "What are you doing spinning that postcard rack, man? Let's hit the road."

While my wife answered the ring of the doorbell, I turned the card over and looked at the photograph on the other side. *Superstition Mountain*, read the caption. I'd never heard of it, but then there were a whole lot of things in Arizona I hadn't heard of. It looked like a big stone beast in slumber.

My wife spoke my name. "Mason."

I placed down my cup of coffee. A rotund but young female police officer was framed in my doorway. I walked to her, hand extended, thinking, and saying, thank God, not before time thcy did something about that dumped vehicle at the end of the street. Hell, it was an eyesore.

The officer's eyes remained semi-hidden under her cap. She said she was sorry, she hadn't come about that. She said she was sorry a second time, then asked if she could talk. I said, "Sure," wondering why she wasn't. When she asked if we could wait until my wife returned from the kitchen, the cogs in my brain turned and I understood that she wanted Jen to be present for this conversation. I immediately thought, well, she has to be if this is the way we are heading. And I knew we were.

It had happened near Sedona.

From what we found out later, they were en route to Flagstaff. Terence had taken his turn at the wheel. Matty had felt tired and unwell, but, typically, was eager not to spoil the vacation by making a fuss. Drowsy, he slumped on Terence's shoulder. Terence remembers him saying, "Soon be there." Then he murmured something, and fell asleep with his eyes open. Those were the last words he said.

When the car stopped at the road side, he couldn't be woken. He had to be carried from the car into Verde Valley Medical Centre, where he was put to bed and a blood test was taken. The results showed "a considerable haemolytic anaemia"—a breakdown of blood platelets, something completely unpredictable in a young man of his age and good health. He died within an hour of arriving there.

Terence was almost invisible in the confusion. Even so, we heard his reaction impressed the entire staff of the Medical Centre. He displayed dignity and strength, signs of a maturity beyond his years. He remained calm and composed. He did not crumble in the face of devastation. The same couldn't be said about us.

Our world imploded, and even as it was happening, I thought how unbecoming it was to the memory of our son, that we owed it to our perfect boy to cling on and survive this, but the overwhelming drive for us both was to do the opposite. Only the thought of hanging onto him, a memory of him, and not letting that go, kept our mouths above water.

The next day another postcard arrived. A sucker punch, right in the base of the guts.

My hands shook as I clanged the mailbox shut, my heart trying to escape my chest as I staggered back to my home, the mundane truth dawning on me, stiff and prosaic and cruel, that our son simply must've sent it before he died. As he'd done dozens, hundreds of unknowable things in those hours before . . .

I took a deep breath and turned over the photograph of *The Manger Desert Sun Motel, Phoenix.*

We sat with our hearts dragged half out of us. Staring at it, steeling ourselves, thinking how something can be a torture and a blessing at one and the same time. But it was.

Mom & Dad

Terence wants to see the Grand Canyon. Decided we're going to go to Flagstaff for a few days, fly back from Phoenix. Will probably beat this card home!

Matty x

We read it, weeping.

Weeping from the roots of our souls because when he wrote those few unremarkable sentences, Matty had no idea what would occur later that day, under that cloudless sky. He was alive in that writing, frozen in time, like a face in an old photograph, and that was the sorrowful joy of it—he was still *alive* in those words.

We clung to that postcard. And when my wife was ready to let go, a decade, a century later, I took it from her hand and gently placed it on the mantel with the others, the smoke from the log fire biting the surface of my eyes.

Foolishly, I thought God had done with us then. I was wrong.

The following day I went to the mailbox and collected a sheaf of letters, mostly junk mail and coupons from a local supermarket or pizza delivery service. Flicking through them as I walked back to the house, I called my wife. Must've sounded something like the cry of a dog.

The handwriting unmistakable.

It threw me at first—of course it would—then I concluded Matty must've sent it the same day as, or even the day before, the last. That had to be it. It was logical. The mail screws up, after all. Christ, they do that all the time.

This time it was a photograph captioned *Desert Donkeys Burros*. Perhaps he bought it from the same truck stop or drug store as the other, I didn't know, but what did it matter?

I called Jen a second time. She looked pale and wobbly coming downstairs, her hand gliding down the rail as I raised up the small rectangle in my fingers.

She held out the flats of her hands. I placed it on them and wiped the perspiration off my skin. I found my glasses. She found hers. The kitchen table beckoned. She said aloud the first three words . . . but not the rest.

Her eyes lost focus. She stared at the table, then the wall. I asked what was wrong. Silence gagged the woman, and it frightened me. I took it from her. Not sure I wanted to. And damn sure, once I'd read it.

Mom & Dad

You probably know by now. I died today. It didn't hurt. It's hard to explain. Don't be sad. Love

Matty x

Jen snatched it back.

The most horrible thing I've seen in my life is her look of pleading puzzlement right then, because there wasn't a thing I could do about it, least of all explain it. I mouthed that it must be from somebody else. Some sick sonofabitch.

"Who?"

"Somebody trying to cause us pain."

"Someone in Arizona? We don't know anyone in Arizona."

"Okay, who? Who do you think it is? Tell me."

"It's him," she said, anger in her frown. "You know it's him. It's obviously him. Don't you recognise your own son's handwriting—Look!" She grabbed the other postcards and threw them down. She wanted me to compare them, and I didn't. I refused to. "You *know* who it is!"

Did I? *Did* I know? If it had ended there, maybe that question would have plagued me. But this was only the beginning.

Greetings from Arizona. The Grand Canyon State.

I took it to the bathroom. I ran the water as I sat and read it, alone.

Mom & Dad

It's so weird. You can see hundreds of miles in all directions across the desert. Over to the west I can see a town, and there are dark clouds over it like you get in cartoons (Road Runneresque) + I can see lightning jab down, and rain. But where I'm standing is dry as a bone.

Don't cry over me. I'm in a good place. I like it here. Met Pops and Grammy. They say hi. Hugs & kisses

Matty x

I don't know why I thought I could keep it from Jen. I couldn't.

After I read it to her, she went for a walk with the dogs, our military Schnauzer and American bulldog, probably in Beebe Woods, or along Surf Drive Beach to the Nobska Light, her usual hikes, and returned, silent then for a long while but happy. Of course she was. Her mother and her father were there with her son. She didn't need to say a thing. I could see it all in her face. I think from that moment, looking back, I knew I almost wasn't part of it anymore.

I remember that night I heard her sitting up in darkness. I checked my watch. She said she was going downstairs to read it again. I pulled on my robe. She said I didn't have to get up. I said, "Yes, I do."

We knew what Matty would have wanted. No black suits. No flowers. No bullshit. No religion. A lead weight lifted when it was all over, but the day you're your son's pallbearer never leaves you. It's against nature and I'd sooner take a bayonet to the skull than go through it again. Afterwards I saw Jen talking to neighbours and friends, my own throat too raw to utter anything but an industrial-level expletive in the form of a howl, resisting that being an extreme act of willpower on my part.

I asked her later why she hadn't mentioned the postcards to Terence as we'd planned. She behaved as though I hadn't spoken, so I said it again. She looked at me like I was stupid and said she'd had the most recent card in her pocket, and took it out in the ladies' room just before she was intending to tell Terence everything, and show him—but there was no writing on it, it was blank; the message from Matty had disappeared. I asked her to let me see it. She took it out of her purse and handed it over.

"I know," she said. "It's there *now*. Exactly. That's what he's telling us, don't you see? This is meant for *us*, not anybody else, just for us."

They came pretty much every day from then on, without fail. And she would wait, standing by the mailbox, all weathers, in a raincoat or wind-breaker, a stone sentinel, only coming to life once they'd arrived.

Desert Scene, Arizona.

It was the one galvanising force in her day. I was jealous, because when I watched it happen my heart sank, just as hers lifted. And I felt I was betraying someone or something and I didn't know what.

Mom & Dad

Great news! Did you know (family secret) Grammy's Uncle Burt committed s/cide beside a tree in Kentucky? And Consolidated Coal said it was "accidental death" 'cos if they said s/cide the insurance wouldn't pay out! Uncle Burt is here too and he's mended. Wish could send a picture—desertnights B.A.-ootiful!

Matty xx

I saw joy in her face as she read this, but it dug into me, the way a grave is dug, that hole getting just deeper and deeper. It wasn't that I was getting pulled down by the sadness, but that I didn't have someone to share it with. To feel, by my side, what was real. She was on a different path, and it helped her, and who was I to deny her that?

At first I thought the solution was to run away.

I switched off my phone, got in the pickup, and drove through the night, several nights, to Flagstaff, to Interstate 17, the Black Canyon Freeway . . . But there was nothing there. How could there be? It was just desert, dust, heat, sun, and a long piece of lifeless, empty road. The second I stopped the car I knew the journey was futile, pointless, irrelevant.

When I drove home to Falmouth I found six or seven more postcards on the mantelpiece, arranged either side of the clock. The fire was burning. I thought at first Jen was kneeling, warming her hands, gazing into the flames, but she wasn't. She was just being near them. She was just being near him. And she had changed.

Maybe my going away and coming back had thrown it into sudden sharp focus, but I realised she wasn't looking after herself; she wasn't dressing most days, she wasn't talking any more, not to me, not to anybody, and she didn't go outdoors for fear of missing the sound of the mailbox. That was all that mattered to her, now. It filled her with wide-eyed expectation, just as it wore me down and made me want to be free of it, in any way possible.

Her life was reading the cards aloud, over and over, as if for the first time, seeking hidden meanings, or asking rhetorical questions of me that I couldn't answer. At first I'd thought the messages brought her joy, or comfort, but now I was certain they were sapping her of her grip on life, or on everything that made life worth living, and that terrified me, because piece by piece it was eroding the person I loved.

I had to do something about it, I knew. And I did a drastic thing. I had no choice.

One chill December morning, my fingers half-frozen, I put my hand in the mailbox, using my body to block her view from the window, as I slipped the latest postcard inside my jacket. I returned to the house and handed her letters from our internet provider and phone company. She looked at me with sickly disappointment. I said there was nothing else.

"There must be." She put on her snow boots and went to the mailbox herself, delving inside with her whole forearm, poking into every corner. She came back in. "He'd never let us down."

"I guess."

"What do you mean you guess? I'm going down to the post office. It'll be down there, you mark my words, on the floor, behind the, the . . . or delivered to the wrong address. What are we supposed to do *then?*" I suggested she put on her body warmer; she was only wearing her night dress. She ignored me and just said, "Those people . . ." And left, slamming the front door. I watched her through the window, striding down the driveway, elbows jutting.

I crouched at the hearth and placed the postcard on the fire. This was the fireplace we used to sit round, the three of us, to watch TV as a family. It was the fireplace where I used to burn the list of presents Matty wrote to Santa Claus, the flames reflected in the convex mirrors of his bright, expectant eyes. I said to myself, if it was good enough for Santa's list, it was good enough for this.

The postcard turned to ash, curling black, then levitating up the chimney, sucked by the draw.

Jen arrived home white and shivering from the cold, complaining under her breath about the lack of cooperation of the U.S. Postal Service, mumbling that she would take it to someone in authority, someone higher up. But her words soon ran aground and she dried up, lost and helpless, slumping onto the couch. I made her soup but she started shouting and took herself to bed.

No postcards were delivered the next day. I closed the empty mail box.

"What does it mean?" Her arms were wrapped around her body. She was bent over in the armchair, rocking.

"I don't know." Lying, or trying to soften the blow at least, I said, "Maybe it means Matty is happy and can move on to the next life."

She said, "What about me? What do I do?"

"You've got life," I said. "You've got it right here."

"No, I don't."

I tried to give her answers, but the guilt was crushing me inside, like barbed wire twisting and tightening, and I couldn't say anything much. I felt sick, but I had to go on feeling sick. It was the only way forward.

The days passed, and no more postcards came.

I watched her check the mailbox every day, every hour. She could hardly tear her eyes away from it, even to eat or drink. She'd take her mug with her—only hot water from the kettle now, never coffee or tea—stand there for hours, with the neighbours passing, dog-walking, trying to start a conversation, failing. One time I heard her say she was waiting to hear from Matty. That Matty was going to tell her some important news real soon.

Then, one day, she didn't go outside. Said it was cold and she didn't want to. I'd not been taking on much work by then. I had to stay in all day looking after her. We'd got money put away. We were fine in that regard, but I couldn't leave her.

"I think he's stopped loving us," she said. "He's stopped remembering us." That was the only thing it could be, she said.

I asked if she wanted me to go to the mailbox.

She thought for a while then nodded her head, weakly.

I came back in and shook my head.

She looked completely blank. Not sad, not happy—nothing.

"Donkey. Pretty donkey." She touched one of the old postcards with the tips of her fingers. The nail polish was cracked and bitty, and her nails were half-chewed. She hadn't washed or cut her hair for months, because she had the idea that if she did, Matty wouldn't know who she was anymore. The tragedy was, I didn't know who she was anymore.

When her sentences didn't make sense and her eye contact was like the stare from inside some inert husk, the diagnosis of a mental breakdown was inevitable. It was obvious that she needed a place to recover and get the proper care. And she did. A wonderful place near Hyannis not a lot different from the rich people's estates on Martha's Vineyard, but this was for people who had nothing, as opposed to everything. The unstable, not the terminally safe and sound. And in all her irrationality, would you believe, the one thing she was fully aware of was she didn't want to go to that place, she wanted to go home. And they were nice people, and they took her, and they said that wasn't unusual, and she'd be all right, I would see, with the medication and the therapy and the attention and the rest, I would see.

But all I could see was that I was alone.

And now I stared into that fire and nothing in the world could get me warm again. Not even the bottles of Jack Daniel's I consumed. Not even the flames as they ate up the cards that had come after his death, one by one.

Desert Donkeys Burros . . . Desert Scene, Arizona . . . Greetings from Arizona, The Grand Canyon State . . .

Did he forgive me?

Did I?

Sometimes I got to thinking her madness was the easy way. The way that made sense. I'd visit and we'd sit facing the trees and she wouldn't say a word, and I'd tell her what I'd done that week, doing some coppicing, or up high on the canopy, overlooking the clap-board houses with their widow's-walks, or Buzzard's Bay. I'd be praying for the hour to be over. Then praying to be back there beside her. Praying for a sentence, a word, an improvement, a smile, a look that brought it all back, intact and wonderful, like it used to be.

She attempted suicide. Twice. Kept talking about it to her psychiatrist. Said Matty wanted her to be with him. Said it was the only place she could be alive: the desert, with the dust, and the sun, and the cloud over that distant, nameless city, with the arrows of electricity falling.

She spoke to him, that doctor, but she didn't speak to me.

Eventually I received a postcard.

Block capitals. Simplistic, sentimental—as if somebody had dictated it word by word to a young child. But I knew it wasn't a child. It was her.

They gradually became more frequent. The writing clearer, more flowing, more open. She was getting better. I could tell. And, in time, they told me she was well enough to come home. Part of me was euphoric. Another part of me, unbelievably anxious, to the point of panic.

The threat of her suicide attempts had hung over me for so long I'd forgotten what it was like to be without them. For over a year I'd lived in terror of getting a phone call in the middle of the night, telling me the inevitable had happened, that she had been successful this time. Every day that I woke to sunlight shining through the blinds, knowing she was still alive, was a day of reprieve.

Now, in a few hours' time, I will be collecting her, and our lives will be able to resume, but even last night I lay awake, convinced that the worst might happen. The phone on my nightstand might bleat its sickening distress call. Its melodious death knell.

I eat my cereal standing up, looking out at the yellow and orange tapestry of leaves that needed raking up. I dress and pocket my cell phone, still not free of the feeling it might ring at any moment. I play out our coming meeting in my mind. Her old voice greeting me, talking like she used to talk, being the person she used to be. Then a part of me imagines walking in to be confronted by the news she has killed herself. I have literally no idea which eventuality it is more likely to be, which to expect.

Buttoning my parka and flicking up the fur-lined hood, I leave the house, passing the mail box just as Virgil, the postman, walks away from it, hailing me with a slight wave before trudging on his way.

I turn back and look inside. I see a postcard. Nothing else.

On the front is a photograph of the Nobska Lighthouse, a picture I've seen a thousand times but it's like I'm seeing it afresh. On the back I read:

Dear Mason

I'm looking forward to being with you. I know I haven't been for a while. Thanks for being there, even when I wasn't. Thanks for believing. I know I'm going to see you soon, but maybe I'll beat this card home!

Jen xx

I climb into the pick-up and start the engine. The interior is freezing, but pretty soon the blast of heat warms my cheeks and hands. The windshield clears, as if the great breath that had misted it moves away.

The postcard in my inside pocket, over my heart, I drive.

Vardøger

The sign ahead read SHEWSTONE HOUSE HOTEL in that ornate English script normally reserved for the titles of Jane Austen films—gold lettering on National Trust green, proudly displaying its four AA stars. *They probably get that for there being a kettle in the room, or a Corby trouser press,* thought Sean. There he was, being negative again. And that's what he didn't want to be. Not this weekend. This was supposed to be a nice weekend. That was the whole point. Get out of the heaviness and grime of London. Leave your troubles way behind you. Rest, fresh air, clean sheets, beds made by some total stranger, and a little bit of how's your father if he was lucky.

The courtesy mini-bus slowed down, turned and entered between two suitably moss-encrusted pillars topped by eagles, or was it griffins? Sean didn't get a good enough look and wasn't sure what griffins were, anyway. Through the rear window the big gates closed automatically as if pushed by invisible, servile hands.

"Leaves on the track. Wrong sort of snow. Something like that," he said. "Still it gave us more time to enjoy the trolley service. Every cloud has a silver lining, know what I mean?"

The driver laughed as they rode down a long, oak-lined avenue which was pretty inadequately described by the word driveway.

"Anyway. Thanks for waiting. Cheers."

"No problem, sir. That's what they pay me for."

Sean smiled at his wife. The sun, streaming in, did ridiculously good things to Alison's cascading blonde hair, making her look like someone off a sixties Athena poster: gossamer-thin summer skirt, massive sunglasses and espadrilles, breast-bone highlighted over the low U of her T-shirt with an exclamation mark of perspiration.

"Even the railway station looks nice out here," Sean said loudly, in order for the driver to hear over the engine. "I half-expected Jenny Agutter and Bernard Cribbins to be there waving at us." He chuckled at his own joke.

"Know what you mean, sir. Not quite, sir."

Ali elbowed Sean in the ribs.

What? He dropped his smile like a brick, took her hand in his. Squeezed it, widened his grin, followed her gaze back out of the windshield ahead, at the looming frontage of the hotel.

"Blimey O'Reilly . . ."

The picture on the website hadn't done it justice. Sean felt his heart beating a little faster. It was pathetic, some deep social inferiority awakened in his DNA. *Bollocks.* But it *was* stunning. History seeped out of its pores. Births, deaths, murders, mayhem. Shagging, no doubt. Generations of it, no doubt.

As they approached he could see the Victorian and later embellishments including a swimming pool and conservatory. *This is the business, this is,* he thought. *God, Americans would wet their knickers over this. Talk about* Downton Abbey. *Shit a brick.* Then, strangely, he thought of how much his mum and dad would be intimidated by a place like this, but sod that. He wasn't them, he was going to enjoy this. These people were going to be serving him, not vice versa. He patted Ali on the knee, excited as a little kid.

Gravel crunched under the tyres as the mini-bus pulled up outside the tastefully discreet arrow pointing to reception. As Sean climbed out, taking in the fenestration open-mouthed, Ali looked behind her at a line of parked Volvos, BMWs, and assorted four wheel drives.

"Modest little residence," murmured Sean, cricking his neck.

"Yeah. On a clear day you can see the poor people," said Alison, equally *sotto voce*, scanning the endless lawns being manicured by a gardener in rolled-up shirt-sleeves phuttering along on his motorised mower. The man raised a gnarly hand of greeting before doing a brisk U-turn.

"Do you think they need some plastering done?" said Sean. "I can always leave my card."

"Don't you dare show me up."

"Shame on you. I thought you were proud of your working class roots."

"Yeah . . . not *that* proud."

"Welcome to Shewstone House." The driver in his slate grey chauffeur outfit and peaked cap had placed their luggage next to them.

"Thanks. Thanks a lot, mate. Er . . ." Sean searched his pockets for a tip, but by the time he had, the driver had got back in the mini-bus and was reversing.

"Damn."

"Every pound a prisoner," said his wife.

"What do you mean?"

She kissed him on the lips. "I'm winding you up. I don't think he was expecting anything. He probably earns more than you do."

"Oh, thanks."

She gurned one of her big, wicked grins at him, picked up their bags.

"Hold on. Leave that, love. Some flunkey'll do that. That's what they're here for. Remember?"

"Sean. I do *not* need some flunkey to carry my bags."

•●•

Sean negotiated the revolving doors with a suitcase in each hand, and a bag under each armpit, going bandy-legged by the weight of it all, Norman Wisdom-like. The look on Ali's face was one he knew of old. *Yes, but you love me really, don't you?* And of course—

bloody fool that he was, pack mule that he was—he did. They reached the reception desk and he plonked them down in a Tower of Pisa.

"So," he whispered, "D'you think they'll know we got this on special offer with those vouchers?"

"Oh yeah," said Ali. "From the tattoos across our foreheads. What are you like? For all they know, you could be one of those eccentric millionaires or something. You know, the scruffy type."

"Scruffy type? You . . ." He tweaked her ribs with hands like crab claws.

A chubby, terminally provincial girl turned from the fax machine with a cloyingly disingenuous chirpiness normally found only within the confines of building society commercials.

"Hello there, sir, madam. How can I help you?"

"Oh. Hi. It's Mr and Mrs Merritt," said Sean. "We're booked in for two nights? Friday and Saturday? Tonight and tomorrow?"

While the girl smilingly went to her computer screen, Ali removed her sunglasses and rotated, absorbing the Tudor baronial decor.

"What do you reckon then?" Sean, out of the corner of his mouth.

"I don't mind slumming it."

Grinning at each other like school kids, they admonished each other wordlessly and went all po-faced. This was way beyond expectations. Secretly they wanted to jump up and down, stupidly, but a little bit of decorum was in order. A few seconds later the girl came back from her computer screen, wiping her nose with a tissue.

"What was the name again, sir?"

"Merritt. M-E double-R I double-T."

"Sorry. Okay . . . Okay, I see. If you'd like to take a seat out on the terrace a minute? I'll just . . ."

"There's not a problem, is there?"

"No, no, no. I'm sure there isn't. You're just not showing on the, ah, computer, Mr Merritt."

"I phoned at least three weeks ago."

"Right. Oh, right, er . . . Do you remember who you spoke to?"

"No. I didn't ask their name."

"Did they tell you to send confirmation in writing?"

"Yes. And I did. I wrote a letter. I've got a copy of it but I didn't think it was necessary to bring it with me."

"It's all right," Ali said under her breath. "Relax."

"Are you sure it was for tonight, sir? The tenth?"

His lips, a straight line, started to whiten. "Yes. Of course I am."

At that point a smooth young assistant manager appeared. A dark, bland suit containing a light bland person. "What's the problem, Karen?"

The receptionist straightened her back. "Gentleman says he's booked in for tonight and tomorrow night, but he's not on the computer and we're fully booked, what with the wedding and—"

"What?" Now Sean was teetering on the brink of alarm.

"If you can just bear with us, sir," said the suit. "I'm sure we can sort this out. If you'd just like to take a seat on the terrace . . ."

"No, I would not like to take a seat on the terrace. I'd like to take a seat in my *room*."

"Sean, don't," said Ali. "God."

Passing hotel guests down-turned their crepe mouths and looked offended by this disruption to their oasis of calm. Sean was all too aware of them thinking him loud. *This isn't loud*, he thought. *I can show them LOUD.* The moon-faced girl was back at the computer screen. It reflected in her glasses. She looked calm, and Sean didn't bloody want her to be, but he bit his tongue. Relax. *Relax . . .*

"Sir? Sir . . . Here we are. I see now . . . There's a booking here for Mr Merritt, a double room with bathroom ensuite . . . ?"

He sighed with relief.

"... booked for Friday the third and Saturday the fourth. That's, ah, that's last weekend, sir."

Ali turned her back to the desk and shut her eyes. Sean leaned his elbows onto it, doing his superhuman best to keep within the limits of some kind of non-berserkness. It was a tall, tall order. Getting taller by the second.

Calm. "Are you telling me I'm not booked in for tonight and tomorrow night?"

"You were here last weekend, sir."

Calm . "I'm here now."

"According to the computer you were here last weekend, sir. You paid your bill."

"No, no, no. Somebody *else* stayed here, obviously. Somebody *else* paid the room bill and there's been a mistake with the name."

The girl turned to the assistant manager. "M- E- double-R I double-T." Pronounced like some esoteric code. The two shared each other's blankness even-handedly.

Sean decided to interrupt their communion with whatever ethereal spirits hotel staff commune with, and said slowly but forcefully, as if speaking to a small child, a small child whose first language was not English: "There. Has. Been. A. Mistake."

The assistant manager stepped forward. "Did you pay this bill, sir?"

"I'm going mad. No. Are you listening? I wasn't *here* last weekend. I'm here *now*."

Ali's cue to butt in. Always the peacemaker. Some things never changed. "Look, it doesn't matter how it happened. But is there something you can do? What are we going to do if there are no rooms?"

"Hang on, hang on," said Sean. "This room was *booked*."

"Nice to see you back so soon, Mr Merritt! Glutton for punishment, eh, sir. Can't keep you away!"

Sean looked down at his hand, which another man, an unctuous clown cut out of the same dough as his pimply minion, was shaking violently, then gazed up at the man's face with a deeply-etched frown of mystification. The smile slid off it like a slate from a roof. The manager's grip went soft, then limp. Sean looked behind the desk at the Lego duo.

"Is—is he taking the . . . ?" Then, after a moment, he laughed. He thought of the jokers he worked with on building sites, always having a laugh. That prank his brother played at the wedding. Those TV shows where they set up members of the public for something stupid and embarrassing. *Trigger Happy TV,* was it called? Noel Edmonds, as was. Jeremy Beadle, as was. (Never found him funny.) "Okay. What's going on here? Are two men dressed as enormous squirrels going to come out from behind that palm tree, or what?"

The manager wasn't laughing. Didn't get it. "Is something wrong, Mr Merritt?"

"I was not here last weekend. I've never seen you before in my life, mate. I've never *been here* in my life."

"Sean. Calm down," said his wife.

The manager darted a nervous glance at Ali as if seeing her for the first time, his mind ticking.

"I—I, yes, I see," he stammered. "I'm so sorry, sir." He gave another semi-furtive glance at Ali. "I must be, ah—must be mistaking you for someone else, clearly. Of course I am." Blushing very slightly.

Ali tugged Sean's arm. He knew she didn't enjoy embarrassment in others, whether they were in the right or in the wrong. She was also, unlike him, innately tolerant, and believed that mistakes happen, and it's no good getting upset about it. Yes she was a bloody saint at times, let's face it, and while the poor man conferred in a huddle with his team, trying to sort things out, Sean found her escorting him out onto the terrace and dumping him in a big wickerwork armchair, where he simmered on a low heat for about fifteen minutes.

• • •

"The perfect bloody start to a perfect bloody holiday, eh?"

"Don't worry." Ali smiled at a waitress who cleared away the longstanding debris of a previous guest's afternoon tea of half-nibbled scones on willow-pattern plates. It was in Ali's nature to smile. Sean didn't, as was his nature also. "It doesn't matter."

"It does. The first time away, the two of us, for four years. Scarborough, 2005. It *does* matter."

She rubbed his knee, smiled a big smile, nodding for him to smile one back, *Go on,* wanting him to say, *Hey, it'll be all right.* But he couldn't. Instead, he sighed. The gloom had descended like a metal curtain. And he knew she hated it, but put up with it. Why she did, he could never quite understand. He saw her head turn as she noticed the manager appearing in the distance, looking round, targeting them.

"Mr Merritt? Mrs Merritt? I think we've solved the big mystery, sir."

The assistant manager had a paper receipt in his hands. "Have you used your Visa card in the last few weeks, Mr Merritt?"

"I think so. Probably." Sean patted his pockets for his wallet. "I'm sure I have."

"You see," said the manager. "We have a signature, which explains why someone would have claimed to be you." Sean dug out his Visa card and laid it flat on the table in front of them. "Somebody must have made a copy of your card some time before last weekend, and used it here along with a fake signature."

The younger one put the signed receipt next to Sean's Visa card, comparing the two. "Did you make any other payments on the third and fourth, sir, do you know?"

"I . . . I don't know. I'll have to take a look at my next statement when I get it."

"Damn," said Ali. "We should cancel it, and phone up that number, stop any more—"

"I will, I will do, give me a chance. I don't know, all sounds pretty farfetched to me. I mean . . ."

"Come on. Credit card fraud. You hear about it all the time. They get your details off the internet, or when your card is swiped at a petrol station, fake a new card, a new identity, spend your money and you never even know about it."

"Anyway," said the manager. "The good news is, we've had a cancellation. So we can offer you a room after all. Double. Ensuite."

Ali exhaled. "Thank God for that. We could see ourselves kipping in the nearest bus shelter, couldn't we Sean? . . . Sean?"

Sean had picked up the credit card receipt and was peering at his signature, comparing it to the one on his card. They were identical.

"Yeah. We could."

• • •

He couldn't relax till he'd cancelled the card, telling the call centre (in a Calcutta fish market, it sounded like) that he thought it had been used fraudulently. They checked his purchases and there didn't seem to be anything unaccountable except the Shewstone House bill, so they reassured him he wouldn't be liable now he'd reported it and said he'd have a new card in five to ten days. *Job done. What was he worried about?* He chopped up his current card into tiny pieces using a pair of scissors from the reception desk drawer. The manager took a key from a hook as Sean signed the hotel registration form Ali had completed. "Thank you, sir. Giles will help you with your bags. And please accept a complimentary bottle of wine with your meal tonight, as a token of apology."

"Oh." Ali beamed perkily. "Thank you very much."

"Not at all, madam. Have a wonderful stay at Shewstone House. Sleep well."

Giles, evidently an Australian student, took the cases, as loaded as Sean had been, but with none of the attending effort. The whippersnapper was clearly in training for a triathlon. He veritably bounced like a springbok up the wide oak staircase while Ali and Sean followed him to their room.

As they ascended into creaky, French-polished history, Sean heard the *ratatat* of the credit card pieces landing in a waste paper bin, looked back over his shoulder at the manager and assistant manager below. The figures were standing like shop window dummies at the foot of the stairs, not looking at each other or even moving—as if both knew something that they were not about to let on.

"Look at these old photos, Sean."

He looked. The atrium of the staircase was decorated all around with huge, dark, impressive Elizabethan oil paintings. *Photos.*

"Bit of a rogues gallery, isn't it?" Giles grinned.

The boards of the stairs protested underfoot as they ascended. A pigtailed little girl in her school uniform—bottle-green blazer outlined with a yellow trim—walked downstairs past them. Sean smiled at the girl but she didn't smile back.

"Look," squeaked Ali. "Henry VIII."

"Not quite," said Giles.

"He could do with signing up with Weight Watchers, whoever he is," said Sean.

"It's the family who lived here," said Giles. "Till the chain took over, that is."

"Gosh," said Ali. "All looking down at us . . ."

"Thinking, 'Who are these oiks trailing muck up my stairs?'" added Sean.

"Here, d'you think it's haunted?"

"It's creaky enough. Five stars in the Good Creak Guide, this place." Sean raised a visor and peeked inside the helmet of a fifteenth-century suit of armour. "Oi! Anybody home?"

The pigtailed little girl in the school blazer who had just passed him came downstairs a second time, and this time she giggled. Sean's eyes followed her and he did a quick double-take as

Giles carried the suitcases on, up, then ran to catch up, before he had too much time to think about what he'd seen.

•●•

Giles entered Room 23 first, stacking the cases, switching on the two bedside lights and opening the bathroom door. The room was straight out of *World of Interiors.* A large ornate mirror virtually covered one wall. Suddenly struck by an afterthought, Sean dug in his pocket and gave Giles a tip.

"Thank you, sir. Enjoy your stay."

Sean saw Ali's grin, remembering the moment with the driver's tip, and refused to get embarrassed all over again. Giles closed the door after him.

"G'day, mate," said Sean.

While Ali was drawn to the bathroom, he switched on the TV with the remote. He always, inexplicably, gave the TV the once-over when they went away. It was some sort of prerequisite. Puffing his chest and slapping his ribs, he wandered to the window to assess the view.

In the garden below, he saw the little girl. No, wait—*two* little girls. Two *identical* little girls playing in the sunlight, playing tag in and out of the screw-coned topiary hedges. *Twins. Obviously.* He almost laughed out loud, now, for not twigging the first time.

"Ensuite!" Ali cried out from the other room. "Oh, I do like me ensuite! Sean, this is fab! Loads of expensive smellies and everything!"

He turned from the window, stretched his arms above him and flexed himself, trying to work off the angst of the last half-hour. Went to the bed, upended himself and lay on his back like a landed whale. In that position, he listened to the water running, and his wife humming "Mud, mud, glorious mud" in the echo-chamber of its tiled ambiance. It was a silly song and it made him smile. She didn't have to do much, when all was said and done, to make him smile. There's a lot to be said for that, he realised. He was a lucky man. He had nothing to be upset about. Ever.

"Al? Listen. I'm so sorry."

"Sorry for what?" she said, echoing and splashy. "It's all sorted."

"You come away. The one weekend. It was supposed to be perfect. It was all supposed to be . . . I don't know . . ."

Staring at the ceiling, he felt soft and philosophical. Unexpectedly, Ali moved into his field of vision, sitting astride him on the bed. She had undressed and put on a white fluffy hotel bath robe.

"I'm not complaining," she said. "Do I look as if I'm complaining?"

She untied the robe and lay on top of him, rolling up his T-shirt, kissing his hairy chest with a mixture of lasciviousness and comic abandon, tweaking his nipples—she knew he *hated* that—and tickling him relentlessly. Sean was overcome with giggles, play-fighting her off, but really wanting her closer. Closer as closer can get.

"I don't know. We come away for five minutes. You want to control yourself, woman."

"No, I don't," she said, her face hovering inches above his.

She got up, pulling him with her by a finger hooked round his trouser-belt, into the bubbling bathroom. A lamb to the slaughter and he knew it.

"Oh, yes. Ensuite!" he cried, succumbing to it all in echoes, in tiling, in the indulgence of Radox. "I do like me ensuite!" Their bubbly foreplay was played out to the soundtrack of the end of *Ready Steady Cook* with Ainsley Harriott, which happened to be on at the time. Sean entered her to the frantic jiggling of pans and drizzling of sauces as the chefs panicked against the clock. Ali moaned to the rising crescendo of suspenseful theme music. He massaged her breasts as the sprig of parsley was snipped off, her going down on him to the choppa-chop rhythm of a knife on basil leaves, fingers rolling potatoes in butter, chocolate licked from fingers as he hit the spot. Hopping excitement as Ainsley whipped the audience into the countdown: *"5—4—3—2—1 . . . Stop cooking!"* The studio audience applauding rapturously.

•●•

Some time later, in a dizzy post-sweaty glow, Sean finished a wet shave in the bathroom mirror.

"Are they all right? They're not playing you up?" Ali lay on her tummy on the bed, wearing the bath robe with the Shewstone House logo on it, mobile pressed to her ear. "You know they've got their granddad eating out of their hand, the old softie."

As she talked, Sean came from the bathroom, sat on the bed beside her, still sexually ravenous (or at least peckish) and slowly lifted the bath robe to reveal her smooth, tightly upholstered behind. She playfully slapped his hand away.

"Well, if Hannah has baked beans, Polly has to have baked beans. That's little sisters for you . . . Pardon?"

Sean kissed each precious buttock. Then he put two paper drinks coasters, one on each cheek of her bottom. Ali had serious trouble keeping a straight face and keeping her voice from wavering.

"Sean? Oh yes. He's having a good time too. He's enjoying himself immensely."

•●•

They went down to dinner, both feeling a little bit like they were wearing signs saying JUST HAD SEX and SEVERAL TIMES, ACTUALLY. It made them think how many other couples were there for just that, and might be thinking the same, sheepishly, hunched over their prawn and avocado starters. The barman put two drinks in front of them. "One gin and tonic, one orange juice."

Sean swapped the glasses. His was the orange juice. He worried, fragmentarily, remembering the earlier mix-up with the room booking, and decided to make a joke of it.

"You've never seen me before in your life, correct?"

Ali smiled. The barman paused, perplexed.

"No, sir."

"Good. Thank you. Cheers."

Sean raised his glass, clinked it against Ali's, and drank.

The dining room was an impressive, candle-lit job with painfully starched tablecloths and silver service, more cutlery and glasses laid out on their one table than they actually owned. Waitresses circulated like monochrome geishas, quietly accommodating, chatty without being intrusive. It occurred to Sean that they were paying over the odds to be made to feel slightly ill at ease, which was a pretty clever trick when you thought about it. Halfway through the meal he looked over and saw the twin girls sitting at a table with their long-necked, swanlike mother. They were playing tug-of-war with a Sindy doll, and as he watched—while Ali was talking to him about something or other—the two girls began yanking it back and forth quite violently. Really, *really* violently. Their mother caught his eye. He quickly looked back at Ali.

"I didn't know Professor Dumbledore was having an affair with Germaine Greer."

Ali looked over her shoulder. Sure enough, there was a couple resembling the hoary old wizard and the hoary old feminist. Tipsy, Ali sniggered. It came out as a bit of a snort, and some of the more stuff-shirted guests looked round in disapproval. She had to bite her lip, cover her mouth to stop a further snort erupting.

"And don't look now but we've got Salvador Dalí's brother in."

Ali followed his nod to an extravagantly moustachio'd man, who could be the surrealist painter's clone, sitting opposite what appeared to be his mousy wife.

She shook her head. "He's probably a hairdresser from Birmingham."

"And she's a librarian. One of those ones in the films where somebody takes off her glasses and says, 'My, but Miss So-and-so, you're beautiful!' No, not for me." Sean broke off to stop the waitress—regulation white blouse, black skirt, black tights—from re-filling his wine glass. But she'd poured some already. "I said 'Not for me.'"

"Sir?"

"I don't drink."

The black-eyed waitress froze. Staring at him. As if flatly disbelieving him at first, then eyes boring into him almost accusingly. Sean stared equally harshly back at her. *What the fuck's going on?*

"I'm very sorry, sir," she said curtly. Too curtly for his liking.

"What do you mean by that?"

She took the soiled glass off onto her silver tray.

"I made a mistake, sir. *Obviously.*" She wasn't just curt, she was sullen now. "Is the table all right for you? I mean, you *did* want the table by the window? Like last week?"

"What do you mean 'last week'?"

The waitress turned on her heel. He grabbed her thin wrist.

"What the bloody hell do you mean—*last week*?" Sean had sprung up without thinking and caught the table-edge and knocked over his glass of water. It didn't break, but there was water washing all over his dinner plate and the table cloth. Ali was mopping at the spillage with her napkin and his, embarrassedly, all too aware of all the eyes now on them.

The little waitress's eyes glared at him hard as nail-heads. "You're hurting me. *Sir.*"

Sean let go, and the waitress hurried out of the restaurant.

"Is this you?" Sean turned on his wife. "Is this your idea of a joke or something?"

Ali had stopped laughing and stopped smiling. She looked right at him with tears of anger and humiliation in her eyes.

"Thank you, Sean."

That was it. That was enough. She grabbed her handbag, got up, snatched up the hotel room key and walked out, leaving her husband alone with the wettened debris, chewing on the anger and frustration he'd dumped on himself till he could learn to behave himself.

•●•

"I'm sorry. I'm sorry!"

"Stop being sorry."

Sean was pacing, yanking off his clothes piece by piece by the light of one bedside lamp as Ali finished undressing, threw herself angrily into the double bed and switched off her light. "You'll just have to tell them, that's all," he said.

"Who?"

"The waitress. And that manager."

"Tell them what?"

"Where I was last weekend. Friday, McDonalds with the girls . . ."

"Saturday, Tesco and football . . ."

"Exactly. Sunday, a lie in. And we went to that carvery in Hackney."

"Sean. I *know* where you were."

"Yes, but *they* don't. *They* think I was here!"

"So who *was* here?"

"Christ knows!" said Sean. "Some geezer! Some bloke who looks like me! How do I know?" He ran his hands through his hair, finding his scalp was unnaturally sweaty. His shoes fell to the carpet with two dull but emphatic thuds.

"Some bloke who looks like you. Who steals your credit card. Who comes here. Why?"

"I have no idea! It was a mix up. She's mistaken. It's two different things. It has to be. Coincidence. It's not impossible. Coincidences happen, don't they?"

Ali sighed. "I don't want to talk about it. I've had enough of it. Can we just not talk about it? Please?"

Sean did as he was asked and shut up. Happy to. Got in bed, switched off the light on his side. Jiggled around for a while trying to get comfortable, then lay stiffly on his back in the hotel darkness, for there is hotel darkness, which is never complete darkness, but has the faint irrepressible glow of the FIRE EXIT sign, and the red wink of the smoke detector light.

In that gloom—external, internal—he sighed a sigh designed to out-do that of his wife. He thought it was a bit too obvious, though, when he heard it himself. He didn't like to be that obvious, personally.

It was hotel warm, an artificial warmth you only get in hotels and coffins, as artificial as the Shake-'n'-Vac carpet cleaner that was meant to be fragrant but, he found, really clawed at the back of your throat. It made him want to gag, often. There wasn't any fragrance any more—not even from the exotic bath salts from the ensuite. And, now, he couldn't believe that the figure in bed next to him was the one he had enjoyed tremendously enjoyable sex with only a few hours previously. Now, a small part of him cried out to touch her skin, but a larger part of him wanted to scream at her.

Possibly another sigh was in order, but he resisted the temptation.

A strong wind was being cultivated outside, and after some time in the shadows, Sean was aware of the finger-tip tapping of rain drops hitting the glass of the window on the other side of the heavy Laura Ashley curtains.

He could picture it. Outside, the hotel floodlit—artificial, again—an island in the storm. A vandal breeze buffeting patio canopies and overturning several identical garden chairs. Trees shuddering. A swing swinging. The light over the main entrance coming on, remaining on for a few seconds, then going off, the same thing happening repeatedly, triggered by the gale which seemed now to be acting like a naughty schoolboy knocking someone's front door and then running off.

Still life.

The digital alarm clock—hotel, artificial—read: 2.15 a.m. Beside it sat Sean's watch, ticking, a thick airport novel, and Sean's open wallet, open at the reject passport photo of Ali he always kept there. Not far from this the enormous, fluffy pillow on which Sean's head rested, or tried to, unsuccessfully. He was used to cheap, flat pillows, and these monstrosities were sprayed with something that unsettled him. Unsettled his sinuses. Alarmed him, somewhat, somehow. *Fragrant.*

Finally he shifted from lying on his front to lying on his back. But even then he was even less comfortable than before, and after the third contortion, less comfortable still. How many times would he change position before becoming a total twisted bloody jelly? *Shit-balls.* In the stillness of the darkened room, he tossed and turned, unable to achieve anything approximating sleep.

He buried his face in the fluff-cloud, but soon his cheek burned like fever and he lay on his back—he never slept on his back—just to get breath. He lay thusly in perspiration—*bloody hotel heating*—but he knew if he got up to wash, he'd revive himself and be awake for hours, and so opted to remain in his sweat and hoped to dream. But he didn't dream, at least thought he didn't.

No mind, however restful, could have cut out all the manifold and dubious sounds of the hotel. Unwillingly, he followed footsteps as some prat had room service delivered above. He wanted to cheer when the footsteps finally faded away to nothing.

Then, in the next room. Footsteps. A door opening and closing. More footsteps. A thump. Bedsprings. Murmurings. Laughter. A man and a woman. A door banging hard and—

Sean's eyes flashed open. Awake.

He turned on his side silently. *Trying* to listen now. He wasn't sure why, but it was impossible *not* to listen.

There was no doubt about the sound he heard. He was being treated to the sounds of someone's lovemaking gently filtered through the wall. He realised he was unable to move, and, very soon, unable to breathe, as the sounds became more passionate, the bed-head knocking the wall more rhythmic, the ghastly springs squealing like a mouse skipping round the innards of a church-organ, the woman's voice pantingly bereft, grasping, bucking, lurching—did he think *lurching?*—then snarling louder and louder...

"No, no, no, uh, uh, uh, uh, uh, uhh, uhhhh . . ."

Eyes trying to stay clamped shut, Sean reached out for the bedside phone and pressed "0" for Reception. He could hear the phone ringing at the other end of the line as the woman in the next room came to orgasm in his other ear. Then the room went quiet.

Nobody was answering the burr-burr of the phone, so in the end he hung up. Let out a long breath. Turned over, impatient. Tired beyond tiredness. Then, after a few beats, he heard voices, almost under the radar, but clear as a bell.

"Did you enjoy that?" A woman.

"Yes. Thank you very much." The man.

A pause.

The woman chuckled.

"What?" said the man. "What's so funny?"

"'Thank you very much.' Like your mum told you to say it."

The woman laughed again.

The man laughed too.

Then it went quiet.

Until the man said: "What's so funny about my mum telling me to say it?"

Pause.

"Nothing. Don't look at me like that. *Nothing's* funny, all right?"

SLAP!

Sean felt like he was slapped himself. Then he heard another *SLAP*—then silence. He wasn't sure if he had imagined it. Maybe it was the sound of something else. Maybe he was mistaken. Maybe he wasn't quite as awake as he thought. He cranked up his head at an angle from the pillow.

There was silence in the next room. He was afraid to breathe.

"No, if it's funny, it's funny," said the man's voice, not raised at all. "If it's funny, why aren't you laughing? Eh?"

Sean sat up in bed, silently, his bare feet touching the floor.

Now the woman wasn't laughing, she was sobbing. She was weeping.

"You're hurting me. You're hurting me!"

He stood up and pulled on his jeans rapidly. He came out into the corridor, barefoot.

At the end of the corridor he could see a pair of lift doors with a sign reading: OUT OF ORDER. He hadn't noticed the sign before. It must have been put there recently. He was in Room 23 and the room next to him was Room 24. That's what it said on the door, the door he was now staring at. It was dead silent in there. He nervously backed away from it, the door, staring at it a few seconds more before going downstairs without shoes on.

The on/off light from outside cast an erratic beat.

On.

He came down the history-riddled, Henry VIII stairs and padded to the desk. *Photos?* It wasn't manned, but the computer was still on, with some super-helix screen-saver spinning round on it hypnotically.

Off.

He walked around the hall area, peering into the bar, then into the lounge. Both looked as deserted as the *Mary Celeste* ... He heard some swing doors open and some footsteps.

On.

The assistant manager had a love bite on his neck which Sean didn't seem to remember seeing before.

"Ah, Mr Merritt, are you happy with your new room?"

Sean looked at him open-mouthed. He blinked like a fish.

"What are you talking about?"

Off.

The assistant manager seemed just as baffled as he was.

"Er . . . The room I just took you to? You rang about ten minutes ago to complain about the noise from the neighbours."

Sean blinked again. "No, I didn't."

The assistant manager laughed nervously, as if Sean was trying to catch him out. But he could see that Sean was deadly serious. In fact the young man didn't enjoy seeing slow, confused horror creep over a customer's face. He did what he was told, and accompanied Sean quickly back upstairs, with the key to Room 24.

"Here. This is it. Open it," said Sean when they got there, realising that he was still bathed in his layer of hotel-bed sweat.

"But, sir—"

"Open it, for God's sake."

The assistant manager turned his skeleton key in the lock. The door opened an inch. The room was dark within. Sean could hear the sound of a woman's muffled groaning, her dry lips parting—a sound as if frightened, hurt.

The assistant manager stepped trepidatiously inside as Sean reached past him in a blur to turn on the light. The woman's breath caught in her throat as light flooded the room. Sean's heart caught in his mouth with shock. He couldn't get his head round what he saw.

He was looking at the mirror of his own room. *Room 23.* This room was identical, he could see that, but the layout was exactly reversed. But that isn't what made him feel someone was standing on his thorax in hob-nail boots. What did that was the fact that Ali, his wife, was sitting up in bed, groggily blinking awake.

"What is it?" More than half-asleep, she seemed to be trying to decipher the blurry, uncertain figure at the door. "Sean? What's happening?"

Frozen and feeling his sweat go unaccountably icy too, Sean switched the light off again. He went to the bed, swathed once again in shadow, leaned over, kissed her and tucked her in.

"I'm sorry, love. Go to sleep."

Seconds later he was back out in the corridor where the assistant manager was fidgeting. Hardly looking at him, Sean went straight to the door to Room 23. *His* room. He pointed at it with a stabbing finger.

"Open it. *Open* it."

Again, the assistant manager did as he was told. Again, he didn't have much choice.

The keys rattled. The rain lashed at numerous panes of glass. Sean started to take some kind of control of his breathing and was momentarily happy when he had. The assistant manager prodded the door inwards and stepped back. Sean stepped in.

Switched on the light.

And found Room 23—what exactly was he expecting?—totally pristine. Untouched. Empty. Uninhabited. Spotless. As if the housemaids had just walked out. Bottled water untouched. Bed and pillows unwrinkled and unruffled, and most definitely un-shagged in.

"I must be going mad."

Sean reversed back out into the corridor. The assistant manager closed the door to Room 23 and locked it. Sean looked at him, trying to find some kind of explanation, but couldn't. The assistant manager smiled. What the hell he smiled for, Sean had absolutely no bloody idea.

With the young man's eyes still on him, Sean went sheepishly back to his room—his new room, the one with number 24 on the door. He felt deeply uncomfortable touching the handle—which felt slimy and hot—but turned it and pressed it shut after him.

He lay in the hotel dark and waited for sleep to come, wondering if the assistant manager was still out there in the corridor, monkey-suited and with the love bite on his neck, staring at the door of the room, smiling, because he hadn't heard his footsteps walk away.

•●•

Nothing like the sound of birds singing brightly to dissipate the blues of bad dreams. Sean drifted up into consciousness with an innate yearning to be an ornithologist, to identify his little feathered friends, to hold them in his hand and kiss them on the little beaks. He sensed a golden glow of morning on the far side of his eyelids. It was only with the waking that he realised how much he had been desperate, really *desperate* to get to sleep, and that (or was it the plush bouncy bed, wide as a kingdom?) gave him a feeling of innate and all-consuming bliss.

The radio alarm had clicked on with an easy listening version of "The Girl from Ipenama". (Was there any other kind of version?) Images of swishing hips in a grass skirt flitted across his mind's eye, stupidly. His face, buried in pillow, smiled more broadly to every imaginary swish. A swallow and gulp of air came before lying on his back in the yellow spotlight that fell across the duvet, forcing his lids to open.

He could hear the bathroom taps gushing indulgently. Craning, he saw that the bed next to him was a rumpled, empty space with the cover tossed back and a dent in the pillow. A wife-shaped dent. He smelled her nice smell of last night's lipstick and night-care skin milk, the one he'd bought for her birthday, and the image of her rubbing it into her legs last thing before bed made his cock tickle.

"That's it," he said, loud enough to be heard in the ensuite. "No more coffee for me. Strictly decaf or nothing!" He put on his watch, noticing the strap was beginning to fray at the hole, making a mental note to buy a new one when they got home the following day. "Ali? Hey . . ." He downloaded the previous night's dream from his memory, more in curiosity, now, than alarm. "Did they give us Room 23 or Room 24 last night?"

No answer was the stern reply, as his mum used to say.

Sean sat up, back creaking a little. He wasn't used to the level of comfort of last night, there had to be a price to pay, naturally. The way of the world. He felt the soles of his feet touch the carpet.

"Ali?"

Still no answer.

He stood up and walked over, only accidentally aware of the daylight and the bright emerald green of the lawns outside the window, and entered the bathroom.

In the parallel mirrors, hotel-sharp and unforgiving, he saw that he was reflected back on himself into infinity, like some childish fairground-ride and it twanged him to infanthood and back like an elastic band. The himself he saw there was older and more world-worn than the person he thought he was, which was why he avoided mirrors at the best of times. He instinctively turned away from them and looked at Ali, ready to make some remark about that, but all he saw was an empty Victorian repro claw-foot bath, with scalding-hot water spiralling down the plug hole. And Ali? Where was Ali? Where was his wife?

She laughed. Ali laughed.

He heard her laughter. It was hers. No question. It sent him back to a weekend in Brighton on a penis-shrinkingly cold winter's day, it flew him sideways to kissing her breast and tickling each other in bed, it slapped his face to walking down the aisle, not that there was an aisle but there was a registry office and a best man dressed as a matador.

It was Ali's laughter and it was coming from outside.

He turned from his endless reflections, rushed, stumbling against unfamiliar furniture to the window, yanking back the heavy drapes, clawing back the multiple layers of net, flattening his hands, his face to the glass, sunlight direct blasting his eyes, looking down, seeing below him the driveway, and then he could see her.

Ali in a raincoat, red high heels, with a man in a black coat beside her. Sean couldn't see his face, he could only see him from the back, and she was in profile now, laughing again. Sean wanted to yell her name but he knew he wouldn't be heard. He felt trapped like an animal in a cage. Their footsteps were silent on the chippings. They were walking now, starting up the long drive, at a leisurely pace. Arm in arm, like lovers.

Sean stared, because he could no more than stare, at first. Because when the man in the black overcoat looked back over his shoulder and then up, up at Sean as if knowing he was there looking down at them, then gave him a knowing little wink as he put his arm around Ali's shoulder, Sean saw with peculiar clarity that his wife was leaving the hotel on the arm of himself. *Himself, grinning.*

He fought with the window latch that sprang into sharp focus now. It was locked with a key. He launched back to the bed, grabbing his jeans and pulling them on, not bothering with underpants or socks.

A sedate octogenarian couple were taking one step at a time up the stairs as this maniac came crashing like a stuntman down at them, through them, blinded by the T-shirt he was pulling over his head, revolving disorientatedly in the reception area now, laces undone.

He ran out of the main doors into a sunlight so bright he thought his cornea blasted to ash. It stopped him dead. His lungs were telling him he'd run several marathons but in fact it was panic constricting his chest like several tightening loops of metal.

The driveway stretched out ahead, a quarter of a mile across the green lawns and immaculate garden to the wrought iron gates. And not a soul in sight.

Sean turned, looked round three hundred and sixty degrees. *Nothing. Nobody.* Just the doddery old gardener examining a rose bush, tending it lovingly with a dribble from a long-spouted watering can.

"There was a man and a woman. Where did they go? Did you see where they went?"

"Morning, sir. Sorry?"

"A man and woman. Just now. Did you see them?"

"Man?"

"And a woman. Yes. Here, just now."

The gardener just stared at him, adopting a frowning, thoughtful blankness. Sean rushed back inside.

He looked round at the various hotel guests milling towards breakfast. Giles, the Australian helper, stood over to one side. Sean had zoomed past him on the way out.

"Giles. Have you seen my wife? Did you see my wife going past you in the last five minutes?"

"No. Have you tried the breakfast room, sir?"

Sean dashed into the breakfast room. Did a quick circuit. Ran out again.

"Can I help you, sir?" The assistant manager.

Sean ignored him, rushed straight back outside. Without pausing he headed up the drive, legs pumping like a sprinter now. He hadn't run like that in years. Couldn't remember when he'd last run like that. The adrenaline was flowing and he had to use it or it would burn up, burn him up.

He'd almost reached the gates when the mini-bus slammed on its brakes. He slapped his hands gecko-like on the wide windscreen. A few shrieks were uttered and as Sean got his breath back he saw passengers beyond the driver, all dressed up in wedding togs, tuxedos and bridesmaid dresses.

"Have you seen my wife?" Sean eyeballed the driver. "You've come on the road from the station? There's only one road, right?"

"Yes, sir."

"Did you see her? With a man."

"No, sir."

"Are you sure?"

"There's no footpath, sir. And I'd notice somebody walking along the road." The driver addressed his passengers. "Anybody see anyone?" There was only a chorus of various phrases in the negative, a lot of shaking of heads, and a bullet-headed guy called Sean a tosser. The guy had the letters spelling L-O-V-E on his fingers. Sean could see it as he tapped the driver's shoulder to get a move on.

• ● •

Head in hands, Sean sat in the manager's office, trying to keep his cool but wanting to go nuts and trash the place with its stupid Habitat desk light and stupid IN and OUT trays, year planner and idiotic office toys. Opposite him sat a WPC in uniform. She was youngish, far too young for Sean's liking. She should be swotting for her GCSEs as far as he was concerned. She was pretty, with straw-like hair and a rural ruddiness to her cheeks, but had a masculine jaw-line and was nobody's fool. He could see her breaking someone's arm with a truncheon at a peace demonstration, no problem.

"You don't think it's likely your wife might have wandered off on her own?" said the WPC, whose name Sean had already forgotten.

"Look. I saw her from the window. With this man."

"So you think they may have gone off together, is that what you mean?"

"Yes. What else would I mean? Yes."

"So have you seen this man before? Do you know him?"

Sean thought for a moment. His head sank into his hands again and he rubbed his forehead vigorously as if trying to remove an indelible stain. What could he possibly say? That the man who made off with his wife looked identical to him?

"No," he said. "I don't . . . *know* him."

"Can you give me a description of him?"

"No. I only saw the back of his head. Look, why don't you put out an APB or whatever the hell it is you people do and just *find* her? Please!"

"Did you try her mobile?"

"Do I look like an idiot?" He pulled it out of his pocket, thrust it out at her. "It was beside the bed upstairs, where she left it."

"Have you checked it for any unusual incoming calls?"

"Yes. There aren't any. Check if you like, if that's what you want to do."

"No, sir," she said. "I believe you."

You—hold on, did you just say what I think you said?

Before he could say anything the WPC looked at her watch. "She's been gone for, what? Eight o'clock-ish? So say, three hours? So she's not exactly *missing*, exactly?"

"So what *is* she, then? *Mislaid* or something? She'll turn up, is that what you're saying? Like a coin down the back of the bloody—"

"You seem unduly anxious, sir."

"I'm not *unduly* anxious. At all. I just—"

"I understand you and your wife had words last night in the restaurant."

"Words?" Then he remembered. No point denying it. He wasn't going to lie to her. "Okay, words. Yes. So?"

"With respect, sir . . . you see, I'm a woman." *Really?* "I know what women are like, how they think, and . . ."

"Yeah." Sean wanted his irritation to go away. "And I'm her husband. I know what my wife is like, and what she would or wouldn't do, thank you very much."

"It's just that, if I had a barney with my husband, I don't know, I might just high-tail it for a while, leave the old bugger to stew for a bit." It was the first time she'd betrayed her country accent.

Sean let out a breath and shook his head, making it plain he disagreed with the local yokel's particular assessment. Not that he had anything spectacular to replace it with.

"And what about the man?" he said.

She looked at him inscrutably.

"What exactly did you see, Mr Merritt? Someone leaving the hotel? A passing joke, perhaps, between two people? Your wife was laughing, you said. Abducted people don't laugh, do they? People in danger don't laugh." The WPC stood up, pocketed her notebook, and put on her gloves. "My money, she'll show up by lunchtime. You can make up. Kiss kiss."

Sean glowered at her.

She put on her peaked cap, aware maybe that she'd stepped over the line into facetiousness, and softened. "I seriously don't think there's any need to panic, sir. Not at this early stage. This isn't the seething metropolis out here. The nearest thing we have to a crime wave here is a stolen bike." Sean didn't smile, if a smile was expected of him, tough. "You stay put here at the hotel. If she hasn't been in touch in a couple of hours, we'll start making enquiries. Okay?" She carefully put her chair under the desk in the position she'd found it. Her eyes fell upon Sean again and she said quietly: "Is there anything else you want to tell me?"

Sean was thinking: *Yes. Yes, the voices in the next room, the slaps, the weeping, the room next door, the Visa card, the mistaken identity with the waitress, the assistant manager's love bite . . . God, Christ.*

But what he said was:

"No. Nothing. I appreciate your concern, officer."

He didn't quite know if the WPC detected his sarcasm before she left.

There was nothing he could think of doing then, except he knew Ali had promised to phone the girls first thing in the morning at her grandparents' to check they were okay, and it wasn't first thing anymore.

He returned to his room and stood by the window, looking out, as he made a call on his mobile. "No. Daddy just wanted to talk to you, darling." As he stared down at the driveway he was afraid even to blink in case he missed something. What could he miss? He'd missed the most important thing already. Ali was gone. His eyes had begun to prickle, he blinked them and the dryness was medicated by a glaze of tears. He listened to his daughter's voice. "No, darling. Mummy . . . Mummy's not here just now. Mummy'll talk to you later, Okay? Yes, promise."

He felt desperately isolated in the big room. A maid moved around, robotically making the bed, straightening the side where Ali slept, freshly tight, tucking it in, and puffing the dent from the pillow as if she'd never been there. It made Sean shudder and he wanted the maid to leave so that he could weep in peace. Not that peace was anything to do with it.

Later he sat on a cold stone bench by a flower bush in the hotel grounds. The prettiness of the garden did nothing to lift his feeling of being out of control. Not him, the *world* was out of control. No wonder he was twitchy as hell. Shell-shocked. *Worse* than shell-shocked—this was not a battlefield wound, this was something inexplicable to others, some punishment targeted at him alone. And even as he thought it, he knew it made no sense: none of it made sense, any of it.

He had ants in his pants. He got up and crossed the drive, looking up the length of it to the far-off wrought-iron gates, willing Ali to reappear by magic since she had disappeared in the same fashion. It didn't happen. Nothing did. The ancient gardener went on pruning. The twins, the two little girls he saw the day before, went on playing croquet, Alice-like, their laughter was horribly delightful. The sun went on shining.

Feeling numb and devoid of hope, he turned and looked over his shoulder up at the hotel.

With a chill he realised he was standing at the exact same

spot where his double had been standing, looking up at the window of his bedroom, just like he had done. It made him feel physically sick.

He turned away, catching sight through the ground floor bay window of a waitress in the restaurant. He recognised her straight away as the same one they'd had the night before. Made a bee-line for her.

She was clearing the last debris of lunch and setting the linen, cutlery and glasses for dinner that evening. She was unaware of him entering the room until he was quite close, and when she did see him she gave a little start of alarm. The cutlery tinkled. Sean didn't move. She didn't say anything, abruptly returning to her work.

"Do I know you?" Sean tried not to sound confrontational. He didn't want to be confrontational. He just wanted to know the truth.

She eyed him with lazy disdain. "After last weekend?"

"What happened last weekend?"

She laughed, like the word *pathetic* was on her lips ready to come out.

"I wasn't here last weekend." Sean attempted to be as non-aggressive as possible. "Do you think I'm somebody else, or what exactly?"

"I know who you are," said the waitress confidently. "Does she?"

"Look, I don't know what you're talking about, but . . ."

"Of course not." She tweaked a red wine glass. "I get it."

"Get *what*?"

"I just didn't have you down as a married man. You were about the most *un*-married man I've ever met."

"So you *have* met me? Someone who looks like me?"

She stared at him hard. Tired of it now, pissed off with him. "Oh, get lost." She tried to walk past him, ending the conversation, but he side-stepped and blocked her.

"No, please. Tell me."

She curled her lip, eyes burning. "This Mr Nice Guy act might work on her indoors, but don't try it on me, all right?"

"Act? What *act*? Wait a minute."

She picked up a full tray and crossed the room to the double swing doors leading to the kitchen.

"Help me." Sean followed her. "Tell me about this man who looks like me. You know about him. Who is he? What's his name?" Tight behind her, close enough to touch, not wanting to let her get away. She span around and looked him in the eyes. He saw toughness, bravery, hurt, and little glinting slivers of pain, little sharp thorns of love.

"His name's Sean Merritt. He said he'd be with me. This weekend. Without fail. He promised. Remember?"

"Look. I've never been to this place before in my life. I swear. You've got to believe me."

"Oh sure," she said. "Believe you?"

"I'm not who you think I am."

She almost swore, but there were other kitchen staff around, maybe her boss, and he was a customer after all. "Is this your idea of 'patching things up?' Shoving your wife in my face?"

"What did he do? Tell me."

"Who?"

"The man who looks like me."

"You're sick." She punched the controls of a dishwashing machine. It rumbled into its wash cycle. She pressed her hands on top of it, as if afraid what she might do with them otherwise.

"He's taken my wife. For God's sake, help me. Please."

Perhaps there was something in his voice made her turn and look at him, properly this time. Perhaps, he thought, it was the face of a man scared and fucking desperate. And whatever she felt afraid of or disgusted by, she didn't see there any more. She saw, he hoped, someone as afraid and hurt and desperate as she was.

The sound of the chef giving his sous chef a bollocking broke the spell. Sean looked down and saw that his own hand was gripping the girl's spindly arm. He let go, held up his palms apologetically, backed away, heading out of chef's realm before it was him who got a roasting. Before disappearing he paused at the double doors to look back at the young waitress.

"Help me," he said.

•●•

A cloth moved back and forth, polishing the surface of the bar. Sean removed his elbows.

"The usual, sir?"

Sean looked up. It was a different barman from the night before, smiling like he had too many teeth in his head. Sean said nothing and felt gnawingly sick again. The barman measured a double Jameson's from an optic on the wall and placed it in front of him. Sean stared down at it.

"What happened to the other barman?"

"Oh, Ian from The Grapes? Last night? He was filling in for me. It was my night off."

Nauseous, Sean got up and left the bar, and the barman, and the whiskey, intact. He passed the reception desk on his way upstairs, but the bank-advert-looking girl hailed him over with a raised, beckoning finger.

"Ah, Mr Merritt? Excuse me. I think you have a message."

Sean back-tracked down the stairs and walked over.

"Is it from the policewoman? Has she got any news?"

The girl gave him an envelope from a pigeon-hole behind her.

"I don't know, sir. I just saw it in the box for your room. Room 24."

Sean looked at the envelope, examined it front and back, then walked out onto the terrace. He sat himself at a patio table. Not far away a bride and groom were posing for wedding photographs against the lush flower beds and fake Grecian statues. She had flowers in her hair. He had gel in his.

Sean opened the envelope and found, firstly, one of the Shewstone House DO NOT DISTURB cards, the ones you hang on the outside door handle of your room. Secondly, a photograph. The passport photograph of Ali he always carried in his wallet.

The bride and groom's chuckling wafted towards him but he felt ice cold in spite of the heat. He looked at the back of the envelope and his heart quickened horribly as he saw a thumb print in red ink . . . *is it* red ink? Or is it—

He walked across the terrace. He stuck his thumb in the soil of a potted plant. Extracting it, he made a grubby imprint beside the red one. He raised it up in front of his eyes, the sun on his back, squinting, focusing. Trying to convince himself and his eyes that the two thumbprints were not—could not be—identical.

More guffaws and high jinks from the photography group made him look up. He hastily put the passport photo and the DO NOT DISTURB card back in the envelope, and the envelope in his inside jacket pocket. He tugged his cuffs and coughed into his hand and walked back inside.

He went up to his room. To Room 24. He went straight to the bedside table, and saw the same still life of alarm clock, airport novel, and his open wallet, still full of money, twenties, tens, but with a space where the passport photograph of Ali used to be.

In the ensuite he rinsed water over his face, rubbing it forcefully into his tired eyes and slicking it back through his hair. He wanted to wake up. He wanted to wake up *from this*. He saw the dirty black soil-mark on his thumb and rubbed it off, grinding it into the palm of his other hand until it was gone.

When he turned off the sink taps he began to hear a faint but distinct noise—a *tap, tap, tap* . . .

It stopped for a moment. He listened more intently. There it was again.

Tap, tap, tap . . .

Stepping out into the bedroom and looking around, he tried to detect where it was coming from. Unsurprisingly, his mind was doing the works on everything since the morning. But this was probably nothing. He was about to turn on the radio to kill the silence when—there it was again.

Tap, tap, tap . . .

For all the world like a witch's crooked finger on a window pane. Yes, that was exactly where it was coming from. The window. He turned.

Beyond the glass something was dangling on a string, like a ghastly pendulum, some object swinging and knocking against the glass repetitively. A plastic doll's face, Barbie-blonde hair hanging, blue eyes open, quickly whipped out of sight—*gone.*

Sean opened the bottom sash and leaned out. He twisted his head, looking up.

Directly above him, a window was open. The twin girls he'd seen before were leaning out, hauling up their Sindy doll, which they had been dangling on a piece of string tied to her ankles. Now the two cheekily grinning faces disappeared quickly inside, Sindy disappearing with them, blonde hair, blue eyes, gone.

Sean ducked back inside his room, closed the window as he heard the window higher up also close. He heard the children's laughter in the room above, getting louder and louder in his head. He stared at the ceiling, picturing the twins tossing the doll one to the other, laughing at him, laughing endlessly at the joke.

• ● •

Darkness didn't exactly fall. Light passed from the sky according to the laws of nature, yes, but Shewstone House was still lit by the floodlights embedded in the grounds, disguised by bushes and bedding plants, bathing its Bath stone glory in a honeycomb hue.

Cracks of inner light shone from a few windows as guests spruced themselves up, or dressed, or watered, or fondled, or frolicked. Already the soundtrack of the evening was being provided by the wedding reception underway in the function room, its own notable light show pulsating in all directions, frightening off prowling vixens and other scavengers. Village People and Take That vied with the night. There were more cars in the car park and wedding revellers staggered round on the chippings outside the hotel, puffing fags or guzzling beer or spirits with loosened collars, dangling ties, and suspect footwork. If they couldn't stagger, they sure as hell couldn't dance, however much George Michael implored them to.

In Room 24, Sean lay on the bed, staring at the ceiling, fully dressed. He was utterly exhausted but knew he would not be able to sleep, or even shut his eyes. The music of the wedding disco was muffled, turning to Ibiza dance music now, an insistent beat which was too much like the hammering he felt inside his skull to think of it as a welcome distraction. It just added to the torture. That and the knowledge there were people down there—married couples down there—enjoying themselves as if nothing had happened. What *had* happened, exactly? A gentle knock on the door broke his thought pattern, and he was grateful to it.

"Yes?"

"Room service," said a voice.

Puzzled, he crossed the room and opened the door. The skinny little waitress he had spoken to in the restaurant stood there. She looked down, resolutely avoiding his eyes, pushing a trolley on which sat a silver salver, napkin in a ring, knife, fork, spoon, glass. As she moved round the bed and started to lay the starched white cloth on the side-table, as was expected of her, it was obvious she was uncomfortable seeing him, didn't want to be there, and it made Sean uncomfortable too.

"I didn't order anything."

She stopped, saying nothing, still didn't look at him. She looked pained and continued laying the table as if he hadn't spoken, or wasn't even there. When she'd finished she held out a slip of paper stiffly. The tongue of a till roll.

"Would you sign this please, sir?"

"No. Talk to me. Please."

She stiffened, aware of the empty bed. "Where is she?"

"She's gone. I told you. He took her." The waitress was already heading to the door. "Please. Don't go."

She stopped halfway, turned back.

"Something's happened to you," she said. "You're not the same."

"I'm *not* the same. I'm trying to tell you. The person you think I am is somebody else. I know it sounds . . ."

"Two people don't look that alike. Not unless they're twins. And you said you were an only child."

"When?" The penny dropped. "He told you that? He knows that about me? What else does he know?"

She didn't answer. He decided not to push her. He didn't want to hurt her, verbally or otherwise. She looked frightened enough as it was. Suddenly he felt like a puppet whose strings were cut and he had to sit down before he fell down. It had built up and built up, this pressure, this pain, this fear, and suddenly it was too much. His head was swimming and he sat down on the bed corner, gazing into space. Lost.

She became even more uncomfortable and adjusted her black, tight, waitress skirt. "They'll be wanting me downstairs."

"Stay. Please."

He didn't dare look up at her. Then he felt the weight of her sitting on the other corner of the bed, not close to him, but close enough. He still felt she didn't want to be there and he wondered why she was.

"He has my wife. I have to know about him. I have to find out what happened." He looked up into her face directly. "What happened last weekend?"

She was gazing past him at the NO SMOKING sign on the wall.

"Have you got a cigarette?"

"I don't smoke."

She tensed. "He does. Rules don't matter to him. Silk Cut. Keeps the lighter tucked in the packet."

Sean looked blank.

"Is this amnesia or something? Have you had a bang on the head?"

"I don't know what it is. All I know is my wife is missing and I saw her with him. With *me*."

She looked like she really wanted that cigarette now. "You said you'd come back and see me. You said you'd be here. You promised it would be good this time." Her throat tightened drily. "I believed you."

Sean realised they were talking in whispers, as if in church.

"What did he say to you?"

She shrugged. "He was alone. Travelling between tournaments. Table all to himself."

"Tournaments?"

"Snooker. You're a snooker player. Professional. Champion. On the telly, you say. Suit worth a bit. More than a bit. Clean hair." Her eyes roamed over Sean, from his forehead to the tips of his toes. "He doesn't sit like that. He sits like he owns the place. Brandy. A few. Montecristo cigar on the terrace. Wants me to have a drink with him . . . Have a *chat*."

He noticed she said *chat* like it was an ugly, obscene word. He stood up and took the wine bottle from the room service trolley. He twisted the corkscrew into it and poured one glass and handed it to her. Her hands had been pressed flat to the bed cover till that moment.

"Restaurant's empty now," she continued as she took it. "No harm in that. Then the brandy bottle's on the table. I say, 'No thanks.' He says, 'Come on. Nightcap.' The bar's about to shut. He says, 'I'm off to my room, then, Monica. Catch up on my beauty sleep.' He puts the brandy bottle on my tray and he looks at me in the eyes and says, 'Room Service?' Just like that." She drank some wine, to get rid of a lump in her throat. Lowered her chin as she swallowed. "And he goes upstairs."

Sean felt his palms prickling.

"Did you fancy him?"

"He's a type. You can tell them a mile off. I know I'm nothing to him. But he wants me. I feel like being wanted, for a change."

"I'm sorry."

"Why?"

"You sound like you've been hurt."

Monica smiled, trying to make it a bitter one but just making it more clear Sean was right. "You can't be sorry for everyone that's been hurt." She wasn't uncomfortable with him any more, he could see, but she didn't like looking into his eyes. *His* eyes. "This is cold." She stood up and took the silver dome lid from the room service meal. A strong smell erupted, catching Sean unawares. "Tiger prawns in garlic sauce."

"I hate prawns," said Sean. "I hate garlic."

Her back to him, Monica stared down at the food in front of her. Tiny waist. Bony shoulders.

"What does he like? What does he hate?" Sean wanted to know something. Anything. "Monica?"

As he watched, she unbuttoned her sleeve and rolled it up to her elbow. Her head tilted to one side, accidentally in an attitude of coyness, and he didn't like that. Gradually revealed was a nasty bruise, purple and livid, running right up the inside softness of her arm. Sean was shocked enough by that. His scrotum constricted and a spasm ran though him. Then she turned to face him and slowly unbuttoned the neck of her blouse. He saw a vivid love bite between one breast and her collar bone. The spasm in Sean's body became a horrid ache, and though it was nothing to do with him—*was* it to do with him?—he was upset and felt somehow responsible. Yes, responsible. Right Said Fred's "I'm Too Sexy for My Shirt" pounded from the disco down below.

"That's not all," said Monica.

She turned her back and lifted up the hair that covered the back of her neck. Sean stood up, moved closer. He saw several brown scars smaller than five pence pieces. He took them at first to be moles, but they were too alike in shape and density. He almost gagged as he realised they were cigarette burns. She didn't turn to look at him as she spoke.

"He did it from behind. I didn't want to. He knew that. He knew I couldn't scream. If anybody knew I was in the room . . . I realised that was why he asked me in the first place. It was his cunning plan." She held the edge of the metal trolley. He couldn't see her face but heard her sniffle back tears.

"My God. I'm sorry, I'm so . . ."

He felt he should do something, not to compensate but as a natural human response. He wasn't sure it was right but he trusted his instinct. He touched the base of her neck with trembling fingers. She turned, unmistakable tears welling up in her eyes now. Tears of anger.

"Have I turned you on, then? Have I?"

"No. God, no."

The tears shone as she whipped her face away.

"You said you loved me. You said you were sorry. You said you'd explain. This weekend you'd come back to the hotel. You'd make it up to me."

"And he *has* come back."

"'Make it up to me.' What does that mean? 'Make it up to me?'"

"But this time it's not you," said Sean. "He's not interested in you. It's Ali. It's Ali he wants to hurt this time. Oh, God. Oh,

Jesus Christ." Suddenly he thought it would be him who lost it, him who would be in tears, and he paced, shaking his head, hands on hips, gulping air.

"You love her, don't you?"

"More than anything," he said.

For several seconds neither of them moved. The disco beat was getting to him again. Maybe it was getting to her, too.

He sat on the bed with his back to her, elbows cemented to his knees, hands cemented to his cheeks. He did not know more to do than that. Only that he had to be alone. He had to shut everything else out, everyone else out, think about Ali. He had to think about *him*. Lost in his thoughts, he expected Monica would leave the room as the music changed to Boney M and Abba, but she didn't. He found that, to his astonishment, she walked around to him and turned his face to hers and kissed him on the lips.

He said "No," but it had already happened. He said "No" again.

"You're not like him," she said.

"Thank you."

Monica gathered the stuff on the trolley, including the bottle and glass of wine, and he could hear her wheeling it off down the corridor. He leaned the front of his head against the back of the door when she'd gone. Hot Chocolate were singing that they believed in miracles. He didn't know what he believed any more.

•●•

He went to the bathroom and washed his face again, and as he dried off with the towel, dripping, he looked at himself in the mirror. At his reflection, at his left cheek then his right. Is that what he looks like, this monster, this madman? He heard footsteps outside his room and he heard Ali's voice saying, "Not like that, like this!"

He ran to the door, flung it open and poked his head out, darting glances right and left.

The corridor was empty. Empty except for the figure of the mother with one of her twins, who was dressed in daffodil-yellow as a bridesmaid. Mum, too, was done up as if for the wedding in a calf-length frock, bent over her daughter like a dentist, half-obscuring the child's face. The child was making guttural noises, standing stiffly with its mouth wide while the mother delved deep into her mouth with two fingers. A gurgling, choking noise continued to be emitted. Aware of being watched, the mother stopped and stood erect, staring at Sean. He forced an embarrassed smile. The mother took her child by the hand and trotted down the corridor in the direction of the staircase. Sean heard their scuffing feet and mutterings fade.

Turning to go back into his room, he felt the give of something spongy under his foot. He moved it aside and looked down and saw that what he had trodden on was the head of the Sindy doll. He thought of picking it up, or calling the mother and twin back, but didn't. Instead, he stepped over it, went into his room and shut the door.

What could be more of priority than lying on the bed with his eyes closed? That's what his body was telling him. Sleep. Though his brain screamed anything but.

A car engine growled outside as the ignition was switched on, its tyres rasping coarsely on the gravel. Its headlights cast shadows round the room like a phantasmagoria as it did a U-turn and headed away up the drive. One of the shadows it cast on the wall above the bed was the upside-down silhouette of a woman's headless torso, turning slowly in the air as if dangling by her feet.

Sean sat bolt upright with a gasp.

There was nothing on the wall. Just the normal shadows of the room in the spill of the floodlights and the light of the moon.

He looked over past the foot of the bed at the closed curtains.

Lifted himself off the bed. Crossed to the window and slid up the bottom sash. Leaned out and looked up above him. The twins' window was closed and the curtains drawn. No light from inside.

He looked down. The faint spill of light from the hotel windows fell on the driveway, the occasional strand of party streamers fluttering on the surrounding bushes. A few stray balloons drifted across the pristine lawns to be gobbled up by the dark beyond the artificial lighting. Half in shadow sat a car with JUST MARRIED sprayed on it in shaving foam. He could see two youngish blokes tying a string of tin cans to its back bumper. Seeing him looking down at them, they made a sibilant "Shshshsh!" in unison with fingers pressed to their lips.

"Sean? Sean?"

A woman's voice. Coming from below, out of sight. Familiar, definitely. The first thing Sean thought was: it was the woman's voice he'd heard in the next room. *God, it was her.*

"Come on, Sean, you old fart! Don't you know how to have a good time? What's the matter with you?"

She was calling his name. Or was it *his* name? He shut the window, turned, looked for his hotel room key—(hell, where was it? It was big enough, attached to that huge plastic tile)—snatched it up in his fist, left his room like a whirlwind.

His name.

Trying to keep panic at bay, not knowing why he was panicking, not knowing why this voice, her voice, filled him with a sense of dread and excitement, he ran to the end of the corridor. The sign on the lift doors still said OUT OF ORDER. *Shit.*

He took a right and hit the stairs, leaping, not afraid of the dark. There were other things to be afraid of than the dark.

Outside, the security light sprang on, brightly illuminating him like the searchlight in some old British prisoner of war movie, dazzling him slightly. He turned right and ran across the parking area to where the lights and the sound of the disco were blaring out. That was where the voice had been coming from, he was sure. That was where he could hear other voices now. That was where the woman was, he sensed. He passed a guy in a morning suit and shirt unbuttoned at the neck throwing up in the undergrowth, two of his pals in top hats pretending to looking after him but in fact more sozzled than he was. Sean saw another drunk man standing nearby, swigging Stella from a can.

"Excuse me," said Sean. "I'm looking for Sean. Is there a guy called Sean here tonight?"

"Sean? You're joking are you? Sean?" The pissed guy invaded his personal space. "Sean's only the bloody *bridegroom*." Swaying, he pointed to the huddle of young men with the one who was retching his guts up in the bushes.

Sean knew the feeling. Bono and the Edge were bashing his head inside out from the function room. He went over to them, the youngsters. They looked too young to get married, all of them. Then he realised they were his age when he'd got married, and just as he realised that, they looked up at him, as if on cue. All except the one who was in a bad way, who remained bent over, his face in shadow, totally in shadow.

"'Scuse me. Can I speak to Sean?"

"Who are you?"

"Are you Sean?"

"I'm the best man. Never mind me. Who the fuck are you?"

"I . . . Hey, no sweat, pal. I just want to talk to Sean a minute."

Sean moved forward, to ease past the bullet-headed best man and get a look at the vomiting kid's face. He needed to see that face. The best man didn't like Sean's hand on his arm and pushed back. Drink had made him belligerent. Sean hated that. Didn't like conflict at the best of times, but his patience was beyond thin, it was non-existent. He put a hand against the man's chest and shoved him aside firmly and that should have been that, but the guy liked that even less and shoved back, harder. Next second they'd grabbed each other by the scruff of the shirt, lurching eyeball to eyeball. And Sean wasn't going to back down, not now, not tonight. He could rip the fucking guy's head off, truth be known. He was prepared for it. He was fucking ready to.

Then the kid, bridegroom, looked up, right into Sean's face.

On.

And Sean's fist slackened on the best man's Moss Bros shirt. Because he didn't see Sean, didn't see *himself*, or anyone approximating himself. He saw a ginger-haired boy with bloodshot eyes and a pallor like death not even warmed up. The groom convulsed again as if reacting to an invisible kick in the stomach, the contents of which flew to the four winds, and he spun away, directing his monumental *hughie* at the geraniums.

Off.

"Sorry . . . Sorry mate." Sean backed away, rapidly, hands up. "I thought you were somebody else. Sorry." Luckily the best man and his mates had lost the lust for a fight and went back to nursing their bilious amigo.

Sean hurried back inside, headed straight up the stairs past the oil paintings—*look at all these photos, Sean*—the man in the ruff with the pointed beard and the woman with no eyebrows and three children, freezing mid-creak as he heard several woman laughing, and like a film going into reverse motion retraced his steps back to the reception area.

The sound—he couldn't make out the words, just the voices, drunken, conspiratorial, disembodied—came from behind the door to the left of the reception desk. *Wives. Girlfriends. Women. Women will know. Women know everything*, he thought. Pictures went through his mind of high heels and chubby calves. Without pausing, he went through. Didn't know where the corridor went because he didn't read the sign with the arrows on. Doors led off, but the sound didn't come from any of them. There was a porthole-window at the far end and a strange sort of wavy light reflecting through it on the surrounding walls so he aimed for that and banged through it into chlorine and echo.

The hotel swimming pool was not exactly sporting dimensions, but big enough for ladies who lunch to do the dog paddle and slag off their husbands. It was brightly lit from below the surface even at night—why at night?—the rippling lines of water dancing around the walls. Sean had the sense of a lava lamp flatlining, and the unadorned surfaces deflected the tiniest sound back at him a hundredfold. It was deserted, except for an inflatable elephant and a pink and green rhinoceros with a gigantic air-filled tusk. The duo bobbed invitingly. The disco, distant, was belting out Tom Jones singing "Sex Bomb" now—which was all he needed.

"I've never been so sober in my life. Honest to God."

Sean turned to see that the woman's voice from before, the one he had heard all along, belonged to this girl, this bride, the one who was posing for the wedding photographer earlier, the one with flowers in her hair, bottle blonde, very much so, more than slightly overweight, slightly tarty-looking even in her white bridal dress too tight across the midriff, boobs like hostages, couldn't wait to get out of it, ready to get out of it. Off her tits with a vengeance.

"I got married today." Syllables up and down in a singsong.

"So I see," said Sean.

The Welsh girl swayed perilously. "I'm a married woman, me. I'm spoken for. It was my wedding day and everybody's got to give me a kiss!"

"I think you've had a little bit too much to drink, love. No offence."

She pulled a face. "What do you mean 'No offence'? Are you going to kiss me or not? I mean it now." Staggering towards him. One high heel on, one missing.

"All right. Calm down. Okay. I don't know you, but—congratulations, okay?" Sean kissed her on the cheek, a glancing blow—as glancing as he could make it.

The bride grinned, then laughed.

Then frowned. "What do you mean you don't know me?"

"I don't know you."

"On the lips! On the lips, it's got to be, or it doesn't count. All or nothing. Come on, it's my wedding day for Christ's sake!" She held out her arms at her side and twiddled her fingers, offering her mouth forward, eyes closed.

Sean kissed her on the lips. The bride didn't let him go. Her arms were round his neck. On his face. In his hair. She hung on for dear life, dear breath, sucking the air out of him. He thought of the inflated elephant. He wanted its air. He felt the sting of stale, cheap wine on her, on his tongue now. He had to pull her off his face like a limpet. As he held her at arms-length he could see her blood-red lipstick smeared all over her chops. Her chest was heaving.

"That was all right, wasn't it?" she panted.

"No, not really."

He backed away, one hand keeping her at bay. She caught his arm and wrist and firmly planted it on one of her breasts. Sean snatched it away.

"No, seriously now. I'm serious." He wanted to get away but she was coming at him, laughing.

"So am I. Look."

Sean followed her gaze down to where he saw that her frilly, insubstantial knickers had been pulled down to her ankles. He hadn't seen her doing it, but there they were. She laughed. She was grinning as she began to lift up her voluminous white wedding dress past her calves, the dimples of her knees, thighs . . .

He ran for the exit without looking back, but the bride kept lifting and kept laughing, he could see her lava-lamp shadows on the swimming pool walls, and for all he knew the elephant and rhino were laughing too because it sounded like the whole crowd at White Hart Lane shouting:

"Sean? Sean! SEAN!"

He ran until, mercifully, he could hear her no longer. This Sean, this *other* Sean she was calling rattled in his head. She was pissed, of course. It was a coincidence, of course. Plenty of people were called Sean. *Get a grip,* he told himself. What was he doing looking for an explanation when everyone was half-cut? He had to wait till morning. Things would make sense in the morning. They had to. He tasted her Chardonnay on his tongue again and squirmed inside. He could feel her sweaty hands over his neck and in his hair. He reached the door to his hotel room, Room 24, and fumbled with his key in the lock.

A clunk made him stop. The clunk of closing doors. A grinding machine-like noise wound and cogged into vertical action. He recognised it with no effort at all. It was the unmistakable sound of the lift ascending from the ground floor.

He turned and looked down to the far end of the corridor, and somehow knew with uncommon certainty what he would see.

OUT OF ORDER.

The lift doors still displayed the sign.

The disco throbbed in the ventricles of his heart.

He fixated on those words, on those letters:

OUT OF ORDER.

Somehow he couldn't look away, though his hand was still on his room key and all he had to do was to turn it. But he couldn't look away. An icy coldness swept up from his belly and he knew if it reached his head he might collapse. When the coldness reached the floor his brain was on, that would be it and he could hear the mechanism as it rose up the shaft and he imagined the digital blink of the numbers, innocent numbers, blameless numbers, rising. Alarm clock numbers. Wake, please wake, please wake.

OUT OF ORDER.

Doors opening.

His exact double was standing inside the lift. The "other" Sean. Leaning casually under the insipid yellow down-light, dressed to the nines in a snooker player's tuxedo and bow tie, with a heavy black overcoat slung over his arm, smuggest of smiles on his face. The face disappearing as the doors slid shut across it.

OUT OF ORDER.

Sean waited for the ice to hit. It didn't. His blood boiled. He was galvanised suddenly, flying down the corridor like a crazy person, hammering his fists on the lift doors, then trying to prise them open, pressing the hook of his fingers into the crack between them, uselessly, then, hearing its smuggest of hums, smuggest of descents, started thumbing and bashing all the buttons, to no effect.

Just as suddenly the hum stopped.

He looked down. Saw that indicator light had stopped on number '1'. Heard the lift doors open on the floor *below.*

He ran to the stairs and didn't stop. Burst into the first-floor corridor from the stairwell just as the lift doors were unhurriedly closing. Jammed in hands, wincing as they crushed them for a second then, blocked, paused a beat, then re-opened. He stood his ground. Tightened his fists. But the lift was empty.

Of course it was empty.

He turned and looked down the length of the empty corridor. It was in darkness except for a single, nondescript FIRE EXIT sign. He saw something on the floor.

He walked over to it, knelt down, and picked it up in his fingers. His shadow, cast by the FIRE EXIT light, was long, the whole length of the corridor, and not man-shaped any more.

The object he touched was a square of blue chalk. The sort snooker players use.

His head jerked as if yanked on a rope at the sudden clack of two snooker balls hitting.

The door only two feet away from him was marked GAMES ROOM.

Sean stood up and moved towards it. The floor felt tacky and glued to his feet, holding him back. He gripped the door handle.

He could hear the sound of *his own* laughter coming from inside the room. *Was* it his own? Why was he even questioning this? He couldn't pause, couldn't stop now. He opened the door.

The only lighting was the downward-pitched cone from a shade overhanging the autopsy slab of green baize. It illuminated at the very edge of its circumference a big fat half-spent Montecristo, resting on the rim of an ashtray on the mahogany surround. Its tip did not glow, but Sean could see smoke rising from it with lugubrious insouciance.

He walked slowly to the billiard table, his eyes fixed on the smoking cigar. He could hear only his own breathing. He was waiting for his eyes to become accustomed to the dark, but that wasn't happening. He passed a snooker cue and a variety of balls arranged on the green baize like a still life. Like atoms. Like DNA. He thought of his own DNA. Of life. Of Ali's life.

As he stared at the green baize, he saw what looked like the perfectly round shadow of a large coin. He thought of the tip he should have given the driver. The memory of Ali's teasing made his throat feel raw. As he looked closer, he began to hear a quiet *bip . . . bip . . . bip . . . bip . . .*

Mesmerised, he reached out the flat of his hand to touch it, to pick it up, if he could pick it up, but the minute his hand hovered over it—*bip . . .*

A splash of red daubed the back of his hand. Bright red. He snatched it back, stupidly, as if he could make it un-happen.

He stared at it, not wanting to touch it, not wanting to smear it, though he knew what it was he didn't want it confirmed. His breath passed quickly through his teeth and back again in quick succession. His chest turned to lead.

His eyes jumped up to the light fitting, the shade, and the chain holding it up at each end. Without thinking, he reached up to the nearest chain and ran his fingers up it and examined them.

His fingers were covered in blood. DNA. Life.

The cigar smoke caught like razors at the back of his throat.

bip . . . bip . . .

He looked up at the ceiling fitting. He could make out what he first thought was a shadow—*shadow of what?*—but then realised was a huge dark, black stain up there, three feet wide.

"Oh my God."

He cannoned out of the games room, bouncing off the far wall, and shot for the stairs ignoring the pain in his crushed shoulder. Physical pain was the least of his worries. He couldn't give a shit about *that*. Half-flying, half-stumbling, he raced up the steps back to the second floor.

He exploded through the double doors and charged, breathless, to the room directly above—his room, Room 24. He thrust his hand deep in his pocket for the key.

It was only then he realised the door was already wide open.

His fingers clasped round the key in his pocket tightly, anyway. Making a fist. He was unable to extract it.

Wide open.

Inside, a store window dummy, no, a suit, no, the manager was standing in the middle of the room, wearing on his head a red fez, streamers bedecking his shoulders, bright coloured streamers, it didn't make sense. It did make sense. The decorations strewn from the wedding reception. He was looking at Sean expectantly. He'd heard his footsteps approaching. He wasn't surprised to see him, but there was something about his expression, something Sean wanted to look away from, he didn't know why.

"Mr Merritt. I'm sorry."

Sean walked into his own hotel room.

"What's going on?"

"You didn't answer the telephone. I knocked the door and there was no answer."

Sean dropped to his knees and, finding a join, tore up the carpet that lay over the spot on the floor which he reckoned was above the shadow. The stain. The blood.

"What are you doing in my room?"

"Somebody complained. About the noise. Naturally we . . ."

There was nothing on the outside of the carpet and nothing on the underside. He folded it back. The tan underlay was pristine too.

"What kind of noise?"

"Er . . . Well, I'm . . . Voices."

Sean pulled up the underlay, popping the tacks, tearing it mercilessly. There was no sign of a stain on it or underneath it on the bare floorboards.

"What kind of voices?"

The manager shifted embarrassedly from foot to foot.

"Having it off," said Sean. "Is that what you're telling me? Making love? Having sex? Screwing? Fucking?"

The manager laughed lightly in acknowledgement. He remembered he was wearing the fez and took it off, reverentially, undertaker-like, and flicked away the inappropriate streamers. Inappropriate to his own discomfort.

"What's that?" said Sean.

The manager turned to look at what Sean was staring at. An overnight bag sat on the slatted luggage table beside the vanity mirror. A two-tone leather overnight bag that Sean didn't recognise.

"What's that doing there? It's not mine."

The manager walked over to it and examined the leather tag.

"It does have your name and address on it, sir. 'S. Merritt, 3 Kay's Road, Finsbury Park.'"

Sean was suddenly aware for the first time that the bathroom taps were running, just like they were running when Ali disappeared. The sound was identical.

"Did you turn the taps on?" he asked the manager, hardly waiting a beat for the answer. "Did you turn the bathroom taps on?"

"No, sir. They were on when I came in."

Sean spun round, taking in the rest of the room, what else was here that shouldn't be here, what else was wrong. The lead-heavy feeling in his chest came back with a vengeance. He saw the room service trolley sitting there, just like the one Monica had wheeled in when they'd had their chat. He went to it. The plate was uncovered, the napkin screwed in a ball, the meal eaten—apart from seven hollow pink tiger prawn shells. He reeled back to the manager. And the two-tone overnight bag.

"Open it."

The manager looked at him.

"Open it."

The manager carefully lifted the bag from the rest and put it on the bed. The bed bounced slightly. The manager folded down the loop handles and slowly pulled the tag of the zip along the length of the top. It rasped in fits and starts, got stuck and he had to ease it on with a bit of manual dexterity and persuasion. His fingers were quite female, Sean noticed. Quite like a surgeon opening a wound.

The manager stepped back from it and looked at Sean. Sean was not about to take over. He could continue, thank you very much. Sean's eyes told him as much. Sean was the one who was terrified, but the manager was the one with beads of sweat in big dots on the back of his neck. Sean stood behind him as the man arched his head forward and looked into the wound.

The manager laughed through his nose. Sean's face didn't show any sign of relief as he moved round to see for himself. The manager was holding up a red snooker ball which had been nestled within, in a bed of white fluffy towels.

His smile faded as he looked back in the bag, taking out one of the fluffy towels. Head bent over, he froze in mid-motion, staring. Sean thought he heard him emit a little whimper. Perhaps that was his imagination but it wasn't his imagination when he watched the man backing away with his hand covering his mouth, stuffed against his teeth.

Sean stood in place of him over the overnight bag, denying the sickening dread that was rising inside. He placed a hand on each side, looping thumbs under each lip, and tugged open the mouth of it.

Ali stared up at him, her severed head neatly packed inside the leather case, love long gone from her staring dead marbles of eyes, an obscenely neat curl falling across her forehead as an added insult, not a mark on her cheeks or perfect skin, a white billiard ball rammed deep in her mouth, filling it, filling her, filling his throat too.

• ● •

In the manager's office, Sean put the empty mug on the desk in front of him. The tea had curdled a small part of him that wasn't curdled already. He felt vague. He felt dulled, dim, semi-absent. Already he wanted them to leave him alone and they hadn't even begun. He didn't even want them to open their mouths, if it meant he had to open his. He'd heard the doctor—one of the SOCO people—talking to the detective, the woman, in a whisper that was nevertheless perfectly audible: "Go easy on him. He's in a state of shock."

"Join the club," she'd responded. As well she might.

He had no doubt the forensics team were all over the games room in their white astronaut-type gear, white paper suits and baby-big shoes, dusting the snooker table and light fittings for fingerprints, using their science fiction black-light tubes to detect any blood stains; all the stuff you saw on *Silent Witness* and *CSI*. The difference was, Sean thought, you couldn't sit back and enjoy this. You couldn't open a beer or go for a pee. You were *in* this. Your wife was dead and her blood was on your hands. And some copper with a swagger and ill-advised facial hair was carrying the overnight bag in his outstretched arms to a vehicle with black windows. And you were sitting in a straight-backed chair, with a mug of hot tea in your hands.

"I'm sorry we have to ask you some questions, Mr Merritt," said the DI, not unpleasantly. She had a good bedside manner. *Corpse-side manner.*

"I know it must be distressing at this time," said her DS. *At this time.* "But I'm sure you want us to do our job." Sean thought he had the look of a rugger player and instantly felt the bloke wasn't on his side. He didn't think *anybody* was on his side. Why the hell should they be? He rubbed his head, having trouble dragging himself into the moment, having *real* trouble with that. Wanting it all go, go away, please, somehow just—

"Can you tell us . . ." said the woman DI softly. She reminded Sean of a terminally dull but earnest woman politician whose name escaped him. "Can you remember anything, however trivial, about this man you followed to the games room?"

Sean shook his head, trying to shake some reality into it if he could. He rubbed his eyes and fell short of slapping his own cheeks. *Concentrate. They're trying to help you. Are they trying to help you? What's easier for them, helping you or—*

"Had you ever seen the overnight bag before?"

Sean shook his head again.

The DS placed a clear plastic bag on the hotel manager's desk. When Sean looked at it he saw that there was a luggage label inside.

"You didn't write this label?"

"No."

"This is your handwriting, sir?"

"I didn't do it. You think I could do that? To my wife?"

"Take it easy, sir," said the rugger bugger, as if the reaction came straight from training school, chapter three, page thirty. "We're not accusing you of anything."

Oh. Right.

Sean stared blankly at the spot he had chosen on the wall, a little bit of damp rot. It served its purpose well. He felt quite safe as long as his eyes didn't drift too far away from it and the enormity of the whole damn world fell about his ears. Hold it. Hold that damp spot, mate, that's it. Aural reminders of the hotel filtered in from afar, only making him shiver because he felt completely elsewhere now. He felt he was in the Arctic. His teeth were chattering like those wind-up Hallowe'en skulls. He wanted to put a fire on. He wanted to switch on that four-bar electric fire, but was afraid to ask. And suddenly waiting in the chasm for their next question was too much to bear.

"It was him," he said, then repeated it slightly louder and more firmly for their benefit, because they looked like they hadn't heard it the first time: "It was *him*."

•●•

In the ensuite bathroom, Sean revolved under the spray of the shower, his fingers combing through his hair. *I do like me ensuite.* Eyes closed, he washed soapsuds from all over his body, trying to let the spray relax him. That's the way he'd been taught; water, switch the shower off, lather up all over, then water to wash it off. He thought it was a penny-pinching habit from his father, to save water, or from his Dad's time in National Service. But habits, even stupid habits, were hard to break. His pores. His skin. His fingertips. He needed them to feel cleansed. It was when he finally switched off the shower he heard a knock at the hotel room door. He wondered if someone had been knocking a while. He stepped out of the cubicle and wrapped a Shewstone House towel round his waist.

His dripping feet left footprints on the carpet. He used a smaller towel to dry his hair. When he opened the door, it was Monica, in civvies rather than white blouse black shirt waitress gear this time. Camouflage jeans, with more pockets than anybody but a forester would need, and a black T-shirt under a purple 'Creighton Prep' hoodie.

He let her in without saying a word. Her hair wasn't tied back now and he saw it came to her shoulders, a touch of auburn in it which he couldn't tell was natural or manufactured, but matched her light dusting of freckles.

He noticed her register his suitcase, which lay open on the bed.

"What happened?"

"They let me go. God knows why. It's all a bit of a blur. I didn't hear half of what they were saying, to be honest."

She sat with her back to the vanity mirror, knees together.

"What did you tell them?"

Sean shrugged. "What *could* I tell them? That there's a man out there who looks like me—*exactly* like me?" He continued packing as he talked. "'What does this man look like, sir?' 'Oh, he's my height, my build, my colour hair, my colour eyes, he's got a mole here, he's got a scar here from falling off a swing when he was six years old, he's got a wedding ring here . . .'"

The horror crept up on him again. He ran out of words and fetched his soap bag from the bathroom. Pressed it flat in the case.

"I'm sorry." She really sounded like she meant it, he thought. Sorry for being a pain, sorry for disbelieving him.

"It's not your fault."

"What did they say?"

"At the end of it all? 'Go home, sir.' Just like that. They said they'd give me counselling, was what they said." Irony rose in him rather than anger. "I don't want counselling. I want my—" Having crept up on him, it pounced. The word. The horror dug in its fangs. He didn't want to show her that, and kept facing his suitcase, bare shoulders hunched.

"I'll go. I . . ."

He didn't protest. She walked silently to the door and opened it, and then heard him say:

"No don't. Please. Don't go."

• ● •

He was bored now. He'd sat for hours and he'd run through his story a hundred times for them. What more did they want to hear? Did they want him to repeat it and repeat it until he made some slip up and they could slam the handcuffs on? Or did they genuinely want to know the truth?

"It wasn't me. I've said it till I'm blue in the bloody *toes*."

"It's this man, who looks like you." The DS made a grimace, a plea to make it easier for them.

"Like Dr Jekyll and Mr Hyde," said the female DI, momentarily thoughtful and momentarily sympathetic. "So you're the 'good' you, and the other one is the 'bad' you?" She took out a pack of cigarettes and offered Sean one.

"It's not allowed, inside the building."

She shrugged. "Let's bend the rules. Shall we?"

He shook his head.

"I don't smoke."

"Don't you? Never?"

"Never have. Ever."

She put the packet away, without having one herself.

The sergeant leaned forward, fingers woven together on the desk, thumbs making a little steeple. "There was this old episode of *Star Trek*. When there was a fault in the transporter, and it produced a good Captain Kirk and a bad Captain Kirk? That sort of thing?" Sarcasm, the twat.

"I know it sounds mad. I know that."

The sarcasm went. The Rottweiler arrived. "What are you playing at, Sean, eh?" It was going to have his arm off.

"I'm not 'playing at' anything! Do you honestly think I'd make this up?"

"'It wasn't me, it was somebody who looked like me.' Come on, mate. Fifty per cent of the prison population of the UK have that catchy little ditty tattooed across their foreheads."

"I know—I *know!*"

"So what's his motive, this double of yours?" said the woman DI. "Why should he want to murder your wife?"

Sean's brain was working overtime. It was a question he hadn't asked himself. Why hadn't he asked himself that? He couldn't believe it. His eyes were flickering. *Wait a minute.* They watched the cogs turning. They weren't going to give him forever. Then the only *possible* truth dawned on him and it came as such a revelation it made him grin.

"He wants to replace me. It's so bloody obvious why didn't I think of it before? That's what it is. That's why he's setting me up. That's it. He wants to *replace* me."

• ● •

Sean methodically pressed his folded clothes into the suitcase. Then he carried over Ali's clothes too and did the same. He arranged them carefully, not wanting to get them wrinkled, and ran the flat of his hands over them meticulously.

"You'll have to tell them, Sean." Monica didn't look up. "You know. Tell them the truth."

"The truth? What good is that? It won't bring Ali back, will it? What does it matter who believes what? What does it matter if he did it, or I did it, or . . ." He stared down at the summer dress in his hands, the one with big sunflower heads all over it, the one she always took on holiday. Spain. Portugal. Italy. That restaurant in Positano at the sea front where they brought out the giant fish and we got talking to that nice American couple, and those backpackers introduced us to limoncello. "You know, she always thought this one made her look fat. Fat? She never looked fat. She always looked . . ." His voice splintered. "Amazing."

He swallowed the feelings, went and steadied himself against the wardrobe. He felt the comfort of Monica resting her hands on his bare, wet back, the feeling of safety as she coiled her arms around his shoulders, holding him tight.

"It's all right. It's all right."

She kissed his skin as his shoulders heaved with sobs, and he could tell she was holding back tears herself.

• ● •

"So this man. This double . . ." The woman DI poured fresh tea supplied by the hotel restaurant. The waiter with a punkish haircut exited, reminding Sean of the normality waiting agonisingly close outside the manager's office door. "If he wants to replace you, why didn't he kill you?"

"I don't know! I don't have the rule book. Maybe he *can't* kill me. If he kills me he destroys himself."

"So if you die, he dies."

"I don't know. You keep asking me and I keep telling you—I don't know!"

"You did it, didn't you?" said the triple-chinned DS matter-of-factly. "You took her out, in the woods round here somewhere. Brought back your little trophy in the overnight bag. Dreamed up this totally unbelievable little concoction, maybe thinking you can get away with diminished—"

"No. No. No!" screamed Sean, finally losing it, not unreasonably, he thought. "It was him! You should be out there looking for *him!*" His fists banged the desk like an infant in a tantrum, but he didn't give a shit any more. The door opened and a uniform WPC looked in.

"Bring the car round, Wendy," said the female DI without flinching. "Me laddo is coming with us."

•●•

Monica crossed the room to get tissues from the box on the vanity mirror. She heard the crunching of footsteps on the gravel of the driveway outside, and as she plucked at each Kleenex she saw through the window in front of her a woman in a police uniform walking off briskly towards a parked police car. She returned to Sean and pressed the tissues into his hand.

"What are you going to do?"

"Go home. House, anyway. Tell the girls, somehow. God

knows how. I have to leave now. Except—I . . ." He paused. "I never like travelling alone."

Monica turned to look out of the window again, faintly aware that there was more activity outside. Voices, not loud. Police, gesturing, she now saw.

He was sitting on the bed next to his open suitcase, still half-empty. He was just sitting there, immobile.

"Have you finished packing?"

"Not quite," he said, without looking at her and without blinking. Then he did look up at her, still unblinking, as if he knew what she was thinking—exactly what she was thinking—and answered by taking out a packet of Silk Cut from the bedside table, taking a lighter from inside it and lighting one up.

Monica felt a slackness in her bladder and a lack of willpower in the muscles of her legs, just when she needed them. But she also thought, almost comically: *No swift moves.* She was justifying the fact that she was rooted to the spot. Cars and footsteps sounded on the far side of the window but she was inside, and she could have spun round and leapt at that window but she had to keep her eyes on Sean's double because he was already coming, already had the flat of his hand (and it hurt, hurt came back to her) over her mouth—hard, so hard her own teeth drew blood, salt sweet on her tongue as he shoved her back against the wall.

• ● •

"I'll radio we're on our way."

"Look, look . . ." Sean was saying to the woman DI as a phone rang on the reception desk. "I can prove it to you! You'll realise it *has* to be my double. Look, look . . ." He took out the envelope, took out the passport photo of Ali. "He stole this off me. Took it from my wallet when I wasn't in my room." He showed them the two thumb prints, one in blood, one in dirt. "This is me, and this is him. Look! Identical. Me. *Him*. Not similar. *Identical!* Look. Explain that. Go on, explain it! You *can't!*"

"Sean Merritt, I believe you are responsible for the murder of your wife Alison Merritt. I am arresting you. You do not have to say anything but anything you do say will be . . ."

But even as he was listening to the caution, Sean was listening to the girl on reception as she spoke. "Certainly, Mr Merritt. I'll have the bill made out and waiting for you. Thank you."

Sean felt an out of body experience.

"—you later rely on in court. Anything you do say—"

Sean jerked the hands off his elbows.

"He's here. Shut up!—he's *here!*"

•●•

Upstairs, the man who looked like Sean gently placed the receiver down on its cradle. His body, still glistening with water from the shower, was tensed, every muscle taut as an anatomical drawing, a flayed man, some Christian martyr beyond-it-all expression. Not of this world. Above it, looking down. Looking down at Monica, held face down by his other hand in the pillow, held by the back of the neck, strong enough to snap it. When the phone had pinged he pulled her up, the way someone lifts a cat by the scruff of the neck and the poor thing is immobilised and scared, and with unhurried pleasure forced the leeches of his lips onto hers.

•●•

Sean grabbed the detective sergeant by the lapels—thank God for policemen wearing suits—and threw him, full force, catching him off-balance, at the woman DI who sprawled backwards as Sean leapt in the other direction. Upstairs.

"Stop him! Don't let him get out!"

The girl receptionist looked blank. A duty manager stood behind her and comprehended, or at least took the initiative, and pressed a button which locked the glass front door with a *ker-clunk*. The WPC outside, returning to the hotel, pressed against glass, found that she was faced by an immovable object.

•●•

In Room 24, Monica thrashed against Sean's double even knowing as she did so it was futile. She could do not much more than a drowning kitten could scratch. Her foot lashed out at the bedside table, *bang, bang,* sending the book and lamp and clock radio cascading, wrecked.

•●•

Sean zigzagged up the stairs, knocking the old paintings—*photos*—askew. He tripped up, fell to his knees. The manager stood in front of him, looming over him, and he could hear the girl receptionist coming up the stairs after him. He elbowed the manager hard in the groin, doubling him up, barging past him.

•●•

The hacksaw flew across the carpet, knocked by Monica from Sean's double's hand. He forced Monica down on the bed. Onto the suitcase. Her hands grasped for something—anything. She lifted a canister of shaving foam and struck him on the forehead. It seemed to make no difference. He grabbed her wrist and twisted it, forcing it out of her hand. It bounced away across the bed.

•●•

Sean burst through the swing doors to the corridor that led to Room 24, caught immediately off-guard by the sight of the twin girls, in pyjamas, fooling around, play-fighting, one laughing uproariously while the other wore a large Elastoplast over her mouth. Two identical, pigtailed heads turned. When they saw him they froze and ran away. Panting, Sean tore the DO NOT DISTURB card off the door handle of his room. He opened the door. Tried to. It was locked.

•●•

Incensed, Sean's double yanked the suitcase away from Monica on the bed. It spilled its contents all over the floor. He slapped her hard across the side of the face. She reeled back, stunned.

•●•

Sean hammered on the door with his fists. It was no good. He stepped back and took a good run at it, using his shoulder as a battering ram (like they do in stupid films) which didn't work, (stupidly, stupid), then tried with his foot.

•●•

He burst in, sprawling into the room, shoulder hitting the wall to see

to see

to see—HIMSELF.

HIMSELF strangling Monica.

—to see Monica, her clothes torn and dishevelled, sprawled across the bed, head upside down hanging over the edge of it, with HIMSELF sitting across her, legs apart, across her hips, HIMSELF posed as if riding her, the rim of the bath towel pushing down on her, HIMSELF with his arms outstretched downwards, squeezing the life out of her tiny throat. Her flicking eyes rolling up into her skull as if looking for something up there long lost, the gurgle in her throat saying, no not there, no not there.

And his double looked up at him.

His double stared straight into Sean's eyes, and Sean stared back as the laughter of his own voice rang mockingly in his ears. Monica's last breath had long departed her body.

Sean stared at the scene, with no capacity to act, only to speak.

"I'm going mad. I'm going mad," he said.

And his *doppelgänger* smiled, still with Monica in his grip and not letting go, and chuckled to himself in delight at his knowledge: "No you're not," said Sean's double. "You're mad already."

Unconditional horror played plasticine with Sean's features as the blood drained away. He was going out of body again, in a bad way, and in less than a breath it had happened and was over, with no tripping a switch and no cutting of a cord and no scream of alarm. Now he was sitting astride her, looking down at Monica beneath him, stretched away from him, chin in the air, bones of her breastbone countable. The U of the middle of her collar bone. He was looking down at *his own hands* fastened round on her tiny throat, *his own hands* not letting go. The beads of bathwater dotting his own forearms. Finding *himself* half-naked now, and crouched on his own bed in the body of a murderer.

Sean looked up startled to where he had been standing, across the room, looking at the bed. He wanted reality to rescue him, but it didn't. There was no-one standing there, where he once was. How could there be? There was no Sean anymore. *Bye bye Sean.*

"No!"

He was across her, fully dressed now, wearing the clothes he was wearing downstairs while he was being interviewed by the police and it popped into his head, this phrase as if someone whispered it. *The old switcheroo.* And he thought of the leering sadistic grin that had been on the man's face, on his face, and it made his own melt like candle wax. He was a blob, but he was Sean. He *was* Sean; but who *the fuck* was he *now*?

"The old switcheroo, matey."

"No," said Sean. At least he knew his voice was still his. "No. *No!*"

The door to Room 24 slammed against the wall as if a SWAT squad had entered. Sean was looking down at his upturned confessing murderous helpless hands. *Someone's* hands. And before he could even look up at who had burst in, they were snatched away.

The assistant manager and the girl receptionist were on top of him like a couple of wrestlers in some tag match of doom. Hurting him. *Leave it out!* Twisting his elbows up behind his back, overpowering him, throwing him off his bed onto the carpet. The air instantly knocked out of him. He couldn't get any back in. Flashes went off like fireworks, poking at his eyes. He felt a forearm heavy as a railway sleeper across the back of his neck. *Now, before I . . . is somebody going to* fucking *tell me what the . . . what the . . .*

Sideways, from Shake-'n'-Vac level (getting into his nostrils, big time), Monica jerked upright, hand to her throat, retching, gagging for breath like a cat with a hair ball. The manager swelled into Sean's screwy comic-strip point of view, fussing to help her. Sean heard him say to her: "I told you, you idiot!" Then, looking down at Sean with a shine of spittle on his lower lip. "Bastard! You bastard!"

"Don't fight it, Sean," said the chubby girl receptionist. "You know not to fight it, don't you?"—and Sean stared up as she held up a giant syringe, needle pointing towards the ceiling, and whipped off the sterile cover. He knew where that needle was going and he didn't like it, but the banal, beige assistant manager was a dead weight on his back. The girl vanished and he felt this sudden spike dig deep in his left buttock, and though he roared he knew it would do fuck-all good, and even as he bared his teeth he felt a warm feeling spread through his muscles and knew that temporarily at least he was kissing this world goodbye, whether he liked it or not.

•●•

When his eyes flickered open, Sean found himself lying alone on the bed in the same room, fully dressed, waking from a deep, untroubled sleep, the best he'd had in years . . . *It was all a dream, a nightmare.* Was it? The corniest of movie clichés, made real? Even as he was feeling it, he wondered why his sense of freedom, relief and elation was cancelled out by a seeping feeling of dread.

All was not right. Or was it? *Don't knock it, son*, he thought.

He heard the warm, far-off phuttering of the lawn mower, the twitter-tweet of songbirds hopping from branch to branch. Ornithology was good, he remembered. Ornithology was great. He ran his tongue over his lips, and found they were unnaturally dry.

He sat up, swaying slightly on the edge of the bed, trying very precisely to work out what he had imagined and what he hadn't. But the main thing was, he told himself, he was *here*, and he was *safe*. The room was as he last saw it. His feet were square on the floor, he felt completely calm and unhurt, and even peaceful. Yes, sod it, peaceful.

"How are you, Sean?"

Monica's voice, but Monica wasn't in the room.

He slowly stood and revolved on the spot, looking into every corner of the room. But there was nobody there but him. If it wasn't coming from the room, he thought, maybe it was coming from inside his head.

"How are you now?"

This time he could tell where it was coming from. He walked over to the ornate mirror, the large Louis Fucking Whatever one that dominated one wall, and touched the cheek of his own worried-looking reflection. He didn't know whether to be reassured that his reflection was there, behind glass, where it belonged, or—

"Are you feeling angry at me?" Monica's voice. "Those are your real feelings, Sean. Don't deny your real feelings."

•●•

In the observation room, Monica switched off the microphone. The hotel manager stood next to her, chewing a thumb nail, wearing a shabby Fair Isle sweater and cord trousers. She herself no longer wore the waitress uniform but a slate grey business suit, and a neck brace fastened round her neck. The two of them watched Sean in the antiseptically-plain, institutional hospital room beyond, touching the glass of the one-way mirror on the other side.

"I've prescribed chlorpromazine for the anxiety and restlessness," said the manager. "Seventy-five mil a day."

Monica frowned. "And have him doped up like a nice little zombie?"

"Look what he did to you."

She rubbed her neck. "He's my patient. I don't want to fight to see his symptoms through some antipsychotic fog."

She stepped out of the room into the plain, lime green corridor of the hospital, with its many identical doors leading off. She had learned by now not to be distracted or disturbed by the patients' peculiar behaviour but adopted the requisite benign smile. Anything else might be interpreted as invasive or inappropriate and you never know what might accidentally set them off. It was a steep learning curve. Professor Dumbledore stood muttering to himself, flitting his hands over each other as if trying to catch a mouse. Germaine Greer sat on a window sill, sobbing over some long lost childhood pet, or the long lost childhood itself. It was best not to dwell on the awful crimes these people had committed, and concentrate on their care. The girl from reception was kneeling on the floor, doing her best to comfort the woman.

"Nurse," said the hotel manager, behind her. "She shouldn't be out of her room. You know too much human contact winds her up."

"Sorry, doctor. She wanted to."

Monica fetched a can of Lilt from the vending machine.

"There was a perceptual leap," she said to her male colleague, returning to the subject of Sean Merritt as she pulled its tab. "A sensory switching to the autoscopic self." She sipped. "It could be the turning point."

"He's a lost cause, Monica."

"He's a lost soul, Paul. But he's not a lost cause," she said.

• • •

Sean looked at her as she came in and sat opposite him. She was in that same ubiquitous black-and-white waitress uniform. He wondered why waitresses all dressed like that, like it was some kind of European Union directive, the 'bistro imperative' or something. He was both relieved to see her again, and irritated. He stopped his fists bunching. He didn't want to show her the extent of his pent-up anger. He didn't move from the hotel room bed and she took residence in the repro Georgian chair by the vanity table. A manila folder rested on her crossed knees, bending slightly, and she made no attempt to talk for a long while. Sean thought two could play at that game. He had a million questions to ask but he was damned if he was going to give her the satisfaction of asking them.

Eventually she gave in, and the first question came from her, when her twiddling ball point pen finally came to rest on the folder.

"What's my name, Sean?"

Sean thought it must be a trick question, and not a very subtle one at that, but he wasn't in the mood to play games any more.

"Monica, of course."

He stared at her. The door opened and the barman, the second barman, entered carrying a DVD player. Monica nodded. The man knelt down and set about connecting it to the TV set in the corner.

"Who am I, Sean?" she repeated. "What do I do?"

"You're a waitress." Sean snorted a laugh, but there was enough sour apathy loaded into his reply without that addendum.

"My name is Dr Monica Chase, Sean. I'm a psychiatrist."

"Don't be stupid."

She leaned forward.

"What happened when you attacked me, Sean?"

"*He* attacked you."

"*You* attacked me. You know that, don't you? You felt it. Something happened in your mind. It wasn't him, was it? It was you."

The barman stood to one side of the television set with his arms compactly folded. His belly made his shirt ride up at the front like a valance. He was squat, shaven-headed and strong-looking and it struck Sean that he was now in the role of some kind of heavy in case of trouble.

He thumbed towards the newcomer. "What's the barman doing here?" Nobody said anything. Sean was getting pissed off now. They were letting him do all the running and not giving anything in return. "What's going on? Tell me."

"Are you ready for this, Sean? I think you are."

She took out a DVD and slid it into the slitted mouth of the player. She picked up the remote control from the top of the set, quickly familiarised herself with the buttons and pressed PLAY.

Monica knew the footage well. CCTV images filmed by security cameras located in various positions all round the building, bleached and blurred in a hundred shades of grey, six-digit time-code running across the bottom of the screen. First shot, a high angle of the iron gates opening electronically, to allow a square, high security vehicle through. Closing after the van has entered. Cut to another camera angle. The square black van, a police vehicle, pulling up outside the entrance. The vault-thick metal doors swinging open at the back. Sean stepping out of it, escorted by two police officers, wearing dark uniforms and peaked caps, into the building. Handcuffed.

"Tell me what you see, Sean."

Sean watched. Thinking it an infantile exercise, he ran his hand through his hair, but for her stupid benefit, he described what he saw:

"I'm arriving at the hotel. With Ali. In the courtesy mini-bus."

Monica knew what the next shot was. Inside, at the admissions desk, where Paul Davenish, the residential psych at the unit for the last five years, first talked to his new patient. Ali was not there on screen, even though Sean could be clearly seen talking to thin air as if someone was standing next to him.

"Me. And Ali . . ." Sean said. "Talking to the hotel manager. All that Visa business."

Next shot, the hospital canteen. This one always filled Monica with sadness, she couldn't help it. There was something heart-string pulling about her patient sitting there and eating alone. Talking to thin air, chuckling to himself as if he were enjoying a romantic meal for two. He seemed so happy that night, she thought. Oblivious to the other mostly doped-up inmates in the canteen all round him. He only had eyes for someone who wasn't even there.

Sean smiled as the memory came back to him. "I'm with Ali in the restaurant. We're joking about the other guests. Having a good old laugh."

Monica watched his expression. She'd have sworn his face filled with a feeling roughly approximating as love, but she knew better than to let that fool her.

Other shots continued in sequence. She knew them by heart. Sean sleeping in his room, tossing and turning. Alone. Occasionally visiting the bathroom. Occasionally holding imaginary conversations with someone on the bed, gesticulating, then nudging up tenderly. Then, later, according to the time code, Sean pacing up and down, with his hand to his face, but no mobile phone held in it.

"That's me, phoning the girls," he said.

Another CCTV camera angle. "The pissed nymphomaniac in the wedding dress." On the screen, Sean was reacting to the invisible advances of the drunken bride, pawing her away, then running. In reality, nobody was there. Just him.

The screen went black and Monica saw that Sean had jumped up and grabbed the remote. He threw it down on the bed, animated now.

"Look, I've had enough of this. I want some answers."

The barman shot her a glance, but Monica didn't react to Sean's change of mood with so much as a tremor. It was important not to. She wanted the realisation, the epiphany, to come from within, not for the blame to rebound on her as the catalyst, which was why she had to be careful. This wasn't shooting a stag—the lobotomy approach—this was catching a butterfly and, hopefully, setting it free. Psychologically, at least.

She opened her folder and took out a set of ten-by-eight black and white photographs. "I'm going to show you some photographs, Sean, and I want you to tell me if you recognise who they are."

She placed the first photograph on the bed.

"The WPC. The policewoman who came out first," he said. To the next photograph, his answer came equally easy: "The twins' mother." Next it was the man-eating slapper in the wedding dress. "The inebriated Welsh bird—what is this?"

Monica smiled. "Indulge me."

She laid down the next ten-by-eight.

"Yeah. The female Detective Inspector," said Sean, exasperatedly. "You know this." Without pausing, Monica next placed down a photograph of Alison, Sean's wife. He looked away, bristling. "Ha, ha . . . very funny."

Next, a photograph of a man.

Sean looked. "Don't know his name. Detective Sergeant something. Okay. Time's up. What's going on here?"

Monica sat carefully back in her chair. Looked at him with the fingers of one hand entwined in those of her other.

"Where do you think you are, Sean?"

"Where do I *think* I am? I'm in a country house hotel. What are you talking about?"

"You're in a hospital, Sean. A secure psychiatric hospital."

He shook his head with laughter. "You're bloody mental. There's nothing wrong with me. There's something fucking wrong with *you!*"

Monica didn't uncross her legs. "You had a breakdown, Sean. A total collapse. It started even before the trial."

"Trial?"

"It was a reaction to what you did. But I happen to think you're on the point of recovery."

"*Recovery?* Recovery from what?"

"Denial. A denial so complete as to lose contact with reality. Mental dissociation. You constructed in your mind a double—we call it an *eidolon*—as a distancing mechanism in order to psychologically cope with the enormity of your crimes."

Sean wanted to yell at her now. Derision wasn't enough, wasn't nearly enough. "Enormity? What *crimes?*"

"About five years ago there began a series of fatal attacks on women in the North London area." She placed a cover of the *Evening Standard* on the coffee table between them. "The police had trouble catching him. It was down to fingerprints in the end. And DNA." Fingerprints? DNA? "A man targeting and killing sex workers and vulnerable women. Brutally." She walked over to the bed and pointed to the photograph of the woman he had identified as the WPC. "Victim number one. Rachel Benn."

"This is a wind-up. All right, nice one."

She pointed to the photograph of the twins' mother. "Victim two. Evelyn Wagner." The photograph of the drunken Welsh bride. "Victim three. Vivienne Spottiswoode. Like the others, sexually assaulted. Mutilated. Her head . . ."

"Crap. Absolute bullshit."

Monica ignored his interjection and indicated the print of the female Detective Inspector. "Victim four. Margaret Louise Cobb. Same MO exactly." Finally she indicated the photograph of Ali, and as the acid rose in his throat and before he could say, *No, don't*, she was already saying: "Victim five. Alison Hind."

Ali?

"His last victim. Wrong place, wrong time. A junior school teacher walking home from night classes in Art History because she'd missed a bus." Monica tugged the picture of the Detective Sergeant on top of it. "Alison had a loving husband. Who came to the Old Bailey and stared you in the eye every day for five months. Do you remember him now?" She watched Sean gaze down expressionlessly at the row of photographs. "A happily married wife and mother of two daughters. Hannah and Polly."

How are you, kids?

"Get—get out of here!"

Sean scooped up the photographs and threw them at the wall. The barman stepped forward ready to restrain him but Monica signalled him to back off.

"A man was arrested, Sean. Unmarried. A loner. No family. The only time anyone saw him was playing snooker at his local boozer. A man with a chaotic childhood, rife with abandonment, violence and sexual—"

Sean covered his ears, didn't look at the new photograph in her hand.

"No. No! No! SHUT UP! *SHUT UP!*"

He upturned the coffee table with the tabloid cover on. He tried to circle the room, but Monica stayed with him, right in his personal space. He couldn't shake her off. He picked up the newspaper and tore it into little pieces.

"Don't fight it, Sean. I'm trying to help you."

"You're *LYING* to me!" He threw the pieces of paper into her face.

"You needed to cope. You needed to escape. Your mind provided the answer. By splitting you into two different selves." She cornered Sean. He couldn't get past her. He couldn't escape. He slid down the wall. *Leave me alone. Leave me alone!* But she didn't leave him alone. She couldn't leave him alone. This was it. This was what he had to hear. This was what he had to accept. "And what did you do? You created a happily married man, the total opposite of the lonely, disturbed, friendless, violent man you really were. You created an identity you craved to be—*prayed* to be, even."

Sean moaned. His arms wrapped over his head now. Rocking, sobbing. "No! No! It was *him!* It was HIM!"

Monica took his hands in hers, unwrapping them from his head, from his mind.

"The double you were afraid of was the real you. That's why he was trying to come through, that's why he was trying to take over. But that's *good!* Because when you can accommodate him, let him back in, when you can acknowledge the responsibility—then we can help you. Then you can get better."

"NOOOOOOOOOO!"

Sean couldn't take it. He started to sob uncontrollably.

•●•

In the observation room, behind the mirror, Dr Paul Davenish, in pullover and cords, was murmuring to himself: "He's not ready. He isn't sodding ready for it, chicken."

•●•

Her voice hushed and soothing, Monica crouched up close to the huddled shape of Sean, foetus-like against the wall with his arms over his head.

"It was a fantasy. A fantasy wife. A fantasy *life*, Sean. Come back to reality. You can do it. I know you can."

The room was still and silent.

"Sean? . . . Sean?"

She stood up and stepped back from him, proud of the fact that she hadn't touched him, even though she was tempted, and he needed it. But what he needed wasn't the same as what was good for his mental health and that was her call and nobody else's. Responsibility was the key. And if he turned that key, that was everything.

She sat on the bed, her flat hands sandwiched between her bony knees.

Sean uncurled from a ball. Sat still for a few minutes. She wondered if he was reacting to the sound of birdsong.

He stood up straight, wiping away tears with the balls of his thumbs.

Monica walked over to him. Had the dam burst? Did he now feel refreshed, renewed and reinvigorated? Was it the resurrection she dreamt of?

She delved into her pocket and took out the pack of Marlboro and lit up. It was sandpaper-like on the back of her throat because she didn't smoke that much, only on special occasions, but this was a special occasion. Nervously, pointedly, she offered him one.

He took it from her between finger and thumb. Considered it as a chimp might, sniffed it, even, then reached out and put it neatly back in the packet.

"No thanks. I don't smoke."

• • •

Breakfast was from seven-thirty to nine and he was one of these people—it was one of the treats of coming away, wasn't it?—you don't want to miss the *breakfast*, do you? He found a jaunty spring returning to his step as he left his room and headed for the staircase, and began to whistle "The Girl from Ipanema". Maybe it was the sunlight through the stained glass. Maybe it was just the mood he was in after a good night's kip. Whatever it was, this morning he felt the stately hominess reassuring, the sense of family and history wrapping him up like a nice warm blanket. Even the paintings, the old portraits seemed to look down more benevolently now. It was always a bit worrying booking a place sight unseen, but now he'd settled in, Shewstone House Hotel was somewhere he felt really at home. The food was good, the service was good, the rooms were good, the staff were friendly and hospitable. In fact, he didn't have a bad word to say about the place. He wondered why it wasn't publicised more, or was it one of those hideaways that people who stayed preferred to keep a closely guarded secret?

Descending the grand staircase, he nodded hello to the Prof Dumbledore lookalike and his Germaine Greer wife. He thought he might strike up a conversation with them later, maybe they weren't as fuddy-duddy as they looked. He might be a nuclear physicist and she a society madam. They could be a laugh. Giles gave him a little salute of recognition and Sean smiled back, hopping down the last few steps with Fred Astaire lightness.

The linen of breakfast shone in the glow from the windows. The restaurant was peppered with guests and waitresses. Sean side-stepped one, right, left, Laurel and Hardy fashion, laughing apologetically, and skipped to the table by the bay window.

Ali sipped her tea as she ran her eyes down the menu card. Sean joined her, unfolded his napkin and lay it across his lap, and poured himself a cup of tea from the pot.

"What happened to you?" she mumbled. "They talk about women in the bathroom. Continental or full English? That's a silly question."

"Black pudding. Fried bread. Double egg, double sausage. The full Monty."

"The full heart attack."

"I'm on holiday. We're here to enjoy ourselves, remember. Remember?"

Ali arched an eyebrow. "Mmm. I've noticed."

He knew what was going through her mind. It was the exceedingly good sex they'd had the night before. He wasn't about to disagree. He had a smile on him like Zippy from *Rainbow,* too. She touched his hand, which was flat on the tablecloth, then he took hers and squeezed it.

"I love you," said Sean.

"I love you too, fat face," said his wife, reaching over to touch his cheek. He felt his stubble stand on end. It was nice that your wife could still do that for you. A voluminous Jamaican waitress asked if they wanted more tea and they said they did, please, and some toast while they were thinking what to order, if that was all right. Half white, half brown. That would be fabulous.

"Look. It's a beautiful morning," said Ali.

"I know."

"I feel as if we've been away forever already. That's the great thing. And the whole weekend stretches ahead of us."

"It does," said Sean. "This is only our first day. This is just the beginning." He leant over and, not caring who was watching, kissed her on the lips, wanting it to last forever and feeling he was the luckiest, happiest man on earth.

A Meeting at Knossos

I FOLLOWED THE STRING, hand over hand, until I emerged from the belly of the earth. The scent of sea lavender and the tang of bergamot tickled my nostrils and made them widen. Blinded, I felt the sun on my fat, flat toes. It tickled the coarse hairs on my shin as I extended my left leg from my prison. They were as little accustomed to the light as I was.

"Theseus, my love."

That last word caught like a nut in the throat of a lark, its beautiful song curtailed in a knot of sudden abhorrence.

I lowered my hands from my eyes, allowing them in slats to endure the blaze of Helios, my grandfather, in the sky. My bull eyelashes fluttered.

A vision as though through water took form. I remembered water, vaguely. Not seen it for an age, other than the cavernous trickle tasting of iron and moss that had been my wine for too many days to count.

I took her first to be my mother, but no. Princess Ariadne, my half-sister. A pip when I'd last seen her. Elaborate hair, long dress, breasts exposed. Always the fashion-conscious one.

Standing there with the ball of twine in her trembling fingers. Chest rising and falling in horror at the monster she beheld.

Hand over hand, I reached her.

She would have planted a kiss on the cheek of her lover, I was sure. But her half-brother? No.

I was not *Theseus.*

I was something else.

The Prince of Athens lay dead at the centre of the labyrinth.

He'd come to dispatch me, but I'd dispatched him. His club had snapped in two across my forearm. I remembered feeling his Adam's apple jiggle against my palm. His neck had grown hot and pulpy. His shiny helmet had fallen off. So much for shiny helmets. He'd crept up on a sleeping creature to murder it. Not very sportsmanlike.

I dropped the ball of twine at my feet. I had need of it no longer.

"Sister," I breathed, as if my first breath.

The dagger fell from her fingers before I realised she had cut her neck from ear to ear.

I backed away so that she didn't splash me, but it was a bit late for that. I watched her girlish frame crumble and her limbs thrash in a scarlet, widening pool under her. Then, after a while, she was still.

I had seen many a dead maid before. It was not new to me. But it was a disappointment. I would have liked to have caught up on old times, after all the years that had passed, but she'd put paid to that, well and truly. I wasn't sure what to do. There wasn't much I could do. So I knelt and lapped up the blood before it dried. No sense wasting it.

The taste reminded me of the time I nipped my mother's breast with my teeth and got a slap for it. I could still feel the sting on my cheek. That was long before being confined to the bellowing dark. Back when I was loved, or thought I was.

Stepping over my sister, and with no destination in mind, I walked north, avoiding the Royal Road with its traffic and people. Crunched olives underfoot, juniper berries, thorns. Nothing smelled as strong as the fiery rot of the sun. My skin was unused to such attention, and oozed, and shone.

Half-cooked and half-exhausted—half most things—I reached the coast and took myself unto the waves, washing away the stuff that stained me. My sister reddened the surf. Poseidon hissed his thanks for the offering by means of the waves combing the sand then retreating.

Just as I turned back to face the beach I saw a strange shape adorning the rocks, so jagged I first took its inelegance to be the buffeted sail and mast of a wrecked ship. Yet it also resembled as much an arm stretching to the firmament.

What creature, then, was this?

I trod carefully closer.

White petals fluttered in the air about me. I caught one. Opened my fist. It was a feather. I snorted and let it off into the wind like a butterfly.

The thing had vast wings but I could not in all honesty call it a bird. And it had a man's head and body but I could not in all honesty call it a man.

Whatever it was, it was dead, I was sure of that.

I leaned closer to see if the meat was fresh. Old habits die hard.

I sniffed its pale cheek. Touched the long bones covered in feathers, thinking I might break off a piece.

The beast flexed its muscles with a rattling groan. The wing flapped out of my grasp.

I fell over backwards, bruising myself, and squatted silently on a rock formation for a while to see if it awakened.

I don't know why I sat there, looking at its shape. Why did it interest me? Perhaps I thought it might metamorphose into a man. Or metamorphose into a bird. Either would have satisfied.

Neither happened, so I dragged it to the beach to prevent it being swept away by the tide. Why that mattered to me, I cannot say.

Only when I laid it flat did I see the straps and buckles that held the wings to its back. I loosened them and they came away in my hands. Not part of the creature itself but an attachment. Not of bone and flesh at all, but of wooden fronds jointed and planed by human hands.

I peeled away the broken wings and tossed them into a feathery pile of cracked beeswax and leather, revealing a man, a youth, blood-soaked from his wounds.

I revealed you.

A sapling of no more than fifteen or sixteen summers.

Straight away you made me feel old, with my skin dry as the bark of a Cypress, while yours was as unblemished as porcelain, decorated only by the marks you had suffered by some physical misadventure yet to be known to me.

You were mystery made manifest.

Perhaps that was what prevented me from entertaining thoughts of eating you. Zeus knows, I had eaten many in my time. Perhaps it was the idle way your arm was thrown up over your eyes, as if you were sleeping. Or the paltry flatness of your hairless chest. Or perhaps I felt sympathy for the nakedness that made you seem such easy prey for vultures and the like.

Possibly the real reason was that you were neither bird nor man, but some strange type in between. As I was in between. And saw in you my reflection.

The boy half-bird and the man half-bull.

One from the sky and one from underground.

Here met, at Heraklion, the shore that serves the great Palace of Knossos, home of my father.

I cleaned the gore from your body.

Arranged your limbs to better serve your comfort.

You winced like a strangled gannet, then lapsed into a wittering delirium, your teeth chattering, arms crossed over your breastbone.

Your lips were cracked. The sun had battered you worse than it had battered me.

I used a scallop shell to cup fresh water to your lips, softening your blisters with my thumbs. Collected driftwood and made a campfire so that you would be warm come evening.

You did not move.

I wondered what you dreamt. If you dreamt at all.

My chin had fallen onto my chest at the fireside when your sudden screaming shocked me. You were struggling to move, to crab away from me on your elbows, but, I could tell, even the smallest movement was torture. Your cries of terror reminded me uncomfortably of the cries of my numerous victims over the years. I was relieved when they gave way to a general, bleating helplessness.

"You do not have to look at me if it is a hardship," I said.

You flinched and shivered, forcing yourself to lay your eyes upon my features. Not finding it easy.

Frankly, I was used to it.

"Be still. You only hurt yourself all the more by squirming. I shall not eat you. Don't ask me why."

But squirm you did, as I shed my robe and tore it in strips to make bandages. I set about binding your leg to a makeshift splint. I supported your useless arm by means of a sling. The worst damage was to your back. I knew that, and so did you. I wondered if you would ever walk again. Let alone fly.

As you continued to lose yourself in a melody of whimpering, I took myself to the nearby rock pools and returned presently with breakfast.

I broke open a sizeable crab and hooked out the contents of the shell with my tongue.

"It is good," I pronounced, offering you the next, my lips glistening with oil.

You shook your head.

As I chewed the white meat with ungulate jaws, punctuated by the occasional belch, I could tell you were appalled at the sight. Sometimes I think that is the meaning of me. To appal.

Your voice, when it came, took the form of a delicate whisper with all the softness of one of the palace seamstresses.

"Every animal I ever saw before this day that sported horns was content to eat grass,"

"I do not eat grass." I snorted. "But I am not content."

I fed you with my fingers. A hungry man always eats eventually. Even a crab will eat a crab eventually.

"What is your name?"

You did not answer.

"I'd tell you mine if I had one. But I am more thing than person. They put a *The* in front of me, as they do all horrors."

"I thought you fearsome," you said quietly, like an admission of guilt.

"Thank you very much," I said.

You pushed away my hand and what it contained, repulsed by it, or repulsed by me. I wasn't sure which.

At the sound of ocean birds gabbling overhead, you twisted your head to look up at them, creating a spasm that shot through your body. You shut your eyes tightly.

I walked away, leaving you alone with your pain, not wishing to tax you with further conversation.

For an hour I listened to the lullaby of the ocean and sat with my arms around my knees, uplifted by the salty breeze of samphire perfumed with rosemary. I felt Helios filling the sky, searing and prickling my bare shoulders, my bovine ears, my hunched back, the lumps of my spine.

A tern with its black cap and red beak wheeled over my head and kept me company, though I doubted that was its intention. It disappeared and squawked a song from its nest on the cliffs. I thought it sang the name of Ariadne, my sister.

Ariadne . . . Ariadne . . . Ariadne.

I thought perhaps the tern *was* my sister. The gods are mischievous like that.

When I returned the fire was diminished.

"You can't let it go out." I poked the embers with a stick and tried to puff them back to life. "Do you know anything? What use are you?"

"Not much. Except for flying."

"And not that."

You sat up as best you could, adjusting a triangle of my robe about your shoulders.

"I'm a story," you said. "If there is any use to that."

The face I looked at pretended to slumber. I knew that you did not.

"The maidens used to tell me stories," I grumbled as I placed twigs in the shape of crosses upon the newly crackling flames. "Enough to keep me up with events in the outside world. Through their terror, of course. Did it to keep themselves alive. Day by day, hour by hour, one story at a time. Their reed-like voices bouncing off the walls of the maze. Then I'd get hungry, and, well, that was that." I wasn't sure if you were listening because your expression didn't change. "The youths weren't so co-operative. They'd tell me to go fuck myself. They'd show off their virility by jumping over me with their staves. Proving who had the biggest balls. But I'd get them all in the end, however cocky they were. Whatever names they called me. I chased them. It kept me fit."

I crooked my arm, let my bicep bulge.

I could see you were not impressed.

"Some killed themselves the minute they saw me. Or their hearts gave out. Which isn't good for a fellow's confidence, it has to be said."

You gazed unblinking into the fire.

"Their bodies lay where they fell. No stories," I said. "Their bones frightened others. Some touched my cheek before they ran away."

My fingertips had found their way to my face. Same old face. Same old ox hide. Stupid gesture. I lowered them to my lap.

"In the dark you say they were nevertheless horrified?"

I grunted. "They brought torches, the better to see their worst fear. Yes, they really were that stupid. The darkness would have served them better."

"I see you in light," you said softly. "There is no shadow here."

"Do not pretend," I said sharply. "I know you would flee in an instant, if you could, from the sight of this monstrosity."

"You cannot know."

"I *do* know. Do not dispute me. Or mock me. A bull angers easily!"

I shot to my feet, towering over you. I could feel blood pumping behind my eyes and drumming in my ears like a call to battle. I knew I could have split your head open in an instant, and let it join all your other broken parts. I could have held it in both hands and twisted it open in two halves like the crab and sucked your brains out. All these things were possible, and desirable, and yet—

Instead, I kicked sand over the embers, dousing the flames.

"There. There! Your wisdom. The fire unattended. Feel the cold of night and see how you like it."

I turned my back on you, my feet sinking in the still-warm sand, my horned head hanging in front of me, elbows jutting as I walked.

"Stay."

I ignored your entreaties. Bull-headed, as they say.

"Do not leave me."

I walked to the west, applying myself to the setting sun. Making a line of footsteps. Not looking back at the shadow I cast behind me, which had the body of a man but the head of a bull.

Then I hesitated.

Ahead of me an ugly, gnarled thing nestled where water and land met.

A dead gull with its organs ripped out.

What had been at it, I could not tell, whether a fisherman's hooks or a fox's teeth. Its yellow feet stuck up from a distended belly. Its eyes were stricken berries. One wing under it, the other splayed like a fan, pointing to the sky, its feathers matted with seaweed.

I turned and hurried back in the direction my shadow was pointing.

It was well and truly dusk by the time I got there and the moon was a silver coin against a purple cloak. I scrambled over the slippery rocks on all fours. Dribble fell from my mouth into the rock pools.

I saw to my surprise that you were wiping tears from your eyes.

"You are safe now, and I have cared for you," I said, perplexed, as I sat. "Why do you weep?"

"I weep because you cared for me," you said, stifling your sobs. "And because my father was a traitor. And that's why we were imprisoned, just as you were."

I was surprised but not alarmed.

"Imprisoned by King Minos. Well, he is a complete bastard. This we know."

"This is serious. Are you not curious?"

"Should I be?"

"Yes."

My smile was washed away by the sound of the waves.

"It is a tale I must tell."

"Then tell it," I said.

"I am not sure you will want to hear it."

"I do now," I said.

You shifted your position, trying to alleviate the pain but failing miserably. You had become pale. Blood had seeped into your bandages.

"My father had done something unspeakable to offend the king."

"I imagined as much."

The embers were grey and I hoped that was what was making you shiver.

"He could not let it stand and sentenced us to imprisonment in the tallest tower of the palace."

"I can think of worse," I mumbled.

"He would have executed him, when he found out. Except he knew that he was the most talented weapons maker in his empire. The army would be at a severe loss without him. And his enemies would take that for a weakness."

"How came you to be birdlike?" I cut in, impatiently.

"My father was a great designer. They say he invented the saw. It's incredible to think that before that nobody had thought of putting teeth on a blade to cut wood. It seems obvious. But he was the first. I'm not saying he was grand about it. He was a humble man. Anyway he was always just Dad to me. Always pottering or playing. Son, look at this, have a go at that. Telling me why a candle flame is yellow at the top but blue at the wick. His room was full of drawings, all kinds. Thousands of drawings of things he saw in his head."

Your eyes rested on the bundle of sticks and feathers that were once your means of travel, albeit briefly and dramatically.

"My father saw me fly my kite one day and his eyes grew bright in that way they did when a new idea was sparked. He told me to gather all the feathers the birds shed on our roof, and we did so, day after day, week after week, month after month. He hammered away in his workshop, carving and drilling, until one day he put his finger to his lips and revealed what he had made. A pair of wings. Two pairs. One set for me. One for him. I knew immediately that he had been devising our means of escape. The king's armies control the land, he said, and his fleet controls the sea, but nobody controls the air. I couldn't believe this was my opportunity to soar over the heads of our captors and be free. I couldn't wait to launch myself off that roof and let the wind take me, but my father was always the sobering influence. Son, he warned me, be careful. Follow me closely once we are up there. Don't fly too low, lest the waves waterlog your wings and weigh you down, and don't fly too high, lest the heat of the sun melts the wax that holds the wings together. I promised him. Of course I promised him. What is there not to promise?

"We stood on the parapet, looking down at the citizens of Knossos going about their business, haggling over the price of melons or whipping the backs of their stubborn donkeys. None of them looked up. My father was lifted as if pulled on a string, like my kite. My own toes stuck over the ledge and, just as he had done, I took to the air, arms outstretched. Before I knew it I was hundreds of feet above the palace walls. Every beat my arms made lifted me higher on an unseen ladder to the clouds.

"It was sensational. I could not stop myself laughing, and wondered if the rooks could hear as they passed me. I didn't care. I squinted at my father as he glided ahead of me, and I felt such love for him as I'd never felt before. I adored my father. But never like this. I felt light-headed. Happiness inflated my lungs with a kind of reckless madness and before I knew it I was looking down at my father below me. I suddenly knew I had done wrong and I wanted him to rescue me but he wasn't looking back. He couldn't see that I was in trouble. He had given his orders for me to follow. But I could feel the wax that held me together melting. My artificial limbs began to feel cumbersome and insecure, wobbling in their fixtures. I could see the wax dripping in gobbets. I kicked my legs, like a swimmer trying to keep afloat, but I was not in water. I wished I was. I tried to gulp air into my chest but it was all I could do to keep flapping my arms. The ground rushed towards me. I closed my eyes tightly. The last thing I saw was the outline of my father, Daedalus, disappearing towards a distant shore."

"*Deadalus*," I repeated, the sound curdling on my tongue, though puzzlement swirled in my brain. "I know that name. As a babe in arms, I tugged his beard. That man designed the very labyrinth in which I was caged. I found his name carved on the wall with a chisel. The artist had signed his masterpiece."

"I know," you said.

"I had grown too large, too surly, too disobedient, too passionate, too ferocious, too—*horned*."

"I know," you said a second time. "My father told me how the king, at his wit's end, consulted the Oracle at Delphi, who told him to build a labyrinth to keep you in. So what was he to do except employ the greatest architect in the land?"

"You *know*?" I thrust my bull head at you. "You *know* my prison walls were drawn by your father's eye and hand?" I grabbed your throat in one fist. My thumb and fingertips almost touched. It was like the neck of a swan.

"Yes. He created you, as he created me."

"As I was forged in that prison, yes!"

"No! I mean he was father to us both. In a way you cannot know."

"Then I had better know soon." I let go of you. "Or these fingers will return to your windpipe and crush the air out of it."

You coughed, gulped, swallowed. Regained your senses.

"It is a tale he told me . . . to unburden his guilt."

"Guilt?"

"It was because of your . . . your fate . . . your very being . . ."

"What can you tell me that I do not know myself, twittering, clucking thing?"

You took a deep breath into your broken chest and let it out slowly.

"I shall tell it the way I heard it. No more, no less. Many years ago, to gain the throne of Crete, King Minos prayed to Poseidon, who dispatched a white bull as a way of conferring his blessing. The king was supposed to sacrifice it to the god, but was so busy celebrating his victory he forgot. Poseidon was enraged by the insult and, as punishment, made Pasiphae, the king's wife, fall in love with the bull. The queen became so unnaturally besotted she privately called upon the services of Daedalus, the cleverest engineer in the court, to help her satisfy her lust. Unable to refuse on pain of death, my father, behind the king's back, constructed a hollow wooden cow for Pasiphae to hide inside, which was wheeled out into the fields to enable the bull to enjoy bestial congress with her. The offspring that she . . ."

"No."

"Let me finish—the offspring she subsequently carried to birth was the hybrid of his mother and father . . ."

"No."

"—with characteristics of both man and bull."

I had been striking one dry stick against another but the fire had not re-ignited.

"So! I am a tale!" I laughed bitterly, wiping slather from my chin. "You are telling me that, but for a wooden cow built by your father, I would not be?"

"The gods also had a hand in it."

"Oh, the gods have a hand in everything!" I threw the sticks into the distance. "But they have truly outdone themselves with this piece of work." I looked down at my thickly muscled arms, my stout, ugly fingers. "This art. This—*toy!*"

"While you languished underground, my father kept his secret. Not because he wanted to save his own life but because he wanted to save mine. My mother, Naucrate, a mistress and slave girl given by King Minos to my father in reward for designing the labyrinth, became jealous of the love between father and son. It wasn't until five years ago she told the king that Daedalus had helped the Queen mate with the Cretan Bull. He was enraged at the betrayal. He had forgiven his wife, Pasiphae, after she'd cured him of a spell by which his seed turned into scorpions and millipedes—little knowing that the spell was cast by the sorceress herself in revenge for the king's own numerous infidelities. No, the betrayal of Daedalus, another man, and a man he held in high regard, cut far deeper. So father and son were imprisoned. Not in the labyrinth—which, as he had designed it, my father could have easily escaped. Instead we were locked up in a tower, so that we could look over creation and see every day how human ingenuity was no equal for that of the gods."

At that moment, I cared nothing for the gods.

It was Daedalus—a *man*—to whom I owed my monstrous existence. Without *him* I would never have been born. I had always held him responsible for my labyrinth alone, but now I could see he was to blame for my bigger prison—*life.* And I hated him for that all the more.

My laughter turned to tears.

"Who am I?"

"One who cares for another," you said. "Do you wish for anything more?"

"Yes!" I struggled to hold back my sobs even though they contorted my every word. "I *deserve* more! I deserve to know my place in the world, as every living creature does, from ant to emperor. But I do not even know my nature. Man or beast."

"Ask yourself, what pleases you."

"What pleases me? Nothing pleases me!"

Your smile sat, indefatigable, on your face.

"Man can ascend."

"You say that, who has fallen?"

"I do. Nothing is beyond us. All is wonder. My father taught me that."

"The same father who saw you drop like a stone to your death? Who watched you and flew away? He did nothing."

"He did everything. He built these wings. I saw the pride in his face as I buckled them on."

"And what did you see in his face as you plummeted?"

That hit you like a blade. As it was meant to.

But you refused to be browbeaten or cowed. Cowed by a cow-face like mine. I could not harm you with words, or anything else. I don't know why. Perhaps you were too tortured already. Where I would have expected to see self-pity through the pain, I never did. I perceived only a good, generous soul in a failing body. You were withering but your spirit was not. Whereas mine burnt with the bile of a vast emptiness.

Who had taught *me* the science of a candle flame? Who had taken *me* to the roof edge and encouraged me to fly?

"You have the brain of a bird," I said, "if you do not feel with every step in life the thorns underfoot."

"I have had the eye of a bird for a passing moment and that is enough. I have hovered above the clouds and gazed down upon them as you look down at the sand. There is a silence there beyond inquiry. And when they clear, and you alight upon an eagle face to face, in symmetry, and converse with cascading geese, and below them stretches a carpet of unimaginable greens and yellows, forests bulging like glorious pillows, rippling sheets of sea with untouched serpents coiling therein in a whole moving tapestry, but a tapestry the like of which could never be captured by human endeavour, and will outlast every king and god, why—it is unbelievable. And yet, belief itself."

I did not like the look on your face.

I think I liked the pain better.

"The air up there is thin indeed," I said. "You have lost all reason. And do not speak ill of the gods. They have the habit of taking umbrage. I think I am ample proof of that."

"You would not wish to see what I saw?"

"No." I shook my big, horned head. "I do not want to fall as you fell, strange as it may sound. Look at you. You are a mess. As an advertisement, you fail. You are not even a man, so stop it with all the wisdom bollocks."

A low grumble made me look to the sky, which had become the colour of flint. Perhaps the titans had heard their playthings jabbering and were annoyed. Let them be, I thought. White sheets had transformed into pregnant bowls ready to dish their wares on our heads. It required no great Oracle of Delphi to see that a storm was imminent.

My arms hooked under your armpits.

"You cannot carry me."

"I can."

"You are my brother." Your heels tracked two parallel lines in the sand.

"Shut up," I said.

The campfire was dead. My horns dripped rain onto my shoulders as the shower commenced.

I had spotted a small cave at the foot of the cliff with enough cover to shelter. High tide did not reach that far.

Your beloved sky had darkened swiftly.

As the rain fell in sheets, I pondered if you were hungry, but if you were there wasn't much I could do about that. If our conversation was over, it was over. I had had enough talk for a lifetime.

You groaned several times so I rearranged your legs. You hissed rapidly through gritted teeth, then became rested. The bandages were sodden and the breathing clotted with a thick paste in your throat I hoped wasn't blood.

"Sleep."

"I am afraid to sleep," came the words, claggy and crooked.

"I am here," I said softly, making it sound like my mother's words, when she would rock me.

"These damp walls remind me of my labyrinth," I sighed, idly tossing pebbles out into the rain.

"You live in hatred, when you could live in wonder."

I stood up and pissed in a corner. It ran out of my pizzle with substantial urgency, gathering in an acrid puddle about my feet.

"He was a great man," you wheezed. "I do not blame him for my fate. I decided upon my own actions. Not he."

"So be it," I said, shaking drips from my penis. "Do you mind if I take a shit?"

"Thank you for asking."

You gave a magnanimous wave of your one mobile hand.

I did the necessary. The stink was abominable. You made no complaint. If you had some superhuman powers granted by the gods, it was that.

I made myself comfortable.

Watched you fall asleep.

You live in hatred, when you could live in wonder.

A noise came out of my mouth. Bull or man, it doesn't really matter.

I thought of all the years I had hunted the seven maidens and seven youths donated by Athens in tribute to King Minos as recompense for the death of his other son, Androgeus—my half-brother—and all the while had thought their fear was my engine, my being, but the truth was, every second I was fearful myself. I had been born to fear. I ate for fear of being eaten. I did not even like the taste of human flesh. It was stringy at the best of times.

"Go to sleep," I said, realising that you already were, and shortly afterwards, so was I. Back in the bleak dungeon. Back among the dead things. The frightened virgins and the cock-wavers. The boredom, the emptiness.

When I woke with a start, it was still dark. The rain had ceased, and you were gone.

I jumped to my feet in panic. I didn't even know your name to call out.

I saw a bloodstained length of bandage.

I followed it outside, as I had following Theseus's ball of twine.

I found you stretched on your back. I could see your skinny chest was moving so I was gratified you were not dead.

Your shins and feet were striped with wet sand.

There were patches on your elbows.

You must have crawled out on your belly.

I could not imagine the slow determination it must have required to haul your protesting carcass all that way onto the sand. And to stifle your cries of pain while doing so—why? So as not to wake me?

I planted my feet solidly either side of your hips.

"You would try to escape? You won't get far."

You laughed, shaking your head.

"Escape *me*?" I said.

"No."

You stretched your arm, as if bemused, pointing your index finger at me. But I realised you were not gazing at me. You were gazing beyond me, at the night sky above.

"I wanted to see it. I had a dream, you see . . . A beautiful dream."

"Yes, well. I slept soundly. Till now."

I took my position at your feet and lifted your ankles as if gripping the handles of a wheel barrow.

"I dreamt I met your half-sister and we had danced."

"Ariadne was ever a good dancer."

I pulled you along a few feet but your face contorted wretchedly.

I was compelled to stop. Only then did it resume its former state of calm repose. One might say even peace. Though what peace you could enjoy, with that map of lacerations all over you, and your insides thrashed like wheat, was beyond me.

"Afterwards she took off her crown and told me she had no need of it. Then Dionysus swooped down and took it from her forehead, and set it in the sky, where it blazed through the dark of space, and as it soared its jewels changed into bright fires, and fell into their allotted places, that she might shine eternally." You stared up at the stars, enraptured. "Corona borealis. You see it? It has all the appearance of a crown, between the kneeling Heracles and the head of the serpent that Ophiuchus holds."

"You would sleep here then? Or inside? It makes no difference to me."

I waited for an answer, but none came, so the decision was mine.

I lay down beside you. My rugged back the wall between us. I would not like to say if I was awake when I felt your fingers touch the V between my shoulder blades where the bristled, hard skin of a bull met the soft flesh of a man. Or whether some puny arm wrapped around me. If it contented you, I let it. And if the dream flitted away with the opening of my eyelids, I let it too.

"Do not let me die alone."

Was it in a dream you said that? And in a dream did I answer?: "I shall kill him for both of us."

The sun came up over my mountainous bulk and illuminated you.

I looked up at the sky in its unforgiving blue and was saddened the stars had gone. But the stars always go. I don't know why it saddened me on that particular morn.

I poked your thigh lightly with a toe. Wakey wakey.

You groaned and roused, sheltered your eyes from the intense glare of the day. I thought it might wither you, the sun, if you were not a plant half-withered already.

I repaired myself to the cave we had formerly occupied, applied my tongue to the libation of the stalactites, using their moisture to wet my armpits and groin.

When I returned, you had lifted yourself up on one elbow and were drawing in the sand like an infant. You looked over your shoulder at me, squinting as the little tune you hummed came to an end.

"I know your name," you said, smiling.

I froze to the spot, thinking this another game invented to fox me.

"Icarus," said a voice behind me, confusing me further.

I spun around to behold first the shadow of a vast sea bird on the side of the cliff, then an old man with wings half as wide as the beach we stood on, or so it seemed. Wings that beat, thrumming, like great flags—adjusted by ropes operated from the old man's wrists—arresting his fall with delicate ease as his bare feet met their own shadows on the ground.

"Father," you said, but I had no need of such information.

The beard was whiter than I remembered it, but the beard was the same.

Daedalus, with tears bulging in his eyes, had found his son. After how much searching far and wide I did not know, but on that day the searching was at an end, and the emotion of reuniting too much for both of you.

By dint of your injuries, you could not move, but neither could he.

He folded the wings under him like a cob swan after landing. His arms extended from the whiteness of his raiment. He showed you his pink and trembling palms and fell to his knees.

"Icarus. O, Icarus!"

Yes, I get the point.

"What took you so long?" I said, making the old chap's lower lip quiver. He was the cleverest man alive, but not as clever as me. He had a beard but I had a breast that was bursting, and a heart afire within it. "I have been waiting for this. Behold."

I picked up a seashell, serrated along one edge. It fitted adequately in my hand. I pulled your head back by the hair and drew the sharp edge from one side of your neck to the other.

The mouth opened in your throat and a fountain of scarlet pumped over your insubstantial chest. Your ribs—those pained ribs—jerked as you tried to suck in air, but into what? Your lungs were already a terracotta jar half-filled with blood. The blood that seven after seven maidens never saw stain their thighs, and seven after seven youths never shed in the name of king and country.

The blood that for centuries had stained many a bull ring and now gathered black as ink in the sand.

I backed away, seeing that my knees and dangling prick were painted with your funeral gruel.

As Daedalus crawled to you, I took myself to a rock pool to wash it off.

As he bawled uncontrollably, I looked down at the shell in my hand. Amused to find the form of it displaying the spiral of the labyrinth, a line I could trace with my fingernail leading inexorably to its centre. I put it to my ear, chuckling in the knowledge that in aeons to come, a little mite would pick it up and do the same, and, even centuries distant, hear, as if trapped within, the mournful bellowing of a bull.

I cast it far out into the waves. A gift for Poseidon—for him to be reminded what passions he had put in train when he conferred his blessing on King Minos with a gift.

Your father's hands became a pillow on which your head lay.

He lavished your brow with kisses, but no trick of any inventor could put life back into those dull, unseeing eyes. They were fixed in wonder forever.

Dripping with seawater, I looked down at the sand where you had been doodling with your finger minutes earlier.

I saw letters, spelling out the word ASTERION. Meaning, star.

"My death would have been enough." Daedalus cradled you on his lap now, your dead cheek held firm against his bony chest.

"Not for me," I said, satisfied that my revenge upon my maker was complete. "Thou art dead now, in suffering, for all thy days."

"I am not as dead as thee," said the old man venomously.

But no venom could poison me now. Least of all his.

While he blubbered and rocked your corpse, with that one skeletal arm of yours jutting out like a whittled branch, and your chin hanging loosely, I gathered up the remnants of your wings.

The wings that had failed you, but brought success to me. Revelation. Truth. Completion. And I would always thank you for that, dear Icarus.

I untied the knots of the straps. Pulled on the shoulder harnesses as the wind lifted the carapace of feathers, buckling the fastenings much as the Palace Guard used to do when they donned their breastplates, thinking briefly of how those soldiers used to amuse themselves by tossing hoops onto my horns as a child, taking wagers on who would win the game.

The contraption felt cumbersome at first, but I knew I would get used to the weight. The gulls seemed to chorus their approval. Or maybe it was the blood that excited them so. On the other hand, perhaps the feathered ones were grieving for the passing of one of their own? No matter.

Without a backward glance, I left Daedalus to bury you. Abandoned him to his obsequies. His designs.

I had executed mine.

"I shall not eat grass," I said.

Loud enough for the old man to hear, and never forget.

In the months and years that followed, I made my way to the city of Inycus in Sicily, where my future opened before me. Slaughtering all comers to the arena—and shocking the crowd when I revealed I wore no horned helmet to take off—I earned myself the trust of King Cocalus, who named me his champion, and, thereafter, general.

Soon, with the bloody sands of Heraklion far behind me, I was being bathed by handmaidens and armies bowed down before me, offering up seven sons and seven daughters to me in order to save their skins. The number became a superstition to me. And often, too much to fill my appetite.

But from their bones I fashioned a beautiful litter.

And those nations that have not yet been ravaged call me *The* . . . and tremble.

I am glad to be known by such a name, now.

I need no other.

Destiny is a fickle beast, but if I know anything I do know beasts, and I knew that sooner or later the day would dawn when I could command a fleet of a thousand vessels to sweep across to Crete and descend upon King Minos, my father.

And so I stand at the prow of the flagship, double-headed axe in hand, my shield adorned with the spiral of the labyrinth, carrying the broken wings on my back, knowing that behind me every warship is furnished with a figurehead half-man, half-bull.

When I kill and eat my father I shall feel nothing. And in reuniting my mother with that hollow, wooden cow I shall feel even less.

For I am the monster they made me, come to claim my birthright.

Nothing but the son returning home.

Sicko

THE MOMENT MARION stepped into the shower the world changed forever. She felt the water hit her forehead and run over her closed eyelids. It had been icy on her fingers when she'd first turned it on. Now it was lukewarm. Good. Cooler was best, to wash away the Phoenix heat. The heat of a long drive. Perspiration the young man may have noticed, but she hoped he hadn't. *Not very ladylike.* But did it matter, really, what the young man thought? She'd never see him again. Apart from checking out the next morning.

She revolved, away from the spray. It hit her shoulders and calmed her, slightly. Didn't get rid of the stress entirely. That would be asking too much. Maybe she wouldn't get rid of that stress in her shoulders for the rest of her life. What a thought! Maybe it would never go away. How about that?

She asked herself what had made her do it in the first place. Was she crazy? Or did those lunchtime sessions with Stan in that featureless downtown hotel room, slats of sun intruding through the blinds, knotted limbs, trading saliva, make her feel crazy a little bit? Of *course* they did. God knows, that's what they were *for*. She needed an escape, or the office would have made her scream. Watching that clock go round. Waiting for you-know-who to come out and hand her back her typing, telling her there was a spelling mistake, not just one, but *I think you'll find . . .* like she's back in school, and his fingernails, too long for a man, they needed attending to, as she nodded, contrite, and smiled sweetly, rolling a fresh sheet into the typewriter.

Her previous shower had been earlier that day, after Stan had been inside her. Not his real name, but the one he wrote in the register. Stanley *Kowalski.* They joked about it! *Streetcar Named*

Desire. "Punk downstairs wouldn't know Tennessee Williams from a hole in the ground." She'd lain there and lit a cigarette, as he did, from his own packet, but she wasn't worried about taking the smell of the cigarette back to her desk. She was worried about taking the smell of him.

Under the shower, back then, a world ago, she'd thought, wet, rotating, dreamy, of those commercials with the perfect housewives who held up for scrutiny their dirty linen and immaculate lives. Who said to her every day: *Don't get jealous, get even. You too can be like me. Seemingly unattainable but actually far more sexually accomplished than you might presume.*

Doris Day. Grace Kelly. If she couldn't *be* them, she could at least look like them. That was a form of advertising, too, really. *A message from our sponsor* . . . Available, but not easy. And if she couldn't afford new stockings, she could use that pencil line up the back of the leg trick her mother taught her.

He'd cupped her breasts from behind, then helped her on with her white *Tide clean* bra, kissing her neck hairs before hooking it up, taking a suck on the cigarette and giving her a halo of smoke. He declared he was hard again. Donning earrings, she'd pointed out with an arched eyebrow she'd just taken a shower.

"Showers are overrated," he'd replied. "I like dirty."

"I know you do." Grinning, she'd pushed him away, splayed fingers against hairy chest.

He'd sat on the bed, one sock on and one in his hands, and his face drooped, as it always did when their liaisons came to an end. He became a little boy again, sad to say goodbye. That saddened her, too, but cheered her at the same time, because she at least meant something to him, and she didn't always feel that with men. Stan was different. Even if they had to sign in under bogus names. That was something of a thrill in a childish way, but it also made it not real, not serious, impermanent, and somehow trivial, like a prank. Something silly, to him. . . . Was it?

She didn't know *what* she thought. It was probably just *too much thinking* getting in the way, like he said it was. Fretting that things could go wrong because they'd always gone wrong in the past, but they wouldn't this time. He'd said he loved her and wanted to marry her, hadn't he? What more did she want?

All they needed, before they walked down that aisle, was some money to settle his debts—and it wasn't like they were *debts,* as such, so much as mistakes, so much as people who had let him down, who promised him things would happen, and hadn't. Stan was too trusting like that. He saw the best in people, and suffered for it. It wasn't fair. But then the world wasn't fair.

This was what she'd been thinking as she walked back to the office earlier that Friday afternoon. As she sat at her desk straightening her skirt, as her boss tapped his watch and she apologised for being two minutes late, it wouldn't happen again, tidying her hair, coughing into her hand, turning the roller of the typewriter. Not even aware of the meeting he'd had behind closed doors with a client, thinking only of Stan's body tangled in a bed sheet, one knee raised, his lips coming closer to hers, until her boss placed the brown paper package on her desk.

Until he said it was a *$40,000 cash payment* for a property, just brought in by a valued customer and friend.

She hadn't even noticed the person leaving. She'd been in a post-coital daze. Her boss had said the name of the customer. He'd said the address of the property. But after he'd mentioned the quantity of cash, which hit her like a weapon—the way money did to those who didn't have it—the rest became a blur, a kind of dull thudding hum in her head, monotonous and overwhelming, like the giant hive buzz of a drag race.

She *did* hear him telling her to *Put the cash in the safe, Marion, please . . . It's the weekend . . . You can take the money to the bank first thing Monday morning.* She did hear *that*—loud and clear.

"Yes, sir. Yes, sir. Yes, sir."

$40,000! House for his baby daughter—a wedding present!

"Yes, sir."

Her boss returned to his office, shaking his head. She could hear him on the telephone as she opened the metal door hidden behind the painting that adorned one wall.

She had her purse with her, the straps over one forearm.

Nobody was watching. The other desk was empty. Wittering Peggy was off buying a wedding dress. (Peggy, so plain, but so full of confidence now she had an engagement ring on her finger.)

Using the combination entrusted to her, Marion opened the safe.

Felt a hollowness growing inside and didn't know if it was her stomach churning or her uterus aching, but part of her was crying out. Crying out for Stan. Crying out for him to tell her what to do. But she knew what to do, didn't she? Didn't she know what to do, all on her own, without a man telling her? *Do it!*

She slipped the brown paper package *not onto the shelf of the safe* but down into her purse. Tugged the zip closed over it. Clunked the safe door closed. Spun the rings of the combination lock with three jerks of her wrist.

Back stiff as a rod, she walked into her boss's office. He looked up, startled, standing, saying she didn't look well. No colour in her cheeks. Gosh. She really didn't look well at all.

"No—No, I don't feel well, actually, sir. I don't. I've got the most awful headache."

Well, gracious . . . In that case, she'd better go home, hadn't she? Go home, Marion, dear. Right away!

But—

She protested, diligent, dutiful. A good employee. (A good actress. Grace Kelly . . .)

"No buts! Go home this instant, young lady!"

Coat. Purse.

$40,000!

"Thank you, sir. Goodbye, sir. Have a nice weekend, sir."

"You too, Marion. And Marion? . . . Do rest up, won't you?"

"Oh, I think I'll be spending the weekend in bed, sir."

The memory of her own small, tight laugh made the sweat come out of her pores again, and she stood with her hands flat against the shower walls.

She remembered stepping out of the office onto the sidewalk, into the oven-hot sunlight, looking back at the word REALTY painted on its front window. Recalled, when she was a little girl of about five or six, and innocent—asking why that shop sold REALITY? And her momma telling her, no, silly pig, it wasn't REALITY, it was *REALTY*, and that meant REAL ESTATE—which somehow, to her mind, back then, still meant something was real and something wasn't.

And walking away with the package in her purse, she'd felt she was leaving REALITY behind. But perhaps that was what *$40,000* bought you. The fantasy you always dreamed of. The perfection of the commercials. The perfect marriage that, in America, only money could buy. And if she didn't deserve it—who did?

Her back was straight. Her poise immaculate. Daring not to run and give the game away, she almost slowed to a stop, and so paused and touched up her lipstick, which didn't need it.

She walked straight home—five blocks, so convenient!—where she packed a suitcase since she'd already decided to take herself and the *$40,000* to Fielden, California, where Stan lived. *Airport check- in closes 3 p.m.* she'd remembered him saying. *Come with me. Hang work.* Fieden, California—where he now sat, or stood at a bar, not even remotely guessing their troubles were over. That black curl hanging over his brow, striking a match, she could smell the phosphorus, she loved that smell, and became deliriously happy for a moment, imagining his face as he rips open the package and sees the wads. His jaw dropping before he grips her face in his hands and smashes her lips with his.

Her Ford Customline slid out into the road.

She drove.

Not that it was easy at first. Just as when she walked back from lunch she thought everybody could see that she'd had sex, now she thought everybody could see she was a thief. Of course they couldn't. Of course there wasn't a great big sign on her vehicle saying STOLEN MONEY ON BOARD.

Of course. Of course. She knew. She knew.

She stopped at a red light. Flexed her fingers on the steering wheel.

$40,000!

Nobody could tell by looking at someone whether they'd done something bad. Not that woman pushing the stroller, not the fat, bald man crossing the crosswalk, not the skinny old man with a moustache who looked a lot like . . . oh *God,* looked *exactly* like—and stopping, doing a double-take, staring right at her. Her boss—*right at her!*

The lights changed and she floored the gas.

Her back sank into the seat as the car took off. She imagined her boss turning his head, perplexed, doubting his eyes, watching her powder blue Ford sedan go. *No, it couldn't have been. Could it?*

Her face was in shadow, she told herself. He'd never have made out her face. Maybe the blonde hair. That was all, she thought, as the city peeled away.

One thing she did know . . . no turning back now. *No turning back, kiddo,* she could hear Stan telling her. Proud of her, taking her hand.

She hit the highway for as long as she could, eyes always flitting to the mirror, too often probably, more there than out front probably, and the steering suffering from her jitters, because she got honked at more than once, and more than one car swerved to overtake her. But she kept her cool. *Relax,* Stan kept saying in her mind. *Just relax, baby. You're doing just fine.* And she *was* doing just fine. If she could just hold it together and keep her eyes on the asphalt.

The one thing she didn't want to happen was to get a fender bender or to get pulled in. If Moustache *had* recognised her, he'd have wondered why she wasn't laid up in bed like she said. He'd have grown suspicious, checked the safe, found the *$40,000!* gone, and phoned the police instantly, so she could be all over the police radio by now.

He didn't recognise you, baby.

I know, but—what if?

What if nothing.

A howl like a bear in a trap went through her. Her eyes flashed wide as a long hood Peterbilt loomed in the back window. Her head almost went through the roof. The wheel spun in her hands. She grabbed it hard. Her tyres whined. The massive bulk of the truck sailed by. Spooked her so much she pulled over to the side of the road.

Her body was telling her to sleep, so she'd best listen to it and catch forty winks or else end up in a ditch. Some broad in the morgue being ogled and prodded by the glee of men perusing the enemy. For what? Money? *Stupid bitch.*

And at her funeral . . . who?

Next thing she remembered, being woken up by the knuckle-rap of a state trooper. Long face filling the side window. Sunglasses filling the face. Herself filling the sunglasses. A blonde hitching herself upright elbow by elbow, tousled hair like a tramp—in both senses. To the black orbits of a skull.

His lips, desert dry. Desert wry. Non-committal.

Questions.

Answers.

Did they satisfy him? Did she satisfy this man? If not, what would it take? Why didn't he wet his lips with his tongue? What was a tongue for anyway? He looked at her from behind the blackness. The look that was always the look. Never scared in the way a woman was scared every day.

But she wouldn't show him she was scared. She wouldn't show him she was powerful either. Men didn't like that, and cops didn't like that especially. They liked, Yes sir. Sorry, sir. I won't let it happen again, sir. I won't do anything this stupid again, sir, said the *widdle girl* to the *big bwave man*.

His face didn't move. His body didn't move. She wondered how he moved in bed. Whether he kept his uniform and sunglasses on.

He touched the peak of his hat, let her go. *Allowed* her to go. She wondered if he wanted to take her to bed the whole time he was talking to her. She wondered whether the whole time he was comparing her to his wife.

She drove, and noticed he was following her at a prowl. At worst, suspicious. At best, protective. *Daddy gonna look after you, sweet pig.* She lay off the accelerator as a mark of obedience. They liked you to obey them. It was the main thing they were interested in, when it came down to it.

Her neck was red hot and damp.

He was still on her tail when she pulled in to the gas station in Blocksville to fill her tank. Paid with her own last few dollars. Considered a while trading in her auto for one with California tags. Then she saw the state patrolman standing, watching her from the edge of the forecourt, leaning against his black and white, arms crossed as she left. Watching him in the rear view as he pulled into the space she left beside the pump, filled his own tank and didn't follow. Grew tiny.

She drove, then the heavens opened. Gushed over her windshield like the water ran down her hips and behind now thinking about it.

Her headache should have told her the air pressure was building and a storm was due. She was a witch like that. Expected it to be a shower—*shower, ha!*—ten, fifteen minute downpour, but it failed to desist after thirty. Forty-five and counting.

The road was layered with a mirror-like sheen pocked by machine-gun holes that refused to relent. *Biblical,* Marion thought. And, as in the Holy Book, lo, did appear a Good Samaritan—or was it the Angel Gabriel glowing up ahead?

Bright illumination broke through the gloom.

Two words. One of them . . . MOTEL.

A letter flickering between life and death, right and wrong. Electricity debating her fate.

The parking lot was empty, its spaces ill-delineated in the dark. Rain sparkling in the glare of the beacon that she saw turn away from her as she arced the Ford to a halt near the cabin at the far end of the chalets, its window the only one lit, and switched off her engine, surprised how loud the rain was on her hood. Louder still on her purse and fingers, her purse being over her head as she ran to the building, throwing herself through the screen door, and shaking the water from her like a dog.

The desk was unmanned. She rang the bell. *Unmanned.* Funny word. Meaning emasculated. In a different context. Obviously in a different context. But no one was there. Not a soul. She could see through to the back—an old typewriter, really old, an Underwood, which made her think of her IBM electric in work, which had made her feel efficient, modern. But she didn't have work anymore, did she? That was behind her. She supposed this was called "the office" was it? She saw a bunk bed of an in/out tray, a spike with checks impaled on it, and a Howdy Doody Ovaltine mug holding pens.

She turned and looked at the rain through the window. Beyond it, a path snaked up to a grotesque, crippled-looking building atop of a slope. Only half-believing her eyes, she squinted then laughed. *The House on Haunted Hill.* Vincent Price would be right at home. She couldn't think anyone else in their right mind would be. She didn't think houses like that existed anymore outside of movies. Moustache, her boss, would have pulled it down in an instant and built a condo.

$40,000!

The screen door banged. The young man used a newspaper as a roof. It was now sodden. He dumped it in the bin next to the umbrella he now held, apologising for not coming out to greet her. She shook her head, shrugged, laughed. It no longer served a purpose in his hand so he put it down, buckling under a little self-applied shame. He hadn't met her eyes with his own. That told her pretty much everything.

He said he hadn't seen it much worse than this. Er, the weather.

She said, I know.

She confirmed—Yes, just one night, please. She had to make an early start in the morning. Had someone she had to meet in . . . *No, don't tell him. If the police come* . . . She quickly replaced the rest of the sentence with a smile. He smiled back, hesitant and gauche. Poor kid. Flummoxed in the presence of a female. Had he ever seen one before? Didn't he go to the high school dance?

He looked up—not at her, *past* her—said she was the only resident tonight. She had the pick of the bunch. "What's it to be?" Like a game show host. She gave him her lucky number. He said that was absolutely fine, though he didn't believe in luck. "Luck is just a word people use to blame something for things going wrong."

She swallowed and said, "Bright boy . . . Man, I mean."

He didn't take offence. Rummaged in his paperwork a while before dangling the key, escorting her under the covered way, unlocking the door to her temporary abode. She expected to hear the army of cockroaches run for cover, but it was well cared for. Clean, but sparse. The bed was soft. The shower worked. As he demonstrated, swishing the plastic curtain back and forth proudly. It was all she wanted right now. A box to rest in.

He tossed the key from hand to hand, then placed it on the night stand. She asked if there was anywhere to get something to eat? He said, "Not really." He said he'd just made a sandwich and she was welcome to have it. She said that wasn't necessary. He said it wasn't a problem, he could make another one when he went back up to the house.

She imagined the kitchen in the house and Vincent Price, or rats, at the very least. Which was stupid.

"That's kind," she said.

"You can watch TV too," he said, "if you want to watch TV." Beckoning her to follow him back to the office.

"No, that's fine. Just a sandwich is fine."

While she eyed the stuffed birds—and they eyed her—he puffed up the cushions of an arm chair. Sat opposite, hands clasped between knees and hunched forward, eager for praise. Egg mayo. What kind of praise was he expecting? *Yum yum.* Did she want a soda? Coffee?

"*Uh-uh.* Coffee will keep me awake."

He produced two bottles of Seven-Up from a refrigerator. Handed her one. Offered to get her a glass. She told him not to worry, she'd drink from the bottle. "Wouldn't be the first time." His eyebrow jumped and he nodded away.

To fill the space, she asked his favourite show.

"*I Love Lucy.* Isn't she great?"

"Sure, she's the best."

"You know she's married to that guy who's her husband on screen? Desi Arnaz? In real life? Can you imagine the money they have? That house . . . I mean that house on TV is incredible, but her house in real life? Do you think she has a swimming pool?"

"Well," she said. "You've got a swimming pool out front, too, if you look."

He didn't understand. Then he did. He said, "You're funny!"

"Sure," she said. "I'm Lucille fucking Ball."

He didn't seem to like the *fucking* and flinched slightly, then pretended it hadn't bothered him, and squared his shoulders, grinning away his unease. The chasm that opened between them filled her with desolation. She rubbed her eyes.

"Look, I'm sorry, I'm bushed. I appreciate your hospitality but I need to hit the sack."

"That's okay." He stood too. "Was the sandwich okay?"

"The sandwich was perfect. Thank you. You're very sweet."

Shit.

With the opening of the screen door the air was cold.

"I'm, er, sorry I wasn't here when you arrived," the young man said, hands shoved in his jean pockets. "Mother . . . she takes a lot of looking after, and I have to split my time between here and the house. If she hollers . . ."

"I get it."

"She's not well. Not at all well. Hasn't been for years. Never gets out. Which means I don't get out much either. I don't mind. That's my job. Caring for her. That's what I'm here for."

"I'm sorry about that."

"Don't be. Not much to expect, is it? In return for a mother's love?"

"I guess not," Marion breathed.

"I try not to worry. About the medical bills mounting up. About the loan from the bank. About the warning letters. About them coming knocking some day. About what I'll do when that happens. When something happens to her. About this place. Where someone stops for one night, then moves on. That must be nice."

That must be nice, she thought later, back in her room, as she turned on the shower. *Must be nice to have a future. Must be nice getting away from being trapped.* Yeah, she knew what *that* felt like. But had she escaped? Had she really? Her boyfriend was out there somewhere, sleeping in his ignorance, but till she hooked up with him, where was she? Pretty alone, that's where.

The spout sounded like a cat with a hairball before the water came, dredged up from who knows where below the Californ-*ai-ay* desert, trilling against the glass.

She let it run as she slipped out of her dress, smoothing it flat on the cheap, ignominious bed. That was her now, cheap and ignominious as she uncoupled her white *Tide white* bra. Thinking of Stan again as she listened to the water outside and in and needing his touch, and hating that she did, sliding her panties down past her knees to her feet.

Naked, she took the money from her purse and stared at it in its fat brown envelope, as if it might impart some revelation to her, or frog-like be prince-like with a wish. She was way beyond that now. Way beyond fairy tales and princes. She wasn't waiting to be rescued. She could control everything. She could have everything she wanted. The rest of her life was just a build up to this moment. This opportunity. And she was going to take it.

She wished to hell she believed that . . . any of it.

As she stepped under the spray everything was just pounding and hurting and deafening and making no sense. If it all made sense and she was doing the right thing, why did she feel like crap?

Because she'd been *selfish*—that's why. It had been total greed that had motivated her. The greed to have a better life. To snatch it up whatever the cost. Was that the person she was now? Hard, callous, uncaring?

Did she need that money more than the poor young guy who ran this motel, with his sick mother and the bank loans mounting up? Did she need it more than Moustache, even—a man nearing retirement, maybe tearing his hair out right now, having a sleepless night, taking his ulcer medication, whose reputation was on the line, whose *responsibility* was to look *after that money,* and what had he done? *Trusted her.* That was his only mistake. *Trusting her.*

And what about the guy whose money it was? *Cash payment* on a house. A *$40,000 house* for his daughter to live in, raise a family in, make love in, have Thanksgiving in—*gone.* Stolen. All of it. Their savings—*$40,000!*—up in smoke. Their futures ruined. *All* their futures, *destroyed.*

She turned to the shower head, shoulders shaking, skin rippling in goose flesh, her tears mixing with the rivulets as she wept.

She couldn't. Couldn't do it. Didn't *have* to do it.

She could change her mind.

Handle on the lever of the shower. It was up to her.

And she thought: *This was where it all changes.* All she had to do was turn around. Go back. Put things as they were. Nothing was stopping her. *Nothing.*

She yanked the controls to OFF and the flow of water cut out abruptly.

Silence fell over her.

Good silence. Happy silence. Decorated only by her breathing. Yes. *Now. Yes.*

The shrill rattle of metal rings along a metal rod.

•●•

She stepped out of the shower.

Drew the plastic curtain closed after her. Quickly wrapped herself in the cardboard-stiff towel—*hey, everything* stiff *here, young man?*—tucking it in over her breasts, like she always did, since a child really, how many thousands of times covering herself up, patting herself down, left arm, right arm, armpits and ass, the time honoured ritual, using the second towel to adorn her head with the flourish of a turban, and, still damp in places, picked up the money, thrust it deep in her purse, dried her hair with rough, impatient hands—still wet, no shape, spiky, a mess, a blonde *mess,* but who was going to see her, who was going to judge?—and, body only half-dry, feeling the patches of water still on her calves and between her toes as she dressed, the frock sticky, not sliding on, plucked and tugged by her fingers to cooperate, she left the room after a circuit of scrutiny, suitcase packed, key fob dangling.

In the motel office a light was on. Inert birds stared from the back room, but the desk was empty. Nobody home. Except he *had* gone home—O, virgin mine—up the wooden hill to . . . Mother.

Plucking a pen and pad, Marion decided to leave a note for him to find next morning. To say thank you, at least. No . . . Explain? No—not explain.

She looked out again at the ghost train pile where an old woman was dying, half a cent from a Halloween joke, crappy clapboard tower of a time long bulldozed, made from every cheated yesterday with how many nails of regret, how many mortared joints that couldn't be undone?

She took two hundred from the first wad her fingers found in the depths of her purse. Reconsidered. Made it a round five. The message she left with the banknotes read: "Good luck." She paused before adding an X.

The parking lot was mirror-like with puddles, but the rain had ceased, as if she'd turned off that flow, too. The night accepted her car back without question. She pictured the young man running down the snaky steps after her, fearing she'd run off without paying. But that didn't happen and she was glad. His surprise would come in the morning and it'd be a pleasant one. She smiled. It was the kind of thing people did if they were a good person. And she was a good person. She was sure of that now, as she drove.

To keep herself awake she tuned the car radio to 90.7 FM. Harry Belafonte singing "Scarlet Ribbons (For Her Hair)." She turned it up, though that voice was so soft you couldn't turn it up. It soothed her like ointment on a graze, and the surrounding darkness now seemed a comfort not a threat.

She hadn't left her name, and realised now that she'd never asked his—the young man's—and he had never given it. To pass the time she asked herself, was he a Roy or a Ray? A Deke or a

Dennis? A Freddie? Fred? Alfred? It didn't matter. She'd never see him again. She might never even *think* of him again, and that made her a little sad. She told herself to snap out of it. Not to go into those *crappy thoughts* again like she always did. Keep firm! Keep a grip of the wheel!

Not long now and it would be over. The record would be off the turntable. The lid would be closed. But for now the music was taking her there.

Phoenix. The sign fled past. *20 miles.*

She almost mouthed it to make it real. But it *was* real.

REALITY.

Frog-hopping from crosswalk to crosswalk, traffic light to traffic light, she crept downtown, where it seemed they'd depopulated the city just for her. Leaving the street she knew so well, she swung round back of the real estate office. Five spaces for her company, five for the liquor store, five for the attorney. The RESERVED FOR sign ballooned in her headlights, then died.

She could've driven straight home, held onto the money for the weekend, and put it back in the safe before her boss came in Monday morning—but what if he came in early? Before her? *Real* early. He did sometimes. How would she do it then, without being noticed? Or explain it, after walking in, if he'd already found the money had disappeared?

No. She couldn't risk it.

She dropped her set of keys on her desk.

Crossed the room. Hinged back the framed copy of Whistler's Mother. Behind it found the bland grey door of the safe. Her mouth an O, she spun the combination to the numbers she knew, back and forth, clockwise and anticlockwise.

What if he had recognised her at the crosswalk, though? No—that hadn't been her. It couldn't have been. *Why, I was at home sleeping off my headache, sir. You must've been mistaken. It must've been someone who* looked like *me.*

The safe opened without protest. The sigh was hers. She reached for her purse. Took out the brown paper package.

$40,000 . . . *less the five hundred.*

She felt light-headed with shock. *God.* He's sure to notice *that* on the cashing-in slip—*$500 short!* How on earth was she going to explain that? Maybe she could doctor the slip on Monday, but he'd still see it on his bank statement sooner or later. How the—?

"Well, well, employee of the month."

Marion span around, holding the brown paper package against her chest.

Stepping out of his office, Moustache switched on the overhead light with a limp hand and it blinded her. She tried not to writhe like a rabbit throttled by a wire. Tried to formulate the story in her head, the answers she'd gone through a million times—

But he knew. She could tell. He *knew!*

"I . . . I just . . ."

"You just *what,* Marion?" Skeleton in a charcoal grey suit. Sallow eyes, so like her father's, gliding closer, so full of disappointment, so full of the feeling he knew it would amount to this. "Just thought you might get away with it?"

"No! No, it was just—just a loan," she stammered. "I just needed to borrow it, for a short while. I can explain."

"Good." Moustache said she could explain everything to the police. He was sure they'd understand completely. Picking up the phone, he'd see what they said about this whole *sorry affair* when they got here.

"No, please!" She killed the call he was dialling. Told him in a rush, a fountain, he'd always been good to her—not a lie—given her a job when nobody else did. Shoe store girl, fired. No qualifications, no good in school. She'd always be grateful for that. His kindness. *And she knew he'd be kind now, when she needed it. Knew he'd understand.* The one person who had faith in her.

His laugh a grunt. "And this is what you do to me?"

"Not to you! *Not to you!*" Feeling his hurt, but feeling her own hurt more. "I . . . I wanted to get married."

He laughed. "Well, congratulations. But I wouldn't set the date just yet. You know you'll do time for this?"

"Please. Listen to me. Please, sir. I'm not a bad person. I just made a mistake, that's all. Is a person not allowed to make a mistake? Have you never made a mistake in your whole life?"

"Like stealing $40,000? No. I can tell you I most certainly haven't! Nor would I!" Skull face filling her vision. Too close. Making her giddy. "I have too much respect for the law, and I have too much respect for myself. And people who don't have that end up where you're going. To jail!" He grabbed the phone off her, trailing it away from her grasp.

"If that happens," she stated, for avoidance of doubt, "my life will be over."

"Well, quite frankly, you should have thought of that."

She showed him her palms, voice breaking. "You know if I go to prison I'll be finished. I'll have nothing."

"Young lady, you *always* had nothing. And you always *were* nothing." He was coming forward—skinny, a Charles Atlas "before" picture under the clothes—and Marion found herself walking backwards, almost tripping over her heels, until her back hit the wall and the breath out of her. "Don't you think I always *knew* that?" He looked down from her head to the tips of her toes, eyeballs rolling over every inch of her. "Look at you," he said, lower lip glistening under that used bathroom-brush. "Yes, I took pity on you because you're easy on the eye, you *decorate* the place. But you're nothing but a cheap tramp with dyed hair and the pretence of a respectable job. The truth is you're not respectable at all, are you? And never will be."

Marion moved to get past him but he caught her forearm, so hard it drew a gasp. He clasped it to his chest like a possession. Nicotine breath reaching her flexing nostrils.

"Relax, dear."

She tried to pull back her anatomy but couldn't.

"Hey, hey. We're both grown-ups, aren't we? There's a way out of this, and you know it. Don't you?" His free hand lifted her chin from her chest. "Sure you do. Look at me."

Not taking puzzlement for an answer. But if she needed a ribbon tied on it . . .

"You need to be nice to me, Marion. I'd say you need to be *very* nice to me indeed."

And then it was clear. She understood, because she was a *cheap tramp* and only had the *pretence of a respectable job* because that was all she deserved—*a lie*—and wasn't expected to be nice—*a thief!*—was just expected to obey. Understood the only way for it all to end, now.

"It's okay. It'll be fine, you'll see," he whispered, mockery of a Romeo, between dry pecks to her mouth.

"Put your lipstick on."

She did.

This was the price, the cost, the punishment she had created for herself.

This opening of gangrenous lips fastening onto hers. This jabbing jaw, once, twice. This odour of aftershave on his collar turned stale with the Arizona sweat. Skin the texture of a turtle's rubbing against her cheek.

This belt unbuckling from the bag of bones—this *respectable* man—draped in the boss's chair under the boss's desk lamp, its glare glinting off his gold tie pin. This kicking off of her high heels. This kneeling on the office carpet.

This blackness in her mind . . . a prayed-for blackness as she shut her eyes but still had the picture in her head of his open pants, the parting of the folds of his underwear like a vagina, having to hold it, having to caress it, for hours, for days, clammy, hot, vile, until she had to . . .

—try to replace the image with memories of Stan, of his body, of their own activities, the nice ones, but the pictures wouldn't stick. Her boyfriend's *Kowalski* smile cut into his seven o'clock shadow and the way he kissed her hand so tender, so true, fingertip by fingertip—*oh baby!*—but her mouth tasted not of him but of the pulsation of corpses. The hands on her scalp placed there like a foul benediction, fingers raking through her platinum curls as something filled her mouth with its flesh.

Scarlet ribbons . . . Scarlet ribbons (for her hair) . . .

After he was done, Moustache gave her the handkerchief he'd used to wipe. Told her she could keep it. Quipped he sure wasn't going to give it to his wife for the laundry. "It's monogrammed. Worth something."

Marion tidied her dress as best she could. Wanted to rinse herself out with bleach, to throw up. Dreamt of doing both as she put back on her earrings, but mainly just wanted to be out of there, gone.

Moustache came back from washing his hands and looked at his watch. "I'd better get home," he said, lifting his jacket from the back of his chair. "I told my wife I was working late, but there's late and late." He placed the parcel of money in the safe, shielding it with his back as he slammed its door and twisted the lock. "I've re-set the combination, so don't go getting any more bright ideas."

His look was one of disdain. Of power. Well, she wouldn't let him have that. Not completely. She took a cigarette from the box on his desk and lit it with his airplane lighter.

"Happy now?"

"Happy?" He actually grinned. "Oh I think happiness is relative, don't you?" He snatched the cigarette out of her mouth and stubbed it out in the ash tray.

"I did what you asked," Marion said. "We made a deal. We forget what happened. Both of us. This is over."

"Oh, you think so?" He smiled with one side of his mouth. A Dick Powell smile. Just needed the tuxedo. "I think that's up to me. I think the terms of our arrangement need to be defined more clearly." He sat on the edge of his desk, knees angular in the baggy pants. "Let's say once a week. Maybe twice. Hell, even three times if I'm in the mood for it and I don't mind looking at that sour mug of yours. What say let's just leave it you're at my beck and call, day and night? That seems fair, don't you think?"

Her stomach turned over. The cancerous smell devoured her again and bile rose in her gullet, hot as a wildfire. *And what if not,* she wanted to say, but she knew what if not. His hand was stroking the phone receiver.

"Now get out."

She did get out. Couldn't wait to get out. Wanting the night air of the parking lot. Thinking of the trail she left and he left, of viscid substances, of liquids. Liquid brimming in her eyes and no, not wanting to give him the satisfaction of that, no way, keeping her cool, her *fucking* cool, her *fucking* strength as she reversed past the Cadillac Eldorado he stood next to, smirk bidding her farewell, smirk saying: *You'll repay my generosity for some time to come, young lady.*

No, that wasn't ALL. Not by a long chalk.

Home, door closed, locked, safe, safe now, and sleep. Her pills saw to that. Tempted to take the whole damn bottle. But Stan, darling Stan—he would be sad. He would pine. She couldn't inflict that on the man she loved. *Love!* That's what she had to remember. Facing her boss the next morning. *Love!* Taking his dictation. *Love!* Touching up her lipstick so she looked presentable. *Love!* Getting the Dick Powell grin again. The glint on the tie pin. Typing a contract when what she wanted to type was—

No. It was private, what had happened. It was their *secret,* the old man's hand on her shoulder said. The liver-spotted hand that had run through her blonde hair, and now patted her shoulder like a father, the father who she never knew much and then was gone. Two years old, and a figment. ***REALITY.***

She wanted to talk to Stan on the phone, so she did, like she always did, except for the night before, when she'd been driving to the motel. He asked how come, and she said, "No reason." After a while he said, "Shoot, you don't have much to say tonight." She said sorry. He said, "In that case I'll go. This call is costing money." The burr of the dead line made her tummy flip again. She hated that sound. The sound of him not being there.

But she couldn't *tell* him, could she?

What would he think of her? Not much. *Tramp. Blonde. Nothing.*

She kept silent for a week.

Even when they hooked up the next lunch time in that same hotel, that same concrete box with the same squeaky fan, in the same unclean sheets, and she kissed, but didn't want to do more, not this time, honey, please. Just wanted to lie there, just hold each other, was that all right? Did he mind just doing that?

But a week later she couldn't hold it inside any longer. The pictures, the sensations, the knotted, horrible feelings carving her empty like a hollowed log from the inside out. Couldn't keep silent with them swirling around in her brain anymore, jostling there amongst the sweetest memories of childhood, tainting those other memories like a stain that spread and spread.

Stan half-lay against the off-white pillow, striped by the sun—Phoenix, 6.09 p. m.—sucking the cigarette to its root as he listened to what she said, then gave a long blue exhale. She wondered if she'd upset him, because when she opened her mouth to speak he showed her his palm.

"Let me think about this for a goddamned minute, okay?"

He sat up, arc of his long spine over the sheet that covered his legs, which he tore off and strode, naked, to the window. Hand through his black hair. Looking out, not looking at her.

She went to the bathroom and washed her face. She'd predicted he'd be angry. Of course he would. She wiped away the salty lines that streaked her make-up. Hitching her breath, applied it afresh, a duty. Max Factor. The way a woman ought to look, wasn't that right? The way a woman needed to look for her man. No rawness in her throat. No horrors in her mind. No sick feeling of worthlessness in her soul. Just like in the movies.

He didn't turn when she walked back in.

"You know what this means? This means we've got him," he said. "Forty grand is nothing to what we can squeeze out of that old goat now."

She frowned.

Almost laughing, he held her by the upper arms—soft, not hard, not brutal—as if about to shake sense into her. "You think his wife wants to find out about what he's been doing? You think his friends in the golf club do? It's called blackmail, baby! And we've got him over a goddamn barrel. We can bleed him for—what? A thousand a week? Three thousand? It doesn't have to stop when I pay off my loan, either. This can go on forever. This is a cash cow, right here! And the beauty is, he'll never go to the police about the money because it'll all come out about you." He held her heart-shaped face in his palms and his lips met hers, but it wasn't the kiss that she'd been waiting for, or the embrace she craved. Instead, he just tittered like he'd backed a winning pony at the races. "This is beautiful. *You're* beautiful!"

Was she? *Was* she beautiful?

White shirt slung on unbuttoned, he asked did she want to go for pizza, dim sum, or a burrito? Her choice, he said, arms wide and magnanimous.

Later, watching the pointed end of a wedge of dough slide into his mouth, and the Bourbon after it, and the grease of mozzarella and pepperoni shining on his chin and lips as he spoke, and the finger that wiped it as he laughed, and as they clinked glasses, she realised he was celebrating. To him it didn't matter whether she was using her body for love or for profit. So what? They loved each other. This other thing was about money. What difference did it make, if it meant they could be happy?

And she thought, *Fuck you.*

Fuck you, and when he looked up, puzzled, she was gone. The chair opposite, empty.

She drove.

Foot on the gas. No suitcase. No map. Passing the city limit signs. Not knowing which highway she was on, whether she was heading for Hollywood or the Grand Canyon. They said that Grand Canyon was deep. Real deep. Maybe deep enough for her.

And her thoughts went round and round till a cop car wailed. The sky in her rear view streaked with the bruises of sundown. The blue lights blasting into her eyes slowed her down to a halt. Her tyres kicked up a cloak of dust as she braked. In her side mirror the figure approached through a sandstorm. Emerging, squat, broad.

"Hands on the steering wheel, ma'am," said a high pitched voice.

A woman's face lowered to the side window, asking politely but firmly if she knew she'd been driving 10 m.p.h. over the speed limit for the last ten miles.

Highway patrol uniform. No sunglasses. Blue gray eyes. Pale skin. Freckles peppering her cheeks. She'd never seen a female one before. Didn't know there was such a thing. Like unicorns. She almost smiled. Almost.

Ma'am, is there something wrong? . . . Ma'am?

Marion opened her mouth, and spoke.

The Naughty Step

One voicemail. Could be worse. Could be ten. She listened as she hurried back to her car, started the ignition, phone pressed to her ear. Instantly recognised comms.

Minor been found at a crime scene. Age about six. Male. Not yet located anyone to look after him. Calling out to EDT to attend scene.

Accelerating, she punched in the post code of the address, already thinking ahead to finding this one a room and food. Ran through her mental rolodex of emergency foster homes she could rely on at a moment's notice. The Hendricks. The Garretts. Those people were godsends.

Not in physical danger ... at least there was that. Even so, Friday after hours you never knew what was going to hit you. Shoplifting at closing time was classic Morag. She'd been needed as appropriate adult during the police interview, then to talk her down before delivering her home to mum and stepdad. Morag was just the sort of teenager who'd disappear through the cracks if you let her. She wouldn't.

You have reached your destination.

The street's dark gullet widened ahead. Neighbours like meerkats at their front gates. Coppers telling them to stay indoors, to not film with their phones please. The rectangles of illuminated screens you get at a rock concert.

She parked, got out.

No tape up, so presumably the crime scene was contained. Forensic people drifted in Arctic white. Two ambulances. Two police cars. A van marked PRIVATE AMBULANCE, which she knew to be an undertaker's vehicle for the removal of a body.

Death was present.

She'd known that from the police control room saying there was nobody to look after the child. One or other parent, she was pretty sure, was in that PRIVATE AMBULANCE. She'd seen it before, too many times. Violent break-up with the kid as piggy-in-the-middle. Wished to God she hadn't.

A female PC—stab vest, tool belt—stood outside the house next to a male with a clipboard making a log. She knew a few, but didn't know her. Afro-Caribbean heritage, which was good. Diversity getting out to the sticks at long last.

"Emergency Duty Team."

The woman in uniform looked over to a skinny man in a suit, who gave her the nod.

Pathetic. Ten years since she started as a social worker and it was still ingrained in the culture. Women deal with the kids. Men deal with the offender. The big, macho guys won't deal with children or domestics. Gay domestics, forget it. Once someone told her about a pair of queens living in a caravan park who used to regularly get into fights. The females were always sent from the station to sort it.

"What happened?"

"Still piecing it together. Neighbours reported shouting. Most likely scenario, a domestic that got out of hand. Woman in her thirties didn't make it."

"Where's the boy?" She peered into the back seat of the parked police car.

"Still inside."

"You're kidding me."

"No, I'm not. We tried to move him, he wouldn't come. Went into a shit fit like you wouldn't believe."

"God."

"We didn't want to push it."

"Good."

Truth was, every cop knew if they laid a hand on him that'd technically be assault in the eyes of the law. The child had done no wrong, they couldn't arrest him, and they couldn't manhandle him. Why risk it and lose your job? Worst case scenario, a public inquiry, tabloids descending like jackals? Pass the buck to Children's Services. Let them be the fall guys.

"Never seen anything like it." The PC shivered in the cold. "Not a word of a lie. He's sitting at the bottom of the stairs. Just staring into space. Won't move an inch. Wouldn't take my hand."

"Was he witness to . . . ?"

"Everything, we think."

"Jesus Christ."

"It wasn't pretty. Still a bit of a mess."

"And you left him in there?"

The PC didn't like that frown of accusation, and tightened defensively.

"CID say you can go in, as long as you limit yourself to the hall and stairs, and put on a suit. DI is understandably keen to interview him as a witness on video as a priority."

"Yeah, well. He needs emergency foster care *as a priority*. Can you imagine what kind of a—?"

"Trauma. We're aware of that."

She could see the officer's taut expression, and felt for her slightly. She had a job to do as well. They were picking up the pieces.

"What state is he in?"

"Unharmed, from what we can see. I've spent the last hour sitting next to him while SOCO do their stuff. Trying to get through to him, without much luck. No reaction. Not a dickie bird. Nothing. Nothing in his eyes."

"What do you mean by that?" She knew what the PC meant. She meant the kid was weird as fuck. She'd heard it all before. *Weird kid. Bad child. Waste of space. Scrapheap fodder.* To her mind, there were no bad kids, just hurt ones.

"I'm just saying. If you ask me, he's not—"

"Thanks." The sarcasm showed on her face.

"Yes, well, you work your magic, if you've got any." The PC moved away.

"Are you going to tell me his name?"

"Sorry. Jared. Jared Simkins. Mother Michelle, deceased."

"Father?"

"Location unknown."

"Anybody got any previous history on the system?"

"Not on ours."

"Grandparents? Uncles? Aunts? Friends of the family?"

"We're working on it."

The PC lifted the flap of the SOCO tent for her. She went in alone, feeling a little guilty, cutting the PC some slack. She'd probably seen the crime scene first-hand. God knows what she'd seen. Or the kid had seen, come to that.

She zipped up the white plastic forensic overalls. Thought of the corpse that had been zipped up in a black body bag hours, perhaps minutes earlier. Put the little plastic booties over her shoes. They made her think of babies.

Jared. Jared. Jared.

She reminded herself of his name as she walked back to the front door. The male PC stood out of the way, allowing her to enter.

The boy was sitting at the bottom of the stairs. Underpants. Bare legs and feet. No sign of neglect. No dirt. No bruises. Blue pyjama top with rockets and stars on. He wasn't looking at her. He wasn't looking anywhere. If he did look up at her, what would she look like? Some sort of alien. ET in the white body suit.

She took her hood down. Removed her pale blue rubber gloves. She could see the SOCO team moving about in the kitchen, silently measuring, fingerprinting. The flash of a camera strobed, the battery buzzing as it recharged.

She sank to a crouch. Put on a soft voice, aware that, though she was born and bred less than ten miles away, her accent was a bit too posh for some of her families on these kinds of estates. Too "minted peas from Waitrose" as one teenage mother put it.

"Hi. My name's Linda. I've come to look after you for a short while. Just to be with you for a bit, is that all right?"

No reaction.

She dredged up her training from the Tavistock all those years ago. How to deal with an elective mute. Don't ask questions. Don't demand that they talk back to you. Just talk until you earn their trust.

She knelt on the floor. Another strobe. Another buzz. She glimpsed a man in white checking the screen of his digital Pentax. Ridiculous she was avoiding trigger words when this was going on all around them. A firework display.

"You know what? I felt a bit lonely outside. I thought I'd come in. I thought I might come in and, you never know, find a new friend, maybe."

No reaction.

No eye contact at all. Autistic? No. Lord knows, kids could be uncommunicative because people like her represented the system and they shut off. She was the one their mum yelled at because they couldn't get re-housed or benefits. The one who was taking them away from the person they loved, sometimes. But it wasn't that either. It wasn't wilful lack of cooperation. She knew what that looked like. This boy was in a state of shock.

"It's a bit cold in here isn't it? I'm freezing." She stroked the radiator. Edged her knees closer to him. Palms resting on her thighs.

She found it disturbing because one thing she liked about dealing with kids was their forthrightness, their honesty. Painfully so, sometimes. She was used to telling them there was nothing to worry about, and they didn't believe it, and, most of the time, neither did she. "You know where I'd really, really like to go? Somewhere comfortable." She extended her right hand, hoping he might take it, but he wasn't even looking. Yet his whole body tightened.

She put her hand back on her thigh, pretending she never meant the gesture in the first place.

The boy's chest was rising and falling rapidly. Jaws locked. Knuckles on his own knees bone-white.

She blew into her hands. Slid her palms under her armpits as if sheathing weapons. Smiling broadly. Some would say inanely.

Made no difference.

She could see what the female PC meant now. He was having none of it.

Jared. Jared Simkins.

Hunched, almost foetus-like. Rigid.

Slowly she edged closer to him, one knee at a time.

Over her right shoulder, the open door to the living room. She couldn't help giving it a quick glance.

Sofa and cushions. Facing a TV set? Did she watch daytime TV? Was she watching daytime TV when it happened? CD covers on the floor. Left there or dropped there? *Pure Heroine* by Lorde. Rag 'n' Bone Man. Christine and the Queens… One of her own favourite albums of late—how strange was that? Did Michelle dance to it, hand in hand with her little boy? Listen to it on the dashboard stereo as she drove to school? Is that what kind of woman his mother was?

Michelle. Michelle Simkins.

She thought of the wallpaper around her. How had they chosen it? Had they had a big fight? Did he leave it to her or was he the controlling type? A bully? She told herself it wasn't always like that. But, surprisingly often, it was.

"Y'areet, big man?"

The child suddenly gasped and covered his eyes with his hands.

A man, big man, almost filled the doorway to the living room. SOCO white. Monstrous to the boy. Rubber gloves. Plastic evidence bag. Carving knife inside it.

"For God's sake—" she said.

The Geordie giant shielded it, turning his back to the boy.

"Children's Services," she explained.

"Does Chris Holroyd know about this?"

For fuck's sake. The DI, she presumed. Gave him an incendiary glare. *What do you think?*

"We'll give you some space, then." Backing off. "Give them a DNA swab when you leave. For eliminations purposes."

"Yes, buzz off now, please."

He went, taking the photographer with him, a woman in a baggy forensic suit that un-gendered her almost completely. They left the front door ajar. Darkness outside. Soundless. Frozen. No radio crackle. No chat. Just the wind gently rustling the white plastic of the forensics tent in the middle of the road.

Linda walked to the door and pushed it shut. The security chain was just like the one she had at home. She didn't need to put it on. How often did Michelle do that, though? Trying to protect herself? Trying to feel safe?

The boy still had his hands over his face.

The idea surged up in her: what the hell had he seen? Had he heard his mum's cries as she was stabbed? Or had it gone chillingly silent? Had he cried out, terrified, and got no reply? No wonder he was in a state of shock. It was incredible he wasn't catatonic. Fight or flight? He couldn't fight, he couldn't fly, so he froze. And to break it, to come out of it, to let reality back in, would be unbearable.

"Sorry. Sorry." She sank down on all fours. "They're gone. They're all gone now. It's all right. Nothing's going to happen. There's nobody here. Just me. Just you. Promise."

Silence.

Then the boy took away his hands tentatively. For a fraction of a second his eyes met hers—then abruptly shot down to the carpet at his feet.

Her eyes fell on a toy car next to the skirting board. Smaller than the Dinky and Corgi toys her brother played with. A red car with fire along the side. Eyes in its windshield.

"This is a nice car. It's not a car, is it? It's a sports car." She turned in a circle, running it along the carpet. "Brooom Brooom." She made a squealing noise of a handbrake turn, taking an imaginary curve on two wheels.

She sensed he was watching her, but as soon as she looked at him directly he looked away.

The length of the hall between them, she pushed hard and made the car run across the floor towards him. Unable to get traction on the carpet, it stopped short, halfway. Beyond the reach of his arm. Unless he moved.

He stared at it. Blank, black eyes. So black she couldn't tell where the irises ended and the pupils began.

"You can play if you want."

Nothing.

"You can even get down on the floor like me if you want."

The boy shook his head.

She crawled closer. Flicked the car with her finger.

It hit the step. He leaned over slowly and picked it up.

"Lightning McQueen." He frowned as he saw her blank expression. "He's called Lightning McQueen."

Turning sideways on the step, one knee raised, he ran the car up his thigh, making it do a jump to the wall. Doing so with no sense of distraction or enjoyment a child normally had in play. She could see only a focussed, insular, hermetically-sealed determination. A force field holding her back.

The bleep of a text. She turned and stood up. Snatched her phone from her pocket, switched it off. Didn't want calls to interrupt her or spook him.

Crouched again, one hand on the bottom step, inches from his bare foot.

"Are you hungry, Jared?"

He shook his head.

"Thirsty maybe?"

Again. Then a nod.

"Do you want a drink of water?"

"Juice."

She should call out. She knew that. Except she didn't want to use her mobile and didn't want to leave him alone to go outside. Not now.

"Where do I get some juice?"

"In the fridge."

"Okay."

She walked past him, down the two steps to the passage to the kitchen. It was the same layout as the house she was brought up in. She thought of the time her mum left the gas on and caused an explosion, just a big FUFF like the air got sucked away, and it took off her eyebrows. There'd been a different explosion here.

Bright red smears on the stable door leading to the garden, tagged with a SOCO sticker with an L-shaped metric reference scale and photo cross-hairs. She tried not to look at the blood on the floor. The claggy smell made her feel sick, but she couldn't be sick, not with the boy there. She had to control herself. Control her stomach. Control her eyes.

In her peripheral vision the windows looked dirty, almost opaque, but she realised they'd been powdered with a Zephyr brush for fingerprints to be lifted.

On the fridge door she read J-A-R-E-D in fridge magnets. A photograph pinned there showed a younger Jared—age two or three—long hair, shining yellow. His mother must've been sad to see it go. Maybe he wanted it off. Maybe he was being teased for looking like a girl. School certificate for Outstanding Schoolmate held by a magnet of the Eiffel Tower. Another photograph of a barbecue chicken sitting on a beer can. Beer can up its arse. So funny. Mum and Dad puckering up, snogging (fake-snogging?) for the lens. Were they happy then, her glasses askew, Eric Morecambe-style? On the old Sancerre? Pink stripe of dye in her blonde hair?

Sleeve of tattoos, small mouth, doe eyes. Him, the nameless one, grinning at a party in the garden, showing his hairy belly button for the finger she inserts, laughing her head off.

Inside the fridge door—milk, orange juice. The shelves were packed. Big jar of mayo. Baby bels for his lunchbox. Cream cheese dippers. Ready meals for the week. Nobody intended to die today.

She separated one of the apple juice cartons from the six-pack, tore the straw off the side, broke the seal to insert it. Hung on the banister, behind and above him. Handed it down.

He slurped eagerly.

"You know I have a favourite place, and sometimes I want to go there and never leave it. It makes me feel really good there."

"I don't have a favourite place."

"It isn't the stairs?"

"The stairs?" Again like she is mad. "Why would the *stairs* be my favourite place?"

"I don't know. I thought you didn't want to leave it."

"I *want* to leave it, but I can't leave it, can I?"

"Why's that?"

"Because!"

"Because what?"

"Because *she* said!" Anger overspilling, he flung the juice carton away down the hall. It tumbled, splashed and lay.

She lowered herself, holding the banisters like prison bars. "What did she say, sweetheart?" He struggled. Sighed. "It's okay." She touched his knee.

He recoiled as if receiving an electric shock. "It's not okay! It's *not* okay!"

"Tell me, Jared love, and maybe I can help."

"You can't! I *know* you can't!"

"How do you know if you don't tell me? You're hurting. I can tell you're hurting inside and I want to do something about it."

"You can't! *Nobody* can!"

Wait. Wait. Wait. Her heart was breaking, but she knew she had to give him time. She had to give him the air to fill with his words. Maybe the space she gave would tug them out of him. Maybe they were ready to come, like a baby tooth that had worked itself loose.

"It wasn't my fault," he said, then it came like a dam burst. "All I was doing was watching Transformers Cyberverse. She *said* I could watch another one, but before it finished she said *come and have your pasta,* and I said, *Mum, Transformers hasn't finished yet* and she said *now!* and *Jared!* and *Jared, listen to me!* and I said *but you promised!* and she said *right, get you-know-where and think about the way you're behaving and don't come back until I . . .*" He stopped, gasping, trying to catch the words. "And I *did.* I went to the naughty step."

And that's what you're doing. Waiting. Waiting for her to call you. Waiting for her to say it's all right. But she never can call you, can she, sweetheart?

"Jared, what if I said it's okay to leave the naughty step now?"

"It isn't."

"Why?"

"Because *she* has to say. That's the way it works. That's the way it *always* works."

But your mum's not going to say anything now, is she, Jared?

Linda heard a tap on the front door. Shape outside. She went and opened it.

"Can I have a word please?"

"Quickly," she said to the female PC, looking back at the boy whose arms now covered his head.

"It would be better if we spoke outside."

The cold hit Linda as she stepped out. The scene was depleted. Fewer cars, fewer officers. Seemed like that. What she was wearing foolish. No coat, no stab vest.

"The father's been found dead. Suicide." The PC turned her cackling radio to mute. "Found by the railway tracks. Use your imagination. There was an allegation against him, apparently. Made by her."

Shit.

"Yeah. Look, CID's going mental. We need to get this kid out of there."

"Great. How do you intend doing that? By force? By sedating him? Dragging him kicking and screaming into the back of a police car?"

"Obviously not."

"What then? He's the responsibility of my department now."

"And what are you intending to do?"

"Stay here." She didn't care whether the PC thought she was mad or incompetent or both. She knew what she was doing and CID wasn't her problem. "He's got to start relaxing, the adrenaline can't last forever. The body will eventually level out. You can't deal with fear indefinitely."

"You're the expert. How long?"

"As long as it takes."

"My shift's over soon. Anything I can do?"

"You can go and feed my cat."

She almost got a smile out of her at that. Almost.

"Wait a sec." The PC disappeared into the dark, her equipment giving her pear-like figure a kind of waddle, reappearing a minute later with a plastic bottle of water and a Yorkie. "It'll keep you going. I've got ten more in the glove compartment." She retreated back into the gloom. "Good luck. One for the memoirs, huh?"

Memoirs?

She supposed it was a joke, smiled, left the night to its own devices and shut the door gently after her.

It was a neat seal, like the door of the fridge. She switched the porch light off, kept the hall light on. The fact the PC had gone home weirdly unnerved her. Her cat would be all right of course.

A vet had told her once it was healthy for a cat to miss a meal once in a while. More like in the wild. Didn't stop the thing whining if she did, though.

"Go. Go if you want to." The boy.

"I don't."

"Why?"

"Because I like it here. Right here, with you."

She held out the bar of chocolate. Head shake. Water. The same.

She leaned against the wall and stripped off her crinkly white SOCO suit and the shiny elasticated slippers, to reveal a green M&S pullover and jeans.

The boy looked at her with curiosity, as if seeing her for the first time.

"Are you somebody's mum?"

"No."

"Why not?"

She thought it best to answer him in a way a child would understand. "Nobody loved me enough, I suppose." She unexpectedly felt tears welling, and blinked them away, fighting them off with a smile. A smile she wanted him to see.

"My mum and dad loved each other."

"I know."

"They did."

"I'm sure they did, sweetheart."

Anger again, bedding down into a knotted confusion. "Why do mums get so angry? Why did she have to get angry and shout at him?"

"Maybe she couldn't help it."

"She *could* help it. All she had to do was stop. If she stopped . . ."

"It wasn't her fault, sweetie."

"I know. I *know*. It was *my* fault. They were arguing about me."

"Don't say that." She sat next to him on the step. Put her arm around him. "Don't think it. Think about nice things."

"What nice things?" A sob escaped. "*What* nice things, though?"

She couldn't say. But felt the soft, almost unnatural warmth of him. The proximity of him like a glow.

Could she scoop him up right now, she thought, when he was upset and vulnerable, less likely to fight back? Could she just hold him to her tightly and make a run for it, get through that door and outside to the police car that was parked in the street?

No. It would feel like the most terrible betrayal. After her earning his trust, it would destroy him. She could imagine him howling in her arms. Trauma heaped on top of trauma. It would destroy *her*. She couldn't . . . But she needed to do something. Soon.

"My dad loved me."

"They both loved you in different ways. I'm sure they did."

Allegations.

"He wouldn't leave me, would he?"

"No, he wouldn't," she lied. Hand on his back. Ready to urge him to stand up. Leaning forward. "Do you think you can come as far as the front door, can you do that for me?"

He stiffened. Went rigid—his back like an ironing board.

"Sorry. Sorry. Sorry—"

"I can't!

"I know you can't, sweetheart. I know you can't."

She sat back down, rubbed his spine. The hotness radiated through her palm. She settled, and let him settle. Let his heart slow down. Let hers.

What time was it? She daren't look at her phone. Was it nine now? Ten? Without the porch light on it was really dark, as dark as she could ever remember seeing, and the house felt cold and unloving. She sometimes felt that when she visited. Toxic relationships, you could feel them, you knew something was brewing, you knew it wouldn't end well, there was going to be no saviour, no knight in shining armour.

His breathing was heavy, guttural, his sinuses blocked.

She wondered if she could creep upstairs to the bathroom cabinet and get him some Calpol. Something that would relax him. It was a sedative. If it calmed him down, that would be a good thing. If it got him to sleep, even better.

He leaned against her, his cheek against her chest. His breath against her heart.

"It'll be all right, you'll see." She cradled him. "A lot of people are here to help you. I'm here to help you." She didn't know if there were, but she knew one thing for sure. She'd stay there till he was ready. "You know, if you want to come with me, that's all right. Nobody's going to be angry with you. Your mum wouldn't be angry. She's never been angry with you for very long, has she?"

Nothing. His face snuffled in closer.

"Sleep. That's it. Sleep, if you want to. It doesn't matter. I'm here."

He was quiet for a long while.

She wondered how often the house was this quiet. This still. This cold.

The letterbox lifted, breathed. The wind had become strong. Gusty. Something began banging, clattering out in the garden. Loose corrugated iron on the roof of a shed, she thought. She wondered if the fence he jumped over when he'd escaped, fearing the neighbours would see him if he went out the front way, was broken. Pictured his wet hand on it. Wet with blood. His wife's blood.

"Sometimes we hear foxes." The little voice next to her chest. "Sometimes they make me scared. My mum says there's nothing to be scared of. They just want to get in our bins. She says they're more afraid of us than we are of them. Is that right?"

"Shshshsh. Don't think about things like that. Go to sleep. Just let it all float away, yeah?" She rocked him. "There were ten in the bed and the little one said roll over, roll over . . ."

When the song was over, her voice a drone, lulling, she heard a long, warm sigh.

He was drifting away but he wasn't off yet. She didn't envy his dreams, poor mite. Or perhaps they were an escape right now. She hoped so.

Perhaps when she was sure he had dozed off she could carry him to her car without him waking up. But what if he woke when she was driving to the emergency foster care? And she didn't know where that was yet. She should've phoned before she got here. She told herself not to get anxious about things that hadn't happened yet. It would all work out, as long as she didn't panic. And there was a team outside to help her—wasn't there?

She heard a bin blown over. A high-pitched dog, if it was a dog.

They're more afraid of us than we are of them.

"It's all right." The voice below her. "I know it'll be all right because he promised."

"Shsh."

"He's going to take me. He said he would. She said no. She said she had enough of him letting me down, but he didn't, he was busy sometimes and couldn't come on time, that's all. She was *wrong* and he was *nice. He* was the nice one. Why did she have to be so *horrible?*"

"Darling—" She felt her insides tighten. Hands knotting them like rope.

"He said we'd go somewhere special." Squirming. "He's going to come back and take me somewhere special!"

"No, nobody's coming, darling. Don't worry."

"He will though. He comes every Friday. He's *got* to come!"

"I'm sorry. He's gone darling. Gone a long way away. He can't touch you now. He'll never touch you ever again."

"No! That's not true!"

"It is true."

"It's not! He's *here*. He's here now! I can hear him!"

The wind outside rose to a whistle. Buffeting against the stable door in the kitchen. She could hear it shake. Something had fallen against it. A tree or branch. Something heavy and unrelenting. Something beyond the bloody fingerprints.

"*Dad?*"

The boy sat up. Alert. Eyes wide. Trying to pull her arms off him. She tried to hold him, but he was like a snake, and she heard herself say the worst thing, and she knew it was the worst thing. She simply didn't know what else to say.

"But you can't go, sweetheart. Remember, your mum said you have to stay here. Your mum said!"

Her arms wrapped around him, trying to hold him tight and still and safe.

"Let go of me!"

"No. You don't understand. Jared. He doesn't love you."

"He does! He does!"

Allegations.

"He called it love but he wants to hurt you and I won't let him."

"Let me *go you fucking bitch!*"

She saw the knife go in. A rolling wave of filth seeped from the kitchen, through the air between them, and she knew that he stood there, in the kitchen, nameless and hairy-bellied. Saliva or snog on his lips. Hand on his knife or his cock.

"I won't let you go! He's not going to have you. I won't let him!"

A vow. A prayer.

She crossed her arms over the boy's body. He kicked. He grunted. He screamed.

She shut her eyes.

Her own father once took her to a hawk sanctuary and she'd sat with a baby bird on her finger, a peregrine with its perfect yellow feet, and it was a day they weren't open, but her father asked them to open just for her. Just for his Lindy. And they did, and the owls had a feeding time and they took these dead mice from the freezer and her dad said not to look but she did, just a little bit. And one of the teenage girls had a leather glove and put the mouse on the back of her hand next to her thumb and the owl flew the whole length of the barn and landed on it, and its eyes were what she remembered now, the rich smell of the dead animals from the freezer and the sawdust. That smell was in her nostrils now.

"Bastard. You bastard."

She wouldn't relent. She would be brave. She would be courageous.

She would do her job.

She would save this little soul, even as she felt the breath of the dead thing on the back of her neck.

"You can't have him. You can't."

•●•

By morning light, the police and paramedics have to prise his body from her. When they examine him, they think his ribs are broken, she held him so tight.

The DI asks them how long it would have taken for the child to stop breathing.

They say the boy probably struggled for some time. They think his face was held against her chest, his mouth and nose pressed against the green sweater probably inhibited his breathing. He suffocated and his little heart gave out.

When they found her, she was stroking the boy's hair. Humming a lullaby. Maybe it was a hymn. Maybe it was Kylie Minogue.

She doesn't answer their questions. She doesn't see them. She's staring. Her arms wrapped around herself now.

They ask her to come with them, but she doesn't move.

Remains sitting on the step.

"Let me talk to her." The female PC crouches level to her face, and finally she speaks.

"I saved him. He's safe now. He won't be hurt any more. I protected him. You see that, don't you?"

"I see that," the other woman says.

Standing aside as men take her.

Watching as she is led into the light, blinking up at a cloudless sky. Put in the police car, smiling, vindicated, content.

And the female PC closes the front door quickly as she leaves, for she felt something looking at her while she stood in the hall, and, whatever it was, invisible, mocking, and wet, it had been holding the small, invisible hand of a little boy.

Adventurous

Carole had wanted a nice house, big enough to grow a family in, nothing luxurious, not five bathrooms or anything ridiculous, just somewhere that looked nice, semi-detached, smart, not too old, not too modern, not needing a lot of maintenance, just somewhere "comfy" as her mum would say, with a driveway to park in, one car, two at the most if she had a job as well, and a garage with one of those swing-up doors, though that could be used for storage, or an extra room, a games room for instance, with a billiard or ping-pong table for the kids, two of those, ideally, one of each, though she didn't really care either way, two daughters or two sons was acceptable, and a couple of wheelie bins with individualised numbers on so that the neighbours didn't nick them, and a cat, or dog, depending what her husband felt about the subject. But, as it turned out, she didn't want any of it, not really.

As for a husband . . . well.

She never expected to get one with 'Isambard' for a middle name. That should have got the old alarm bells ringing for a start. That, and his penchant for watching films about steam trains. Not any old films about steam trains, mind. They had to be certain journeys to certain destinations, and the length of the film had to be the *exact* length of the train journey, and it had to be shot from the point of view of the driver, without any cutaways, or there was no point.

She didn't think any of this as she gyrated on the dance floor at the Christmas party. She didn't think anything, much, or tried not to, as she flung herself at Roxy Music with abandon, not caring too much what Bryan Ferry thought, or Fergal "I-couldn't-possibly-be-homophobic" Daxter in his pink shirt, or that snooty cow *Deb-o-RAH* from the top floor, with her athletic calves and Comic Relief collecting box, face on her like she'd rescued the starving in Africa personally, one by one.

Carole's perspiration glued her dress to her body but she didn't care much about that, either, taking the opportunity to partake of the free booze, intending with no little gusto to get slaughtered under the multicoloured heat of the disco lights, which was when, propping herself for a much-earned breather at the buffet table, she noticed someone watching her. *Watching?* Was that too strong a word? Eyes in her direction, anyway. Eyes behind slightly askew glasses, too Specsavers to be stylish, pint held against his sternum, resting on the shelf of an incipient pot belly, the way men hugged their libations, more protectively than they ever did their wives. Top three buttons of his shirt undone, a sign of availability that was achingly desperate in a chap so young. Anyway, she went for it. Went for him. Heat-seeking. Mince pie in each hand, the two objects floating as if she was a child using them to mime a pair of flying saucers, till she stopped, swaying, trying not to look as pissed as she evidently was.

"Hello, you. I'm Carole. Have a mince pie," was her opening gambit, more an order than a request. Not surprisingly, the suit trembled.

"You're all right. Not keen on them, to be honest. Sorry."

She thrust one at his lips. "Go on, they're gorgeous!"

"No, no, really."

"Go *on!*"

The tin foil almost hit Colin Tweedie's front teeth and he recoiled into a green, unforgiving spotlight. Colin from Finance, originally from Potter's Bar. All the girls said he was a virgin, or gay, didn't have a girlfriend, lived with his mum, supported Arsenal, but Carole thought he was just shy, and she liked that. Better than a blabbermouth who thought corned beef of himself.

He wasn't bad-looking, she thought, if a bit spotty, and with a terrible Lego man haircut. And skinny. You could be skinny and a nice person, though, couldn't you? Sexy, even, at a push. It wasn't all about physical attributes anyhow, she told herself. She didn't want a stud. Some gym-addicted Adonis who'd ultimately have her crying into her pillow. What *did* she want? She wasn't sure. But she was still talking, and Colin, taller than her by about a foot, and younger than her by about ten years, wasn't listening, and neither was she any more, the music being too deafening, as he squinted down at his watch and, bending over, lips close to her ear, had to shout he'd better be going home, like, and was sorry again, like, and she shrugged, mince pie filling her cheeks by now, flecking the crumbs from her breasts, turning away and returning to the dance floor, arms in the air.

Come the morning and paracetamol, Carole saw him through the glass doors, gawky as a schoolboy. Straightened her back as he approached her desk past the other females, looking like a newly-conferred eunuch entering a harem. Carole wondered if he'd lain awake all night in his Arsenal pyjamas, surrounded by Arsenal posters and memorabilia, thinking about her, maybe even having exotic dreams of her nakedness, imagining her bare thighs, which in his dream would be smooth, muscled and tan, the stuff of an instant coffee commercial. Then the thought of masturbation on his part surfaced and she told herself to shut up. Even that inner reprimand, though imaginary, hurt her synapses and she cringed and hid her face. Rising from her desk, she walked to the stationery room, past her bitchy, small-minded colleagues who were probably thinking *virgin,* thinking *gay*, thinking *Arsenal supporter*. Colin followed restlessly, bending over to pick up a paperclip from the floor, examining it minutely as he said he wanted to email her but didn't know her surname, there were lots of Carols in the organisation, and . . .

"Car*ole*," she corrected, emphasising the *hole* part, realising as she heard it out loud that, with her dry throat from the night before, it sounded husky and seductive. "Spinks," she added, somewhat killing the illusion. She took a blue ballpoint from a fresh box and wrote down carole dot spinks at the name of the company dot com on a scrap of paper.

Colin, top row of teeth digging into his lower lip, stared at it in his hands as if it was a winning lottery number, or at least a scratch card, at least a possibility, at the very least that, as he backed away gratefully without another word.

Ten minutes later, an email. Subject line blank: **Hello! Would you like to go for a drink some time? Colin.**

She typed **Yes**, but quickly deleted it. Didn't want to be too eager. Paused. Then wondered why. Why couldn't she be forthright? *Forthright.* She thought about the word. *Fourth.* What did the *fourth* part of it mean? And *right.* Was that *right* or *write*? She always got mixed up: was it *playwright* or *playwrite*?

She'd be it anyway, for once in her life, and wrote, impulsively: **Tony is up in Stoke tomorrow. All day. Not back till late. Come around at 2 p.m. This is the address.** She typed it, three lines, complete with the post code. Clicked SEND before she could change her mind, then waited nervously for a reply. To distract herself, she unwrapped the ream of paper she'd fetched from the stationery room and was bent over, replenishing the printer, thinking you could say he was *lean* rather than *skinny*—yes *lean,* she preferred that—when she heard a ping.

Got a meeting over lunch. Can we make it 3?

Her heart beating fast, she typed: **Great**, then deleted it with the backspace key and typed: **Fine**. Smiling as she typed excitedly: **I'll put the kettle on, and not much else.** Then deleted that with the backspace key and typed nothing.

• • •

"I've, er, parked up the, er, road, just in case . . ."

Colin wiped his feet on the welcome mat, his sentence running out of steam. *Steam.* She wished he hadn't made her think of that. The big framed poster of the Forest of Dean Railway on the wall was more than enough. He stepped in front of it, over her son's muddy trainers and held up a bottle. She'd have sworn the lenses of his glasses were clouding; probably just him coming in from the cold air outside. Not his passionate ardour exuding from his biological interior.

"I didn't know if you like white or red."

It was white.

"That'll do," Carole said, tightening the belt of her dressing gown and fetching a corkscrew from the kitchen drawer, then dangling it from a hooked finger. "Bring it upstairs. Follow me. Sam's got football practice and Donna's got ballet lessons. We've got till about six. Is that all right?" Colin nodded. She looked for two glasses. "Good." She was surprised how formidable she sounded, because that wasn't how she felt at all. It was just that small talk would make her feel bad and she didn't want to feel bad, so better get on with it.

Twenty-seven, she thought, or twenty-eight, max. Living with his mum in Potter's Bar. In his room watching porn while his mum watches *Newsnight*. Was this his first time? Could be his bloody last.

She saw him looking around the room and wondered what he saw, what he really saw, what he made of it, what he made of her. The thirty thousand pound kitchen with marble work tops. The fridge magnets holding the kids' latest school reports in place. The old ginger cat that passed them as they climbed the stairs.

When the two glasses were empty, she closed the curtains, slipped off her dressing gown and got into the double bed. He turned away, not with any great meaning but to unzip and drop his trousers, making a mess of pulling them off over his shoes and socks. A six-year-old would have removed the shoes and socks first, which Carole told herself was an endearing lack of forethought rather than the sordid portent of disaster.

She watched him remove his shirt and put it on the back of a chair, over his jacket. She noted a bulge in his Marks & Spencer underpants. Eagerness to get on with it, she deduced. Her bare shoulders felt chilly. She wished she'd advanced the heating, which was set to come on at 3.30, but she hadn't. He had no chubbiness at all, other than two pouches above the elastic on his lower back, his pale Potter's Bar skin neither hairy nor hairless but sort of nondescript in the hair department.

He jumped into bed, and he was freezing too, making comic mileage out of his teeth chattering, which made her chuckle.

"This is nice," he said, and she said it was too.

"You're not intending to keep them on, are you?"

He peeled off said underpants and tossed them onto the carpet, lying next to her until she hooked her arm around his neck which he must have taken as a come-on, because shortly afterwards his body was on top of hers and his lips were on hers and dry. She took off his glasses and placed them on the bedside table.

"Now I can't see you. Now you're all blurry."

"My best feature," she said.

He kissed her again, wetter and with more suction this time. They were warming each other, gradually, but there was no hurry. She felt activity down between her legs. Saw him gazing deeply into her eyes as if expecting a verbal caution which didn't come. Instead, Carole, more from impatience than lust, guided his mouth to her right nipple, a movement which was accompanied, unexpectedly, by a piping voice from downstairs.

"Mr Macrae is off sick so we got sent home! Result!"

The slam of the front door juddered through her entire body and stiffened Colin—though not in the way Colin wanted to stiffen. He jerked up on straightened arms with a gasp. Quick as a flash upon hearing the thunderous footsteps on the stairs and the swiftly approaching "Mum? Mum?" he darted into the only place he could see, given he saw no lock on the bedroom door—no lock, no key. *Crap!*

"Mum?"

Colin stepped in and pulled the wardrobe door shut after him—

... Exactly as the bedroom door swung wide to reveal freckles, curls and the premature insouciance of an eleven-year-old.

"*Mum* ... can I go round to Finlay's? We're going to do our homework together."

"Yes, that seems highly likely," Carole mumbled, elbows propping her up from the pillow, feigning being woken from sleep rather than *coitus interruptus*. "D'you ... d'you want something to eat before you go?"

"No, his dad's outside in the car, waiting."

"Fine. Have a nice time." The door closed. "Text me when you want picking up."

"Okay!" The door opened again, halfway. "Mum? Er ... What are you doing in bed?"

Carole's eyes still hadn't opened. "I had a headache, and I didn't sleep well last night. I was up at four."

Shrug. "Okay."

The bedroom door closed again—with a finality this time.

Soon after, the front door followed suit, just as Carole's eyes fell on the clothes on the chair by the window—the suit jacket, trousers, shirt, tie. *Shit!* Her son hadn't seen them. The sudden, gut-hollowing sense of relief made her want a wee.

"Colin?"

No answer.

"It's all right, you can come out now."

Carole sat up on the side of the bed, bare feet with freshly painted toenails sinking into the beige carpet.

"Very funny. Don't play silly buggers."

Was he deaf or something, as well as being a virgin and/or gay?

"Colin?"

Annoyed now, she stood up, pulled on her dressing gown, and rapped the wardrobe door with a crooked finger.

Nothing.

The bottle of white sat on her vanity table. She uncorked it and refilled one glass. Good job her son hadn't noticed *that* either.

"Two can play at that game. Cheers."

After a second mouthful, she shook a cigarette from her packet, lit it, but crushed it out in the ash tray without taking a second drag.

"Right. I don't know how you get your kicks, but this is not exactly a turn on. Not for me, anyway."

She turned the handle of the wardrobe and pulled it open.

As if he was leaning against it on the other side, Colin fell out, shoulder-first—or, more like, was thrown out. Or, even more like—was running at full pelt for two hundred breathless yards and barrelled through the door with someone or something at his heels, to tumble, almost knocking her off her feet, then sprawled, panting, onto his knees, scrambling up onto her bed, gibbering.

"Bloody hell. Fucking *bloody* hell on a bike!"

"What?"

"Shut it!" Colin yelped, and she thought he was telling her to be quiet, till he added, pointing madly, jabbing his finger in the direction he'd come: "Shut the door!" So she did, as he wrapped himself in her duvet, backing as far as he humanly could into the corner. Away from it.

"Are you feeling all right?"

"No! Do I look all right? Fucking hell!"

His eyelids were pulled back, his face a polished surface of sweat, his hair lank and oily as if from a ten mile run, his voice no more than a whimper, his vision fixed unblinkingly. Fixed on the wardrobe door.

"What's the matter?"

Colin didn't answer—huddled, shuddering like a man plucked out of an icy pond, but was laughing, as if the laughter was being hooked out of him with a spoon, or a pitchfork. It frightened her to death. Not least because he was turning aubergine. Her prospective toy boy was going puce.

"Are you having a heart attack?"

"I hope not."

"I'll call an ambulance."

"No! Don't you dare!" He swung his legs off the bed and shot to his feet. Pulled on his underpants with alarming speed and determination. (No bulge any more, she noticed. Far from it.) "I need to go, I need to get out of here." He had his back to the wardrobe and shot a wary glance over his shoulder at it. "That place. They, they, they . . . What time is it? What *day* is it?"

"Wednesday."

"Oh, for fuck's sake."

"Have a drink." Carole filled the other glass with wine. "Calm yourself down."

"Calm down? You must be joking."

Nevertheless, Colin took it from her and sank it in one. And once he was dressed, he was gone. Carole didn't even get a chance to ask him to stay, if she'd wanted to. And she wasn't sure she did, she thought, as she rinsed the glasses and placed them back on the shelf where they'd come from. If he wasn't having a heart attack, what *was* he having? *Qualms?* A surge of disgust at what he was doing? At *her?* Was *that* it? Some elaborate way for her frightened virgin, her Arsenal fan, who lives with his mum, to head for the hills, and not see her again?

Bloody funny way to do it, she thought, once she was alone with her puzzlement, but, then again, she never understood men at the best of times. Or was it some—what did they call it—psychotic episode? Maybe that. Or a stroke. Or brain embolism. In some ways, she wished it was.

In some ways, that would be a hell of a lot easier to understand.

•●•

Anyway, she didn't expect to hear from him again, but she did.

"Look," he said on the phone, with the surprising authority of a courage plucked up.

"What?" she snapped, curtly.

"Can I come round tomorrow?" More meekly, now. "Sorry. Sorry . . . I . . ."

She sighed, thinking she was going to be an idiot for agreeing, but he sounded at a loss. He sounded desperate. Like a smacked child. And her husband was off again on one of his away days. And she wanted an explanation. And she could ring in sick again. So she did.

•●•

He cleaned his feet on the welcome mat even more vigorously the second time. She went on tiptoes to kiss him on the cheek. His eyes were fixed on the stairs.

"Can we . . . ?"

Carole accompanied him to the bedroom. He gazed around it furtively, treating the wardrobe like an unexploded bomb.

After clearing her throat, she said: "Second time lucky."

Colin looked like he didn't understand the inference. She kissed him again, this time on the lips. His face showed total disinterest. He pretended otherwise but his eyes were continually drawn to the wardrobe.

She took off her top. He stripped to his underpants and socks, which were chocolate brown with lime green stripes. Daring for a man, she thought. Or perhaps she was out of touch with what constituted men's tastes, of late. She took off her skirt and hung it up on a hanger.

"I'm sorry," he breathed.

"Doesn't a man usually say that after sex, not before? This is a first."

His shoulders sagged, making his concave chest even more so. "It's no good. I don't expect you to understand. Nobody can. It's not possible."

"Try me, Colin."

"It's a duty now, okay?"

"What the hell are you talking about?"

"A solemn pledge. A mark of honour. Of, of chivalry, of . . . There's a girl, a woman, who—"

"And what am I, Colin? A lump of meat?" Carole sat on the bed in her not inexpensive, specially purchased underwear.

"It's not that." His face contorted with genuine conflict. "There's just something I've got to do. Can't you just accept that?"

It was pointless arguing. "Bloody do it then."

He'd looked troubled, and she couldn't bear that. The pity he wanted to extract from her that she didn't want to provide. She wanted to explain that to him, if she could, but it was already too late. He'd stepped into the wardrobe and closed the door after him.

Alone in the room, Carole put her ear to its door, her cheek to the mirror, but could hear nothing, not even the gentle rattling of wire coat hangers you might expect, if you expected a person to be in your wardrobe.

She sighed, remembering how Tony would tell her not to sigh like that, and ran a bath, which she thought might relax her, but it didn't, not really, though she became drowsy and her eyelids grew monumentally heavy, and she was starting to think of somewhere far away that was safe and nice and sandy and warm, somewhere they'd gone on holiday once, Sorrento or something, and she could almost smell the sun tan lotion when she heard a THUD from the bedroom and, eyes flashing open, wrapped in a bath towel, leaving wet footprints, she found Colin in a heap, the door of the wardrobe swung wide, and he was lying there in his socks and underpants, gasping like a big fish on dry land.

She saw cuts. Blood. She bent over him. Not cuts. *Claw marks.* Parallel. Four of them. Deep. Raked across his shoulder blade. *Gouges.*

"Heck! We need to get you to A&E!"

"No way. Get me some antiseptic and Elastoplasts, I'll be fine."

"What if you need a Tetanus jab?"

"It's not some rusty fucking *wire*, Carole. Jesus!"

"Pardon me for breathing."

"Well, don't. You have no idea." Touching his shoulder was a bad idea because it caused a jolt that ran though him like an electric current. His jaws locked. He hissed his words through a clamped wall of teeth. "That . . . *fucking* thing! It won't die. No wonder they . . . Jesus! It's incredible."

"What's incredible? Colin?"

"Everything!"

•●•

Carole thought that would be the last of it and, to be truthful, part of her wanted it to be. Colin had been terse and rude and she didn't know where she was, in any shape or form, really, and didn't think it was fair. She hadn't asked for this, whatever it was, she really hadn't, and thinking about it was doing her head in. But two days later, just after lunch, an email pinged up, from you-know-who.

I'm sorry.

Carole stared at it for a full minute and ignored it for a few more full minutes, and even went for a cup of tea from the vending machine, and came back to her desk, before replying, then deleting the whole thing and ringing him.

"No. Not good enough. This is over, Colin. I can't do this."

"You can. You have to."

There was a pause. Quite a long one. She could hear a little mewling noise like a cat at the other end and she was going to ask him if he was crying, but if he was crying because he loved her she didn't want to ask, in case he said no.

• ● •

This time he wore walking boots rather than black business shoes, and a green anorak over his suit, the tail of the jacket extending two inches below its rim. His spine was straight and he didn't seem skinny any more. The glasses weren't steamed up and his eyes were clear with resolve behind them. No, not resolve—*purposefulness,* if that was a word.

As Carole stepped aside, he carried in something long and wrapped in a blanket which she took to be either a fishing rod or golf clubs, being the only things she could remotely think of that would fit the bill. So when Colin unveiled a medieval broadsword on the living room carpet, it came as a bit of a shock.

"You're not bringing that in here. I have children in this house."

"Where?"

"Not now. Obviously not *now.* But generally."

"*Generally* doesn't matter. Not to me. Not with what I've got at stake, I promise you." Colin lifted the weapon in both hands, rehearsing a swipe or two in the air above a bowl of artificial fruit. "There's no alternative, see? Its scales are thick. Its claws are deadly. And if I don't get in there, well . . . To be honest, I don't like to think *what* might happen."

"What are you talking about, Colin?"

He pressed the blade's tip into the floor and leaned on it like an umbrella. "The virgin! The Princess!"

"The who?"

He winced visibly at her inability to grasp the details. "Look, it *has* to be me. Don't ask me why, but that's what they all tell me. The prophecy says. The witches say."

"The what?"

"The wise women, priestesses, the oracle, the king, the chamberlain—everybody! The crowds in the street, thousands of them, the townsfolk, the peasants cheering."

"Cheering who? You?"

"Well, don't look completely astonished."

"Sorry. But, well."

He shrugged off her scepticism. "Look, they're all trapped in a state of fear. Terror. Frozen. Bewitched. No, not bewitched. Enchanted. Can I have one? I'm gasping."

She tossed her packet of cigarettes to him. Didn't know he smoked. Didn't know anything about him, actually. Apart from the *virgin/gay* business, and Potter's Bar, and his ambivalence on the hirsuteness front, and the Marks & Spencer underpants, which, now she added it up, was quite a lot to know about someone, actually.

He lit up, sucked in and breathed out, leaving little trails of smoke to come out of his nostrils. "It's lain waste the land. Devastated crops. Taken maidens every seven years. Ravished them. Eaten them. They thought they could satisfy its hunger, see. Do what it wanted. Ritual sacrifice, to save the city."

"Sounds positively medieval."

He gave her a hard, sour stare until the hurt of the remark abated. "It's got to stop. Don't you get it?"

"No. I don't. Why is this your business, all of a sudden? You're a young guy with a promising career in financial planning."

"Am I though? Am I *really,* Carole?" His eyes shone. Not his glasses. His eyes. "Thanks for the fag. I thought I'd given up. Spent a fortune on flaming NiQuitin patches." She took the ashtray with his dead cigarette stub and emptied the contents into the swing-topped bin. "Anyway, I'd better go. They'll be waiting." He looked over at the staircase.

"Do you need me to come—"

"No, you're all right."

He stood up, took his sword, which had been leaning against the washing machine, and went upstairs.

Carole settled on the sofa and leafed briskly through a November 2018 copy of *World of Interiors* to take her mind off what Colin might be up to, before switching on morning telly, which she didn't watch as a rule, as it tended to be wall-to-wall with middle-aged Cockney men pretending to be chefs, or repeats of people going up the Amazon to find the world's biggest eel.

An hour later, when Colin arrived back, waking her up from a semi-snooze, he didn't look well at all, and had a slight limp.

"It's worse than I thought," he said, wiping thick scarlet blood from his sword with some kitchen roll. "It has magical powers. And it's growing."

• ● •

Carole decided it was best at that stage to put a little distance between them so that they could both reassess the relationship, if that was what it was. She felt bad that she had to tell Colin it wasn't convenient for him to come round to her house on a whim of his choosing (or in fact for some time afterwards). But not that bad. He was gutted, and a bit petulant, but there was Christmas, after all, and, of course, New Year. Then, in January, her husband mentioned taking the kids to Disneyland Paris for the weekend. Going with his sister's kids in tow. Carole didn't get on with the sister, or the woman's obnoxious kids for that matter, spoilt brats who'd pulled her up on her lasagne at one point, so that was an easy thing to get out of, without too much obvious duplicity. Still, she was fairly ill-prepared for how Colin turned up on her doorstep that Friday evening.

She opened the front door to a vision.

Full suit of armour, white-plumed helmet with a visor, breastplate, the lot. Shield. Battle axe. Gauntlets. Chain mail. The full *Ivanhoe.*

Her first thought was to make a quip about fancy dress, but he very firmly said—"*Don't.*"

She sighed.

"I'm sorry, Carole." His eyes were frozen with a conviction visibly tinged with abject terror. "There's no other way. I promise you there isn't."

•●•

Shortly afterwards he was sitting with her at the kitchen island, armour-plated feet long and pointed on the crossbar of his stool. Carole was a little worried his gauntlets might leave scratches on the black marble, which would make Tony hit the roof.

"Can I make you a coffee? I've just de-scaled the Nespresso machine."

"Go on then. Can't hurt."

Colin's plume bobbed slightly and his metal elbow joint creaked as he raised the tiny cup to his lips.

"Will you be careful?"

"As careful as you can be with a fire-breathing monster that weighs as much as fifteen double decker buses, Carole."

"No need to be sarcastic."

"Perhaps there is. Perhaps I need a little more support than someone undermining my confidence."

"I've never done that."

"Haven't you?"

Colin's mood shifted from tetchy to recalcitrant—again, with a degree of metallic creaking. "I'm sorry. You're right. That was unfair."

He shoved up his visor, which, irritatingly, tended to slip down over his forehead with a squeak. "I'm under a lot of stress at the minute."

She could see that. "Would you like a sandwich to keep you going?"

"No, ta. I think that's a bad idea. What do boxers have before a big fight? Raw steak. Bit of that might go down well. I'm kidding. I think if I had so much as a Twiglet I'd throw up." A little laugh salted the atmosphere.

"Colin, if I ask you something, will you answer honestly?"

He nodded. "If I can."

She wasn't sure if she should say it, but she did. "Are things going to go back to normal when all this is over?"

"I don't know. I really don't."

For all his faults, she did believe he was telling the truth when he said that, because he looked sad. Sorrowful. What's the difference between *sad* and *sorrowful*, she wondered? Except *sorrowful* sounded better. Almost like a good thing.

Halfway up the stairs, looking like a clanking astronaut ascending the ladder to his module, he paused and turned around. "Goodbye, Carole."

"You haven't got a trusty steed outside, have you?" she joked.

"Don't be silly."

Carole smiled.

She couldn't help but follow him up to the bedroom, hesitating as she observed him in his contemplations before the wardrobe mirror. Sensing he was being watched, he looked back to find her standing on the landing.

"You know I have to, don't you?"

She nodded. "Wait a minute."

She knelt and looked for something in one of the drawers, wiped the dust off it, and handed it to him. It was a glove. A mitten she wore in winter. Something that kept her warm.

"Thank you," Colin said, tucking it behind the U of his breast plate. She could smell the metal tang of chain mail as he pressed his lips to hers and held her body to his.

Turning sideways to accommodate his battleaxe and shield, he stepped, clinking like rattled saucepans, into the wardrobe, and she closed the door after him, carefully turning the latch to secure it, almost afraid to let go.

When she turned it back the other way and opened the door a second later, he was gone. She reached her hand inside, knowing what she would find.

Nothing.

Just her own clothes on hangers. No false panel. No door. No portal.

He was gone.

•●•

Carole sat with her husband listening to tales of Disneyland. Of fairytales. Of castles. Her children were excited, transported, and their happiness brushed off on her. How could it not? She wouldn't have been much of a mum if it hadn't. She enjoyed hearing their voices so much she held their soft hands as they talked, thought every syllable beautiful as a bird.

The weeks passed. Colin never reappeared.

The wardrobe became a wardrobe again.

In work, new rumours circulated. That he'd had a rich mistress. That he was married all along. That he was an international criminal. They asked Carole what had happened. She knew him, didn't she? "No," she said. "Not really. Not at all." But she thought of him every time she opened the wardrobe door. Thought of what he went to do, to save that land, that kingdom . . . And over the next few weeks, and months, as the season changed colour and became renewed and supple again, the memory of him faded—but not completely . . . *never* completely.

"Tony," she said to the man she'd married, as they lay in bed one night, reading separate books under separate reading lamps. "I want to move. Somewhere exciting. Not even exciting. Somewhere different. I want to *be* different. Both of us. We can, you know. We can, if we try, and we want to, if we want to enjoy life. Enjoy each other, like we used to. We can be . . ." She paused.

"What?" asked her husband.

". . . Adventurous," she said.

The Flickering Light

THEY HAD THEIR ALLOTTED ROLES. Her realm was the kitchen, and, once they'd agreed the choice of courses, usually over a period of days, recipe books decorated with Post-It notes breeding on the dining table, he more or less left her to it, not micro-managing at all until the final, tasting stages, when she was grateful for a second opinion of her beetroot gazpacho.

His job, meanwhile, was to lay the table and make the room look its best. The collection of antique laboratory glass needed to be freshly washed and sparkling. The junk mail, which Bell habitually let gather on a chair, had to be put in recycling, or shredded. The wood burning stove prepared. Above all, choice of tableware was key. Black dishes were his choice for seafood pasta, but the plates with graphic renditions of iconic British buildings—Battersea Power Station, The Shard—were more suitable for tonight. They'd set off the tomato and onion tart Bell had made to a tee, just as the pale blue Nigella Lawson bowl would be perfect for the pre-cooked green beans, mange tout and hazelnuts.

Piet liked things to look nice. No, he liked things to look *right*. In fact, he often said that he felt anxious, and sometimes physically ill, if they weren't. He couldn't bear to see a painting that wasn't hung straight, and felt compelled to adjust it, or, if they were in a public place, had to sit in such a way that it wasn't in vision. She'd often laughed, and he never minded that, sometimes joking, huddled in his Gulag-style overcoat, that it was an affliction. One that had helped to earn him a living. Respect. Fame, even. *Piet Nuyens* was a brand now after all. Like Richard Rogers, like Norman Foster. A name people used as shorthand to convey a near-ascetic, almost punishing, post-Mies van der Rohe minimalism.

He hadn't liked the low-cut teal and pink frock she'd first put on, with ankle boots, and had asked her to change into something he thought smarter and less frivolous: the black Issey Miyake dress he always preferred. Less flesh on show, he'd said. More stylish.

He reminded Bell again to put on some make-up, it helped her complexion, and she was applying her lipstick, and he was lighting the candles, evenly-spaced around the room, when the first guests arrived, heralded by the beam of headlights on the grass beyond the picture window.

Hilton and Dora had met at Glastonbury, which, Piet said, is exactly what anyone with half a brain cell would guess by looking at them. Hawaiian shirt and white-flecked goatee, he was an immaculate carpenter with the delayed reaction but basic harmlessness of a dedicated marijuana smoker. She hung on his arm like a cowboy's wife abducted as a baby by the Apache. They came with Australian wine and chocolates, which Bell thanked them for, and Piet took their frosted coats. Hilton hastily reclaimed a tobacco pouch from his pocket as if it were life-sustaining medicine, which possibly it was.

Jacquetta and Spence's lateness was a given. Bell thought it was a Bristol thing, because every Bristolian she knew had the same habit. You could either get uptight about it or forget about it, so she decided on the latter. And as soon as she saw them, entwining both of them in hugs, it didn't matter. Jaquetta big and mad in her fake fur coat and garish scarf, a Weight Watchers femme fatale. Spense a hero just for enduring.

The prosecco bottle empty, Bell served up the gazpacho with warm bread from the local artisan bakery, while Piet directed people to their assigned seats, went to the iPhone dock and selected Jóhann Jóhannsson's *Englaborn*—the evening's playlist carefully preordained—and was turning down the spotlights to create the desired refectory-in-a-monastery glow when one of the bulbs flickered.

"Uh-oh."

It seemed it was going to expire, but unexpectedly clung to life and remained on.

"Ah!"

Piet sat himself at the head of the table and peered across the meniscus of his newly-poured Shiraz.

Bell tugged at her collar to cover the skin on her neck, which she felt redden."What?" Jacquetta asked.

"Nothing."

"Bell."

"She has a thing about lights at the moment." Piet smiled asymmetrically. "Tell them."

Bell shook her head with a quiver. "It's silly. Help yourself to bread." She thrust out the wire basket. "Take a piece and pass it round. There's—"

"A few days ago I heard a hell of a thud upstairs. Like the house was falling down."

"Wasn't *that* bad," murmured Bell.

"Felt like it." Smile more of a smirk now. "The whole house shook. I'm not exaggerating. I shouted *Jesus fucking Christ! What the hell's happened?* And this little voice came back from upstairs: *Sorry!*"

They laughed. Bell almost wanted to laugh too, but could only tug her mouth into a smile as her husband continued.

"'I was standing on the bed trying to fix the light,' she said. 'What's wrong with the light?' I said. 'Haven't you noticed? When you switch it off, instead of going off immediately it retains a bit of a glow that fades off slowly. Not much, but . . . haven't you noticed?'" He presented a theatrical shrug to the guests, earning him titters. "'No. I haven't noticed.' 'Well go and have a look.' 'You're telling me you were jumping off the bed because you were checking a light bulb?'"

More laughter, through bread and wine.

"Yes," Bell said. The redness had spread to her cheeks now. Perhaps it was the Prosecco. "It must have been the new bulb we put in the other day. We'll have to get an electrician."

"I said 'Why are you doing it now? It's ten o'clock at night!'" Piet was working the audience. "She said 'Because I went up to the bedroom to put my dressing gown on and it was right in front of me, and I thought, if I didn't do it now, it won't get done.'"

"Familiar," Jacquetta grunted. Spence turned to her with a double-take and a frown.

Hilton went, *Ha!*—pointing a gotcha finger.

"I don't suppose it's anything to worry about."

Piet lifted Bell's hand and kissed it. "'That's the thing with my wife. She *will* worry about trivialities."

"Come on," said Jacquetta quickly. Bell could always count on her as an ally. Especially where Piet was concerned. "World famous architect needs his house's wiring checked out. I'm phoning the fucking *Daily Mirror*."

"The *Daily Mirror* hasn't heard of me, darling. They've barely heard of architecture."

"Well, I'll say you're one of the cast of *Love Island*. I reckon there's fifty quid in it for me." Jacquetta was the only person in the world who could take the piss out of Piet and get away with it. On holiday in Barcelona she'd once wound him up by driving round a roundabout three times because he was in a foul mood. If Bell had done that, he wouldn't have spoken to her for days.

"What's *Love Island*?" Piet said.

They'd bathed in separate bathrooms earlier. That was one thing he'd been adamant about. Insistent about, all along, in the design of the house, his pride and joy, five years in the planning, down to the radiators, coat hooks, underfloor heating—every latch, every door knob. A bathroom for him. A bathroom for her. She remembered him saying he couldn't see why any civilised person would share one unless they had to. Not when they were creating all that space from scratch. And it was designed specifically for them to live in. *Him* to live in, he meant.

Civilised. She supposed the word meant different things to different people. To her, it meant decency and kindness. To him, she thought, it meant security and timeless values such as beauty, the very things denied his ancestors who'd been driven out of country after country. The opposite of a father with no passport who'd deceived and absconded, taking any remnant of affection with him. Piet had only spoken once, with a certain cold distance, of finding his mother in tears of helplessness after being left alone with two children to bring up. Bell had put her palm on his back and felt his chest catch as he breathed.

Now she stared up at the spotlight across the room—the offending one, which was flickering again. Within a minute or two it had breathed its last. Though no-one else noticed, to her it felt almost like a cue.

"You know what it is?" All eyes turned to her, quizzical, anticipatory. Surprised by her sudden interjection. So out of character. She had no idea what the subject of their conversation had been at that point, and didn't much care. "The light bulb thing earlier. I'll tell you what it is . . ." She sipped her wine, then her water. Somehow not even interested if they were listening, any of them. Not even looking up. Running her fingers round the edge of her plate, straightening her knife and fork as she spoke. "When my sister and I were kids, back in Barbados, I remember lying in bed side by side. It was soon after Papa had his heart attack and was in the hospital, and the two of us were frightened. We had no idea what was going to happen. Our father would live forever, wouldn't he? Doesn't everybody think that, at that age? I was ten and Triss was—what? Seven? That's right. She'd been born with a twisted spine. Scoliosis. She'd been in hospital most of her life, in callipers and getting operation after operation, so it was a huge excitement, her coming home. I was excited about having a sister, but guilty too, because I'd been happy and something bad had happened."

Bell looked up a fraction at Spence, who had muscular dystrophy, and had written a science fiction book called *Rhombus* and a folk horror novel called *Baby Forester*, about a child found in the middle of an ancient wood.

"She was crying and I was trying not to. Mrs Briar was babysitting because Mama was at our father's bedside, naturally enough. We were told not to be naughty for Mrs Briar and to go to bed and go to sleep but we couldn't. We lay there, staring up at the ceiling, knowing we couldn't sleep. Then the light bulb started flickering on and off. And we were staring at it, and I said, I don't know why . . . it was a nutty thing to do really, and it was nasty. I didn't mean to be nasty, but she was always playing me up, you see—poking me, needling me—she knew what buttons to press the way sisters do, and perhaps I thought it was my turn or something. I don't know, but the light was going on and off, off and on, over our heads, and I said: 'If that light goes out, you know what it means, don't you? It means Papa's died.'"

Bell felt the table tense, but she herself didn't shudder, though she heard a tremor in her voice.

"I don't know why I did it. And she got upset. Of course she did. And I got upset too, myself—even though I'd said it. And the light did go out, you see. And Papa did die."

Dora invaded the silence that loomed. "That night?"

"I don't remember."

"So maybe not that night," said Piet.

"But it did happen. The light flickering. My father dying." Bell stared in the candle glow, not blinking, hands clasped, making a chin rest. "So it was a bit . . . weird, is all I'm saying. The light bulb upstairs. It made me think of it." An unconvincing smile broke. Wanting to move on now. Thinking better of what she'd said. Spouted. Stupidly.

"You're not superstitious, are you?" said Hilton, the super-chilled one.

"No. I don't believe any of that nonsense."

"I do," said Jacquetta. "I believe in something. Otherwise what's the point?"

"Plenty of point." Piet stood to uncork a fresh bottle, wedging it between his thighs. "We procreate. Our genes live on."

"Plus it's fairly enjoyable," added Hilton. "Procreation."

"How would you know?" said Dora.

"Perhaps not with you. Generally."

A groan circulated in mock outrage. They were safe in each others' company. They knew that. Banter was banter.

"Matisse created a beautiful chapel in Vence because he was a consummate artist with an exceptional eye," said Piet. "Not because he was a religious man nearing the end of his life who believed in supernatural forces. I go along with Richard Dawkins. I can look at a flower and appreciate its beauty by random mutation of natural selection just as I look at a beautifully designed Eames chair or Maserati. I don't have to believe in a big, bearded God in the clouds."

"Maybe ghosts don't believe in God either," said Bell. "Maybe they're totally atheistic ghosts. They just exist. Like grass. Like the air."

Piet snorted. "Yes well, that's enough of that. I think you've done enough talking, darling. You're starting to make yourself sound stupid."

He squeezed her hand and she shut up. He was probably right after all. She did sound stupid. She didn't know why she'd spoken at all. He was the intelligent one. The well-read one. The one who could quote Socrates or Ovid. What was she? Just a painter who didn't paint anymore, because he'd told her she wasn't good enough to cut the mustard.

The remnant of her smile flickered as if it might vanish. She rose, straightening her back. Jacquetta was looking at her and she knew that. If she'd met her eyes, that would have been it. Instead, she gathered the empty plates as Piet changed the music to Ólafur Arnalds' *Re:member*, holding court about the album's "blissful serenity" and the fact they'd seen the composer at the Forum, an exceptionally moving experience for both of them.

Bell took the plates to the kitchen, stacking them in the dishwasher with a cloudy head and prickly eyes.

The memory now sparked, she thought of the way she used to cuddle into the curve of her sister's spine, like they were meant to fit together. Seven years in hospital. She'd had a picture of Triss in her head, but it was like that of a story book character, a legend, a work of imagination, till she arrived home. And when she did come home, it wasn't the same. Bell had been jealous. She could see that now. People visiting, bringing gifts, telling the little one she was beautiful. And they all brought toys. Loads and loads of toys filling the parlour. Even a Raleigh bicycle. And she'd wanted that Raleigh bicycle so much, and Mama said they had to give everything to the orphan's home because it wasn't fair and they didn't need charity. But she wanted that bicycle so, so much.

Lemon polenta cake with vanilla ice cream. As she placed it down, Piet touched her bare, soft forearm. He demonstrated smiling. She demonstrated back. The cake was sliced.

She sat down and chased a spoonful around her plate. You never felt hungry, really, when you'd been doing the cooking all day. It was as if your taste buds deserted you. She thought about the dark outside the shutters and the dark outside the windows when she was a child in the Caribbean. It seemed that they couldn't be the same dark.

"So is somebody going to die tonight?" said Spence, glanced up at the dead spotlight pointing blindly in his direction. "You said the light flickered the night your father died. So . . . do you think someone's going to die tonight?"

They ate silently. Until Dora spoke.

"We passed a crash at the side of the road. It was why we were late. The car was really stove in on one side. We didn't see much.

There was an ambulance and a police car, and a recovery truck. Someone might have died, for all we know."

"Or they'd hit a fox," said Piet. "Alas, poor badger. We knew him, Horatio."

"Maybe they didn't," said Hilton, manufacturing a roll-up. "Maybe it's just some ninety-eight-year-old fucking numpty who should have had his license taken away from him years ago."

Bell said nothing. She'd been told to say nothing, so that's what she did.

Jacquetta lay down her fork and leaned her elbows on the table. "Last Sunday we went up to Cheltenham to see a friend of ours. We haven't seen them for ages, really—I knew them from London days—but then Sophie got in contact by email about six months ago to say Abe had been diagnosed with some sort of blood cancer. He'd gone for an eye test and the optician, friend of his, had said, you need to go and get this checked out, like, immediately. Next thing he knew he was up in Manchester seeing an oncologist who was telling him he had this rare blood disease and it was terminal. There were tumours at the back of his eye. He went into surgery the next day and they took it out. When we met him in the summer he had a glass eye. Same old Abe, laughing and joking. 'Don't get me wrong,' he said, 'I have my dark nights of the soul.' I remember when they left at the end of the evening, I said, like you do: 'We'll see you soon, yeah?' and he laughed and said, 'You'll have to!' That was a killer. I keep thinking about it." She took a mouthful of wine and took time to swallow. "Spence and I got another email last week from Soph. The doctors were saying he'd only got a few days left. We thought he'd have months. Years. You don't imagine it happening quickly. I think you go into denial. Which is nothing to what Soph and the children must be feeling. On Sunday he was on a recliner watching the rugby with Jonno, his son—big lump, handsome, rugby mad, both of them. We talked about stupid things. Telly, the weather. What's important when you're dying? I don't know. We just wanted to be there. Show ourselves. He looked terrible. Yellow. Holding his son's hand. His grown up son's hand." She held her breath then let it out slowly. "We heard this morning he'd died, with his family gathered around him."

"Christ," said Hilton, lowering his Zippo from his unlit spliff.

"Maybe that's what it picked up on . . ." Dora looked pale. "That's what the light flickering meant."

"The light bulb was psychic." Piet curled his lip sourly. "Almost certainly."

"Fuck off," spat Jacquetta without restraint. "He was a lovely guy. A super person. Kind. Generous. Loving." She directed the words at Piet like arrows.

Piet offered his arms to the air in a *mea culpa*.

"Awful," breathed Dora, shaking her head.

"Fucking dreadful," said Hilton. "Here's to him." Glass to the heavens. "Please let me go rapidly, if not instantaneously, with as little fucking agony as possible."

"I think you've got a bit of catching up to do, mate," said Dora. "You haven't been inside a church since . . . what?"

Hilton thumbed through an imaginary diary. "Er, let's see . . . Never. How does never suit you?"

Bell thought about being with her father when he had his heart attack, in the Cricket Club. She liked going there. Everyone made a fuss of her. No one made a fuss of her at home. Her mother called her dirty and told her she wasn't pretty. But Papa lifted her up and showed her the nice paintings on the walls. Sometimes he got paid in paintings, because his customers had what you'd now call *cash flow problems*. Her mother would call him stupid for getting paid in paintings like that, but to him they were special, she could tell. He was nothing more than a builder, a quiet man, but he liked to look at beautiful things.

She'd been playing cricket in the corridor with the other men when she thought he'd been an awful long time in the toilet, and one of the men went in and found him unconscious. She remembered being in the back of a car crying as they followed the ambulance, asking if her papa was going to die, and nobody said yes and nobody said no.

The sound of clapping brought her back to the present.

Like a stage magician displaying an egg he is about to make disappear, Piet was holding up a light bulb newly extracted from its cardboard container. He stood on his chair, unscrewed the dead one and replaced it with the new. As the fader was turned up and the fresh bulb burned brightly a new round of applause spontaneously arose and Piet gave a bow before getting off the chair.

"Coffee?"

That was one of his allotted roles, and Bell let him commandeer the Nespresso machine whilst she arranged the champagne truffles on a Grayson Perry dish emblazoned with wankerish but witty aphorisms about art. Spence elected to join Hilton in a Calvados.

Bell imagined that Piet was embarrassed by what she had shared. She knew he didn't think her life was very interesting, and her theories about life after death, if they existed, must surely be inane and worthless. As her guests left, she wondered if she should apologise, saying she hoped they'd enjoyed the rest of the evening apart from her, what?—stories?—but thought that would be yet another thing that she'd do wrong.

As she kissed Jacquetta's cheek, she felt her hand squeezed. Her friend looked her deep in the eyes and gave an intense little frown meant for her alone. "We'll meet up, yeah? Let's meet up, just you and me. The two of us. Yeah?" She didn't let go of Bell's hand until she nodded.

After blowing out the candles, Bell was tired and wanted to go to bed, but Piet turned up the spotlights and said if they stacked the dishwasher and set it running there'd be less to do in the morning.

"You looked beautiful." He kissed her cheek as she passed. "And they really enjoyed the food. Did you notice? Nobody left a crumb. It was a tremendous success. Well done, you."

He collected the glasses and washed them by hand while she used a credit card to scrape up the drips of dried candle wax from the table top, and a damp cloth to mop the red crescents from the bottom of the glasses. Hell to get off if you left it.

"Are we done?" Sleeves still rolled up, he dried his hands on a tea towel and switched off the lights.

"I think so," she said, following him upstairs.

She switched on her electric toothbrush. Removed her make up with swabs. The callousness of the strip lighting always poured scorn on her physical failings, and she considered whether that was the real reason he didn't want them to share a bathroom. The truth was he didn't want to look at her unadorned.

She remembered flowers and surprises.

She remembered tactile, effortless moments. Of release. Of fondness. Of unknowing, but of finding out . . .

She didn't think he hated her—not yet—but he tolerated her, and in some ways that was worse. She had gone from being an obsession to a trophy to an irritation. He probably thought it was better than being alone. But was that what she wanted her marriage to be: *Better than being alone?*

She padded barefoot to the master bedroom. The reading light was off on his side and he was naked under the duvet, lying on his side with his eyes closed, head immobile, sunken in the scarlet pillow below.

Bell hung up her dressing gown on the hook on the back of the door and kicked off her slippers. She switched off the overhead light and stared at the bulb's faint illumination as it refused to go out immediately, as it was supposed to, instead slowly fading, but hesitating, as if reluctant to take the room to darkness.

Something had died, she was certain. But she wasn't sure what it was.

Bad Language

> *"But how could you live and have no story to tell?"*
> Fyodor Dostoevsky
> "White Nights"

I'VE USED DEATH once or twice. To get me off the hook. Buying me time when a deadline loomed, after I'd been staring out the window for too many days, or weeks, waiting for that self-punishing kick up the backside to finally motivate me. I've certainly got through five or six grandmothers over the years. Heart attack. Cancer. Stroke. After all, only a monster would expect pages under such circumstances. Only someone with a heart of ice would crack the whip when someone is grieving the loss of a loved one. That was the idea.

I'm wondering if I can use it now, to postpone the imminent Skype meeting tonight with those two illustrious morons with an "in" at New Line. The one with the draw-string pants and hideous tan slip-ons, and the other leather-skinned silver fox who insists on wearing white slacks so tight they segregate his testicles. But this time the family bereavement tactic doesn't feel right.

Because, this time, my mother is actually dead.

Predictably, it's scheduled for 3.00 p.m. LA time, 11.00 p.m. in the UK. No doubt they've enjoyed a couple of Cobb salads for lunch, the bill coming to more than they're giving me for an option. But hey, it's my job not to discuss that. It's my job to smile and be professional.

Hi. Hi. Hello.

Hello! Paul Taberner!

My name in full. As if to prove, impressively, they know who they're addressing.

Hi! How're you guys? I ask. I'm not interested. They appear fuzzy. An improvement. The pleasantries are mercifully short. The usual apology for the time difference. Some banter about the weather. Sunshine in Los Angeles. *You're kidding me*, I joke.

Shall we dive straight in, Paul?

I wonder, what if I say no? But soon they're telling me they've talked through their individual notes together and, guess what, Daffy Duck and Pluto agree on everything. So it's a case of doing another pass and getting it in super-fast to the studio, where everybody's really excited.

Of course they are.

I listen, leaning forward, as if hanging on their every word. Frowning, hands in a praying position now, fingertips touching my mouth, so they probably think I'm concentrating very deeply on the pearls of wisdom they're imparting. I'm not.

I'm not thinking about them at all, or their observations about the first act turning point being five pages too late.

I'm thinking about my mother again.

How my partner and I would take a drive over there, the two of us, across the Severn Bridge, ninety minutes each way, of a Sunday, and sit in that living room with the gruesome seventies wallpaper, us trying to make conversation, my mum facing the TV set, and finding that we never had much to offer. Affie would always make more of an effort than me and, with his brilliant smile, usually get a story out of her, probably because he was a new audience. I'd heard them all before, and he was a good listener. She'd always liked him. Called him "cariad"—which was ironic, because Affie meant "darling" in Kenya. Sometimes we'd take her out for a treat, to Penarth for posh fish and chips at *The Fig Tree* and a walk up the newly renovated pier. She was always grateful for a day out of the house, and her thanks always made me feel sick with guilt that I couldn't wait to leave behind the home I grew up in.

Each year she'd come over to us for a day or two. While she insisted, to the point of tedium, she didn't want to be any trouble, it was nevertheless a strain. "Do you want a cup of tea?" was always met with: "Are you having one?" And "Do you want tea or coffee?" with "Whatever's easier." Driven mad, I'd end up saying: "Mum, both are equally easy, which do you want?" Then I knew I was raising my voice, and sounding like I didn't want her there, which wasn't true, and wasn't fair.

There was nothing wrong with her. She was lovely. She'd always been a fantastic mother, and always put other people first, whether it was her parents, or my dad, or my Auntie Rita when she was poorly, or my brother's boy when he was in junior school. She effortlessly took on the role of serving other people, and when I was young, to my shame, I really didn't understand how someone could do that. Where was her ambition? Didn't she want to *do* something with her life? As I grew older I became less dismissive. Realised she didn't want the things I wanted, and that was fine. She didn't want a career, or success, or material wealth, or to travel the world to exotic places, or need artistic expression to justify her existence—why should she? Her ambition was that her two sons would be safe and happy. That wasn't such a bad ambition to have, and she achieved it.

Maybe I envied that. I don't know. The simplicity of a life of giving. What did I have? A life of fretting. A life of being told I'd done something wrong.

Perhaps the guilt of moving so far away from home was what sat heavily on my shoulders. Realistically, there was no question of her living with us, in Wiltshire. She'd have been a total fish out of water. She had nice neighbours who were on her wavelength, small kiddies next door she could dote on, a man who cut her grass, and she'd always been more than emphatic she was *all right on her own*, *we didn't need to worry about her*. So when we asked her to come to ours for a few days, we had to couch it as something *we* wanted. And by the time I was watching her making a mess of doing up her seatbelt, giving a big theatrical sigh and appealing to me with pathetic big puppy dog eyes, I was regretting it.

The final time she came over—though we didn't know it then—we sat and watched *The Monuments Men* together, a film about American soldiers getting back priceless works of art from the Nazis. It wasn't far into the movie before she piped up. "I know him. Who is he?" I said, "George Clooney, Mum." Five minutes later: "I know this bloke. What's his name?" "George Clooney." Every ten minutes: "Who's this feller, now?" "George Clooney." As the final credits rolled, she said, "Now, I'm sure we had this, didn't we? What is it?" Trying to disguise my fatigue, I said, "World War Two, Mum."

It was pretty obvious by then her memory was going, long before we heard the term "vascular dementia". Long before the painful visit to the GP where—after getting a blood test to rule out something simple like low iron or low B12—he gave her IQ puzzles she couldn't do, and started crying, and tried to leave, and he made her an appointment at the Memory Clinic at the hospital, and we got her up there on false pretences. Then she saw the sign saying PSYCHIATRIC UNIT—bloody hell—and we had to lie to her, saying it was just the side entrance to the nurse's office. But she knew. God, if she didn't know anything else, she knew something was up.

Years ago, she'd tripped on the stair carpet and hit her head, and that might have been a contributing factor. We didn't know what was or wasn't a contributing factor, to be truthful. Diet? Mental stagnation? Physical inactivity? Loneliness? Emptiness? Worthlessness?

She'd been a bit rudderless after Dad died, but not nearly as rudderless as we'd anticipated. She'd been terrified how she'd cope with bills and everything, but my brother showed her how to write a cheque and use a credit card, and before long, you could tell, she felt she could deal with this. She even took up reading again—potboilers, library books, chick lit—nothing demanding, but she said she hadn't read a book since she was pregnant with me, and it was great to see her enjoying them.

I'd always sent them copies of the books I'd written, of course, over the years. The short stories, written on the side, between screenwriting gigs. But my father only read the sports pages of the *Western Mail*, and had two hardbacks to his name, a biography of Margaret Thatcher and *First Among Equals* by Jeffrey Archer. After he died, I saw my book on his shelf of the bureau in the middle room, and could tell from where the spine was broken he'd only got a quarter of the way through. I was surprised he'd opened it at all.

Over time, though, her enthusiasm waned. The books she'd read sat in a pile near the door. Her memory problems must have rendered them gradually out of reach. It was a slow decline, and one, in some ways, we refused to see happening, even though we knew it was.

She'd tell me she hadn't seen my brother, Lyn, for weeks. Then I'd find out from him that he'd done her shopping and sorted out her tablets the day before. He'd get upset and call her a liar. Looking back, it was more of an indication that her ideas of what had, or hadn't, occurred were all of a jumble. I tried to react less emotionally then he did, but could see why he'd be hurt. He was taking on the lion's share of keeping an eye on her and I was over in England. Out of sight, out of mind. If he resented that, I wouldn't have blamed him. But that was just the way it was. He'd stayed in Ponty, got a job as a surveyor, and I'd gone off to film school. Neither of us accused the other of anything. In fact, we pussyfooted around each other, desperate not to clash when it came to Mum, or anything else.

But even Affie had to bite his tongue on occasions. Like, how many times did she have to ask what day it was? Once he said to her, "Miriam, what difference does it make what day it is? It isn't like you have to get a train to London, or run a marathon." She looked confused for a moment, and said, "I just like to know." Of course. Why wouldn't she?

That last time she visited, after we'd watched *The Monuments Men* in the afternoon, I suggested we went for a walk before dinner. I wanted some fresh air, to be truthful, but Mum had to be persuaded. "You go. I'll be all right here." I said, "All right then." Affie gave me a look. Mum said, "How far?" I said, "Not too far. Ten minutes. Just for some fresh air. You've been in all day." "I'm always in all day." Behind her back, I rolled my eyes. "It'll do you good." She agreed, finally, on sufferance. "As long as it's not uphill. You know I can't do hills." I said, "It won't be."

Ten years earlier, I'd got a phone call from my dad. *Nothing wrong, nothing to worry about . . .* His usual mantra. Of course, there was. She'd been rushed into East Glam. My brother texted me she was in the coronary care unit. "You've had a heart attack," they said. Her ECG was regular but they couldn't let her go home in pain. She needed an angioplasty. The way she described it, you go into this huge room, there's a blackboard, twelve doctors, and TV things to see what's happening. "I didn't want to see, mind." She said she felt hands behind her head, then they went into the artery in her groin, sent this balloon up—*right up.* "You'll experience some pain now." *"Crikey Moses!"*

That night she woke up to find the bed was swimming in blood, all over her feet and everything. She pressed the buzzer and a nurse came and tidied her up. "It looks worse than it is," the doctor said. They gave her an inhaler with instructions to use it if she got a pain in her chest. She was warned not to exert herself, but kept to her obsessive housework regime—cleaning the windows, dusting high and low—in spite of Dad shouting at her. He'd call her bloody mad, and she'd say she took two puffs halfway around, as if that exonerated her.

Hence the wariness of hills. But there weren't any in Bradford, not really. We just wanted to take her over the pretty town bridge, and down beside the river, where she could see the swans and ducks, or the blue dart of a kingfisher if we were lucky, even a prehistoric-looking heron. The gorgeous Cotswold limestone of the houses glowed at dusk, so different from the red brick and concrete abortions that afflicted the rebuilding of my home town in the sixties, the cheek of it slashed by the razor of a bypass. It had become a dump, but I couldn't say that and it didn't need saying. I was lucky enough not to have to live there, but she did.

We passed the swimming pool, doddering along at her pace, Affie with his hands in his pockets slightly ahead of us, pointing out one of the cheeky squirrels who lived by the riverbank. A couple of pink-faced winos in hoodies sat in the country park, but a man with a Scottie dog doffed his cap to my mum and said it was a glorious evening, which pleased her. She said she could see why we liked living here. "Bit different from Ponty." I said, "Plenty of good things in Ponty. You like it there." She turned her face up towards the setting sun, half-blinking, and for a moment it made her skin golden.

I knew it was too much to expect her to accompany us on our usual walk to Avoncliff and back, so we took a right near the Tithe Barn to cross the Pack Horse Bridge, where a wartime pill box nestled secretively in undergrowth. I took her arm as we crossed the railway line and mounted the steps to Barton's Orchard. This was where I'd forgotten there was a short slope before we reached the flat, and Mum baulked at the prospect like I'd committed a crime, making it abundantly clear she was already out of breath. I said, "There's no hurry. Take your time." Affie strode ahead and she ignored my advice with typical stubbornness and hurried after him, pausing to gasp after every four or five steps as if to rub my nose in it. I glowered at her, hands on hips. She waved me away with a flick of her hand. "Your father, you are."

It levelled once we were at the gate to the meadow. Trees hung low over the gravel path and more grey squirrels scampered on the stone wall, arguing over the ownership of nuts. Mum chuckled to see them playing, as if they were children. Then they were gone. There was no way we were going to take her up the steep path to Tory, so cut across Newtown to Mason's Lane, where the pavement started to curve downhill. I took my mum's elbow and looked both ways as we crossed the road. Not a vehicle in sight until there was one.

The 4x4 appeared from nowhere, doing thirty, forty miles an hour as it took the corner, all its weight on the outer tyres as if it was in a rally. Mum was still walking. I thought that was it. The car was going to hit her.

The driver's grip on the wheel wobbled. The mass of metal swerved. The side window was open, and a thick slab of a forearm rested there, decorated by a sleeve of tattoos. A face bulged from the aperture, swelling like a boil. Its expression like nothing I had ever seen in my life. One of pure, bilious rage.

"Fucking CUNT!" it yelled—into my mother's face.

She reeled back on unsteady feet. It might as well have been a physical blow. I grasped her elbow again, steadying her. She looked bewildered. Light-headed.

"What did he say?"

"Nothing," I said. "Just rubbish."

The car was already at the bottom of the hill, at the mini-roundabout, then gone, in the direction of Trowbridge.

Affie asked if she was all right. Without answering, she crossed the road and I kept up, admonishing her there was no need to rush. She always went like a bull at a gate. It drove me mad. At the zebra crossing she paused to lean on a Belisha beacon and rubbed her sternum, making a face.

"It's probably indigestion. You had a big lunch."

She took her angina spray out of her handbag and squirted the contents onto her tongue, twice in rapid succession.

I didn't want to make her any more agitated, and luckily, it seemed, she hadn't heard what the odious gorilla in the 4x4 had said. So I zipped my lips and tried not to look as angry as I was feeling, for her sake.

When we got in we cooked Affie's fish and yam stew. Mum used to tell us she didn't want garlic in anything, but now she didn't bother. We got the usual, "Good God, I can't eat all that. What do you think I am?" Polished it off, though, in spite of being worried about her weight. My nephew used to say it was ridiculous for his nan to be worried about her weight at her age. She should be happy to be "nan-shaped".

"Too full, I am." She undid her slacks. Watched TV. Nine o'clock, sloped off to bed in the spare room, giving us a few hours to ourselves. *Not wanting to be any trouble.*

I remember looking down at her slippers, those awful, cheap velour jobs. Beige, like her entire wardrobe. Colourless. Screaming out that she wanted to blend into the background like a transparent ghost. One Christmas we bought her a lavender blue cardigan, not too flamboyant, perfect for her complexion and silver hair, but we never saw it on her. One birthday, a scarf she never wore. Affie thought if she'd got a decent haircut she'd have looked like Judi Dench, but there was no chance of that. She didn't want to look like Judi Dench. She didn't want to be noticed at all. It was maddening, but perhaps just me wanting to turn her into something she wasn't, as opposed to accepting the person she was comfortable being.

"Do you think she's enjoying herself?" Affie asked, cross-legged on the carpet, cheek resting on my knee.

"Yes. Of course she is. I just think it's a bit much for her. She's probably done more walking in two days than she's done in two years."

"You're a good son." He kissed my thigh. "You do your best."

"Do I?"

The next day we went for a run in the car to Bruton, for a spot of lunch at an artisan bakery-cum-pizza parlour type place in a converted chapel, all whitewashed walls and lancet windows. Posh, my mum would think. But if you can't treat your mum occasionally, what can you do?

She enjoyed her glass of white wine, but I noticed her giving a sharp intake of breath and rubbing her sternum from time to time, a punctuation in the conversation that got me anxious, then started to annoy me. I asked, irritably, if she wanted something from the chemist. She shook her head. Typical martyr. I said it was only over the road, I could be there and back in less than a minute. I know I sounded pompous, but how were any of us supposed to be enjoying ourselves? She didn't answer, so I got up from the table and went anyway, coming back with some Rennie which she obediently ingested. Bruton was famous for its public school, and the place was full of well-off parents and their snooty-sounding children. The walls echoed with the braying of the English upper class types I loathed, and I could tell my mum thought I was one of them now. I wasn't, but I wasn't the boy from Ponty I used to be, either.

She mimed that she needed the loo. I accompanied her, since it was in the basement, down some steep stairs she'd never negotiate on her own. I waited in the corridor. The door was half-open and I remember seeing her looking at herself. Not brushing her hair or applying lipstick, not doing anything in any way, just looking.

She came out, skin like chalk. I asked what was wrong. She pulled a face. I told her to sit down on the nearby bench. She made some guttural noises and I told her to take some deep breaths. Then she wasn't answering me anymore and suddenly her eyes rolled back in her head and she looked like she was going to faint.

A waiter appeared and I asked him to call an ambulance. He

came back within ten seconds and got her to lie flat on the floor. He was only young, about twenty, but he talked to her beautifully, soothing her in a way I couldn't. He said it was probably the heat in the restaurant, it had happened before, meaning with people her age.

Once the paramedics arrived I felt a surge of relief because somebody knew what they were doing. Her eyes were open but she was still lying on her back. I asked if she'd had a stroke or heart attack? They said, it doesn't look like that. "She's had a turn." It was as medically unspecific and galling as that. We had to drive to Yeovil hospital, which was in the opposite direction from home.

When we arrived there we could hear her voice behind a screen. The doctor, when he came, was Polish or Eastern European, singularly abrupt with her, which I knew would have upset her. All the questions I could have answered: what's your name, what happened, which I doubted she'd remember. Perhaps that was why they asked them, as some way of assessing potential damage to her brain. She was told her blood sugar was a bit low. He asked her what medication she was on. I knew she wouldn't know. ("What's that thing I have?" "Diabetes, Mum.") I had a list in my wallet. My brother did too, in case of emergencies. Funny thing is, I can recite them even now, like a prayer in Latin.

Isorbide mononitrate. Lansoprazole. Glicazide. Atenolol. Lisinipril. Atorvastatin. Metformin Hydrochloride.

"Look at the shape of me." She sat propped up in the hospital bed. Dark-rimmed panda eyes, looking pitiful. We told her not to worry. If there was something wrong, she was in the right place.

The nurse who adjusted her pillows had extensive tattoos. It triggered something, and I saw the toad in the 4x4. That screwed-up face. The mindless hatred spewing from that flaccid tongue and black throat.

Fucking CUNT!

I felt rage brewing, perhaps from hearing the doctor's voice, perhaps from the situation generally. I found my fingernails digging into my palms while I was talking. I suppose I felt I had no control. Perhaps you write because you want to be in control of things, and in the real world you can't. That has always been scary to me.

Affie asked if I was okay to drive. I said yes, of course I was. He couldn't drive anyway. What were we supposed to do? Get a taxi?

At the hospital I'd tried to shake the rubber face in the 4x4 from my head. Now, with the monotony of country lanes in front of me, and no conversation to distract me, the Neanderthal infested my thoughts all the way home. I tried to break out of the trap by saying to my mum that I wasn't best pleased how that doctor was talking to her. "Who?" "The doctor." "He was all right. He was nice. We had a bit of a laugh."

That made me even more furious. Did she have no conception of what had just occurred? Or did you get like that when you reached eighty? A severe medical crisis is just something you get up from, dust yourself off from, and go back to normal? It could be argued, what the hell alternative do you have?

She sat in the back. Quiet. Docile. Actually, in the reflection in the rear view mirror, she had more colour than I'd seen her have in months. I reassured myself that she'd been checked out, and she was fine. I don't know if I really believed that, or if I was deluding myself, looking back on it, but I do know that, as I drove, I fantasised punching that driver's face in, like a maverick cop in a TV series. I wanted to take him to a cellar like a macho, undercover CIA operative and attach the wires of a car battery to his balls. Oh, I could make up all sorts of horrible things to do to him. I was good at that. I could do what I wanted in my head. I could kill who I wanted, and get away with it. I had done. It was my living, after all.

Fucking CUNT!

I can see his face, and I'm listening to the producers. They're saying here's another thing they want changed, because the studio won't like it.

Your protagonist, Paul. She says fuck way too much!

No A-list actress is gonna want to play this role!

Look at it. Fuck . . . Fucking . . .

Every page! Every page!

I bite my tongue and say calmly, but with undeniable sarcasm, she *is* battling alien creatures at the time. She could be forgiven for saying the odd *fuck* under the circumstances.

The aliens are taking over the world and nobody believes her. They're coming through a portal into our dimension and they're out to kill her. Plus her husband has just been thrown off a tall building and ended up as strawberry jam.

Yeah, but we have to make her likeable, Paul, and she's just not LIKEABLE!

Always, always the note from the most horrible producers on the planet.

I want to ask them, these slime balls, do they ever think of how likeable *they* are? How *relatable* their own *redemptive character arc* might be, consisting as it did of regular duplicity, insincerity, distrust, double-dealing, and numerous instances of ass-fucking writers like me? Guys, honestly, what's *LIKEABLE* about *you?*

Take out all the fucks, Paul. See how it reads!

Christ. Really? Have they even *seen* a sci-fi or horror movie in the last ten years? Don't they know wall to wall *fucks* and *fuckings* go with the territory? The genre audience was raised sucking that teat, you self-basting fools. We're not aiming it at Mary Poppins. We're not aiming it at—*my mother.*

I must've been thirteen when I went with her to see *Cabaret* and she visibly withered at the single use of the f-word. She hated swearing—*proper* swearing—at the best of times. At home I never heard anything worse than "bloody" or "bugger," or "God" or "Christ," which populated my father's vocabulary with copious regularity. I didn't realise this for years, but my brother told me Dad once let out the word *"fuck"* by accident when they were driving to Iceland, and it was like a grenade had gone off in the car. Mum didn't speak to him for weeks.

And a "prick," I think there's a "prick" somewhere . . .

There's a "fucking prick."

We can lose the "fucking prick."

"Asshole?"

"Asshole" is fine.

I'm beyond arguing. An asshole is not a prick, but as I'm dealing with an asshole and a prick, I don't give a fuck. Except I do give a fuck about my work, and I sense this double act of the damned are killing the project every time they open their mouths, as surely as Moby Dick chewed up the hull of *The Pequod* and sent it in a slow but steady spiral to the bottom of the briny.

And if I didn't know it before, I know it now: my project is dead. I'm grinning, I'm nodding, but part of me is dead, too. Not for the first time, and not for the last. The LA shitmeisters are killing me, sentence by sentence, note by note. Bringing me back to life, then killing me all over again.

After the incident in Bruton, we drove Mum back to Wales without any relapses or repercussions. I thought the crisis was over, but it wasn't. It never is, when your parents get to a certain age, and I remember when Dad was ill, the threat of the telephone ringing in the middle of the night, as it sometimes had done, created a palpable physical dread that's still a muscle memory for me, a Pavlovian stiffening at the sound of the phone. Similarly, I'd reached the stage when my stomach flipped whenever my mum's number came up on the LCD screen.

I picked up after taking a deep breath. Why did it have to be so arduous, just speaking to her? Why did it upset me? I suppose because I couldn't make everything all right. I couldn't make her happy with the wave of a magic wand like I wanted to.

She told me she'd seen an acquaintance down the shop who told her she looked terrible. *Friend of your father, you remember*

Rhodri, down the cricket? He said, good God, Miriam, you need to get that checked out. I said, "Mum, you *did* get it checked out. They checked out everything." "Who?" "The doctors, who d'you think?"

It was almost like she wanted something to go wrong. Just to show me. To show me what, I don't know. To show me I wasn't there? I already knew that.

And two weeks after that last holiday with us, she had the fall.

Nice young couple next door were returning from work about six and heard her shouting. She'd gone out the back yard for some reason, had slipped and ended up on the ground and couldn't get up. God knows how long she'd been there on the cold paving stones, calling out. Hours, probably. They called my brother, finding his number in the notebook beside the phone in the front room, and said they'd already called an ambulance.

She was pumped with morphine by the time we got there. They'd done an X-ray and detected a broken hip, but remarkably, considering the legendary NHS waiting lists, they operated the next day. I wasn't complaining. When she came out of general anaesthetic she was groggy and talking complete gobbledegook. Martian. She had no idea she'd just had surgery. Kept wanting to get out of bed to make us a cup of tea, thinking she was at home. The nurse explained sometimes the anaesthetic affects people like that. They call it post-op delirium. Low blood sugar could add to her confusion, so they'd altered that. The doctor was more brutal.

She took me to a small room and said that some people get over it, some don't, depending on their state of mental health. It felt like a sucker punch. My mind was in overdrive trying to read between the lines of what she was saying to me. She wore flat shoes and a very obvious black wig, which I took to mean she was Jewish. She looked up my mother's file on a grubby, out of date computer, one an average secondary school would have junked years ago. I can never get my head around religious people who obey a book thousands of years old using things like computers and phones. Peering at the screen, she asked outright if my mother had dementia. I said I thought she did, but we hadn't had it diagnosed yet. We'd been waiting five months for an appointment with a consultant, and the irony was, our appointment was for two days' time. She gave an exasperated sigh and said that wasn't acceptable, she would see to it that Mum was diagnosed by a psychiatrist immediately, and we'd see how we went from there.

I wondered, where *would* we go from there?

"You know she isn't going to get better," she stated as fact, adding it was a one-way street, and we all had to be prepared for that. She said vascular dementia was like all little explosions going on all over the surface of the Death Star. I couldn't believe that the doctor was a *Star Wars* fan. I expected to be blinded by science, not blinded by science fiction. It was almost a joke, but there was nothing funny about it. I felt nauseous, keeping my feelings at bay, and at the same time memorising every detail to pass on to my brother, who'd be sure to interrogate me.

I returned to my mother's bed and she was resting, dull eyed, with the man beyond the curtain next to her wittering and calling hello. The nurse for some reason told us she'd spent £800 buying her son video games for Christmas, which I thought was ridiculous on a nurse's salary. What was going on in her head? "Have you been up Prince Charles?" It sounded like a piece of ghastly Julian Clary innuendo, until I realised she was comparing the various merits of local hospitals. "It's lovely up there." My mother's mouth hung open behind the oxygen mask, thin lips devoid of lipstick.

Three weeks she was in that hospital bed. We kept asking when she'd get a physio to help her walk, and they said that was being done, but she wasn't being very cooperative. I asked what they meant by "cooperative". They said they couldn't force people to do things they didn't want to. Patients had rights. Which was frustrating on the one hand, and reassuring on the other.

When it became clear she would soon be ready to leave, I remember going in for a meeting with a social worker. They'd assessed her capacity, and we'd been told then she'd likely end up as a placement, i.e. need 24-hr care. Hence the Discharge Planning Meeting (DPN).

I was surprised at the efficiency of the whole thing. Someone from every department was there. The nurse to talk about her medical needs, which they went through in detail, nutrition, mobility, CT scan, Mental Health report. Then there was an advocate simply there to speak on the patient's best interest, because she couldn't herself. Then there was the family—us four. Two brothers and their partners. The social worker looked like a PE teacher in his too-tight Cardiff City jersey open at the collar. The meeting lasted over three hours and covered absolutely everything. Given Mum now had a dementia diagnosis, it was a case of where she was going to go, and who was going to look after her. We knew she'd never allow carers to come into her home, so that was a no-no. But we all knew she couldn't look after herself either. There'd been an incident with her leaving the gas on that put the fear of God into me and Lyn, and we weren't at all sure she was eating properly. She'd say she'd had beans on toast for lunch—*dinner*—but when we looked, there'd be no can in the bin.

The social worker made a little diagram of Pros and Cons. Pro care home, Anti care home. Then my brother muscled in and said they'd just converted the garage into an annexe which could easily be a granny flat, and she could move in there. He said he'd never forgive himself if we didn't try. I thought it was a terrible idea—she'd be alone while my brother and his wife were out at work, imprisoned there staring out of the window all day—but I didn't argue. He was adamant he wanted to give it a go, and if it didn't work out, we'd think of something else. He then asked a question about the unhelpful physio and why our mother was unable to walk, which got the nurse's back up and she left the room.

The social worker said, "It's all right, she's upset." I said, "Hang on, with respect, this is about our mother. It's us who should be upset, not her." They all went quiet at that point.

As it transpired, we didn't need to see how it worked out.

Mum had a heart attack and died overnight. Apparently she'd woken, and forgetting she couldn't walk, got out of bed, probably to go to the loo. Then her leg had given way, and she'd fallen like a ton of bricks. Why someone wasn't keeping an eye on her I didn't know. It seemed the shock had triggered her attack. Her second fall was on the linoleum of the hospital ward, amongst all those geriatric strangers, at night, and that was that.

For all the talk of mini-strokes, cause of death: heart attack.

I didn't cry or break down or anything. I'm not that kind of person. I'm self-aware enough to know I turn things inwards. I don't talk about my feelings. I type them in the form of stories. They come out that way, if they come out at all. Affie, of course, wanted to hold me, to goad it out like raking an oyster from its shell, but I wasn't interested. I told him it didn't mean I wasn't grieving. I'll do it in my own way, not anybody else's. He said: "I know."

I tried to get back to normal. I tried to grasp it, but there was no normal any more. Some part of me knew that.

I tried to box away the experience, the way I did old projects once they were produced, or, more often, unproduced, but dead. We use that word: *"It's dead."* Well, she was the dead project now. I had to put it behind me, but the image was difficult to eradicate. The picture of her in her nightie, keeling over, hitting the floor with a crunch of pain. A brittle, immobile stick figure with frightened eyes on the cold linoleum as her heart went into spasm.

Fucking CUNT!

The epithet cut through me like a rusty knife.

I couldn't edit it out. That sliver of time. Those four or five seconds. What came before. What came after. The avalanche. The tsunami. Before it? Peace. A plateau of un-knowing. The squirrels on the wall. My mother's weightless arm crooked around my elbow.

Fucking CUNT!

I couldn't stop it.

Couldn't stop thinking of my mum standing there on the pavement, looking both ways, like she was in the Tufty club or something, hanging on my arm and starting to cross, and the 4x4 coming round the bend, that face framed in the window, that wind tunnel of a mouth, shouting.

Fucking CUNT!

Two words. That was all

Two words—but that was when it all started going downhill.

The *inciting incident* for everything that followed. The pain in her chest. The scene at the restaurant the next day. The dash to Yeovil hospital. Her fall in the back yard. The hip replacement. The final, fatal heart attack on the ward . . . I could see it all now, absolutely clearly, laid out in my mind's eye like the fifty index cards that went into planning the structure of a screenplay, scene by scene.

Fucking CUNT!

If not for those two, stupid, verminous words, I thought, my mother might still be with us. If not for that one stupid, ignorant idiot . . .

In that long meeting we'd had with the social worker I'd known what was going through my brother's mind. I knew why he was agitated. He wanted to find someone responsible for what had happened. To apportion blame. But I'd sat there in silence. Because I knew who to blame all along.

Considering he'd been so outspoken at the hospital, Lyn didn't want to say anything at the funeral, which didn't surprise me. He'd even broken into a sweat giving the speech at his wedding. Fine. I'd put words in people's mouths for twenty years. I'd even written a fair few funeral scenes in my time.

That moment when the pallbearers stand back and bow their heads at the coffin always gets to me, I don't know why. The simple act of respect for the dead. I looked away. Didn't want to lose it. Not that early, anyway.

When my father passed away, two hundred people sang "Jerusalem" and raised the roof like a male voice choir. Not as many turned out for my mum, which was to be expected. He had a throng of sports cronies. She had a sprinkling of family from Merthyr, most ailing or on Zimmer frames. Too many people at my dad's funeral had said they'd meet up with her, be sure to pop in for a cup of tea and a chat, but never did.

I wrote the part about her early life myself. Her father, George, had been a collier and later ran several pubs in the area alongside his wife Ruby—small, "chopsy" and ginger. My mum, when she was old enough, used to help behind the bar, having left school, which she absolutely hated, early. She used to tell the story that one of the teachers caught her daydreaming one day. "Miriam Griffiths, you're not that clever you can afford to stare out the window!"

I chose another story she loved to tell—or I loved to hear, anyway. The time Monty, her dog, stole somebody's dentures and ran off down Taff Street with the false teeth in this mouth, looking like he was grinning madly. Another concerned her father being paid with a live hen, and having to kill it himself in the yard behind the pub—at which point the chicken started running around without its head.

We were the custodians of those memories now. They were our stories to tell.

She used to play piano in the bar, entertaining her brother Maldwyn and his mates. One night some fool made faces behind her back, while the pals all hooted with laughter. "Who was that dull bloke acting the goat?" she asked her brother. Didn't like him much. Married him all the same. We were left to our thoughts as a threnody played. "The Blue Danube." Piano version.

I did two short readings: Clive James' poem "Japanese Maple" which I'd heard the author read on TV and found very moving, though I concentrated too much on not fluffing any lines to do it justice. Then a piece from "Grief is the Thing with Feathers" by Max Porter, a sad and strange book about two boys who have lost their mother. I took pause a few times and stopped dead once. A chasm.

The Humanist celebrant—none of us were religious, and Mum certainly wasn't—said we were there to celebrate her life and mark it in time, and to take a moment to remember what a good and kind woman she was, and that family and children were everything to her. Which was true.

The exit music was one I remembered from sitting with my mother as a child watching *The Glenn Miller Story* on TV, starring James Stewart and June Allyson. A real Hollywood weepie. Indeed, Mum had displayed tears on her cheeks as she watched it. Dad had tut-tutted from behind *The Echo*, saying she was bloody soft to get upset over a film. Mum had said "Yes, well, I don't start crying when somebody kicks a ball into the back of the net, like some people."

We left the building to the strains of "Moonlight Serenade". Thinking of her tears at a soppy black and white movie, holding back our own.

When we got home Affie and I went to bed. It was only three in the afternoon, but we were exhausted. He made me tea. I told him I wasn't an invalid. The restless, angry, numb feeling didn't go away. I wanted somebody to explain how I was feeling now I didn't have any parents and was alone in the world, but nobody could. It was something I was going to have to work out all on my own.

Then one evening, weeks later, everything changed.

Affie was away in Nigeria—his work at the National Museum in Benin, organising exhibitions of the famous "Bini" sculptures, had led to his current job as Curator of Ethnography in Bristol—

so I was rattling around in my own cage. Not getting the page count I wanted done. Not able to concentrate. Wasting too much time scrolling through Twitter, which just got me more uptight, instead of less. I ordered a pizza by phone and decided to take a walk beside the river for the requisite twenty minutes before collecting it. Fresh air would do me good. I hadn't been outside the door all day, which wasn't unusual when I was under the cosh.

I stretched my shoulders as I headed down the hill, the quiet cul-de-sac where we lived, off the town centre. The pub on the corner had been called The Kings Arms when we moved in, then was pitifully rebranded The Sprat and Carrot, filled with mindless regalia such as lobster pots and tin signs from a bygone era, then, equally inexplicably, reverted back to being The King's Arms again.

I instantly recognised the lumpen, golf ball head of the figure lolling in its porch. Superdry tracksuit top and matching white jogging bottoms. Stains on the leg. Lurching, pissed. Red flip-flops. Benidorm chic. Voice a rancid crackle from a life support of fags. Pink neck pencilled with white scars. Shades like an Alice band atop the shiny pate. Undecipherable growl revealing misshapen, peg-like teeth blackened by plaque. Gums full of ulcers courtesy of long term heroin usage.

Fucking CUNT!

I slowed down, but not much, before the oik whose face I'd seen in the window of the 4x4 flicked away his dog end and ambled down towards the mini-roundabout, with an oily, unshaven *confrère* in tow whose greasy hair fell to the shoulders of his motorcycle jacket, making him look like a sad refugee from a heavy metal tribute band.

Fucking CUNT!

His words smouldered in my memory as I watched him put up his hand to slow down a driver so that he could cross the road, a second cigarette shaking from packet to palm. Tats everywhere. Adorning himself like a Maori warrior when his own cultural identity didn't go much further than pissing in a bus shelter after ten pints.

Staggering through town, he zigzagged over the ancient stone bridge, a visual assault on the prettiness of the buildings around him, houses where generations of hardworking citizens, weavers and Huguenots, had lived and worked and loved. I felt sick. Sick he was walking the earth and my mother wasn't.

Perhaps some might say I lost my reason at that point, but I would say I very much found it. Either way, I didn't want to look at him anymore. It was too upsetting. I turned back.

The pizza was like cardboard. I threw it in the bin. I sat at my laptop and told myself to type, just type, just type anything.

EXT. PUB—DAY

I stared at it. The cursor kept winking at me. A wink that said, I know you of old. You can't do this stuff. You never could do this stuff. It was all an illusion. I thought of the TV scripts I'd done—*Proctor*, that had got an RTS award, two seasons of *Hellbent*—the plays like *Assisted Crying* and *Bloody Lefties*, and the movies; *By the Light of Darkness; Dead White Men.* Then I was swamped with all the ones that hadn't come to fruition, the children that ended up in an early grave. *Zugun. Sergeant Bertrand. Rabbit on a Chair. Diddums* . . . the list was endless. My life story. Made up of stories that hadn't happened.

But this story *could* happen . . . *This* story could be real.

I was counting on the fact he was a regular. The following afternoon I went in, ordered a Diet Coke, and sat reading my book, *The Collected Stories of Flannery O'Connor*, having chosen a table at the back, in the shadows, but a good vantage point to observe the door.

I'd read five stories and was about to leave when the creature from the 4x4 rolled in. Spruced up, but not much. Stepped-out-of-the-shower redness. Been on the tiles, had a skinful, slept till noon. Now he wanted a few pints to take the edge off. Hair of the dog. What a miserable existence.

He smoked outside the window while his pint was pulled. Through the dust I saw him blowing smoke, chattering on his phone, hopping from foot to foot, jangling, looking at himself in the reflection in the window pane. Loving himself. Glasses on. Glasses off. Hanging up with a poke of the finger as if he wanted it to go in somebody's eye.

Came back in. Nasty mood now. *Get it down you,* said the leather-bound *confrère*, his own face a prize-winning ad for virulent acne. 4x4 took a long slurp, wiped his upper lip, nested his rump on a stool, shaking his head.

What he was thinking about I didn't know. All I knew was he wasn't thinking about my mother. He wasn't thinking about that coffin going behind that beige curtain in that very *beige* crematorium to the sound of Andrea Bocelli singing "Con Te Partiro". I was positive he hadn't thought about her for an instant since that day when the car swerved to avoid her. She meant nothing to him.

He was on his phone again, poking it like a chimp. Laughing, joking.

The pint was followed by cider. Then another pint. Whiskey at the side. Peanuts into the gob. More cider flowing into the drain.

I was well aware he might look over at me at any minute, so I kept my head down, but he never did, or if he did, I had my nose in my paperback. Not that he'd notice anyone like me. His type didn't, unless it was to bash our faces in.

I turned pages. He ordered drinks with an imbecile grunt.

I saw them mount up. Guinness with a short, lager with a short. Always at least one glass in front of him.

Two teenage girls in the corner suffered a swagger of repulsive banter. How the cretin thought he might in any way be attractive was beyond my faculties of perception. But that's where his barely hominid brain took him, immune from any sense of rejection, failure, shame, or embarrassment. Animal through and through. I almost expected a hoof to paw the ground when the girls left. He gave the blonde one a lingering look up and down, felt his crotch as he turned back to the bar and said he wouldn't mind if he did. *Don't think much of yours. Mind you, bet her hole's had a bit of cock. Be like throwing a chipolata through a barn door, that one.*

The barman laughed, called him a fucking pig under his breath.

Oik unruffled by the accusation. Perhaps flattered. His friend absented himself about six-thirty, with better things to do. He himself indulged in a quick Bell's and exited soon after. By then I knew what I was going to do. It was just a question of how I was going to do it. I'd been pretending to read the book, but I hadn't been taking in a word. I had my own plot to figure out.

Handing over my empty glass as I left, I asked the barman who the feller was with the shaved head. I said I kept seeing him around town. "Character."

"He has his moments, does Aidan." He mopped up the piss-head's spillage with a cloth. "Been banned from every pub in town, but he's going through a bad time of it at the moment. Wife's left him. Lives on his own down Berryfields. Someone's got to take pity on him."

Boo hoo, I thought. Chronic alcoholic and shit-faced junkie. Fact he probably roughed her up on a regular basis was a given.

"Thanks."

Outside, I watched the bubble-gum pink skull atop jogging gear get turned away from The Bear. Followed as he veered into the Grocery Basket, emerging with a six pack of Stella and a bottle of Johnnie Walker red label.

Provisions. Loser.

He stumbled out of the town centre, down the Trowbridge Road. I kept a safe distance, but he clearly wasn't in any state to notice anyone or anything short of a bomb dropping. For most of the route he kept his head down with a forward tilting gait. Wise move.

I wasn't surprised he lived in Berryfields, the kind of nondescript, aesthetic-free modern estate property developers erect in a matter of months, down by The Beehive, bordered on the other side by the Kennett and Avon. Populated mostly by housebound retired couples, with a small number of residences begrudgingly put over to social housing and the odd cannabis farm.

He headed towards a tiny house with the pathetic design feature of a canopy over its front door, as if that was an artistic flourish that might appeal to anyone but the brain dead. Key in the lock, he was inside. A dog had deposited a pyramidal shit on the path, maybe the same one that was barking somewhere. Still, the place was a lot nicer than this knuckle-dragger deserved. I wondered how much he was getting from social services to keep himself in the manner to which he was accustomed.

The light came on. I saw the coloured shapes of widescreen HD. What was on? I looked at my watch. Five to seven. I reckoned *Hollyoaks.* Stone the crows. *If you have been affected by any of these issues* . . . Yes, I have. It's a pile of crap with rubbish acting. That's my issue.

I walked back home, unable to remove the image of the oik with the remote in his hand peeling off his fetid T-shirt to expose a corpse's skin, hard line between his sunburned neck and a torso looking as if it had never seen daylight. Horribly, he'd run his podgy fingers over his flaccid breasts and belly. I'd nearly puked at the notion of another person touching that repellent surface.

Waste of fresh air.

The phrase had been used on a cop procedural I'd been watching on TV—*Bosch*, on Amazon Prime, based on the novels of Michael Connolly. The dialogue was sharp, authentic, and Harry Bosch, as the morose and troubled central character, was full of spiky angst and a back-story chock full of trauma, from PTSD in the Iraq war to seeing his prostitute mother murdered as a child. That's what he, the acerbic Los Angeles police detective, had called some low life in one episode:

A waste of fresh air.

I spent an hour at home. Long enough to collect what I needed and look up what I wanted on the internet. My mind was racing, but everything was falling into place extremely neatly.

I got in the car. Reversed out of our parking space. Drove.

Not to Berryfields. In the opposite direction. Actually went north, towards the M4, into Gloucester. Felt right to aim for a different county. Technically I didn't need to travel that far, but I did. I don't know why. Maybe I wanted to distance my normal life from the act I was about to undertake.

Around Stroud, in one of those Laurie Lee valleys I sometimes went with Affie to find a cream tea place, I found a track off into some woods, about as far from CCTV coverage as could be reasonably imagined. Police investigations are all CCTV footage, DNA matches, and number plate recognition. That's what hundreds of hours in front of cop shows and *24 Hrs in Police Custody* did for you. I didn't want any rookie blunders to trip me up.

I took the five litre—one gallon—plastic jerry can from the boot. I'd known there was one in the cellar amongst the residue of Affie's abortive attempt to make home brew, and it would do nicely. I'd watched a video online, surprisingly easy to find, and had learnt how to extract fuel from my tank in the absence of a siphon pump, and without getting a mouthful of unleaded. It didn't look that complicated.

I unscrewed the cap, inserted a length of tube and put the other end into the plastic container. I'd cut a second length of garden hose, and put that in the tank, wrapping a cloth around both and making sure it was wedged well in. I blew through the shorter tube, and, after two or three attempts, the petrol came out in a steady flow. I screwed the cap back on tightly and threw away my rubber gloves. The jerry can securely in the back, I started the ignition and made my way back to the main road. Gratified that the fuel gauge had hardly dropped, yet I had more than sufficient for my purpose.

I drove back to Bradford, feeling strangely energised. The radio was going over the news repetitively, so I put on a CD of *Deluge* by Jocelyn Pook. Entering town, I didn't take a right as I usually did up our cul-de-sac. I kept going straight, across the mini-roundabout and over the bridge, following the Trowbridge Road.

I didn't like the look of where I was intending to park—by the patch of greenery next to the towpath. No other cars were parked there, and I'd stand out like a sore thumb, so I kept on driving, really just keeping on the move for the sake of it, till it got dark, which it did, at about ten o'clock. My hands got clammy on the steering wheel and the heater seemed to be pushing dusty air back at my face so I switched it off. I ate a Picnic and read *The Guardian* I'd picked up at a local newsagent's earlier. Some god-awful opera getting five times the coverage as the previous night's telly. It was ever thus.

I pulled into a side street—no cameras—adjusted my chair, and snoozed for an hour, or tried to. Didn't drift off. Didn't fully expect to. The smell of the petrol was pungent. Nevertheless, I rested my eyes for a while, and when I opened them it was dark, and chilly. I started the engine. The dashboard clock said it was past twelve, so I must have dozed off after all.

I drove to Berryfields. The coast was clear. No joggers or dog walkers. No drug deals in progress. I got out of my car and zipped up my body warmer, pulled up the hood of the sweater I'd selected to wear underneath. I'd removed the branding from the material. Black in colour.

Street lamps now cast a bilious sheen. The horse-shoe of dwellings sported petals of vehicles in driveways.

A light shone upstairs. The man who killed my mother had gone to bed. I wondered if he was sitting up reading Proust. Or was it Aldous Huxley? Camus, perhaps? The light went out. I thought of him wanking off into a pair of soiled underpants, then coiling up under his putrid, flea infested duvet, an illuminated manuscript of blood, urine and spunk.

A waste of fresh air.

Back in my car, I turned on the radio again. One of those turgidly unfunny programmes that Radio Four produces on a regular basis, broadcast from some crèche of Footlights rejects, had me lunging for the off switch, but it had already started to make me anxious, as if I wasn't already.

I sat in silence for a while and thought about what I was about to do. A stray song lyric entered my mind about Peter Lorre "contemplating a crime" but I couldn't identify the song. Other thoughts intruded, which I tried to shut out. I needed to keep calm. Weirdly, I *was* calm all of a sudden. I think, for me, stress comes from anticipating the worst, but when it happens the tension dissipates. For instance, I hate travel, but when our luggage was lost by Air France that time, I became uncharacteristically Zen about it. So it was that night as I climbed out of the car into the still, empty air between me and the house.

The walk to the front door took about a minute. I soaked an old rag in petrol—nothing that could be identified, not a T-shirt or anything. Gently wedged the letterbox open with some folded cardboard from an old Amazon package. Using the same technique I'd used with the fuel tank, I extracted the contents of the container, and let it flow through the tube onto the floor of the hall.

I could hear it spreading indoors. I was terrified the smell would wake him, but after all that booze I was pretty sure he would be sleeping like a rock.

I lit the rag with my Zippo—a birthday gift from Affie—then stuffed it through the letterbox. It dropped with a fuff of smoke and for a horrible moment I thought it had gone out. Patting flames from my fingers, wiping my gloves on my jeans, I extracted the piece of cardboard quickly but carefully so the letterbox didn't snap, and backed away.

The light didn't come on.

I chose not to run, in case by some fluke someone saw me, but walked, shooting a glance over my shoulder to see a substantial flickering glow beyond the textured glass of the front door.

The bedroom light still didn't come on.

I didn't look back a second time. I reached my car, twisted the key in the ignition, and drove home. Not with any undue acceleration that might attract attention to the vehicle. That would be disastrous, potentially. I pulled back my hood and unzipped my body warmer. Both were going to go into a black bag and out with the rubbish. The cardboard from the Amazon delivery would go in the recycling.

I sniffed my fingers and washed them thoroughly as soon as I got in. Nails brushing palms. Rubbing the valleys between fingers, then circling the wrists, the way surgeons did. I could still smell petrol so put on sanitiser, then hand cream. My skin absorbed it in seconds.

I poured a Bushmill's. Ice, no water. Put on music—Bronski Beat, "Smalltown Boy". The synthesisers took me away to another place. I remembered standing in the kitchen at home—the home I was born in—and my mother saying she thought that singer, Jimmy Somerville, was "you know". That was when I told her I was too. "*You know.*" She didn't look at all shocked. I asked her if Dad would be angry. She shrugged and said he wouldn't be bothered. "He'd be more bothered if you announced you were playing football for England."

I took out an old photo album. Weird to think youngsters don't have them these days. There is no record. Just the narcissistic fragments digitally captured on their phones. Not the actuality of these rectangles with white borders we used to collect from Boots the Chemist.

There she was, hand on hip, head tilted. I turned the page. Same tilt of the head. Hair a little tossed by the wind. No grey. Not yet. Brecon, it looked like. Dad grinning, but then he always was. For the camera anyway. Shot of them in our garden, holding up the BAFTA I'd got for *The Black Faced Sheep*, looking really happy. She always liked to know what I was up to, whether anything was being filmed. Mostly she wanted to know what actors I'd met. Thrilled when it was someone she'd seen on *Midsomer Murders* or *New Tricks*. She'd settle in her armchair like a hen on her eggs. "Right, that's one I'll just happen to slip into the conversation when I go down the shop tomorrow."

Isorbide mononitrate. Lansoprazole. Glicazide. Atenolol. Lisinipril, Atorvastatin. Metformin Hydrochloride . . .

It would be self-serving to say I couldn't sleep, but I did. Spark out. I was shattered.

Four, five hours later, wide awake. Prone in blackness. Craning to hear a fire engine or police siren. Feeling my throat clogged up, almost expecting to smell smoke in the air. Sitting up to get phlegm out into a bedside tissue.

As an oily sun started to seep in through the blinds, I opened my laptop. Saw that Affie was online, posting silly things on Facebook. I sent him a message. We hooked up by Skype. It was good to see his face. He has a nice face. I think he looks like a child. I can't imagine him looking any different when he was six years old.

I asked him what Oyo was like. He returned with a question about what I felt like when I went to Wales. Nigeria was a romantic destination to me, it was where we'd met after all, but to him it was somewhere parochial and narrow. He'd gone for his sister's wedding, and taking me was a bad idea since they were devout Christians. I asked him how the festivities had gone. "You know. Christians," he said. I said, "Nigerians." He said, "Nigerian Christians," like it was the worst combination, and hooted with laughter.

He said one of his cousins had got drunk and flicked a piece of wedding cake at him. He never liked the cousin and picked up a thick wedge of cake, on its plate, and threw the whole thing, plate, fork, everything, at the guy's head. "You've never seen anyone move so quickly in your life."

I laughed, wondering if it sounded like an effort, or false. Actually it wasn't an effort, or false. He asked what I'd done.

"Nothing much."

"Tell me."

"Boring."

"Bore me."

"Went out for a meal."

"Went out for a meal," he repeated with that lovely drumbeat of an African accent.

I fabricated a trip to a pub. Fish, nice cod, and thrice-cooked chips. Tartare sauce. Mushy peas. Bottle of Sol. Bread and butter pudding.

"You are the king of bread and butter pudding. You are going to have love handles by the time I return."

"Long as you return."

"Hey."

"I love you," I said.

He said it too. It was nice to hear, even at that distance. Even disembodied. "Let's go to the pub when I come back. Same pub. Same fish and chips."

It was a plan we stuck to. Five days later I picked him up from Gatwick. We were too tired to cook, so decided to go down the hill and order food at The King's Arms. Piss poor choice of wine, so we opted for two San Miguels. I asked Affie if he was feeling culture shock getting back. He said yes. "Lack of." I laughed and told him to put a bone through his nose, that'd go down well. He said he thought of going the full Rorke's Drift.

I smiled. "Zulu the musical."

"I've seen worse."

I said, "I've written worse."

While he used the loo, I went to the bar to order another round. The first hadn't touched the sides. While I waited I picked up a copy of the local newspaper that happened to be sitting there, folded in half.

KILLER BLAZE

Dad and two daughters killed in Bradford house fire
Murder probe launched as three found dead

A father and his young daughters have died after a blaze erupted at their house in Parfitt Close on Friday night.
The tragic family, named locally as Aidan Chronister, 42, his daughter Hettie, 8, and her sister Daisy, 5, all died inside the property.
Police said it is believed to be an isolated incident.
Fire crews were initially called to the home at around 2.30 a.m. Saturday and police arrived at the scene a short time later.
A joint police and fire investigation has been launched. It is not yet clear how the fire started.
Mr Chronister had worked as a drayman but was currently unemployed.
His former wife Caroline, who works at a supermarket, is reported to have posted on social media: "I have lost my whole family."
One neighbour described the moment he saw smoke pouring out one of the windows of the three bedroom house in Berryfields.
The 67-year-old man said: "I just looked out of my bathroom window. I didn't see fire, just smoke. I got straight on the phone to the emergency services."
Another resident said that parents had recently split up, but Mr Chronister always looked after the girls at the weekend. "Caroline would turn up at 8.30 on Friday to drop them off. He was a good dad. They were always laughing and smiling. We were shocked. You don't expect things like this to happen on your own doorstep."
Detective Inspector Rob Cernow of Avon and Somerset Major Crime Unit said: "Our thoughts are with the family and friends of the three people at this difficult time."
Police described all three deaths as suspicious and have launched a murder investigation, but indicated that there was unlikely to be a threat to the wider community.

I folded the newspaper in two and placed it down again on the wet beer mat.

My credit card bleeped contactlessly as I paid for the drinks. I looked over at Affie, who was pointing down at the plates, beckoning me to join him back at the small, round table. The food was there and it was getting cold. I sat down on the stool, then got up.

"What's the matter?"

"Salt and vinegar," I said. I didn't want him to see my face. I didn't want him to see my eyes. "I forgot the salt and vinegar." But within minutes I was telling him I didn't feel well and wanted to go home.

In bed I felt his cold body against mine, frosted by the chill of night, his breath salt sweet as he kissed me, and felt the sudden urge to wrap him in my arms. I clung to him like driftwood, holding the back of his neck and pressing his chin to my shoulder so that he couldn't see the tears running down my cheeks. But he could hear me trying to hold them back.

"Hey. Hey. Hey."

His voice, his sympathy, his love, crushed me. The sobbing gushed out. I thought it would never stop. It continued for minutes. Relentlessly. He held me in his arms, I think for hours. In bed, downstairs, in the kitchen. Every time it surged up afresh, he was there. Arms outstretched. He didn't let me go. His generous soul encompassed me and accepted me, even when I was wrecked. Broken. In dead of night.

"It's good. Let it out," he said. "This is good. This is good. This is what you needed."

I could not tell him the truth. Tell him what I had done.

I could not tell him about the children.

Children . . .

He held my downcast face in his hands, turned it up towards his own, and wiped the tears from my red raw eyes with his thumbs. He was happy the dam had burst. He was happy I had emerged from my cocoon of grief over my mother at last.

"A new beginning. A new you," he said, magnificently.

I nodded, rubbing my eyes with the heels of my hands like a four-year-old. Knowing even as he pulled me into his vast embrace, that whatever I might share with him in the years we might have together, I could never share the secret that would blacken and scorch my heart forever.

And the producers are talking, still, but I'm not listening.

Reg? What kind of name is that for her husband? Reg! It's a weird name.

It's an English name. I've never heard it. Have you heard it?

Roy. Let's call him Roy.

Roy is good.

Everyone knows a Roy.

I've long given up caring, but as my US agent always tells me, never walk, always wait till they fire you. Think of the money.

So I'll get the notes and I'll do the notes, and *Reg* will transform into *Roy*, or *Chuck*, or *Jack*, and I'll press DELETE on all the *fucks* and *fucking* and *motherfuckers* and *motherfucking* because—hey, it's only the end of the world, and my hero/heroine/star will be *likeable,* kind, sweet, gorgeous, slim, all of which is sure to add up to a box office slam dunk. Hell, she'll be even *more* likeable at the end than she was at the beginning, and she was kind to children and rescued injured animals in the first five pages! And in the third act she saves the whole of mankind!

Enough of a character arc? Probably not.

But I'll bank the cheque, tot up the WGA residuals—and take to the Bushmill's if I have to . . . and take to the photograph album if I have to—and be free of another round of idiot meetings with millionaire plankton who know nothing about, and care nothing about, story, character, meaning, life, or what makes people do things, and I'll be finished, at last, on this, at least, and the work will be done. *FADE OUT.* Press SEND, and you know what? Live to write another day. Nobody died.

As they say.

As my US agent says, from his office in the Avenue of the Stars, from Tinsel Town, where the sun never stops shining.

Hey . . . Nobody died.

Agog

AGOG SITS NAKED upon a hump, a fort as was, battlements now ghosts, where once a beacon burned in celebration or warning of some foreign foe, his bare arse nestled in a soft cushion of brambles and blackthorn, evicted sparrows having scattered, his thighs as hairy and filthy as his history.

Agog is the last of Albion's giant race, and, being the last, both proud and melancholy under the burden of his loss. His towering ancestors are now still, now grime. His forebears lucky if they are bones. Though he had known them but briefly, his memory of them cuts deep. His Maw. Her vast, hanging breast. How it obliterated the sun, and was very tasty.

Agog looks down upon the moon-bathed eiderdown before him. The flat pelt of the Levels, broken only by the erection of the Tor. This hillock under him, once residence of chieftains, is his favourite place. It has been his perching spot for aeons as he watches generations come and go, the land flickering from season to season, ploughed brown changing to emerald green, twinkling with frost or shimmering with damp.

Agog sits atop of it, arms wrapped around his shins. Bony knees against his chest, scabbed and dusted by dry skin. Legs the envy of tree trunks. Balls like boulders. Feet like funeral barges. Toenails like the dulled shields of weary knights.

Agog hears his tummy rumble. It shouldn't do. He'd eaten that cow for din-dins. Indigestion, methinks. Wind to the wind required. He lifts one buttock and lets rip. Better out than in. The fart floats like a wraith over hill and dale.

Agog couldn't say the land comforted him, nor was he comforted by it. But it was *his* land. The certainty of that ran in his blood. Sometimes they conversed. Sometimes the land was uncommunicative. Sometimes a chatterbox.

Agog wonders if men ever have such conversation. They never seemed to. Men dig, and discover, and use, and move on, to discover more. Use more. They never pause. That's the thing about men, he has noticed. Giants pause all the time. Their lives are one big pause, in fact.

Agog gives a sigh. Watches it ripple through the valley below. It rustles bushes for a full five minutes. When they have settled, he winks at a passing vixen, who looks startled and flits away to her cubs. He likes it when the moon gives life to the earth, when the hustle and bustle comes, gossipy and rummaging, and is sad when it is dampened at the rise of the sun, who always arrives officious and parent-like.

Agog likes hours like these, slow as a grandfather slug.

Agog likes being alone. It doesn't worry him, he tells himself.

Agog likes his own company. It's the only company he can get, aside from slithery things and the odd antlered beauty. Only a fool would crave what he can never have. The thought is as regular as the toll of a church bell o'clock. He's even bored by the gloom of it, but can't bat it aside. Maybe only a fool tries to.

Agog doesn't think he is a fool, but it's a debate he carries on his shoulders every day. To give up the craving, would that make him happier? He doesn't know. But when he hears the hum coming from the other side of the forest, he can't help himself. His back straightens and he sniffs the acorn and pine air. His optimism gets the better of him. His optimism is the one thing that the centuries have not worn down.

Agog rises to his feet. Squints. He can see it now. Its lights flickering between the black bars of trees on the fringe of the hill opposite, weaving along the course of the snaking road down into the dip where the pleasure boats glide, the cream teas are served, and the parking is situated. Without hesitation, he lumbers thunderously down the slope, sending rabbits packing.

Agog plants his feet in the path of the car. The headlights illuminate the corns and warts in bilious yellow, the cracked and crusted nails, the bristly hair of his ankles. Body. Face.

Agog sees the driver yank the steering wheel to the left and is spot-lit no more. The vehicle veers into darkness, skidding into a soft patch of spraying gravel and mud. The brakes abruptly stop it hitting a looming, brightly burned-out dry stone wall.

Agog straightens his spine, rubbing the small of his back. The run and a jump over that last five-bar gate took it out of him. He is breathless, but exhilarated. His scrotum shakes as he laughs and claps his hands, disturbing nocturnal wildlife for miles around.

Agog hears the driver shouting that she'd seen something in the middle of the road, had swerved to avoid hitting it. She asks the man if he'd seen it too. He says he hadn't. Of course he hadn't! There was nothing! She'd taken her eyes off the road! She hadn't been concentrating, woman! He called her Woman. She was one, after all. Woman said there was. There really was something in front of her! Man, standing in the road now, looks all around and asks her where it is now, then, eh, eh? Where is it? Woman can only repeat that it was there. Woman *saw* it!

Agog, invisible, nods in agreement. Creaks to a crouch, scratching at the pattern of tyre marks on the tarmac with his index finger, then scratching his armpit and thereafter feeling obliged to smell his fingers, which are sour.

Agog frowns, and finds his face sagging as he listens to the duo argue. One see. One not see. One blind. The other mad. He could roll the dice as many times as he liked, but the number would always be the same. She had sensed him, even glimpsed him. A beautiful occurrence. A rare occurrence! He could add up the number of times that had happened on the fingers of one hand.

Sensed? Yes, sometimes! A tremble at his presence? Yes, often! *Seen?*—almost never. But now her doubts had set in and the shutters had come down. She perceives him not—only shadows.

Agog's heart plummets. He wants to beg her to stay, to be with him, just for a minute, a moment, but the only sound that comes out of him is the lowing of a bull. The words of giants are unheard by small people. They are deaf as well as blind. He should know that by now. But a giant can dream . . . can't he?

Agog hears Man say, those brake pads will probably need replacing now. Man says, that's going to be a trip to the repair shop I can do without. Woman says it's not her fault. Man asks whether it was his, then? Answers question himself: *No, it wasn't!* Getting back into the car, in the passenger seat now, Woman tells him, thank you for a lovely night out. The giant looks down through their sun roof as she clips on her seat belt. Both do. The ignition starts and they are gone, and so is he. Destined to be a figment.

Agog, abandoned to darkness as his shoulders droop, sighs again. He looks at his hands, front and back. Centuries ingrained there. Remembers washing off the mud of the Somme in the stagnant pool of a shell crater. Gone to war to defend his country, just like the little ones. They'd lied about their ages; he couldn't count his in numbers that small. Remembers marching beside those khaki battalions—towering over them—but not one of the soldiers looking up at him. He'd looked down to see them, though, with their eyes fixed forward, at the enemy, seeing death, but not seeing the glorious giant in their midst, whose footfalls smashed the enemy gun emplacements harder than any cannon fire. He had done his bit. He was unseen, but he was with them. What more could he have done?

Agog didn't know then, and doesn't know now. He only knows that an invisible existence is hard to bear. He could have touched them . . . that was it. Looked into their eyes. Shared their pain, at least that. Or did he want them to share his?

Agog trudges back to his vantage point, swatting bats from his penumbra, splashing through a stream as he recalls the trenches and the victory parades. Swimming home alongside ships full of Tommies, as he had once swum beside Merlin's fleet to Ireland when another enemy threatened, but Merlin, for all his supernatural powers, saw him not. Though once mistook the wake for that of a whale. On their return from rugged Eire, Agog had lifted up and placed those Saracen stones atop the henge on Salisbury Plain, the wizard taking all the credit. Claiming levitation by his magical arts to be the cause, his juddery arms outstretched to make a drama of it. Once primed, the engine of the stones kept the forces of evil at bay—though Agog had a hand in it too. Not wishing to brag. It was his job, and purpose in life. His vocation, if you will. The protection of his native Isles from invaders. As had been that of all his kind before him.

Agog often wondered why, hand-in-hand with that duty thrust upon him, there'd come a curse. A curse to be forever outside the reach of human eyes and minds. To be beyond all human grasp, let alone tenderness. To be huge, yet nothing.

Agog had grown accustomed to that role, nevertheless, though it never gave him peace. At a low ebb, he once asked the rooks if he was created by The Devil. The rooks never replied. A god, then? They choked on their laugher, and have done ever since.

Agog had accrued hundreds of years unseen and unloved. And, while it is true that giant's years and human years pass differently, the unhappiness of that condition can be imagined by most. No co-ogre shared his star-lit bed. No small man, nor small woman, had ever whispered in his ear, or combed his beard with the spine of a narwhal, or lovingly extracted his ear wax.

Agog had never once laid eyes upon a she-giant with whom to mate—for, in all his travels, he'd found none existed, outside of graves. Nevertheless, he found himself aroused by observing morsels in the act, their mousy ruttings intoxicating. As they were intoxicated, generally, themselves. On these occasions he took to the icy waterfalls of the Highlands to dampen his ardour. When he washed—once a decade, whether he needed to or not—he saw his reflection, and occasionally it made him ponder those who looked like him and had been lost. The only other, now, gazed back at him, disappearing in concentric circles as his fist struck the surface of the pool.

Agog, in his time, had trodden the battlefields of Agincourt and Waterloo. Saved the day at both, or given a substantial contribution. Not that he liked to be big-headed about it. Though his head was—hard to avoid the fact—big. Waist-deep in the English Channel, he had punched holes out of the hulls of the Spanish Armada, though Drake put the success down to—surprise!—himself. So be it. History was written by men, for men. It would be nice to be acknowledged once in a while, but Agog didn't dwell on it. He'd discovered time and again that the little fellows always had a natural explanation, even when the cause of things was an unnatural one. He learned more of men every day, and yet understood them little, still. And they understood him even less. In fairness, could he expect it any other way? He should be happy that once in a blue moon the bonkers, or gifted, or both, perceived, or thought they perceived, *something* of him, if only through a glass, a curdled glass of milk, dimly.

Agog, up on his green hill, thinks again of the woman in the car, the half-seer, and how she might have made a giant-wife, if three times taller. If she had been, he'd wrestle her like a shot. Respite to his woes.

Agog's kinfolk, you see, had been keen wrestlers. His father, Gogmagog, rolling him as a nipper in the moss and flint of Dartmoor, throwing him into the sponge of a bog. He'd learned to tangle and untangle under his father's might. He also learned, through bedtime stories told in the caves they populated, the origin of his race. How the king of a far-off land had thirty-three unruly and disobedient daughters, and married them off to thirty-three husbands to keep them under control. But the thirty-three daughters baulked at this, and plied the thirty-three husbands with drink, and cut their throats while they snoozed, for which misdemeanour the king put them on a raft and set them out to sea. How, after floating for many weeks, the fierce murderesses landed on a wild and deserted island in the far north west, which they named Albion (after Albina, the eldest, their leader), and there set about playing mothers and fathers with demons—never a good idea. The result of which hanky-panky was born a race of prodigious giants. These first true patriots took it as their purpose to protect the nation of their birth from all comers. And did so, successfully, for many generations, though at a cost. For, by the time Agog was born, they numbered, in all the country, only twenty-four. And, if the rest was a story, he knew that at least to be true. Because he had counted them. And knew their death throes, for he had witnessed them with his own eyes.

Agog shuddered as he remembered that fateful day, at the age of no more than five, when he overheard Gogmagog, as chieftain, tell the elders, all gathered in a circle, their beards reaching the ground, that Brutus and his followers, the descendants of the survivors of the fall of Troy, had been spotted coming up the River Dart.

Agog had never heard so much as a tremor in his father's voice, but now he heard fear. And felt it too.

Agog pleaded with him afterwards, saying he wanted to go with the twenty-four to fight, but Gogmagog held his son back with a hairy outstretched arm and roared in his face like a lion. Tears on his cheeks, the boy-giant did as his father demanded, cowering behind a rock, only able to watch as his clan fell upon Brutus's troops at Tottenesse, where they first landed, almost wiping out the entire camp in one brutal swoop. But the tide turned as quickly as the grey clouds turned black, and the sprightly Trojans, superior in numbers and armour, hurled back mercilessly with spear and dart at the creatures that loomed over them. The strength of the giants was no match for the skill of the Trojans, and all, male and female alike, were slaughtered, except one, the hugest, who was reserved alive, and overcome by many hands.

Agog takes in a sharp gasp of night air, the picture in his brain never less than shocking when resurrected—that of his father hobbled by chains, dragged with ship ropes, severely wounded in the leg, half-throttled. The "one detestable Gogmagog!" as the soldiers round him jeered—twelve cubits in stature (or twenty, as they later said, as anglers are wont to puff up their catch), and of such strength he could, at one shake, uproot an oak and brandish it as if a hazel wand.

Agog watched aghast from his hiding place as they put their captive to the test, as befits a leader, even a leader of monsters; releasing him so that the largest of their own breed, a barrel-chested warrior named Corineus—giant-sized, though born of man and woman—could wrestle him. Sport, you see. Brutus declaring that whosoever came off the conqueror shall be proclaimed ruler of all the western land.

Agog, though but a chubby child, knew his father would have been a fool to believe for a moment that they told the truth, or that he could win his freedom. Sport, you see.

Agog watched the proud chieftain raise his chin to the sky and pray to his gods, and the Trojans laughed. He dared not blink as the two enormous bodies crashed into each other, shaking the very ground under their feet, causing the walls of nearby buildings to crack. The twisting, strangling and pounding seemed to last forever, and, though he was bigger than any of the human whelps cheering, Agog felt little and lost. The lad heard three loud cracks, as if of branches snapping. Gogmagog had broken the Trojan's ribs in a bear hug. Enraged, Corineus lifted Gogmagog onto his shoulders, ran to the cliff edge, and threw. As his son stifled a cry that may have rocked the heavens, Gogmagog fell headlong and shattered into the sea, staining the ocean red. And from that day hence it was called Langoemagog, which is to say "Giant's Leap", at which place, from time to time, the frothy waves lapping the shore, even now, turn the colour of blood.

Agog heard Brutus give orders to his men to spread out and kill any giants they came across. Soon they came upon Agog himself, and he was sure they would do him in, but to his astonishment they saw him not, even though he was right under their Trojan noses. The boy realised his dad had asked the gods to make his son invisible. To save him. But why had Gogmagog not used his prayer to save *himself?* It was a question to which Agog could find no answer, to this day. Perhaps the gods were fickle. Devious. Mean. Perhaps they had their reasons. He'd like to ask them outright, but he didn't know their names. (He didn't even know the name of the king of rats.)

Agog, back then, that scar of an afternoon, had wept for his mother, who'd cradled him after he oozed from her womb like a pip from an orange. He'd wept for Partholón and Pantagruel, and Sasnol, and Kruunuvuör, and Rodochra, and Villeumauhh, and Ckrót. But none did he weep for more than Gogmagog, whose loss was a bottomless hole in the world, and cleft him like an axe.

Agog thinks he knew from that moment, even though it took him a while to prove it, that he was alone. But sometimes he found that, though his race was gone, eradicated, extinct, expunged from this world, they were not entirely forgotten. For morsel-men told stories too.

Agog had blinked when he watched the parade at the coronation of The Virgin Queen, and saw the tall, unstable effigies of two giants lumbering towards him, as if striding from dream sleep. They had passed level with his slack-jawed face, though they dwarfed the cheering crowd. He had heard them called "Gogmagot the Albion!" and "Corineus the Briton!" But even the ignorance, that day, served to warm the cockles of his heart.

Agog, later, saw the same two figures, knocked up in pasteboard and wickerwork, grace many a Lord Mayor's show, year on year, becoming known as "Gog and Magog"—splitting his father in two—two names better than none, he supposed. Better than surf the hue of a slit gizzard washing up on crab-ridden rock pools. These "two valiant giants who had defended our realm" (as was). Legend said that Brutus, founder of London, his New Troy, had brought two giants to serve as porters at the palace gates. But Agog knew legend to be wrong. Even so, he felt a prickly sort of pride when the twins of those guardian statues stood at the Guildhall enjoying all the esteem of the Municipality's gratitude, and there remained—a hop and a skip from the Griffin holding the City's coat of arms—until one of Hitler's bombs dropped on their heads. *Kaput.*

Agog had looked skyward at the sound of doodlebugs, had seen the ants scatter into their holes, seen the buildings burn, heard the sirens blotting out the wailing of mothers and patriotic songs. He had fought to protect Albion, as he always fought, swatting bombs from populated areas. Smashing a low-flying Fokker to smithereens. Good show.

Agog's next sigh is extensive. He rubs snot from his nose. Briefly examines its moonlit snail-trail on the back of his paw. Looks at the journeys mapped out by the blue, subterranean veins. All those long, lolloping walks from the low chalk hills of Cambridge to the dragon-steeds of Uffington or Cherhill. Thumbing his nose at barbarians across the Channel. Beating his chest atop the white cliffs of Dover.

Agog's mind inevitably drifts back to the time those first two figures were destroyed by fire. The time he had to fend off an enemy as invisible as he was. A foe more deadly than anyone or any thing of flesh and blood. His mind conjures the scene. He cannot steer the stubborn bullock away from it. Though he wants to, badly.

Agog had found the city of Londinium much as a child finds a discarded, much loved plaything in a gutter. And gutter it was;

not a gilded palace of wealth and promise but a huddled tramp of a town, full of vinaigrettes and nosegays. His visits to towns and villages in their devastation had prepared him somewhat—but not enough. The air was a filthy, poisonous miasma. His misbegotten muckiness matched it in a way, his dirty frame as soiled as the stockings of the wretches hauling sedan chairs. In another way, even invisible, and safe from small man's pestilence and pock marks, he felt he did not belong. The place was too *material* for his liking. He too lumpenly ethereal to fit. The pall of a black cloak covered all. Half-frightened, he'd slid around from street to fetid street, rubbing shoulders with snotty beggars and snooty how-d'ye-do's. He'd peeked through windows and seen beds buckling with a Kelpie's stroke. Whether the occupant was making life or losing it was anyone's guess. His own big-bastard bulk, lathered at the best of times in slime and grit, could only roll from alley to rancid alley like a stinking foetus seeking timely exit from its prison.

Agog had thought the place a long-handled profanity. Not to put too fine a point on it. But he had work to do. Not that he knew how to do it. This was not something in the handbook of giants. This was hideously, and irredeemably, new.

Agog wandered down avenues of doors marked with red crosses. Thought to himself, the paint must be getting scarce. While he squatted to shit, he saw bundles carried out onto the cobbles. The big bundles one thing, the tiny ones another. Carts soughed under the weight of them. The bonfires didn't go hungry. Nor did the pits. London was all pits. Amongst them, plague doctors roamed with their snouts in drains, examining tongues and wallets. But even those with diplomas and spectacles were blindfolded when it came to the giant standing amongst them. Dogs barked at him, and cats hissed and arched their backs, but then they always did. He was no phantom to animals. But now sheep ran from his approach with stricken eyes, and pigs ignored his outstretched hand with squeals fit for the abattoir. Here he could smell all the friends of fear.

Agog lolled drunkenly from the over-imbibing of death. Stepped over daisy-chains of children. He had faced every heathen that threatened these shores, but now he was flummoxed. This, he could not comprehend. Was *this* his fate, then? . . . To be witness to the death of the incumbent race of Britain, now, as well as its former?

Agog closed his eyes tightly, not sure his heart or soul could withstand another such purge. His shoulders fell back against a dwelling. Catching his breath, he heard another's, faintly, from inside. The sound was unlike a human voice, more resembling the whistle of a bird. Perhaps a marvellous bird, he thought. It seemed to beckon him. And he heard weeping, too. A weeping that reminded him of his own the day his father died. The mouth of the front door lay ajar, to let good air in, and bad air out.

Agog was curious. By narrowing his shoulders and crawling on all fours, he could just about squeeze along the coffin-tight passage, having to twist like a well-fed python to slither up the stairs to one landing, then the next. Groaning and panting, he lay on his side to insert his frame through the door to the attic bedroom. Luckily the rest of him followed with some shuffling of hips. Still on his hands and knees, brushing a powdery layer of daub from his scalp, he felt the harsh smoke of chair legs and banister rails in his nostrils. The family, entirely oblivious to his ungainly entrance, were trying to burn the fever out. Draw it like pus from a sore. But the whole child was a sore.

Agog could see that now, as he crouched in the corner, wedging himself between a crooked wardrobe and the wall, knuckles pressed to the floor. He watched the sweat-sodden blankets stripped off to burn. Before they were replaced with clean, he glimpsed the skeleton-doll, halfway to a tombstone angel, the bag of sticks within a scratch of being an epitaph.

Agog stared at bed and boy while skinny parents floated downstairs like mourners already. Only the two of them remained in the room. He could have left, but something kept him there.

Agog, of all creatures, knew what it was to be alone.

Agog, hardly moving, nestled as the hours passed, and tried to rest, but failed, even though his eyes were heavy with their burden. Time crunched like a millstone. Candles came and went. The coughing abated, but not for long. Soft flannels were applied to a fluttering birdcage of ribs. The grown-ups glided away again, hiding tears behind their hands, and presently he heard a cry from the street, accompanied by the tolling of a hand bell. Not a rag and bone merchant, the crier wanted what was inside the rags.

Agog shut his eyes. The giant thought of his bleak, green hillock, far away, but did not want to go. Even sitting, pig-skinned, he filled the room, pink feet like furniture. Knees touching the ceiling. Shins forming a V, with stiff arms an eleven between them, the way a cat sits. Or a boy watching a wrestling-match from behind a rock while the gods titter up their sleeves. When he could bear his thoughts no longer, he opened his tortoise lids and watched a rat circumnavigate the wainscoting.

"That's a wee one, that is."

Agog gave a snort of alarm at the sound. The sprat could barely turn his head, but had done. Did the little one know that someone was in the room?

Agog poked his nose from the shadows. The lad's eyes were closed. The fragile body motionless. Agog moved his sausage lips carefully, in words as deep and groaning as a shipwreck.

"Poor egg . . ."

"I'm not an egg, or poor," came the croak. The boy lifted himself half-up. "My father wouldn't take kindly to hear you say that."

Agog couldn't even manage a snort a second time. His heart raced. The boy could see him. Not sense, not dimly comprehend, not intuit, but—*See* him! Not only that, could *hear* him too!

Agog found himself robbed of speech. Now, when it was required above all else, his lips would not part. Noble daddy, he thought, was *this* what morsels talked about when they talked of miracles? Agog always thought they meant *mackerels*, but now felt too light-headed to rustle up a sentence in reply. Luckily, he didn't have to.

"Have you come to take me?" The boy's voice struggled to climb above a reedy whisper, just as his eyes fought to stay open. "You do not resemble an angel."

"Don't insult me, whippersnapper."

The boy folded upwards, a gargantuan task—even in the eyes of a gargantuan. Half a nod to the crust on a plate at his bedside.

"You can have my bread if you wish."

Agog did not know if the boy thought him famished. He frowned. The boy reached over, tore off a chunk and threw it weakly in the giant's direction, but it did not reach, and he fell back, defeated, into his pillow.

Agog thought him like a trout gasping on dry land. It wasn't that he wasn't hungry. He was always hungry. It didn't seem the right thing to do. Fill his cheeks.

"I do not want thy bread, cousin."

The boy squirmed back onto his elbows. Eyes becoming slits as he assessed the grubby giant in his bedroom. (A first, it is safe to presume.)

Agog saw his buboes. The rings of roses.

"I will not eat thee."

The boy chuckled thinly. "You would not eat a primrose."

"Is that what you are?"

In cruel imitation of laughter, the boy's broken bellows piped like a curlew. Soon he found the balm of silence, but with it, sadness.

"They keep me indoors. I cannot see the sun."

The giant shrugged. "It is the same sun you saw when last outside. The sun is not partial to change. He is boring like that. I prefer the moon."

"Why?"

"The moon is my darling. Danger. Thrillin'. Makes heart quick."

"You feel something."

"I do."

In the thoughtful pause the boy took, Agog wondered what the young one considered of the matter. Perhaps he considered nothing. Perhaps he had other considerations on his mind.

"Big One?"

"Yes?" Agog said, reasoning he was the only one present.

"Will the moon light my way when I go?"

Agog wasn't certain, but he was kind. "You can trust the moon."

The boy must have thought him foolish, though.

"You fat thing!" he giggled.

"You wood louse!" Agog threw back, smiling.

"You rat dropping!"

"You flea!"

The boy laughed, and so did the giant. But when coughing rent the room like stabs of forked lightning, what smile was left was scraped from the giant's face.

Agog turned when he heard the bedroom door open, allowing in the parents swathed in their premature grief. He felt guilty, the invisible spectator to their woes, though visible all too clearly to the reason for them.

"How can I care for him? I am his mother. It is my duty, husband. O perfect one, know that you were longed for and loved, if but for a little while." The wan she-person placed down the arm thin as a corn stalk and walked to the far corner of the room, not knowing she spoke now directly into the giant's countenance, which was inches from her own: "O Lord, take me instead, I beg of thee."

"Shsh, quiet," whispered the master of the house, now at her shoulder. "It is God's choice, not ours. God must choose."

"And chooses those without sin?" hissed the wife bitterly.

"If he must. All we can do is pray."

"To what? One who is invisible?"

"Hush, woman. We can only do what we must."

Agog watched them turn their backs on him, return to the bed, and read from the Book of Job, proffering all the lies of tenderness therein. At nightfall their son roused, briefly, with slight but enthusiastic animation.

"Mother, I fancied a book I might write. Or poem. Which has the most words? Book or poem?" He looked at the giant directly. "I have much in my head. Wild imaginings. But my ink pot is almost empty." The man in the periwig and frayed cuffs rushed about frantically to fetch the youngster paper and ink. But no sooner had he wrapped the child's pale fingers around the quill, than the tousled head sagged. The pen rolled from the writing-tray to the floor.

"Praise the Lord. Praise the Lord. Shed tears of joy, wife. For he has gone to a better place."

Agog shed tears. Unstoppable ones. He couldn't help it. They were neither bidden nor habitual. They formed a pool on the floorboards. The boy's father said the water had not been there a moment earlier, and so was inexplicable. He made the sign of the cross.

Agog, in his rage, hit the wall with his fists. "Hark!" the boy's father shouted; "The knocking of spirits!" And people gathered. Servants and passers-by and neighbours. And the giant struggled to get out, past them, for he wanted to look upon the little corpse no longer. And even then, some said they felt a presence, and thereafter it was said, on many lips, the house was haunted.

Agog was alone once more. The flea was dead. The night air was no medicine. In his rage, he strode through the city of coughs and blisters and coffin carpenters blowing into fingerless gloves, making his hibernaculum in a bakery in Pudding Lane, alternating between sobbing and stuffing his belly with loaves. Upturning a candle in the process. Fire bloomed. Blossomed.

Agog could not have known the consequence, but, due to his action, the plague was seared away, cauterised like a wound. Smoke rose from the roofs at his back as he fled. An inferno wracked the sky, but he'd had enough of London. He ran, and a giant covers ground pretty quickly.

Agog was back in the West while the embers were still warm. In rugged Curnow with its horizontal trees and constantly peckish gulls. Cornwall—named after Corineus, the very captain under Brutus who had been given that foot and ankle of Britannia as a prize after killing his late, brave father.

Agog, though, had first breathed air in that place, long before the first king of Britain planted his feet there, and the reign of Great Giants ended, and the lineage of Troy took their hold. It was his family plot. Where the salt in his hair and sea spray on his eyelids meant home.

Agog saw London rebuilt and replenished. Gog and Magog reinstalled in the Guildhall. Resurrected. The legend, lie, intact. Stories being the real protectors.

But it stayed with him, that one day out of thousands. The time a piccolo voice spoke to him, he answered, and a small boy listened. The pup had had a story to tell that no-one would read. A picture to paint that no-one would see. A song to sing that no-one would hear. But he had seen wonder, if just for a minute. He had seen the unknown thing that evaded the eyes of others. That others could not—or would not—open their spirits to believe in. He had seen the impossible, if only for a heartbeat, if only for a gasp, if only for a breath.

Agog, in his dreams, sometimes kneels at the boy's bedside again, and, leaning over, offers the chap his thumb, that grimy thumb with the black and broken nail, the thumb that had poked and delved where it's best not to know, and the beautiful child grasps it, and clings to it, and closes his eyes.

Agog, for all his sobs, when he dreams that, does not want to wake.

Orr

Temperature 75°. Sunny. High 75F. Chance of rain 0%. Humidity 38%. Clear. Wind SSW at 8 mph.

Orr threaded his belt through the loops of his pants and, breathing in, tightened it to a notch that was too unrealistic. He optimistically loosened it to the next, a vain hope, then the next, wishful thinking, then, abandoning self-delusion, the next two were swiftly skipped over and he opted for the last—which he had created himself with a pointed awl in his garage only a month before. Actually, he had created all three of those last three holes, in a rare instance, for him, of forward planning.

Full length mirrors. To be avoided by any but the svelte. Relaxing his abdominal muscles, he could already feel the leather cutting into his belly, but told himself it would be a mere few hours before he could loosen himself from Purgatory. Besides. He had no other belt and no other pants. Not to mention, no other him.

The uniform looked good, though, even if its occupant didn't. He'd worn it receiving the Pacific West Region Harry Yount Award, recognised for his overall record of accomplishments: Long service and commitment to performing the wide cadre of duties of a National Park Ranger "effectively and consummately" in the multifarious roles expected of him. Shouldn't forget that. Got a write-up in *Sierra News*. Twenty years ago. Gone by like a flash. Hadn't had to hold his gut in then.

Well . . . not so much.

Orr combed his hair and checked his shoulders for dandruff.

Plucked the strands from the tines and let the thin white clouds float down to the water in the john before flushing.

"Showtime."

He put the all-important bag under his arm—mustn't forget *that*—took his entry card from the plastic slat next to the door, and, in the second before the room went dark, wanted to crawl into that bed with fresh-laundered sheets and just sleep. Or get in his car and drive straight back to Sonora. The survivors wouldn't mind. The survivors could do this without him. Sure they could. As he let the heavy hotel room door close after him, he wondered why the hell he was there, but he had come now, so maybe he would find the hell out.

Downstairs, as he crossed the cavernous lobby, the ping of the elevators behind him sounded like wind chimes in a Buddhist temple. The area was scattered with mannequin-like women and fastidiously well-groomed men. Orr reminded himself it was an industry town where looks meant everything. Only in LA could you have a street called Avenue of the Stars.

He followed the sign with the arrow he'd seen when he checked in, down a long corridor to another signpost with the familiar acronym.

SMLS-USA.

He straightened his tie. Voices echoed. He went in.

Next to the door was a small, unmanned desk where the lanyards were laid out in the time-honoured manner. He spotted his name amongst the five remaining and hung the red loop around his neck, straightening the plastic rectangle that rested on his paunch to face outward. To his right, a long table with a spread of white, empty cups and saucers. Coffee jugs sitting on warmers. A bowl of creamer sachets. Another of sugar packets. Further along, wine glasses. Bottles of Chardonnay and Merlot already opened. Iced water in jugs. Tall glasses for that. OJ in pitchers. Children—they looked like children to Orr—serving and circulating with nibbles.

The people—attendees, if you will—didn't fill the room. Twelve, fifteen tops, gathered at the far end, by the window. Many he knew from last time. Some he recognised instantly, even with their backs to him. Some not—which worried him. Were they new, or was it due to erosion of the head on his part? Orr lived in fear of mental decline. Of faces deserting him. Names taking to the sky when he wanted to grasp them. It terrified him, day by day. He liked not to think about it, but it made him nervy in gatherings such as this. More anxious than he ever was when young and had a grip on the world. Or so he believed.

Orr took some water to fill his hand, walked over to a line of empty chairs against the wall and placed upon one of them the thing he had under his arm, the plastic dry cleaning bag containing his broad-brimmed ranger hat.

Nearby he saw an island of freshly-printed paperbacks, each with identical gold-embossed covers emblazoned with the title *Touched by God*. Clouds behind the lettering broken by shafts of light. The author's name: Amor Roberts. Of course it was. That name and lipstick he *did* remember.

"Hey, big man!"

Dick Hanselaar in a golfing sweater. Looked like a used car salesman or a televangelist, but actually a lawyer for Shell. Dick had been hit on a beach in Cancun, staring at fish swimming between his feet. Ten days in hospital and a flight home by Medicare before he opened an eyelid. Handshake now like an auto crusher.

"Hey guys. Look who's here. What are the odds?"

That old joke. Their rallying cry. Their motto. *What are the odds?*

Dick had a predilection for easy laughter which made Orr vaguely suspicious of him rather than warm to him. Perhaps, deep down, he envied that Dick was content in his own flesh.

"The legend!" An impish man with little or no neck scuttled up, boyish even in his forties, hand extended.

"I don't know."

"I do! *Guinness Book of Records.* You kidding? I brought a copy, special. Mind if I take a selfie?"

"Be my guest," said Orr.

He always wore the uniform for just that purpose, after all. The one in the photograph. The one that had appeared everywhere. He thought tonight the photo opportunities would come after, but it didn't matter. Let the man get pleasure where he may.

The imp nestled up close, head against Orr's shoulder and held up his phone.

He wore a Brooks Brothers suit and loafers with argyle socks. Another oil and gas trumpeter, Orr thought, as he signed the requisite page in the *Guinness Book of World Records*. Scrawled boldly with the Sharpie over his likeness in grainy, old school black and white. Thought he looked sadder in that shot than he recalled being at the time. Holding his ranger hat like that. "Remarkable Humans" the headline read across the whole double page spread.

"Much obliged."

"No problem."

"Any objection if this goes out into the ether?"

"Not at all."

Orr had forgotten the guy's name. The man could perceive that.

"Cheech Gerlach, from Wisconsin."

"Cheech. Pleasure."

Orr remembered now. Just needed a prod, mostly.

Cheech had been flipped off his Kawasaki on Route 425. Orr remembered the story was his wife had said that while the paramedics were looking for a pulse, a mystery woman arrived by the side of the road dressed all in white, carrying something on a tray covered in a white cloth. The woman just said her husband was in good hands, and when Cheech's wife looked up a second time she was gone. Way he told it, Cheech woke up in Emergency and hadn't seen a thing. Paramedics hadn't either.

"Still think that cover of *National Geographic* is a peach."

"Yeah," said Orr. "My wife liked that one, for sure."

"I'll show you the camera I had on me in the Rockies. Melted like a fried egg," said Dick Hanselaar. The imp wandered off laughing in the direction of the guacamole dip.

Orr felt Dick's hand, glistening with silver hair, on his arm. "Man, good to see you again. Five years."

"Circumstances."

"I get it. We all get it." Over his shoulder, to the room now. "I'm saying We Get It!"

More people moved closer. Some with saucers resting on their palms.

"Hello stranger," said a woman. She kissed Orr's cheek, her lips causing a faint abrasive sensation against his stubble. She smelled of mimosa. Honey, violet and almonds. "My husband left me since last we met."

"Know the feeling."

"Younger, slimmer model."

"Cancer."

"I know."

Orr didn't need to look at her name badge. Renée Mancuso, bound in a raiment of fuschia. Not a strand of grey hair that hadn't been attended to. Wearing mauve glasses to give herself the illusion of being more radiant and spirited than she was. She'd been walking across a runway at Logan, he thought. Had a picture in his mind of her holding her purse over her head to keep off the rain when a second later her life changed forever. Consequent medical repercussions. Then the second time, in Des Moines, he believed.

"Jerry talking about his appearance on Leno." She teetered on too-tall high heels, pointing a thumb over her shoulder.

"Some things never change."

Orr glanced over at Jerry Gold. More a jockey's dimensions than a cowboy's, dressed in a Texan shirt with arrows stitched on the pockets and a Stetson for avoidance of doubt of his origin, even though he now built condos for a living. True to character, Jerry held the semi-circular crowd with unabashed entitlement to their attention. The rodeo story, no doubt. An oldie and a goodie, it had to be said. He'd hit the booze, Orr could see, or more accurately, the booze had hit him. Orr knew what that felt like. It was his own prehistory for a time, and not a source of pride, or much enjoyment. Made him think of other survivors who'd gone down that route over the years. The self-destruct of the non-destructed, or something. If that didn't get me, maybe this will.

Orr could hear Jerry saying he'd been a nice guy, the talk show host. Real natural. Real friendly. *What you see is what you get with Leno.* The usual spiel. *Everybody treated me great. Green room, they call it. Jennifer Lopez? Let me tell you. The audience laughed so hard at my jokes, Leno said, hey, who's the comedian here?*

Everyone standing around him laughed. They'd all heard it before. No one minded hearing it again. It was the least they could do. In some ways, it was why they were here. To hear the same old stories again. There was a comfort in that.

Orr remembered he himself had gotten inquiries from all over the world when he hit his nine iron. Japanese TV desperate to interview him. Fly him to Tokyo, no expense spared. Spouse included. He hadn't been interested. Gretchen had, and was cranky with him for weeks. She was always more interested than him in travel broadening her horizons. Orr always thought there was more than enough to see in America for one lifetime. He'd said in the end, "Listen, it's not you has to face the cameras, and I don't want to." And there it ended.

"You've grown a beard," said Renée Mancuso as Jerry's Texas real-estate twang wrapped around the words *Discovery Channel, for a special.*

"No law against it. When I last looked."

She touched Orr's sleeve and moved away, smiling.

"I like it." Standing a few yards away, a girl of twenty or so. The age of one of his grandchildren.

"You do?"

Sweater sleeves covering her hands. It probably belonged to her boyfriend, dad or mom. The collar was baggy. Scars on her neck, he noticed—burn scars. Plastic surgery. A good job, but he could spot that texture. They all could. It had got her bad, then. He could see that. And the dark rings around her eyes. Sleeping problems, or—he didn't like to think—drugs, of some ilk.

"You should lose the moustache though. It would look cool. A beard with no moustache, like an Amish person."

"Okay, I'll do that."

"You'd do it because I say so?"

"Yeah. Why not? What have I got to lose?"

"Upper lip hair."

"Upper lip hair grows back. Worse comes to worst."

"You're a philosophical soul."

"I ain't that," said Orr. "What brings you to this illustrious shindig?"

"Accident while hiking. Up on Half Dome."

"My old stomping ground." Yosemite's tallest granite peak. Five thousand feet. "They let people up there with a storm comin'? That's remiss."

"Not really," the girl said. "There were four of us. Trekking all day."

"You would be."

"We were fine going up the chains. Weather changed real fast. The others wanted to film it on their phones when the clouds came over. We heard the thunder real close. They panicked and hid in a sort of a like rocky enclave." Orr wondered why she didn't say *cave*. "I decided to run. Reckon I stayed alive because my feet weren't touching the ground at the time."

"Narrow escape, that comes under."

"Sure does."

Orr sipped his water and didn't ask if any of her friends were killed or had life changing injuries. He remembered his own bruises. The tingling. Multifarious pain. Years of flu-like symptoms and headaches.

"They get you down okay? I guess they did, because you're here."

"Messed up, but yeah."

"We're all messed up, honey," said Renée, coming back with a drink in her hand, aloft like a prize. "My math is shot to hell."

"I'm a newbie," said the girl. Under thirty was a girl to him.

"How many times?" Orr asked.

"Two. Got out of my car to mail a package. Overcast was all. Caught by a side flash. Hit the flag pole of the post office." She chuckled with a vein of nervous embarrassment. "Got on CNN."

"All right, then."

"You?"

"Nine," said Orr, aware that the casual way he said it sounded boastful. Wasn't meant to be.

"Awesome."

"Awesome indeed," said Orr. He didn't want to monopolise the girl's time and had no more to say. He pointed to the coffee contraptions. A polite way to escape, and she knew it, and perhaps was grateful, he imagined, and smiled. Renée extended her arm around the girl's shoulder and they moved away together towards other people, turning their backs.

Orr turned his attention to filling a cup with coffee. Alone in that pursuit, he felt more at ease.

"When you gonna make it ten, Howie?" The man in the disabled scooter sported a MAGA baseball cap, and a metal cylinder that piped oxygen through a tube to both nostrils. "Not gonna let those Ruskies beat us, are ya?"

"This is not the Olympics, Hank," said Dick Hanselaar, smiling and placing a hand on the shoulder of the old man's flying jacket.

"Not the moon landings, either," said Orr, plucking a sachet of Sweet 'n' Low and wiggling it in the air before tearing off a corner.

As the two men talked, he looked back at Renée and, seeing her glance back, wondered what she was telling the girl about him. Renée had tried to entrap him in a one night stand when she was drunk that time in Atlanta, and failed. Somehow, since then, Orr always thought she saw him as something of a dope. But that was her problem. When was that? Ten years ago? Twelve? His memory. Who cares, anyway? His wife didn't. Gretchen was gone. That misbegotten flirtation did no damage any more, except to him, if he let it.

The girl had a slightly bent up walk. She carried her injury in every step. A lot of them did. He didn't mean the walkers, or the disabled buggy. He meant scarred under the business suits, the North Carolina Tar Heels sweatshirts. Or ailments you couldn't see. Psoriasis. Nerve damage. Ongoing concerns, seen and unseeable. Jitters. Anxiety. Wendell Blackwell, over there, hands shaking with a tremor. He'd been fishing on Caddo Lake, Louisiana. Sky the colour of bluebells. Frank Markovitz, next to him, one arm useless and stuffed in his left pocket after a stroke. Repairing a roof at the time the strike happened, in Priam, Wisconsin. Not even his own goddam roof, either.

They were a wonder of sorts, all of them. People who had seen the burning bush and suffered a power outage. Or worse.

Renée worked as cabin crew for Delta and therefore knew how she looked and used it. Orr nevertheless thought that was why she acted so super confident: the great celestial finger had given her a life lesson. Darn near blotted her out. The power in her soul or her spirit had been sucked away by happenstance and all that was left to cling to was pretence. Orr wondered if that was what her husband couldn't deal with. Maybe there was no "younger, skinnier model"—just the person Renée used to be. The person her husband was in love with. Lost in a segment on the local news.

Orr reflected on what *he* had lost, nine times over.

He looked down at the face of his Luminox. The only watch he could wear that ever kept time. The rest—birthday gifts, Christmas—all gave up the ghost when he put them on. All, ironically, except this one—the one he was wearing his first time. Since then he'd had to avoid any and all types of damned gadgets. Garage doors, laptops. Flashlights would go flat on him with predictable regularity. University doctor at a barbecue once said, it could be that Orr had some brain damage from the incident. Could be that he simply forgot to replace the batteries. Orr had given him a long, hard look in the eye and said, "I like my version better."

Dick Hanselaar was in his element arranging chairs in a circle, lanyard dangling, miming directions as if conducting an orchestra, his expansive gestures scooping people in towards the seating area.

Orr finished his coffee and joined them. Glad to take the weight off.

From his seat, past the people directly facing him, he could see a furled Stars and Stripes in the corner. It made him wonder what other clubs and societies booked this room for gatherings. Civil events. Weddings. Funerals. He realised then that for all the bonhomie, *that* was what this felt like. The walking on egg shells. The attempts to create ease where there was none. The finger food. The cheap, tepid coffee and cheap, tepid conversation. Had he been a different person, he'd have felt like asking out loud who had died . . . but the fact was, they were there for the exact opposite reason. None of them had, and they ought to have done.

So it was a celebration of life. Correct? Perhaps it was just him, then. Fish out of water. Not used to breathing on dry land. And that wasn't anyone's fault but his.

He couldn't say people weren't convivial. Most were smiling. Chatting merrily. Most people were happy to be there. High point of their month. Hell, of their year. He used to feel at home with them, but wasn't sure any more. Same as he fitted the park ranger uniform no longer. Same as it felt uncomfortable to his very structure, so did this.

Maybe he was to blame for how he felt. He didn't know. He did know he wanted time to pass quicker than it was. But here they were—again—facing each other in the round, ready to declaim their souls. Like him, though, they knew by now better than to join hands. Had learned from past experience that the accumulated static would be asking for trouble.

"I got one from the door handle."

"Door handles are a bitch."

Speaking over the murmurings, Dick introduced the proceedings, typed sheet in hand. Dick was a typed-sheet kind of person. Welcomed everyone to this meeting of the "SMLS-USA."

Survivors of Multiple Lightning Strikes. Augie Baxter had called it *The Zap Club.*

Orr smiled. Good old Augie. No longer with us. It definitely was a club, though—if not of like minds, then of like individuals, with like experiences. Gretchen used to call it an AA meeting of oddities. "Human lightning rods," as they were often called by journalists—*USA Today*, the *Orlando Bugle*—too lazy to coin an alternative.

After reeling off the health and safety regs, and listing absentees, Dick asked the assembled to please observe a minute's silence, as they had done since Tampa in '98, in memory of "those they had lost" in the previous twelve months. "Lenny Soto, a good friend of this organisation," said Dick, "passed only two weeks ago. There's a book near the door, over by the flowers, to leave your words of condolence. I'm sure you have them in abundance."

He bowed his head and the rest followed suit.

Orr closed his eyes and dropped his chin, but didn't want to think of those people too hard, or of those under permanent medical care who weren't present, or those who struggled worse than he did, because it made him feel relentlessly sad, abominably lucky, and guilty as hell.

"We are gathered here in spirit of support and love, to share and share freely. Remember, there are no wrong answers." Dick always said that, and enjoyed doing so. It was his catch phrase. His trade mark, like the expensive dentistry. "Now, who wants to go first?"

Orr looked at the people and looked at the girl who had come up to him earlier in particular. She was not going to speak first, he was certain. Maybe she wasn't going to speak at all. That wasn't unusual for a "newbie", as she called it. She looked like it was a severe effort just to be sitting there, bony knees pressed against each other as if wanting to overlap.

Amor Roberts announced her name and credentials in the bashful way of a five-year-old about to sing a party piece, before holding one of her paperbacks up against her chest and turning it right and left for everyone to see. She said she was really excited, it was a *dream come true*—the incredible story of enduring *five* lightning strikes, one at sea, one in the air, and in three different states!—and it would be launched next month with extensive nationwide publicity. As if giving away top secret information in the strictest confidence, she whispered that the SMLS-USA got a *thank-you* in the Acknowledgements, and that every single one of those present—"newbies" excepted, sorry!—got a mention, because they were her rock, her guidance and her lodestar.

Orr thought she probably got "lodestar" from the dictionary.

Amor talked some more about it and herself, then made her hands into a prayer shape before saying the book would be available at Barnes and Noble, Books-a-Million, all good book stores, and on Amazon dot com. At the end of this session she'd also be happy to sign some of the copies she'd brought with her for the discounted price of $10—reduced from $14.99.

Orr crossed his arms and thought to himself there'd be a stampede.

Amor shifted back in her chair, reluctantly backing out of the limelight, and Trinessa Roos announced after her name and "three times and counting, sweet Jesus"—she'd had, well, another set of steel rods inserted into her legs, and (cough) they seemed to be taking, after the first ones had given her an infection, they'd remember. She could walk now—in pain, of course, but not so much. Time was, she couldn't so much as raise her ankle off the floor. They did remember that, and it got her a round of applause.

Orr applied one hand to the other also.

Trinessa coughed again, excusing herself, splayed a hand on her chest with pink fingernails, long and artificial, saying she was sure now, without a shadow of doubt, that her fourth lightning strike had healed her from the damage done from the third, which had happened in her kitchen in Idaho, when she heard a huge blast of thunder and discovered herself displaced to the foot of the stairs without having got there by ambulation. The following time, she related in no small amount of detail, she'd felt a tingling like a thousand needles in her crippled right leg, and suddenly felt full of vitality. "Vitality and verve" were the words she used. Whereupon she stood up fine and could walk, and prayed every night and every morning till she was hoarse.

Everyone clapped again, more vigorously this time, Amor Roberts with her book balanced on her knees, meticulously remote and blonde as a Fox News anchor, and Orr watched the girl in her twenties clapping as if it was the thing to be done, which it was. She was cottoning on fast.

Two fingers in his mouth Jerry Gold gave a racetrack whistle. Orr felt curmudgeonly not doing the same. Trinessa'd had a spiritual awakening, after all. But there was always one. Orr didn't feel uncharitable towards her when she said she saw golden particles in the air, or that she felt "immersed in God". Whatever gets you through the night, Orr thought.

Zachary Clait from Jackson, Mississippi—"one time to add since last conference"—piped up, finger raised, with a story he said he never knew. His mother told him only a month ago. Said he was born during a thunderstorm. A real Humdinger. That's what they called him as a child, he said: "Humdinger!"

Everyone laughed, except the MAGA hat guy, whose hands were sequestered in his armpits. Orr noticed white tufts on the man's throat where he had failed to shave and wondered why there was no-one in his life to point that out.

"That shows you, sweetie. You were special right from the start," said Susan Tratnik. Orr had to squint to read her name tag. Oh, yeah . . . He remembered her well, now his eyeballs focused. Susan had developed psychic abilities ever since a lightning bolt struck her when she was sheltering under a tree at 17th Street and Pennsylvania Avenue. She was the one who heard sonatas composed by the dead. Wrote them down, recorded them. Put them on her YouTube channel. Had seen occasional angels, subsequent to her third and fourth electrical experiences, though more infrequently. And, as she had said herself in the past, "That's not normal. It ain't."

Orr listened as she explained, ass wider than the chair, how she was currently helping people through palmistry and numerology. Not to mention aiding the police with a missing person investigation.

Susan said she'd awakened one night with the wind blowing through the room and the Venetian blinds wrapped round her and the bed in flames. At that moment, she knew *for sure* a child was somewhere in peril. And the day they found the body, well that was the day she got a shock from an electric socket due to a second-hand refrigerator being faulty. That was more than mere coincidence.

Orr was watching the girl in her twenties mimicking the others nodding, then seeming to nod of her own volition.

She was skinny, he observed now. Thigh bones like sticks, the figure-hugging jeans loose. He pictured her pushing her food round her plate instead of eating it. He wondered if she sometimes said her mother and father didn't understand what it was like in her head. They just didn't.

"Things happen in life for a reason," Susan Tratnik continued, with conviction. It was just about the dumbest thing Orr had ever heard coming from a human being's lips, and that was saying some.

A few of them had seen God, or found Him. This came as no great surprise to Orr. Personally, he thought if God had anything to do with this, He was a hell of a comedian. Especially as a lot of people He picked out for this particular treatment—a bolt from the blue—ended up dead as concrete.

Some had taken to ministry over the years. He couldn't say he blamed them. They'd been singled out, if not by a loving higher being, then by something mindless and all-powerful as hell. Probably a good move to consider it a blessing, rather than the simple "WTF" moment it truly was.

He could see why people liked the idea of heaven, too. Didn't take an Einstein to figure it out. Certain folks just wanted somewhere to go where they'd be loved.

He felt tired at that thought, then, and wished he'd had a nap in the afternoon instead of sitting in his underpants on the corner of the bed staring at the TV screen showing movies he remembered as a kid.

Rusty Canavale, UPS delivery guy—"five times, boy and man"—hair like a bush, was talking now. Saying he wanted to thank it—whatever "it" was—'cause it got him his girlfriend, and his girlfriend was now his wife. Sure broke the ice at parties, he could say that! I mean, girls never looked at him before! But that strike, the third one, man, it was like Cupid's arrow, right there!

"I was never special but, I dunno, soon as that happened, *everything* happened. Everything *good.* I mean I had nothin' going for me, and now I've got a whole lot. I'm not just some surfer bum any more. I've got a story, you know?"

Orr wondered what the heck story that was, worth a crap. Which was unkind. But the boy was too damned happy. Happiness didn't endear people to Orr. It was a failing he was working on.

Rusty'd been ordering pizza on a land line when the heavens opened. The line had cut out and the youngster'd watched white light crawling up his body from his feet, football-shaped—classic ball lightning. Then a spike came from the handset and knocked him into the wall. Hell, Orr could see why women in Tallahassee would swoon.

"Now I *am* somebody," Rusty said, and everyone clapped, because, Orr guessed, that meant they were somebody too.

"That's why each one of us is special, even if we don't think so," said Amor Roberts, clutching *Touched by God* like Elmer Gantry clutching his bible. "As I say in my penultimate chapter, we should get strength from this. It's not a weakness. We are not victims. We will not be victims." She was playing to the crowd. If she wanted a bigger reaction, Orr thought meanly, she should have chanted "lock her up". For all he knew, maybe she had. Recent TV coverage had soured him. And he was sour enough before that. Maybe it was due to the toe he'd lost, black and snapped off like a twig that time down in Yosemite Village. And barely overcast. The day he got that hole in his hat, singed hair, and lost an eyebrow.

Wouldn't have been human if he hadn't been changed. They all had.

Orr thought of the story of one of the earliest survivors. Digs Dauncey. Trombone player with Duke Ellington. Age fifty-three when lightning struck, and not of the inspirational variety. Digs had undergone a vast personality change. Started robbing banks. Wearing false moustaches. Different ones. Handlebar. Prussian Cavalry. Salvador Dalí. Got caught. Shot a woman. Death row. Faced Old Sparky. Said: "I'll go out of this world the way I entered it. Electricity." And he did. Wife planned to commit suicide the same day, by shotgun. She failed, and shot half her jaw off. Lived another twenty years. Digs left two wives, four daughters from the first, four sons from the second. A myriad of complexities.

Orr considered perhaps Digs Dauncey was their patron saint. Sure deserved to be. They were all saints in their own minds. Saints or sinners. Headlines or footnotes. They were a club, yes. An exclusive club. But the thing was, for all that united them, they were all incomparably alone. What had happened to them, to each of them, had put them at the centre of their universe. Maybe it had to. Maybe that was how they survived. Not by questioning it, but by having answers.

A guy with a prominent Adam's apple and his hair in a man bun was saying that tribal cultures have known for millennia that people struck by lightning have cheated death, therefore have a unique relationship with the gods. "They know what the shamanic path to enlightenment means. It means giving yourself to the will of a higher power. It means being symbolically reborn. It means arriving at a new self though trauma. It means being chosen."

Amongst the Sioux, he said, such people were called *Heyoka* which meant "thunder dreamer" and these medicine men had visions featuring what they called *Wakinyah* which meant "thunderbirds" or "thunder beings". He held up a photograph.

Black Elk. Lakota holy man who "followed the path of Heyoka".

Orr fought the compulsion to sigh. Lifted his elbows from his knees. Wished he could undo the buttons tormenting his waist. Martyrdom had lost its appeal.

Dick Hanselaar, suddenly animated, asked if anybody knew of a scientific study of whether there's something *physiological* that attracts lightning to certain individuals. (Orr was impressed that he endowed the word "physiological" with the heft it deserved.)

Laura Nemes—of North Randall, Ohio, a 'fivesie'—perked up, undaunted by her lack of scientific authority. "I definitely feel that the magnetic force of my body draws lightning toward me. I'm no expert, but when you magnetise something it *stays* magnetised until you demagnetise it. Well, that's what has happened to me! I'm not demagnetised!"

"We're electrical beings, man," declared Rusty, the former surf bum, with equal certainty. "It's like our superpower!"

It wasn't a super power to Orr. It wasn't super-anything, except a super pain in the ass. He didn't need that Marvel comic, *X-Men* bullshit.

"What if we're not special?" he said, almost not knowing it came out loud till it did. "What if it doesn't have meaning? What if shit just happens?"

Silence.

The old hearing-a-pin-drop number. Bigtime.

Shit.

Orr felt he'd insulted someone's mother. All their mothers.

"It's got to mean something," said Laura Nemes, frowning in righteous perplexity.

"What if it doesn't?" said Orr, straightening his punishment of a spine in the chair. "In my opinion, after a good many years on this planet—some might say too many—meaning is a sorely overrated commodity."

The faces he looked at seemed hurt. Disappointed. Disapproving. Downright affronted by the notion, though none called him on the declaration, though some shifted in their seats uneasily.

He saw in their expressions that they had bedded down in their preconceptions and were about to concede to no man in the matter. Especially not him.

He felt bad. Did sigh, now.

He knew they were tender creatures. He was a tender creature too. So raw he felt sometimes his nerve endings were showing through his skin and hurting just by touching air.

"Howard Henry?" Dick offered him the floor, magnanimously.

Orr didn't stand. None of them had done, so far, so he thought it incumbent on himself to do likewise.

He had it all worked out, what he was going to say. About his wife. How she'd gone. It was all in his head.

"Started with a cough. Chest infection. Chest infection lifted with some meds, got pain in her back now . . . Didn't think anything of it. Thought it would pass. It didn't . . . Stage four lung cancer. That's the worst. That's terminal. Means you'll die of it, but they don't tell you when. I said to her—*you're gonna get treatment, and you're gonna get over this thing*. People do. You hear about it all the time. Oncologist said it was extensive and she needed to put on some weight because the treatment would be tough. He asked if she wanted to know the prognosis—meaning how many months, how many weeks. She said 'No, I do not.' Well . . . She never did get that treatment. One night she couldn't get her breath. I called EMS. They took her in. I sat with her. Oxygen mask on her face—she needed it. Looked real weak, but she was tugging off that mask and talking. Nurse told her to stop it. My daughter and son came. The other two were planning flights. I told them not to. Things would be fine. Their mother just needed to shake this bug and get her treatment. 'Pneumonia,' Gretchen said to me. 'Pneumonia and cancer'—like I didn't know it. My daughter held her hand. I let her have the chair beside the bed. After two hours doing nothing I got up and said to them I had a conference to go to in San Diego, and couldn't let my friends down. They'd be expecting me. I said nothing's going to happen in a hurry and I'd be down and back by Monday morning and by then she'll be sitting up in bed and laughing. My son and daughter stayed. They didn't say anything and they didn't argue. They didn't want to say what they were thinking in case they were right. And they were. So I was away in San Diego, five years ago, at a SMLS meet-up just like this one when I got the phone call that she'd passed. Voices on the phone, all weeping and hollering and sobbing . . . I didn't see. I didn't know. I was stupid. Maybe I knew I was running away. I don't know. It hit me hard. Harder than I can put in words. And that's why I haven't done this thing for five years, but I'm doing it now, and I don't know why, except to say it's my last one."

Orr did not say any of this.

Instead, he stared down for a long while, looking at the sorry shape of his hands, thinking of what he wanted to impart, debating if he had the right to go against the status quo—the status quo being that they were all so special, that they were good, and they hurt, much more than anybody else hurt, and that they were God's people.

"If I've got anything to say, it's this one thing," he said. "I'm not a hero or a legend. I'm a man who was in the wrong place at the wrong time. Nine times running. Some of you want to explain that by mysticism or by miracles, and that's fine, but did I ever feel that? No. It just hurt a hell of a lot, is what it did. And I'm sorry."

Nobody spoke.

"You get afraid to step outdoors." He avoided their eyes lest they look into his own. "You check the forecast. Maybe the forecast is wrong. You look at the sky. Never stop looking. That's the tough thing. And that's the thing you've got to learn, if you get through this. The fact of not knowing if it's a good day or the day when the boot falls."

When he did look up, he looked at the skinny girl, who was now chewing the sleeve of her sweater. The girl who lost her electric virginity on Yosemite's Half Dome. How many more strikes did she have to look forward to? Would she survive the next one? Or the one after that? Or would the next one never come?

"You've got to live with it," Orr said. "Live with the fear, each and every day. Living with the possibility. That's the worst thing. That's all I got to say."

Dick Hanselaar started clapping like he was warming his hands on a camp fire. The rest took him up, but it was out of politeness, Orr could tell. Dick stood up and rescued the energy in the room, saying, if everyone was happy they'd have fifteen minutes for photographs then make their way to the Kirk Douglas restaurant, where their pre-ordered three course meal was about to be served. And, yes, the vegan option was taken care of. "If we can please end with our customary vow of allegiance."

Orr stood up along with the other survivors. Heads bowed—Orr thought of funerals again, unavoidably—they intoned in ragged unison the verse cobbled together, he thought, from various self-help mantras:

"I am a beautiful and unique spirit. I love myself and I am worthy of love. My worth is untarnished by my imperfections or the way others see me. I am worthy of good things. I am strong. I am positive. Each day I work towards being the person I want to be. I seek to surround myself with those who support me and do not question or undermine me. I am the creator of my own destiny."

"Amen," said a voice.

"God Bless America," said someone else.

Before they dispersed, Dick Hanselaar quickly corralled them, sheepdog-like, for the requisite group photograph, arranging them like props—*tall at the back, please, short at the front, that's it*—against the picture window with the swimming pool, topiary and cloudless blue sky beyond. Orr stood in position and smiled, but felt somehow he'd punctured the occasion. Deflated its balloon. It didn't make him feel good, and he over-compensated by grinning, feeling lousy about that in turn.

After that a few people wanted a photo call, predictably, with him and his hat. Orr unwrapped it and held it against his chest for the cameras. Scorch hole over his heart. It was the least he could do, after throwing cold water over the proceedings.

Cheech Gerlach, the imp, was handing out business cards profligately, though it was anybody's guess what his business actually was, and Orr could see the anorexic girl peering fixedly at her cell phone, typing a tweet or some such with frenetically jabbing thumbs. She wore a fixed smile but her eyes were glazed.

"One point eight million Instagram followers," said Renée Mancuso. "Three point two on Twitter."

"I don't understand 75% of those words," Orr said flatly, though in fact he did, and she knew it.

She offered him her arm. He shook his head. Said he was going to bow out of the meal. Said he felt tired. He wrapped up his ranger hat in the cellophane bag and made his way towards the elevator without saying any goodbyes.

Orr could see Dick Hanselaar making for him and held up a hand to stop him. "This holy man has to go pee." He punched in his floor number, but Dick was standing behind him at a distance.

"You'll be missed."

"I guess," said Orr, before the elevator doors closed. Had he made it clear he wasn't coming back? He couldn't remember. Anyway, it didn't matter now.

As he travelled in vertical seclusion, he stuck his nose in the dry cleaning bag and inhaled the smell of embers, pine and the John Muir Trail. Only when he got to his room and loosened his pants did he realise he'd written nothing in the Book of Condolences for Lenny Soto.

He felt queasy. He didn't know why. Maybe the coffee. Maybe the creamer. Maybe the stuffiness of the room now. Hotels were always way hotter than he liked. He switched on the air con. Something was loose inside, because it chirruped like a bird.

Lying on the bed, one wrist on his brow, Orr wondered if they liked him now. He wondered why the hell he cared any more. He'd spent all his life worrying if people truly liked him. He wasn't special in that regard, or in putting on weight as the years mounted up. He'd boxed in his youth, in the Navy. He'd been taught to roll with the punches, but he realised he'd never learned how to do that. Not really. And even before he was asleep, he felt the day had been a dream.

• ● •

Temperature 78°. Sunny. High 80F. Chance of rain 0%. Humidity 11%. Clear. Wind SW at 5 mph. Sunrise 5:48 a.m. Sunset 8:08 p.m.

Only one trip to the bathroom during the night, courtesy of his enlarged prostate, but he hadn't stood waiting for a trickle, so that was a win. Orr dressed in chinos and the black and red check "lumberjack" shirt his wife had bought online without consultation. Gretchen'd had strong opinions on what shirts he wore. He was a void of such opinion himself, and always had been.

He didn't wish to encounter any of the survivors at breakfast, to endure their catechisms or be subject to their interrogation, and eschewed the delights of the breakfast bar for a diner half a block away.

His deceased wife ventriloquised as he ordered granola and yoghurt, but afterwards he succumbed to his own will and called over the waitress (Korean) to request crispy bacon, eggs, lightly scrambled, and pancakes with maple syrup. Just a trickle, like Gretchen, dead, was watching him. *His* health. Crazy, when you thought about it.

On his refill, he watched a lean, bristle-haired boy in a camouflage jacket, wrapped up like it was winter. Orr didn't notice the cold. It could dip to below zero and he'd be fine in a T-shirt. Twenty below didn't bother him. Once, he and Gretchen'd had some cold nights working alongside Christians handing out food parcels to the homeless. One of the poor unfortunates had recognised him as the "Lightning Guy" from TV and didn't want to touch him, or the food he'd been offered. When they sat in the car afterwards, Orr had said to his wife, "I'm not good for much, am I?" Gretchen was her usual straight-talking self. "You don't need to be good for anything. You just need to be good."

He thought of that now, and of her, and the little ones. Not so little these days. His children were scattered. Two on the East Coast. One in Florida. One in Houston. Grandkids innumerable. He lost count. Forgot their names sometimes, even looking at their faces. They got bored on FaceTime. Didn't know what to say to their papa. Had other more important things to do. Way back, naked in a paddling pool, one of them had said, "I'd like to be struck by lightning, to see what it's like." Orr had told them firmly "No. You wouldn't."

Check-out time was eleven. He paid by the touch of a Mastercard. The checkout woman was clearly transitioning from being a man. That didn't bother him. Everyone had their battles. He was asked, pleasantly, "Would you like to sign up for our newsletter and frequent stay offers?"

"No, thank you."

She told him that was fine, but if he changed his mind he could always do so via the website.

Well, that's a hell of a relief, thought Orr.

Before he left, he asked if she could do him a favour and put something in the trash for him. She said sure, and he handed her his ranger hat in the dry cleaning bag. She put it somewhere, he didn't see where, and told him to have a great day. Orr said he'd try to.

When he'd driven from North Hollywood, he usually figured five hours but had done it in under that, starting out from the McDonald's near Lankershim/Vineland and Riverside Drive. But the friend he used to visit was there no longer. Still, he stuck to old habits, there being little else to stick to, and went through the Grapevine, taking the road on up to Merced, was the intention.

He saw the sign for Bakersfield, which reassured him, then stayed on the 99 through Tulare, Selma, and Fresno, to Chowchilla, where he didn't need to top up with gas, but chose to, at the Merced Truck and Auto Plaza, ten miles from the highway, but he was sure as hell it used to be on it. Maybe they moved the highway, just to mess with him.

Not much more to the store than sodas, chips, jerky, and beer, so he stocked up on those. Wasn't sure what he had in the refrigerator. Chips, jerky and beer sounded fine.

His oxblood Plymouth Trail Duster had more dents and scratches than when he last unscrewed the cap, but he had no abiding desire to touch them up. They could be touched up when he was dead and gone.

At the pump he saw a scruffy black and white mongrel in the front seat of a pickup. A second before he realised the steering wheel was on the far side, he'd thought the thing was in the driver's seat, which would have been a heck of a thing. As he filled his fuel tank, the creature nevertheless fixed him with a gaze of aloofness and thinly-veiled hostility. Something he'd only, so far in life, perceived in the human species, and was glad to be rid of the mutt's casual disdain.

Taking the on-ramp back to the 99, he was pressing down on the gas as he passed a figure wrapped in blue-green robes walking at a steady and unhurried pace in the same direction as he himself was travelling. The figure was slight and the silk, or cotton, whatever it was, billowed in spite of the lack of breeze. The gait was assured, the spine straight, the neck held high. The face, as he overtook it, that of a Middle Eastern woman. It took a second before Orr realised she was carrying a baby. Teal was the colour he was trying to remember the name of. *Teal.*

Orr found himself braking. He could see in his rear view there were no cars behind him, and in his side mirror, no-one but the Middle Eastern looking woman, walking at the same, long-legged, languorous pace.

When he'd stopped, he reversed, stopping before he got to her. A few seconds later she appeared framed in the side window. He guessed her eyes were a question her lips couldn't deliver, so he nodded.

She got in. Didn't say thank you. Said nothing. Gently tucked back the cloth over her baby's forehead. Orr looked at the child, then the woman looked at him, so he looked away.

He put the car in drive and rejoined 99. Presuming that was what she wanted, but all he got was silence.

"Where you going? I live in Sonora. That's north."

"North."

If he expected more, he didn't get it.

"I drop you somewhere?" Orr ventured. "You say stop, okay?"

"Stop."

Was she Middle Eastern, or North African? He couldn't tell. Maybe he should be able to tell. He didn't know.

As Orr drove he tried not to stare, but in the periphery of his vision he could see her complexion and thought it to be smooth and unblemished. He wondered if chocolate when referring to skin, or coffee-coloured, were deemed offensive now. If he'd been asked on pain of death, he'd have said hers was a warm reddish-yellow, like the heartwood of elm. He couldn't see a whole lot. A headscarf, perhaps they called it a *burqa*, encircled her face. He thought a *burqa* covered the face, and this didn't. Maybe the word was *hijab*—for Muslims anyway. But he didn't know if she was Muslim. He didn't know if she was anything.

She was a woman with a baby, dressed in silken robes, that's all he knew.

Turquoise, lilac and cerulean.

He'd noticed when she climbed in she'd been carrying a shopping bag, which now sat between her feet. A green Save Mart bag with a design on it reading: "Okie Dokie Artichokie", which was brimming with vegetables and fruit. Out of the corner of his eye he could see a pineapple, eggplant, bananas, mango.

Her feet were bare.

Was she a Los Angeleno? No. Didn't think so. But it wasn't impossible. It didn't look like she spoke the language, but that didn't mean anything. The whole economy ran on people who didn't speak English, he knew that.

If she was a newcomer, perhaps she was a refugee.

Perhaps she had no home.

Perhaps this was it.

He didn't know.

From time to time he looked across and smiled at her, to relieve the lack of conversation, in case the Grand Canyon of silence made her feel uncomfortable, but clearly it didn't. The one who was uncomfortable was him.

The child didn't cry, that was a thing, and he wondered if it was sleeping. She nestled it gently against her chest, rocking it almost imperceptibly, her shoulders shifting a little from side to side, and it seemed content. A part of her. An extension to her being. Young enough to be that, still. Unformed, as it were, though he thought children came out pretty formed, in his recollection. He couldn't remember any blank slates in his brood. They all had plenty to say from the get-go.

Still. The simplicity of it. She seemed to carry her motherly responsibilities without undue tension. He hadn't observed that for a time.

"You mind?"

Tired of the drone of the asphalt, he slipped a DIY compilation CD in the dash.

The woman's eyes drooped slightly—perhaps she was tired, long time on the road—but she shook her head. No she didn't.

And so they listened—or at least he listened—to Duke Ellington, "Take the 'A' Train". After that, "Mary's Boy Child" by Harry Belafonte, during which Orr looked down at the baby and smiled through his white whiskers.

"First record my mother ever owned," he said, not knowing if she understood. "My father bought it for her birthday. 'We're going to get her that song.'" The music played a while longer and when the song came to an end, he said: "Harry Belafonte. A rare talent."

The woman offered neither agreement nor counter-argument. Perhaps none could be conceived, thought Orr to himself, and the smile stayed on his face as he drove.

She wore one small jewel in the lobe of the ear on the side of her face he could see. When it caught the sunlight it shone a microdot somewhere between blue and green. She might have been twenty. Might have been forty. It was hard for him to pin her down. Her appearance to him did not speak of the Sierra Nevada, or of California north or south, even of Hollywood, for all its creation of wild and exotic places and planets far away, but spoke of some desert, some vast Sahara, or Yemen, with endless sand dunes and sphinxes, or somewhere—

Yes . . . *Biblical.*

And, not desiring to, Orr thought of his father.

A Pentecostal pastor in Pulaski, Virginia. Used to take a block of wood and three nails to the congregation every Sunday. Bash those three nails into the wood with a hammer—*BAM! BAM! BAM!* . . . Sure got their attention. Not to mention frightening his young self pretty much to death, every time.

Orr remembered, too, how the family used to drive into the next state to get rid of his dad's liquor bottles, so none of his parishioners would see them. Even as a child, Orr wondered if it might shake their faith if they had. His own was on unsafe ground while he was still in short pants.

His daddy used to take him on fishing trips for what he called "Man Time". When he cast his line he would say that his job was like Jesus's—"fishin' for souls". Returning from one such jaunt, Orr, being about six or seven, saw a bum by the side of the road, thumb extended. He asked, "Daddy, if we're fishing for souls, why didn't we stop and give him a ride?" His father had said nothing, just stopped the car without looking at him, reversed it right up beside the hobo, and let him get in. When they'd gotten home, his father had rolled up his sleeves and disinfected that car. Hosed it down with bleach from top to bottom. Took a yard brush to the seats, ran a soap and cloth over every inch of it. Orr never forgot that, and didn't know why it came to him now.

Hitchhiker, he guessed.

It was seventeen miles and a twenty minutes' drive, absent of communication other than the above, before they reached Merced. Orr knew that Merced to Sorora took sixty minutes, so knew he was an hour from home.

"Not sure if I should keep on the 99 to a rest stop."

The woman didn't turn her head.

The baby seemed asleep now. Both of them immobile.

He decided to keep to his route. If she couldn't converse, that was her problem. She didn't look surly. She didn't look worried. He guessed the word was impassive. Which would be a nice thing to be. To let the world roll over you like waves, long as there's someone there to drive you to your destination.

It shouldn't vex him. He hadn't asked for company, so why should he be riled now he didn't have it?

Still . . . Hell of a thing.

In Merced, with no instruction to the contrary, he exited G Street, remembering G for Gold Country as he always did. The exit lane swirled around and about since he was coming off the freeway, then he came to a traffic signal where it intersected. He turned right and followed it, out of town, north, knowing it would become the Snelling Road, but the official J59 was something like P or R Street and tangled through Merced so badly it was a real time waster and headache.

By now Orr could foresee this woman being with him all the way home, which he didn't want particularly, his charitable actions having their limit, so when he saw a Walmart with a large parking lot, that was where he headed for and pulled in. It was that or the In-N-Out Burger.

He applied the handbrake. The baby murmured slightly, and the woman pressed the knuckle of one finger to its gums, but showed no intention of getting out, and gazed at him as if he'd done it for his own purposes and not hers.

"Okay," said Orr.

Once they were back on the J59, he felt he could relax. It wasn't built up like LA. There was some beautiful countryside at first, like the puckie brush of Wyoming, then into oak studded rolling hills. His finger went to the dashboard.

"Sorry." Not that she'd reacted. "Used to be signs all along this stretch of road telling you to turn off your A/C to avoid overheating," he said. "They do that when you get desert or climbing elevation. I don't think you need it with modern vehicles and all their bangs and whistles. But I can't help it. Better safe than sorry, I say."

The woman hadn't moved.

"Air conditioning," he explained.

She gave a long blink, but didn't look at him.

"Some say let the car do its job. I say, sure, you wear those pants without a belt, you see if they fall down."

Perhaps it was wishful thinking but he saw his smile reflected on her lips, which were pink and arid-looking.

"You okay?" Orr said then, in a stutter. "I, I mean . . . you are okay?"

The woman rolled her head slightly towards him, and nodded microscopically, like she was weary. There wasn't an ounce of fat on her, he noticed, but her cheeks were not hollow and her eyes not sunken. He wondered what she looked like not covered up and wondered if she could be on some fashion catwalk—but as soon as the idea came to him he found it repulsive. Obscene.

His CD played The Foundations—"Build Me Up Buttercup".

He sang along with it, tapping the steering wheel with his fingertips.

The baby didn't wake.

"Good kid," he said.

Immediately east of Snelling, about five hundred feet east of a pretty little cemetery and the elementary school was where he knew to make a left, north, to follow the J59. It was marked but easy to miss. Turning into La Grange Road, he followed it all the way to Stanislaus County and then into Tuolumne County, by which time they were travelling across the foothills of the Sierra Nevada.

Not a word had been spoken.

The rocks changed colour.

He thought of Yosemite. That granite valley carved out by glaciers. He thought of the volcanic rocks. The basalt flows, latite tuff, and lava flows. The Inyo Craters, south-east of the park—volcanoes that erupted three thousand to forty thousand years ago. Those things put you in your place.

He thought of the lower montane forests along the western boundary. The California black oak, the butterscotch aroma of ponderosa pine, incense-cedar, and white fir. Then the ancient, giant Sequoias and redwoods off Wawona Road. All the days and years he had spent amongst the oldness of wood. He missed it now. Missed the humility.

Silver Apron. Emerald Pool. Vernal Falls. Liberty Cap . . .

His first time there, he'd never forget. He'd driven up what used to be called the Priest grade, really steep winding road, never been on that kind of road before, and it was raining hard. He kept thinking if he went off this road, nobody would ever find him—these were the days before cell phones—and he hadn't left word with a soul. By the time he reached the valley, it was all socked in and it was dusk. He didn't know where to go so he went to the lodge. "I'm working here." They said "Who are you? Who with?" Orr said "The Park Service." So they called park dispatch and Jeff Tillinghast pulled up and brought him over to the Ranger Club. Jeff became the best buddy he ever had. That night, he didn't know where he was, sleeping in this log structure, small room, woken up by a noise like strangulated children. Never heard coyotes before. Year later he recognised that sound as a kill, but back then he didn't, and it had a real effect on the bladder.

Orr never did get back to sleep that night. Found his eyes wide open so went walking and was up and about as the clouds broke and the sun came up, and the falls were there, he could hear them, and there was snow halfway down the Valley floor. Spectacular.

Up till then he had no idea such places existed outside of storybooks. And he was going to work there. He walked around the whole day with his head up. Never ate breakfast, never ate lunch, just went from one place to another, had a plate of something for dinner, out to watch the moon. Crazy. Beautiful. Couldn't get enough of it.

A series of PG&E power lines curved low over the road.

Orr saw towers silhouetted on the escarpments, against the sky.

The Middle Eastern woman looked out into the emptiness. What she saw there he couldn't surmise.

Perhaps that kind of place was home to her.

Her eyes wrinkled against the sunlight, which whited out the window that framed her. Her elbow rested on the ridge at the bottom of it, and her long brown fingers were splayed on her brow, but not with any semblance of distress.

He guessed if she wanted him to know what she was thinking, or who she was, she would have told him by now, or would have tried to. He decided not to question that, or let it concern him anymore.

Five minutes later the infant gurgled and Orr noticed its mother was looking at him, not with any curiosity or with any demand, just an action she had taken. One arm cradled the baby, the other curled under it and lay limply across her chest. The hand was incredibly perfect.

"You want to stop?"

The Middle Eastern woman nodded. The road ahead was long and straight. There was no traffic in either direction, and no habitation for miles around.

"Here?"

She nodded again, though not forcefully or with urgency, as if she knew he would do what she wanted without coercion. And she was right.

Orr pulled the car off the highway into a sandpit, kicking up dust. He rolled to a halt and put on the brake.

"Here?" he asked again. In the middle of nowhere?

She opened the passenger side door and swung herself out, carrying the baby in the sling of her garment and lifting out her bag of groceries from the foot well with her other hand.

Barefoot, he thought. Not even sandals. What the heck?

"Here?" he said a third time, but, without smiling at him, she pushed the door shut. His CD had finished and ejected itself. He quickly snatched it, placed it in its sleeve, tossed it in the glove box and slammed it closed.

Why this place? Who would come for her? Too many questions to contemplate. Maybe there were no questions at all. Maybe he was just tired and not thinking straight. Maybe it made sense to anyone with half a brain and it was him, with less than that.

Orr put the car into drive, and paused. Watched her in his side mirror.

The tall figure walking away from him, unhurriedly, facing nowhere, holding her offspring in her arms, coils of the sand he had kicked up curling in the air, surrounding her like a sentient murmuration, making her semi-transparent, a ghost.

He put on his sunglasses and immediately took them off again.

On the passenger seat there sat a large orange.

He grunted.

Payment for a good Samaritan, he guessed.

He thought of getting out, then, suddenly, and not leaving her there, of doing something, his hand finding the door handle, but he looked back in the side mirror and the veil of sand still clung to the air, but she was nowhere to be seen.

•●•

After forty-five minutes of the J59, he crossed the series of railroad tracks and dropped down a hill to the T-intersection where it met Highway 120/180 which he always took as a signal he was almost home, even though it was another sixteen miles to go to Sonora, Queen of the Southern Mines, in the heart of Gold Country, with a surfeit of wine tasting and fine eating establishments to die for, though he never went to them. Never needed to. His wife's cooking was better than anything out of a freezer rustled up by a stranger who wanted to take your money. He figured, at least.

On the 120, Orr took care to keep to the speed limit of fifty-five, unlike some jackasses. Not only it being unsafe for you and other innocent drivers you could smack into, but you risked by dint of foolishness getting stopped by the CHP, so it was a no-brainer. What's the god-damned hurry about everything, anyhow?

Mist veiled the conifers that fringed the loop of his driveway on Ahwahnee Road.

Getting out of the car, stretching his back and glad to get home before sunset, he inhaled the sweet smell of lupine, then a pungent waft of Californian bay laurel.

The air was fine, damp, warm.

Orr took out his iPhone and poked the weather app, which elicited a grunt. At least the thing hadn't given up on him.

Temperature 52°. Low 52F. Chance of rain 30%. Humidity 48%. Heavy cloud. Wind W at 5 to 10 mph. Moonrise 10:04 p.m. Moonset 7:05 a.m.

It forecast for an hour's time a little cloud icon with rain, changing around 1:00 a.m. to a cloud icon with a cute little lightning symbol. Those things persisted through the night, it looked like.

Orr pocketed the contraption, picked up his bag of groceries from the backseat. He'd forgotten something, came back out to zap the auto lock off again and stretched over to fetch the orange from the passenger seat.

He unpacked his paltry supplies in the kitchen, remembering, unbidden, that time he and Gretchen had gone shopping and someone asked for his autograph in the parking lot outside Yosemite Lakes Country Store in Groveland. "Better stand back while I do this," he'd joked to the happy couple, pointing at the sky. The couple laughed and so had he. "You proud of me?" he'd asked his wife while they drove, afterwards. "For what?" Gretchen had said.

He'd started as an Entrance Fee Ranger at Tioga Pass, and a Field Training Officer and Education Instructor in Tuolumne Meadows. That's where they'd met. She was also a National Park Ranger. They'd lived in Yosemite Valley, till they didn't.

The beer and jerky were suddenly an unappetising prospect, and Orr opened a can of tuna and ate it with a fork from the tin. No sense in dirtying a plate.

The TV showed footage of a black guy on the ground being hit by police officers with batons. A human being. His life, like that. Animals. No, worse than animals. Animals only acted on instinct, those people *chose* to act like that. Orr thumbed the off-button and tossed the remote at a throw pillow.

He took his pills, took himself to bed. Amitriptyline. One at night time, to help him sleep, to relax the muscles. That woman doc with the piled-up hair had told him "They used to prescribe this for depression, but they found it really works well as a muscle relaxant. I'm not giving it to you as an anti-depressant." He'd said, "Fine by me." *Do not drink alcohol,* he noticed—though he must have read it before. An instruction, or rule for life? If the latter, a damn good one. He took a big white dollop of moisture balm—he liked that word, *balm*—and slathered it over his lower legs and forearms. The dryness of his skin sucked it up in an instant. Another rule for life, according to Gretchen, and she was right about it, for once. Not for once. She was *always* right, and always told him she was always right, in case of confusion on his part.

Lying alone in the king-size bed, Orr missed running his hand over her warm back. It didn't give him peace that she went on ahead of him. She'd needed little from him in life, but he wished he had given more. His navigation was lacking.

Orr failed to get to sleep in the first half-hour and always knew that was a sign he'd get very little. The drive had made him concentrate and had taxed his eyes and now all he could see when he shut them was the road disappearing into the horizon and cars passing by.

At midnight he heard the rain getting heavier, tapping ever harder on the glass of the skylights as if needing his attention.

The roads wouldn't leave his mind, or the Middle Eastern looking woman who plagued him now with unknowns.

Why did she not speak? Who was she?

Was she a ghost?

Did he remember her from a news bulletin?

She seemed so close, so familiar, yet far distant.

Where was she going?

Who was she going to meet?

What was her purpose?

Did she have a purpose at all, or was she lost, like the best of us?

He remembered the coverage on the news he had only half-watched. Perhaps it was Syria. Perhaps it was a city called Aleppo. That name popped into his head. *Aleppo.* He had heard it many times. On CNN, just as the skinny girl with the Instagram followers had been on CNN.

Images of a devastated city resurfaced in Orr's mind. Images like Dresden after the firebombs, except not in grainy black and white, filmed in colour, hand held, or by a phone. The place was a body with no bones. Incredible that people could still thrive in such a cemetery. Could still breathe and love and touch and mend wounds and play there—children in the street, with nothing, no fathers or mothers. Smears of cement dust on their cheeks and in their tousled hair. Coughing it up through insurmountable grief.

The question now, unbidden but inevitable . . . was the baby her only child?

Or had there been another, far away, in a foreign land, covered in rubble, buried under sheets of concrete, with anguished men scampering desperately to dig it out?

And . . . Did she have a husband, or was he left behind? Lying bloodied on a road someplace? A doctor, medical man, saving lives. Did they both make it to the border? Did they both make it across the ocean?

Orr ached with the possibilities.

Perhaps it was easier for him to accept she was dead than that she was alive and suffering in the world. The supernatural always being the more comforting option.

A respite from the world as it really was.

He thought of her child lying amongst rubble. A little hand or arm scuffed by dirt. The bombs blind, unthinking, descending. The things she might have seen that he cannot.

And the child in her arms.

Was it safe? Was it hungry?

Who would it grow up to become?

Would it be hated or loved?

He could not know.

Nobody could know.

That was the agony that didn't go away.

Orr pressed his bare feet to the bedroom floor. Sat and listened to the storm, shoulders hunched. The tamping of rain had ceased, perhaps temporarily, nevertheless a *rom-pom-pom* of thunder drummed as the weather front moved across from the Bay Area.

Through slatted eyes he saw his Luminox on the night stand. Brought it up close to his face. Read 3:00 a.m., gazed ceilingward, and rolled the crunchiness in his neck.

He rose and descended to the kitchen, heavy-limbed, in pyjama shorts and *Eat, Sleep, Repeat* T-shirt, taut across his belly, shorter with every machine wash. He knew the do's and don'ts of a thunderstorm—*duh!* Of course he did. One was to stay put and not to move around till it was over, but the other thing was to check everything was switched off, including the lights, so that's what he did.

He bent over, grunting, and yanked the plug out of the socket at the foot of the stairs. In his den, the antique Dell that begrudgingly served as his desktop needed attending. An upright fan stood a few feet away and he disabled that too, as well as his printer. The chest freezers in the basement could take their chances.

When he had unplugged everything—the kitchen utensils, toaster (wedding gift), coffee maker, TV—Orr looked around the kitchen in case he'd missed anything.

The orange that had been on the passenger seat was the sole piece of fruit in the fruit bowl. He'd never been a fruit person. It was always Gretchen made him have his "five a day". If it was up to him he'd have none a day.

Orr picked it up, feeling its weight for a second, tossing it lightly and catching it, then took it to the worktop. He found a knife and cut it in half, then half again. The four segments rocked gently as he placed them on a dinner plate.

Orr carried it to the sliding doors beyond which he could see shadowy branches and stepped out into the garden, his and his wife's garden, which they had cultivated from dirt and sand and stones, where the wind was wet and refreshingly chill.

Orr felt spots of water hit his arms and shoulders and neck and hair and scalp, by no means a downpour, by no means even rain. More like little apologetic tapping reminders of things forgotten.

Orr sat down at the picnic table with the plate in front of him. He couldn't see to the end of his property, but he knew there was a wildness beyond. Another *rom-pom* sounded, another hint of the symphony to come.

Orr brought the first segment of orange to his mouth and bit deeply into its juicy flesh. Its taste filled his mouth, enveloping his dulled, half-sleepy senses completely.

Another beckoning rumble wheeled across the blackness of the sky. Night's grand hesitation. Starless. Welcoming.

Orr picked up the second segment of orange. It rested in the cradle of his fingers, so bright it shone. He did not know from what source it owed such brilliance.

Orr closed his eyes and kept them closed as he sank his teeth into its beauty, its offering.

He waited for his next lightning strike to happen.

Perhaps it did.

STORY NOTES & ACKNOWLEDGEMENTS

MANY PEOPLE, in their different ways, helped these tales come to fruition:

Foz Allan, Peter Atkins, Andrew David Barker, Ruth Baumgarten, John Clewarth, Ray Cluley, Andy Cox, Dan Coxon, Ellen Datlow, Dave Elsey, Peter Engelmann, Gary Fry, Christopher Golden, Andy Hedgecock, Stan Hey, Charlie Hey, Sarah Howard, Michael Kelly, Tim Lebbon, Steve Lockley, Johnny Mains, Emily McMahon, Antone Minard, Mark Morris, Matthew Parry, Ray Russell & Rosalie Parker, Jae Prowse, Maria Pilar San Roman, Steven Shiel, Matt Stephens, Jo Taylor, Steve Toase, Cath Trechman, Frank Turner, Patricia Volk, Sean Wallace and Sylvia Morena-Garcia. They know what they did, and I thank them deeply for it.

In particular I must single out Ray Cluley and Cliff McNish who read many of the stories herein and gave generous and perceptive feedback, and Priya Sharma for her insightful and sensitive introduction. My respect and admiration must also extend to Pete and Nicky Crowther, Mike, Tamsin, and the whole team at PS Publishing, including, not least, Pedro Marques for designing the book you hold in your hands.

The following words were primarily written as notes to myself, for myself, on the origins of these stories. Some readers find such addenda interesting—others, quite understandably, find them superfluous. If you're in the latter camp, by all means pass them by. The author will not think the less of you for doing so.

The Holocaust Crasher

As anyone who follows my work will have noticed, I am extremely interested in stories about hoaxers and deceivers, self-deceivers, and the psychology and motivations of such individuals. In recent memory, you will recall, no doubt, the anonymous "Nick" who asserted to the police that he had been repeatedly abused by a "VIP paedophile ring" including former home secretary Leon Brittan and ex-prime minister Edward Heath. Believed hook, line and sinker by the Metropolitan Police to be "credible and true". Carl Beech's tales were found by a later investigation to be a complete fabrication.

Another outstanding example—one that almost beggars belief—is that of Tania Head, whose name frequently appeared in media reports of the attack on the World Trade Centre on September 11, 2001, to the extent that she joined the WTC survivor support group, later becoming its president. However, Head's story was a hoax. Real name Alicia Esteve Head, she was not even in NYC on Sept 11th, let alone in the South Tower when flight 175 hit. She never crawled through flames on the 78th floor and she had no husband called "Dave" who died in the North Tower. Nor did she take a dying man's wedding ring to give to his widow. On Sept 11, 2001, she was in a class studying for her master's degree in her home city of Barcelona. In fact, she didn't even travel to the USA for the first time until 2003. Nonetheless, Head was photographed with Mayor Michael Bloomberg, former mayor Rudy Giuliani, and former NY Governor George Potaki, and regularly escorted groups attending Ground Zero. Only when fact checkers at *The New York Times* found that her supposed employer in the South Tower, Merrill Lynch, had no record of her did the fantasy collapse.

This extraordinary case prompted me to wonder what would be the most extreme and most inexcusable deception imaginable in terms of invented victimhood. This story is the result.

I agree with Professor Felix Weinberg (author of *Boy 30529: A Memoir*) who said fictional accounts masquerading as true stories of the Holocaust are "tantamount to desecrating war graves", and I have no wish either to contradict or dilute his moral repugnance.

If any reader thinks the subject should have been left well alone, I can only say I follow my instincts, whether an idea is unpalatable or not—and sometimes *because it is.*

Furthermore, if any reader thinks, not unreasonably, that the idea of anybody cashing in on the Holocaust in some depraved quest for attention is so inconceivably horrid as to be impossible, I regret to be able to point out instances where exactly that took place.

Joe Corry claimed in his memoir published by Simon & Schuster, that he assassinated a Nazi scientist with a crossbow, rescued Robert Oppenheimer from Holland, witnessed a Nazi experimental extermination camp where a rabbi approached him and kissed his hand, and saw inmates ripping the flesh from a dead horse. None of this was true.

In 1996 Herman Rosenblat appeared on Oprah Winfrey's TV show with an incredible story of being imprisoned at Buchenwald, and throwing apples over the fence to the young Jewish girl who would one day be his wife—of later meeting her, even more incredibly and movingly, on a blind date in New York. The story sold to Berkley Books, an imprint of Penguin, and a £17 million feature film was gearing up, when Holocaust scholars pulled the rug from under Herman's story, saying it could never have happened. Rosenblat claimed in his defence, however, that he had wanted "to make good in the world".

Similarly, Misha Defonseca, who published *Misha: A Memoir of the Holocaust Years* in 1997, claiming she survived the Warsaw Ghetto and was raised by wolves, justified it, after being exposed as a fake, by saying "it's not the *true* reality, but *my* reality."

What makes someone create a past that is profoundly distasteful and cruelly distorting of history, knowing their raw materials are the horrors other people *really did* suffer? Why would they be led to do something so profoundly shameful? I didn't know—and perhaps I shouldn't have asked—but I felt a strong urge to explore it.

As a curious and distasteful footnote, while I was writing "The Holocaust Crasher" in August 2020, there emerged the Tik-Tok "trauma porn" trend of social media "influencers" pretending to be Holocaust victims, dressing in striped pyjamas with dirt-smeared faces, talking to camera as if from heaven. Interestingly, when Tik-Tok was contacted, the company said the videos did not constitute a violation of their guidelines, due to their "educational nature". To quote a Rufus Wainwright song—what a world we live in.

The great American writer Flannery O'Connor's work was said by one critic to be "all about the operations of supernatural grace in the lives of natural men and women". I was reading her complete short fiction while I was working on this story, so I wouldn't be surprised if some of that rubbed off. What makes us human, or indeed inhuman, is various and delicate. Moreover, the "voice" of the story—first or third person, past or present tense—was tricky to find in this case. Only in watching Alan Bennett's *Talking Heads* monologues did I discover how it had to be. The banality of evil, indeed.

The Airport Gorilla

The catalyst for this one was a famous photograph which appeared in the UK and international press, showing the debris of an air crash (Malaysian Airlines Flight MH17) in rebel-held East Ukraine, and a man in uniform holding up a child's cuddly toy monkey. I wondered what happens next to that cuddly toy? Did he take it home to his child?

It was a horrible idea, but didn't seem enough. Then I thought, perversely, of the toy telling the story. I'd really enjoyed the 2009 novel *Me Cheeta* by James Lever, told as it was in the first person from the famous Hollywood chimpanzee's point of view—to comic, and surprisingly moving, effect. That still wasn't enough to make it a story, for me. Then, thanks to a chat with Steve Lockley, I thought of the granddaddy of all monkey stories, "The Monkey's Paw" by W. W. Jacobs—one of the best known horror tales even written—and that gave me the final piece of the jigsaw: the three wishes.

The House That Moved Next Door

This story wouldn't exist if Johnny Mains hadn't encouraged me to write something to celebrate Robert Aickman's centenary. Thing was, I wasn't sure how to approach the task. Yes, I was a fan—but by no means an expert on the legendary master of the strange tale. I remembered vividly, however, a fascinating interview about him with Jeremy Dyson (of *Ghost Stories* and *League of Gentlemen* fame) at the Halifax Ghost Story Festival. Rather than a pastiche, I wanted more to capture that sense of enigma Dyson had described as being often central to the author's work (together with "the cruelty of fate" and "an existential dread", as someone recently put it).

These descriptive phrases only apply to my story in hindsight, of course. I began to write it with little idea where it was heading, but trusting it to become peculiar in its own way, with the psychological fleshing-out and details of character emerging in the second draft. Above all, I hope with this one that I've achieved that Aickmanesque trick of any real and complete understanding being ever-so-slightly beyond one's grasp. And, hopefully, the story is the more chilling for that.

Unchain the Beast

A werewolf story in a political setting was an idea I had been playing around with for years. I was thinking of Paul Naschy's movies featuring the Waldemar Daninsky character and Franco's regime in Spain, and the film *Mephisto*, where an entertainer falls under the thrall of Hitler, with inevitably tragic consequences. Other influences were undoubtedly *Kiss of the Spider Woman* and Harold Pinter's chilling *One for the Road*.

I'm fascinated how dictatorships want to take control of, and fear, culture—especially culture that is challenging, and how, in those circumstances, the artist has to make a fundamental choice, whether to toe the line or speak from the heart. Shostakovich wrote that the Stalinist government systematically executed all the Soviet Union's Ukrainian folk poets, and when Pinochet took power in Chile in 1973, muralists were arrested, tortured and exiled. In 2015 the artist Danilo Maldonado, known as El Sexto, was held for ten months in Havana for producing anti-Castro art. And if that feels far removed from our comfortable lives in the West, we should remember President Donald Trump's vitriolic castigation of the "Hamilton" cast after it issued a fairly tame commentary directed at Mike Pence. Eve L. Ewing's article "Why Authoritarians Attack the Arts" (New York Times, April 6, 2017) is telling.

Seeing a documentary about Mexican folk art, the brightly coloured *alebrije*, and reading both about protestors on the streets of Mexico City in 1968 and the banned film *El Grito* made me want to set my story in that country. It also fitted nicely with the rise of Mexican directors like Guillermo Del Toro into the Hollywood A-list today. The massacre I describe is a fictionalised account of something that really happened. The politicians are fictional too—though, as we all know, Margaret Thatcher was photographed with Pinochet.

Incredibly, the genius that is Dave Elsey—he of the endlessly impressive SFX credits, including *Mr Holmes* and Moffat and Gatiss's *Dracula*—helped by sharing with me his tips on how to create a "Wolf Man" make-up, sixties style, even showing me some of the astonishing preparatory drawings of Hammer's Roy Ashton. Always lower dentition fangs, never upper like vampires. And ears, or no ears? The eternal dilemma!

The Little Gift

Murder, by definition, curtails lives—but we seldom read stories about the lives curtailed, or diverted, by such extreme and aberrant acts. This novella—and I didn't know it would be more than a short story, going in—began with the image of the dead bird. Our cat, even though a pet, has the pure animal instinct to kill, and I wanted to riff off that into the wider idea of predators, and, down the grey scale, into the so-called "normal" relationships between men and women.

As far as crime fiction goes, I'm more interested in innocent bystanders than the standard fare of loner cop hunting a killer. Reading a recent interview with Edgar award-nominated crime writers, I found it puzzling that they talked of the role of the genre to be "restoring order from chaos". Really? In my crime stories the chaos, if anything, gets worse. I don't really believe that fiction has to offer "a dream of justice" (as Jill Paton Walsh puts it)—in fact, I think it's the duty of a serious writer not to give spurious comfort at all. Crime impinges on lives deeply and sometimes in unexpected ways, the abnormal usurping the normal, and my characters tend to contribute to the mess rather than do the tidying up. They're part of the mystery, not the solution.

Certainly, the most tired of crime fictional tropes is the nameless dead young woman on the mortuary slab—an image that still perpetuates in too many cop stories, alongside the ubiquitous clever and charismatic serial killer. In "The Little Gift" I wanted to turn both on their heads. I wanted a victim that was a fully-fledged, multi-faceted character with volition and a story, before it is cut off. And I wanted to play with the unintended consequences of a violent act. Even the perverse thought that something "good" can come from something irrevocably evil and mindless.

The last image in the story, I should point out, came from a documentary about Kieslowski. The great director was describing how he knew exactly how long to hold the camera on a cube of sugar dissolving in the surface of a cup of coffee. The shot stayed with me, and ended up here.

Outside of Truth or Consequences

The title came during the final draft when I noticed a strangely named town in New Mexico, but this idea occurred to me ages ago and went in and out of a drawer many times in exasperation before I felt it began to work. It may have been inspired by Boris Karloff, either in *The Sorcerers* or *The Man Who Changed his Mind*, or indeed anything involving the swapping of minds, or bodies, not excluding the obvious influence of *The Fly*. (By the way, am I alone in preferring the old, surreal Vincent Price movie, with its nightmarish ending, rather than the Cronenberg remake?) The flavour here is, I hope, pure *Twilight Zone* or one of those deliciously enjoyable Amicus portmanteau films that always involve poetic justice. If the story works no more than on that level, I will be happy.

The Black Cat

I've never liked our cat. It isn't a good pet. It never shows affection. I spend my time cleaning out its litter tray and feeding it, even though it regurgitates most of it on the carpet. My days are spent trying to work with the background soundtrack of its incessant whining (like right now). No surprise, then, that I think of Poe's tale, "The Black Cat", on a daily basis, and identify fully with its protagonist. The internet is full of people who treat their pets as children—which I must admit I find peculiar, so these two things combined in my head with the notion of the cat in Poe's story symbolising a child. Pushing it further, I wondered, thinking the colour of the animal as no accident: what if it symbolised a black child?

Immediately I realised this might be contentious, and many might say, straight off the bat, I am not entitled to write about such a subject as racism. I cannot say whether that view is justified, only that I was drawn to the idea, as a way of expressing my disdain for one of the most horrendous things that has blighted human history, and indeed does so to this day. In fact, for that very reason I thought it my duty not to abandon the tale—which would be revealed to come from a racist's point of view.

However, I did decide that, if I was to write it at all, I needed to grasp, firstly, what Poe actually thought about race, and what his intention with "The Black Cat" actually was.

Importantly, at the outset, I found it is simply too sweeping (if tempting) to define Poe as a racist. Toni Morrison said, "No early American writer is more important to the concept of American Africanism than Poe", yet many critics have acknowledged the slippery way in which he deploys genre not only in the examination of race but also of gender and class. G. R. Thompson says "Almost everything in Poe is qualified by or controlled by a prevailing duplicity or irony".

I was intrigued to read that Leland Person and Lesley Ginsberg interpret "The Black Cat" solely as the re-enactment of the Nat Turner rebellion of 1831, while to Hannah Walker it "depicts the injustices of slavery and ultimately shows how slavery damns the South". It is hard after reading her analysis not to see the image of the hanged black cat as that of a lynched slave. Joan Dayan makes a similar compelling argument that the story is about the mutually destructive effects of slavery on both slave *and* master. It was Poe's political intent and personal attitudes, she says, that anchor the story. In this context (according to Walker) the narrator's wife has a pivotal role, representing Northern abolitionists in their fight to abolish slavery. It is she who takes a "solid stand" against the violent narrator/slaveholder, making Poe's tale a racial allegory and "an omen of the damning effects to come if the South continued to unleash aggression towards slaves and Northern abolitionists".

With all this in mind, I wrote my own "Black Cat" story (spurred on, at least in part, by remembering President Trump's horrid invective that there is "good and bad on both sides" when talking of white supremacists).

As a footnote: Amariah Brigham was, indeed, superintendent of Utica, New York, in 1843 and his aim was to make a model institution for the care of the insane. The writer of the letter and his patient in the story are entirely fictional, while the legend of Herakles as a baby throttling a python in his crib is taken from Oliver Stone's outstanding memoir of film making, *Chasing the Light.*

Beat the Card Home

Ten Word Tragedies was a book edited by Chris Golden and Tim Lebbon, subtitled *19 Stories inspired by one Frank Turner song*. In the lyrics of the song in question, musician Frank wanders through the snowy streets of New York and stumbles across a thrift store selling postcards by the yard: he "bought a mile and shipped them home . . . Ten thousand ten-word tragedies." It struck the editors as a great premise (and title) for an anthology. But when Frank told the guys it was a true story, it was a slam-dunk. Tim sent me three of the postcards in Frank's collection and I was free to do what I chose, inspired either by the image on the front or the written message on the back. One mentioned in a PS that the person who'd written it would probably "beat this card home" and the phrase struck a chord. What if the postcards kept on coming after something terrible had happened? It hit me as a wonderful metaphor for reaching out beyond the grave, in the most mundane yet personal form imaginable, and soon became about how we deal with grief. I once saw a film—John Sayles' *Limbo*—that ended with a couple seeing a rescue plane coming, and waving at it, but not knowing if it contained their enemies or their saviours. Then the screen cut to black. I wanted to end this story the same way, with two outcomes left possible in the reader's mind.

Vardøger

A *doppelgänger* story is nothing new, but hopefully this is a new spin on it. *The Non-Paying Guest* first saw light of day as a storyline for the BBC, when I worked on it with *Ghostwatch* producer Ruth Baumgarten and script editor James Saynor for the sadly ill-fated second run of the anthology drama series of *Ghosts* back in 1995. By a circuitous route, after a hiatus, it was further developed under the auspices of producer Foz Allan at BBC Wales (again to no avail, though in some tweaking I gained the wedding guest scene I've loved ever since). The television version having died a death, I decided to reconfigure it as a novella—which was, happily, picked up by Gary Fry to publish under his late, great Gray Friar Press imprint in 2009 as one of the Gray Matter Novellas series. It was deemed interesting enough to catch the attention of the British Fantasy Awards and The Shirley Jackson Awards, which is why I think it deserved a second outing in this volume. I should point out, that the original published version has been revised with numerous tweaks and cuts for reprinting here, hopefully not to its detriment. It will come as little surprise that the catalyst for this story was the notion of someone like

Peter Sutcliffe, The Yorkshire Ripper, being incarcerated in Broadmoor, and what the inner life of a serial killer *in denial* might be like.

A Meeting at Knossos

I have been fascinated by the Minotaur for as long as I can remember. It's always struck me as the archetypal monster story and I could never understand why it hadn't ever, to my knowledge, been exploited in cinema. I first pitched *The Minotaur* as a film idea to Milton Subotsky (the producer of the classic Amicus horror and fantasy films) way back in the seventies when I first came to London. I thought you could update the Greek myth, much as Hammer had done with *The Gorgon*, by setting it in their beloved mitteleurope world of 19th century gothic. Subotsky was far from convinced, so that was that.

More recently, visual influences rather than literary ones have brought it to the front of my mind. I think it's exceptionally hard to draw or sculpt a human figure with a bull's head and make it work, let alone have it embody the horror and pity imbued in the legend. The artist Beth Carter succeeds in this brilliantly, and her *Sitting Minotaur* and *Minotaur Reading* are direct catalysts for this story, even though I know that such artists as Michael Ayrton and, obviously, Picasso, have been obsessed by the character before.

The double idea that Daedalus not only created the labyrinth but fathered Icarus sparked me to put pen to paper. I had no idea where the meeting of the fallen Icarus and the freed Minotaur would lead, but it turned out to be about someone who has the chance of redemption—of *change*—and refuses it. I wanted to save the poor creature but I couldn't. Like Victor Frankenstein's creation, he was damaged not so much by an accident of birth but by the way he'd been treated, and the die was cast.

Some of this was, I'm sure, influenced by my reading of *The Devil You Know* by Dr Gwen Adshead and Eileen Home. Adshead is a forensic psychiatrist who has worked on the rehabilitation of violent offenders at Broadmoor hospital. I was struck when she described such patients as having been "witness to a trauma; the trauma which is their own life". That could be said to be the autobiography of my Minotaur—a retelling that I hope releases the age-old monster to be interpreted in a new way.

Sicko

For many years, in the back of my mind, I had a version of *Psycho* where the murder didn't happen. I was so disappointed by Gus Van Sant's shot-for-shot remake that it made me think: what would *Hitchcock* do if *he* were remaking *Psycho*? He'd tell us he was making a shot-for-shot remake, sure. But he'd then, mischievously, do something *completely different*—maybe avoid his most famous scene entirely! So what might happen if Marion *wasn't* killed in the shower—the most horrifying and pivotal scene in American cinema history? She would return the money, fine ... but what then? I realised I wanted to re-tell the story from a modern #metoo, post-Weinstein perspective, to show perhaps that monsters don't lurk in creepy houses next to highways, but might be the person you work with every day, or even the man you are in love with. Importantly, I wanted to empower Marion (arguably the most famous dead woman in movies) in the end. Hence the only person who will listen to her story is another woman.

The Naughty Step

Mark Morris asked me for a story for *After Sundown*, the first volume in an ongoing series of horror anthologies to be published by Flame Tree Press. I had the simple premise and title in mind, though I'd been thinking of it as a two-hander drama or short film, but decided on impulse it would be interesting to try it out on the page. Of course, the vulnerability and unknowable inner life of children has been rich territory for horror since forever; from Henry James's "The Turn of the Screw" and Saki's "Sredni Vashtar", right up to and including *The Exorcist*. I especially liked the enclosed nature of my set-up—no escape—and the fact that the whole thing happens on top of a crime scene.

Adventurous

In the tradition of the Brian Rix Whitehall farces, the adulterer is often surprised—usually with his pants down—by the husband arriving home early, and has to hide in the wardrobe. Much hilarity invariably ensues. This combined, unbidden, in my head with the legendary wardrobe through which the children in C. S. Lewis's books disappear to Narnia. The juxtaposition of an Arthurian/St George/*Game of Thrones* mythic fantasy world with a banal suburban affair was just too bizarre not to start writing straight away. Surprisingly, it yielded more of a serious theme than I expected it to, and I was pleased it did. A very different type of story for me, but writing it was fun.

The Flickering Light

This is one of those stories that's a compendium of true life detail woven into something not true at all. The "flickering light" in the bedroom is something my wife remarked upon. Her subsequent telling of the story about her father's death, of sharing the bed with her disabled sister who had spent many years in hospital, and of her father dying after a heart attack in his club, is all absolutely true. Even the bit about the toys and the Raleigh bicycle happened. It's also true that, back in the present, soon afterwards, a light bulb flickered above our heads at a dinner party. Sadly, the death of a good friend of ours from cancer as described in the story is completely factual too, and happened around New Year's Day 2020, when I wrote this story. So I would like to dedicate this tale to my old neighbour and late friend Andrew Fleming. His good humour and loud laughter will be much missed and never forgotten.

Bad Language

Ralph Robert Moore has said "Misunderstanding is a powerful theme in horror. And life." That, of course, is at the core of this one. The way the protagonist offloads his inner guilt/responsibility by making the "waste of fresh air" Aidan Chronister more and more monstrous (and "other") as a way of justifying his actions: the horrible tragedy being that he doesn't know the full picture.

Much of the mother/son relationship is autobiographical here, though, as Eric Morecambe said of Grieg's Piano Concerto, the notes are not necessarily in the right order. I'd had the idea for this story knocking around for years, and, with some cruel synchronicity, had started to write it when my mother died on 23 April 2020 of pneumonia and Covid-19. It became fitting—if not compulsory, in my mind—for me to make my story authentic in every way I could. Consequently, I think it developed into more than the short, sharp shock of a story I set out to write. The shout from the car was a real event (though directed at my father years before), and the incident in Bruton and its consequences more or less described accurately, though they weren't the following day. I play somewhat fast and loose with chronology. The stories and quotations are true to what was said at my mother's funeral on May 12th 2020. A strange and dubious tribute, to use all this in fiction, you might say, but to me, I would be a coward to have shirked it.

It would be cowardly, too, if I didn't admit that my rage at Dominic Cummings' controversial and inexcusable lockdown jaunt to Durham didn't contribute somewhat to the idea of blame and revenge in this story. (Perhaps, it just occurred to me, a parallel with the writer's hunger for retribution in Dennis Potter's TV swan song, *Karaoke*.) Whether *Bad Language* helps me come to terms with *my* grief, I don't know. But I know I had to write it this way, for good or ill. However, the worst parts of the main character are not me. Or I'd like to think so.

Nathan Ballingrud says: "I believe self-interrogation is a key to strong fiction. You should write about what you are ashamed of. You have to be merciless with yourself. That's why I like to write about characters so easy to hate. Writing fiction is, in no small part, about practicing empathy: and if there is a noble purpose in literature, it's that." I concur with that philosophy. And if you cannot tell whether a protagonist is a good person or a bad person, I feel I've done my job.

Agog

A real smörgåsbord of influences went into this one; the image of Goya's *Seated Giant*, William Blake's *Ghost of a Flea*, and sculptor Ron Mueck's oversized naked man in a room, almost filling it. I always wanted to write about a giant, probably since reading "The Drowned Giant" by J. G. Ballard, but they always seemed too big and blunt a figure for horror. Even so, the idea of something huge and mythic but *invisible*—as stories are—got hold of me, and the writing shaped it. I'd had this word *Gogmagog* in my head. It was a great title, but who was Gogmagog? Bypassing Biblical references, I discovered about a giant race, ancient protectors of Albion. All gone . . . But what if not? The story seemed simply descriptive at that stage, linguistic fun, treading here and there through history, but going where? I struggled to write this in March 2020 during the first Covid-19 lockdown, and had no desire whatsoever to write about a pandemic, but the image of a boy dying during the Black Death, and a giant in the room with him, bubbled up from somewhere, and was irresistible, so I didn't resist.

Orr

Thunder and lightning are possibly the most ubiquitous and tired tropes of the horror genre. We picture tridents in the sky above the Villa Diodati or Frankenstein's laboratory, and remember Ray Bradbury's evocative use of a lightning rod salesman in *Something Wicked This Way Comes*. A bolt from the heavens has inspired a sense of fear and wonder undiminished since the dawn of time, when it first made us consider powers beyond our understanding. I didn't realise it until I wrote this story, but lightning has always been, in a way, on the hazy boundary between us and the supernatural. Yet I wouldn't class this as a horror story.

It was inspired by my reading an article on "Human Lightning Rods" by Louis Proud which appeared in *Fortean Times* #330 and led with the tragic life of Roy Cleveland Sullivan, Guinness World Record holder for having been struck by lightning more times than any other human being. Sullivan was a ranger in Shenandoah National Park for twenty years, and tragically died in 1983 aged 71 from self-inflicted gunshot wounds. The local geography was said to funnel thunderstorms down a particular route he worked on, though many people worked the same district and were never hit. The US National Weather Service puts the odds of a person being struck by lightning at one in 10,000, but Sullivan was hit an astonishing nine times over his life span. What made him such a unique individual remains a mystery, and was the spark (sic) of this story, which went through many abortive attempts, ending with consignment to the bin, until my wife, Pat, asked me to tell her the story I was clearly getting so frustrated trying to write. I don't know why, but I told her *not* the version that had just got me in a funk, but a previous version I'd junked, and she really loved it. Which sent me straight back to my keyboard with a spring in my step. This is the third story herein that was written under the Coronavirus lockdown in Spring/Summer 2020, so, unsurprisingly, it shares a common theme or themes with the others. Namely, mortality.

It wasn't until I shared "Orr" and "The Holocaust Crasher" with my good friend Ray Cluley, and we exchanged emails, that I realised that, by coincidence, the stories that I'd designated to open and close this collection have one very obvious thing in common—they are both about survivors.

Which reminds me of a line of dialogue I wrote for the TV series *Afterlife* (Season 1, Episode 6: "The 7.59 Club"), which in many ways summed up *Afterlife* for me—and, in some ways, sums up this collection, much of which was written during a time of uncertainty:

"People get obsessed with whether we survive death. But that's not the real question, is it? The real question is how we survive *life.* But we do."

Stephen Volk
Bradford on Avon, June 2021

The Holocaust Crasher © Stephen Volk 2022 appears for the first time in this collection

---

The Airport Gorilla © Stephen Volk 2018 was first published in *New Fears 2*, edited by Mark Morris, Titan Books

---

The House That Moved Next Door © Stephen Volk 2016 was first published in *Supporting Roles*, the companion volume to the limited edition of *The Parts We Play*, PS Publishing. It was reprinted in *Best New Horror 28*, edited by Stephen Jones

---

Unchain the Beast © Stephen Volk 2019 was first published in *Black Static* #68, edited by Andy Cox, TTA Press

---

The Little Gift © Stephen Volk 2017 was first published as a standalone novella by PS Publishing

---

Outside of Truth or Consequences © Stephen Volk 2022, appears for the first time in this collection

---

The Black Cat © Stephen Volk 2022, appears for the first time in this collection

---

Beat the Card Home © Stephen Volk 2019, was first published in *Ten Word Tragedies*, edited by Christopher Golden and Tim Lebbon, PS Publishing

---

Vardøger © Stephen Volk 2009 was first published as *Gray Matter Novella 5*, Gray Friar Press. Shortlisted for the Shirley Jackson Award. Shortlisted for the British Fantasy Award

---

A Meeting at Knossos © Stephen Volk 2022, appears for the first time in this collection

---

Sicko © Stephen Volk 2020, was first published in *Black Static #73*, edited by Andy Cox, TTA Press. Reprinted in *Best Horror of the Year #13*, edited by Ellen Datlow, Night Shade Books

---

The Naughty Step © Stephen Volk 2020, was first published in *After Sundown, The Flame Tree Book of Horror*, edited by Mark Morris, Flame Tree Press

---

Adventurous © Stephen Volk 2021, was first published in *Weird Horror #2*, edited by Michael Kelly, Undertow Publications

---

The Flickering Light © Stephen Volk 2020, was first published in *Strange Tales: Tartarus Press at 30*, edited by Ray Russell and Rosalie Parker, Tartarus Press

---

Bad Language © Stephen Volk 2022, appears for the first time in this collection

---

Agog © Stephen Volk 2020, was first published in *The Dark #62*, edited by Sean Wallace and Sylvia Moreno-Garcia

---

Orr © Stephen Volk 2022, appears for the first time in this collection

ArtScroll® Series

Rabbi Nosson Scherman / Rabbi Gedaliah Zlotowitz

General Editors

Rabbi Meir Zlotowitz ז״ל, *Founder*

on the Haggadah

By Rabbi Avrohom Meir Weiss

Edited by Rabbi Yosaif Asher Weiss

UNGER FAMILY EDITION

הגדה של פסח נהר שלום
מאת הרה"ג שלום ראובן פיינשטיין

Reb Reuven Feinstein

Published by

ArtScroll
Mesorah Publications, ltd

FIRST EDITION
First Impression ... March 2024

Published and Distributed by
MESORAH PUBLICATIONS, LTD.
313 Regina Avenue / Rahway, N.J. 07065

Distributed in Europe by
LEHMANNS
Unit E, Viking Business Park
Rolling Mill Road
Jarrow, Tyne & Wear NE32 3DP
England

Distributed in Australia & New Zealand by
GOLDS WORLD OF JUDAICA
3-13 William Street
Balaclava, Melbourne 3183
Victoria Australia

Distributed in Israel by
SIFRIATI / A. GITLER — BOOKS
POB 2351
Bnei Brak 51122

Distributed in South Africa by
KOLLEL BOOKSHOP
Northfield Centre, 17 Northfield Avenue
Glenhazel 2192, Johannesburg, South Africa

ARTSCROLL® SERIES
REB REUVEN FEINSTEIN ON THE HAGGADAH

ISBN 10: 1-4226-4026-4
ISBN 13: 978-1-4226-4026-5
ITEM CODE: HRRH

Typography by CompuScribe at ArtScroll Studios, Ltd.
Printed in the United States of America.
Bound by Sefercraft, Quality Bookbinders, Ltd., Rahway NJ

We dedicate Reb Reuven Feinstein on the Haggadah
to the memory of the person
who made it all possible,

Rebbetzin Shelia Feinstein ע״ה

חוה שרה בת ר׳ אברהם הלוי ע״ה

our beloved Tante Shelia, who was so close to us,
our children, and our extended family,
all of whom she treated like her own grandchildren.

We were blessed to have known her, and to have spent
Sedarim with her and יבל״ח, Uncle Reb Reuven, שליט״א.

It is our fervent wish that Tante Shelia has a tremendous
nachas ruach from the glimpse Klal Yisrael gets
from this Haggadah into the *mesorah* that she and
Uncle Reb Reuven built, the *hashkafos* they shared,
and the link in our *mesorah* that they together
continue to represent to this day.

We miss her dearly, and await the arrival of
techias hameisim, when we will all rejoice
with a *shirah chadashah.*

Itsik and Etah Unger

We feel humbled and privileged to help dedicate
the Rosh HaYeshiva, R' Reuven Feinstein's
insights into the Haggadah
in memory of our beloved grandparents

ר׳ צבי בן ר׳ משה לייב ז״ל
חיה שרה בת ר׳ שלמה הלל ע״ה
ר׳ אריה לייב בן ר׳ יעקב ז״ל
נעמי בת ר׳ צבי הירש ע״ה

ר׳ יהושע בן ר׳ ברוך נתן ז״ל
חנה פייגא בת ר׳ אליהו לייב ע״ה
ר׳ נפתלי בן ר׳ יהודה אריה ז״ל
שאנעט בת הרב גוטל אהרן ע״ה

The Haggadah represents the quintessential example of the transmission of the Jewish Mesorah from one generation to the next. We stand on the shoulders of the giants of previous generations whose uncompromising principles and personal example provide the inspiration for us to look toward the future of Klal Yisrael.
May the lessons from this Haggadah be a *zechus* for our grandparents, parents עמו״ש, and family and for all of Klal Yisrael.

Raphael & Tamar Sacho
Tzvi, Avital, Sara, Chana, Chaim, Aryeh,
Naftoli, Yehuda, Yitzchok, and Noam

SIMANEI HASEDER DEDICATORS

KADEISH ❖ קדש

Dedicated by Pinky and Miri Friedman
והגדת לבנך — In honor of our precious children

URECHATZ ❖ ורחץ

Dedicated to the memory of
ולעילוי נשמת דוד מרדכי בן שמואל הלוי ע"ה

KARPAS ❖ כרפס

Dedicated by Eli and Sirki Lax,
in honor of Rabbi Avrohom Meir Weiss

YACHATZ ❖ יחץ

Dedicated by Eliyahu and Rebecca Berger in memory of Julius Berger
יחיאל נתן בן שרגא דוד הכהן ע"ה

MAGGID ❖ מגיד

The heart of the Haggadah and the fifth step of the Seder, Maggid,
is dedicated to Moreinu v'Rabbeinu, the Rosh HaYeshiva, shlit"a,
and his beloved Rebbetzin Shelia, a"h.
The grateful LES Community Participants of the Rosh HaYeshiva's
Shulchan Aruch Shiurim spanning over 40 years
at the Renowned Bialystoker Synagogue:
Rabbi Yehudah Blank, Mr. Norman Dawidowicz, Mr. Dovid Dinter,
Mr. Raphael Ehrenpreis, Mr. Shlomo Fishelis, Mr. Shmueli Friedman,
Dr. Aron From, Rabbi Yesocher Ginzberg, Mr. Dov Goldman,
Mr. Shlomo Goldstein, Mr. Ari Gruen, Hon. Shlomo Hagler,
Mr. Chaim Meyer Mermelstein, Mr. Joseph Peretz, Mr. Moshe Rosenbaum,
Mr. Avraham Rothman, Hon. Martin Shulman, Mr. David Sitzer,
Rabbi Shaul Small, Rabbi Moshe Tuchman, Mr. Chesky Tuchman,
Rabbi Menachem Tuchman, Mr. Joey Warren, Mr. Avi Zomberg

RACHTZAH ❖ רחצה

Dedicated by Mr. Yank and Mrs. Avigail Stoll
לזכר נשמת שלמה פישל בן אהרן

MOTZI ❖ מוציא

Dedicated by Mr. and Mrs. Goldman,
in honor of Rabbi Nechemia and Mrs. Rivkie Weiss

MATZAH ❖ מצה

Dedicated by Mr. and Mrs. Goldman,
in honor of Rabbi Nechemia and Mrs. Rivkie Weiss

SIMANEI HASEDER DEDICATORS

MAROR ❖ מרור

Dedicated in memory of
ולעילוי נשמת
שמואל בן אריה ליב, אליעזר יעקב בן חנינה משולם
מיכאל בן יעקב, יהודה זונדל בן יעקב

מאת משפחת רייזמאנן

KOREICH ❖ כורך

Dedicated in honor of the Rosh HaYeshiva, shlit"a,
for all that he does for our family
ולזכות רפואה שלימה בעד רוחמה פעסל רבקה בת פערל דינה

by Zvi and Faygie Bokow, Binyomin and Shima Cooper,
Shmuli and Chaya Hartman, Chananya and Bracha Leah Pearl,
Aron and Eliyahu Moshe Bokow

SHULCHAN OREICH ❖ שלחן עורך

Dedicated by Naftali and Leah Solomon,
in honor of our dear Uncle Reb Reuven, shlit"a

TZAFUN ❖ צפון

Dedicated by Mr. Yank and Mrs. Avigail Stoll
לזכר נשמת פנחס בן חיים יוסף ראובן

BARECH ❖ ברך

Dedicated by Mr. Chesky and Mrs. Miriam Rosenberg
לזכר נשמת יוסף יוספא בן חזקיהו פייבל
ולזכר נשמת מנחם מנדל בן יוסף יוספא

HALLEL ❖ הלל

Dedicated in memory of
ולעילוי נשמת ר׳ יוסף אריה ליב בן אליעזר יעקב ז״ל
איש ירא שמים אהוב לכל ונחמד לבריות
By the Lower East Side Community

NIRTZAH ❖ נרצה

Dedicated in memory of
ולזכר נשמת אבי מורי ר׳ זלמן פנחס בן שמחה ז״ל
איש ירא שמים ואוהב תורה בשעות פנאי
שקד על דלתות התורה בחשק גדול
וכל חייו קודש לחינוך זרעו
נלב״ע כ׳ תמוז תשע״ה

ניסן וגיטל הירש ומשפחה

Preface

I have had a treasure for my whole life, and I want to share it with you.

Since I was a child, I have been privileged to join one of the *Gedolei HaDor* for at least one *Seder* on most years, and sometimes for both. Of course, when I was young, I had no idea that what I was experiencing was anything out of the ordinary. To us grandchildren, Bubby and Zaidy's house was just that — a place to join our cousins, receive presents from our grandparents, and enjoy special Pesach recipes. And sure, we all knew that Zaidy was (and is) the *Rebbi* of our fathers and uncles, so perhaps everyone respected him a bit more than the average Zaidy. But all in all, we thought our experience was like everyone else's; spending the *Sedarim* with a Bubby and Zaidy who wanted to hear their *einiklach* say the *Mah Nishtanah,* and give them *Afikoman* presents.

As we got a little older, we realized that Zaidy is a *Rosh Yeshiva,* to whom lots of people look up with tremendous respect, and ask all of their important questions. Bubby, *a"h,* too, was a very well-respected *Rebbetzin* and *mechaneches.* We started to appreciate that maybe our grandparents were not exactly typical. But still, there are many *Rabbanim* and *Rebbetzins* in the world, and we thought that surely there were many people that shared the type of experiences that we have.

It is only now, as an adult, that I look back and realize that what I have merited to experience, and *b'ezras Hashem,* still do to this day, together with my own family, is completely unique, and incredibly special. Zaidy walks us through *Yetzias Mitzrayim* as a carrier of the *mesorah* of Klal Yisrael, passed on to him through his father, *Rabban Shel Kol Bnei HaGolah, Maran Reb Moshe, ztvk"l.* He walks us through the *minhagim* of the *Seder* with the clarity of a senior *poseik,* also in the footsteps of his father. Personally, I can attest that the lessons that he teaches ring so true, it is as if they are coming directly from the mouths of *Chazal* and straight into my ears, and into my heart, if I merit to internalize them. Zaidy is not just a grandfather, not just a *Rebbi,* not just a *Rosh Yeshiva,*

and not just a *poseik*. Zaidy is a carrier of the *mesorah,* and is a person about whom it can be said that the *Shechinah* is *medaberes mitoch grono*. I am sure that my eyes will only continue to be opened to this more and more, and that it will be decades before I can fully appreciate it, *b'ezras Hashem*.

What I therefore undertook to do in this *Haggadah* was to give you, the reader, the chance to share in what I have experienced. To invite *Reb Reuven, shlit"a,* into your home, and to spend the *Seder* with him; to watch his *minhagim,* to hear his anecdotes, to learn his *hashkafos,* and most importantly, to walk away knowing what it means to live as a Jew who is free to serve Hashem.

Writing this *Haggadah,* spending hundreds of hours on the material, hearing it, working on it, and going over it with Zaidy, *shlit"a,* who takes it so very seriously, has been nothing short of awe-inspiring. With this *Haggadah,* you have brought an illustrious guest to your table; and be prepared — your *Seder* may never be the same. Let him hold your hand as he explains the history of *galus Mitzrayim,* the origins of our salvation from it, and what it means to be a free *eved Hashem*.

You are bound to be fascinated. And, if you are lucky enough to allow the words of the *Rosh HaYeshiva, shlit"a,* to live with you, this *Haggadah* can change the way you view your relationship with Hashem. And if *that* happens, we have accomplished something great indeed.

In earnest, I can say that my desire to write this *Haggadah* was fueled by a desire to pass on to our entire generation, and the next, what the *Rosh HaYeshiva, shlit"a,* teaches on the *Haggadah*. My father and Rebbi, *HaRav Yosaif Asher Weiss, shlit"a,* has imbued within me the passion to teach — a quality which he himself possesses because of the attitude of his own father, *z"l*. In truth, the bulk of "my *mesorah,*" as it were, is really from my two *Rabbeim* — my Zaidy, the *Rosh HaYeshiva, shlit"a,* and my father, *shlit"a*. It is only fitting, then, that the work I have merited to do writing this *Haggadah,* encompassing what I could glean from the commentary of my grandfather, the *Rosh HaYeshiva, shlit"a,* is a tribute to my father and Rebbi, *HaRav Yosaif Asher Weiss, shlit"a*. In every way, anything that I have accomplished is a direct result of the foundation that he and my mother, *Rebbetzin Ahuva Weiss, shetichyeh,* have laid. And in the arena of the *harbotzas haTorah* of the written word, my parents are humble giants. Together, they read, edited, and proofread the entire manuscript, and their efforts are apparent on every page.

Why was I *zocheh* to bring to light the commentary of the *Rosh HaYeshiva, shlit"a,* on the *Haggadah?* At least in part, the answer is clear to me. During the development of this *Haggadah,* one of the resources that was never far from my hand was the *Vayaged Moshe Haggadah,* published by ArtScroll in 1991, with the *Rosh HaYeshiva, HaRav HaGaon Reb Moshe Feinstein, ztvk"l's* comments on the *Haggadah.* At some point, I turned to the Acknowledgments of that *Haggadah,* and I read what my father, *shlit"a,* wrote 33 years ago:

"Reishis kol, I wish to dedicate the English portion of this *Haggadah* in memory of my father, *R' Aharon Tzvi ben R' Meir, z"l,* who, even during his final illness, encouraged me to begin and continue this work. May this *sefer* be a *zechus* for his *neshamah.* A project such as this requires many hours of work, sometimes into the wee hours of the morning. I wish to thank my devoted wife, Ahuva, *shetichyeh,* for patiently listening, advising, typing, discussing, etc. Without her help, this *sefer* would not exist." And a little later on in those Acknowledgments: "It is my fervent hope that this volume will help to bring the Torah of the *Rosh Yeshiva, zt"l,* to many more members of Klal Yisrael."

It is so clear to me that my wife, Leah, and I are *zocheh* to be involved with the Torah of the *Rosh HaYeshiva, shlit"a,* because my own parents, *shlit"a,* forged that path for us, with their own *mesiras nefesh* to spread the Torah of the *Rosh HaYeshiva, ztvk"l.*

Acknowledgments

Hodu laShem ki tov, ki l'olam chasdo! This *Haggadah,* containing the Torah of my grandfather, the *Rosh HaYeshiva, shlit"a,* is our latest effort to disseminate his Torah to the Klal. There are a great many people without whom this *Haggadah* would simply not exist.

It would not be possible for me to learn, write, or teach Torah without the support of my *eishes chayil,* Leah. She demonstrates *mesiras nefesh* for Torah on a constant basis, allowing me to prepare and say *shiurim,* prepare manuscripts, and learn in *Kollel,* all while she supports our family and runs our household. To anyone who learns anything from this *Haggadah,* I must tell you — *sheli v'shelachem, shelah hi.* May we merit to continue to enjoy our portion of the Torah, see success in spreading it, and have *nachas* from our family.

In our efforts of *harbotzas haTorah,* Hashem sent us the perfect partners, our dear cousins, Itsik and Etah Unger. This *Haggadah* is just

another example of Itsik and Etah's efforts to help Klal Yisrael, which, as anyone who knows them can attest, is the goal of so much of what they do. *Baruch Hashem,* they do so, so much good, and may they merit to see only *nachas* from their family, and success in all that they are involved in.

Dr. Raphael and Mrs. Tamar Sacho and their family joined the Yeshiva of Staten Island community a few years ago, and quickly took to the *Rosh HaYeshiva, shlit"a's* guidance and became supporters of his Torah. It is an honor for us that they have chosen to support this project. May they too merit to see *nachas* from their family and success in their endeavors.

The initial support for this project was provided by the *Simanei HaSeder* donors, most of whom joined our ranks during the parlor meeting made earlier this year. It is an eternal credit to Rabbi Geilan and Mrs. Gittel Tova Grant and Rabbi Nechemia and Mrs. Rivkie Weiss, who put the meeting together, and enabled us to begin what ultimately became this *Haggadah.* They were the *Nachshon ben Aminadavs* of this project. May they merit to see *nachas* from their families and success in all that they do.

My good friend and partner in the *harbotzas haTorah* of the *Rosh HaYeshiva, shlit"a,* is the founder of TCP, and the transcriber of all of the *Rosh HaYeshiva, shlit"a's* recordings — R' Yisroel Dovid Akerman. May he and his *eishes chayil,* Rochel, merit to be rewarded with continued success in all of their endeavors, and to see *nachas* from their family.

Some of the *divrei Torah* in this *Haggadah* were adapted from the *Rosh HaYeshiva, shlit"a's Nahar Sholom* series on *Chumash.* I once again express my gratitude to the entire *Nahar Sholom* team, and specifically to Rabbi Moshe Feinstein and Mrs. Vori Shachter; this project was directly aided by all of your efforts.

I have the *zechus* to be able to consult with a great many *talmidei chachamim,* who freely share their knowledge and counsel when called upon. In alphabetical order, I owe a debt of gratitude to R' Avrohom Yosef Birnbaum, whose ability to locate *mareh mekomos* is phenomenal; R' Shlomo Eisenberg, my esteemed cousin and *chavrusa,* who was always available to discuss the intricacies of the *Rosh HaYeshiva, shlit"a's* words; R' Gabi Fried, one of my *Rebbeim* in *machshavah,* whose understanding of the words of the *Rosh HaYeshiva, shlit"a,* is profound; R' Chaim Friedman, my longtime *chavrusa,* who helped me (not for the first or second time) calculate *chatzos* properly; R' Geilan Grant, whose encyclopedic knowledge always provides insight into any subject; R'

Shmuel Goldstein, who took the time to discuss and clarify to me the *Rosh HaYeshiva, shlit"a's* halachic rulings; R' Menachem Lomner, another of my erudite *chavrusas,* constantly lent his deep perspective; R' Nechemia Fogel was always available to discuss a topic; R' Moshe Weiss, who translated and edited the *Rosh HaYeshiva, shlit"a's* work on *Avos, Pirkei Sholom,* as well as other ArtScroll works, was aways available to help clarify and sharpen a *vort*; R' Yisroel Weiss, who together with his *Rebbetzin,* Mrs. Rochel Weiss, prepared the *Rosh HaYeshiva shlit"a's Divrei Sholom* on *hashkafah,* was similarly always available to clarify the *Rosh HaYeshiva, shlita's divrei Torah*; and R' Reuven Wolf, who, with his piercing questions, inspired my writing. You each have a share in what we have, *b'ezras Hashem,* accomplished here.

R' Yitzchok Yehuda Weiss does so much for the *Rosh HaYeshiva, shlit"a,* including running all facets of *darcheisholom.com;* live-streaming his *Chumash shiurim,* and much more. He was also a valuable resource when *mareh mekomos* were needed. R' Yaakov Lustiger is *meshameish* the *Rosh HaYeshiva, shlit"a,* and I appreciate that he was able to be so accommodating. Azaryah Dov Rotberg was very helpful when it came to recalling past *divrei Torah* of the *Rosh HaYeshiva, shlit"a,* and Yehoshua Matanyah Weiss aided us in many ways — fielding my calls, bringing manuscript drafts to Zaidy's desk, and so much more. The photo credit for the *Rosh HaYeshiva, shlit"a's* cover photograph is theirs as well. You all have the special *zechus* to be *meshameish* the *Rosh HaYeshiva, shlit"a,* and may it stand you in good stead.

I owe a debt of gratitude to the various siblings, cousins, uncles, and aunts who helped me gain an even fuller picture of the history and *minhagim* of our family. I hope that you all find this *Haggadah* and the *mesorah* it contains reflective of your own experiences, as I know I do.

A special thank you to my dear cousins Shlomo and Ahuva Gurwitz, whose support of my *harbotzas haTorah* allows me to focus on ambitious projects such as this one while still learning as much as I possibly can.

I owe a tremendous debt of gratitude to my mentors at ArtScroll, all of whom are close to the *Rosh HaYeshiva, shlit"a.* It has been nothing but a pleasure to work with R' Gedaliah Zlotowitz, who stands faithfully at the helm not only of ArtScroll, but also the board of MTJ; R' Nosson Scherman expertly guided us regarding how to present the words and *minhagim* of the *Rosh HaYeshiva, shlit"a*; R' Sheah Brander poured his *lev v'nefesh* into presenting the words of the *Rosh HaYeshiva, shlit"a,* in a pleasing and aesthetic way, guiding us along every step of the project, and making it his own, with his customary unmatched attention to

detail. Together, all of you have created a tremendous *kevod Shamayim* — *Yehi ratzon shetishreh Shechinah b'maaseh yedeichem!*

R' Shloime Brander worked at his father's side, burning the midnight oil, to produce a final product that is something to be proud of; R' Eli Kroen, a master of his craft, designed the beautiful cover. R' Avrohom Biderman's advice was timely and on point. Mrs. Mindy Stern proofread the entire manuscript with her trademark efficiency and accuracy, and made many important corrections. I have had the pleasure of meeting, and befriending, R' Yisroel Besser, whose *chizuk* was much appreciated. *Yeyasheir kochachem!*

Finally, I must express my boundless *hakaras hatov* to my Zaidy, the *Rosh HaYeshiva, shlit"a,* for granting me the opportunity to spread his Torah. In writing the Torah, *minhagim,* and *hashkafos* in this *Haggadah*, I have been gifted the opportunity to work on them and clarify them, and the experience has been life-changing for me. On behalf of everyone who worked on this and other projects involving the *Rosh HaYeshiva, shlit"a's harbotzas haTorah,* I wish to extend my *birchas hedyot* that the *Rosh HaYeshiva, shlit"a,* continue to guide Klal Yisrael in good health and with strength, until we are *zocheh* to eat the *korban pesach* together with the coming of *Mashiach, bimeheirah beyameinu, Amen.*

Avrohom Meir Weiss
Adar I 5784 / March 2024

Introduction of the Rosh HaYeshiva, shlit"a

The *Haggadah* is not just the story of Klal Yisrael leaving Mitzrayim — although surely the Exodus is discussed extensively in the *Haggadah*. When we say *Vehi SheAmdah,* we thank Hashem for saving us in every generation, and at the conclusion of the *Haggadah,* the *piyutim* discuss various other times throughout history that Hashem redeemed Klal Yisrael. We see that the *Haggadah* is more than just a story of a long-ago occurrence; in fact, the *Haggadah* is much, much more than that.

The *Haggadah* is the background for the development of our relationship with Hashem. Every time Hashem protected us throughout our history, He further shaped us; He added another brick to the castle that is the story of our survival as the eternal nation. Thus, the *Haggadah* is the fabric of the story of the growth of every individual in our nation, from the lowest levels to the very highest level we can reach. Hashem always watches over us, and we, as His servants, attempt to fulfill the mission of bringing out His lessons and His teachings to His world, and thereby improving it and sanctifying His Name.

The *Haggadah* tells us that we must each view ourselves as having left Mitzrayim. This obligation, when viewed properly, is an incredibly personal insight into each person's own connection to Hashem. Each person has to feel as if he himself was saved from Mitzrayim, in the sense that he realizes that his journey of *avodas Hashem* starts with his own experiences and in his environment. Each of us, as *avdei Hashem,* can reflect upon the events through which we have lived, and analyze what their effects have been upon our lives and surroundings along the way.

I have seen this in my own life, from my own vantage point. Throughout the history of my lifetime — the small slice of Klal Yisrael's history that it represents — I can see the greatness of Hashem and how He leads our nation, and how He cherishes us and takes care of us. I was born

in 1937, just before World War II and the decimation of European Jewry during the Holocaust, and I have lived to merit seeing the glory of Klal Yisrael grow, and it *baruch Hashem* continues to grow. Many people who emerged from the concentration camps developed to become people who influenced Klal Yisrael greatly, and built their own stories of salvation and dedication to *avodas Hashem,* effecting the continuity of the covenant between Hashem and us, His servants.

I look back at my life, from when I was a little boy with big dreams and aspirations, all the way until now, and at who I have become at this point in my journey. Through the occurrences of my life and how He constantly guided and protected me, Hashem has taken me from a low level of understanding and raised me up. He gave me the strength to overcome challenges that I faced; it was Hashem who gave me that strength. And I see from my own failures in the past what I must still improve, to hopefully continue to grow, with Hashem's help. I reflect on everything Hashem has given me throughout my lifetime, and I reflect on the occurrences that the world has seen over that time. My personal growth, the *kavod* Hashem has given me, and the family into which he put me all shaped my relationship with Him, and helped me understand how He wants me to relate to Him. Hashem gave me my wife, *Rebbetzin Shelia, a"h,* and to both of us He granted my children, *ybl"c,* and Hashem has granted them all the ability to influence Klal Yisrael for the good. He has given us grandchildren, who continue on the path we forged, as do their children, *sheyichyu*; and He has also given me, *b'ezras Hashem,* the *zechus* to begin to see the generation of their children, who I pray will continue on this path as well. This is the eternity of Klal Yisrael, of a single family, or even a single person in Klal Yisrael. I am only a *pashute yid,* but I have been able to realize this. I merited to grow as an *eved Hashem,* and to raise a family of *avdei Hashem.*

This is what each individual in Klal Yisrael must see in the *Haggadah.* After the *Seder,* we have time for a little reflection, to recognize that we can see the commitment that Hashem had to us in not only the miracles of *Yetzias Mitzrayim,* but all of the miracles with which He saved us, generation after generation. And the commitment lives on! This is the mission of each one of us, as we pine to leave exile together. The *Haggadah* is not merely a story of something that happened. It is rather the blueprint for the way we live — the way we *must* live — for accomplishing the ultimate purpose for which we have been given the gift of living in Hashem's world. It contains the key to how we pass on this sacred covenant we have with Hashem to our children, and thus continue Klal

Yisrael's mission until the end of time, to serve Him, as established when He redeemed us and freed us from Mitzrayim. Moreover, the *Haggadah* contains the guarantee between us and Hashem — that He loves us and will always care for us, and that we will be able to accomplish our mission in this world.

We find ourselves, in the year 5784, in a world full of danger, and the hatred of the world toward us is on full display. And yet, our success as a nation — the blessing that Hashem has given each one of us — is virtually without parallel. *Nissan* is the season of renewal, the season when we are encouraged to renew our commitments to Hashem. So many great miracles happened in this season, and we look forward to the Final Redemption, *b'ezras Hashem,* in *Nissan,* the month of *Geulah.* Let us be assured of Hashem's commitment to us, and grow together in our *avodas Hashem,* so that we merit to join *Mashiach!*

Chag kasher v'same'ach,
Sholom Reuven Feinstein
Adar I 5784

About This Haggadah, and How to Use It

Ever since he was a young *bachur,* it has been *HaRav HaGaon Reb Reuven's* practice to refer to his illustrious father, *Maran HaRav HaGaon Reb Moshe, ztvk"l,* in the third person, as "The *Rosh Yeshiva."* As a grandson and *talmid,* I grew up my entire life hearing *Reb Moshe* referred to as "The *Rosh Yeshiva, zatzal."* This is how my Zaidy, Reb *Reuven,* refers to his saintly father, and this is why in his *sefarim,* rather than being referenced by name, *Reb Moshe* is almost always referred to as the *Rosh HaYeshiva, ztvk"l.*

It is only fitting, then, that a similar reverent practice be adopted when discussing *Reb Reuven* himself. Now, the *divrei Torah* in the *Haggadah* are written in the first person, from *Reb Reuven's* own perspective. The *minhagim* which are recorded in the *Haggadah,* however, are written in the third person, and *Reb Reuven* is referred to in these as "the *Rosh HaYeshiva, shlit"a."*

The pages of this *Haggadah* are brimming with the *Rosh HaYeshiva, shlit"a's* anecdotes, historical perspectives, thought-provoking *peshatim,* eye-opening *hashkafos,* and perceptive *mussar;* many of them are not short. Because the entries are sometimes lengthy, and not necessarily concise enough to be enjoyed at the *Seder,* we arranged this *Haggadah* using a somewhat unique format.

Before each *devar Torah,* we have provided bullet points that summarize the content of the piece which follows. These are extremely brief synopses, and are there for two reasons. The first is to help the reader recall a thought or *peshat* that the *Rosh HaYeshiva, shlit"a,* teaches. Even if there is not time at the *Seder* to read the entire piece, the bullet points will serve as a reminder, summarizing what has been read previously. And secondly, they are meant to draw the attention of a reader who is as of yet unfamiliar with the Torah of the *Rosh HaYeshiva, shlit"a,* on that

particular subject. The bullet points are intended to provide the opportunity for a novel thought to catch one's eye; for example, that the *eino yodei'a lishol* is on a higher level than the *chacham,* that the less bitter the *maror,* the more preferable it is, or that there could be a *mitzvah* of *sippur Yetzias Mitzrayim* even into the morning. Every bullet point is expanded upon in the *divrei Torah* themselves.

We have attempted to tailor the instructions in this *Haggadah* to mirror those practiced at the *Sedarim* of the *Rosh HaYeshiva, shlit"a,* and we have described his own *minhagim,* as well as several of the *Rosh HaYeshiva, ztvk"l's minhagim* where appropriate. [These appear in boxes at the appropriate points during the *Seder.*] Reading these *minhagim* will serve to connect the reader to the *Rosh HaYeshiva, shlit"a,* providing insight to the reader into the way his personal *Sedarim* are conducted.

There are many references throughout the *Haggadah* to *Nahar Sholom,* which is the name of the *Rosh HaYeshiva, shlit"a's* published *sefarim* on *Chamishei Chumshei Torah. Nahar Sholom* on *Chumash* is available for purchase at ArtScroll.com; it is also available at *darcheisholom.com.* [For those who want to experience the Torah of the *Rosh HaYeshiva, shlit"a,* firsthand, his Friday *Chumash shiurim* are available on Zoom each week — the contact information for the *shiur* is also available at *darcheisholom.com.*]

It was a tremendous pleasure and *zechus* for us to bring this *Haggadah* to life, from thought to print, and we are confident that Klal Yisrael will find it a pleasure to use, and more importantly, to learn from.

Before Pesach

Bedikah

The obligation to perform *bedikas chametz* begins thirty days before Pesach. Therefore, if one leaves his home more than thirty days before Pesach (for example, to go to Eretz Yisrael) and does not plan to return until after Pesach, he does not have to make a *bedikah*.

If one leaves home within thirty days of Pesach, but before the night of *bedikah* (that is, the night before Erev Pesach), he should make a *bedikah* on the last night he will be home, but he does not make a *berachah*. Thus, a *yeshiva bachur* leaving for *bein hazmanim* should be *bodeik* his dormitory room on the last night of the *zman,* without making a *berachah*.

During the years that the *Rosh HaYeshiva, shlit"a,* lived on the Lower East Side and spent Pesach in his Staten Island Yeshiva apartment, he would make the *berachah* on his *bedikah* in Staten Island on the night of *bedikah,* and then (without being *mafsik,* unless necessary) he would travel to the Lower East Side, accompanied by a grandchild, so he could also be *bodeik* his apartment on the East Side the same night, after which he would return to Staten Island.

Many people have a *minhag* to put out ten pieces of bread around the house before making the *bedikah*. The *Rosh HaYeshiva, shlit"a,* does not have this *minhag*. He explains that even if one has already cleaned the house thoroughly and does not expect to find any *chametz,* there is no issue of a possible *berachah levatalah,* as the *berachah* made before the *bedikah* (*al biur chametz*) refers not only to the *bedikah,* but also to the burning of the *chametz* that is done the following morning.

For the laws of *bedikah* and *bittul* that apply to one who is going away for Pesach to a hotel, or family, see Appendix A.

Selling Chametz

Selling one's *chametz* to a non-Jew before Pesach ensures that any *chametz* that one has forgotten about at his workplace, his summer home, his Yeshiva dorm room, his young children's school knapsacks, or any other place that he owns cannot cause him to transgress the prohibition against owning *chametz*. It is recommended for everyone to sell their *chametz* to a non-Jew for this reason, even if he is not keeping any *chametz* foods. [*Bachurim* or other family members who wish any *chametz* that they own to be included in their family's *mechiras chametz* should make their parent a *shliach* (agent) to sell their *chametz;* if the sale has already been made, they should sell or give their *chametz* to their parents before Erev Pesach, so it will be included in their sale.]

Many *bnei Torah* follow the *minhag* of not selling any *chametz gamur* (actual *chametz,* such as cookies, pasta, or the like) to the non-Jew. The primary reason for this *minhag* is to prevent the leniency of allowing the sale of *chametz* (as opposed to destroying it) from degrading the seriousness of the *chametz* prohibition in people's eyes. Certainly, this is a worthwhile *minhag*. However, the question often arises as to whether one who does not sell *chametz gamur* can sell alcoholic beverages such as whiskey or beer.

The *Rosh HaYeshiva, ztvk"l,* who did not sell *chametz gamur,* would sell whiskey, but not beer. He explained that the alcohol in liquor is distilled, and is identical to alcohol that is produced from non-*chametz* sources. Although it is *derived* from *chametz,* it is not actual *chametz.* From the fact that the Gemara has to expound a separate *posuk* to teach us that *chametz* derivatives and *chametz* mixtures are forbidden on Pesach, we see that the Torah does not consider a *chametz* derivative to be the same as actual *chametz*. [This is unlike the law that applies to other forbidden foods, where a mixture containing a forbidden food is automatically forbidden unless the forbidden component is nullified, and no special *posuk* is needed.] Since the *chametz* derivative (in this case, the whiskey) is in a different category than *chametz gamur,* even one who will not sell *chametz gamur* may sell whiskey to a non-Jew before Pesach. However, beer is not distilled, but rather it is brewed. Thus, the actual essence of the *chametz* — its "juice," so to speak — is in the beer, and it can be considered *chametz gamur.*

It is important to note that even one who does not sell *chametz gamur* should certainly have the intent, when he sells his *chametz,* that any *chametz gamur* that he does own, but has forgotten about, *should* be included

in the sale. Otherwise, one of the major benefits of the sale will have been lost! Also, if one will be traveling to a different time zone for Pesach, he should be sure to tell this to the *Rav* who sells his *chametz* for him.

Checking Cosmetics and Toiletries

As a rule, any cosmetic product or medicine that contains *chametz* should not be used on Pesach; such items should be put away and included in the sale of one's *chametz.*

However, when it comes to shampoos, soaps, and the like, most of them do not contain *chametz.* Furthermore, any *chametz* that may be present in soaps and shampoos is *chametz nukshah,* at most, and these items are not ingested. We do not presume that there is any *chametz* in such products. In certain cases, though, a product specifically states that it has wheat or the like in it; such a product should not be used on Pesach. Generally, though, a product that contains grain will advertise itself as such, or reference this in the name. [For example, Aveeno moisturizers contain oats. The name Aveeno is derived from the Spanish name for oats, *avena sativa.*] There is no reason to assume that a soap contains *chametz;* any that would contain *chametz* are likely to be specialty soaps, not regular soaps.

Perfumes should be checked before Pesach, to determine the source of the alcohol they often contain. There are many extensive lists available from the various *kashrus* organizations and the dedicated *Rabbanim* who devote countless hours to determining which items may be used.

Makeup, like soaps and shampoos, generally does not contain *chametz,* and there is no reason to suspect that makeup contains *chametz* (unless the presence of the *chametz* is known or advertised). Nevertheless, it is recommended that one use a new lipstick on Pesach, because of concern for the possibility that a previous application during the year might have picked up a minute amount of *chametz* from the lips, which can then inadvertently be reapplied to the lips on Pesach. [The same reasoning can be applied to toothpaste and toothbrushes, as well as bottles of mouthwash, if one uses the cap of the bottle to rinse with.]

The preceding notwithstanding, if one wishes to be exceedingly scrupulous in these matters, the aforementioned lists provide the ability to procure cosmetic products that are definitely free of any hint of *chametz,* and many companies now produce special cosmetics just for Pesach. However, using only these is a stringency rather than a requirement, for the reasons described above.

Checking Medications

The preceding applies to cosmetics, which are not ingested. Medications, which are actually swallowed, should be treated more stringently (even though, halachically speaking, ingesting medicine is not the same as eating). Liquid medications (such as cough medicines) often contain alcohol, which can come from *chametz;* and the inactive ingredients that hold pills together can include starches that are *chametz.*

For these reasons, the following precautions are recommended. When one is taking over-the-counter medications (such as antacids, cough medicines, or analgesics), it is best to consult the available guides, and obtain medications that are known not to contain *chametz* (the vast majority of the most common medications, such as Tylenol, Advil, and the like, are *chametz*-free). Furthermore, if one knows that an over-the-counter medication that he usually takes during the year contains *chametz* (lists of such medications are also available from the aforementioned *Rabbanim*), those medicines should be put away and sold with the *chametz.*

One is permitted to use medications that contain *kitniyos,* even if he is not of Sephardic descent. [It is also permitted for all to use baby formula that is *kitniyos* on Pesach, but one should avoid bringing it to the table, or washing the bottles together with Pesach dishes, if he is not of Sephardic descent.]

All this applies to over-the-counter medications. **However, prescribed medications, especially those that are taken for a chronic condition (heart medication, asthma medication, blood pressure medication, etc.), even if it is not a potentially life-threatening condition, should never be discontinued on Pesach unless both one's *Rav* and one's doctor are consulted first.** If one finds that a prescribed medication that he usually takes is on a *chametz* list, and his doctor can provide an equivalent substitute that is not on the list, it is best to switch for Pesach; if, **for any reason,** this is not feasible, one should never endanger himself in order to be stringent in this matter, and **the medication should be taken (unless both one's *Rav* and doctor are consulted, as above).**

Checking Sefarim

One is not required to check through the pages of his *sefarim* looking for *chametz,* as any crumbs which may be present have already been nullified through *bittul.* However, one should not bring any *sefarim* to

the table to use there on Pesach, since such crumbs may fall out of the *sefer* he is using into his food. [If a *sefer* has *never* been used near food, or one *never* uses his *sefarim* near food, this is not a concern.]

Braces

The *Rosh HaYeshiva, ztvk"l,* would advise people who had non-removable braces not to eat any hot *chametz* starting twenty-four hours prior to the time when one may no longer eat *chametz* on Erev Pesach, so that any *chametz* flavor absorbed into the braces would already be *pagum* (spoiled) by the time the prohibition begins. [Removable retainers or other dental appliances can be removed and *kashered* for Pesach.]

Shemurah Matzah

The *halachah* is that on the night of the *Seder,* the *matzah* that is eaten needs to be *shemurah, guarded;* that is, produced especially for the purpose of the *mitzvah* of eating *matzah*. The rest of Pesach, however, there is no requirement to eat only *shemurah matzah*. Still, the *Rosh HaYeshiva, shlit"a,* eats only *shemurah matzah* that was produced by his *chaburah* the entire Pesach. This was also the practice of the *Rosh HaYeshiva, ztvk"l*. Additionally, any food that is prepared for him by his family that contains *matzah* meal (the *Rosh HaYeshiva, shlita"a's minhag* is to eat *gebrokts* on Pesach) is made using *shemurah matzah* meal that is produced by grinding *matzos* that were baked by his *chaburah;* the same *matzos* that he eats the rest of Pesach. [He points out that this stringency only makes sense for one who does not eat any other *matzah* (such as machine *matzah*) on Pesach; there is no reason to be stricter with regard to *matzah* meal than one is with regard to *matzah*.]

Special Pesach Foods

Included in the preparations for Pesach are certain special foods that are prepared at this time of the year. One of the beloved Pesach recipes that comes from the *Rosh HaYeshiva, shlit"a's* kitchen is *matzah farfel kugel* (which, when prepared for him, was made using broken-up pieces of *matzos* baked by his *chaburah*). The proper *berachah* on the *kugel* is *mezonos,* even though it is made from pieces of *matzah*. The reason is that the *matzah* pieces are first soaked in water, and they lose their *tzurisa d'nehema, form of bread*. The *Rosh HaYeshiva, shlit"a,*

explains that once the water in which the *matzah* is being soaked turns whitish (which takes about half an hour), the *matzah* has soaked long enough for this purpose (see *Orach Chaim* 168:11).

Another favorite Pesach recipe was *the Rebbetzin, a"h's matzah latkes* (which she would make as a special treat on other Yom Tov afternoons as well), made from *matzah* meal. The *Rosh HaYeshiva, shlit"a,* explains that because the pieces of *matzah* meal are so small, and the *latkes* are fried, no soaking or waiting time is required to make their *berachah mezonos,* even though they were originally baked as *matzah.* [However, the *Rosh HaYeshiva, ztvk"l,* would only partake of these *latkes* if he was in the middle of a meal where he had previously washed and made a *Hamotzi.*]

In addition to personally preparing the *charoses* for the *Seder* (see below, *Seder Preparations*), the *Rosh HaYeshiva, shlit"a,* also makes a special [and very large] coleslaw that he distributes to his extended family as well (these days, aided by his grandchildren and great-grandchildren, *kein yirbu*). He explains that the recipe was originally developed based on a halachic concern, although it was not an issue pertaining specifically to *hilchos Pesach.* Many years ago, mayonnaise was not a popular or well-known condiment, and if it was visible in a recipe, it had the appearance of cream, which is *milchig.* Now, the *halachah* is that if a person is eating almond milk with meat, he needs to make a *siman* — for example, by placing almonds in or near the almond milk. The *Rosh HaYeshiva, ztvk"l,* ruled that there would need to be a *siman* that the mayonnaise was not cream. To remove the need for a such a *siman,* the *Rosh HaYeshiva, shlit"a,* developed a special recipe, where French dressing was added into the coleslaw together with the mayonnaise, so it would have an orange appearance, and not look at all like cream. Nowadays, mayonnaise is a very common condiment and ingredient, and a *siman* would not be necessary in any case. But, the recipe stuck, and the *Rosh HaYeshiva, shlit"a,* still makes it this way for Pesach.

Going to the Mikveh

The *Rosh HaYeshiva, shlit"a,* cites the *Rosh HaYeshiva, ztvk"l,* who held that before each of the *Shalosh Regalim,* as well as before Shemini Atzeres, men should go to the *mikveh* because of the obligation of *chayav adam letaher atzmo b'regel.* This applies to Pesach as well; thus, men should go to the *mikveh* on Erev Pesach (and if Erev Pesach is on Shabbos, men should go to the *mikveh* on Friday). There is no need to go to the *mikveh* before the second days of Pesach.

ערב פסח
Erev Pesach

בדיקת חמץ

The *chametz* search is initiated with the recitation of the following blessing:

בָּרוּךְ אַתָּה יהוה אֱלֹהֵינוּ מֶלֶךְ הָעוֹלָם, אֲשֶׁר קִדְּשָׁנוּ בְּמִצְוֹתָיו, וְצִוָּנוּ עַל בִּעוּר חָמֵץ.

Upon completion of the *chametz* search, the *chametz* is wrapped well and set aside to be burned the next morning, and the following declaration is made. The declaration must be understood in order to take effect; one who does not understand the Aramaic text may recite it in English, Yiddish, or any other language. Any *chametz* that will be used for that evening's supper or the next day's breakfast or for any other purpose prior to the final removal of *chametz* the next morning is not included in this declaration.

כָּל חֲמִירָא וַחֲמִיעָא דְּאִכָּא בִרְשׁוּתִי, דְּלָא חֲמִתֵּהּ וּדְלָא בִעַרְתֵּהּ וּדְלָא יָדַעְנָא לֵהּ, לִבָּטֵל וְלֶהֱוֵי הֶפְקֵר כְּעַפְרָא דְאַרְעָא.

לִבָּטֵל וְלֶהֱוֵי הֶפְקֵר כְּעַפְרָא דְאַרְעָא — *Should Be Nullified and Become Ownerless, Like the Dust of the Earth*

❒ We search for *chametz* and destroy it. Whatever *chametz* we may have missed is still not in our possession on Pesach, because of our *Kol Chamira* declaration.

❒ In *Kol Chamira*, we declare that our *chametz* is both *hefker*, ownerless, and also *k'afra d'ara*, valueless (literally, *like dust of the earth*). These are two different descriptions, and according to my understanding of *Rashi's* opinion regarding the commandment of *tashbisu*, they accomplish two different things.

❒ We declare the *chametz* to be valueless because Hashem has declared that, on Pesach, *chametz* has no value. We raise our perception above the viewpoint of the physical world, where *chametz* is valued, and treat it as the Torah does, as completely devoid of value. According to *Rashi*, this is the main objective of the mitzvah of *tashbisu*; to be able to look at the physical entity and place the Torah's valuation on it in our own minds.

❒ We also declare the *chametz* to be ownerless. This way, just in case we cannot rise to the mental clarity that *chametz* on Pesach is worthless, or if we falter during the holiday and momentarily place a value on *chametz*, we are still not in violation of the prohibition to own *chametz*, for we have declared that it does not belong to us.

The Search for Chametz

The *chametz* search is initiated with the recitation of the following blessing:

Blessed are you, HASHEM, our God, King of the universe, Who has sanctified us with His commandments and has commanded us concerning the nullification of *chametz.*

Upon completion of the *chametz* search, the *chametz* is wrapped well and set aside to be burned the next morning, and the following declaration is made. The declaration must be understood in order to take effect; one who does not understand the Aramaic text may recite it in English, Yiddish, or any other language. Any *chametz* that will be used for that evening's supper or the next day's breakfast or for any other purpose prior to the final removal of *chametz* the next morning is not included in this declaration.

All *chametz* or leaven that there is in my possession that I have not seen and have not removed should be nullified and become ownerless, like the dust of the earth.

During the *bedikah* and the *biur* of our *chametz,* we twice recite a declaration rendering our *chametz* as *battel.* The word *battel* means nullified. This is an idea that we need to study well, for not everyone really understands quite what it means.

In the text of the *Kol Chamira* recitation, we declare that any leaven we may possess should be *hefker* and like *afra d'ara;* ownerless, and like the dust of the earth. Surely, most people utter these words and presume that they are expressing the concept of ownerlessness in two ways. But, if we actually analyze the words, their meanings are quite different. For while a state of *hefker* is indeed defined as not being owned by anyone, the expression of *afra d'ara* connotes worthlessness. These two descriptions are actually at odds with each other. For when something is declared *hefker* by its owner, its value has not changed at all. It simply passes from the possession of its owner to not being owned by anyone. But, by definition, it still has a value; for if it did not have a value, it would not need to be declared *hefker.* On the other hand, one who says that his *chametz* is like the dust of the earth is not relinquishing his ownership to the public, but is rather *devaluing* the *chametz.* Once it has no value, it cannot be owned, and so it leaves his possession. So, does our *chametz* have the status of being given away as *hefker*, which would mean that it retains its value, or is it like the dust of the earth, which means that it has no value at all?

In order to answer this question, we must first ask another. Why is it that we recite *Kol Chamira* in the first place? To get rid of our *chametz.* The *mitzvah* to destroy the *chametz* (called *biur*) is known as *tashbisu,* from

ביעור חמץ

The following declaration, which includes all *chametz* without exception, is to be made after the burning of leftover *chametz*. It should be recited in a language that one understands. When Pesach begins on Motza'ei Shabbos, this declaration is made on Shabbos morning. Any *chametz* remaining from the Shabbos-morning meal is flushed down the drain before the declaration is made.

כָּל חֲמִירָא וַחֲמִיעָא דְּאִכָּא בִרְשׁוּתִי, דַּחֲזִתֵּהּ וּדְלָא חֲזִתֵּהּ, דַּחֲמִתֵּהּ וּדְלָא חֲמִתֵּהּ, דְּבִעַרְתֵּהּ וּדְלָא בִעַרְתֵּהּ, לִבָּטֵל וְלֶהֱוֵי הֶפְקֵר כְּעַפְרָא דְאַרְעָא.

עירוב תבשילין

It is forbidden to prepare on Yom Tov for the next day even if that day is Shabbos. If, however, Shabbos preparations were started before Yom Tov began, they may be continued on Yom Tov. Eruv Tavshilin constitutes this preparation. A *matzah* and any cooked food (such as fish, meat, or an egg) are set aside on the day before Yom Tov to be used on Shabbos, and the blessing is recited followed by the declaration [made in a language understood by the one making the *Eruv*].

If the first days of Pesach fall on Thursday and Friday, an *Eruv Tavshilin* must be made on Wednesday.

In Eretz Yisrael, where only one day Yom Tov is in effect, the *Eruv* is omitted.

בָּרוּךְ אַתָּה יהוה אֱלֹהֵינוּ מֶלֶךְ הָעוֹלָם, אֲשֶׁר קִדְּשָׁנוּ בְּמִצְוֹתָיו, וְצִוָּנוּ עַל מִצְוַת עֵרוּב.

---

the *posuk* (*Shemos* 12:15), *tashbisu se'or mebateichem, you shall destroy leaven from your house*. In *Pesachim* (4b), there is a dispute among the *Rishonim* pertaining to the optimal way to perform *tashbisu*. All agree that we seek out and destroy *chametz*, and all agree that we perform *bittul*. The question is which of these steps is the fulfillment of the *mitzvah*, and which one is done as a precaution.

Tosafos (Pesachim 4b, *d"h Mid'Oraisa)* learn that the *mitzvah* of *tashbisu* is optimally performed when one destroys his *chametz* (*biur*). The reason we also perform *bittul* is that just in case we missed some *chametz*, we do not want to be implicated in the prohibition against owning *chametz*, so we disown any *chametz* we may have missed. But *bittul* is not an actual fulfillment of the commandment to destroy the *chametz*. *Rashi (d"h b'bittul b'alma)*, on the other hand, understands that one who has been *mevateil* his *chametz* has actually fulfilled the commandment of *tashbisu*. Now, *Rashi's* view is somewhat puzzling. How can a declaration that something

Burning the Chametz

The following declaration, which includes all *chametz* without exception, is to be made after the burning of leftover *chametz*. It should be recited in a language that one understands. When Pesach begins on Motza'ei Shabbos, this declaration is made on Shabbos morning. Any *chametz* remaining from the Shabbos-morning meal is flushed down the drain before the declaration is made.

All *chametz* or leaven that there is in my possession that I have seen or I have not seen, that I have removed and have not removed, should be nullified and become ownerless, like the dust of the earth.

The Eruv Tavshilin

It is forbidden to prepare on Yom Tov for the next day even if that day is Shabbos. If, however, Shabbos preparations were started before Yom Tov began, they may be continued on Yom Tov. Eruv Tavshilin constitutes this preparation. A *matzah* and any cooked food (such as fish, meat, or an egg) are set aside on the day before Yom Tov to be used on Shabbos, and the blessing is recited followed by the declaration [made in a language understood by the one making the *Eruv*].

If the first days of Pesach fall on Thursday and Friday, an *Eruv Tavshilin* must be made on Wednesday.

In Eretz Yisrael, where only one day Yom Tov is in effect, the *Eruv* is omitted.

Blessed are You, HASHEM, our God, King of the universe,Who sanctified us by His commandments and commanded us concerning the commandment of *Eruv*.

---

has no value be the fulfillment of a commandment to destroy it, when it has not physically changed at all?

The answer is that, according to *Rashi*, the goal of the Torah's directive is not to physically destroy the *chametz*. It is rather to raise our minds above the physical world, and to recognize with certainty and clarity that if the Torah devalues *chametz*, then that means that the *chametz has* no value. Period. Even if yesterday, a person paid a thousand dollars for his *chametz*, and it held great value for him, once the *zman biur chametz* arrives, a person places no value on it at all, because the Torah has declared *chametz* valueless. According to *Rashi*, then, the *mitzvah* of *tashbisu* is not merely to save a person from the possibility of transgressing the prohibition of owning the *chametz*, but it is rather an exercise that requires us to view the *chametz* the way Hashem does.

However, this is a high level to reach. Many people cannot detach the

בְּהָדֵין עֵרוּבָא יְהֵא שָׁרֵא לָנָא לַאֲפוּיֵיו לְבַשּׁוּלֵי וּלְאַצְלוּיֵי וּלְאַטְמוּנֵי וּלְאַדְלוּקֵי שְׁרָגָא וּלְתַקָּנָא וּלְמֶעְבַּד כָּל צָרְכָּנָא, מִיּוֹמָא טָבָא לְשַׁבְּתָא לָנָא וּלְכָל יִשְׂרָאֵל הַדָּרִים בָּעִיר הַזֹּאת.

---

market price of their *chametz* from the *chametz* itself in their minds, and thus they cannot transcend the physical world in this manner. And even if they can, upon serious introspection, reach this level, they may stumble when they come upon a delicious morsel of *chametz* on Pesach. To ensure that this does not happen, we must also seek out and physically destroy any *chametz* in our possession, so that we will not come across any such delicious morsels, and discover that our nullification was not sincere.

To accommodate those who cannot perceive the *chametz* as actually being ownerless, we include the expression that the *chametz* is *hefker, ownerless,* in *Kol Chamira* as well. This way, in the event that a person does assign value to the *chametz*, he will still not transgress any prohibition, for the *chametz*, even if it has not been either physically destroyed nor nullified, does not belong to him any longer.

Through this *Eruv* may we be permitted to bake, cook, fry, insulate, kindle flame, prepare for, and do anything necessary on the festival for the sake of Shabbos — [this permit is] for ourselves and for all Jews who live in this city.

Accordingly, it emerges that *Rashi* would understand, in direct opposition to *Tosafos,* that the true *mitzvah* of *tashbisu* is fulfilled when we perform *bittul,* devaluing the *chametz* in our minds. The only reason that we also physically destroy the *chametz* is to protect ourselves in case we cannot reach or maintain this high level.

[See *Nahar Sholom, Devarim* 7:25-26, where we explained that the Torah bids Klal Yisrael to recognize that idols have no value, even though the world might prize the precious metals and gems from which they are fashioned. When the Torah declares something valueless, it is the Torah's intent for us to internalize that this defines the item, even if in the physical world it is sought after and many would pay great sums for it. We are charged with viewing idols, and *chametz* on Pesach, according to *Rashi,* the way Hashem views them; as being completely devoid of value — *k'afra d'ara.*]

Seder Preparations

Charoses

A day or two before Pesach, the *Rosh HaYeshiva, shlit"a,* makes the *charoses* for his *Sedarim* (and also for those of several of his children, grandchildren, and a few neighbors). He explains that the *halachah* is that apples make up part of the *charoses* mixture because they recall the *posuk* (*Shir HaShirim* 8:5), *tachas hatapu'ach orarticha, under the apple tree I aroused you.* Now, there are several thousand varieties of apples, so we are not attempting to replicate a specific taste. Moreover, the *Rosh HaYeshiva, shlit"a,* explains that *tapu'ach* might not translate precisely as "apple," but rather to the general category of fruit known as "pome" fruits — fruits that contain cores inside their flesh with small seeds. Apples and pears are both pomes, and indeed, the *Rosh HaYeshiva, shlit"a,* uses both apples and pears in his *charoses.* [The other ingredients include crushed almonds, ground cinnamon, and grape juice.]

HaRav HaGaon Reb Dovid, ztvk"l, writes in his *Laws of the Seder* that there is no reason to use ground cinnamon in the *Charoses,* because the reason we add cinnamon is as an allusion to the straw that was made into bricks, and ground cinnamon does not resemble straw; only sticks of cinnamon do. The *Rosh HaYeshiva, shlit"a,* however, maintains that ground cinnamon can also serve to remind us of the straw, because when we taste it, we can picture in our minds what cinnamon sticks look like. Larger slivers or sticks of cinnamon would not be edible, and his opinion is that all of the ingredients we use for the *charoses* should be edible. [Presumably, *HaRav HaGaon Reb Dovid, ztvk"l,* was unconcerned about this because the *charoses* is mainly for dipping, and there can be non-edible components that add flavor to the rest of the mixture. In the *Rosh HaYeshiva, shlita's* family, *charoses* is eaten as a condiment throughout Pesach.]

Maror

Depending on how strong the grated horseradish is, the *Rosh HaYeshiva, shlit"a,* will sometimes leave it uncovered for several hours prior to the *Seder* so it will not be overpowering. With regard to checking romaine lettuce, see below, *Minhagim,* p. 270.

Matzah

The *Rosh HaYeshiva, shlit"a,* gets his *matzos* from the Yeshiva of Staten Island's *chaburah,* which is run by R' Yisroel Weiss. The *chaburah* gets its *matzos* from the Boro Park Shemurah Matzah Bakery. The *chaburah* does not bake the *matzos* themselves; rather, they supervise the process, and then select the choicest *matzos* from among those that are baked while they are there. They inspect each *matzah* for [among other things] *kefulos,* an area where the *Rosh HaYeshiva, ztvk"l,* was more *machmir* than some others. The *Rosh HaYeshiva, shlit"a,* does not insist upon specifically using *matzos* he checked himself — anyone in the *chaburah* can check for him as well.

The *Rosh HaYeshiva, ztvk"l's minhag* was to use only two *matzos* at the *Seder,* in accordance with the opinion of the *Gra.* This is the *minhag* of the *Rosh HaYeshiva, shlit"a,* as well. The *Rosh HaYeshiva, shlit"a,* often notes that the two *matzos* he uses are sufficient to provide all of the *kezeisim* necessary for the *Seder* (*Motzi Matzah, Koreich,* and *Afikoman*) for two people — and this is certainly so if one uses three *matzos*!

If the only person who has *matzos* before him is the head of the household, then everyone else will end up having to supplement their *kezeisim* from other *matzos* upon which the blessings were not recited. The *minhag* of the *Rosh HaYeshiva, shlit"a,* is that each man and boy who has reached the age of *chinuch* has *matzos* set before him at the *Seder,* and each one of them provides *kezeisim* from his *matzos* to a woman or girl as the *Seder* progresses. In this way, there is usually enough *matzah* upon which the blessings were recited at the *Seder* to supply all of the participants. [A girl who has reached the age of *Bas Mitzvah* should not be paired with a boy under *Bar Mitzvah,* because she cannot be *yotzei* with his *berachos.*]

In a situation where the women and/or girls outnumber the men and boys, and there is not enough *matzah* from the "*Seder matzos*" to provide all the *kezeisim* for all the participants, other *shemurah matzah* may

be used to supplement the required amounts for each person. In such a case, each person should receive at least a little piece of each of the *matzos* over which the blessings were recited.

Setting Up the Ke'arah

The reason that the *Rema's* opinion is to set up the *Ke'arah* with the *karpas* and saltwater closest to the person, then the *matzos,* then behind them the *maror* and *charoses,* and only then the *zero'a* and the *beitzah,* is because of the idea that *ein ma'avirin al hamitzvos, we do not pass over mitzvos.* Thus, when a person is taking *karpas,* he should not have to reach over the *matzah* or the *maror* to do so. Although, in general, the *Rosh HaYeshiva, shlit"a,* sets up his *ke'arah* following the *Rema,* no contemporary *ke'arah* is ever set up with the *matzos* in between the other items. Sometimes they are underneath them, but often they are completely separate, in their own *matzah* cover. Because they are set apart from the other items in the *ke'arah* and they are covered, there is no issue of *ein ma'avirin* when one is reaching to the *ke'arah* to take *karpas.* There is thus no need to design a special *ke'arah* that would have a place for the *matzos* on it.

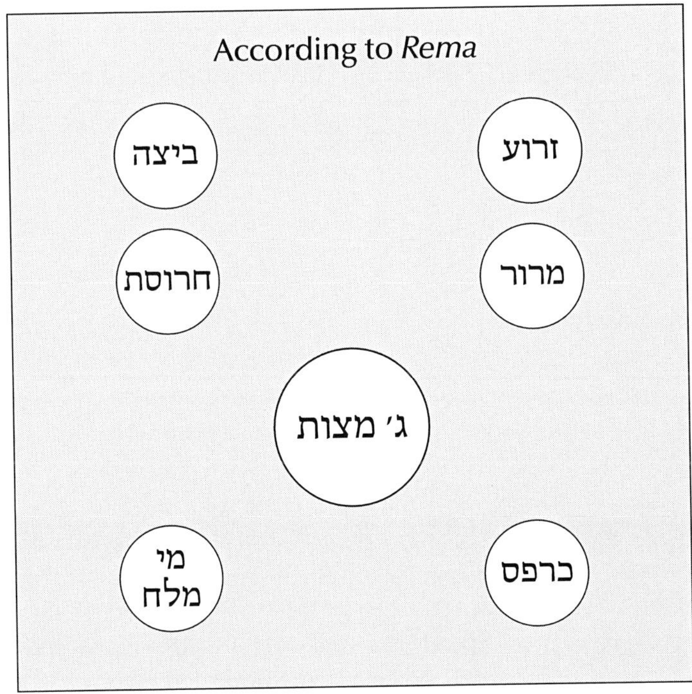

Setting the Table

Rebbetzin *Ahuva Weiss, shetichyeh,* recalls that the *minhag* of the *Rosh HaYeshiva, shlit"a,* was to set the table before the *Seder* (with *kosos,* water glasses, *matzos,* and the *ke'arah* — the rest of the tablesetting was done after *Koreich*) himself. [This was not a special Erev Pesach practice; rather, this was something that the *Rosh HaYeshiva, shlit"a,* would do every Erev Shabbos and Shabbos morning.]

Wearing a Kittel

The *Rosh HaYeshiva, shlit"a's minhag* is that a *chosson* during *shanah rishonah* wears a *kittel* at the *Seder.* A person in *aveilus, lo aleinu,* does not wear a *kittel.*

Hallel

The *Rosh HaYeshiva, ztvk"l's minhag* was not to recite *Hallel* after *Maariv* in *Shul* on the first two nights of Pesach, and this was the *minhag* in Mesivta Tiferes Yerushalayim as well. When the *Rosh HaYeshiva, ztvk"l,* would *daven Maariv* with the *Dembeker Rebbe,* whose *minhag* was to recite *Hallel* after *Maariv,* the *Rosh HaYeshiva, ztvk"l,* would also do so, and he would make a *berachah.* See also *Igros Moshe, Orach Chaim* 2:94, where he writes that if one is *davening* in a *minyan* that is reciting *Hallel* and he is *davening* for the *amud,* or even if he is not, but it will be obvious to others that he is not reciting the *berachah,* then he should recite the *berachah.* [However, one should not seek out a *minyan* in order to recite *Hallel* if this is not his *minhag.*]

A Note From the Writer Regarding Shiurim

The *Rosh HaYeshiva, shlit"a,* is a world-renowned *poseik,* and anyone who has ever had a *Seder* in his presence was able to ask all of their questions about *shiurim,* and have them answered with clarity. Nevertheless, the *Rosh HaYeshiva, shlit"a's* goal in putting out this *Haggadah* is not to write a *Sefer* on *shiurim.* This is first and foremost because his older brother, *HaRav HaGaon Reb Dovid, ztvk"l,* wrote extensively on the topic, and there is not very much to be said after *Reb Dovid ztvk"l* rendered his *pesakim.* [For further details, the interested student is referred to the *Kol Dodi Haggadah,* and *The Laws of the Seder,* both published by ArtScroll/Mesorah.] Nevertheless, the *Rosh HaYeshiva, shlit"a,* gave us permission to cite certain basic *shiurim,* and a few examples of anecdotal evidence related to *shiurim,* throughout the *Seder.*

The Four Cups

The *shiur* of *reviis,* which is necessary for the Four Cups, can be calculated in two ways. We can derive the size of a *reviis,* which equals 1.5 *beitzim,* by measuring an egg. In the *Kol Dodi Haggadah, HaGaon Reb Dovid, ztvk"l,* determined a *reviis* to be 2.9 fluid ounces. The second way is to use the Gemara's formula, that 2 *etzbaos* by 2 *etzbaos* by 2.7 *etzbaos* equals a *reviis.* According to that calculation, based on the *Rosh HaYeshiva, ztvk"l's* measure of an *amah, HaGaon Reb Dovid ztvk"l* determined a *reviis* to be 4.42 fluid ounces. For *mitzvos d'Oraisa,* we use the larger *shiur,* and for *mitzvos d'Rabbanan* we use the smaller *shiur.* The Four Cups are *d'Rabbanan,* with the exception of *Kiddush* when the *Seder* falls on a Friday night.

Because there is a dispute among the *Rishonim* of how much of each cup one must drink and how quickly one must drink it *lechatchilah,* it is better not to use a cup that is larger than necessary.

Matzah

The *shiur* of a *kezayis* for *Motzi Matzah* can also be calculated in two ways. One should eat a large *shiur* of *matzah,* for two reasons; firstly,

because it is a *mitzvah d'Oraisa,* and secondly, because there is an *inyan* to eat a *kezayis* from each of the two *matzos*. However, to fulfill that *inyan,* it is enough to eat a small *kezayis* from each *matzah*. Thus, one can eat half of a large *kezayis* from each of the two (or if using three *matzos,* from the top and middle) *matzos*, and in that way he will fulfill the *inyan* of having a *kezayis* from each. [The *kezayis* that one uses for *Koreich* can be somewhat smaller, as it is only a *minhag d'Rabbanan*.]

The *matzah* that the *Rosh HaYeshiva, shlit"a,* has used for many, many years comes from the Yeshiva of Staten Island's *matzos* that are baked in the Boro Park Shemurah Matzah Bakery. There are generally between 6 and 7 *matzos* per pound. The *Rosh HaYeshiva, shlit"a,* says that two of those *matzos* contain enough *kezeisim* to provide all the *matzah* that a couple needs to fulfill all the *mitzvos* of the *Seder* that require *matzah;* that is, *Motzi Matzah, Koreich,* and *Afikoman*. He and the *Rebbetzin, a"h,* would share two *matzos,* and were able to get all of the required *kezeisim* from them. This was also the case at the *Sedarim* of the *Rosh HaYeshiva, ztvk"l,* many years ago. [If one uses thinner *matzos* and there are more *matzos* per pound, this may not be the case, as a larger piece of *matzah* would be needed for each *kezayis*.]

For *Motzi Matzah,* it was the practice of the *Rosh HaYeshiva, ztvk"l,* not to measure out a *kezayis,* but rather to just eat *matzah* for three minutes straight. [The three minutes begin when one swallows his first bit of *matzah*.] By definition, since the *zman achilas peras lechatchilah* has passed by then, he must have eaten a *kezayis* — and if he did not, eating more *matzah* after *kedei achilas peras* would not help. The *Rosh HaYeshiva, shlit"a,* said that one may employ this method even if he drinks some water during the three minutes that he is eating the *matzah*. [While this method surely works, it may not be the best method for someone who does not want to eat any extra *matzah* at all.]

The *Rosh HaYeshiva, shlit"a's minhag* is to break his *matzah* into small, disc-like shapes, approximately the width of the widest part of an egg, then to pile them approximately as tall as an egg, and to eat this volume of *matzah*.

For *Afikoman,* it is best to eat the same large *shiur* as one eats for *Motzi Matzah*. Here, too, there is an *inyan* to eat two *kezeisim,* in remembrance of both the *korban pesach* and the *korban chagigah,* and we fulfill this by eating twice as much as the smaller *shiur* of a *kezayis,* as explained above.

הדלקת נרות

The candles are lit and the following blessings are recited. When Yom Tov falls on Shabbos, the words in parentheses are added.

בָּרוּךְ אַתָּה יהוה אֱלֹהֵינוּ מֶלֶךְ הָעוֹלָם, אֲשֶׁר קִדְּשָׁנוּ בְּמִצְוֹתָיו, וְצִוָּנוּ לְהַדְלִיק נֵר שֶׁל (שַׁבָּת וְשֶׁל) יוֹם טוֹב.

בָּרוּךְ אַתָּה יהוה אֱלֹהֵינוּ מֶלֶךְ הָעוֹלָם, שֶׁהֶחֱיָנוּ וְקִיְּמָנוּ וְהִגִּיעָנוּ לַזְּמַן הַזֶּה.

It is customary to recite the following prayer after the kindling. The words in brackets are included as they apply.

יְהִי רָצוֹן לְפָנֶיךָ, יהוה אֱלֹהַי וֵאלֹהֵי אֲבוֹתַי, שֶׁתְּחוֹנֵן אוֹתִי [וְאֶת אִישִׁי, וְאֶת בָּנַי, וְאֶת בְּנוֹתַי, וְאֶת אָבִי, וְאֶת אִמִּי] וְאֶת כָּל קְרוֹבַי; וְתִתֶּן לָנוּ וּלְכָל יִשְׂרָאֵל חַיִּים טוֹבִים וַאֲרוּכִים; וְתִזְכְּרֵנוּ בְּזִכְרוֹן טוֹבָה וּבְרָכָה; וְתִפְקְדֵנוּ בִּפְקֻדַּת יְשׁוּעָה וְרַחֲמִים; וּתְבָרְכֵנוּ בְּרָכוֹת גְּדוֹלוֹת; וְתַשְׁלִים בָּתֵּינוּ; וְתַשְׁכֵּן שְׁכִינָתְךָ בֵּינֵינוּ. וְזַכֵּנִי לְגַדֵּל בָּנִים וּבְנֵי בָנִים חֲכָמִים וּנְבוֹנִים, אוֹהֲבֵי יהוה, יִרְאֵי אֱלֹהִים, אַנְשֵׁי אֱמֶת, זֶרַע קֹדֶשׁ, בַּיהוה דְּבֵקִים, וּמְאִירִים אֶת הָעוֹלָם בַּתּוֹרָה וּבְמַעֲשִׂים טוֹבִים, וּבְכָל מְלֶאכֶת עֲבוֹדַת הַבּוֹרֵא. אָנָּא שְׁמַע אֶת תְּחִנָּתִי בָּעֵת הַזֹּאת, בִּזְכוּת שָׂרָה וְרִבְקָה וְרָחֵל וְלֵאָה אִמּוֹתֵינוּ, וְהָאֵר נֵרֵנוּ שֶׁלֹּא יִכְבֶּה לְעוֹלָם וָעֶד, וְהָאֵר פָּנֶיךָ וְנִוָּשֵׁעָה. אָמֵן.

Lighting the Candles

The candles are lit and the following blessings are recited. When Yom Tov falls on Shabbos, the words in parentheses are added.

Blessed are You, HASHEM, our God, King of the universe, Who has sanctified us through His commandments, and commanded us to kindle the flame of the (Shabbos and the) Festival.

Blessed are You, HASHEM, our God, King of the universe, Who has kept us alive, sustained us, and brought us to this season.

It is customary to recite the following prayer after the kindling. The words in brackets are included as they apply.

May it be Your will, HASHEM, my God and God of my forefathers, that You show favor to me [my husband, my sons, my daughters, my father, my mother] and all my relatives; and that You grant us and all Yisrael a good and long life; that You remember us with a beneficent memory and blessing; that You consider us with a consideration of salvation and compassion; that You bless us with great blessings; that You make our households complete; that You cause Your Presence to dwell among us. Grant me the merit to raise children and grandchildren who are wise and understanding, who love HASHEM, and fear God, people of truth, holy offspring, attached to HASHEM, who illuminate the world with Torah and good deeds and with every labor in the service of the Creator. Please, hear my plea at this time, in the merit of Sarah, Rivkah, Rachel, and Leah, our mothers, and cause our light to illuminate that it not be extinguished forever, and let Your countenance shine so that we are saved. Amen.

סימני הסדר
The Fifteen Steps of the Seder

Kadeish	Reciting *Kiddush*	קַדֵּשׁ
Urchatz	Washing Our Hands Without a *Berachah*	וּרְחַץ
Karpas	Dipping a Vegetable in Saltwater	כַּרְפַּס
Yachatz	Breaking the Top (or Middle, if There Are Three) *Matzah*	יַחַץ
Maggid	Recounting the Story of *Yetzias Mitzrayim*	מַגִּיד
Rachtza	Washing Our Hands With a *Berachah*	רָחְצָה
Motzi	Reciting *Hamotzi*	מוֹצִיא
Matzah	Reciting the Blessing on the *Matzah* and Eating a *Kezayis* of *Matzah*	מַצָּה
Maror	Reciting the Blessing on the *Maror* and Eating a *Kezayis* of *Maror*	מָרוֹר
Koreich	Making a *Maror* Sandwich and Eating It	כּוֹרֵךְ
Shulchan Oreich	Eating the Meal	שֻׁלְחָן עוֹרֵךְ
Tzafun	Eating the *Afikoman*	צָפוּן
Bareich	Reciting *Bircas HaMazon*	בָּרֵךְ
Hallel	Reciting *Hallel*	הַלֵּל
Nirtzah	Praising Hashem	נִרְצָה

- *Chazal* organized the *Seder* into fifteen steps. Why did they do so? In order to pique the curiosity of the children, by stressing that each thing we do on this night is significant. This sharpens their focus, and encourages them to notice the things that are out of the ordinary.
- This is the theme of the *Mah Nishtanah* as well. In the four questions, the children are noting practical departures from the normal Shabbos and Yom Tov meals. These questions all point the child to recognize that there is something different about the night of the *Seder*, which encourages their participation as we fulfill our obligation of *vehigadeta levincha*.
- The manner in which we organize the *mitzvos* of *matzah*, *maror*, and *Afikoman* is intended to arouse curiosity, even though the reason we do these *mitzvos* is not related to the children's curiosity, but rather to our obligation to fulfill them. Perhaps we can better understand this in light of Rabban Gamliel's edict that one who has not discussed *pesach*, *matzah*, and *maror* has not fulfilled his obligation of *sippur Yetzias Mitzrayim*. Rabban Gamliel requires not only that these *mitzvos* be fulfilled at the *Seder*, but also that they are part of the discourse of the evening. In this light, it is perfectly understandable that these *mitzvos* would be presented at the *Seder* in a manner that causes the children to wonder about them.

There are many additions to the Yom Tov meal which occurs on the first night (or first two nights, in *chutz la'Aretz*) of Pesach. It is interesting that on a regular Shabbos or Yom Tov, we do not have a formal "five-step meal," even though we always recite *Kiddush*, wash our hands, make *Hamotzi*, eat the meal, and recite *Bircas HaMazon*. And on Succos, we do not add a "sixth step" of reciting the blessing of *Leisheiv BaSuccah*. Yet, on Pesach, *Chazal* enacted a *Seder*, *an order*. On Pesach night, the five parts of every holiday meal are categorized as steps, and ten additional steps are added to it, for a total of fifteen distinct components. Was this really necessary? Technically, we could have enumerated only the ten steps that are added on Pesach. Or, we could have not enumerated any of them at all, and *matzah*, *maror*, and *Afikoman* could have been seen as additional courses of the meal, the way we view a fish and salad course, followed by soup, followed by a main dish. But this is not the way *Chazal* enacted the *Seder*.

The reason for this was that one of the overarching themes of the *Seder* is to involve the children, by piquing their curiosity. Not only is what *actually occurs* on the *Seder* night different, but even the *manner* in which we do everything, as distinct steps in a longer process, draws their attention to each detail of the *Seder*. Many people sing the steps of the *Seder* as it is beginning, and many people announce each step as it is reached. These are good

customs. The teaching of the children and the passing of the *mesorah* of Klal Yisrael's relationship with Hashem, as viewed through the prism of its very forging at the time of *Yetzias Mitzrayim*, is the main focus of the evening.

This is clear from the formatting of the four questions in the *Mah Nishtanah*. They do not contain questions about slavery in, or salvation from, Mitzrayim. Rather, they contain very practical questions about what is happening at the present time, from the perspective of a young child. The theme of the *Mah Nishtanah* is for the child to note that tonight we are acting in an unusual manner. The *Seder's* deviations from what a child would consider standard behavior at a meal are intended to cause them to ask, "Why is tonight different?" When a child notes that we are eating only *matzah* tonight and *chametz* is nowhere to be found, that the evening's herbs are bitter, that we are ceremoniously dipping our *karpas* and *maror,* and that we are leaning when eating the *matzah* and drinking the *kosos,* and he or she questions these behaviors, they are unwittingly following the script written by *Chazal* for the evening. *Chazal* wished for the children to note, in the more ways the better, that things are different on the night of the *Seder*.

When the connection between our *Seder* is in sync with our children's live experience, the opportunity is ripe to pique their genuine interest, which leads to a proper fulfillment of *vehigadeta levincha*. My granddaughter once asked me at the *Seder* that as a girl, and therefore someone who is not leaning at the *Seder,* she should not be required to ask the *Mah Nishtanah!* Clearly, she felt that the *Mah Nishtanah* must not be written for girls, if not all of the practices it notes are observed by women. See below, where we discuss the *Mah Nishtanah,* for the lessons I gleaned from this question. But it really brought home to me the chemistry between the observations of our children at the *Seder,* and the genuine curiosity we expect and hope that they will exhibit.

One further note on this subject: Many, although not all, of the additions to the *Seder* over a regular meal are due to the *mitzvos* of the evening. Eating *matzah, maror, koreich,* and the *Afikoman* are added into the *Seder* because they need to be done. And yet, we observe from the separation of the steps in the *Seder* that their additions into the meal were intended to arouse the curiosity of our children. This might be because part and parcel of the obligation of *vehigadeta levincha* includes explaining *pesach, matzah,* and *maror* to our children, as Rabban Gamliel maintains. Moreover, from the fact that the *posuk* commands us to retell the story of *Yetzias Mitzrayim* specifically when there is *matzah* and *maror* before us, we see that the lessons we are gleaning from the *pesach, matzah,* and *maror* are indeed a segment of what we are required to pass on to our children. [Indeed, there are those who maintain that the source of Rabban Gamliel's ruling is this *posuk*. See below, where we will discuss Rabban Gamliel, and present a second possibility as to the source for his ruling.]

Kadeish / קדש

Kiddush should be recited, and the *Seder* begun, as soon as possible after one comes home from *Shul* — however, not before nightfall. The cups should be washed before pouring the wine. Each participant's cup should be poured by someone else, to symbolize the majesty of the evening, as though each participant has a servant.

Each one of the Four Cups must be free of cracks, filled to the brim, and must hold at least a *reviis*. If the *Seder* falls on Friday night, the person reciting *Kiddush* (or, if everyone is reciting *Kiddush*, then everyone) should be sure to use a cup that contains at least 4.42 fluid oz. If it falls on any other night, or for those not reciting *Kiddush*, the cup need only contain 2.9 fluid oz. This volume is sufficient for the other three cups as well, even on Friday night.

For very small children, the cup they are given can be very small. When a child reaches the age of *chinuch*, one should give them a cup that contains 2.9 oz.

Those who are sensitive to wine can dilute their wine with grape juice, as long as the majority of the mixture is wine.

Although, when it comes to *Kiddush*, grape juice is generally considered wine, the *Rosh HaYeshiva, ztvk"l*, was of the opinion that the wine used for the Four Cups should be alcoholic, as using such wine is a mark of freedom.

The *Rosh HaYeshiva, shlit"a*, does not have the *minhag* to say the *Hineni Muchan U'Mezuman* prayer before drinking each of the Four Cups.

Each participant at the *Seder* raises their cup while the leader of the *Seder* recites *Kiddush*. Many have a custom that each of the participants recites *Kiddush*. In that case, any women who have already lit *neiros* should omit the recitation of the blessing of *Shehechiyanu* during *Kiddush*.

MINHAGIM

The *Rosh HaYeshiva, shlit"a's minhag* is to use a silver cup. He prefers that the cup not have a stem, because if it does, the body of the cup is not really resting on the palm. What he does when making a *berachah* under the *chuppah* at a *chasunah*, where they virtually always use stemmed glasses, is to slip the stem between his middle finger and ring finger, so that his palm supports the cup on one side and his fingers on the other.

[The above applies only to a *kos shel berachah*. The *Rosh HaYeshiva, shlit"a*, when holding a *kos shel berachah*, will hold the cup from the bottom, and hence the above applies. However, regarding a cup over which only the blessing of *Hagafen* is recited, like *Kiddush* made during the day on Shabbos and Yom Tov, or the cup over which the Kohen makes a *Hagafen* at a *Pidyon HaBen*, the *Rosh HaYeshiva, shlit"a's minhag* is that those cups

קַדֵּשׁ — *Reciting Kiddush*

❒ ***Kadeish*** **contains two elements. The first is the *mitzvah* of *Kiddush,* which is a *mitzvah d'Rabbanan* if the *Kiddush* is only for Pesach. If the Seder falls out on Friday night, then it fulfills the *mitzvah d'Oraisa* of *Kiddush,* and if it falls on Motza'ei Shabbos, then it also fulfills the *mitzvah* of *Havdalah.***

❒ **The second element of *Kaddish* is that it is the first of the *daled kosos,* the Four Cups that we drink at the *Seder.* Each cup commemorates a different level of freedom that Klal Yisrael experienced during the Exodus from Mitzrayim.**

We know that the *daled kosos,* the Four Cups of wine that we drink at the *Seder,* correspond to the four expressions of *geulah, redemption,* that Hashem uttered to Moshe Rabbeinu when He commanded him in the beginning of *Parashas Va'eira* (*Shemos* 6:6-7), to go tell Klal Yisrael that He would redeem them. Surely, there must be a deeper meaning to this, for if there had been, say, ten expressions of *geulah,* would we drink ten cups of wine at the *Seder?* Rather, these four words are not mere expressions, but rather they allude to progressively greater degrees of freedom that Klal

MINHAGIM

are held from the side, and therefore it would make no difference if there is a stem. This distinction was a *chiddush* of the *Rosh HaYeshiva, ztvk"l,* and highlights the importance of the requirement for specifically a *kos shel berachah* to be held *in* the hand, as opposed to *with* the hand.]

The *Rosh HaYeshiva, shlit"a,* acknowledges that there is a well-known *inyan* to use wine that is not *mevushal* for the Four Cups. He cautions, however, that one who wishes to practice this *chumra* should do so only if all of the participants at the *Seder* can touch it without consequence; however, if there are family members or staff present who are irreligious or non-Jewish, this can lead to problems, and it would be smarter to use *mevushal* wine.

The *Rosh HaYeshiva, shlit"a,* adds that as per the *psak* of the *Rosh HaYeshiva, ztvk"l,* if a wine is pasteurized, then it is *mevushal,* even if the label says that it is non-*mevushal.* This pertains both to the leniency of being able to have anyone touch it, and to the *chumra* that it is not considered non-*mevushal* for the Four Cups. [He points out that there are some wines made in Eretz Yisrael that are not even pasteurized, and such wines indeed qualify for this *chumra.*]

The *Rosh Yeshiva, R' Dovid Beinish, shlit"a,* recalls that when he was growing up, there were many different people at the *Sedarim* of the *Rosh HaYeshiva, shlit"a,* often including the non-observant. He specifically recalls one Erev Pesach that the *Rosh HaYeshiva, shlit"a,* was busy boiling the wine, to ensure that there would be no issues with non-*mevushal* wine at the *Seder.*

On Friday night begin here:

(וַיְהִי עֶרֶב וַיְהִי בֹקֶר—quietly)

יוֹם הַשִּׁשִּׁי וַיְכֻלּוּ הַשָּׁמַיִם וְהָאָרֶץ וְכָל צְבָאָם. וַיְכַל אֱלֹהִים בַּיּוֹם הַשְּׁבִיעִי מְלַאכְתּוֹ אֲשֶׁר עָשָׂה, וַיִּשְׁבֹּת בַּיּוֹם הַשְּׁבִיעִי מִכָּל מְלַאכְתּוֹ אֲשֶׁר עָשָׂה. וַיְבָרֶךְ אֱלֹהִים אֶת יוֹם הַשְּׁבִיעִי וַיְקַדֵּשׁ אֹתוֹ, כִּי בוֹ שָׁבַת מִכָּל מְלַאכְתּוֹ אֲשֶׁר בָּרָא אֱלֹהִים לַעֲשׂוֹת.[1]

Yisrael experienced; and each one is commemorated with a cup of wine that we drink at the *Seder*. There are several points throughout the *Seder* where we perform *mitzvos*, and *Chazal* decreed that the Four Cups of wine should be connected to four of these *mitzvos*. They are *Kiddush*, the blessing of *Ga'al Yisrael* at the conclusion of *Maggid*, *Bircas HaMazon*, and *Hallel*. [The fact that Klal Yisrael was redeemed in stages rather than suddenly and all at once helped them adjust to their new reality. See further, *Nahar Sholom, Devarim* 15:14, where we have contrasted the *mitzvah* of *hanakah* with the situation that arose after the emancipation of the slaves in America.]

The first expression, *"vehotzeisi" eschem mitachas sivlos Mitzrayim, "and I will take" you out from under the burden of the harsh labor of the Egyptians*, means that Hashem was promising to save Klal Yisrael from the torturous physical labor they were being forced to do. Of the many factors of Klal Yisrael's enslavement, this was the most physically pressing, and the need for relief from it was surely the most immediate. This was the first level of freedom, and it is commemorated by the first cup, which we drink at *Kiddush*.

MINHAGIM

The *Rosh HaYeshiva, shlit"a's minhag* is not to recite the words *Vayehi erev vayehi voker* at all, but rather to begin *Kiddush* with the words *Yom HaShishi*.

The *minhag* of the *Rosh HaYeshiva, shlit"a*, is that during the Friday night *Kiddush*, one stands from *Yom HaShishi* until *la'asos*, and sits for the blessings of *Kiddush*. When the *Seder* is on a weeknight, he sits for the entire *Kiddush*. The *Rosh HaYeshiva, ztvk"l*, explained that, in reality, all authorities agree that this would be the optimal thing to do; it is only that the *Mechaber* held that one should stand for the beginning of *Kiddush*, as it is *eidus, testimony*, that Hashem created the world, and we do not bother people to make them sit down in the middle, while the *Rema* held that one must sit at the end of *Kiddush*, and we do not bother people to make them stand initially, as they already have said their testimony when they recited *Vayechulu* during *Maariv*.

On Friday night begin here:

(quietly— And there was evening and there was morning)

The sixth day. Thus the heaven and the earth were finished, and all their array. On the seventh day, God completed His work which He had done, and He abstained on the seventh day from all His work which He had done. God blessed the seventh day and hallowed it, because on it He abstained from all His work which God created to make.[1]

(1) *Bereishis* 1:31-2:3

The next expression, *"vehitzalti" eschem mei'avodasam, "and I will save" you from their work,* alludes to a broader salvation, and represents the cessation of any work at all that was being done by Klal Yisrael on behalf of Mitzrayim. This was essentially an emancipation, declaring Klal Yisrael to no longer be slaves of the Egyptians, but rather a free people. This is the second level of freedom, and is commemorated by the second cup, over which we recite the blessing of *Ga'al Yisrael* at the conclusion of *Maggid.*

The third expression, *"vega'alti" eschem bizro'a netuyah u'vishphatim gedolim, "and I will redeem" you with an outstretched arm and with great judgments*, was an assurance that Hashem would raise the status of Klal Yisrael in the eyes of Egyptian society. Because of the might Hashem would employ on behalf of Klal Yisrael, they would no longer be viewed as a subhuman race, or even as second-class citizens. The stigma of such a long slavery would not affect the nation. It would become clear to the Egyptians that Hashem protects His children, and that not only are they not to be oppressed in any way, but that they are actually fine, upstanding, productive members of society. Yet, even at this point, the terms of society would still be defined by the Egyptians. To illustrate: There was a time that here in America, a Jew was welcome to become a professional in the workplace, because all Americans are equal. However, college exams took place on Shabbos, and a *yarmulke* was not permitted in the workplace. [See *Nahar Sholom, Vayikra* 18:3 (2), where we cite the *Rosh HaYeshiva, ztvk"l's* explanation of how it came to be that head coverings were once prohibited in public places.] A Jew was thus free to join society as a first-class citizen... but only on strictly secular terms. Nevertheless, this is a higher level of freedom than simple emancipation, in that the Egyptians would welcome the Jewish people to integrate into their society as equals; and this is commemorated by the third cup, over which we recite *Bircas HaMazon.*

The fourth term used here, *"velakachti" eschem Li l'am, "and I will*

On all nights other than Friday night, begin here.

סַבְרִי מָרָנָן וְרַבָּנָן וְרַבּוֹתַי:

בָּרוּךְ אַתָּה יהוה אֱלֹהֵינוּ מֶלֶךְ הָעוֹלָם, בּוֹרֵא פְּרִי הַגָּפֶן.

On Friday night, include all passages in parentheses.

בָּרוּךְ אַתָּה יהוה אֱלֹהֵינוּ מֶלֶךְ הָעוֹלָם, אֲשֶׁר בָּחַר בָּנוּ מִכָּל עָם, וְרוֹמְמָנוּ מִכָּל לָשׁוֹן, וְקִדְּשָׁנוּ בְּמִצְוֹתָיו. וַתִּתֶּן לָנוּ יהוה אֱלֹהֵינוּ בְּאַהֲבָה (שַׁבָּתוֹת לִמְנוּחָה וּ)מוֹעֲדִים לְשִׂמְחָה חַגִּים וּזְמַנִּים לְשָׂשׂוֹן אֶת יוֹם (הַשַּׁבָּת הַזֶּה וְאֶת יוֹם) חַג הַמַּצּוֹת הַזֶּה, זְמַן חֵרוּתֵנוּ (בְּאַהֲבָה) מִקְרָא קֹדֶשׁ, זֵכֶר לִיצִיאַת מִצְרָיִם. כִּי בָנוּ בָחַרְתָּ וְאוֹתָנוּ קִדַּשְׁתָּ מִכָּל הָעַמִּים, (וְשַׁבָּת) וּמוֹעֲדֵי קָדְשֶׁךָ (בְּאַהֲבָה וּבְרָצוֹן) בְּשִׂמְחָה וּבְשָׂשׂוֹן הִנְחַלְתָּנוּ. בָּרוּךְ אַתָּה יהוה, מְקַדֵּשׁ (הַשַּׁבָּת וְ)יִשְׂרָאֵל וְהַזְּמַנִּים.

Continue on the next page.

---

take" you to Myself as a nation, connotes a freedom to openly serve Hashem in the society in which Klal Yisrael were living, among the Egyptians, without needing to bend to their way of life in order to join their society. In the above example, that means that a Jew has a right to wear a *yarmulke,* and a Jew can take makeup exams on a weekday. The society respects the right not only of the Jew to live as an Egyptian would, but also to live as a Jew, and provides equal opportunities for Klal Yisrael. [This is similar to the level of freedom we have merited to experience here in America, *b'ezras Hashem,* from approximately the 1950s to the present day.] This was the pinnacle of freedom that a Jew could possibly hope to achieve in Mitzrayim. There were many, many Jews who felt that this degree of freedom to serve Hashem as an Egyptian Jew was perfect. We must ask ourselves, though; is this enough? Is it what Hashem really wants from us, and is it the proper manner in which we are intended to practice our religion? Many Jews in Mitzrayim genuinely thought so...

On all nights other than Friday night, begin here.

By your permission, my masters and teachers:

Blessed are You, HASHEM, our God, King of the universe, Who creates the fruit of the vine.

On Friday night, include all passages in parentheses.

Blessed are You, HASHEM, our God, King of the universe, Who has chosen us from all nations, exalted us above all tongues, and sanctified us with His commandments. And You, HASHEM, our God, have lovingly given us (Shabbasos for rest,) appointed times for gladness, feasts and seasons for joy, (this Shabbos and) this Feast of Matzos, the season of our freedom (in love), a holy convocation in commemoration of *Yetzias Mitzrayim*. For You have chosen us and sanctified us above all peoples (and the Shabbos,) and Your holy festivals (in love and favor,) in gladness and joy have You granted us as a heritage. Blessed are You, HASHEM, Who sanctifies (the Shabbos,) Yisrael, and the festive seasons.

Continue on the next page.

---

and it was these Jews who died during the *makkah* of *Choshech*. Why? Because they had no desire to leave Mitzrayim.

The members of Klal Yisrael who did leave Mitzrayim, however, were those who were not satisfied with this degree of freedom. They wanted the true and absolute freedom to live in a Torah society, where the morals of Hashem and His Torah, beautiful and perfect in every way, would define everything in their lives. Not merely to live in a foreign culture according to the Torah, but to live completely with the Torah, in every sense of the word. This could only be accomplished with an exodus from Mitzrayim. They yearned to leave, to receive the Torah, and to establish a Land where Hashem's word reigned supreme, in the way that their forefathers, Avraham, Yitzchak, and Yaakov, had dreamed that it would. The Torah would not simply *accompany* life, but would rather define, shape, and mold what Klal Yisrael's society would be like. It would be a lifestyle geared toward *dveikus baShem, connecting to Hashem,* focusing on the Torah and on Klal Yisrael's relationship through it to Hashem. [See also *Nahar Sholom, Shemos,* comments to 12:42, as well as *Devarim,* comments to 16:1(2).] *This* level of freedom was the ultimate goal of the Exodus from Mitzrayim, as is evident from the words of the next *posuk*

On Motza'ei Shabbos, add the following two paragraphs:

בָּרוּךְ אַתָּה יהוה אֱלֹהֵינוּ מֶלֶךְ הָעוֹלָם, בּוֹרֵא מְאוֹרֵי הָאֵשׁ.

בָּרוּךְ אַתָּה יהוה אֱלֹהֵינוּ מֶלֶךְ הָעוֹלָם, הַמַּבְדִּיל בֵּין קֹדֶשׁ לְחוֹל, בֵּין אוֹר לְחֹשֶׁךְ, בֵּין יִשְׂרָאֵל לָעַמִּים, בֵּין יוֹם הַשְּׁבִיעִי לְשֵׁשֶׁת יְמֵי הַמַּעֲשֶׂה. בֵּין קְדֻשַּׁת שַׁבָּת לִקְדֻשַּׁת יוֹם טוֹב הִבְדַּלְתָּ, וְאֶת יוֹם הַשְּׁבִיעִי מִשֵּׁשֶׁת יְמֵי הַמַּעֲשֶׂה קִדַּשְׁתָּ, הִבְדַּלְתָּ וְקִדַּשְׁתָּ אֶת עַמְּךָ יִשְׂרָאֵל בִּקְדֻשָּׁתֶךָ. בָּרוּךְ אַתָּה יהוה, הַמַּבְדִּיל בֵּין קֹדֶשׁ לְקֹדֶשׁ.

On all nights conclude here:

בָּרוּךְ אַתָּה יהוה אֱלֹהֵינוּ מֶלֶךְ הָעוֹלָם, שֶׁהֶחֱיָנוּ וְקִיְּמָנוּ וְהִגִּיעָנוּ לַזְּמַן הַזֶּה.

The wine should be drunk without delay, while reclining on the left side. [Women are not required to recline.] It is preferable to drink the entire cup. One may do so in a few gulps, as long as the cup does not leave his lips. At the very least, most of the cup should be drunk. If this is too difficult, even when using the smallest cup that holds a *reviis*, one must, at the very least, drink a cheekful.

---

there, *Shemos* 6:8. The *posuk* states, *Veheiveisi eschem el ha'aretz asher nasasi es Yadi laseis osah leAvraham, leYitzchak, u'leYaakov, venasati osah lachem morashah, Ani Hashem, And I shall bring you to the Land that I [swore] to give to Avraham, Yitzchak, and Yaakov; and I have given it to you as an inheritance, I am Hashem*. This was not merely "extra credit" for those Jews who wished to be even more dedicated than required. This was literally Hashem's stated goal of *Yetzias Mitzrayim!* This is also clearly reflected in the last *posuk* we say in the final passage of *Shema*. The *posuk* (*Bamidbar* 15:41) states: *I am Hashem, your God, Who took you out*

MINHAGIM

The *Rosh HaYeshiva, shlit"a,* advises that rather than resorting to drinking only a cheekful of a larger cup, it is better to ensure that one is using the smallest possible cup. Often, a person who cannot drink most of a large cup will have no problem drinking most of a small cup that contains only 2.9 fluid ounces.

On Motza'ei Shabbos, add the following two paragraphs:

Blessed are You, HASHEM, our God, King of the universe, Who creates the illumination of the fire.

Blessed are You, HASHEM, our God, King of the universe, Who distinguishes between sacred and secular, between light and darkness, between Yisrael and the nations, between the seventh day and the six days of activity. You have distinguished between the holiness of the Shabbos and the holiness of a festival, and have sanctified the seventh day above the six days of activity. You distinguished and sanctified Your nation, Yisrael, with Your holiness. Blessed are You, HASHEM, Who distinguishes between holiness and holiness.

On all nights conclude here:

Blessed are You, HASHEM, our God, King of the universe, Who has kept us alive, sustained us, and brought us to this season.

The wine should be drunk without delay, while reclining on the left side. [Women are not required to recline.] It is preferable to drink the entire cup. One may do so in a few gulps, as long as the cup does not leave his lips. At the very least, most of the cup should be drunk. If this is too difficult, even when using the smallest cup that holds a *reviis*, one must, at the very least, drink a cheekful.

---

of the land of Mitzrayim to be for you a God; I am Hashem, your God. This goal was achieved when Klal Yisrael left Mitzrayim, received the Torah, and entered Eretz Yisrael.

If this was the pinnacle of Klal Yisrael's freedom, why do we not commemorate this fifth and highest level of freedom by drinking a fifth cup of wine at the *Seder*? The answer, of course, is that the cup of Eliyahu HaNavi corresponds to the word *veheiveisi*, and represents this fifth expression of *geulah*. And why do we not drink this cup, as we do all the others? Because it represents a degree of freedom that is not possible to achieve completely until *Mashiach* will arrive, and the *Beis HaMikdash* is rebuilt. So, symbolically, we drink the Four Cups in commemoration of the first four degrees of *ge'ulah* we have merited to experience, and we pour the fifth cup in anticipation of a day when we will merit the Final Redemption, and will once again be able to serve Hashem in complete and total freedom.

ורחץ

All participants in the *Seder* wash their hands as they would before eating bread [pouring water from a cup, twice on the right hand and twice on the left hand], but without reciting a blessing. It is preferable to bring water for washing to the head of the household at the *Seder* table.

וּרְחַץ — *Washing Our Hands Without a Berachah*

- **The *halachah* was, in the times of the Gemara, that before partaking of a food that is being dipped in liquid, one must wash their hands.**
- **There is a dispute among the *Rishonim* why this was so: *Rashi* maintains that it was a decree to prevent *terumah* from contracting *tumah;* thus, it was similar to the decree to wash for bread, and *al netilas yadayim* was recited. *Tosafos* holds that it was a decree to prevent a person's body from contracting *tumah,* and no *al netilas yadayim* was decreed.**
- **It emerges that nowadays, when we are not particular about contracting *tumah, Tosafos* holds that one need not wash. *Rashi,* however, would hold that we do wash, in the same way we wash on bread.**
- **If one wishes to act stringently and wash, a *berachah* cannot be recited, because *Tosafos* holds it would be a *berachah levatalah.***
- **According to *Rashi,* we understand that at the *Seder,* we wash. But according to *Tosafos,* why do we wash at the *Seder?***
- ***Chok Yaakov* explains that according to *Tosafos,* not only is *Karpas* performed to pique the curiosity of the children, but also the fact that we wash before *Karpas* — something we do not do any other time we eat food dipped in liquid — was instituted to arouse their curiosity.**
- **From stories which happened with *R' Pesach Broyde, shlit"a,* and my son, *HaRav Dovid Beinish, shlit"a,* we know that the *Rosh HaYeshiva, ztvk"l,* held like *Tosafos.***

Why do we wash our hands before *Karpas?* And why, if we are washing, do we not make a *berachah* as we usually do for *netilas yadayim?*

In order to address these questions properly, some background information is required. The Gemara (*Pesachim* 115a) writes that *kol shetibulo bemashkeh, any food that is dipped into liquid,* requires one to wash his hands before eating it. There is a *machlokes Rishonim* why this is so. [See *Beis Yosef* (*Orach Chaim* §158).]

Rashi and *Rashbam* there understand that just like the decree to wash before bread, this decree was instituted so that a person's hands would not render the food he touches *tamei.* Since a person's (unwashed) hands have the *halachic* status of *sheni'im letumah,* they cannot cause the food they touch to become *tamei* (unless it is *terumah,* which can become a

Urechatz

All participants in the *Seder* wash their hands as they would before eating bread [pouring water from a cup, twice on the right hand and twice on the left hand], but without reciting a blessing. It is preferable to bring water for washing to the head of the household at the *Seder* table.

---

shelishi). Nevertheless, if the hands of a person would come in contact with a liquid, there is a *Rabbinic* decree that the liquid would become a *rishon,* which would then render any food dipped into it a *sheini.* To prevent food from becoming a *sheini,* the decree to wash one's hands before partaking of dipped foods was enacted.

Rabbeinu Yonah explains this further: The decree to wash for bread was enacted so that a person's hands, which have the *halachic* status of *sheni'im letumah,* would not make the bread of *terumah* into a *shelishi.* This decree does not involve any dipping at all. But, this decree did not apply to anything other than bread. He explains that this is because on a Biblical level, there are only three types of *terumah* — in the words of the Torah, *deganecha, tiroshecha, v'yitzharecha, your granary, your winepress, and your olive vat.* The products of grapes and olives are liquid, and are thus usually consumed from a vessel rather than being touched directly. It is only regarding the products of grain, which are usually made into bread, that we need to worry about their becoming *tamei* by being touched by impure hands. So, *Chazal* decreed that anything similar to *terumah* bread — i.e., all bread — requires washing before eating it. But any other *chullin* food would not require washing.

However, if one is dipping food into a liquid, the food *can* become a *sheini,* as explained above. If any food were to become a *sheini,* there exists a danger that it will then come in contact with *terumah,* and render that *terumah* a *shelishi.* To prevent the transfer of *tumah* to the food to begin with, *Chazal* enacted a new decree that anything which is dipped into liquid requires one to wash his hands before eating it. [It emerges that according to *Rashi,* this decree is rooted in the suspicion that *terumah* may contract *tumah,* and it therefore warrants a blessing of *al netilas yadayim.*]

Tosafos there (*d"h kol shetibulo*) poses several questions to *Rashi's* approach, and argues, presenting his own understanding of the Gemara. He explains that the decree of *kol shetibulo bemashkeh* has nothing at all to do with the *food* becoming *tamei.* Rather, the concern is that perhaps the person will touch the liquid, render it a *rishon,* and thereby become *tamei himself* (on a *Rabbinic* level) when he consumes the *tamei* dip. Accordingly, *Tosafos* note that since nowadays we are not careful to refrain from contracting *tumah,* there is no reason for us to adhere to this decree. Furthermore, according to *Tosafos,* anyone who recites a *berachah* of *al*

netilas yadayim when washing before dipping a food is guilty of making a *berachah levatalah.*

Now, because there is a *machlokes Rishonim* whether one recites a *berachah* when he washes for a food he will dip in liquid, we cannot make that *berachah.* [See, however, *Gra,* cited below.] But what about washing without a *berachah?* Should we or should we not wash before partaking of a *davar shetibulo bemashkeh?*

The *Shulchan Aruch,* both in §158:4 in *Hilchos Netilas Yadayim,* and in §473:6 in *Hilchos Pesach* (regarding *Karpas*), rules that one should wash without making a *berachah. Taz* (*Orach Chaim* §473:2) notes that we wash before partaking of the *karpas,* and therefore harshly criticizes those who do not keep a similar practice all year round, writing that they are clearly not being careful regarding the matter. He dismisses the notion that the holiness of the holiday should somehow change the *halachah* in this regard — see further there. *Mishnah Berurah* §158:20 indeed rules that one should not be lenient in regard to washing before eating something that is *tibulo bimashkeh.*

However, *Chok Yaakov* (§473:28) cites *Tosefos Yom Tov* (*Divrei Chamudos*), who rules in accordance with the abovementioned *Tosafos,* and therefore holds that nowadays there is no reason to wash before eating a food which is going to be dipped in liquid. He notes that this is also the opinion of the *Maharam MiRottenberg* (*Tashbatz* 99, cited by *Tur* in §473). And still, *Maharam* did wash on the night of the *Seder* before eating *karpas,* albeit without making a *berachah.* Accordingly, *Chok Yaakov* explains that the reason we wash our hands before *karpas,* even though we never do so for any other *davar shetibulo bimashkeh* the entire year, is because this is one of the things we do differently at the *Seder* so the children will ask what is different about this night. In my humble opinion, this sentiment is bolstered by the fact that *Urechatz* was codified in the fifteen steps of the *Seder.* It is obviously intended to be noticed by the children, so that they might ask why we act unusually in this regard on this night.

It emerges, then, that there is a *machlokes Acharonim,* rooted in a *machlokes Rishonim,* why we wash before *Karpas.* According to *Rashi,* the *Shulchan Aruch,* the *Gra,* and the *Taz,* we partake of *Karpas* in order to evoke the curiosity of our children; and once we are doing so, we are required to wash our hands because *Karpas* is a *davar shetibulo bemashkeh.* However, according to *Tosafos,* this decree does not apply today. Thus, the *Maharam MiRottenberg,* the *Tosefos Yom Tov,* and the *Chok Yaakov* will maintain that the reason we wash our hands at *Urechatz* is specifically in order to further pique the curiosity of the children.

What is the *halachah lemaisah?* As mentioned above, *Mishnah Berurah* §158:20 rules stringently, and writes that one should wash whenever partaking of a food which is *tibulo bemashkeh.* He also cites the *Gra,* who

maintains that even nowadays, a *berachah* is recited — both by *Urechatz,* as well as all year round when partaking of something that is *tibulo bemashkeh.*

But what did the *Rosh HaYeshiva, ztvk"l,* hold regarding this matter? One of our *chavrei haKollel, R' Pesach Broyde, shlit"a,* recalls that as a *bochur,* he once asked the *Rosh HaYeshiva, ztvk"l,* what he should do in regard to items that are *tibulo bemashkeh* in general. Is it proper to be *machmir* in accordance with the *Mishnah Berurah's* ruling? The *Rosh HaYeshiva* replied to him that one should *not* wash before eating a *davar shetibulo bemashkeh.* He explained that we generally do not wash on things that are dipped in *mashkeh,* and it is only at the *Seder* that we wash *Urechatz,* and we do it so that the children will ask; but if we would always wash before partaking of a *davar shetibulo bimashkeh,* this would not present a curiosity to the children at all!

Clearly, the *Rosh HaYeshiva, ztvk"l,* held like the *Chok Yaakov,* who maintains that we wash by *Urechatz* only as a part of the effort to arouse the curiosity of the children. Moreover, there is reason not to adopt the "stringency" of washing for *davar shetibulo bemashkeh,* for this would come at the cost of eroding any potential curiosity the children would have at the *Seder* when presented with *Urechatz.*

There is another *halachah* that is closely associated with the decree to wash on bread, and that is that we do *not* wash before eating fruit. Even though it is true that fruit can also be *terumah,* since the status of fruit *terumah* is *deRabbanan, Chazal* did not decree that one must wash over *chullin* fruit. R' Nachman holds that one who does so is displaying haughtiness (*Chullin* 106a). Now, what happens if the fruit a person is eating happens to be wet? As far as exposure to liquid — rendering it a *davar shetibulo bemashkeh* — there might be reason to wash, but we also do not wish to appear haughty. There are those who suggest drying the fruit before eating it, as the decree to wash was only made when the food will be eaten wet (see *Shevet HaLevi* 10:15). What did the *Rosh HaYeshiva, ztvk"l,* hold regarding this advice?

My son, *Harav Dovid Beinish, shlit"a,* was once with the *Rosh HaYeshiva, ztvk"l,* in camp, when they brought some large grapes to the *Rosh HaYeshiva,* and the grapes were wet. The *Rosh HaYeshiva* was eating them. My son Dovid took some grapes, and attempted to dry them on his shirt. The *Rosh HaYeshiva* noticed, gave him a funny look, and asked what he was doing. Dovid explained that he had not washed, and so he was drying the fruit. [*HaRav Dovid Beinish* explained to me that he had assumed that the *Rosh HaYeshiva* had washed his hands within the last short while, and knew they were clean.] The *Rosh HaYeshiva* told him, *"Mir firt nisht azoi,* we do not do this."

From this story, we see two things. Firstly, that the *Rosh HaYeshiva* held

כרפס

All participants take a vegetable (preferably one other than *maror,* which is eaten later in the *Seder*) and dip it into saltwater. A piece smaller in volume than a *kezayis* should be used, and it should be eaten while reclining.

Before the blessing is recited, the one leading the *Seder* should tell the participants to have in mind that the *Ha'adamah* blessing also applies to the *maror* that will be eaten later on in the *Seder.*

בָּרוּךְ אַתָּה יהוה אֱלֹהֵינוּ מֶלֶךְ הָעוֹלָם, בּוֹרֵא פְּרִי הָאֲדָמָה.

---

like *Tosafos* that nowadays we do not wash our hands when eating a *davar shetibulo bemashkeh.* This is a *maaseh rav* which corroborates the story that occurred with *R' Pesach Broyde* that was mentioned above. And secondly, we see that even in a scenario where being stringent and taking the opinion of the other *Rishonim* into account would not affect the food we are eating (for rather than forgo our dips, all we would be doing would be drying off the water our fruit was washed with), there is still no reason to do so.

It is important to note that this matter, along with many others, is really rooted in the practices of the various communities in Europe. The *Chofetz Chaim* maintains that it is proper to be stringent, and this was likely the *minhag* in Radin. However, where the *Rosh HaYeshiva* was from, the *minhag* was not to be stringent, and he felt very strongly that changing the *minhag* would be improper. And in the specific case of *davar shetibulo bemashkeh,* it would also be an example of a *chumra* that would result in a *kula,* because the children would no longer be curious at the *Seder.*

MINHAGIM

The *Rosh HaYeshiva, shlit"a,* recalls that when he was a child, the *Rosh HaYeshiva, ztvk"l,* would use potatoes for *Karpas,* which was the *minhag* in Russia. [In the town of *Kubrin,* where *Rebbetzin Shelia, a"h's* parents were from, they used onions for *Karpas.*] When his older brother, *HaRav HaGaon Reb Dovid, ztvk"l,* brought to light his opinion that the *Karpas* should be both a raw vegetable and a green vegetable, the *Rosh HaYeshiva, ztvk"l,* had celery brought to the table also, in his honor. But certainly, cooked potatoes were the *minhag* in his town, and they can be used. [The reason to use a raw vegetable is that one of the reasons we eat *Karpas* is in order to whet our appetites, and *Tosafos* (*Eruvin* 55b, *d"h kol ir*) maintains that only raw vegetables do this; cooked vegetables, on the other hand, while serving to prevent hunger, do not increase one's appetite. The reason to use a vegetable that is green is because the term used for the vegetable is *yerek,* which literally translates as *a green.*]

Practically, one may use celery, potato, parsley, or any other vegetable. [See further, *Magen Avraham* to §473, *se'if katan* 4, regarding the *minhag* to use

All participants take a vegetable (preferably one other than *maror,* which is eaten later in the *Seder*) and dip it into saltwater. A piece smaller in volume than a *kezayis* should be used, and it should be eaten while reclining.

Before the blessing is recited, the one leading the *Seder* should tell the participants to have in mind that the *Ha'adamah* blessing also applies to the *maror* that will be eaten later on in the *Seder.*

Blessed are You, HASHEM, God, King of the universe, Who created fruits of the ground.

כַּרְפַּס — *Dipping a Vegetable in Saltwater*

- **In Russia, the *minhag* was to use a potato for *Karpas,* and so this was the *minhag* of the *Rosh HaYeshiva, ztvk"l,* as well. There are many, including the *Rosh Yeshiva, shlit"a's* brother, *HaRav HaGaon Reb Dovid, ztvk"l,* who held that it is better to use a raw, green vegetable. [His *minhag* was to use celery.]**
- **There is profound symbolism in using a potato, which is grown in the dirt, for *Karpas.* For we are demonstrating the elevation of this lowly vegetable, via saltwater, to a dish partaken of by aristocrats. This alludes to the fact that Hashem raised Klal Yisrael from their unspeakably terrible predicament through the merits of their tears, and gave them the freedom to serve Him.**

There is profound symbolism in the dipping of the *Karpas* into saltwater. There is the fact that we are doing something out of the ordinary, both by dipping before the meal, and by dipping twice at the *Seder.* The saltwater evokes for us the tears of the Jewish people in Mitzrayim as they suffered, which contrasts with the fact that, at the *Seder,* we are dipping vegetables and leaning, in the manner of free men. In this same vein, I see another level to the contrast between slavery and freedom demonstrated through *Karpas.*

There are several reasons why a vegetable is used for *Karpas.* It is my humble opinion that we specifically use a vegetable because, by its very definition, a vegetable grows low to the ground. While this is true of any

MINHAGIM

potatoes.] The *Rosh HaYeshiva, shlit"a,* notes that children definitely prefer the potatoes!

Many wryly note that when it comes to a *kezayis* of *matzah,* the *kezayis* is somehow much larger than they expect, while when it comes to a *kezayis* of *Karpas,* the *kesayis* is much smaller! On a serious note, the *Rosh HaYeshiva, shlit"a,* recalled that the *Rosh HaYeshiva, ztvk"l,* when he was brought a danish or the like in Yeshiva, would eat only a very small piece, because he wanted to avoid the situation of a doubt as to whether he had eaten a *kezayis* or not.

Each person at the *Seder* who has *matzos* set in front of him (see above, *Seder Preparations,* p. 37) breaks a *matzah* in two, as follows: If one is using two *matzos,* as the *Rosh HaYeshiva, shlit"a,* does, the top *matzah* is broken. The smaller part is then placed atop the remaining whole *matzah.* If one is using three *matzos,* the middle *matzah* is broken. The smaller part is then placed between the two whole *matzos.* This smaller broken piece of *matzah* is the *lechem oni* over which *Maggid* will be recited. The larger part of the broken *matzah* is wrapped up and set aside for later use as the *Afikoman.*

---

vegetable upon which we make a *ha'adamah,* it is *especially* true of potatoes. For the edible part of the potato plant — the tuber itself — actually grows *underneath* the ground. Indeed, it is a physical manifestation of the lowliest possible produce. This is a parable for Klal Yisrael, who, when Hashem heard their cries — the *tears* they shed at the hands of the Egyptians — were raised up, not only over their oppressors, but indeed, over all of humanity.

Thus, when we take a lowly potato and use saltwater to improve its taste, and eat it while reclining, we are reenacting the very salvation about which we will be teaching our children. For Hashem took us from our impoverished state, and in the merit of our tears, made us into His nation, and granted us the freedom to serve Him.

יַחַץ — *Breaking the Top (Or Middle, if There Are Three) Matzah*

- ❒ **Which *matzah* we break is the subject of a *machlokes Rishonim.* Some hold that we use three *matzos* at the *Seder,* and we break the middle *matzah.***
- ❒ **Other *Rishonim* hold that we use only two *matzos* at the *Seder,* and they maintain that the top *matzah* is broken.**
- ❒ **The *minhag of the Rosh HaYeshiva, ztvk"l,* was to use only two *matzos,* in accordance with the opinion of the *Gra,* and that is the *minhag* of the *Rosh Yeshiva, shlit"a,* as well.**
- ❒ **The *Rosh Yeshiva's* brother, *HaRav HaGaon Reb Dovid, ztvk"l,* used three *matzos.***

The question of how many *matzos* to have at the *Seder* is one that goes back to the time of the *Rishonim.* One should follow his family's *minhag* in this regard.

The rationale to require three *matzos* is that after one *matzah* is broken at *Yachatz,* there are no longer two *sheleimim* (whole *matzos*) for *lechem mishneh.* Thus, a third *matzah* is added, so that even after one *matzah* is broken, two complete *matzos* will still remain.

Yachatz

Each person at the *Seder* who has *matzos* set in front of him (see above, *Seder Preparations*, p. 37) breaks a *matzah* in two, as follows: If one is using two *matzos,* as the *Rosh HaYeshiva, shlit"a,* does, the top *matzah* is broken. The smaller part is then placed atop the remaining whole *matzah.* If one is using three *matzos,* the middle *matzah* is broken. The smaller part is then placed between the two whole *matzos.* This smaller broken piece of *matzah* is the *lechem oni* over which *Maggid* will be recited. The larger part of the broken *matzah* is wrapped up and set aside for later use as the *Afikoman.*

Others maintain that there is no need to add a third *matzah*. On Pesach, when we are required to partake of *lechem oni, bread of affliction,* the broken piece of one *matzah* counts as a complete *matzah,* and thus, only two *matzos* are required to have *lechem mishneh*. Moreover, this opinion maintains that if one were to add a third *matzah,* he would not be considered to be partaking of *lechem oni;* for two and a half loaves is certainly more than the two loaves ordinarily used! Thus, they maintain that it is best to have only two *matzos*.

The *Rosh HaYeshiva, ztvk"l,* followed the *minhag* of those *Rishonim* who used only two *matzos,* and this is therefore the *minhag* of the *Rosh Yeshiva, shlit"a,* as well.

[Regarding *Yachatz,* the *Rosh Yeshiva, shlit"a,* would often relate the following story:]

When I was a young child, I was *zocheh* to sit at the corner of the table, right near my father, the *Rosh HaYeshiva, ztvk"l.* This was my seat, no matter who was joining us. I know that he used only two *matzos* — I saw this with my own eyes. My brother, *HaRav HaGaon Reb Dovid, ztvk"l,* used three *matzos* at his *Seder.* And yet, the *Rosh HaYeshiva, ztvk"l,* did not object to this.

I presume, then, that the *Rosh HaYeshiva, ztvk"l,* chose not to correct *Reb Dovid* because he presumed that *Reb Dovid* had decided that it was correct to follow the opinion of those *Rishonim* who hold that we use three *matzos*. Because the *Rosh HaYeshiva, ztvk"l,* did not do this, my *minhag* to this day is to use two *matzos,* as he himself did.

From this, I observed a very interesting practice of the *Rosh HaYeshiva, ztvk"l,* pertaining to the *chinuch* of his children. I saw that if there was a situation where he had a *minhag* based on one *shitah* in the *Rishonim,* and one of his children followed the view of the other *Rishonim,* if it was a situation where he did not have any personal *psak* on the matter, he would not say anything. [Obviously, if he himself *paskened* on the matter, he would have felt that his children and *talmidim* should follow him in this regard.] I presume that this was because if he were to tell the child to adopt his *minhag,* he would essentially be telling him or her that the *Rishon* who

מגיד

The broken piece of *matzah*, which is the *lechem oni*, is now lifted up for all to see, and the participants begin the recitation of the *Haggadah* with the following declaration, which emphasizes that we are still in exile, and are still in need of the Final Redemption.

הָא לַחְמָא עַנְיָא דִּי אֲכָלוּ אַבְהָתָנָא בְּאַרְעָא דְמִצְרָיִם. כָּל דִּכְפִין יֵיתֵי וְיֵכוֹל, כָּל דִּצְרִיךְ יֵיתֵי וְיִפְסַח. הָשַׁתָּא הָכָא, לְשָׁנָה הַבָּאָה בְּאַרְעָא דְיִשְׂרָאֵל. הָשַׁתָּא עַבְדֵי, לְשָׁנָה הַבָּאָה בְּנֵי חוֹרִין.

---

held the opposite view was incorrect; and he did not want to do that. [This is because we cannot ever prove the view of a *Rishon* as definitively incorrect; see the second *hakdamah* of *Milchamos Hashem* to the *Rif*.]

Keeping the Children Awake and Involved

- **The *minhag* to steal the *Afikoman* developed as a way to keep the children awake and entertained throughout the *Seder*.**
- **In my own family, I have found that singing *Chad Gadya* with all of the children, supplying the accompanying sounds, does an even better job of accomplishing this goal.**

We are all familiar with the *minhag* of stealing the *Afikoman*. The reason for it is, of course, to keep the children awake until the end of the *Seder*. Even though the actual theft of the *Afikoman* takes place early on, because the father has to negotiate with the child during *Tzafun*, the hope is that he or she will stay awake for the bargaining session.

Some have criticized the *minhag* because it involves theft, which is not something to which we want our children to become accustomed. At the end of the day, it is a *minhag Yisrael*, and I also have an *Afikoman* that is stolen at the *Seder*. [It is not even really "stolen," so much as it is merely officially "taken" from its place.] But, is it effective? I have not necessarily found it to be so.

First of all, what of the other children, who did not steal the *Afikoman?* What keeps them up? We have all seen that the flurry of excitement in the beginning of *Maggid* dies down after someone steals the *Afikoman*, and for the next few hours, the children are not really gripped by it; so is it accomplishing the goal of keeping the children up?

We are also all familiar with the famous stories where a boy asked for something exorbitant, and his father replied that he has no need for the *Afikoman* anyway, because he saved himself a piece! What can I say? As a *pashute Yid*, I find these types of dynamics to be too shrewd for me.

Maggid

The broken piece of *matzah*, which is the *lechem oni*, is now lifted up for all to see, and the participants begin the recitation of the *Haggadah* with the following declaration, which emphasizes that we are still in exile, and are still in need of the Final Redemption.

This is the bread of affliction that our forefathers ate in Mitzrayim. Whoever is hungry, let him come and eat! Whoever is needy, let him come and celebrate Pesach! Now we are here; next year, we shall be in Eretz Yisrael! Now we are servants; next year, we shall be free men!

Many years ago, my wife, *Rebbetzin Shelia, a"h,* and I decided that everyone in the family would get an *Afikoman* present — how could anyone be left out? Now that everyone would be getting a present, there was no need to be the one to actually steal the *Afikoman*. On the other hand, there was certainly less urgency to stay awake for a bargaining session.

My daughter, *Dr. Malkie Eisenberg, shetichyeh,* at her family's *Sedarim,* would give out parts to the children to sing during *Chad Gadya* at the end of the *Seder*. One would be the sheep, another the cat, and so on. My wife and I adopted this *minhag,* and we found that it was very effective. It gave the children something exciting to look forward to at the very end of the *Seder,* and it was funny for them to see and hear the adults (myself included) joining them in making the various silly noises. We found that for our family, this was a way to keep the children awake that was far more effective than stealing the *Afikoman* ever was.

So, in the times of the Mishnah, they would give the children nuts to keep them awake, and the *minhag* of stealing the *Afikoman* developed for the same reason. In our family, we sing *Chad Gadya* and take turns making interesting sounds. The idea is the same — we are trying to accomplish the goal of keeping our children awake, so we can pass the *mesorah* we have from our forefathers on to them.

הָא לַחְמָא עַנְיָא — *This Is the Bread of Affliction*

- **We open the recitation of the *Haggadah* by declaring that the *matzah* is the *bread of affliction,* and recalls the days of our persecution in Mitzrayim.**
- **Why do we extend an invitation to those in need to join the *Seder* at this juncture? Because nowadays, if there is a need, guests can join us at the last minute. But when the *Beis HaMikdash* is rebuilt, we will not *be able* to have unplanned guests, because the groupings for the *korban pesach* need to be arranged before its slaughter; nor will we**

need to. For all of Klal Yisrael will be free aristocrats, and everyone will have somewhere where they belong.

- **Thus, our invitation at this juncture serves to establish that we are in a similar plight to the one our ancestors were in. They sought to be free of cultural influences and to live in Eretz Yisrael, completely free to serve Hashem. We also wish to have this, and eagerly await *Mashiach*. But, for now, we partake of the *bread of affliction* with any guests who need a place to spend the *Seder*.**

We begin *Maggid* by declaring that the *matzah* we are eating tonight is *lechem oni, bread of affliction,* that our ancestors ate in Mitzrayim. Why?

We are setting the scene for the *Seder,* and specifically for the recitation of the *Haggadah*. To do so, we draw a parallel between the generation of *Yetzias Mitzrayim* and our own generation. On the most basic level, we declare that we are partaking of a bread that is similar in nature to the food that was eaten long ago in Mitzrayim, in Klal Yisrael's times of suffering. In doing so, we set the tone for a serious discussion of the precarious predicament Klal Yisrael was in during those times.

But then we continue, declaring that anyone who lacks food or a place to spend the *Seder* is welcome to join us. Surely, this is a beautiful practice. But why is it codified in the text of the *Haggadah?* Are there not many preparations for the *Seder* that are necessary, i.e., baking *matzah,* grinding *maror,* searching for *chametz,* to name but a few, that are not explicitly mentioned in the *Haggadah's* text?

I believe that the answer is that the invitation we issue to join us in our *Seder* further serves to define the *matzah* as *lechem oni,* and thereby also serves to connect us to the plight of our ancestors. How so?

The factor that connects us to the Jewish people in Mitzrayim, more so than any other, is our lack of freedom to serve Hashem completely, in the manner He wishes us to serve Him. Just as they were prisoners to Egyptian culture, we too are prisoners to the cultures of the nations among whom we are dispersed. The ultimate goal of the Jewish people who left Mitzrayim was to be freed from any foreign influence and to serve Hashem in Eretz Yisrael according to the *hashkafos* of the Torah, with all of our hearts and souls, with no distracting influences detracting from this mission — and this is exactly what our goal is today as well! So much of the *Seder* is about the quest to be truly free to serve Hashem. And this quest is as relevant to us at our *Sedarim* as it was millennia ago.

There will come a time when the *Beis HaMikdash* will be rebuilt, when we will not need to invite anyone for the *Seder*. This will be not only because we will not be *allowed* to — after all, one must be joined in a *chaburah* before the *korban pesach* is slaughtered — but also because we will not *need* to do so. As a nation in exile, there are always those who are needy, and there are also those who need company. But when the Final Redemption

arrives, and we are all free to serve Hashem as we wish to, everyone will be in a perfect situation. Free, rich, people do not ever *need* a place to go. Will we gather together to celebrate Pesach? Of course! But we will not do it because we have no other option, or no other place to go. We will *plan* in advance to be together, and join one another because we *want* to.

But, alas, today we are still in exile. Our *matzah* is still very, very much the *lechem oni* it was when we left Mitzrayim, and too many among us are lonely or destitute. Today, therefore, we invite them to join our *Seder.* But one day soon, we will merit to finally experience true and unfettered freedom to serve Hashem. And it is with the acknowledgment that we are still in exile that we begin the recitation of the *Haggadah.*

❒ **Another lesson of the *matzah* is this: Partaking of the *lechem oni,* which is a lowly and humble food, together with the *korban pesach,* reminds us that even though we must feel accomplished about our commitment to serve Hashem — symbolized by the requirement to eat the *korban pesach* when we are satiated — we must always remain humble, remembering always that we are not yet on the level that we aspire to reach.**

A second, unconnected lesson can be derived from the fact that the Torah refers to the *matzah* with the term *lechem oni,* literally, *bread of affliction* (*Devarim* 16:3). In the previous *posuk*, in delineating what animals can be used for the *korban pesach*, the Torah uses the words *tzon u'vakar, sheep and cattle.* Of course, cattle cannot be offered as a *korban pesach. Rashi* (*d"h u'vakar*) explains that the reference is to the *korban chagigah.* The reason to offer a *chagigah* with the *pesach* was so that the *korban pesach* could be eaten *al hasovah*, when one is full. From this law, we derive a lesson: The *pesach* is to be eaten when one has already had a meal, and is satisfied. This is because Hashem wants a person to be *satisfied* when he eats the *korban pesach*; and physical satisfaction is a parable for spiritual satisfaction. The *pesach* should bring a person a degree of satisfaction, in the realization that he has accomplished something significant with his commitment to *avodas Hashem.* And yet, the *matzah* he is supposed to eat together with it is called *lechem oni.* Here, we are taught that the sense of accomplishment from our commitment to Hashem that is represented by the *korban pesach* must also be joined with the lesson of the *matzah* that is ingested together with it, which is a bread of humility. We must set our goals high, and at the same time, realize, with humility, that we still have work to do.

Thus, partaking of the *lechem oni* together with the *korban pesach* reminds us that even though we must feel accomplished about our commitment to serve Hashem (symbolized by eating the *korban pesach* when we are satiated), we must remain humble, remembering always that we are not yet on the level which we aspire to reach.

The *matzos* are covered, and the second of the Four Cups of wine is poured fully, but not to the brim. The youngest child present asks the *Mah Nishtanah,* the "Four Questions" regarding the unusual proceedings of the evening. Afterward, all present recite the *Mah Nishtanah.*

מַה נִּשְׁתַּנָּה הַלַּיְלָה הַזֶּה מִכָּל הַלֵּילוֹת?

שֶׁבְּכָל הַלֵּילוֹת אָנוּ אוֹכְלִין חָמֵץ וּמַצָּה,
הַלַּיְלָה הַזֶּה כֻּלּוֹ מַצָּה.

שֶׁבְּכָל הַלֵּילוֹת אָנוּ אוֹכְלִין שְׁאָר יְרָקוֹת,
הַלַּיְלָה הַזֶּה מָרוֹר.

שֶׁבְּכָל הַלֵּילוֹת אֵין אָנוּ מַטְבִּילִין אֲפִילוּ פַּעַם אֶחָת,
הַלַּיְלָה הַזֶּה שְׁתֵּי פְעָמִים.

שֶׁבְּכָל הַלֵּילוֹת אָנוּ אוֹכְלִין בֵּין יוֹשְׁבִין וּבֵין מְסֻבִּין,
הַלַּיְלָה הַזֶּה כֻּלָּנוּ מְסֻבִּין.

מַה נִּשְׁתַּנָּה — *Why is This Night Different*

- **The thrust of the Four Questions is essentially that there is a difference in how we act on other nights and how we act at the *Seder,* which the child can observe. In certain ways, we commemorate royalty, and in other ways, we recall suffering. This is the theme that we wish the child to observe, and ask about.**
- **In point of fact, there are those to whom all four questions may not personally apply. Nevertheless, the observations are still pertinent. For they are still observing the discrepancies taking place, which indicate that there is something unique about the *Seder* night.**

MINHAGIM

The *Rosh HaYeshiva, shlit"a,* notes that although only one person who understands the questions of the *Mah Nishtanah* needs to ask them to fulfill the requirement to recite the *Haggadah* in a question-and-answer format (and truthfully, it does not even have to be the youngest), this is the time for many children to shine, and each of the children or grandchildren should have the opportunity to ask the questions with the spotlight on them alone, including children who do not really understand what they are asking. At his *Sedarim,* each one of the children gets a chance to recite the *Mah Nishtanah* on his or her own, and then the adults all recite it simultaneously afterward. The questions are applicable for adults also, as a gateway into the discussion of freedom from Mitzrayim, which will be discussed as the *Haggadah* progresses.

The *matzos* are covered, and the second of the Four Cups of wine is poured fully, but not to the brim. The youngest child present asks the *Mah Nishtanah,* the "Four Questions" regarding the unusual proceedings of the evening. Afterward, all present recite the *Mah Nishtanah.*

Why is this night different from all other nights?

1) For on all other nights, we eat *chametz* and *matzah*; but tonight, we only eat *matzah.*

2) On all other nights, we eat all types of greens; but tonight, we eat *maror.*

3) On all other nights, we do not even have to dip once, but on this night, we dip twice.

4) On all other nights, we eat either sitting or leaning; but on this night, we all lean.

❒ **Since our *minhag* is that women do not lean, some young girls may feel excluded from the fourth question. After all, they are taught the *Mah Nishtanah* just like the boys, and yet it does not seem to apply to them! The true answer to this question is that even someone who does not lean — i.e., a *talmid* before his Rebbi — is still obligated in the *mitzvah* of *sippur Yetzias Mitzrayim.* The question about leaning is appropriate because a *talmid* sees his Rebbi, and a girl sees her father, leaning in a non-customary fashion.**

❒ **It can happen that a girl actually feels excluded from the proceedings. We should tell this girl that she is *just as obligated* in the *mitzvos* of the *Seder* as the boys are! The point is not the leaning itself, but rather the discussion of why leaning takes place at our *Seder.* Furthermore, when it comes to those parts of Torah that girls must know, we must teach them just as we teach boys.**

I was once asked by my then five-year-old granddaughter (who is today a noted *mechaneches* in her own right) why she needs to say the *Mah Nishtanah* if it does not apply to her anyway, because she does not lean at the *Seder*?

Now, the truth is that simply because one does not lean is not a reason that they should be absolved from asking the *Mah Nishtanah.* After all, a *talmid* is not allowed to lean in his Rebbi's presence, and still, he asks the *Mah Nishtanah!* It is rather the *talmid's* observation of his Rebbi's behavior, and the girl's of her father's, which prompts the *Mah Nishtanah* to be asked. True as this may be, I still heard in my granddaughter's question her feeling that she was less a part of the *Seder* than the boys. So, I sought to find the words that a young girl would understand, and therefore feel a part of

The *matzos* are uncovered. If one is using two *matzos,* the broken *matzah* is already on top, and is revealed. If one is using three *matzos,* the broken middle *matzah* should be pulled out, so that it is visible even though there is another *matzah* on top of it. The *matzos* are kept in this position as everyone recites the *Haggadah*. The *Haggadah* should be translated if necessary, and the story of *Yetzias Mitzrayim* should be elaborated upon.

עֲבָדִים הָיִינוּ לְפַרְעֹה בְּמִצְרָיִם, וַיּוֹצִיאֵנוּ יהוה אֱלֹהֵינוּ

the *Seder,* even though she is not leaning. What follows is the *dvar Torah* I told her; obviously, the degree of depth to which one can explain this to his daughter or granddaughter will depend on her specific age and acumen. At any rate, there is an important message of inclusion for our girls here, to help them understand that they have an important place in *yedias haTorah*.

In *Shema,* we find two distinct directives to teach our children Torah. The first is in the *parashah* of *Ve'ahavta* (*Devarim* 6:7), which states, *veshinantam levanecha, vedibarta bam, and you shall teach them to your children, and speak in them*. The second is in the *parashah* of *Vehayah Im Shamo'a* (ibid. 11:19), which states, *velimad'tem osam es beneichem ledabeir bam, and you shall teach them to your children to speak in them*.

What is interesting is the manner in which *Chazal* interpreted these two directives. *Sifri* expounds the first *posuk* (ibid 6:7), *veshinantam levanecha, and you shall teach your children,* to include teaching one's *talmidim*. And the Gemara (*Kiddushin* 30a) expounds from the words of the second *posuk* (*Devarim* 11:19), *velimad'tem osam es beneichem,* that *beneichem velo benoseichem, your sons, but not your daughters*. The question which arises is this: Is there any reason why the first *posuk* was the *posuk* expounded to include *talmidim,* and the second was expounded to exclude daughters? Theoretically, might *Chazal* have been able to reverse these *derashos,* and exclude daughters from the first *posuk,* while including *talmidim* in the second?

The answer, I believe, is based on the words that follow each directive. In the first *posuk,* the Torah commands us: *Veshinantam levanecha, and you shall teach them to your children,* followed by a second command, *vedibarta bam, and speak in them*. Who is this directed at? The father! He is obligated both to teach his children Torah, and also to speak in Torah constantly. Let us contrast this with the second *posuk*. There, the Torah writes, *velimad'tem osam es beneichem ledabeir bam, and you shall teach them to your children to speak in them*. This is a single commandment, for a father to teach his children. What should he teach his children? To speak in Torah constantly!

From this distinction, we can see that the two *pesukim* are really discussing two entirely different "teachings." The first *posuk* makes no mention of teaching the children to speak in Torah all the time, but rather

The *matzos* are uncovered. If one is using two *matzos,* the broken *matzah* is already on top, and is revealed. If one is using three *matzos,* the broken middle *matzah* should be pulled out, so that it is visible even though there is another *matzah* on top of it. The *matzos* are kept in this position as everyone recites the *Haggadah*. The *Haggadah* should be translated if necessary, and the story of *Yetzias Mitzrayim* should be elaborated upon.

We were slaves to Pharaoh in Mitzrayim, and HASHEM, our God,

---

discusses the obligation to teach the children Torah. This means teaching them the Torah's laws; the *mitzvos asei* and *lo saaseh,* and the *halachos* pertaining to their observance. The second *posuk,* on the other hand, discusses the obligation to train the children to learn all the time. The *mitzvah* to learn constantly is that of *Talmud Torah, Torah learning,* and is its own obligation. Even if someone knows all the laws of the Torah with clarity, he still has an obligation to learn Torah constantly.

Having drawn this distinction, it is clear to us why *Chazal* expounded the latter *posuk,* rather than the former, to exclude the teaching of one's daughters. For it is indeed true that women are exempt from the *mitzvah* of *Talmud Torah*. But girls *are* obligated to know the laws of the Torah which pertain to them, and so they could not possibly have been excluded from the directive of the first *posuk*. There, the obligation for a father to teach his child the Torah's laws is being discussed, and one *must* teach his daughters the laws they need to know, in order to enable them to observe the Torah!

And how much of the Torah is it that applies to girls? Most of it! The entire *Choshen Mishpat,* most of *Yoreh Deah,* and a significant part of *Orach Chaim!* When *Chazal* taught us that *veshinantam levanecha* does not exclude our girls, they were telling us that it is indeed our obligation to teach our girls what they need to know in order to live according to the Torah.

A girl who is not leaning at the *Seder* should not feel as though she is not part of the *Seder*. The *mitzvah* of *vehigadeta levincha* applies *equally* to boys and girls. For the obligation for a father to teach his children about *emunah* and *bitachon* through recounting the experiences of *Yetzias Mitzrayim* applies to the girls just as much as the boys!

עֲבָדִים הָיִינוּ — *We Were Slaves*

❒ **We answer the *Mah Nishtanah* by explaining that our actions tonight reflect both freedom and slavery, for we were, in fact, slaves to Pharaoh, and Hashem freed us. We tell the children that if Hashem had not done so, we and our descendants would still be slaves to Pharaoh.**

❒ **Does the *Haggadah* mean that we literally would have been serving the Egyptians? But all of the empires of the world, from then until now, have eventually fallen. Why would we presume that Pharaoh would have lasted longer than any other dynasty or empire?**

מִשָּׁם בְּיָד חֲזָקָה וּבִזְרוֹעַ נְטוּיָה[1], וְאִלּוּ לֹא הוֹצִיא הַקָּדוֹשׁ בָּרוּךְ הוּא אֶת אֲבוֹתֵינוּ מִמִּצְרַיִם, הֲרֵי אָנוּ וּבָנֵינוּ וּבְנֵי בָנֵינוּ מְשֻׁעְבָּדִים הָיִינוּ לְפַרְעֹה בְּמִצְרָיִם. וַאֲפִילוּ כֻּלָּנוּ חֲכָמִים, כֻּלָּנוּ נְבוֹנִים, כֻּלָּנוּ זְקֵנִים, כֻּלָּנוּ יוֹדְעִים אֶת הַתּוֹרָה, מִצְוָה עָלֵינוּ לְסַפֵּר בִּיצִיאַת מִצְרָיִם. וְכָל הַמַּרְבֶּה לְסַפֵּר בִּיצִיאַת מִצְרַיִם, הֲרֵי זֶה מְשֻׁבָּח.

Rather, I believe the *Haggadah* is referring to something else. The freedom from labor had occurred on the Rosh Hashanah prior to *Yetzias Mitzrayim*. What we celebrate on Pesach, then, is the freedom from Mitzrayim's culture, which enabled us to leave unfettered by the *hashkafos* of a foreign society.

❒ It is this freedom that we would not have achieved, even after millennia. For even if another empire would have taken over Egypt and either enslaved the Jewish people or emancipated them, Klal Yisrael would never have achieved the separation of culture and society that was needed to give them their own, unadulterated *hashkafos,* gleaned from the Torah.

❒ Now that we are once again in exile, we must spend time analyzing the true meaning of freedom. We must also analyze what we would do with the ultimate freedom if we could have it. And we must spend time discussing and contemplating the values we have inadvertently, or even deliberately, absorbed from the foreign cultures to which we are exposed. The greater in Torah one is, the more there is to explore and discuss. For the Sages can guide the nation, explaining which *hashkafos* are true and Torah-sourced, and which are false. This is why the Sages stayed up all night on the night of the *Seder,* and is also why *Avadim Hayinu* is followed by the story of those Sages. In our own exile, there are many examples of *hashkafos* that we, as American Jews, have picked up from the society around us, and which we need to fix. Some examples are (1) How we define murder; (2) how we view the study of *halachah;* and (3) how we look at sports competition.

Avadim Hayinu is the answer that we give the children to the four questions they have posed in the *Mah Nishtanah*. Essentially, we explain that some of what we do on the *Seder* night recalls slavery — eating *matzah* and *maror* — while other practices we engage in connote freedom and aristocracy — dipping our food and leaning while eating. The *Haggadah* notes that without Hashem's intervention on our behalf, Klal Yisrael would *never* have broken free from the grip of Pharaoh, and we would have

took us out from there with a strong hand and an outstretched arm.[1] And if the Holy One, blessed is He, had not taken our forefathers out of Mitzrayim, behold, we, and our children, and our children's children would have been subservient to Pharaoh in Mitzrayim. And even if we were all wise, all understanding, all elders, all knowing the Torah, there would still be a commandment for us to discuss *Yetzias Mitzrayim*. And anyone who increases in the discussion of *Yetzias Mitzrayim*, this is praiseworthy!

(1) *Devarim* 6:21.

---

remained slaves to his empire to this day. This we must impart to our children; if not for *Yetzias Mitzrayim,* we, the fathers, and you, the children, would still not be free.

Certainly, I concede that the words of *Chazal* are absolutely unassailable, and if indeed their intent here in the *Haggadah* is to state that, in a literal sense, our nation would still be slaves to Pharaoh today, then as unlikely as it may seem, it is surely true. It is certainly fact that the falling of all of the world's empires through the centuries was due directly to Hashem's intervention; if Hashem had left Pharaoh alone, he would, by definition, have lasted longer than all the others. However, even if Hashem would not have freed us, I presume that He would almost assuredly have terminated Pharaoh's reign by now, as He did for all other dynasties and empires. After all, in the time that has ensued, empires at least as powerful as Mitzrayim have risen and fallen. No governing body has survived these millennia. Is there any reason to think that Pharaoh would have done what no other empire could? It seems unlikely. I think there is another meaning to these words — a meaning that I am sure will ring true to many.

The journey from slavery to freedom, as we have noted above (see *Kadeish*), took place in several stages. The final step, which was *Yetzias Mitzrayim* itself, was the freedom from the shackles of the ideology of our host nation, who happened to be Mitzrayim. It was at the time of *Yetzias Mitzrayim* that Klal Yisrael experienced the freedom to have their own identities, uninfluenced by the culture that surrounded them. As we know, this freedom was not afforded to them in a vacuum — it was rather gifted to them, to enable them to be ready to accept the Torah and serve Hashem without any hindrances at all.

But, consider if this emancipation had never occurred. Perhaps then, several centuries down the line, Pharaoh's empire would have been crushed by the Babylonians or the Romans — who is to say? And, perhaps the Jewish people would have been taken as slaves by their new masters, or alternatively, they might have been emancipated. But regardless, we

would have forever remained slaves to the ideas of Mitzrayim first, and to whichever country hosted us afterward, next. Never would we have experienced the separation from our host culture to realize, feel, and know with clarity that we are *not* part of a foreign culture, and we do *not* want the things they want. When would our own identities emerge, our own culture develop? Never... we would still be waiting.

In reality, Klal Yisrael had been freed from all physical labor the Rosh Hashanah prior to *Yetzias Mitzrayim*. So, what occurred on the night of Pesach, the night we commemorate for all time with the *Seder?* Why are we directed (*Shemos* 13:3) to remember *yom asher yetzasem miMitzrayim, the day that you departed Mitzrayim?* The physical labor had ceased months before! Also, it would seem appropriate to refer to the Exodus as *Yetziah MiMitzrayim,* which literally means *departure from Mitzrayim*. Why is it referred to as *Yetzias Mitzrayim?*

These questions answer each other. *Yetzias Mitzrayim* means *the departure of Mitzrayim* —from within ourselves. On the night of our physical departure from the land of Mitzrayim, our dream of complete independence from Mitzrayim's beliefs, ideals, culture, and society was finally complete. And it is this freedom that we would never have achieved without our departure, no matter what was destined to happen to the Egyptian Empire.

On the night of the *Seder,* we strive to focus on the fact that we *did* leave Mitzrayim, and when we did, we were reborn as free people. We accepted the Torah, and began an eternal relationship with Hashem. But, now that we are once again in exile, it is incumbent upon us to rediscover this freedom from the cultures that surround us. Even in the societies that are favorable for Jews to exist in, we must realize that we are still subject to cultures that are not inherently our own, and this affects the way we act and think.

Accordingly, we can now appreciate a fantastic insight into why it is so vital to continue to discuss *Yetzias Mitzrayim* all night. How many *peshatim* can one say and hear on the *Haggadah?* The material, though vast, is finite, and surely if one was a great Torah scholar, who knew the entire Torah, it would not take all night to review. But to know what freedom really is, what we potentially can gain from it, and how our relationship with Hashem should change when we attain that ultimate freedom, are topics that can, and should be, spoken about and delved into all night.

Freedom is not a concept that is absolute and clear cut. To illustrate: There were those who escaped communist Russia in the 1970s, and yet after arriving in America, decided to return there. They realized that their newly gained freedom to vote in an election in New York was not worth the trade-off of not being able to walk in their neighborhoods after dark. They felt that being prisoner in their own homes every night was more restrictive to their freedom than not being able to vote. [And in consideration of that viewpoint, it must be pointed out that millions of people simply

do not bother to exercise their right to vote.] They cared less about who governed their country, and more about their personal freedoms. Were they right? What is real freedom? Freedom from fear of harm, or freedom from having the will of another imposed upon you? The discussion of what constitutes true and unfettered freedom is complex and far-ranging.

We have explained that part and parcel of the *mitzvah* of *sippur Yetzias Mitzrayim* is to focus on the influences that have seeped into our own "Torah society" from the outside; and after identifying them, understanding the Torah's actual viewpoint on these matters, and striving for freedom from these foreign values. This is an ongoing, always developing and evolving discussion, and nobody is overqualified to join such an important conversation. Just the opposite; the elders and the Sages in every generation are perhaps the ones who should spend *the most* time discussing these ideas. For the older generation always possesses the memory of how things were before a particular idea became popular, and can explain its origins. And it is the Torah scholars who possess the clarity of the Torah's perspective, and who can accurately separate between an authentic Torah idea and one that has been adapted from foreign society, and they can perhaps provide those around them with insight into how to return to the ways of the Torah. It is they who can explain why the children of this generation are not the same as those in previous generations, and figure out how they are "slaves" to the society in which Klal Yisrael find themselves. This is why the Sages would stay up all night discussing *Yetzias Mitzrayim.*

Surely, such conversations will involve discussion of the various miracles Hashem performed for Klal Yisrael, in order to gain an understanding into just Who Hashem is, and how we are to relate to Him. The *makkos* and all the other *nissim* of *Yetzias Mitzrayim* were performed by Hashem to make us realize Who He really is, and the greater and more concrete that realization is to us, the more we will be able to strive for the freedom to be exclusively His servants, which will bring us closer to Him.

There are many ways that how we think and feel is affected by the society around us. I will point to three such examples, which many people do not even realize stem from ideologies absorbed from our environs. The first is our attitude toward murder. If you ask a young American what "murder" is, he will likely tell you that it is a premeditated act, where the killer acted with forethought, and planned to kill his victim. What about a case of drunk driving, where a pedestrian is killed? An American will likely tell you that although it was terrible negligence to drive drunk, the act cannot be termed murder; at best, he will say it was negligent manslaughter. We may hear this and think that it is reasonable, but it is really only because we are Americans that we can even accept it.

The Torah charges us to act responsibly, and to ensure the safety of those around us from our actions. If a person was chopping wood in what

he thought was an empty forest, and the head of his axe accidentally flew off and killed his fellow, he is called a *horeig beshogeig, an inadvertent murderer.* The act he has committed is one of murder; if a *goy* were to commit it, he would be *chayav misah.* Now, if a *harigah* was not considered to be murder, but rather "an unintentional act that unfortunately resulted in a person's death," we would not inflict such severe punishment upon one who caused it. [See further, *Nahar Sholom* to *Bamidbar* 35:24.]

A second example is the motive with which people often learn *halachah.* In American law, the reason to know the law is to maximize your rights; to determine precisely what you can do and still be within the boundaries of legality. Attorneys specialize in areas of law specifically to advance their clients' best interests while remaining inside the framework of the law. Torah, however, is intended to imbue a person with the understanding of his obligations to those around him and to Hashem. The more Torah he knows, the more he should respect those around him. Torah is intended to be a vehicle by which to connect to the way Hashem thinks, not a tool to enable those fluent in its rules to be wealthier or more powerful. But, in a society of academia, there are those who study *halachah* and specialize in aiding people to find *halachic* loopholes — which is not what Hashem wants.

And finally, a third example of something we have absorbed here in America is the penchant for victory in competition. In sports, nothing but winning matters. Injuring a competitor is not frowned upon, and is even often encouraged. Not only in violent sports like boxing and football, but even in baseball, where a player is taught to slide into second even if this will threaten the health of the defensive player. This is a very American idea, with which the Torah disagrees.

It once happened that the *Rosh HaYeshiva, ztvk"l,* visited the sixth-grade class of *Rabbi Lomner, zt"l,* in MTJ. He asked the boys what they thought that they should be spending their time doing. One boy spoke up, saying that they ought to be learning Torah. The *Rosh HaYeshiva, ztvk"l,* told him that, no, they could play ball, too. [These were young boys, under *Bar Mitzvah* age.] "But," he warned them, "you need to play like a *Yid.*" Never lie for an advantage, embarrass someone, or cause harm to another person.

You may ask: What difference does it really make? It makes a *world* of a difference! For in a true Torah society, there would never be any distracted driving, for this would be seen as a murderous act. But now, to our sorrow, people do not take potentially murderous actions seriously. In a true Torah society, there would never be a *to'ein* who could be hired to advance *halachic* loopholes on his client's behalf, because no *to'ein* would

It once occurred with R' Eliezer, R' Yehoshua, R' Elazar ben Azaryah, R' Akiva, and R' Tarfon, that they were leaning

---

ever be willing to utilize the Torah in this manner. And if we were in our own society, we would all view sports as nothing more than an opportunity to experience camaraderie, exercise our bodies, and enjoy ourselves, without turning them into competitions that mean anything more.

These realizations do not occur in a vacuum. In order for them to happen, Klal Yisrael need to be free from society's views on these issues, so that we can freely analyze them according to the Torah perspective. And there are many more examples than the three we have briefly discussed here. This discussion can easily last the entire night, and it is a *mitzvah* to participate in such a discussion!

[When *Yetzias Mitzrayim* occurred, Hashem did us the favor of decimating the entirety of Egyptian society, so that we would have no misgivings about leaving their society behind. This was the gateway to our true freedom from their culture as we departed. Although Hashem does not always decimate our host society as we leave, He often, one way or another, puts a very foul taste in our mouths for that nation. Our hatred for them allows us to separate from their culture, and makes it repulsive to us, freeing us from the shackles of that particular place. Even today, many people react with disgust at the thought of buying a German-made product. More recently, people were calling French fries "freedom fries," out of their antipathy toward France. See below, *Vehi She'amdah,* second explanation; see also below, *Vanitzak.*]

מַעֲשֶׂה בְּרַבִּי אֱלִיעֶזֶר — *It Once Occurred with R' Eliezer*

❒ **From this story, we see that even the greatest Torah scholars of the generation should busy themselves with *sippur Yetzias Mitzrayim*. Not only that, but the greater the scholar, the more he should engage in it!**

❒ **Why did the *talmidim* come? And when did they come? If they came to tell their *Rebbeim* that the time for *sippur Yetzias Mitzrayim* had passed, then they likely came at *alos*. But if so, why did they say it was time for *Shema,* rather than simply saying that it was no longer nighttime? Also, *alos,* which marks the end of the night, is really too early to recite *Krias Shema* according to R' Eliezer! And if we posit that they actually came at *misheyakir,* and the reason they came was to announce that it was time to recite *Shema,* we have two questions: First, why was there even a *mitzvah* of *sippur Yetzias Mitzrayim* once *alos* had passed? And second, once we explain why there was a *mitzvah,* why were they not exempted from reciting *Krias Shema* because of the rule that *osek b'mitzvah patur min hamitzvah?***

בִּבְנֵי בְרַק, וְהָיוּ מְסַפְּרִים בִּיצִיאַת מִצְרַיִם כָּל אוֹתוֹ הַלַּיְלָה. עַד שֶׁבָּאוּ תַלְמִידֵיהֶם וְאָמְרוּ לָהֶם, רַבּוֹתֵינוּ הִגִּיעַ זְמַן קְרִיאַת שְׁמַע שֶׁל שַׁחֲרִית.

- ❒ **Perhaps we see from here that we do not apply the dictum that *osek b'mitzvah patur min hamitzvah* to *Krias Shema* when the *mitzvah* that is pushing it off has already been fulfilled, even if it could be extended.**
- ❒ **There is also a rule that *ein ma'avirin al hamitzvos,* we do not pass over *mitzvos.* Once we know that, it would seem that we would never interrupt a *mitzvah* we are already doing to perform another *mitzvah.* What, then, does the additional rule of *osek b'mitzvah patur min hamitzvah* teach? The answer is that if a person is busy with a *hechsher mitzvah,* the rule that *ein ma'avirin al hamitzvos* would not exempt him from a new *mitzvah.* But, the rule that *osek b'mitzvah patur min hamitzvah* would exempt him, even if he was busy only with a *hechsher mitzvah.***

Although it seems obvious, it is worthwhile to mention that the main reason why this story became a part of the *Haggadah* is because it demonstrates so clearly that no matter how old or how wise one is, it is incumbent upon him to perform *sippur Yetzias Mitzrayim.* Moreover, these were some of the greatest men of their day, and they spoke the entire night! This shows us that, actually, the greater one becomes, the *more* he should be involved in the discussion, as we explained above.

What bears closer examination, however, is why the *talmidim* approached their *Rabbeim* and stopped them from continuing their *sippur Yetzias Mitzrayim* even longer. And, as a part of that exploration, we need to consider exactly when it was that the *talmidim* came, as the issue of their timing is surely directly related to the reason they came.

Most people, I think, assume that the reason the *talmidim* interrupted the *sippur* of their *Rabbeim* was because morning had arrived. As we will see below (*Yachol MeiRosh Chodesh*), the time for the *mitzvah* of *sippur Yetzias Mitzrayim* is at the time when there is *matzah* and *maror* before you, which of course is the night of the *Seder.* Once the night passes, there is no longer any *mitzvah* of *sippur Yetzias Mitzrayim.* If this was indeed the reason the *talmidim* came, it would seemingly mean that they came at *alos,* which is the time that *mitzvos* of the night end (see *Megillah* 20b). However, if they came at *alos,* their statement of *higi'a zman Krias Shema shel Shacharis* would seem to have been imprecise; first, because the reason they approached had nothing to do with the arrival of the new *mitzvah*

[together at the *Seder*] in Bnei Brak, and they were speaking about Yetzias Mitzrayim all that night, until their talmidim came and said to them, "Our *Rabbeim*! The time to recite the morning *Krias Shema* has arrived."

---

of reciting *Krias Shema,* and everything to do with the expiry of the time for the old *mitzvah* of *sippur Yetzias Mitzrayim.* They should simply have noted that the night was over! And second, because, in fact, although one can recite *Krias Shema shel Shacharis* right after *alos,* it is not the preferred time to do so. The Mishnah (*Berachos* 1:2) records that one should recite *Shema* when he can differentiate between blue and white, and R' Eliezer rules that he should be able to differentiate between blue and green. This time is known as *misheyakir.* Now, R' Eliezer was a senior Tanna. Who would have had the absolute temerity to knock on the door and announce, *"The time to recite Shema has arrived!"*, knowing full well that according to R' Eliezer, one should not recite *Shema* until *misheyakir?!* So, although it is possible that the *talmidim* came at *alos* and meant to announce the departure of the night and the arrival of the day, there is some difficulty with this interpretation.

Another way to understand this would be that the *talmidim* came not at *alos,* but rather at *misheyakir,* to tell their *Rebbeim* that the time for *Krias Shema shel Shacharis* had arrived. However, there are some difficulties with this interpretation as well. For if the *talmidim* arrived at *misheyakir,* that means that when *alos* had come some time earlier, they saw no reason to interrupt their *Rabbeim* to tell them that the time of the obligation of *sippur Yetzias Mitzrayim* had passed. Why not? Seemingly, because there was still a reason for the *Rabbeim* to be discussing *Yetzias Mitzrayim.* And once we determine why there was a *mitzvah* of *sippur Yetzias Mitzrayim* even after *alos,* we must ask: Why did that *mitzvah* give way to the obligation to recite *Krias Shema shel Shacharis?* The rule is that *osek b'mitzvah patur min hamitzvah,* if a person is occupied in the fulfillment of a *mitzvah*, he is exempt from performing another *mitzvah.* Why did that rule not apply here?

Perhaps it can be suggested that the directive mandating the time for *sippur Yetzias Mitzrayim* at the time that we have *matzah* and *maror* before us is only telling us the *beginning* of the time for this *mitzvah.* But, theoretically, the *mitzvah* could continue past that time. This could answer another question as well. R' Elazar ben Azaryah, one of the participants at that *Seder* in Bnei Brak, is of the opinion that the *Afikoman* must be eaten before midnight. Clearly then, according to him, after midnight is no longer a time when there is *matzah* before us. And yet, he was engaged in the *mitzvah* of *sippur Yetzias Mitzrayim* throughout the second half of the night! But, if we explain that once the *mitzvah* of *sippur Yetzias Mitzrayim* was begun during

אָמַר רַבִּי אֶלְעָזָר בֶּן עֲזַרְיָה, הֲרֵי אֲנִי כְּבֶן שִׁבְעִים שָׁנָה, וְלֹא זָכִיתִי שֶׁתֵּאָמֵר יְצִיאַת מִצְרַיִם בַּלֵּילוֹת, עַד שֶׁדְּרָשָׁהּ בֶּן זוֹמָא, שֶׁנֶּאֱמַר, לְמַעַן תִּזְכֹּר אֶת יוֹם צֵאתְךָ מֵאֶרֶץ מִצְרַיִם כֹּל יְמֵי חַיֶּיךָ[1]. יְמֵי חַיֶּיךָ הַיָּמִים, כֹּל יְמֵי חַיֶּיךָ הַלֵּילוֹת. וַחֲכָמִים אוֹמְרִים, יְמֵי חַיֶּיךָ הָעוֹלָם הַזֶּה, כֹּל יְמֵי חַיֶּיךָ לְהָבִיא לִימוֹת הַמָּשִׁיחַ.

---

its proper time, the *mitzvah* continues for as long as we are discussing the topic, R' Elazar ben Azaryah's participation can be explained.

But we still must understand: Why were the Tannaim obligated to stop the *mitzvah* they had been busy with to perform the *mitzvah* of *Krias Shema shel Shacharis?* Why did they not apply the dictum of *osek b'mitzvah patur min hamitzvah?*

Perhaps the answer is that even though the dictum of *osek b'mitzvah patur min hamitzvah* applies to *Krias Shema* in other cases, here, the *mitzvah* of *sippur Yetzias Mitzrayim* cannot push off *Krias Shema.* This is because even though it is true that the *Krias Shema* recital is going to stop the *mitzvah* of *sippur Yetzias Mitzrayim* from continuing, that *mitzvah* has been fulfilled. True, it could have continued for longer, but mandating that *Krias Shema* be recited now does not in any way change that the *mitzvah* of *sippur Yetzias Mitzrayim* was fulfilled and completed, albeit earlier than it otherwise would have been. This idea is similar to one we find pertaining to *Talmud Torah.* A person is obligated to learn every waking moment. *Talmud Torah* is also equal to all the other *mitzvos.* And yet it does not supersede any of them. When the time to recite *Krias Shema* arrives, one must stop learning and perform the *mitzvah,* even though the time he was not learning will never be replaced. There as well, the *mitzvah* of *Talmud Torah* is fulfilled – the fellow learned during all of his available time. Even though he learned for less time, the *mitzvah* to learn was fulfilled optimally. The desire to fulfill the *mitzvah* of *Talmud Torah* for more time is unable to push away the obligation to recite *Krias Shema.*

While we are on the subject of *osek b'mitzvah patur min hamitzvah,* I think it is worthwhile to explain how this dictum differs from the rule that *ein ma'avirin al hamitzvos, we do not pass over a mitzvah.* This principle tells us to place our *tallis* closer to us than our *tefillin shel yad,* which, in turn, should be closer than our *tefillin shel rosh,* so we do not have to pass over one *mitzvah* on the way to carry out another. This principle is also on display on the *Seder* night, when we place the *karpas* and saltwater closer to us on the *ke'arah* than the *maror* and the *charoses,* so that we should

Rabbi Elazar ben Azaryah said: I am like a seventy-year-old man, but I could not succeed in having *Yetzias Mitzrayim* mentioned every night, until Ben Zoma expounded it, for the verse states: "In order that you may remember the day you left Mitzrayim all the days of your life."[1] The phrase "the days of your life" would have indicated only the days; the addition of the word "all" includes the nights as well. But the Sages declare that "the days of your life" would mean only the present world; the addition of "all" includes the era of *Mashiach*.

(1) *Devarim* 16:3.

not have to reach over the *maror* to access the *karpas*. Seemingly, once it is true that we are not supposed to pass over a closer *mitzvah* in favor of a more distant one, we should certainly not be *interrupting* a *mitzvah* we are *in the middle of performing* to do a *mitzvah* whose opportunity of fulfillment has arisen only just now! And if that is true, why do we need the principle of *osek b'mitzvah patur min hamitzvah* at all? We already know not to stop and do the new *mitzvah,* because the one we are in the middle of is definitely "closer," and *ein maavirin al hamitzvos!*

I believe that the distinction between the two principles is found in a situation where the person is not actually busy performing the *mitzvah* itself, but is rather busy with a *hechsher mitzvah;* an action that is being performed in preparation for the *mitzvah* being carried out. A good example of this would be the case of *perutah DeRabbi Yosef*. The person caring for the lost object is not actually returning it right now. He is rather engaged in the care of the object, so that when he does eventually find its owner, it will be in pristine condition. This is not the actual performance of *hashavas aveidah,* but is certainly a necessary *hechsher mitzvah*. And yet, when a pauper comes collecting, the fact that the *shomer aveidah* is busy with the *aveidah* does indeed exempt him from giving charity. This is because he is *osek b'mitzvah*. When one is *actively busy* with even a *hechsher mitzvah,* we apply the rule that *osek b'mitzvah patur min hamitzvah*.

This is different from the rule that *ein maavirin al hamitzvos,* which would only tell us to prioritize the *mitzvah* whose performance is closer at hand. But if the actual *hashavas aveidah* is not being performed, but rather only a *hechsher* for it, such as caring for the lost object, *ein maavirin* would not tell us to prioritize that *hechsher mitzvah* over the actual *mitzvah* of *tzedakah*. As such, we need the principle that *osek b'mitzvah patur min hamitzvah* to explain why it is that even when a person is only doing a *hechsher mitzvah,* he is still exempt from performing another *mitzvah* which comes his way.

בָּרוּךְ הַמָּקוֹם, בָּרוּךְ הוּא. בָּרוּךְ שֶׁנָּתַן תּוֹרָה לְעַמּוֹ יִשְׂרָאֵל, בָּרוּךְ הוּא. כְּנֶגֶד אַרְבָּעָה בָנִים דִּבְּרָה תוֹרָה. אֶחָד חָכָם. וְאֶחָד רָשָׁע. וְאֶחָד תָּם. וְאֶחָד שֶׁאֵינוֹ יוֹדֵעַ לִשְׁאוֹל.

— כְּנֶגֶד אַרְבָּעָה בָנִים דִּבְּרָה תוֹרָה

The Torah Anticipates [and Commands a Father to Teach to] Four Different Types of Children

- **We are commanded several times in the Torah to teach our children about *Yetzias Mitzrayim,* and *Chazal* understood from the various *pesukim* describing these children and the father's replies that different children are being addressed with each *posuk.* We will discuss each of these categories of children.**
- **Of particular note is the fact that while one child is labeled a *ben rasha,* there is no *ben tzaddik.* This means that the *ben chacham,* although demonstrating a thirst for Torah, is not necessarily a *ben tzaddik.***
- **We must realize that even our "good kids" require our supervision and our input, in order to ensure they are indeed on the path that they appear to be on, to help them grow and mature into righteous adults, and to make sure they do not falter.**
- **We learn from the fact that the *korban pesach* needs to be roasted — a method of preparation that requires the constant attention of the chef — that *chinuch* requires parents to be involved with their children's upbringing all the time, without lapses or blindspots. This is the only way to ensure that *all four* categories of children have a chance to develop into true *tzaddikim.***

In describing the four children who need to be taught about *Yetzias Mitzrayim* by their father, the *Haggadah* lists the wise child, the evil child, the simple child, and the child who does not know how to ask. *Chazal* understood that the Torah speaks to four different children because there are several *pesukim* where the Torah foretells that Klal Yisrael's children will ask about Pesach, and what the father should reply. [We will discuss each child separately below.] Of particular note, however, is that *Chazal* did not explain any of the *pesukim* as referring to a *ben tzaddik, a righteous child.* Rather, the proverbial "good boy" is referred to in the *Haggadah* as the *chacham, the wise son,* while the proverbial "bad boy" is referenced as a *ben rasha, an evil child.* Why is there no allusion in the *Haggadah* to a righteous child?

In the *Haftarah* to *Parashas Chayei Sarah* (*Melachim I* 6:1-31), we read

Blessed is HASHEM, Blessed is He! Blessed is the One Who gave the Torah to His nation, Yisrael, Blessed is He! The Torah anticipates [and commands a father to teach to] four different types of children: One is wise, and one is evil, and one is simple, and one does not know how to ask.

---

the episode of the rebellion of Adoniah. In my humble opinion, one of the greatest lessons in proper *chinuch* is revealed to us within this story.

If we examine the *pesukim,* we are told precious little in the way of a "back story" regarding Adoniah and his decision to take the crown for himself. There is only a single *posuk* describing Adoniah's relationship with his father, David HaMelech, and that is 6:6; *All his life, his father had never saddened him by saying, "Why do you do this?" Moreover, he was "tov to'ar me'od," and he was born after Avshalom.* What is the intent of this *posuk*, and how can it explain what triggered Adoniah's actions?

In order to understand the answer to this question, we must first explain the phrase *tov to'ar.* What is the difference between *to'ar* and *mareh*? We can understand the distinction based upon *Rashi's* explanation of the Torah's description of Rachel Imeinu. Of Rachel, the *posuk* (*Bereishis* 29:17) states, *v'Rachel hayesah yefas to'ar vi'fas mareh, and Rachel was beautiful in to'ar and beautiful in mareh. Rashi* there explains that *to'ar* refers to the physical form of a person's features, whereas *mareh* refers to the shine of one's countenance.

Based upon this distinction, we can explain the word *to'ar* as an allusion to something concrete and noticeable — such as a person's physical features, or actions that we can observe them performing. These things, when observed, contribute to a person's *to'ar.* On the other hand, *mareh* is what we call things that we cannot clearly observe. A person's countenance can be vibrant or ordinary, and the difference is not easily detectable physically. A beautiful countenance is a quality that is almost intangible. Similarly, a person who is always out of the limelight, never observed — his value as a person is also intangible; no one sees him in action, so nobody has a positive picture of how good a person he really is.

I would like to present a parable by which we can better understand the difference between *to'ar* and *mareh.* Suppose there are two *bochurim* in Yeshiva. One of them is always coming in to *davening* with great fanfare, displaying true zeal in rushing to his seat. He can never be missed — his clear pronunciation, as well as the feeling with which he imbues his prayers, can be heard throughout the entire *beis medrash.* The second *bochur* is quieter. In fact, nobody really sees when he comes in to *daven* — he just always seems to be there. He is not loud, and does not seem to be outstanding at all. But he appears to be a nice boy. The first *bochur*

חָכָם מָה הוּא אוֹמֵר? מָה הָעֵדֹת וְהַחֻקִּים וְהַמִּשְׁפָּטִים אֲשֶׁר צִוָּה יהוה אֱלֹהֵינוּ אֶתְכֶם[1]? וְאַף אַתָּה אֱמָר לוֹ כְּהִלְכוֹת הַפֶּסַח, אֵין מַפְטִירִין אַחַר הַפֶּסַח אֲפִיקוֹמָן.

---

has a good *to'ar*; that is, we can identify tangibly what we feel are his merits, based upon observation in the real world. The second boy has only a good *mareh* — his actions are not providing a true picture of his merits. Now, if we would look "behind the scenes," we would realize that the second *bachur* never makes an entrance to *davening* because he is always there early. If we would be able to see what was going on in his mind, his concentration might astound us. But we see none of this. It takes a little bit of *to'ar* — a "crack in his armor" of nondescript behavior — to reveal to everyone just how great this boy's *mareh* truly is. If he comes late to *davening* just one time, but rushes in with the same zeal with which we always see the first *bochur* arriving, this will serve as a window into his *mareh,* and will help us begin to recognize the person he really is.

Rachel Imeinu is described by the Torah as having beautiful *to'ar* and *mareh.* In regard to her actions, this means that she had beautiful actions that people were able to see, and also beautiful actions that remained hidden. Rivkah Imeinu, however, is described by the *posuk* (*Bereishis* 24:16) as *tovas mareh me'od;* but there is no mention of her *to'ar.* I believe that this is precisely because of what we are positing here. With beautiful *mareh*, a person's true righteousness remains hidden from view. Rivkah faced a unique challenge growing up in Besuel's house. How could she practice *chessed* under her father's roof? Rivkah therefore developed her *mareh* — her unassuming way of just happening to be where people needed her; never making it obvious that she had planned to be available to perform *chessed.* In this way, she exhibited no *to'ar* at all, thus preserving her guise. This was a very great level of *mareh,* and thus the Torah refers to her as *tovas mareh me'od.*

Now, let us examine the *posuk's* description of Adoniah. Adoniah was the exact opposite of Rivkah. The *posuk* calls him *tov to'ar me'od,* as opposed to Rivkah's *tovas mareh me'od.* This means that Adoniah developed his *to'ar.* Aside from the normal behavior of a person, from which it is apparent to others if he is righteous, Adoniah practiced *to'ar me'od.* How so? He made a show of everything — on purpose. He specifically came just a drop late to *shul,* so his piety would be noticed by all. He made all the right moves, always looked the part of the righteous little prince, and invested all of his energy into showing David just how sincere he was in serving Hashem with love and fear, and adhering to the Torah.

David HaMelech never questioned Adoniah's actions, and more importantly, his motives, when he was a child. Why? Because Adoniah was

The wise son, what does he say? "What are the testimonies and the laws and the ordinances that HASHEM, our God, has commanded you?"[1] And also you shall say to him all of the laws of the *pesach*; [concluding with the law that] we do not partake of anything after the *Afikoman*.

(1) *Devarim* 6:20.

---

tov to'ar me'od — everything he did was picture perfect! He was like that dream child in *shul,* always praying with visible fervor, pointing to the place. He was like the child whose homework was always done perfectly, who always cleaned up his toys, and everything else you could imagine a child doing exactly right. And where does the *posuk* teach us that this led? To a rebellion against his own father! How can this be?

This is the vital message for parents of apparent little angels. What the *posuk* is teaching us here is that all children, no matter how angelic, are still children. Even when they seem to be acting like little *tzaddikim*, there are still childish motives behind their actions. These motives need to be examined by us, the parents. And we cannot examine what we do not know. So, it is important to realize — not suspect, but know for a fact — that totally perfect children do not exist, and it is always proper to discuss with a child what his or her motive is, even if they are acting appropriately. Through discussion, a parent will be able to (1) keep the child on his or her toes, so they do not think that they can get away with anything untoward should they feel like it; and (2) correct and/or implant more mature ideas and morals in the mind of the child. We must not simply rely on their *to'ar* — which is only an illusion of perfection — and be complacent that our children are being raised properly through osmosis from their environment.

David HaMelech treated Adoniah as if he was a *ben tzaddik,* and the lesson Adoniah taught us is that while he might indeed have been a *ben chacham,* there truly is no such a thing as a *ben tzaddik*. The true *yetzer tov* does not exist in children, and that means that their good behavior is for ulterior motives. There is nothing wrong with this, of course! But for a father to believe that his child is a *tzaddik* when he is not can lead to disastrous consequences. [See further below, *Va'omar lach bedamayich chayi,* below, where we will discuss a valuable lesson in the proper manner in which we must be *mechaneich* our children.]

חָכָם — *The Wise Son*

❒ **The *ben chacham* is inquisitive, and seeks to understand the *content* of the Torah. The *Haggadah* notes that we have not completed our mission in teaching him until his appetite for Torah knowledge is**

sated, when he has received all the information we have to give him. However, if we examine the *pesukim* that the Torah bids us to say to this son in response to his query, it is clear that while our obligation *extends* to offering this knowledge, it by no means *begins* there.

- In order for this child to be able to appreciate the Torah that he seeks, he needs to understand the import of the Torah. Thus, we must first explain to him that what he is about to learn is incredibly important!
- We teach him that Hashem liberated us from physical slavery, and also from the desire to be similar to Egyptians in any way. This left our minds free to think and feel the way Hashem wants us to think and feel. This allows him to love Torah and *mitzvos,* and to enjoy them. This, in turn, will not only give him a wonderful life in this world, enjoying his mission, but will also give him the ability to truly enjoy his share in the World to Come.

In *Parashas Va'eschanan,* the Torah records (*Devarim* 6:20) that there will be children who will ask, "What are the testimonies, the laws, and the ordinances of the Torah?" The father is instructed by the *pesukim* to respond with a historical perspective of the import of the Torah.

The *chacham* will ask what the content of the Torah is because he is curious, and perhaps eager, to learn about the Torah and its *mitzvos.* In the context of the *pasuk,* the *chacham* may not even be asking about the laws of Pesach per se; he is simply inquiring into Torah and *mitzvos* in general. [It is perhaps for this very reason that the *chinuch* of the *chacham* appears in *Va'eschanan,* while the *chinuch* of the other children appear in *Parashas Bo.* Although the way we teach all four children has an application on the night of the *Seder,* it is in the context of the *Seder* that the Torah teaches us how to relate to the other three children. The *ben chacham,* however, is curious about all of the Torah. As we will see, *Yetzias Mitzrayim* features prominently in how we address him; and certainly, on Pesach night, he is taught in his own way. But because his curiosity is not central to Pesach, the topic of his *chinuch* is written elsewhere.] Of course, we will tell the *ben chacham* everything he wishes to know about what is in the Torah. But before we do so, the Torah teaches us that it is imperative that he gain an appreciation of what it means to keep the Torah; what it meant to Klal Yisrael in the Wilderness; what it must mean for him in his lifetime, and what it will mean for him in the World to Come. Accordingly, the Torah tells us to answer him with the *pesukim* from 6:21-25.

We begin by telling this child that we were slaves to Pharaoh in Mitzrayim, and that Hashem removed us from there with great strength. With this declaration, we mean to point out three things: The first is that Klal Yisrael had, over the course of the exile in Mitzrayim, lost the *mesorah* of the Torah that they had accepted from Avraham Avinu. Thus, Klal Yisrael needed to become Hashem's servants all over again, so to speak. The torturous

pressures that were inflicted upon them by the Egyptians for so long had rendered it impossible for the nation to dedicate themselves to the service of Hashem. This is why we begin the lesson on the centrality that the Torah must play in the life of the *chacham* with our servitude in Mitzrayim.

The second point the Torah is teaching us is that Hashem took us out from there with a strong arm, by performing signs, wonders, and awesome punishments against Pharaoh and his people. This too is critical for the *chacham* to hear. The point that the *pesukim* are making to the *chacham* is that, more important than the fact that Klal Yisroel was freed from slavery, is the fact that the Egyptians were decimated. This point is further emphasized when we realize that, in fact, the forced labor that the Jewish people had undergone actually ceased on Rosh Hashanah — more than six months before *Yetzias Mitzrayim*. And yet, on which day do we celebrate *Yetzias Mitzrayim* — Rosh Hashanah, or Pesach? Clearly, the celebration of Pesach is intended to commemorate the moment when Klal Yisrael was released not from their physical shackles, but rather from the shackles of the notion that Egyptian society was something desirable.

Throughout history, whenever Hashem moved the Jewish people from place to place, He arranged for the local populace to drive them out. This had the effect of leaving a bitter taste in Klal Yisrael's mouths and prevented them from desiring to take the foreign culture with them. This is the third point the Torah is making: After suffering at the hands of Mitzrayim for so long, Hashem destroyed Mitzrayim with the *makkos* and at *Krias Yam Suf*. When the nation was ready to depart on the fifteenth of *Nissan*, they were ready to depart from Mitzrayim both physically and also culturally. And now that their heads were cleared from Egyptian ideals and goals and morals, they were ready to allow their minds and hearts to ascend, and to aspire to a better existence.

So the *chacham* is to be taught that the *mesorah* began anew with the formation of Klal Yisrael, when the nation was separated from the culture of Mitzrayim, and when they became Hashem's people. As the next *posuk* (6:23) states, *And us, Hashem removed us from there, in order to bring us, and to give us the Land that He promised to our fathers*. Hashem did not free Klal Yisrael simply because they were slaves and He felt that they should be free. Hashem freed Klal Yisrael from Pharaoh so that they could band together and become His people, His nation, and live in His Land. It is only after He brought us to a situation where we would be free to accept His Torah as His people that He charged us with its observance; as 6:24 states, *And Hashem commanded us to perform all of these laws, to fear Hashem, our God, etc.*

But this is not all. The *posuk* ends with the phrase, *for our good, all the days, to keep us alive as this day*. Torah and *mitzvos* — *Yiddishkeit* — is *good!* It is enjoyable, and the *chacham* must learn this lesson if indeed he is going to adopt a Torah lifestyle. He is charged with being able to find the joy in a

רָשָׁע מָה הוּא אוֹמֵר? מָה הָעֲבֹדָה הַזֹּאת לָכֶם[1]? לָכֶם וְלֹא לוֹ, וּלְפִי שֶׁהוֹצִיא אֶת עַצְמוֹ מִן הַכְּלָל, כָּפַר בְּעִקָּר — וְאַף אַתָּה הַקְהֵה אֶת שִׁנָּיו וֶאֱמָר לוֹ, בַּעֲבוּר זֶה עָשָׂה יהוה לִי בְּצֵאתִי מִמִּצְרָיִם[2]. לִי וְלֹא לוֹ, אִלּוּ הָיָה שָׁם לֹא הָיָה נִגְאָל.

---

blatt of Gemara or in a *Rashba*. He is expected to gain a feeling of appreciation for an *esrog mehudar,* and to feel good when connecting with Hashem through *tefillah*. These are pleasures that a person experiences in this world.

And finally, we tell the *chacham* that if he will learn to love *ruchniyus* in this world, he will love the share of *Olam Haba* that he will earn! 6:25 states, *It shall be tzedakah for you, when you guard to observe all of these commandments, before Hashem your God, as He has commanded you.* This is an allusion to the fact that the observance of the Torah's laws will stand the *chacham* in good stead as a merit in *Olam Haba*. Once he has gained an appreciation for *ruchniyus,* and for a relationship with Hashem, he will enjoy the reward for Torah and *mitzvos* that he will receive in the World to Come.

In *Avos* (4:21), the Mishnah compares the relationship between this world and the next to a corridor before a banquet hall. *Rabbeinu Yonah* there explains this simply, to mean that the merits that one accumulates in this world acquire for him access to the World to Come. *Rashi,* however, seems to take a different approach. He writes that just as one combs his hair and fixes his beard in the corridor before he enters the hall, so too this world contains what is needed to reach great spiritual heights in the World to Come. See *Pirkei Sholom* there, where we explained that *Rashi* is deriving from the Mishnah a very profound lesson indeed. A person is meant to train himself in this world to develop a taste for *ruchniyus,* through which he can enjoy what lies ahead for him in the World to Come!

So, when the *chacham* approaches his father and asks for details of the laws of the Torah, it is not enough to give him the information he requests. Rather, the father must seize the opportunity to imbue into his inquisitive child the *meaning* that the Torah has to Klal Yisrael as Hashem's chosen nation. When the child gains an appreciation of the import of the Torah, the details of its laws will have a far greater impact upon him, and can serve to help develop him into the *ben Torah* that Hashem wishes for him to become.

All of the above, of course, begs the question: Why does the *Haggadah* instruct us to tell the *chacham* all of the laws of the *korban pesach*, up until, and including, the law that we do not eat anything after the *Afikoman?* What about the other important lessons that the Torah tells a father to impart to this son in response to the young man's query?

The wicked son, what does he say? "What is this service to you?"[1] And because he removed himself from the congregation, he has demonstrated denial of basic tenets of Judaism. And you, too, shall blunt his teeth, and say to him, "On account of this, HASHEM did for me when I left Mitzrayim."[2] "Me," and not him; for if he had been there, he would not have been redeemed.

(1) *Shemos* 12:26. (2) 13:8.

If we look at the words of the *Haggadah* carefully, they do not exclude these lessons at all. Rather, the *Haggadah* instructs the father to present the whole picture of the *korban pesach* to his son, from beginning to end. The *Haggadah* tells us that the "end" is the last law pertaining to the *korban;* but that definitely does not mean that the "beginning" is the first law! The beginning is the background of why there is even a nation of Klal Yisrael, and why they offer this *korban* to begin with. What is the freedom which the *pesach* commemorates, and how, in what merit, and for what purpose did Hashem save His people in Mitzrayim? Once these lessons have been transmitted to the child, we can begin with the *halachos* of the *korban,* which culminate with the law of the *Afikoman.*

רָשָׁע — *The Wicked Son*

- **This child needs our *chinuch,* and it is our mission to impart it to him. Tonight, we have a *mitzvah* to do just that.**
- **When Moshe Rabbeinu informed Klal Yisrael that one day, their children would ask them about *Yetzias Mitzrayim,* and they bowed down in thanks to Hashem for this good tiding, the son Moshe was talking about was none other than the *ben rasha.* We do not despise the *rasha;* on the contrary, we love him and cherish him. Accordingly, our reply to him is not intended to shun the *ben rasha.* In fact, we embrace him and the challenge he brings us, for this is the very essence of the lesson of the *korban pesach* — that a Jew always has potential to do what Hashem desires him or her to do.**
- **In our reply to him, we do not seek to harm the *ben rasha,* nor to reject him. Rather, the idea of "blunting his teeth" is to show the child with our strong reaction how very unacceptable his approach to the *Seder* and everything surrounding it is.**
- **This tactic will only be effective if our relationship with this child is positive. Then, when we react in this extreme manner here, the child will think, "Why would such a loving parent react this way? I must have crossed a line." But, if our relationship with this child is already negative, he will glean no lesson at all from our reaction, and instead**

תָּם מָה הוּא אוֹמֵר? מַה זֹּאת? וְאָמַרְתָּ אֵלָיו, בְּחֹזֶק יָד הוֹצִיאָנוּ יהוה מִמִּצְרַיִם מִבֵּית עֲבָדִים.[1]

וְשֶׁאֵינוֹ יוֹדֵעַ לִשְׁאוֹל, אַתְּ פְּתַח לוֹ. שֶׁנֶּאֱמַר, וְהִגַּדְתָּ לְבִנְךָ בַּיּוֹם הַהוּא לֵאמֹר, בַּעֲבוּר זֶה עָשָׂה יהוה לִי בְּצֵאתִי מִמִּצְרָיִם.[2]

---

say to himself, "Here goes my father again, making fun of me and my opinion, like he always does."

In *Parashas Bo,* after issuing the laws of the *korban pesach,* Moshe Rabbeinu commanded (*Shemos* 12:24) that this *korban* be offered annually. He instructed Klal Yisrael to carry out this service when they arrive in Eretz Yisrael. Then, Moshe Rabbeinu tells the nation that it shall come to pass that they will have children who will ask, *Mah ha'avodah hazos lachem, What is this service to you*? This is the question which the *Haggadah* ascribes to the wicked son. It would follow, then, that the reply that we give the wicked son in the *Haggadah* should reflect the words of the Torah there (12:27) which read, *"And you shall say, this is a pesach offering to Hashem, for He skipped over the houses of Bnei Yisrael in Mitzrayim when he smote the Egyptians, and our homes he saved."* However, as we know, this is not at all what the *Haggadah* tells us to say to the wicked son. Rather, the *Haggadah* teaches us to blunt his teeth (with words), saying to him, "If you had been there, you would not have been redeemed!" What is the explanation for this discrepancy?

The truth is that the question of the wicked son is actually very depressing. We are talking about a situation where Klal Yisrael is living with Hashem, during a time when His Presence is felt throughout Eretz Yisrael and the entire world, and when we have the *Beis HaMikdash.* In that situation, it is certainly going to be all the more heartbreaking for a father to hear from his son the derisive and exclusionary question of, *What is this service to you?* The father might think to himself that this child is so evil that there is no hope for him at all! In that moment, what is the father to say to himself? He must remember that the *korban pesach* itself commemorates Hashem skipping over the houses of the children of Avraham, Yitzchak, and Yaakov, and smiting the homes of the Egyptians. And when did this take place? Soon before the splitting of the *Yam Suf,* at which the angels exclaimed to Hashem, "These (Egyptians) serve idols and these (the Jewish people) serve idols!" We must remember that Hashem looked past our evil deeds at the time of *Yetzias Mitzrayim,* and saw in our essence that we were different from the other nations because we were Klal Yisrael, the descendants of the *Avos*, and we had in our core the attributes of our

The simple son, what does he say? "What is this?" And you shall say to him, "With a strong hand, HASHEM took us out from Mitzrayim, from a house of slaves."[1]

The son who does not know how to ask — you open for him, as it is stated: "And you shall tell to your son on that day, saying, 'On account of *this* HASHEM did for me when I left Mitzrayim."[2]

(1) *Shemos* 13:14. (2) 13:8.

forefathers. Even when a Jew is evil, he is not the same as an evil idolater. [An example of this dichotomy is the difference between two infamous mass murderers, Trotsky and Stalin. Trotsky was an evil killer, but his murderous ways were rooted in the belief that he was fighting to better the world, and he had to kill people to make that happen. Stalin, on the other hand, killed simply to consolidate his own power.]

This is a message for the father who is being confronted with the question of his *ben rasha.* He must tell himself, "Look past your disappointment and see the potential in the wicked child, as Hashem saw the potential in Klal Yisrael at the time of *Yetzias Mitzrayim*! There is hope for him; it just needs love and teaching to bring it out." This explains why the response we give the wicked son in the *Haggadah* is different from the reaction described by the *posuk* — precisely because the *posuk* is telling the father what to say to *himself,* while the *Haggadah* tells the father what to say to his son.

The *Haggadah* tells the father to "blunt his son's teeth" by telling the son sharply, "Had you been there, you would not have been redeemed." This is meant to open the eyes of the wicked son. It is important to remember that if a father *always* acts this way toward his son, this behavior will have no positive effect — it will only reinforce the opinion that the wicked son has (albeit perhaps incorrectly) of his father's "intolerant ways." The only way a shock like this can work is if it is an obvious departure from the norm. This means that if a father is usually loving and tolerant, when he reacts this way, he sends a clear message to his son that a line has been crossed. This will hopefully get the young man to think, "Why did my father, who is usually so level-headed, react so sharply? It must have been something I said..." This is the goal of the *Haggadah*'s response. Not to show anger and not to carry out discipline, but rather, to take a sharp tone, in order to set the wicked son on a path to reconsideration of his incorrect attitude.

תָּם וְשֶׁאֵינוֹ יוֹדֵעַ לִשְׁאוֹל — *The Simple Son, and the Son Who Does Not Know How to Ask*

❐ **The *tam* is a child who is on a simple level, and understands his obligation to serve Hashem through the prism of what he "owes"**

Hashem. This *madreigah,* while not at all evil, is a lower level, and a generation where Klal Yisrael at large feel this way would not merit to enter Eretz Yisrael (although if they were already dwelling there, it would not cause them to be exiled).

- ❒ The *she'eino yodei'a lish'ol* is not an infant or toddler, who cannot ask. Rather, he or she is a child who seeks to grow from the childish relationship they share with Hashem now — that of seeking reward and avoiding punishment — to actual love and dedication to Hashem. The term *she'eino yodei'a lish'ol* is used to describe them because they are clueless as to how to develop such a relationship with Hashem.
- ❒ When a child expresses this type of interest, the father must be on a high *madreigah* in order to be able to properly introduce to his child the concept of a life of dedication to Hashem. When Klal Yisrael is comprised of such people — fathers who are holy, and children who strive to be — Klal Yisrael can merit to enter Eretz Yisrael.
- ❒ The formula for attaining holiness, through which a father can properly be *mechaneich* his *she'eino yodei'a lish'ol,* is gleaned from the *pesukim* that precede the Torah's prescribed reply to the *she'eino yodei'a lish'ol.* In summary, he must:
  - Separate from foreign culture and realign with the values of the Torah;
  - Cease any sinful behavior;
  - Understand *teshuvah* — that it is both possible and necessary;
  - Understand the potential of a Jew;
  - Begin to perform *mitzvos* optimally;
  - Develop to a point where his previous improper actions are not recognizable when looking at him.

Who is the *she'eino yodei'a lish'ol?* In many of the illustrated *Haggados* of our youth, the child was portrayed as an infant sucking his thumb. This reinforces the impression that this child is one who is too young to be asking any questions at all. Indeed, many understand that the point that the *Haggadah* is making is that the *chinuch* on the *Seder* night is for all children who are old enough to understand the story if we tell it to them, even if they are not old enough to ask on their own. In my own humble opinion, however, the *she'eino yodei'a lish'ol* is not that child at all. Rather, the *she'eino yodei'a lish'ol* is a child who is striving to set out on the path of holiness, to dedicate himself to the service of Hashem, and who is seeking direction.

I arrive at this understanding based upon the answer which the *Haggadah* instructs us to tell the *she'eino yodei'a lish'ol,* which is *Shemos* 13:8: *And you shall tell your son on that day, saying, "On account of this*

Hashem did for me, when I left Mitzrayim." The placement of this *pasuk* in the Torah is striking. It does not appear in a vacuum; rather, it is the eighth *pasuk* in a series of *pesukim* that outline the blueprint Klal Yisrael are to follow in order to attain holiness (see below). This indicates that it is only a father who has followed this blueprint, and who is himself on a high level of holiness, that can properly guide this child, the *she'eino yodei'a lish'ol.*

The *she'eino yodei'a lish'ol* is a good boy or girl — a child that has grown up with good *chinuch.* Every normal child, even a good child, needs to be raised to either serve Hashem out of fear, or the positive equivalent, of being encouraged by the prospect of reward. Both methods are really rooted in the fact that the child serves Hashem for a purpose other than just serving Hashem — either reward, or avoidance of consequences. This is necessary because a child is born with a *yetzer hara,* and no *yetzer tov.* However, when a child is maturing, and needs to take the next step — the step of beginning to serve Hashem for Hashem's sake — the child is *eino yodei'a lish'ol;* he or she has *no idea* how to attain the concept of serving Hashem for His sake, for it is beyond them. They need a practicing adult to guide them by opening the discussion for them. It is that father, the father with such precious, good children, who needs to introduce them to the concept of serving Hashem in a way they never before have, who must be on a holy level to make that introduction to them. And if he attains this level, he will be successful in imparting the message to those children who are seeking to understand what it means to live a life of serving Hashem for His sake, and that the entire purpose of life is to serve Hashem.

Allow me to explain what I mean when I say that the *pesukim* in *Shemos* 13:1-8 contain a blueprint for Klal Yisrael to achieve holiness. In *Shemos* 13:2, Hashem commanded Moshe to sanctify the *bechorim, the firstborn sons.* It is interesting, then, that Moshe did not simply go to Klal Yisrael and issue a command along the lines of *"vehiyisem li kedoshim, and you shall be holy to Me."* Rather, Moshe's reaction to the command of Hashem was to tell Klal Yisrael 13:3-10. Why was this? Additionally, none of these *pesukim* so much as *mention* the concept of sanctification!

My understanding, because of these questions, is that Moshe responded to Hashem's command that he sanctify Klal Yisrael by affording them a blueprint — a formula, if you will — by which they could sanctify themselves to Hashem. With this idea in mind, let us proceed to examine the entire passage. The words of the *pesukim* here, as well as their specific order, will guide us through different concepts and *hashkafos* to understand the path that Moshe Rabbeinu laid down for Klal Yisrael to study and emulate. Certainly, this lesson was especially pertinent then, but of course it is timeless, and thus applicable now as well. [Perhaps on account of the eternal nature of the lessons found in these *pesukim,* this passage is one of those that we put in our *tefillin.*]

The first step to those aspiring to reach a level of holiness is, as Moshe states in 13:3, *Remember the day you left Mitzrayim.* It is interesting that Moshe focuses on remembering the day we left Mitzrayim, which was Pesach, and not the day on which we became free from the harsh labor of Mitzrayim, which was six months earlier, on Rosh Hashanah. The reason for this is because in the realm of growing in our mission to serve Hashem in holiness, the thing about remembering *Yetzias Mitzrayim* that matters most for the future is our ability to remember what we left behind. In other words, surely, physical liberty is necessary for us to serve Hashem properly, but that was only a one-time occurrence; and even if we would never remember the fact that we were once slaves in Mitzrayim, we would still now retain the physical freedom we were given. What is far, far more important to remember constantly is that *we left* Mitzrayim. Why?

In every society, no matter how much we strive to block it out, the values of the surrounding culture invade the sensitivities of Klal Yisrael. The examples of this are literally too numerous to count. Say a person lives in a place where the sport of boxing is popular. Even if he himself shuns the sport and really has nothing to do with it, the general culture around him will have a certain tolerance for physically hitting another person. And although the sport of boxing does not affect a person on a daily basis, the way society views the hitting of another person does. Slowly, a person's regard for this kind of behavior shifts from the Torah's attitude of *rasha, lama sakeh rei'echa* (*Shemos* 2:13), which identifies one who strikes his fellow as wicked, to his society's take on it, which is, "hitting another person is bad, but not so bad." This sort of shift in our sensitivities can, and does, happen in a myriad of different ways. The very fact that we have in our own society the concept of "the American dream," and how closely we associate this with a real goal is proof positive that we, too, suffer this malady of adopting, by osmosis, the attitude of the culture in which we reside. It becomes impossible to be properly tuned to the Torah when we do not accurately share in how the Torah views the world, and our own lives and goals. Here, Moshe Rabbeinu tells us that step number one in attaining sanctity is to remember that we were removed from Mitzrayim. The values we picked up from them through hundreds of years of cultural osmosis are *not* our values, but were rather imposed upon us. We are now free from that influence, and must always remind ourselves that Hashem has given us the freedom to understand what the Torah view is regarding everything in our lives, and not to be swayed by any other societal "norms." It is perhaps this very idea that is meant when we use the expression *Yetzias Mitzrayim* to describe the Exodus. Saying *Yetzias Mitzrayim,* the *Exit "of" Mitzrayim,* perhaps alludes to the fact that upon our departure, the culture of the Egyptians did indeed leave us as well.

The *posuk* continues by warning against eating *chametz.* Obviously, the

simple interpretation of the *posuk* is that on Pesach, the day on which we are remembering the day we left Mitzrayim, we are not permitted to eat *chametz*. If we look a little deeper, the *posuk* is revealing the second step in becoming holy; and that is not to sin, which, of course, includes the directive not to give in to one's *yetzer hara*. [See *Berachos* 17a, where the Gemara refers to the *yetzer hara* as leaven.] Not eating *chametz* is thus understood to mean refraining from negative behavior. [The concept of putting *sur meira, turn away from evil,* before *asei tov, do good,* is applied here.] Once a person has recalibrated his definition of right and wrong to align with what the Torah requires of him (step 1 above), he knows what he must stop doing, and the next step is to see to it that he does so.

13:4 continues by stating that *Today you are leaving, in the month of the spring*. This is the third step in becoming holy. Just as the spring is the actualization of the physical rejuvenation of the world, so must a person realize that this is also possible with his spirituality. Hashem created the world with the principle of *teshuvah,* and expects us to utilize it. The concept of spiritual renewal is *vital* for attaining holiness, for it allows us to be separated from our past misdeeds. The truth is that the idea of spiritual rejuvenation is part and parcel of the concept behind the *korban pesach*. The *korban pesach* commemorates that Hashem took us out of Mitzrayim and killed the Egyptians, even though we had sunk to the forty-ninth level of spiritual impurity, because Hashem saw in us the spark of our *Avos* — *kedushas Yisrael* — which gave us the potential to become holy servants of Hashem. After we have shed the values of the nations in favor of the Torah's values, and after we have stopped acting incorrectly, it is time to repent and abandon our foolish ways. Remembering *Chodesh HaAviv* gives us the strength to realize that this is possible, and that it is what Hashem wants from us in order that we may become sanctified.

This leads right into the fourth step to becoming holy. The *parashah* continues with 13:5, instructing Klal Yisrael that when they enter Eretz Yisrael, they must perform the service of the *korban pesach*. [See *Rashi d"h es ha'avodah hazos*. That we must bring the *korban pesach* is mentioned in the *parashah* even before we have reached the point at which we are commanded to eat *matzah,* in 13:6, which is the parallel to the concept of *asei tov, do good*.] As mentioned above, the very concept of the *korban pesach* was that Hashem saw our potential and saved us, even though we were guilty and stained with sin at the time. The Torah bids us to internalize this lesson, and to rededicate ourselves to the idea of becoming better, and to teaching this lesson to our children. This is so vitally important because there are those among Klal Yisrael who are like the wicked son. They do not identify with us in this service of Hashem — and indeed, in our goal to become holy in His service. The Torah wants us to internalize the lesson of the *korban pesach*, which was that Hashem takes

us, even when we are wicked, and cherishes us, because He knows who we are and the greatness we can truly attain. With this attitude, we can show love and acceptance to the wicked among us, and focus upon how to reach them with Hashem's word. [See *rasha,* above. In fact, when the verse (*Shemos* 12:27) tells us that Klal Yisrael bowed, one of the reasons they did so was in gratitude at having been informed that they were going to have children — and the children that the Torah speaks of there ask the question of the wicked son! And yet, the prospective parents were grateful and happy.] We can, and we must, work with such children to help them grow in their love of Hashem.

The fifth step on the spiritual climb to holiness is found in 13:6; to eat *matzah,* which is symbolic of the instruction to do good. This is perhaps the most obvious of all the steps — clearly, to grow in spiritual sanctity, one must perform the *mitzvos* properly. This is the step of *asei tov, do good.* Our moral compass has been properly aligned, and we have stopped sinful and otherwise bad actions and behaviors; we have realized that spiritual renewal is within our grasp, and rededicated ourselves to the goal of properly serving Hashem and teaching our children to do the same. Now, we are ready to actually go do it!

This leads us to the sixth and final step in Moshe Rabbeinu's plan. Interestingly, immediately after the command to eat *matzah,* the Torah reiterates in 13:7 that we are to eat *matzah,* as well as (at first glance) the prohibition against *chametz.* Now, we have already been told not to eat *chametz,* in 13:3! Why is this directive seemingly repeated here? The answer is that the Torah does not say, as it did above in 13:3, that we may not eat *chametz.* Rather, it states here that you shall eat *matzah...* no *chametz* may be seen in your possession, nor may leaven be seen in your possession, within any of your borders. This means that we must reach a level of optimal performance of *mitzvos* and of service to Hashem, so that we totally erase all remembrance of our past misdeeds. Whereas above, in 13:3, the directive was not to *eat chametz* — which we have interpreted as not to act sinfully — here, in 13:7, we are commanded that when we eat *matzah* (do good), the *chametz* — or evil deeds — must not be *seen* with us at all. This fits well with the understanding we have set forth, that one must grow to such a high level in his doing of good that nobody — he, or anyone else — can see any remnant of his past evil deeds when they look at him. This is indeed a lofty level, and is indicative of how radical a shift in *hashkafos,* and in actions, an individual might have to undertake in striving for true holiness.

In the *Haggadah,* the answer we give to the *she'eino yodeya lish'ol*, the son who does not know how to ask, is the next *posuk,* 13:8. Why does the answer to a child, and specifically this child, follow Moshe Rabbeinu's blueprint for achieving holiness? The answer is that if a person has indeed

reached the place where his good deeds have rendered the sins of his past to be completely forgotten and erased, he is finally ready to honestly say the words, "*Because of this, Hashem did for me, when I went out of Mitzrayim.*" As *Rashi* (*d"h ba'avur zeh*) explains, the word *this* refers to the performance of Hashem's commandments; for example, *pesach, matzah, and maror*, which are before a person on the *Seder* night. If we have been able to attain a level where our own performance of *mitzvos* is optimal, we can show this to our inquisitive children and explain with the utmost sincerity that the entire purpose of our existence is the pursuit of proper service of Hashem, with proper intent, because we love Him. This is the purpose of life, and nothing else really matters. Finally, in 13:9, we are bade to include this passage (*Shemos* 13:1-10) in our *tefillin.*

It is interesting that above, in 13:2, where the holiness of the *bechorim* is mentioned, there is no mention of redeeming that holiness. Additionally, there is no reference here in 13:9 that the *tefillin* are to be worn on the weaker hand (as opposed to 13:16 below, where just such an inference is expounded by the spelling of the word *yadcha*). These are both due to the fact that a true *eino yodei'a lish'ol* is so holy that his sanctification need not be removed, and he need not wear his *tefillin* — which is a reminder of his commitment to Hashem — on his weaker hand, but rather can do so on his stronger hand, symbolizing that his commitment is strong. Now, it is obvious that nobody, not even the best among us, can wear their *teffilin* on their more dominant hand, nor is anyone exempt from redeeming their *bechor.* This is because, to our chagrin, none of us are truly on the level of the *she'eino yodei'a lish'ol.* None among us are really, truly, completely on a level where our *entire existence* is lived only for the sake of Hashem. Rather, the Torah is giving us the picture of a true *eino yodei'a lish'ol,* and requiring us to "aim for the stars" in being *mechaneich* our children.

Finally, in 13:10, Moshe bids Klal Yisrael to guard "this law" each year. This can be understood, in the context of the above discussion, as a hint that the mission of rededication and resanctification is constant — we never truly reach the level of complete holiness. Hashem knows we are but human, and puts us in the world to come ever closer to perfecting ourselves. Our goal is to constantly strive toward it, not necessarily to reach it. [This concludes the discussion of the passage of *kadesh li,* and the *she'eino yodei'a lish'ol.*]

After the Torah discusses the *she'eino yodei'a lish'ol,* it begins a new *parashah,* that of *vehayah ki yeviacha,* which contains the question of the *tam, the simple son,* and his father's answer to him. This *parashah* is also included in our *tefillin.* 13:11 speaks of Klal Yisrael arriving in Eretz Yisrael, 13:12 speaks of the holiness of the *bechorah,* and 13:13 speaks of the need to redeem that holiness. Finally, in 13:14, the Torah recounts the question of the *tam.* His attitude is not one of exclusion or malice;

יָכוֹל מֵרֹאשׁ חֹדֶשׁ, תַּלְמוּד לוֹמַר בַּיּוֹם הַהוּא[1]. אִי בַּיּוֹם הַהוּא, יָכוֹל מִבְּעוֹד יוֹם, תַּלְמוּד לוֹמַר בַּעֲבוּר זֶה[1]. בַּעֲבוּר זֶה לֹא אָמַרְתִּי אֶלָּא בְּשָׁעָה שֶׁיֵּשׁ מַצָּה וּמָרוֹר מֻנָּחִים לְפָנֶיךָ.

---

he simply wants to know: Why we are so invested in serving Hashem? Why is it so important? Our reply to the *tam* is that Hashem took us out of slavery in Mitzrayim, and when Pharaoh hardened his heart, Hashem killed all of the *bechorim* of the Egyptians and their animals. Accordingly, we redeem the firstborns of our children and our animals. Essentially, we have given this child a simple explanation of the reason we serve Hashem. We have tried to help him understand that we "owe" Hashem for what He did for us, and that is our reason for living our lives in accordance with His Torah. This is certainly a low level of service to Hashem — that we are, as it were, "paying our debt to Hashem" — but it is one that a child on this level will comprehend. [It is true that we find that the *sifrei Mussar* discuss the attribute of *hakaras hatov*, and it is a very exalted *middah* indeed. But *hakaras hatov* is lofty when the focus of what Hashem does, and has done, for a person brings him to love Hashem. Through the gifts bestowed upon him by Hashem, a person can realize how much Hashem loves him and cares for him, and can try his best to serve Hashem with that same level of love and fervor. But if the driving force behind a person's service of Hashem is simply that he feels that he owes Hashem a debt, and there are no feelings of love attached to this recognition, it is a low level indeed.]

We may ask: Why does this passage open with a setting of the *tam* inquiring of his father specifically after Klal Yisrael has already settled in Eretz Yisrael? Seemingly, neither the question of the child nor the answer the father is instructed to give him are germane to being in Eretz Yisrael! I believe that the reason the Torah gives this introduction to the *tam's* question is to hint to us that his attitude, while not evil, is lacking, to the point that a nation of people with such an attitude would not merit to inherit Eretz Yisrael. Still, if Klal Yisrael will come to develop this outlook after they have already come to Eretz Yisrael, they will not lose Eretz Yisrael on account of this. This is in contrast to the *she'eino yodei'a lish'ol* discussed above; the passage that discusses his *chinuch* begins outside Eretz Yisrael, and continues with the entry into the Land. This is because people who are on the level of the *she'eino yodei'a lish'ol* — or are at least striving toward the level of the *she'eino yodei'a lish'ol* by utilizing the steps outlined in the passage of *kadesh li* (*Shemos* 13:1-8), as explained above — are holy, and

You might think that this mitzvah can be performed as early as Rosh Chodesh (Nissan). Therefore, the Torah writes, "On that day."[1] If it needs to be performed on that day, you might think that it can be performed during the day. Therefore, the Torah writes, "on account of this"[1]; I only said on account of "this," at the time that there is *matzah* and *maror* before you.

(1) *Shemos* 13:8.

---

can merit Eretz Yisrael. Additionally, the passage ends with the requirement to include this passage in our *tefillin*. Here, because the *tam* is not on a high level, he is required to keep his *tefillin* on his weaker hand, as indicated by the spelling of the word *yadchah*. Additionally, this passage, when mentioning the sanctification of the firstborns, mentions that the *kedushah* must be redeemed. The allusion of both of these points — the wearing of the *tefillin* on the weaker hand, as well as the redemption of the *kedushah* of the *bechorim* — is indicative of the inferiority of the attitude of the *tam* as compared with that of the *eino yodei'a lish'ol*.

יָכוֹל מֵרֹאשׁ חֹדֶשׁ — *You Might Think That This Mitzvah Can be Performed as Early as Rosh Chodesh (Nissan)*

- **The *mitzvah* of *chinuch* always applies. The *mitzvah* of *sippur Yetzias Mitzrayim,* however, must be performed at a specific time, under specific circumstances.**
- **This is because the ideas that we are charged with passing on to the next generation are going to take hold only if we emphasize them properly. When we set aside an entire night, complete with the symbolism of the *Seder,* to teach our children what it means to be a free Jew, we are able to impart this vital message to them.**

The *Haggadah* tells us that the *mitzvah* of *vehigadta levincha* applies only to the night of the *Seder.* Now, the core of this *avodah* is to raise our children properly. Is it possible that *chinuch* is only a *mitzvah* on one night a year? Of course not! *Chinuch* is always applicable, at every time and circumstance. So, why is there a special time for *vehigadta levincha?*

We are dealing here with very specific subject matter, and to properly discuss these issues with our children, the Torah has identified a time and a setting. We aim to pass on to the next generation what the philosophy of leaving Mitzrayim really is. We want to explain to them in as real a manner as we can what freedom really, truly means to a Torah Jew. In order to accomplish this, the Torah mandates a certain environment.

מִתְּחִלָּה עוֹבְדֵי עֲבוֹדָה זָרָה הָיוּ אֲבוֹתֵינוּ, וְעַכְשָׁו קֵרְבָנוּ הַמָּקוֹם לַעֲבוֹדָתוֹ. שֶׁנֶּאֱמַר, וַיֹּאמֶר יְהוֹשֻׁעַ אֶל כָּל הָעָם, כֹּה אָמַר יהוה אֱלֹהֵי יִשְׂרָאֵל, בְּעֵבֶר הַנָּהָר יָשְׁבוּ אֲבוֹתֵיכֶם מֵעוֹלָם, תֶּרַח אֲבִי אַבְרָהָם וַאֲבִי נָחוֹר, וַיַּעַבְדוּ אֱלֹהִים אֲחֵרִים. וָאֶקַּח אֶת אֲבִיכֶם אֶת אַבְרָהָם

The Torah set aside one night a year — the *Seder* night — as the time when we focus on the transmission of this tradition to the next generation. We give the *mitzvah* the time it needs — the entire night — to enable it to be explained seriously and explored thoroughly, in order that it may affect the children properly. The ceremonial setting that the Torah mandates us to arrange includes the *matzah* and the *maror,* which, with their many lessons, hold the symbolism of *Yetzias Mitzrayim.* With the right amount of time and the correct environment, we are ready to impart this critical message to our children.

Vehigadta levincha is not just a directive for a father to read a declaration to his children. Nor is it merely a directive to make sure they understand the *Haggadah.* Rather, it is, optimally, a directive to discuss *Yetzias Mitzrayim* and to apply it to one's own life and the lives of one's children. This will allow them to gauge their dreams, hopes, and goals, and to realign them with what the Torah's goals for Klal Yisrael really are. This is why it is given a special time, despite the fact that *chinuch* is a constant obligation.

מִתְּחִלָּה עוֹבְדֵי עֲבוֹדָה זָרָה — *Originally, Our Forefathers Were Idol Worshipers*

- **מִתְּחִלָּה עוֹבְדֵי עֲבוֹדָה זָרָה — The *Hagaddah* opens this passage with a declaration recognizing that the origins of Klal Yisrael were from idolaters, and that they subsequently sprouted into Hashem's people. This, according to Rav, is the fulfillment of the Mishnah's dictum that on the *Seder* night, we "Begin with our detriment and conclude with our praise." He maintains that the detriment the Mishnah alludes to is the fact that we are descended from idol worshipers. The *Haggadah* proceeds to cite *pesukim* that Yehoshua uttered to Klal Yisrael which encapsulate this idea. Each phrase of these *pesukim* contains important lessons.**
- **וְעַכְשָׁו קֵרְבָנוּ הַמָּקוֹם לַעֲבֹדָתוֹ — This alludes to the nation Klal Yisrael became through their travails in Mitzrayim and their sojourn in the Wilderness. [See *Rambam, Hil. Chametz U'Matzah* 7:4, where it is**

Originally, our forefathers were idol worshipers, and now, HASHEM has brought us close to His service, as it is stated: "And Yehoshua said to the nation, So says HASHEM, the God of Yisrael: On the opposite side of the river your forefathers dwelled; Terach, the father of Avraham and the father of Nachor, and they served foreign gods. And I took your father, Avraham,

---

clear that he understands that these words are where we "conclude with our praise."]

❒ תֶּרַח אֲבִי אַבְרָהָם וַאֲבִי נָחוֹר, וַיַּעַבְדוּ אֱלֹהִים אֲחֵרִים — Even though Terach, Nachor, and their families served idols, they still somehow merited to be the grandfathers of Klal Yisrael. What merit did they posses which granted them this association? It was the attribute of kindness, which Terach's family practiced. However, it was an unrefined attribute. They would apply it too loosely, for example, by removing the gods they believed in to make another person comfortable. Furthermore, when their own personal gain was at stake, they would not practice it. So, their kindness was unprincipled, to be sure. But it was a merit that gained them closeness to Klal Yisrael.

❒ וָאֶקַּח אֶת אֲבִיכֶם אֶת אַבְרָהָם — What made Avraham special? His recognition of Hashem, and his commitment to follow him. This elevated him above the rest of Terach's offspring and is why Klal Yisrael emanates from him. Because of his belief, Avraham refined his attribute of kindness with principles. His principles were based on right and wrong, which are rooted in belief in Hashem and adherence to His word. [The *Imahos*, who were the righteous women who emerged from Terach's household, followed the beliefs espoused by Avraham, and thus also refined their attributes of kindness.]

Sippur Yetzias Mitzrayim is supposed to begin with our detriment, and end with our praise. Rav is of the opinion that the detriment alluded to is the statement, *Mitchilah ovdei avodah zarah hayu avoseinu,* wherein we recall that Klal Yisrael emerged from a society, and indeed, an ancestry, of idolaters. The service of idols is considered to be the low point of our ancestry not merely because it expresses belief in falsehood and defies belief in Hashem, meaning, that the worshiper does not know *who* Hashem is. It is rather also because the very idea of idol worship reveals that the worshiper does not have a real concept of *what* Hashem's power is, and what it can mean to relate to Him.

The very idea of idolatry is patently absurd. How did such a ridiculous concept come to exist? The *posuk* (*Bereishis* 4:26) tells us that in the

מֵעֵבֶר הַנָּהָר, וָאוֹלֵךְ אוֹתוֹ בְּכָל אֶרֶץ כְּנָעַן, וָאַרְבֶּה אֶת זַרְעוֹ, וָאֶתֶּן לוֹ אֶת יִצְחָק. וָאֶתֵּן לְיִצְחָק אֶת יַעֲקֹב וְאֶת

---

days of Enosh, people began to call out in the Name of Hashem. *Rashi* writes (*d"h az huchal*) that this refers to the fact that at that time, people began calling certain people by the name of "god" — thereby creating the first worship of foreign deities. Perhaps we may suggest that what drove Enosh to serve other people was the fact that he was the first person of what we would consider regular height. [See *Nahar Sholom, Bereishis,* comments to 4:25, where we discuss this as one of several possibilities.] This perhaps caused him to focus unduly on his inferiority as compared to the others of his time, always looking up to them, because they were taller than he was. As he sought God, Who he understood to definitely have been greater than himself, Enosh also encountered people who were greater than he was. He therefore began to serve all who he felt were superior, treating them as godly; this included all the people of the previous generation, and the children of Kayin. [It should be noted that it is possible that this attitude was not merely born of an incorrectly conceived inferiority complex, as above, but of the natural inclination that Hashem built into the psyche of a person, so that he be equipped to seek out his Creator. Either way — whether he simply developed this fascination with superiority on his own, or if he misused the drive to serve what is greater than the self that Hashem had given him — the result was that Enosh deified people, which is *avodah zarah*.]

This was the first instance of idolatry in the world, but certainly not the last. Throughout history, people have struggled with exemplifying different concepts, and turned to idolatry to actualize and represent them. Take, for example, Terach. Terach was a merchant of idols. He crafted them with his own hands, and thus most certainly knew that they were not gods. Rather, his business model was to create idols for his customers in a way that brought out, alluded to, or in some other manner represented a certain idea or principle. The idol was thus meant to represent an ideal in which his customer, the worshiper, believed.

Later on, the Greeks had another variation of idolatry. They struggled with the many emotions and inclinations of the human psyche. Rather than categorize certain things as good or evil, thereby declaring a morally "right" and "wrong" course of thought and action, they chose an easier route. They created many gods, each one representative of a human characteristic. In this way, no thought or action could be called intrinsically evil. Rather, it was the service and characterization of a particular god — be it jealousy, gluttony, lust, greed, thievery, murder, anger, etc.

from the other side of the river, and I brought him through the entirety of the land of Canaan, and I increased his offspring, and I gave him Yitzchak. And I gave to Yitzchak, Yaakov and

---

A person could thus possess any of these character flaws and still be emulating a god.

Praying to an idol or image, no matter what it represents, is something that Hashem does not want us to do. When prayer needs an image to be present, it means that the relationship between the worshiper and the worshiped exists only at the time of worship, in the presence of the image. Hashem desires that we develop our relationship with Him to the point that we live with Him, in His service. Furthermore, an image or representation of Hashem limits Him in our minds to what we can visually experience. This is incorrect, as Hashem is limitless and infinite in every way.

Klal Yisrael emanate from people whose understanding of deities was so limited that they believed that idols could have power, that they could only relate to their deities in limited fashion, and that they could visualize in some manner the power of Hashem. But Hashem, in His mercy, developed Klal Yisrael from our *Avos,* and made us a nation of believers in Him, who possess a finely tuned understanding of the potential of our relationship with Him.

As mentioned, Terach was an idolater, as was his son, Nachor; they are both mentioned here. By the same token, his grandson, Besuel, and his great-grandson, Lavan, were idolaters as well. And yet, each of these men merited to be a grandfather of Klal Yisrael. [Nachor was Sarah's father (although the Torah does not trace her lineage back to him, alluding to her in the context of Nachor's daughter by the name Yiskah), Besuel was Rivkah's father, and Lavan was Rochel and Leah's father.] What merit did they possibly have that gave them the *zechus* to be associated with Avraham Avinu and his progeny? Avraham found Hashem, and committed to serve Him, and to raise his children with this idea. But what was the merit of his idolatrous family?

We know that when it came time to search for a wife for Yitzchak, Avraham sent Eliezer specifically to Nachor's family. Similarly, when instructing Yaakov to find a wife, Rivkah sent him to Lavan. There was something that the *Avos* and *Imahos* saw in the descendants of Terach which was special. What was it?

When Eliezer arrived at the house of Besuel, Lavan made it his priority to remove the idols from the house. Nobody asked him to do so; it seems as though he was doing it so that Eliezer would be comfortable staying there. We can thus observe a general attitude of accommodation and

עֵשָׂו, וָאֶתֵּן לְעֵשָׂו אֶת הַר שֵׂעִיר לָרֶשֶׁת אוֹתוֹ, וְיַעֲקֹב וּבָנָיו יָרְדוּ מִצְרָיִם[1].

---

hospitality among the children of Terach. [See *Nahar Sholom, Bereishis* 24:16, where we explain that Rivkah developed the attribute of kindness that her family possessed and attached principles to it, much in the same way Avraham had done with the natural kindness he inherited from his father.] It was the affinity to be kind which was the default attribute exhibited by Terach's family (indiscriminately, even when they should have taken a firmer stance; and of course, only when they did not stand to lose money).

Kindness is the cornerstone of matters pertaining to *bein adam lachaveiro,* and exemplary *bein adam lachaveiro* is a trait which goes a long way before Hashem. In the generation of Achav, despite the fact that idolatry was rampant, Klal Yisrael enjoyed security from their enemies because no one spoke *lashon hara*. The generation of Noach, on the other hand, was destroyed because they stole from one another. The family of Terach possessed a potential to be kind and good. This "raw" attribute served as a merit for Terach's descendants, and is perhaps why Klal Yisrael emanates from them. The unpolished attribute of kindness was sought out by the *Avos* because it is preferable to a total lack of kindness, and is one step closer to perfect and principled kindness. [See below, where we will suggest that the difference between Lavan's lack of principles and Rivkah's very clear principles was mirrored in Yaakov and Eisav.]

- ❐ **וָאֶתֵּן לְעֵשָׂו אֶת הַר שֵׂעִיר לָרֶשֶׁת אוֹתוֹ — There were two plots of land that the Chivi nation inhabited: Har Se'ir outside the land of Canaan, and the area of Shechem, inside the land of Canaan. Eisav was given the right to inherit both of these plots. However, he chose to inhabit only Har Se'ir, and to abandon the area of the city of Shechem. He did so because he did not want to be included in the decree upon Avraham's descendants to suffer in a foreign land for 400 years.**
- ❐ **וְיַעֲקֹב וּבָנָיו יָרְדוּ מִצְרָיִם — Klal Yisrael, who did merit the Land of Eretz Yisrael, were subject to the decree of the *Bris Bein HaBesarim*, and so they needed to endure the exile of Mitzrayim.**

The *posuk* mentions that Yitzchak Avinu had both Yaakov and Eisav, and that Eisav inherited Har Se'ir, and Yaakov and his children went down to Mitzrayim. There was a direct connection between the fact that Eisav inherited Har Se'ir and the fact that he and his descendants were free from the decree that Avraham Avinu's descendants would need to go down to Mitzrayim.

Eisav. And I gave Eisav Har Se'ir to inherit it, and Yaakov and his children went down to Mitzrayim."[1]

(1) *Yehoshua* 24:2-4.

There are a total of only four nations to whom Hashem promised inheritance in the Torah. These four nations are Edom, Ammon, Moav, and of course, Klal Yisrael. What is the commonality between these four nations?

Avraham Avinu was promised the Land of Eretz Yisrael at the *Bris Bein HaBesarim,* and this was passed to Yitzchak Avinu, to the exclusion of his other children — Yishmael and the children of Keturah. [Nevertheless, the *Zohar* (*Va'eira* 32a) writes that Yishmael is given the territory of Eretz Yisrael when Klal Yisrael are not inhabiting it.] Edom and Yisrael are of course the children of Yitzchak Avinu, and therefore the reason why each was promised inheritance is clearly understood. Why did Hashem promise Ammon and Moav that they would receive land? The answer is that they received an inheritance because they are Lot's children. Lot merited his share when Sarai was captured by Pharaoh, and Avram told Pharaoh that he was Sarai's brother. It is safe to say that Lot would not have contradicted this claim, as Avram was his Rebbi. But Lot could have made a face, or even flinched, upon hearing it emanate from Avram's mouth. As Sarai's biological brother, Lot could have felt that the gifts that were given to Avram by Pharaoh were truly his own, and he could have easily "blown Avram's cover" with just a small reaction. And yet he stood unwaveringly by Avram's side and did not question him at all. For this, Lot merited that his descendants would enjoy a portion of land, and thus Ammon and Moav were assured a territory, as written in the Torah. So, the four nations who were promised territory all received their portions on account of Avraham Avinu — two because they are his descendants, and the other two because their progenitor aided him.

But which lands were promised to which nations? At the *Bris Bein HaBesarim,* Hashem promised the lands of ten nations to Avram. *Rashi* there (*Bereishis* 15:19, *d"h es haKeini*) points out that although ten nations are listed, only the territories of seven of those were promised to Avram; the other three — the lands of the Keini, Kenizi, and Kadmoni — were promised to the nations of Edom (Eisav) and Ammon and Moav (Lot's children). Although the *posuk* there (*Bereishis* 15:19) lists the lands of the Keini, Kenizi, and Kadmoni as being given to Avram, which seems to indicate that he would receive these lands with the rest of Eretz Yisrael, *Rashi* there explains that the intent of that *posuk* was that those nations — Edom, Ammon, and Moav — would cede their territories to Klal Yisrael only *le'asid lavo, in the Future to Come.*

The territory that would be given to the Keini (Edom) was that of the Chivi, also known as the Chori. [For a discussion of how we know this, see further below, *Hallel HaGadol*.] The Chivi's territory was partially in Eretz Yisrael, and included the area approximate to Shechem (as we know, Shechem and Chamor were of Chivi descent), and separately, in Har Se'ir, where the Torah tells us that the Chori lived. Because Eisav was entitled to the entire territory of the Chivi, both of these sections of land ought to have become his inheritance. However, Eisav made the decision not to exercise his claim to the portion of land that was in Eretz Yisrael proper. Rather, as stated here, he limited his claim to only the segment of the Chivi's land that was outside Eretz Yisrael, i.e., Har Se'ir. Why?

The reason why Klal Yisrael went down to Mitzrayim was in fulfillment of the decree Hashem had issued to Avram at the *Bris Bein HaBesarim*; this will be discussed in detail immediately below in the *Haggadah*. Eisav voluntarily forfeited to Yaakov the claim on this part of the Chivi's land in order to exempt himself from the four-hundred-year exile that had been decreed upon Avraham's descendants (see *Bereishis* 36:7, with *Rashi d"h mipnei*). The parcel containing Har Se'ir, though, remained with Eisav and his descendants, and is their inheritance.

Now, what was the difference between the two parts of the Chivi's land? Why was it that forfeiting the one in Eretz Yisrael proper resulted in Eisav not having to go through four hundred years of exile? *Metzudas David* to *Yehoshua* 24:4 points out that this inference can be made from the decree at the *Bris Bein HaBesarim*. For the *posuk* states, *"And the fourth generation shall return here."* This means that it was only the descendants of Avraham whose fourth generation would return to the land of Eretz Yisrael who were going to suffer the exile. But this proves merely that Eisav's calculation was correct. *Why* was it so? What was the connection between living in Eretz Yisrael and suffering in exile?

In *Parashas Shoftim*, the Torah relates that it was on account of the various forms of magic, necromancy, and divination that Hashem banished the Canaanite nations from Eretz Yisrael (see further, *Devarim* 18:11-12). The question arises: Non-Jews are not commanded in regard to these prohibitions! Why, then, should such actions result in their exile? The answer is that we can see from these *pesukim* that the very fact that one is close to Hashem — living in His Land, regarding which the *posuk* (*Devarim* 11:12; see *Rashi d"h tamid einei Hashem Elokecha bah*) tells us that Hashem is always tending to its needs — obligates trust in Hashem to the exclusion of anything else, even if technically one is not forbidden to practice magic or the like.

Thus, Eisav knew that living in Eretz Yisrael would obligate him to be on a higher level, and would require that he be purified through exile. As

he wanted no part of that, he chose to inhabit only the portion of his land that was outside Eretz Yisrael.

What was one of the main differences between Yaakov and Eisav which drove Eisav to make such a decision; a decision which Yaakov would never have considered? Perhaps we can explain that Eisav, following the example set by his evil uncle, Lavan, never developed his attribute of kindness with any sort of moral structure or guiding principles. Yaakov, however, followed the path of his mother, Rivkah, who developed her attribute of kindness, and refined it into a tool with which to serve Hashem. [See *Nahar Sholom, Bereishis* 28:5. There we discuss why the *posuk* describes Lavan as *the brother of Rivkah, mother of Yaakov and Eisav. Rashi* (*d"h eim Yaakov v'Eisav*) comments that he does not know what the Torah is teaching us by saying that Rivkah was the mother of Yaakov and Eisav. In my humble opinion, we can suggest as follows: The *posuk* is describing Lavan. Who is Lavan — this model of unprincipled kindness? He is the brother of Rivkah, who is the mother of Yaakov and Eisav. Lavan, who possessed the unrefined seeds of the attribute of kindness, was willing to be a nice guy — even happy to be a nice guy — as long as the niceness would not stand in the way of personal gain. His selfish nature ensured that he would be a cutthroat when it came to turning a profit, and a generally kind man when it made no difference to him. Rivkah, on the other hand, had refined her attribute of kindness, honing it to the point that it was a tool for Hashem's service. She used it to train herself to behave selflessly — indeed, to love doing so. Perhaps this *posuk* is explaining that a major difference between Yaakov and Eisav was that Yaakov chose to emulate Rivkah, while Eisav, like his uncle, Lavan, ignored any potential for refining his gift of natural kindness, instead utilizing it only when it made him feel good, and making no attempt to hone it for *avodas Hashem*.]

So much is hinted to in these short *pesukim*: That Terach and his descendants were idolaters, and that even so, they merited association with Klal Yisrael, due to their innate, albeit unrefined, tendency toward *chessed*; that Avraham arose from among them to recognize and serve Hashem, and that Hashem blessed him with children; that Eisav chose to distance himself from the relationship he could have shared with Hashem, and as such chose to abandon his share in Eretz Yisrael; and finally, that Klal Yisrael, who would inherit the Land, went down to Mitzrayim. But perhaps the most important question we must ask, the most pressing for the night of the *Seder*, certainly, is this: What is the connection between receiving Eretz Yisrael and suffering in exile in Mitzrayim? We will discuss this immediately below, with the *Haggadah's* citation of the *pesukim* of the *Bris Bein HaBesarim*.

בָּרוּךְ שׁוֹמֵר הַבְטָחָתוֹ לְיִשְׂרָאֵל, בָּרוּךְ הוּא. שֶׁהַקָּדוֹשׁ בָּרוּךְ הוּא חִשַּׁב אֶת הַקֵּץ, לַעֲשׂוֹת כְּמָה שֶּׁאָמַר

בָּרוּךְ שׁוֹמֵר הַבְטָחָתוֹ לְיִשְׂרָאֵל — *Blessed is the One Who Keeps His Guarantee to Yisrael*

❒ The *Bris Bein HaBesarim* occurred, in my humble opinion, following Avram's request for children so that his service of Hashem would be able to endure, in the way that Adam's and Noach's had not been able to. Hashem told Avram that he would have children. Avram then asked what merit Klal Yisrael would have to live as the eternal people of Hashem, in His Land, according to His Torah. Hashem answered that it would be the merit of the *korbanos,* which is to say, in the merit of relating to, and with, Hashem.

❒ Hashem also told Avram that there would be a great and terrible exile that would last four hundred years — longer than any religious campaign until that point in history — and his descendants would emerge from it believers, the children of believers. In this way, Mitzrayim was to serve as a demonstration that Avram's children were different from others who had come before; Klal Yisrael would be Hashem's nation forever.

❒ Thus, the enslavement of the Jewish people did not occur in a vacuum. It was rather in fulfillment of the aforementioned Divine edict issued to Avram one hundred and ninety-eight years before Yosef's descent to Mitzrayim, at the *Bris Bein HaBesarim.* At that time, Hashem not only issued the decree that we would be enslaved, but also foretold of the redemption that would follow. This demonstrated the most basic understanding of the guarantee that Hashem would save Klal Yisrael, and we bless Hashem that He adhered to it. But there is more to it than that.

❒ In His infinite mercy, Hashem began the counting of the four hundred years from the birth of Yitzchak. In this manner, the four hundred years expired two hundred and ten years after Yaakov's descent to Mitzrayim. If Hashem would not have done this, Klal Yisrael would have reached such a low level that they would not have merited to leave Mitzrayim, and so Hashem extracted them early. This is a deeper level of commitment to Klal Yisrael — for Hashem not only saved them, but sought out a way to save them in a manner that would benefit them.

❒ At the *Bris Bein HaBesarim*, Hashem told Avram that He "took" him out of Ur Kasdim to give him Eretz Yisrael. There are two lessons

Blessed is the One Who keeps His guarantee to Yisrael, Blessed is He. For The Holy One, blessed is He, calculated the time of the redemption, in fulfillment of what He had said

---

for us here. Firstly, that Hashem was guiding Avram every step of the way, no matter what it may have looked like. And secondly, that Hashem chose Avram to be the founder of Klal Yisrael, who would live with Him, in Eretz Yisrael, as His eternal nation — the ultimate freedom that was sought by those who departed from Mitzrayim, and the freedom that we will one day experience. This relationship began, then continued to develop throughout history, and deepens further with each passing generation. This was the inception of Hashem's guarantee to Klal Yisrael, but was by no means its culmination.

❒ **The exile in Mitzrayim was a double testament; it was a testament to the fact that Klal Yisrael would survive whatever they would face, and always emerge as the people of Hashem, keepers of His Torah. And it was also a testament that this is due not only to Klal Yisrael's tenacious dedication to Hashem, but is also because Hashem will not allow them to face a situation where their survival is not possible. This, then, is a third facet of Hashem's guarantee to Klal Yisrael: He guarantees that we will not face a situation that we cannot survive as a nation.**

The *posuk* in *Yehoshua* that the *Haggadah* has just cited states that Yaakov and his children went down to Mitzrayim. The *Haggadah* now gives us the background for how and why this came to pass. The key to this issue lies in the *pesukim* of the *Bris Bein HaBesarim,* and we will delve into these *pesukim* momentarily. But, we must realize that if all the *Haggadah* wanted to do was impart that information to us, it would appear that simply citing the *pesukim* of the *Bris Bein HaBesarim* would have been sufficient. The reason that this paragraph opens with the phrase, "Blessed is the One Who keeps his guarantee to Yisrael, Blessed is He," is because the *Haggadah* is pointing out to us that we must not merely identify the guarantee we are discussing, but also focus on the incredible kindness that Hashem performed for us in how He calculated the time for the redemption from Mitzrayim, and thank Him for it.

To address the question of the connection between inheriting Eretz Yisrael and suffering in Mitzrayim, we need to present a bit of background. There is more than one way to understand how Hashem and Avraham arrived at the conversation at the *Bris Bein HaBesarim.* The passage of the *Bris Bein HaBesarim* begins with *Bereishis* 15:7 and concludes with 15:21. And in those *pesukim,* Avram posed the question, *bamah eida?,*

לְאַבְרָהָם אָבִינוּ בִּבְרִית בֵּין הַבְּתָרִים, שֶׁנֶּאֱמַר, וַיֹּאמֶר לְאַבְרָם, יָדֹעַ תֵּדַע כִּי גֵר יִהְיֶה זַרְעֲךָ בְּאֶרֶץ לֹא לָהֶם, וַעֲבָדוּם וְעִנּוּ אֹתָם, אַרְבַּע מֵאוֹת שָׁנָה. וְגַם

---

which is often translated as, *How will I know?,* and was then told of the future exile in Mitzrayim. On its surface, then, it might seem as if Avram was being punished — perhaps for asking Hashem for a guarantee that his descendants would inherit Eretz Yisrael (which is how some interpret *bamah eida*) — through this terrible decree against his descendants. We will see, however, that this is not at all what occurred, in my humble opinion.

We know that the *Bris Bein HaBesarim* took place when Avram was seventy years of age; this is clear from *Rashi* to *Shemos* 12:40 (*d"h shloshim shanah*). Now, the *pesukim* which immediately precede the passage of the *Bris Bein HaBesarim* — *Bereishis* 15:1-6 — may or may not have occurred immediately before the *Bris Bein HaBesarim.* For it is clear from *Rashi* to *Bereishis* 15:1 (*d"h achar*) that those *pesukim* took place in the immediate aftermath of Avraham's victorious campaign against Kedarla'omer. *Tosafos* (*Shabbos* 7b, *d"h v'lo*) cites the *Seder Olam,* who calculates that at the time of the war with the four kings, Avraham was seventy-three; accordingly, 15:1-6 occurred a few years after the *Bris Bein HaBesarim.* However, in my humble opinion, the war with Kedarla'omer occurred when Avraham was seventy.

The issue of when the war took place centers around the understanding of the words of the *posuk* (*Bereishis* 14:4), which states, *shteim esrei shanah avdu es Kedarla'omer, u'shlosh esrei shanah maradu.* The way the *posuk* is rendered by *Seder Olam* is that for twelve years they served Kedorla'omer, and for thirteen years they rebelled. Sedom and its sister cities were founded when Avram was forty-eight, and if we add to that the twelve years of peace and thirteen years of rebellion, it emerges that Avraham was seventy-three when Kedarla'omer arrived to quell the rebellion.

However, I understand the *posuk* to mean that *in the thirteenth year* they rebelled. [This rendering of the *posuk* finds precedent in *Bereishis Rabbah* 42:6, where it is actually the preferred understanding of the *posuk,* as well as in *Ibn Ezra* to the *posuk.*] As such, if we suppose that the twelve years of servitude began only when Avram was fifty-seven, the rebellion occurred when he was seventy. Thus, it can certainly be that the discussion between Hashem and Avram which occurred in 15:1-6 did immediately precede the *Bris Bein HaBesarim,* recorded in 15:7-21. Armed with this understanding, let us begin to shed some light upon the conversation that took place between Hashem and Avram.

to Avraham Avinu at the *Bris Bein HaBesarim*, as it is stated: "And He said to Avram, Know with certainty that your offspring will be sojourners in land that is not their own, and they will serve them, and they will oppress them, for four hundred years. And also

---

In the immediate aftermath of the war with the four kings (see *Rashi d"h achar*), Hashem appeared to Avram and told him not to worry, and that his reward would be exceedingly great. Avram responded to Hashem with the following statement: *"Hashem, my God! What [more] can You give me, seeing that I go childless, and the steward of my house is the Damascene, Eliezer?"* Then, without any reply from Hashem, the *posuk* again states *"vayomer Avram"* — implying a second statement of Avram: *"Behold! You have not given me children, and behold, the occupant of my house (Eliezer) will inherit me."* This is curious indeed. First of all, both of Avram's statements seem to make the same point — namely, that Eliezer would inherit Avram — and second, the format is unusual, in that Avram is seemingly speaking twice without any reply from Hashem. What is the explanation of these *pesukim*?

The *Rosh HaYeshiva, ztvk"l,* explained that in these two *pesukim,* Avram was expressing two very different sentiments. At first, Avram spoke in terms of what he assumed and expected was going to happen — that Eliezer would be the next leader of Avram's followers. *Chazal* interpret the word *damesek* as a contraction of the phrase *doleh u'mashkeh, he would draw and water* from the Torah of his master — i.e., he would learn from Avram, and teach what he learned to the masses (see *Rashi d"h damesek*). Avram thought that Eliezer, who faithfully followed his leadership, would be able to lead a people to believe in Hashem and carry out His will. Thus, he said to Hashem, *"Hashem, my God! What [more] can You give me! And the steward of my house is the Damascene, Eliezer."* Knowing that the path of belief in Hashem and service thereof would continue after Avram's own lifetime was truly a special and treasured piece of knowledge. Avram assumed it would be Eliezer who succeeded him, and asked for nothing more than that.

However, Avram realized — even before Hashem responded to him — that this was really not enough. Not because it did not fulfill Avram's personal desire, but rather because Avram realized that if Eliezer were to actually take the reins after Avram's passing, the religion would not survive. He recognized that there had been periods in the world's history up until that point when mankind as a whole had known the undisputed truth of Hashem. Both immediately following Creation, in Adam's days, as well as in the period immediately following the *Mabul,* there was no doubt

as to the existence and the Omnipotence of Hashem. Yet, in both of these instances, it was only a matter of two to four hundred years until the world was completely overrun by idolatry or heresy — a complete departure from the values and principles held so dear by Adam and Noach. Avram understood the blueprint that these traditions had followed; and, in that moment, as he stood before Hashem, he identified the factor that had ultimately caused their breakdown.

When a senior figure transmitted a tradition, the people who subscribed to that tradition never had to worry about what they were expected to do, because all they needed to do was ask for clarification whenever they were unsure. When that leader became unavailable, another person tried valiantly to fill the vacated shoes of the founder of that tradition. [It is true that Adam lived well into Enosh's generation, and Noach lived through the *Dor Haflagah*. Still, with a world population of millions (or even perhaps billions) of people, they were simply inaccessible to the average person, who, as a result, sought out lesser people to whom they could address their questions.] However, any time an issue arose as to what the tradition mandated in a specific, unforeseen circumstance, or any other issue of doubt, the new leader was forced to rule stringently, because he had no instructions on how to deal with the particular case in question. This phenomenon played out repeatedly, and was further compounded when the second leader was replaced with a third. Eventually, the original tradition was so far from its original form (not to mention extremely cumbersome) that the following generation could not be convinced that it was either possible or even praiseworthy to adopt. This led to the truth of belief in Hashem being lost, and hidden once again, until Avram reawakened the people of the world to the knowledge of Hashem.

Avram reasoned that if Eliezer were to lead after him, this scenario was bound to repeat itself yet again. This was because, although Eliezer was a faithful recorder, and indeed, a faithful broadcaster, of Avram's beliefs and teachings, he was still just that — a recorder and a broadcaster. He did not make Avram's Torah his own, acquiring it as "Eliezer's Torah," but rather simply passed on the traditions he had received.

This principle is illustrated by the story that appears in the Gemara (*Pesachim* 51a), wherein Rabbah bar bar Channah told his son, "I, who witnessed R' Yochanan partake of the fat of the *yisra* (the piece of fat covering the straight part of the stomach), am permitted to partake of it, whether I am in R' Yochanan's presence or not. You, however, whether or not you are in my presence, may not eat it." This was because of the possibility that Rabbah bar bar Channah's son might transgress the Biblical prohibition of eating *cheilev*.

What is the explanation of this Gemara? If Rabbah bar bar Channah was permitted to eat the fat of the *yisra,* how could his son have been forbidden

to do so? The answer is that anytime a bona-fide *safek d'oraisa* (matter of doubt regarding a Biblical prohibition) is at hand, one is required to rule stringently. Now, as the generations pass, and the questions get more technical and more complicated, even the most faithful recorders of the tradition will be forced into adopting new stringencies, simply out of doubt. The only way out of this situation is for every generation to acquire the Torah *for themselves* — to delve into it to such an extent that they are not merely passing on tradition, but rather they *are* the tradition. This means that although some ruled stringently, in the eyes of R' Yochanan (and his own disciples, who he ruled for) there was no doubt — the fat of the *yisra* was completely permissible. How can this be, if in Bavel it was held to be problematic? Because R' Yochanan studied the topic in depth and with clarity, and in his view — the view which was his own Torah — there was no doubt. This same allowance also held true for R' Yochanan's students, who received the halachic ruling of their Rebbi. Rabbah bar bar Channah's son, however, was not a *talmid* of R' Yochanan. Thus, because he had heard both views, and had not decided based on his own study that one was correct over the other (nor had his own Rebbi ruled for him on the matter; his father, Rabbah bar bar Channah, had issued no ruling on the matter at all, and was merely following the directive of his own Rebbi, R' Yochanan), he was obligated to abstain, based upon the doubt which had arisen. This is the difference between one who has acquired the Torah as his own and one who merely passes on what he has heard. [See further, *Dibros Moshe, Shabbos, Siman* 10.]

Avram realized that in order for a religion to have continuity in its undiluted form for many generations — to endure the test of time — it would require something more at the leadership level. It needed the innovation of a person who, even if he would not be greater than his predecessor, would at least be capable of building on the understanding of that leader, further developing the concepts he had believed in and the views he had espoused. In this way, this new leader would, in his own right, be capable of deciding issues that arose regarding the tradition, because he was not merely transmitting the tradition, he was also helping to continue it. Avram realized that the declaration he had just made — that Eliezer would continue his holy work — was precisely the reason that past movements to serve Hashem had lost steam and petered out. Avram did not want this to happen to his own mission. He did not wish that after a few hundred years would pass, his tradition would be lost, and belief in Hashem would again lie dormant, until Hashem would "find" yet another righteous person to spearhead the campaign. Avram therefore changed his mind, issuing his second statement to Hashem, which was, *"Behold! You have not given me children, and the occupant of my house (Eliezer) will inherit me."* In this manner, he begged Hashem to indeed give him children, so that he

might raise a child who would be capable of continuing to forge the path of Avram's beliefs, building on his teachings after he was gone. To this, Hashem responded with 15:4-5; he assured Avram that he would have children, and that they would be as numerous as the stars.

Concurrent with the explanation of the *Rosh HaYeshiva, ztvk"l,* I believe that there is also another message hidden in Hashem's guarantee to Avram. When Hashem showed Avram the stars, He said to him, *ko yihiyeh zar'echa, so will be your offspring.* Not only was Hashem blessing Avram with numerous children, He was also addressing the concern that Avram had expressed in his second sentiment. Hashem was telling him, *so will be your offspring* — they will be forever as you requested — always acquiring the Torah as their own, and never merely repeating what they heard from the previous generation and passing it on to their children. Rather, each generation will add their depth of knowledge and understanding to the tradition of the Torah, thereby ensuring that it continues forever.

[As we discuss the concept of the need for the leaders of the generation to "make the Torah their own," and to leave their indelible mark on the legacy of the eternal existence of the Torah, it is imperative to draw a very clear line of demarcation between what we are describing and the movements of those who seek to "modernize" the Torah and its laws. We are *not* referring to any changes based upon public or private perception that the Torah's laws are archaic, too hard to keep, insensitive to women, too trite, or any other complaints certain deviants might have against the Torah, who therefore attempt to effect changes in its transmission, splitting off from the accepted *mesorah* that we have from Sinai. We are rather simply explaining that what was necessary for the continuity of the *mesorah* was to have leaders in every generation who could figure out what Hashem's will is in any scenario that presents itself. By acquiring the Torah as their own, they possess the deep knowledge of what the Torah — through the explanations of the Gemara, *divrei Chazal,* the *Rishonim,* etc., — requires or allows in any given situation. Thus, they are not restricted to unclear guidelines which they cannot clarify, which only grow vaguer and less relevant with the passage of time.]

As we have explained, the above-mentioned conversation led right into the *pesukim* of the *Bris Bein HaBesarim,* which begin with Hashem declaring that He had taken Avram out of the fire of Ur Kasdim with the express intent of giving his children the land of Eretz Yisrael. This is a commitment that Klal Yisrael will flourish, and will indeed exist forever. Thus, Avram asked: "How can I know that my children will reach the level of greatness necessary to ensure that the religion will truly endure forever?" His question was, "What should I concentrate on teaching them — what specific merit do they need, a merit by whose virtue they will remain faithful to their belief in Hashem, no matter what evil may befall them?" To that, Hashem

answered that the merit of the *korbanos* that Klal Yisrael would offer to Him would stand them in good stead. [See *Rashi* to 15:10, where he explains that the various animals which were split during the *bris* allude to the eventual destruction of the nations of the world, while the bird which was left undivided alludes to the immortality of Klal Yisrael.] The *korbanos* offered at the *Bris Bein HaBesarim* were alluding to various future offerings that Klal Yisrael would merit to offer to Hashem. [See *Rashi d"h vayachshevehah,* as well as *Rashi's* commentary to 15:9.] The concept of offering *korbanos* is, simply put, to connect to Hashem. Various *korbanos* bring out various messages in different ways, but the focal point of *korbanos* is to emphasize that we live with Hashem. The reality is that *tefillah,* which is called *avodah shebeleiv, service of the heart,* and has taken the place of the *korbanos* in our era of exile, also accomplishes this same goal, when exercised properly. When a nation is living their lives with Hashem, no amount of *tzaros, lo aleinu,* can make them abandon their faith. Rather, they will always seek ways to see the light through the darkness, to search for Hashem through the pain, to be *matzdik* the *din*; but they will not forsake Him.

Hashem then told Avram that his children would be subjected to four hundred years of discomfort, imposition, and even persecution — a period longer than the totality of any other religious campaign that had previously existed — and they would emerge believers, the children of believers. Through the crucible of Mitzrayim, Avram's children would demonstrate that their bond with Hashem would be eternal, and merit Hashem's commitment that He would always maintain His relationship with them as well.

Although Hashem had decreed that the Jewish people would suffer for four hundred years, and, as we have explained, this would demonstrate the permanence of their servitude to Hashem, no explanation was given as to how exactly these travails would allow the nation to flourish into the true servants of Hashem that Avram wished his descendants to become. Hashem did not inform Avram exactly why the long exile and suffering would be good for them. Yet, Avram did not ask. Rather, he trusted Hashem explicitly that this course was the very best one for his descendants.

Bearing in mind all we have mentioned, let us return to the *Haggadah's* citation of the *pesukim* of the *Bris Bein HaBesarim* for a moment. We bless Hashem for being true to His word, and keeping the guarantee which He had issued to Klal Yisrael. What was Hashem's promise? That after four hundred years, He would redeem us, punish those who subjugated us, and that we would leave with great bounty. As we have learned, this redemption would take place against the backdrop of Klal Yisrael's budding eternal relationship with Hashem. And Hashem kept this promise then — this is the subject of this paragraph of the *Haggadah*. [Hashem also keeps His guarantee to Klal Yisrael throughout history; see below, *Vehi She'amdah*.]

It was through incredible Divine mercy that the redemption took place when it did. For as we are all aware, the exile in Mitzrayim did not last for four hundred years. It was a "mere" two hundred and ten years after Yaakov's descent to Mitzrayim when the redemption took place. Although there was a Divine decree that Avraham's children would be displaced for four hundred years, Hashem, in His infinite mercy, began the count of four hundred years from the birth of Yitzchak Avinu.

We must realize that it was not necessarily Hashem's plan to calculate the exile in this fashion. In fact, if we had been able to withstand the travails of Mitzrayim and hold onto our faith, He would have allowed us to suffer longer. Why would this have been beneficial for us? Let us remember that there were millions of casualties in Mitzrayim; those among the nation who did not wish to achieve freedom from Mitzrayim's culture, and who wished to keep living in Mitzrayim as Egyptian Jews — they perished during the *makkah* of *Choshech*. The enormity of this tragedy — the loss of either eighty percent of the nation, or perhaps an even larger percentage than that — cannot be overstated. If Moshe and Aharon would have had the opportunity to have more time, more Jews could have been shown the light, and joined the righteous among Klal Yisrael in their desire to leave Mitzrayim, and more would have been saved. However, when Klal Yisrael sank so low, and were in danger of disappearing completely, Hashem acted, and saved all those who were ready to be redeemed.

It is interesting to note that according to this interpretation, we can perhaps understand how history might have been altered had Pharaoh honored Moshe and Aaron's request to spend three days in the desert with the entire Jewish people, sacrificing *korbanos* to Hashem. It is possible that the merit of these offerings — the byproduct of offering *korbanos* in the proper manner — might have enabled the Jewish people to have the spiritual endurance they required, enabling them to survive an additional one hundred and ninety years of slavery, and completing the four hundred years according to their most basic interpretation. But because Pharaoh did not honor this request, the Jewish people, who had fallen to the very depths on the scale of spiritual existence, needed to be rescued far sooner; thus, Hashem redeemed them after a far more lenient reckoning of the counting of the four hundred years.

How can we explain, on the one hand, that the exile in Mitzrayim would demonstrate that nothing could break the Jewish faith, and on the other hand, express the sentiment that if Hashem would have left us a moment longer in the clutches of Mitzrayim, Klal Yisrael would have perished? Are we unextinguishable, or are we not? The answer is that the reason we are unextinguishable is precisely because Hashem guarantees our survival. He guarantees that His nation and His Torah will survive. It is this guarantee that the Torah Jew can completely rely upon; it is the very reason why

Hashem, in His mercy, calculated the time of the redemption the way that He did. Klal Yisrael will survive, no matter what.

We have before us, then, three facets of Hashem's guarantee to Klal Yisrael that He fulfilled. The first was that He redeemed us from Mitzrayim after four hundred years, as He told Avram he would. Secondly, because the exile in Mitzrayim took place against the backdrop of demonstrating to Avram that his children would have an eternal relationship with Hashem, His guarantee to redeem them served as an example for the relationship He was forging with them; He would allow Klal Yisrael to exist in that relationship forever. And thirdly, the *manner* in which Hashem redeemed us — by calculating the years in a novel fashion, so that we would not cease to be able to be His nation — was a fulfillment of the guarantee to Avraham that He will see to it that Klal Yisrael can always survive.

The *posuk* states (*Shemos* 12:40), *And the dwelling of Bnei Yisrael that they dwelt in Mitzrayim was four hundred and thirty years.* As *Rashi* (*d"h shloshim shanah*) explains at length, from the time of Yaakov Avinu's descent until the redemption was only two hundred and ten years. *Rashi* therefore explains that the four-hundred-year exile was considered to have begun with the birth of Yitzchak, and thirty years prior, Avram was told of the decree. Thus, it had been four hundred and thirty years from the time of the issuance of the decree, and it is these four hundred and thirty years that the *posuk* alludes to as the time Klal Yisrael dwelled in Mitzrayim. The question, of course, is why?

Perhaps one might suggest that because Avram and Sarah went to Mitzrayim and did not leave of their own volition, but were rather evicted by Pharaoh, the Torah considers it as though Avram lived under Mitzrayim's subjugation from that moment. The problem, however, is that Avram went down to Mitzrayim after the command of *Lech Lecha*, when he was seventy five, five years after the *Bris Bein HaBesarim*. I am unaware of anyone who places Avram's journey to Mitzrayim after the *Bris Bein HaBesarim*, five years before the command of *Lech Lecha*, and such an approach would seem extremely difficult to fit into the *pesukim*. [See *Nahar Sholom, Shemos* 12:40.]

Perhaps another approach to explain this *posuk* might be that from the very moment Avram began to suffer the consequences of the decree, it was considered to have been in effect. This would not subtract anything from the total of four hundred years, as he had not had Yitzchak yet (and the decree concerned his children). But this was enough for the Torah to describe it as the beginnings of an exile; i.e., to say that it was from that point forward that the Torah began counting time to when the decree would be fulfilled. In the end, four hundred of the four hundred and thirty years between the *Bris Bein HaBesarim* and *Yetzias Mitzrayim* were able to be counted.

To understand this better, let us review how the four-hundred-year exile

אֶת הַגּוֹי אֲשֶׁר יַעֲבֹדוּ דָּן אָנֹכִי, וְאַחֲרֵי כֵן יֵצְאוּ בִּרְכֻשׁ גָּדוֹל.[1]

can possibly be calculated from Yitzchak's birth. Did Yitzchak ever suffer in Mitzrayim as a slave? No; he never even left Eretz Yisrael! Rather, the explanation is that there were several stages of the exile to Mitzrayim. The first was that Avraham's children would be in a land not their own, the second was that they would serve their captors, and the third is that they would suffer oppression. There thus existed at least the possibility that the number four hundred would not be applied only to the servitude and suffering, but also to the years Klal Yisrael would be on foreign soil. This is indeed how Hashem mercifully interpreted the decree. Yitzchak lived on a foreign land, the servitude in Mitzrayim began with Yosef, and the suffering began with the nation's enslavement after the death of the *Shevatim*. But why was Yitzchak considered to be living on a foreign land? Did he not live in Eretz Yisrael?

The answer, of course, is that Avram did not take possession of the land in his lifetime, precisely because he wished to enable the count of the decree to begin as soon as possible. [Not that he necessarily wished for this to occur; he merely wished for the possibility to be there, in case it would be necessary to count the years from an earlier date, which indeed came to pass.] This is why in 15:7, Hashem said He would give the Land to Avraham, while in 15:18, Hashem says, *To "your children" I have given.* [See *Rashi d"h lezar'acha nasati* regarding the tense of the *posuk*.]

We mentioned that there were three distinct levels of discomfort which Klal Yisrael would experience, which are alluded to in the *posuk*. The first is that the Jewish people would be in a foreign land. This is akin to what we experience here today, in America. We are free, but in a land that is not our own. The second level is that of servitude. This does not have to be unbearable — Daniel and his comrades served Nevuchadnetzar, and did so in relative comfort. The last level is that of suffering. It was in regard to this final stage of exile that Hashem tells Avram in the next verse that He will judge those who perpetrate it. This judgment pertained to the motives of the Egyptians — to determine if they acted solely to fulfill Hashem's command, or for other reasons of their own.

Hashem then promised Avram that his children would emerge from exile laden with riches. Clearly, they would acquire the riches of the nations they would defeat in their conquest of the Promised Land. Thus, presumably the riches collected in Mitzrayim were not necessary — rather, they were an extra gift, a kindness from Hashem, to end the exile on a positive note, and an expression of Hashem's love for the descendants of Avraham.

the nation that they serve, I will judge. And afterward, they will leave with great wealth."[1]

(1) *Bereishis* 15:13-14.

One final note on the subject of the *Bris Bein HaBesarim* deals with the reason why Hashem chose Avram. 15:7 states, *And He said to him, "I am Hashem, Who took you out of Ur Kasdim to give you this land to inherit it."* Why does the *posuk* make specific mention of the fact that Hashem "took" Avram from Ur Kasdim? Why does it not simply say that Hashem helped him there, enabling Avram to leave that place in peace?

The answer is that the Torah is stressing to us the fact that Avram was *taken* from there. For while to our eyes it might appear as if Avram voluntarily left Ur Kasdim after having been subjected to the tribulations of the fiery furnace there, or perhaps he was forced to leave by the move of Terach to Charan, the reality was that there was Divine Providence behind his every move. What appears to us in our daily lives to be the result of our own decisions or the decisions of others to which we are subject, is, in reality, Hashem pulling the strings behind the scenes. It is He Who controls everything that happens to us, and any circumstances that cause us to react, are, in reality, set in motion by Hashem, to bring about the result that He desires.

Furthermore, the expression, *took you out of Ur Kasdim to give you this land,* can be understood as follows: Avram went into the fire of Ur Kasdim with one intention, and one intention only — to be burned alive, because he had no desire to live in a world that was so thoroughly corrupted by idolatry. And when Hashem saw this, He (so to speak) said, "This is the person I want to remain in My world, to spread My influence and to stand as a bastion of goodness for all mankind." So Hashem *took* Avram from there, not only with extreme Divine Providence, as above, but with Divine forethought to accomplish the mission — the *eternal mission* — of founding Klal Yisrael, dwelling in Eretz Yisrael, according to the Torah — the ultimate freedom we will one day experience. Truly, then, we can understand that the *Bris Bein HaBesarim* was the inception of an eternal guarantee that Hashem will protect and preserve Klal Yisrael.

וְאַחֲרֵי כֵן יֵצְאוּ בִּרְכֻשׁ גָּדוֹל — *And Afterwards They Will Leave With Great Wealth*

❒ **Moshe argued that the vast wealth that Hashem had granted Klal Yisrael when they left Mitzrayim was the reason they sinned in making the *Eigel*. Why did this not constitute a lack of appreciation for the good Hashem had bestowed upon Klal Yisrael?**

The *matzos* are covered, and the cups are lifted, as the following paragraph is proclaimed joyously. When the recitation is concluded, the cups are put down, and the *matzos* are uncovered once again.

וְהִיא שֶׁעָמְדָה לַאֲבוֹתֵינוּ וְלָנוּ, שֶׁלֹּא אֶחָד בִּלְבָד עָמַד עָלֵינוּ לְכַלּוֹתֵנוּ. אֶלָּא שֶׁבְּכָל דּוֹר וָדוֹר עוֹמְדִים עָלֵינוּ לְכַלּוֹתֵנוּ, וְהַקָּדוֹשׁ בָּרוּךְ הוּא מַצִּילֵנוּ מִיָּדָם.

❒ **Because Klal Yisael did not need the money in the Wilderness, as Hashem was miraculously caring for them, it emerges that Hashem gave them these riches not because they were needed, but rather mainly in fulfillment of the promise to Avraham Avinu at the *Bris Bein HaBesarim*. Accordingly, it was not a favor for Klal Yisrael per se, and Moshe argued that it resulted in aiding their sinful course of action.**

When Hashem confronted Adam about his partaking of the fruit of the *Eitz HaDaas,* the *posuk* (*Bereishis* 3:12) relates that he replied to Hashem, *The woman whom You gave to be with me, she gave me of the tree, and I ate. Rashi* (*d"h asher nasata imadi*), citing the Gemara (*Avodah Zarah* 5b), explains that Adam was being a *kafui tov*; he was ungrateful to Hashem, Who had given him Chavah, his perfect counterpart and companion. His words *the woman whom You gave to be with me*, expressed the sentiment that it was somehow Hashem's fault, as it were, that Adam had sinned, because "His creation" led Adam astray. If Adam truly appreciated that Chavah was intended solely to be his perfect partner, and was created expressly for that purpose, he never could have "blamed" Hashem in this manner; after all, Hashem created Chavah only for Adam's benefit! Adam's words thus betrayed his ungratefulness.

Now, the truth is that we find that Moshe Rabbeinu made a similar comment to Hashem as well. As the Gemara (*Berachos* 32a) tells us, Moshe claimed before Hashem that the sin of the Golden Calf was able to come about as a result of the tremendous amount of gold with which Hashem had endowed the Jewish people at the time of the Exodus. This seems very similar to Adam's comment; in both cases, Hashem had done something positive, and in an attempt to avoid punishment, both Moshe and Adam seemingly paint the picture of Hashem's benevolence as an accessory to the sin. As such, why do we find no complaint against Moshe that his comment, too, reflected ungratefulness?

It would seem that the difference between the two is that Adam was guilty of not showing the proper appreciation for an action that Hashem undertook for his immediate benefit — he was a direct beneficiary of Hashem's kindness. He could not have found inner peace without having

The *matzos* are covered, and the cups are lifted, as the following paragraph is proclaimed joyously. When the recitation is concluded, the cups are put down, and the *matzos* are uncovered once again.

And this is what has stood for our forefathers and for us; for not merely one nation rises up against us to destroy us, but rather in each and every generation, they rise up against us to destroy us; and HASHEM saves us from their hands!

---

found his perfect mate, without Hashem creating Chavah for him. Moshe, on the other hand, was commenting on the great wealth that Hashem bestowed upon the Jewish people when they left Mitzrayim. Truth be told, there was no need for the tremendous amount of booty they collected, at least economically speaking. In the Wilderness they were supported completely by the hand of Hashem, with the *mon*, the *Be'er Miriam,* etc. Why, then, did Hashem make the Jewish people so fabulously wealthy? In order that His promise to Avraham Avinu that his children would leave Mitzrayim *birchush gadol* would be fulfilled. But to the Jewish people themselves, there was no obvious or immediate benefit brought about by their newfound wealth. In fact, if Hashem had desired to give the Jewish people fabulous wealth in a manner that it would be of immediate use to them, He could have bestowed the treasures upon them upon their entry into Eretz Yisrael. However, He chose to supply them with riches, beyond their ability to spend or otherwise use, as they left Mitzrayim, when it was of no immediate use to them, and was nothing more than a burden at that time! Moshe thus noted that the treasure had only brought the Bnei Yisrael to a *nisayon,* and that Hashem could be said to be partially, "responsible," as it were, for their indiscretion. This position did not reflect ungratefulness on Moshe's part, because Hashem had not, in fact, intended the riches he gave to them as a benefit for them as much as for a fulfillment of His earlier promise.

וְהִיא שֶׁעָמְדָה לַאֲבוֹתֵינוּ וְלָנוּ — *And This Is What Has Stood for Our Forefathers and for Us*

❒ **The *Haggadah* states that there is a guarantee that Hashem will always save Klal Yisrael from their enemies. The word *vehi, and it is,* clearly alludes back to the aforementioned promise that Hashem would save us from Mitzrayim. But where is there any indication from that guarantee that Hashem will continue to do this again and again, for our entire history?**

❒ **The answer is that at the *Bris Bein HaBesarim,* Hashem established a relationship with Avram which would last for eternity. We would be**

living in Eretz Yisrael, with Hashem, according to His Torah. Hashem told Avram then, that in the merit of the *korbanos,* and later, of *tefillah,* Klal Yisrael would merit to continue this relationship.

- It was against this backdrop that Klal Yisrael were going to suffer in Mitzrayim. It would be a demonstration that they would remain committed to Him through their exile. Moreover, it would be a demonstration that Hashem would remain committed to Klal Yisrael.
- Hashem thus not only saved Klal Yisrael from Mitzrayim, but also thereby demonstrated the first of many salvations He would visit upon His nation. Furthermore, the manner in which He carried out the redemption from Mitzrayim — wherein He calculated the four hundred years from Yitzchak's birth — was specifically in order that Klal Yisrael would be able to continue as His people. In this, He showed that He will always ensure that Klal Yisrael can continue to exist.
- A second component of *Vehi SheAmdah* is that the same way Hashem separated Klal Yisrael from Mitzrayim culturally, He does so for each society in which we are becoming assimilated. Just as when we left Mitzrayim we were left with absolutely no desire to remain associated with them or their way of life, it has been the same throughout our long exile. Hashem does this to save us from the *hashkafos* that we pick up through the osmosis of living among those who do not adhere to the Torah. Soon, when Hashem brings the Final Redemption, and there will be a *milas halev,* we will finally be freed of any such influences. Until then, *Vehi SheAmdah* assures that Hashem arranges for us to hate the nations into whose cultures we have been tempted to assimilate.

The *Haggadah* explains that the guarantee which Hashem kept when we were slaves in Mitzrayim was in force throughout our history, remains in force to this day, and will continue until the Final Redemption. It is this guarantee upon which Klal Yisrael can rely that we will always survive. Of course, the obvious question we must address is where Hashem issued this guarantee. True, He promised that after four hundred years, the fourth generation would return to Eretz Yisrael. But can it not be argued that this was a limited guarantee, specific to the redemption from the exile of Mitzrayim? Where in the *Bris Bein HaBesarim* do we see any hint of a guarantee for any future redemption?

In the *Haggadah Anah Dodi,* my older brother, *HaRav HaGaon Reb Dovid, ztvk"l,* explains that the guarantee which the *Haggadah* is alluding to here occurred when Hashem told Moshe Rabbeinu to tell Klal Yisrael, *Ehyeh asher Ehyeh* (*Shemos* 3:14), which alludes to the fact that Hashem was with Klal Yisrael in their current travails in Mitzrayim, and also that He would be with them through all future travails. True, this is a clear

guarantee from Hashem that He would save Klal Yisrael in the future. But when did Hashem commit to be with Klal Yisrael in their distress in Mitzrayim and all other situations in which they would find themselves throughout history? If the answer is the declaration of *Ehyeh asher Ehyeh* itself, why is this referred to in the *Haggadah* as *Vehi SheAmdah, and "this" is what stands?* After all, the guarantee of salvation from Mitzrayim as told to Avram Avinu seems to have been distinct from the guarantee issued to Moshe Rabbeinu, which covered all future travails as well!

The answer is as follows: Above, we explained that the *Bris Bein HaBesarim* occurred against the backdrop of Avram having asked Hashem for children so that his mission to serve Hashem would survive, and not peter out like the movements of Adam and Noach had. Hashem promised that Avram would have children, and He compared these children to the stars. He told Avram that his descendants would inherit Eretz Yisrael, and that, in fact, this was the goal that He had had in mind when He saved Avram from the fire of Ur Kasdim. Avram asked what merit his descendants would possess which would allow them to endure, and Hashem revealed to him that their merit would be *korbanos,* which means living with a relationship with Hashem. The Gemara (*Taanis* 27b) reveals that Avram asked further, that while the *korbanos* would be the merit of his descendants while the *Beis HaMikdash* stood, when it was not standing, what would be their merit? Hashem replied that when Klal Yisrael would recite the passages of the *korbanos,* He would consider it as if they had been offered; see further there. Clearly, the relationship which was being established here was for all eternity.

And of course, all this means is that not only did Avram commit to build an eternal relationship between his descendants and Hashem, but also that Hashem committed at the *Bris Bein HaBesarim* to keep a relationship with Klal Yisrael forever. What did the beginnings of that relationship look like? Hashem informed Avram that his descendants would suffer in Mitzrayim for four hundred years — longer than any other religious campaign to that point had lasted — and that He would then redeem them. When He would do so, they would emerge as *maaminim bnei maaminim, believers, the children of believers.* We see this redemption as a fulfillment of Hashem's promise, for He did as He foretold He would do. But is this the *extent* of the relationship forged at the *Bris Bein HaBesarim*? Of course not! It was merely the *beginning* of that relationship, which would last for all eternity. Thus, not only was Hashem's salvation in Mitzrayim a fulfillment of the specific promise He issued at the *Bris Bein HaBesarim* to save His nation, but it was also the first example of His commitment to Klal Yisrael that the nation would eternally be His people.

Furthermore, Hashem calculated the four hundred years from the earliest possible time; from Yitzchak's birth. He did this in order that Klal

צא וּלְמַד מַה בִּקֵּשׁ לָבָן הָאֲרַמִּי לַעֲשׂוֹת לְיַעֲקֹב אָבִינוּ, שֶׁפַּרְעֹה לֹא גָזַר אֶלָּא עַל הַזְּכָרִים, וְלָבָן בִּקֵּשׁ לַעֲקוֹר אֶת הַכֹּל. שֶׁנֶּאֱמַר:

Yisrael would survive, and not fall to the level where they would not merit salvation. If Hashem's guarantee was merely to keep the letter of the law of His promise, He could have waited until the four hundred years of slavery were up. However, He specifically carried out the promised redemption in a manner that ensured Klal Yisrael's survival. Why? Because this is part of the relationship He committed to at the *Bris Bein HaBesarim* — that Klal Yisrael would always be His nation, forever. Hashem *took* Avram from Ur Kasdim with Divine forethought to accomplish the mission — the *eternal mission* — of founding Klal Yisrael and dwelling in Eretz Yisrael according to the Torah — the ultimate freedom we will one day experience.

Truly, then, we can understand that the *Bris Bein HaBesarim* was the inception of an eternal guarantee that Hashem will protect and preserve Klal Yisrael. Over the last two thousand years, Klal Yisrael has endured many Mitzrayims: the Inquisition, the Crusades, the Nazis, and so, so many more. The destruction visited upon us as a nation, over and over, has been terrible beyond description. Yet we survive, because Hashem saves us. He saves us because we are the children of Avram, and for our part, we remain *maaminim bnei maaminim.* We have no *Beis HaMikdash* within which to offer any *korbanos.* It is rather the collective power of *tefillah* that infuses the blood of Klal Yisrael with belief and trust in Hashem, come what may. This relationship, which was also expressed to Moshe Rabbeinu as *Ehyeh asher Ehyeh,* can clearly be traced back to Hashem's instruction to Avram at the *Bris Bein Habesarim.*

There is also a second lesson hidden in *Vehi SheAmdah,* which bears pointing out. It is a sad fact that the downfall of Klal Yisrael in so many instances was their desire to assimilate, to become important in a society, or to adopt the values of a given culture. Hashem protects against these dangerous attitudes by making host nations react with utter disgust and rejection of the Jew. This causes them to persecute the Jewish people, which, in turn, causes the Jewish people who survive to hate the culture from which they are escaping with an incredibly fierce animosity. This has been, over and over, the point which has allowed Klal Yisrael to escape not only the physical subordination of a given nation, but also to purge themselves of the cultural subordination of that nation that they did not even realize they were suffering from.

True freedom to serve Hashem can only be accomplished when a person is free from the influences of a non-Torah society. This is a level we

Come and learn [the extent of] what Lavan HaArami sought to do to Yaakov Avinu. For Pharaoh only decreed that the males [be killed], but Lavan sought to uproot the entirety [of Yaakov's family]. As it is stated:

---

can only begin to understand. In *Parashas Nitzavim* (*Devarim* Ch. 30) the Torah speaks of Klal Yisrael repenting. 30:2 tells us that Klal Yisrael will repent with all of their hearts and all of their souls, and 30:3-5 speak of the incredible bounty Hashem will shower upon Klal Yisrael when they do so. Then, 30:6 states, *And Hashem, your God, shall circumcise your heart, and the hearts of your children, to love Hashem, your God, with all of your heart and with all of your soul, so that you may live.* This is closely followed by 30:8, where the Torah foretells that Klal Yisrael will return to Hashem. But this is difficult to understand: Had they not already repented, as stated in 30:2 above?

The answer is that there are two stages of *teshuvah*. 30:2 alludes to the level of *teshuvah* that is possible even when a person is still under the influence, to some degree, of foreign cultures. For when Klal Yisrael is exposed to other cultures, invariably, some of the values of those cultures affect the way they think and feel. There is thus a degree of impropriety to which a person is numb, and he does not even recognize that it is something wrong, requiring correction and repentance. Hashem then performs *milas halev,* and does Klal Yisrael the service of separating them from the *impurities of their hearts,* which are the influences that had affected and confused them, allowing them to truly *live* their commitment to Him. Once the Torah's *hashkafos* are clear to a person, he can then do *teshuvah* in a more complete fashion, for his picture of what is truly right has been made clear.

With Hashem's help, soon, in our days, we will merit to experience *milas halev,* and He will separate us completely from the cultures to which we have been exposed for these last millennia. This will be the pinnacle of *Vehi SheAmdah;* Hashem's guarantee that we will live in His Land, as His people, only according to His Torah.

מַה בִּקֵּשׁ לָבָן הָאֲרַמִּי לַעֲשׂוֹת לְיַעֲקֹב אָבִינוּ — *What Lavan HaArami Sought to do to Yaakov Avinu*

❒ **Lavan had a unique opportunity, as the grandfather of all of the *shevatim*. He could have aided them, and made it easier for them to serve Hashem, thereby sealing his place in history as one who aided in the development of the nation. But he squandered the opportunity. Instead, he sought to destroy the budding nation because Yaakov's**

existence made him uncomfortable. He was a person with basically good *middos,* and when he saw others that were similar to him, yet different, he sought to eliminate them. This was rooted in haughtiness that his way was correct, and in the fear that Yaakov's continued existence would begin to influence him, or show that Lavan's way was incorrect. We must realize that if we are not comfortable greeting Jews who are a little different than we are, we are suffering from the influence of our Aramean grandfather, and must uproot this influence.

❒ Why does the *posuk* connect Yaakov's time with Lavan to his descent to Mitzrayim, which took place over thirty years later? The *Rosh HaYeshiva, ztvk"l,* answered that what gave Yaakov the confidence that he would be able to raise a Klal Yisrael in Mitzrayim was the fact that, in a somewhat similar setting, over three decades earlier, he had fought the influences of Lavan on himself and his family, and emerged unscathed.

❒ Pharaoh sought to eliminate the baby boys of Klal Yisrael, in order that their savior not survive to interfere with his rule. Why did he not simply attempt to wipe out the nation? If it was because the Egyptians were actively using the Jewish people as slaves, he surely wished to preserve the slaves for as long as possible. But if the Jewish people were only building useless cities, why did Pharaoh feel that he needed them around? It may have been in order to continue to benefit from the monies which the Jewish people were pumping into the Egyptian economy by purchasing building materials for the never-ending projects which with they were tasked.

❒ Pharaoh initially sought to have Shifrah and Pu'ah kill the unborn babies, which would absolve him of deserving the death penalty for killing them himself. Someone who wants to act wrongly, but within the letter of the law, is a *naval birshus haTorah,* someone who acts repugnantly, but technically within the confines of the laws of the Torah.

We begin to expound the *pesukim* at the beginning of *Parashas Ki Savo.* These *pesukim* contain a synopsis of the exile to and the redemption from Mitzrayim. The *Rambam* (*Hil. Chametz U'Matzah* 7:4) writes that it is praiseworthy to expound this passage.

The passage (which is also read when one brings *bikkurim*) opens with the statement that Lavan attempted to destroy our father, Yaakov Avinu.

An Aramean sought to destroy my father, and he went down to Mitzrayim, and he sojourned there, few in number. And he became there a nation, strong, and numerous.[1]

(1) *Devarim* 26:5.

The *Zaide Lavan,* as my son, *R' Avi, shlit"a,* likes to call him, was the grandfather of all twelve of the *shevatim.* But, rather than being a figure who contributed to the welfare of Klal Yisrael (as Yisro did) and potentially having a positive effect upon his grandchildren, which could have aided in the perfection of the *shevatim,* Lavan wanted to destroy Yaakov and his sons. He squandered the opportunity to be involved with Klal Yisrael, and instead tried to annihilate them. This is why the Torah mentions him in the context of Klal Yisrael's early history.

What was it that caused Lavan to express such depravity, and to desire the extermination of his own daughters and grandchildren? Even Pharaoh, who practiced infanticide in order to preserve his kingdom, did not kill any of the females of Klal Yisrael. What was it about Lavan that made him seek to uproot the entirety of the fledgling nation?

There are many people involved in the field of *kiruv,* bringing Jews back to the ways of the Torah. Often, people who gravitate toward *kiruv* will busy themselves with *rechokim* — people who are totally unaware of Judaism, or who do not keep Shabbos, eat *kosher,* or read Hebrew. But, those same people will sometimes avoid *kiruv kerovim;* the people who are from *frum* backgrounds, but who are different than they are. Similarly, people are wont to greet a Jew who is not observant at all, but can be loathe to greet Jews who are religious, but are different than them. If they are *litvish,* they might be somewhat hesitant to say "Good Shabbos" to a *chassidishe* person, or perhaps to a Sephardic Jew. [This is not to say that most people are this way; only that it is a phenomenon with which I am familiar.]

Why? Why is a person drawn to those who are far from his station, and repelled by those who are more similar to him? I believe that the answer, deep, deep down, is that people are afraid of being influenced by those who are similar to them, and the fear of that influence creates distance between people. While a person knows he will continue to keep Shabbos and eat *kosher,* he is afraid that he may start changing his ways if he associates with religious Jews who are different than he is. Unfortunately, it is this fear that keeps us from being friendly to everybody, and eager to help everyone.

Lavan was a person with basically good *middos,* and who practiced *chessed* (see above, *Mitchilah*). But his *chessed* was unprincipled. When he was hosting another person, he would clear his house of the gods he believed in to make them comfortable; this we see from what he did when

Eliezer visited. But when someone crossed him, his haughtiness was such that he felt, "If you are not doing it my way, it is not worth your doing it at all!" In his unprincipled mind, he would do anything for a person he liked, and anything to one he disliked. When he saw Yaakov was different than he was, and that Yaakov acted according to the morals of the Torah while Lavan himself was an idolater, he felt threatened; for Yaakov was a living demonstration that, in fact, Lavan was not living the best, most moral type of life. Once he felt that Yaakov had "crossed" him, he was his enemy; and Lavan would do anything to an enemy. His reaction to this discomfort was *bikeish laakor es hakol,* to try and destroy all of Klal Yisrael. This is a *middah* of Lavan, and we must be sure to eradicate it from our midst — because it is in our midst, as Lavan was a grandfather to every single one of us; it is thus our mission to uproot it. While we surely want our *mesorah* to be intact, and are not interested in adopting the *mesorah* of others, this should never stop us from greeting happily those who are slightly different than we are. We cannot allow the fact that other Jews are different than we are to foster distance between us.

While the above lessons serve to explain why the Torah alludes to Lavan's attempted destruction of Klal Yisrael, we are left wondering about the connection between that statement and the one that follows. For Lavan's evil plans do not seem to have anything to do with Yaakov Avinu's sojourning in Mitzrayim at all. Consider that Yaakov fled from Lavan's estate when he was approximately ninety-seven years old, and he only arrived before Pharaoh in Mitzrayim when he was one hundred and thirty years old, more than three decades later! Why, then, does the *posuk* seem to associate the evil desire of Lavan with the exile to Mitzrayim?

The *Rosh HaYeshiva, ztvk"l,* would answer that the Torah is explaining that when Yaakov Avinu went down to Mitzrayim into exile, he felt he had the ability to do so because he had already survived the travails of the time he spent with Lavan. After going through the adversarial relationship that he had with Lavan and emerging intact in his faith in Hashem and his observance of the Torah, and after seeing that despite the negative influence of their *Zaide,* his children emerged perfectly unscathed, Yaakov felt as though they were ready for further challenges. As *Rashi* to *Bereishis* 32:5 (*d"h garti*) comments, Yaakov's triumph when he departed Charan was that he had been able to learn and observe the Torah and its *mitzvos* while he was with Lavan. Yaakov thus viewed his descent to Mitztrayim thirty-three years after departing from Lavan as another journey into the grasp of an enemy who sought to assimilate him, and he felt that he was ready for it. Why? Because of the seeds Hashem had sown for him and his young children so many years prior, when they lived with the *Zaide* Lavan.

Yaakov's descent to Mitzrayim was the beginning of Klal Yisrael's exile there. The exile ended with the emergence of Klal Yisrael as Hashem's

nation, and the acceptance of the Torah. Clearly, whatever success Yaakov and his sons had in their ability to be *mechaneich* the generations that followed in adhering to Hashem's will led directly to the preservation of the nation, and to the ultimate achievement of receiving the Torah and inheriting Eretz Yisrael. Without the strength Yaakov had garnered from his years with Lavan, he would have lacked that ability. We can see from here that Hashem equipped Yaakov with the tools he would need in Mitzrayim to be able to survive there all those years earlier, when he was spending time with Lavan. We never know why Hashem will give a *nisayon* to us, and we never know how an experience might aid in shaping our relationship with Hashem.

We must note that all we are saying here is that to whatever extent Yaakov Avinu and Klal Yisrael were successful in Mitzrayim, their success had its roots in surviving Lavan. Still, the fact remains that Yaakov Avinu did not go down to Mitzrayim with full confidence; see *Nahar Sholom, Bereishis,* 46:1, where we have explained that Yaakov Avinu was made aware by Hashem, via a dream, that sobering times lay ahead. After that revelation, Yaakov reassessed what he could accomplish with Klal Yisrael as they began their exile, and the reality of this task took away some of Yaakov's strength and confidence. The *shevatim* were unaware of the dream, however, and so they did indeed go down brimming with confidence.

It is also true that despite the great success of Klal Yisrael who left Mitzrayim, there were many, many casualties who chose not to leave, and perished. We therefore do not mean to say that Yaakov and his sons' efforts in Mitzrayim were a complete success because of their experience with Lavan. Rather, what we are saying is that the confidence which Yaakov did go down with, and the *chinuch* he did manage to impart to the portion of Klal Yisrael who were indeed redeemed two hundred and ten years later, can all be traced back to the experience Yaakov and his children gained when they suffered at the hands of Lavan.

The Torah then alludes to the plot of Pharaoh to kill all of the male children of Klal Yisrael. Pharaoh knew that the savior of the Jewish people was going to be born, and sought to solidify his reign by making sure that this savior would be killed. Even so, he clearly was not interested in wholesale destruction of the Jewish people. For if he had been, it would seem that he would have targeted the girls, not the boys. The logic for this is as follows: If we assume that Pharaoh really tried to eradicate either all of the females or all of the males of Klal Yisrael, he would presumably only be, at most, 99.99 percent successful. It is logical to assume that at least one or two people would slip through his extermination plan, being as he was only human. Accordingly, if he targeted the women only, and one or two women survived his purge, it stands to reason that he could still eventually wipe out the future population. This is because a few women,

no matter how they try to procreate, are limited to a handful of potential children in a matter of years. These, in turn, could be slowly found and disposed of for the annihilation to be completed. However, if the plan was to destroy the nation by eradicating the men, and one or two men got away, it could theoretically take them only a short time to repopulate. Two men, when introduced to an entire population of surviving women for even a very short time, can father many, many children. Yet Pharaoh still chose only to attack the males of Klal Yisrael, leaving the females undisturbed. Why?

Now, if Pharaoh was interested in maintaining a slave population, the fact that he wasn't eager to wipe out all of Klal Yisrael quickly is understandable. However, if the workforce was simply being tasked with useless work (see *Pisom and Raamseis,* below), and Pharaoh seemingly had no real use for the Jews, why wouldn't he have simply killed either the females, as above, or else the adult males? Either way would seemingly be more efficient than going after babies as they were about to be born!

Perhaps the reason was that Pharaoh did not want the Egyptian economy to take the hit of losing the influx of Jewish money it was getting by having the Jewish slaves purchase all the materials they needed for their useless projects from Egyptian merchants. He was therefore content to wipe the nation out more slowly, assuming that by the time he was successful, all of the money would have already all been put back into Mitzrayim's economy.

In his endeavor to do away with the baby boys, Pharaoh initially sought a manner in which he would not have been liable to a death sentence. He ordered Shifrah and Pu'ah (Yocheved and Miriam) to kill the baby boys borne by the Jewish women. Now, Klal Yisrael was, by this time, quite numerous. It was only approximately eighty years before *Yetzias Mitzraim,* at which time Klal Yisrael left with six hundred thousand men between the ages of twenty and sixty. This represented only a fifth, or perhaps even a fiftieth (or, according to one opinion, as low as one five-hundredth), of the entire population (see further, *Shemos* 13:18, with *Rashi, d"h chamushim,* as well as *Mechilta* to *Parashas Beshalach, d"h vachamushim,* with *Biur HaGra* there). Additionally, many of the people of those times married when they were under twenty years old, and would have required midwives. Even if the population did boom exponentially over the next eighty years, it is certainly reasonable to presume that the workload would have been unmanageable for only two midwives for all of Klal Yisrael. So, how could he have thought that his orders to only two women would have been effective at eliminating the *moshian shel Yisrael?* Perhaps we can say that

And he descended to Mitzrayim — He was forced, by Divine decree.

---

they were the most senior among Klal Yisrael's midwives (or that Yocheved was, at any rate; she was the wife of the *gadol hador,* Amram, and was almost one hundred and thirty years old, while Miriam, her daughter, was a mere six years old) and thus they dictated policy to all of the other Jewish midwives. Therefore, Pharaoh called them before him when he desired to issue instructions to all of the midwives, and it was their job to pass on these directives to their fellow midwives.

As above, Pharaoh intended to skirt around the prohibition against murder as he attempted to rid himself of the savior of the Jewish people. He knew that for a non-Jew to kill a yet-unborn child was halachically considered to be murder, and thus was forbidden, carrying the penalty of capital punishment. However, for a Jew to do this, while still Biblically prohibited, is only a negative commandment that does not incur capital punishment. Pharaoh therefore commanded that the Jewish babies be exterminated by the Jews themselves, so that he would not deserve capital punishment; at this point, this still mattered to him. [See further, *V'es Amaleinu,* below.]

Here, Pharaoh demonstrated a fundamental difference between the way Hashem wants people to act and the ways of the wicked. The Torah specifies punishments for sins, and Hashem expects us to use the Torah as a guide from Hashem to categorize right and wrong. Thus, it is not merely the punishments of the Torah that we seek to avoid, but rather the behavior itself that the Torah renders punishable, for this behavior is obviously incorrect in the eyes of Hashem. [Indeed, in addition to specifying the punishment for a sin, the Torah generally writes a second verse as an *azharah, a warning,* that the act is forbidden.] Pharaoh, however, was quick to commit the crime of murder by way of killing the unborn children — the morality of the matter did not bother him. It was the technical issue of the accompanying punishment that gave him pause, and this he wiggled out of by ordering Jews to do the deed for him. When a Jew acts the way Pharaoh acted here, he is considered to be a *naval birshus haTorah,* someone who acts repugnantly, but technically within the confines of the laws of the Torah.

אָנוּס עַל פִּי הַדִּבּוּר — *He Was Forced, by Divine Decree*

- **Hashem controls everything that occurs to anyone. As such, why is Yaakov's descent to Mitzrayim singled out as an event that was a result of a Divine decree?**
- **Perhaps the *Haggadah* is alluding to the fact that Yaakov's descent was in fulfillment of Avraham's prophecy at the *Bris Bein HaBesarim.***

וַיָּגָר שָׁם. מְלַמֵּד שֶׁלֹּא יָרַד יַעֲקֹב אָבִינוּ לְהִשְׁתַּקֵּעַ בְּמִצְרַיִם, אֶלָּא לָגוּר שָׁם. שֶׁנֶּאֱמַר, וַיֹּאמְרוּ אֶל פַּרְעֹה, לָגוּר בָּאָרֶץ בָּאנוּ, כִּי אֵין מִרְעֶה לַצֹּאן אֲשֶׁר לַעֲבָדֶיךָ, כִּי כָבֵד הָרָעָב בְּאֶרֶץ כְּנָעַן, וְעַתָּה יֵשְׁבוּ נָא עֲבָדֶיךָ בְּאֶרֶץ גֹּשֶׁן[1].

❒ **Or perhaps the allusion is to the fact that Yaakov himself was told by Hashem, as he began his descent to Mitzrayim, that the exile was beginning. As such, he was literally forced to go down, knowing that he would not return alive.**

In truth, everything that happens to anyone in his entire life is *forced by a Divine decree.* The issue of free will is limited to whether we will act correctly or incorrectly, but what happens to us is up to Hashem. So, what was special about Yaakov Avinu's descent to Mitzrayim that would warrant the *Haggadah* stating of it that it was the result of a Divine decree?

Of course, the Gemara (*Shabbos* 89b) tells us that if Yaakov Avinu had not gone down to Mitzrayim voluntarily, he would have gone down in chains; he was destined to fulfill the decree of the *Bris Bein HaBesarim* in Mitzrayim, whether he chose to do so or not. So, perhaps one way of understanding the *Haggadah* here would be to suggest that the Divine decree which necessitated Yaakov's descent, no matter how it was to occur, was the prophecy of the *Bris Bein Habesarim.* This was distinct from our everyday lives, where even though things happen because Hashem decided that they should, no prophecy has been issued foretelling them.

Alternatively, I believe that the Divine decree that Yaakov was to descend to Mitzrayim to which the *Haggadah* alludes is unique because it was issued to Yaakov himself. For as Yaakov began his descent to Mitzrayim, the *pesukim* (*Bereishis* 46:1-5) state that he first went to Be'er Sheva to offer *korbanos* to Hashem. There, he experienced a prophetic dream, wherein Hashem revealed to him that the exile in Mitzrayim was about to begin (see further, immediately below, *Vayagar Sham*). Thus, in its plainest sense, the descent of Klal Yisrael began with an edict to Yaakov that the exile was beginning — he was thus forced by Divine decree to descend, even though he now knew that he would never return alive. According to this approach, it is fitting that the *posuk* says, *and "he" descended to Mitzrayim,* rather than the plural, "And they descended to Mitzrayim." For it was indeed only Yaakov who was made aware that the exile was about to begin, and thus, it was only he who was, in this sense, *forced by Divine decree.*

And he sojourned there — This teaches us that Yaakov Avinu did not descend to become settled in Mitzrayim, but rather to sojourn there, as it is stated: "And they said to Pharaoh, To sojourn in the land we have come, for there is no pasture for the sheep that belongs to your servants, for the hunger is very heavy in the land of Canaan; and now, let your servants settle in the land of Goshen."[1]

(1) *Bereishis* 47:4.

— לָגוּר בָּאָרֶץ בָּאנוּ. . . וְעַתָּה יֵשְׁבוּ נָא עֲבָדֶיךָ בְּאֶרֶץ גֹּשֶׁן
"To Sojourn in the Land We Have Come... and Now, Let Your Servants Settle in the Land of Goshen"

❒ Yaakov went down to Mitzrayim with the intent to return after the end of the famine. However, Hashem told him in a dream that he would not return to Eretz Yisrael alive, as the exile was beginning. Hashem told Yaakov not to worry. When someone says not to worry, you know that there is something to be worried about! Although Yaakov's own mind was weighed down by the prospect of exile, he did not reveal to his children that they would be living in Mitzrayim long-term. Thus, he allowed them to descend brimming with confidence.

❒ When the *shevatim* appeared before Pharaoh, they mentioned that they were only there temporarily, that they and their forefathers were shepherds, and they asked to live in the land of Goshen.

❒ Yaakov tended sheep because it allowed him the opportunity to contemplate, which gave him the fortitude he needed to stand up to the challenging influences of Eisav and Lavan. The *shevatim* adopted this profession as well, because it afforded them ample time to learn together.

❒ Yosef was intent on making his brothers appear to be outcasts, so that the Egyptians would not want to have anything to do with them. He hoped this would keep the Egyptian influence on Klal Yisrael at bay. He thus instructed the *shevatim* to tell Pharaoh that they and their forefathers tended sheep — a despicable practice in Mitzrayim. Pharaoh countered this by asking Yosef to have them guard his own sheep. Pharaoh hoped that the association with him would serve to elevate the *shevatim* in the eyes of the populace.

❒ Yosef also instructed them to request to settle in Goshen, which was near him and apart from the main Egyptian cities. This was also an effort to stave off integration into Egyptian society. Pharaoh, however,

wanted Klal Yisrael to settle in the main cities in Mitzrayim. Eventually, he ordered Yosef to settle them in Goshen, but to give them other estates in Mitzrayim's main hubs, so that they could reside there when they wished. Yosef was forced to do so.

- ❒ **Yosef warned that even occasional vacationing among the Egyptians would result in assimilation. Perhaps initially his warning was heeded by his brothers. But eventually, the nation began to ignore this advice, and Pharaoh's plan began to come to fruition.**

The *Haggadah* cites the *posuk* in *Bereishis* 47:4 to illustrate that Yaakov and his sons originally intended to stay in Mitzrayim for only a short time. However, although this was indeed their intention, Hashem had decreed that this descent would be the beginning of the exile. He informed Yaakov Avinu of this as he began his journey, and thus Yaakov was made aware that the exile was beginning. Simultaneously, Yosef was endeavoring to secure spiritual salvation for Klal Yisrael, knowing full well that no matter how long his brothers might be in Mitzrayim, Pharaoh was intent upon having them assimilate into the Egyptian culture. Let us explore both the idea that Klal Yisrael was destined to begin their exile now, and the idea that Yosef was trying his hardest to protect them from Pharaoh's influence.

First, the decree. When Yaakov finally accepted that Yosef was alive, he decided to accept the invitation to go and see him. He was, at that time, still under the impression that he was going to return to Eretz Yisrael after the famine would end. His spirit was reawakened, and he traveled to Be'er Sheva to offer *korbanos*. When the Torah speaks of the beginning of this trip, Yaakov is called "Yisrael," the name of Yaakov Avinu that connotes strength, confidence, and fearlessness.

That night, while in Be'er Sheva, Hashem came to "Yisrael" in a dream — and called him, "Yaakov." He told Yaakov not to fear the descent to Mitzrayim, that Klal Yisrael would become a great nation there, that He would be with Yaakov in exile, that He would bring Yaakov back to Eretz Yisrael (for burial), and that Yosef would close his eyes when he died (in Mitzrayim). This dream let Yaakov Avinu know that his plans for a short stay in Mitzrayim were not going to come to fruition. Rather, the exile of Klal Yisrael in Mitzrayim was going to be long-term, and Yaakov, personally, would live out his days there. And although Hashem had told him not to worry, that was the best indicator that there was something that was potentially worrisome on the horizon. This is obvious. When someone says "Do not worry," it does not mean that there is no reason to worry; rather, it means that worrying is not the correct thing to do in response to the potentially worrying circumstance one is about to face. Rather, one should compose himself and act; and in this way, manage the perhaps difficult situation as best as possible.

Hashem was letting Yaakov know that until now, there had been an opportunity to ingrain the principles of faith in Hashem and Torah observance into his family as best he could, to help Klal Yisrael survive the exile intact. The window for optimal *chinuch*, however, was coming to a close, as the exile was beginning. Hashem was telling Yaakov not to fear his descent, because there would be a Klal Yisrael that would survive. It would not be everyone, unfortunately, but a portion of his children would survive this exile. Hashem was telling Yaakov that worrying about this now would be pointless. He should instead use his time and energy to instill in Klal Yisrael in exile as much positive influence as he could. The more he could do this, the higher the percentage of Klal Yisrael's spirituality that would survive the length of the exile would be.

When Yaakov awoke, the Torah calls him by his weaker name, Yaakov. The revelations of the dream had taken his strength and confidence down a notch. However, it is interesting that the *posuk* (*Bereishis* 46:5) then states, *and the Children of Yisrael carried Yaakov, their father.* While Yaakov was sobered by the realities of what lay ahead, this did not affect the confidence and strength of his children, who were even now called after Yaakov's stronger name. Yaakov had sent Yehudah to found a place of Torah learning, and was still going to stand at the helm of Klal Yisrael as their Rebbi as long as he remained alive. But although he was sobered by what lay ahead, he did not reveal the dream he had dreamt to his children, who, ignorant of the perils that lay ahead of them, marched onward, brimming with confidence, *the Children of Yisrael.* [See *Nahar Sholom, Bereishis* 46:1, where we have discussed several scenarios where it is proper to refrain from sharing information with someone.]

Why were the *shevatim* shepherds? It is interesting to note that the *posuk* before the one cited here by the *Haggadah* states, *And Pharaoh said to his brothers, "What is your trade?" And they said to Pharaoh, "We are shepherds — we and our forefathers."* The *shevatim* informed Pharaoh that they and their ancestors were in the business of rearing flocks. While Avraham Avinu and Yitzchak Avinu certainly maintained plenty of flocks, we do not have any reason to assume that they themselves were the ones tending to their own sheep. The Torah writes explicitly that Avraham had shepherds, and so presumably, he was not a shepherd himself. Yitzchak Avinu also had a lot of sheep, and also had servants to tend to them. Of all of the *Avos,* it was only Yaakov about whom we are explicitly told that he chose to be a shepherd; and Moshe Rabbeinu did as well. Was there any particular reason that they chose this to be their profession, and why was it specifically they who did so?

Avraham was a man with a mission; his personality exuded his beliefs, and his life's goal was to educate the people of the world about Hashem's existence and sovereignty. Avraham was an educator of the masses.

Although it is certainly true that Avraham worked on his character and his attributes (after all, the attributes of *rachmanus, baishanus,* and *gemilas chassadim* all come from his sterling character), this was not his main avenue of service to Hashem. Rather, spreading the truth of Hashem to others was Avraham's principal occupation. Yitzchak, who was an *olah temimah,* was of perfect character. Accordingly, it would seem that his principal mode of serving Hashem was not in honing his already perfect character. Yaakov, however, had faced a challenge unlike those of Avraham and Yitzchak — growing up together with Eisav. Certainly Avraham was subjected to living among evildoers, but he was not sharing a childhood with Eisav. The challenge presented by this potential influence runs deep, and can affect a person in many different ways — Eisav was basically the worst of the worst as far as bad influences go. Similarly, Moshe Rabbeinu was raised in the palace of Pharaoh, among terrible *resha'im.* This was certainly for Moshe's own benefit (see *Nahar Sholom, Shemos* 2:11); nevertheless, growing up in an environment such as that one was fraught with the potential for Moshe's character to be adversely affected. As such, both Yaakov Avinu and Moshe Rabbeinu required a fair amount of *hisbodedus, introspection,* to be able to sift through the exposures to which they had been subject, to block out the objectionable influences that had infiltrated their childhoods, and to cling to the pure influences of those childhoods — the influences that had come from their holy parents.

Thus, when they set out to choose a profession, both Yaakov and Moshe gravitated toward shepherding, which allowed for this *hisbodedus,* as it is an occupation that comes along with much free time to think without compromising the quality of the job being performed. Eventually, Yaakov became known as the *bechir sheb'avos,* and Moshe Rabbeinu became the greatest prophet in history. We see, then, that their goal of eliminating these foreign influences was realized. [We find that the *shevatim* were shepherds as well. Unlike Moshe and Yaakov, they did not choose to do this to have time for *hisbodedus,* to weed out bad influences from their personalities. Rather, they grew up watching Yaakov do this job, and learned it at a young age. Additionally, when they all did it together, shepherding afforded them an opportunity to have a Yeshiva of sorts, being that they were all there, and had plenty of time to learn together!]

This leads us to the second point, which also has to do with tending sheep. Yosef understood Pharaoh's agenda of assimilating his brothers and their families into the Egyptian culture. One stratagem he employed in an attempt to protect them was that he told Pharaoh that his family's occupation was shepherding, and he instructed his brothers to do the same. They were to tell Pharaoh not only that this was the family business, but that it had been for generations.

Yosef wished to present his family this way because there existed a

stereotype in Mitzrayim in those times against people who utilized sheep for their own purposes. Now, the Egyptians themselves were accustomed to owning sheep — this is evident from the fact that during the famine, the *posuk* (*Bereishis* 47:17) tells us that they traded their sheep, among other things, for food. And if they had sheep in their possession, they must have looked after the sheep. But, they did not do it in a commercial manner, by assigning as many sheep as they could to a lowly worker, or perhaps even a slave, to look after.

Rather, the Egyptians who tended their sheep probably wore honorable clothing and tended to just a few animals each, and treated them with respect — not like a shepherd, who would treat the sheep like animals. This bred a stigma against "regular" shepherds in the eyes of Egyptian society, despite the fact that the Egyptians certainly cared for their own sheep. The repulsion they felt for those shepherds probably infiltrated the subconscious, to the point that they hated them without remembering why they did; much like people remove their hats today to show respect, but do not realize anymore why this in fact demonstrates respect. [See *Nahar Sholom* to *Vayikra* 18:3, second entry, where this is discussed further.] As herders were typically held in low esteem in the society of Mitzrayim, Yosef hoped that this would make it all the more difficult for Pharaoh to arrange for the *shevatim* to be held in high regard by the general populace. By marking them as outcasts, Yosef was building a protection from the influences of Egyptian culture.

Even before his brothers came to Mitzrayim, Yosef had employed this strategy to protect himself and his immediate family from becoming absorbed into the Egyptian culture. Although he could never be cast as deplorable, as he was, effectively, the ruler of the country, he made an effort to mark himself as different in the eyes of those around him. We can see this from the fact that when the *shevatim* were taken to his home, the *posuk* tells us that Yosef ate apart from the Egyptians, because they found it abominable to eat meat. Now, if the Egyptians found it so offensive, why did Yosef do it at all? And if he really had a hankering for meat, why could he not eat it when they were not around? Rather, I believe that Yosef specifically engaged in eating meat when the Egyptians were present, so that they would think that he was barbaric, and would consciously distance themselves from him. This created a barrier of sorts between his family and the general society. Yosef strove to emulate this model and create a similar barrier between his brothers and Pharaoh and the whole of Egyptian society. [Yet, even though the Egyptians were repulsed by Yosef, this did not cause them to dismiss his authority. Even though diminished respect can, in some cases, be the source of diminished authority over one's subjects, the Egyptians obeyed Yosef's orders. I presume that they found the capacity to allow his rule over them because they convinced

themselves that it was really Yosef who was working for them, and not the other way around.]

Another strategy Yosef planned to employ to combat assimilation was that he arranged for Yaakov and the *shevatim* to live in Goshen. Yosef planned on settling his family in a manner that would allow them to remain apart from the culture of the Egyptians. For this reason, he told his brothers that they would live in the province of Goshen (*Bereishis* 45:10). I understand Goshen to have been a location that was set apart from the main metropolis — a quieter, more suburban area, where Klal Yisrael would be able to minimize their interaction with the society of Mitzrayim. Pharaoh, on the other hand, had a vastly different idea in mind for the family of Yosef. He saw that Yosef himself had been so invaluable and beneficial to Egyptian society thus far; how much greater would the effect of an entire group of people with similar strengths and influences be for Mitzrayim! Thus, Pharaoh bade Yosef to invite his family down to Mitzrayim, and to dwell in the best of the land of Mitzrayim (*Bereishis* 45:18). Pointedly, Pharaoh did not offer Goshen, which we have explained to have been set apart from the general population. Rather, he instructed Yosef to offer them *the best of the land of Mitzrayim*. This refers to the prime real estate, in the heart of Pharaoh's metropolis. In this manner, Pharaoh hoped to assimilate Klal Yisrael into Egyptian culture, and thereby enhance the entire society by way of the many improvements that the Jewish people were bound to introduce.

We see this idea in play in *Bereishis* 45:20 as well. There, Pharaoh instructs Yosef to tell the *shevatim* not to worry about their possessions in Eretz Yisrael, because when they come down to Mitzrayim, everything would be provided for them. While on the surface it seems that Pharaoh is magnanimously offering to provide for all their needs, it was all really part of his vision for the integration of Klal Yisrael into Egyptian society. How so? Because the less that Yaakov and his children arrived with, the more reliant they would be forced to become on the civilization around them. It would be more difficult to live farther apart from the main cities of Mitzrayim if they needed to constantly visit those cities to obtain the supplies they needed. Additionally, they would need to forge relationships with Egyptian merchants and suppliers of goods, which would further expose them to the societal influences of the Egyptians. However, if Klal Yisrael were to bring all of their possessions with them, Pharaoh knew that they would be able to remain that much more apart from the general Egyptian populace.

Both Pharaoh and Yosef danced around the issue of where Yaakov and his sons would be settling, each never revealing his true agenda to the other. That is, I believe, until *Bereishis* 47:6. There, after the *shevatim* requested of Pharaoh that they be allowed to settle in Goshen, and Pharaoh

allowed them, perhaps begrudgingly, to do so, Pharaoh finally made his intentions clear to Yosef. He said, *The land of Mitzrayim is before you — from the best of the land, settle your father and brothers. They shall settle in the land of Goshen, and if you know that they are skilled in their profession, appoint them as shepherds over my flocks.* On the surface, this is an enigmatic *posuk*. Pharaoh orders the *shevatim* settled in Goshen, yet seems to offer the *shevatim* any land they might desire. And, even though Yosef had made it clear that the *shevatim* practiced a profession that was despised by the Egyptians, Pharaoh specifically asked Yosef to appoint them over his own flocks. What was going on here?

I believe that it was here that Pharaoh finally expressed his plan to Yosef, and explained what it was that he wanted to happen. As we explained above, the words *meitav ha'aretz, the best of the land,* which Pharaoh offered, alluded to the metropolis of Pharaoh, where every luxury and pleasure was available on demand for his royal guests. The word *hosheiv, settle*, is in the form of *tzivui, command tense*, and connotes a person giving orders to settle someone. Thus, Pharaoh charged Yosef with settling Klal Yisrael in the main metropolis of Mitzrayim. However, Pharaoh also noted that *yeishvu b'eretz Goshen, they will settle in the land of Goshen. Yeishvu* connotes that they will *choose to settle.*

Pharaoh told Yosef that despite the choice that his family was making to separate from Egyptian civilization, he wanted Yosef to help integrate them, and support his objective to have them take a more central role in Egyptian society. He wanted Yosef to offer them alternate residences in the fanciest neighborhoods of Mitzrayim, where they could vacation whenever they pleased. [Eventually, in the more than a century between their descent to Mitzrayim and their enslavement, these residences became the places from which the Jewish people would operate their businesses, and where they indeed did interact with Egyptian society. Pharaoh had correctly predicted this shift. Later on, during *Makkas Bechoros,* there were Jews whose only residences were among the Egyptians, aside from the main community of Goshen. This is evident from the fact that Hashem had to skip over the houses of the Jewish people during *Makkas Bechoros* — clearly, there were those Jews who were living among the Egyptians at that time.]

In this manner, by offering dual residences to Klal Yisrael, they were effectively being settled among the Egyptians without ever making any choice to do so. Additionally, Pharaoh realized that the profession of the *shevatim* was seen as abominable in Mitzrayim, posing a challenge to his goal of integrating them into the higher tier of Egypt's elite wealthy citizens. He wished to counter this stigma (which Yosef had worked to cultivate). He therefore told Yosef that if they were up to the task, he should appoint his brothers to look after Pharaoh's own sheep. He hoped

this would provide prestige to them in the eyes of Egyptians, despite the actual line of work in which they engaged.

Continuing this theme, I believe that we can understand the *posuk* in *Bereishis* 47:11 to be telling us that Yosef carried out Pharaoh's instructions as he was ordered to do. The *posuk* begins by stating *Vayosheiv Yosef es aviv v'es echav, and Yosef settled his father and his brothers.* Left to our own devices, we would assume this settling to have occurred as per Pharaoh's instructions that *yeishvu b'eretz Goshen, they will settle in the land of Goshen.* However, the *posuk* continues by stating, *vayitein lahem achuzah b'eretz Mitzrayim b'meitav ha'aretz, b'eretz Rameseis ka'asher tzivah Pharaoh, and he gave them estates in the land of Mitzrayim, in the best of the land, in the land of Rameseis, as Pharaoh had commanded.* Can it be that Yosef ignored the right Pharaoh had given his brothers to dwell in Goshen? Firstly, he would never have given up Goshen, seeing as it was a defense for Klal Yisrael against assimilation. And secondly, we know that the Jewish people did settle in Goshen! (see *Shemos* 8:18).

Rather, I believe that the answer is that the first part of the *posuk,* which states that Yosef settled his brothers, is alluding to the fact that Yosef indeed did settle them in Goshen, where he had planned to settle them the entire time. The next phrase of the *posuk,* which discusses the fact that Yosef gave the *shevatim* land in the preeminent locales of Mitzrayim, was, as the end of the *posuk* states, to fulfill the order that Pharaoh had issued. This is why the *posuk* ends with the words *as Pharaoh had commanded him.* Yosef wanted the *shevatim* to have no exposure to the estates he was gifting them — he thus gave them those estates only because he was required to fulfill Pharaoh's command.

Now, we noted above in the context of *Bereishis* 47:6 that the word *hosheiv, settle,* carries a connotation of being commanded to do so against the will of the subject. We explained that Pharaoh directed Yosef to concede to the wishes of the *shevatim* to live in Goshen, but to force them to be exposed to the pleasures [and evils] of Mitzrayim's society by giving them additional estates. Here, the similar word *vayosheiv, and he settled,* is used in the context of settling Goshen. Why was settling Goshen something Yosef needed to *command* his brothers to do? Was this not their preference?

Perhaps we can suggest that Yosef indeed had to settle his brothers in Goshen "against their will." He warned them that they were not to take advantage of the vacation homes and estates they were being gifted by Pharaoh — even occasionally — lest they suffer spiritually. This might have been against their will, because even though they were aware of the dangers of assimilating into Mitzrayim's culture, they might have thought minimal exposure at these estates would not affect them at all. Yosef

cautioned them that even a limited exposure would eventually grow into a great influence, and would lead to potential assimilation. We do not know precisely how long they heeded his warning, but eventually, perhaps even after the passing of the *shevatim,* Klal Yisrael began to take advantage of their vacation homes. From that point, it was only a matter of time until Pharaoh's vision of assimilating the Jewish people into Egyptian society turned into a reality.

Yaakov Avinu might have been unique in that Hashem told him that his plans were changing by way of a prophetic dream. But in no way was he unique in that his journey did not end up going the way he planned it. This happens to so many people, for so many various reasons. Many times, people travel somewhere intending to stay for a short time, but something happens — good or otherwise — that makes them stay long-term. Other times people may have intended to stay until a certain goal is reached, and they keep extending their stay in the hopes that their goals will finally be realized. Other times, people are not intent on relocating to a place at all, but their journey takes them there, and they end up staying. Yaakov Avinu went to Mitzrayim only until the famine would end. Nevertheless, Hashem decreed that he would be staying there permanently.

The relationship between people's plans and what they actually do is thus somewhat involved, for the reality of people's lives does not always reflect the plans they have. The *Rosh HaYeshiva, ztvk"l,* has an interesting *psak* regarding the following situation. Suppose a couple resides in Eretz Yisrael, and their support, which has thus far come from their parents in America, is expiring. This couple does not know where they will put down their roots and build their family. If the man is offered a job in America, he would take it, but if he was offered a job in Eretz Yisrael, he would take that job. If they visit America for Yom Tov, they adopt the custom of the place they are in, and keep two days of Yom Tov. Conversely, if they stay in Eretz Yisrael for Yom Tov, they keep only one day. Why? Because they cannot be considered people from Eretz Yisrael, nor can they be considered people from *chutz la'aretz.* These are people without a permanent locale, and thus follow the custom of wherever it is that they find themselves. If, however, the couple planned to keep living in Eretz Yisrael (like Yaakov did before he had the dream in Be'er Sheva), they would keep only one day of Yom Tov even in America, and vice-versa. This would be true even if they were delayed for some time in America; since at the end of the day, they intend to return and live in Eretz Yisrael, they keep one day in America. Should it happen that they make a decision that they would stay in America if a job comes up, and certainly if they decided to remain in America (as Yaakov was told he would be doing in Mitzrayim), they would then begin to keep two days of Yom Tov.

בִּמְתֵי מְעָט. כְּמָה שֶׁנֶּאֱמַר, בְּשִׁבְעִים נֶפֶשׁ יָרְדוּ אֲבֹתֶיךָ מִצְרָיְמָה, וְעַתָּה שָׂמְךָ יהוה אֱלֹהֶיךָ כְּכוֹכְבֵי הַשָּׁמַיִם לָרֹב.[1]

בְּשִׁבְעִים נֶפֶשׁ יָרְדוּ אֲבוֹתֶיךָ מִצְרָיְמָה — ***With Seventy Souls Your Forefathers Descended to Mitzrayim***

- **The *Haggadah* mentions that seventy people came down to Mitzrayim, mirroring the number the Torah gives in *Parashas Vayigash.* Famously, only sixty-nine names are presented there. The way *Rashi* presents the question is that the Torah lists thirty-two descendants of Leah, and yet states that there were thirty-three. He does not ask that the tally of sixty-six descendants of Yaakov's wives and Yosef, Menasheh, and Ephraim, does not equal seventy. But, the way *Rashi* asks the question makes it apparent that the missing person is descended from Leah.**
- ***Rashi* is showing us that if we have a choice between asking a question in a very understandable manner which will make the answer harder to accept, or to ask the question in a less apparent way, but the answer will be more readily accepted, the latter approach is preferred.**
- **This is in keeping with the requirement to use *shemen zayis zach* for the Menorah. The Menorah represents Torah, and it must be transmitted without any *shemarim*, sediment — in as clear a manner as possible.**

In *Parashas Vayigash,* the Torah lists the people who went down to Mitzrayim. Famously, there are only sixty-nine people listed there, divided into four groups — those descended from Leah, Rochel, Bilhah, and Zilpah. The Torah first lists the descendants of Leah, and then records that the sum total of her descendants was thirty-three people. *Rashi* (to *Bereishis* 46:15, *d"h shloshim v'shalosh*) writes that if one counts the descendants of Leah that are listed there, the number of names listed is actually not thirty-three, but rather thirty-two. He explains that Yocheved was born as Yaakov and his family entered Mitzrayim, and it is she who is the thirty-third of Leah's descendants.

Now, if I were choosing a place to highlight the discrepancy in the Torah's counting, I think I would have chosen another place to do so. Why? Because in 45:8-15, in order to be bothered by *Rashi's* question, one would have to count all the names that appear on that part of the list, compare that total to the number that the Torah gives, and realize that there is a discrepancy of one. However, in 45:26-27, I think the discrepancy is much more glaringly obvious. Let me explain:

Few in number — As it is stated: "With seventy souls your forefathers descended to Mitzrayim; and now, HASHEM, your God, has made you as numerous as the stars of the heavens."[1]

(1) *Devarim* 10:22.

There are really two counts that appear in the passage. In the first count, recorded in *pesukim* 8-25, the Torah records thirty-two descendants from Leah but gives the number thirty-three. The Torah then records sixteen descendants from Zilpah, fourteen from Rochel (including Yosef and his children), and seven descendants from Bilhah. If we total these together, we of course will get seventy (33+16+14+7=70). Thus, the only way for us to realize that the number is off, then, is to actually count the names and realize that only sixty-nine names have been listed.

The second counting is recorded in 45:26-27. 45:26 states that the total number of Yaakov's descendants who went down with him to Mitzrayim was sixty-six. [Clearly, this reflects the number of actual names that have been listed above for all of the families (except Yosef's), and not the totals given for each of Yaakov's wives' descendants enumerated in the previous *pesukim*. That is, thirty-two from Leah, sixteen from Zilpah, eleven from Rochel, and seven from Bilhah totals sixty-six.] 45:27 then adds that Yosef and his two sons were already in Mitzrayim, for a total of seventy. Anyone can see, without counting any names, that sixty-six and three does not equal seventy! Here, I would have thought, would be the place to ask that we seem to be missing one of the seventy people, and to answer that Yocheved was born between the walls of Mitzrayim (in other words, there were actually thirty-three descendants from Leah). So why does *Rashi* ask the question earlier?

I assume that *Rashi* specifically asked the question where he did, in the context of the first counting, because by doing so, he draws the focus to the children of Leah. If the question had been asked later, although the question would have been more obvious, it would not be immediately clear that the missing person of the seventy was a descendant of Leah. Why not? Because the count of sixty-six plus three correctly reflects the amount of names the Torah has listed. It is the seventieth person who is unaccounted for — and that person might be descended from any one of Yaakov's wives. Now, however, that *Rashi* zeroed in on the less obvious discrepancy in the first counting — namely, that the Torah says that there were thirty-three descendants of Leah while listing only thirty-two names — it is obvious that the missing person must have been from the descendants of Leah.

Even though this lesson does not seem germane to *Yetzias Mitzrayim,* it is very important when it comes to *chinuch* — and Pesach night is

all about *chinuch. Rashi* is demonstrating a concept here that applies to teaching in general. That is, that if a Rebbi has a choice between explaining a question in a very clear manner, but thereby making the answer harder for his *talmidim* to understand, or else presenting the question in a less obvious manner, but in this way, the answer he will present will be more palatable to the students, the second option is the preferred one.

Moreover, *Rashi* armed the reader with the answer to the question in his comment to 45:15 before the reader will likely even be bothered by it (as he will probably not count the names). It will only be when the reader reaches 45:27, when the totals do not add up, that the discrepancy will bother him. In this way, *Rashi* has preempted the question the student may have, supplying the answer. Now, when the student reaches 45:27, he will already know that the answer to his question is that Yocheved was born on the way down to Mitzrayim, and she completes the count of 70. Had *Rashi* not presented the information in this matter, the potential might have existed for a student to be so bothered by the question he would face in 45:27 that he might have more trouble accepting the answer. [Of course, *Chazal's* answer to this question is accurate. We are only discussing the most optimal way to pass on the teachings of *Chazal* in a way that they will be accepted.] When we teach our children, one of our goals needs to be to teach them in the way that is most effective at assisting them to be able to understand and accept what it is we are teaching them.

This is a lesson that we can also learn from the requirement that the oil for the Menorah needed to be *shemen zayis zach*. The *Rosh HaYeshiva, ztvk"l,* explained that the reason why the *mitzvah* to use *shemen zayis zach* for the Menorah is written in the beginning of *Parashas Tetzaveh*, before any mention of the *Kehunah* or the *begadim* of the *Kohanim,* is because *shemen zayis zach* is representative of the need for the absolutely pure transmission of the Torah. After the *Mishkan* was built, and we had a place for *Hashraas HaShechinah,* Moshe Rabbeinu turned his attention to the Torah, and came and asked Hashem to tell him who would be the one to shoulder the responsibility of teaching the Torah to Klal Yisrael. Hashem told him it was going to be Aharon who would make sure that the Torah had an everlasting place among the people. This would have been so even if Aharon and his children never became *Kohanim* serving in the *Mishkan*. The main purpose, then, of Aharon's becoming the *Kohen Gadol* was to teach the Torah to Klal Yisrael; his *avodah* in the *Mishkan* was only secondary to that mission. Accordingly, the Torah mentions the *mitzvah* of pure olive oil even before Aharon and his children were sanctified as the *Kohanim* of Hashem. But we must understand: What is the connection between *shemen zayis zach* and teaching Torah to Klal Yisrael?

The idea of *shemen zayis zach* when it comes to learning Torah is that just as there must be no *shemarim* (sediment) at all in the oil, so too in the

teaching of Torah, there must be no cloudiness at all. Torah must always be crystal clear; when it is taught, Torah needs to be clear to the point that there are no doubts or questions. But what does this mean? Surely there are always questions. What it means is that a Rebbi must never create a lasting doubt; never build up a question so much that the answer does not satisfy the listener quite enough, which will result in the *talmid* walking away with *"shemarim"* in his mind, not fully grasping the truth. The Rebbi who does this creates a *safek* in the *talmid's* mind, and the student will never be able to fully appreciate the Torah.

Now, what should a Rebbi do if he comes across a question that seems better than its answer? If the Rebbi truly believes that his answer is correct, then he should present it in a way that does not emphasize the question. For example, the Rebbi can bring up his novel approach indirectly. He can first raise a different problem, and answer that other question with his novel approach. Once he has introduced the novelty, and demonstrated to his *talmidim* that it has value and answers a question, he can then say, "And by the way, according to this novel approach, a certain question that I had might also be answered," and only then bring up his difficult question. Bringing the answer to light first, and making it concrete in the minds of the *talmidim* as an answer that addresses something else, will make it easier to teach it to them as the answer to a more difficult question as well.

וְעַתָּה שָׂמְךָ ה׳ אֱלֹהֶיךָ כְּכוֹכְבֵי הַשָּׁמַיִם לָרֹב — *And Now, Hashem, Your God, Has Made You as Numerous as the Stars of the Heavens*

❒ **The *Haggadah* cites Moshe Rabbeinu's contrast of the number of Jews who descended to Mitzrayim — seventy — with their multitudes when they departed. However, the *posuk* does not mean that Klal Yisrael were similar in number to the stars at *Yetzias Mitzrayim,* for we know that they were "only" six hundred thousand men, or approximately three million people in number, at that time.**

❒ **In *Parashas Devarim,* Moshe gave Klal Yisrael a blessing that they would increase a thousandfold, to approximately three billion, and that eventually, Hashem would fulfill His blessing that they would be as numerous as the stars. And according to the simple meaning of the Gemara, they eventually reached these astronomical numbers.**

❒ **Thus, the plain meaning of the phrase, *you are as numerous as the stars of the heavens,* cannot possibly be that Klal Yisrael had such explosive numbers, because when Moshe uttered the *posuk,* their population was not so great. But, it is possible that when this part of the *Haggadah* was composed, during the era of the second *Beis***

HaMikdash, Klal Yisrael's numbers had exploded to the point that this comparison could actually be made.

- ❐ Alternatively, perhaps the reference that the *Haggadah* is making here is that in Mitzrayim, prior to the *makkah* of *Choshech,* Klal Yisrael had reached the astronomically high number that Moshe, in this *posuk,* blessed them to reach again in the future.

The *Haggadah* seeks to contrast the state of Klal Yisrael at its inception, when they were a small family, with their state later in their history. The *Haggadah* therefore cites a *posuk* in *Parashas Eikev,* where Moshe Rabbeinu made this very contrast; explicitly mentioning that upon its descent to Mitzrayim, the nation contained a mere seventy people, and a few hundred years later, they were a very numerous people. It cannot be said, however, that the nation was so expansive as to be compared to the stars of the sky at the time Moshe Rabbeinu uttered this *posuk.*

In *Parashas Devarim* (*Devarim* 1:10), Moshe says, *Hashem, your God, has multiplied you, and you are today as numerous as the stars of the heavens.* See *Rashi, d"h vehinchem,* who notes that at the time Moshe made this declaration, Klal Yisrael numbered approximately six hundred thousand men; nowhere close to the number of stars in the sky. He therefore explains the *posuk* as follows; *Hashem, your God, has multiplied you, and you are* compared to *the day*; that is, the sun, moon, and *stars,* which will last forever. And, as the commentaries explain, he understood that the word *larov* means that, in addition, there will come a time in the future that you will be *as numerous* as the stars. Accordingly, it would seem that this *posuk* in *Parashas Eikev* should be similarly understood; at the time of Moshe Rabbeinu's utterance, Klal Yisrael were compared to stars in that they are eternal; but their time of being incredibly numerous had not yet arrived.

I would humbly add that the *Haggadah* was (at least partially) composed during the Second *Beis HaMikdash* era. Although certainly, in Moshe Rabbeinu's time, Klal Yisrael's numbers could not have been compared to the number of stars, in the time of the *Haggadah's* composition, it is possible that they could have been.

The Gemara (*Gittin* 57a) gives astronomical numbers for the population of Klal Yisrael at or near the time of the *Churban.* It speaks of a place called Har HaMelech, where there were six hundred thousand cities, each containing a number of people equal to those who left Mitzrayim. Even if we conservatively estimate that number at six hundred thousand per city (i.e., the number of men between the ages of twenty and sixty), the totals for that locale would be approximately three hundred and sixty billion people. Just to provide a frame of reference, the world population now is approximately eight billion — one forty-fifth of the number given for the population of that one area! Certain historians also place the total numbers of Jewish people in that era as greater than any other nation.

If we are to understand the Gemara at face value, it is possible to suggest that the *posuk* was cited as a reflection of the reality of Klal Yisrael's explosive growth in that era. Although even those numbers are, perhaps, not literally the same as the amount of stars in the heavens, it is certainly appropriate to compare the incredibly large population of that time to the number of stars.

In *Devarim* 1:11, immediately following Moshe Rabbeinu's statement that Klal Yisrael would one day be as numerous as the stars, he said, *May Hashem, the God of your forefathers, add to you a thousand times yourselves, and bless you as He has spoken of you.* Moshe Rabbeinu seems to mention two distinct blessings here. First, he expresses to Klal Yisrael the wish that they will increase a thousand-fold, and afterward, he blesses them that they should merit to increase to the number that Hashem had promised they would. *Rashi* (*d"h yoseif aleichem*), citing *Sifri,* notes this inconsistency, and explains the *posuk* as follows: Moshe Rabbeinu offered a blessing that Klal Yisrael would increase in size by one thousand times. When Klal Yisrael heard that, they objected. They said to Moshe, "Are you putting a limit on the blessing we can receive? Hashem has already blessed us that we will be much more numerous than that!" This was based on the fact that Hashem had already told Avraham Avinu (*Bereishis* 13:16) that his children would be as numerous as the dust of the earth, which the Torah itself refers to as uncountable! [Similarly, in the previous *posuk,* Moshe recalled Hashem's blessing that Klal Yisrael would one day reach a number comparable to the stars.] Moshe explained to the nation that the blessing that they multiply by a factor of one thousand was his own; and then he blessed them that they should indeed also merit that Hashem do for them as He had told Avraham Avinu that He would.

This *Rashi* needs to be explained. Why did Moshe give Klal Yisrael a different blessing than Hashem? And if Moshe wanted to give his own blessing, why did he choose to bless Klal Yisrael that they multiply by only a thousandfold? We can begin to explain by examining Moshe's expression, when he said, "This is my own." What about Moshe's blessing was "his own"? We must realize that often, when we are confronted with a large group, we do not correctly assess its true size. If we see a large group of people, a school of fish, or a flock of birds, we tend to estimate their numbers, often wildly inaccurately. [The same can be true of someone's wealth. I was once told by a wealthy man that because people do not really understand the potential of a dollar, his wealth is often grossly overestimated. He explained that while people think he has a hundred million dollars, in reality, he only had ten million. But because all he needs to run his business is ten million dollars, his net worth was constantly being inflated by those who would discuss it.] These examples demonstrate that we are often not conditioned to properly understand massive

numbers for what they actually are, and so we paint ourselves a picture in our imaginations of what the number probably represents. At the time of *Yetzias Mitzrayim,* the population of Klal Yisrael stood at approximately six hundred thousand men. Adding the women, children, and elders, the nation could easily have comprised a total of three million people. A thousand times that number is three billion. Three billion! We barely have a grasp of the concept of that number. We certainly do not have a handle on what it would mean when applied to the nation of Klal Yisrael. The sheer number of *Yeshivos, Kollelim, batei din, shochtim, mohalim* — and the list goes on and on and on — that would be required to support such a populous nation is certainly beyond our perception. But it was not beyond Moshe Rabbeinu's perception. A blessing is not a joke. When Moshe blessed Klal Yisrael, he truly had in mind, without any exaggerations, that every single facet of his blessing would come to fruition. Who can imagine seriously blessing such a large group to increase even twofold? Moshe had the mental capacity to bless Klal Yisrael that they would increase a thousandfold, and was able to do so without any hyperbole. Thus, this was uniquely Moshe Rabbeinu's blessing, for it reflected precisely the expanse of blessing that his great mind could encapsulate. The reason he did not bless the nation with an even greater blessing was because even Moshe Rabbeinu's own understanding had a limit. To offer a blessing beyond his own comprehension would have been to exaggerate, and to have his words not reflect his thoughts accurately.

When Klal Yisrael heard Moshe Rabbeinu "limit" their potential blessing, they were perturbed. But Moshe reassured them that his blessing was only a reflection of his own understanding, and an expression that his understanding would come to fruition. However, the blessing that had been issued to Avraham Avinu, which was that Klal Yisrael expand without quantifiable limits, remained unaffected. Why did Moshe see fit to offer his own blessing, seeing as it was already completely included in the blessing that Hashem issued to Avraham Avinu? The answer is that Moshe believed that the blessing of Hashem was going to come to fruition at some point. However, when it would happen was unknown. Moshe thus offered his own blessing — in as expansive a manner as he was able to — in order to quickly bring to fruition at least the part of Klal Yisrael's expansion that he could understand. More than that was beyond Moshe Rabbeinu's ability to comprehend, and therefore he did not include it in his blessing. But when Klal Yisrael objected, Moshe reassured them that his blessing was not limiting Hashem's blessing at all. It was only helping it along, as much as Moshe was able, so that Klal Yisrael might reap a portion of the blessing

And he became there a nation — This teaches us that [Klal] Yisrael excelled there.

---

that Hashem had issued to Avraham Avinu sooner, rather than later.

It emerges, then, that Klal Yisrael, who originally stood at only seventy people, left Mitzrayim with three million people. They received a blessing from Moshe that they would grow to three billion, which was only a stepping-stone to their eventual population, where three billion people was *less than one percent* of the Jewish people who lived in *one region*!

Of course, there are many who explain the Gemara in *Gittin* as an obvious exaggeration. According to those commentaries, we might explain the *Haggadah's* reference to the astronomical number of Jewish people in the following way: As we explained, the intent of Moshe Rabbeinu when he uttered this declaration in *Parashas Eikev* was to point out that Klal Yisrael are eternal like the stars, and that in the future — according to this approach, a future that is yet to come — they would also be similar in number to the stars. But, the *Haggadah* is citing this *posuk* in explanation of the phrase *bimsei me'at* of the *posuk* describing the descent to Mitzrayim. In that context, the *Haggadah* tells us that during the two hundred and ten years from when they arrived in Mitzrayim until just before the *makkah* of *Choshech,* their numbers had indeed exploded astronomically. We know that during the *makkah* of *Choshech,* Klal Yisrael's numbers were severely reduced. *Rashi* (*Shemos* 13:18, *d"h vachamushim*) explains the phrase *vachamushim alu Bnei Yisrael* to mean that only a fifth of the nation departed from Mitzrayim, while the rest perished during the *makkah* of *Choshech,* for they did not want to leave Mitzrayim. There are Midrashim (see *Mechilta* to *Parashas Beshalach, d"h vachamushim* with *Biur HaGra* there) that place the percentage of Jewish people who left Mitzrayim not at twenty percent, but either at two percent, or at .2 percent, or at .02 percent. According to this final opinion, only one out of every 5,000 Jews left Mitzrayim — and three million multiplied by five thousand equals fifteen billion. If indeed Klal Yisrael in Mitzrayim were so incredibly numerous, the *Haggadah* might be borrowing the *posuk* that describes this number *at some time in the future,* just to show us that, in fact, when Klal Yisrael suffered in Mitzrayim *in the past,* they were similar in number to what is described in the *posuk.*

מְלַמֵּד שֶׁהָיוּ יִשְׂרָאֵל מְצֻיָּנִים שָׁם — *This Teaches Us That [Klal] Yisrael Excelled There*

❒ **Klal Yisrael excelled in commerce, and they grew in strength and importance in Mitzrayim. But they were also abandoning their fidelity to the *mesorah.***

- **Yaakov Avinu and Yosef had done a lot to attempt to stave off assimilation. But the attraction of economic opportunity that the Jewish people experienced exposed them to the glamour of Egyptian society, and assimilation began on a large scale.**
- **Ultimately, many of those who assimilated never wanted to leave Mitzrayim, and perished during the *makkah* of *Choshech.***
- **As the Jewish people became wealthier and more influenced by Egyptian society, the Egyptians hated them, were jealous of them, resented them, and were fearful of them, more and more.**

The *Haggadah* sees in the words, *And he became there a nation, great, mighty,* that Klal Yisrael developed in more than just numbers. Their economic strength grew, and thus, their importance on a national scale grew as well. They had become not merely an immigrant minority, but a bona-fide nation. The narrative of the *Haggadah* continues, telling us that the Egyptians perceived the Jewish people as a threat, which led to our enslavement. But, there was another, *extremely* significant development that was occurring along with the growth and prosperity Klal Yisrael was experiencing — and that was that most of Klal Yisrael were falling away from the *mesorah.* Ultimately, most of Klal Yisrael, by any accounting, did not leave Mitzrayim. Let us explore this further.

Yaakov and Yosef tried their hardest to make Mitzrayim a place where Klal Yisrael could flourish in exile. With this goal in mind, Yaakov had sent Yehudah to establish a Yeshiva ahead of his own arrival. *Rashi* (*Bereishis* 46:28, *d"h lefanav*) cites the Midrash that Yehudah was charged with instituting a *beis talmud*, from which halachic decisions would emanate. This effort was valiant, but it was really a case of help being too little and too late. With different planning, perhaps Yosef could have set aside a magnificent campus for Torah, with all the trappings that the Yeshiva was going to need to serve as a base for Klal Yisrael through the exile of Mitzrayim. But, a combination of the fact that Yosef did not realize that he needed to do this, coupled with the fact that they had no idea how long they were going to be in Mitzrayim, led to this ideal not being realized. Yehudah could only do so much in his short time of preparation, and the Yeshiva ultimately was not enough to save the (at least) four-fifths of Klal Yisrael who did not leave Mitzrayim. [It seems to me that if Yosef had remembered his dreams during the *entire time he was ruler*, rather than just the last couple of years, and realized that it was only a matter of time until Klal Yisrael was going to join him in Mitzrayim, he could have been the one to establish a Yeshiva properly. Over nine years, he could have arranged for the Yeshiva to function optimally, and perhaps by the time of the Exodus from Mitzrayim, Klal Yisrael would have been on a higher level. This would presumably also have resulted in less Jewish people

perishing during the *makkah* of *Choshech,* and would have then been the ultimate interpretation of Yosef's dreams. See *Nahar Sholom, Bereishis,* 46:28, for further discussion of this point.]

Yosef, for his part, was actively preparing Mitzrayim to be a place where the Jewish people would be welcome and comfortable, and would have the best chance to flourish spiritually. [See above, *Lagur BaAretz,* where we explained that Yosef actively distanced himself socially from the Egyptians by eating meat, which they found objectionable. That also was done to further his ultimate goal of halting the progression of assimilation.]

As part of this effort, Yosef also arranged for all the Egyptians to relocate. The *posuk* (*Shemos* 47:21) tells us that Yosef had the entire population of Mitzrayim move to new cities. What did this accomplish? *Rashi* (*d"h v'es ha'am he'evir*) explains that Yosef did this so that all of the Egyptians would remember that they did not own their own land. *Rashi* further comments that Yosef had another motive here as well. He wanted to make the *shevatim* more comfortable in Mitzrayim by removing from them the stigma of being *golim, exiles.* Now that the entire population was exiled from their former homes, they were *all* new to their locales, and would feel just as out of place as would the *shevatim.*

I would like to add some insight into these rationales. Perhaps it is possible to understand the comment of *Rashi* as one long explanation; that is, Yosef desired that the Egyptians remember that they did not own the land specifically in order that they not look down at the *shevatim* and refer to them as exiles. However, it seems to me that *Rashi* really intends to make two distinct, but related, points.

One of the factors that can lead to a rebellion against a ruler is when his subjects feel a sense of entitlement — deserved or otherwise — and feel that they are being taken advantage of. One of the circumstances that can lead to this feeling is when people are in a situation where they feel that everything is being taken from them. For example, if a farmer is obligated to part with a large percentage of his crops as a tax every year, he will invariably entertain the thought that the government is taking what is rightfully his. Even if he pays the tax, he will resent those who are taxing him. As this sentiment spreads to farmer after farmer, a large segment of the populace will eventually be only one good inciter away from a revolt. The root of this entitlement is the feeling that one's homestead is his own. It is from that perspective that the farmer looks outward, and calculates in his mind whether the government is doing as much for him as he does for it.

In my humble opinion, Yosef sought to nip this attitude in the bud. Now that the entire country and all of its citizens were the actual property of Pharaoh, Yosef foresaw a situation where the people might tire of this arrangement, especially after the famine would pass. So, he decided to

move everyone around. By doing so, he arranged that everybody would realize that they were living on an estate belonging to Pharaoh, which was essentially being rented to the citizens in exchange for a twenty percent tax on crops. This made it crystal clear that each citizen was only a guest on Pharaoh's land. It did not allow for the Egyptians to cultivate the sense of entitlement that we described above, and in this way, ensured that the people would continue to be subservient to Pharaoh. [It is perhaps this very logic that Sancheirev employed, although he did it on a far larger scale, when he moved the entire populations of the nations he conquered to new countries and settled them there.]

This brings us to the discussion of the second part of Yosef's idea. As *Rashi* continues, Yosef had in mind to make the *shevatim* more comfortable, by arranging matters so that no one would refer to them as exiles. This concept also is more profound than it sounds. Let us explain: During the Second World War, the Nazis, *ysh"v*, were not the only enemies of the Jewish people. It is well known that the Polish people were virulent Jew-haters. One of the factors that fueled the enmity of the Poles against Polish Jewry was the economic success enjoyed by many Jewish people in Poland. Certainly, a part of this hatred can be attributed to simple jealousy. However, the Polish peasants were not nearly as jealous of their fellow Poles who were wealthy. So, what was special about Jewish success which caused it to be so reviled by the Polish?

A large part of the answer is that the Poles, peasants though they were, possessed a nationalistic pride. In identifying with their country, the peasants adopted as their own (in their own minds) all the wealth and opportunity that Polish society had to offer. So, despite the fact that these boors had not a motivated bone in their bodies, and despite the fact that they drank away their lives, they identified with the success of other Poles. But, when the "outsider" — the Jew — became successful, the Poles felt as though this success had been usurped from Poland itself, and was happening for the Jewish people "on the back of all good Poles." The fact that the Jewish people had made an honest living and worked hard for what they got was totally beside the point. All the riches in Poland should belong to Poles, these peasants reasoned, and if the Jewish people had wealth, it was rightfully really theirs.

This would be the feeling of the citizens of a country who looked upon Klal Yisrael as foreigners. Yosef, therefore, sought to prevent the Egyptians from ever developing this attitude in the first place. Although he kept them all in Mitzrayim, Yosef accomplished this by moving them from their homes to other cities. How so? By keeping the people on rented estates, they would be constantly reminded that they did not own land in Mitzrayim at all, and that they were merely government property. This would keep them from adopting an identity as citizens of Mitzrayim. And if they would

not identify with Mitzrayim, they, in turn, would not resent the successes of Klal Yisrael.

Another factor that contributed to Klal Yisrael's success in Mitzrayim was the desperate plight of the Egyptians when Yaakov and his sons arrived in Mitzrayim, after only two years of famine. There is an interesting sequence of *pesukim* toward the end of *Parashas Vayigash*. In 47:13, the Torah mentions that both the lands of Canaan and Mitzrayim wearied on account of the hunger. 47:14 continues with this thought, explaining that Yosef, in selling food to these populations, collected all of their money, and brought it all to Pharaoh. 47:15 begins the same way; *And the money was all spent in the land of Mitzrayim, and in the land of Canaan*. However, mid-*posuk*, the Torah suddenly stops discussing Canaan altogether, turning instead to focus on the effect that the continuing hunger had upon the inhabitants of Mitzrayim alone, stating: *all the Egyptians came to Yosef and said, Give us bread; for why should we die in your presence? For the money is gone*. Why does the Torah only discuss what the Egyptians were experiencing after having focused on both the economies of Canaan and Mitzrayim for the last few *pesukim*?

One answer is that the *pesukim* that appear in this entire passage are meant to help us gain an understanding of the circumstances facing Klal Yisrael at the beginning of the exile. Part of this equation was the downfall of the common Egyptian citizen, and part of it was the great success the Jewish people were having there — the great opportunities that awaited them, of which they took full advantage. Once Yaakov had departed from Canaan, what was occurring there was inconsequential to the narrative, and so the Torah stops discussing it. Yes, perhaps they too were offering Yosef their very lives in exchange for food, but our narrative continues in Mitzrayim. In order to bring this point to the forefront, the Torah first expresses the utter poverty that the Egyptians were experiencing. In 47:17, we learn that they were trading their livestock for rations, and in 47:19, when the famine was already close to ending on account of Yaakov Avinu's arrival in Mitzrayim (see *Rashi* there, *d"h v'sen zera*), they offered their lands and their bodies to Pharaoh in exchange for food to stay alive. The desperate picture is presented to us so that we can understand the circumstances that existed at the time when Klal Yisrael arrived in Mitzrayim. [For another understanding, see *Nahar Sholom, Berishis* 47:15.]

Accordingly, when the Jewish people arrived, they found a country of people who were working for their king, on lands they did not own. The passion for the Egyptians to enrich themselves was gone; they were clinging to survival, and capitalism was far from their minds. This environment was ripe for the arrival of the Jewish people; a people who still owned their own assets, and, moreover, who were one of only two groups in the country who were not slaves to Pharaoh (the other being Pharaoh's priests).

While Yosef was successful in keeping his brothers away from Mitzrayim, and settling them in Goshen, the next generations were not able to withstand the temptation to swim in this capitalistic ocean of opportunity. Whether it was retail, services, or banking, the Jewish people began to take advantage of the fact that Mitzrayim was existing without a middle class by filling the gap themselves. Before long, they had amassed significant wealth.

It is noteworthy that a similar, although not identical, phenomenon followed the Jewish people throughout our centuries in Europe. Whenever the Jewish people would enter a new land — having been virtually always expelled, often penniless, from their previous country — they would search for jobs to fill. In the Middle Ages, when feudalism ruled, a Jew was prohibited from owning land, so farming was generally not an option. Jewish people were thus left with no other societal role than to assume middle-class duties such as retail and banking. These positions led them to be a natural buffer between peasants and lords, which often got them into significant trouble with one side or the other. [Similarly, when Hitler, *ysh"v,* was in talks with the Japanese, the Japanese at one point were intent on bringing Jewish people into their society, to serve as a middle class between the samurai class and the peasants.]

The "perfect storm" of the Jewish people arriving at a time when the Egyptians were so downtrodden led to incredible economic success, as the *Haggadah* tells us here. In our long and bitter exiles, there has not been a time when Klal Yisrael enjoyed such great economic success since our exile to Mitzrayim — until our current exile in the *medinah shel chessed, country of kindness*, the United States. Why? Because the United States of America, similar to Yosef's Mitzrayim, is itself a country of immigrants. It is only the native Americans who retain any semblance of an ancestral claim to the land, and such claims are largely adjudicated by the Tribal Reservations and the U.S. Government; the average citizen has nothing to do with those claims. The actual citizens of the USA are, for the most part, children, grandchildren, great-grandchildren, and great-great-grandchildren of immigrants. Thus, everyone has the same nationalistic pride as everyone else, and when a Jew employs honest means and is successful, it does not feel to the "host population" as though the success in being stolen from them. [This is not to say that there is no anti-Semitism in America, nor that Jewish success is not met with jealousy. I am only explaining that one very significant contributor to such anti-Semitism is not present, for the most part, in our society. Certainly, though, anti-Semitism is nevertheless widespread, and a Jew must always act in a manner that will not incite his or her non-Jewish acquaintances or neighbors to resent Jewish people.]

But there were some other consequences of this success as well.

Because his plan was so successful, Yosef inadvertently caused the conditions of the Jewish people in Mitzrayim to become harsher sooner than they might otherwise have. For, as we know, Avraham Avinu was promised that his descendants would be subject to an exile of four hundred years. The *posuk* (*Bereishis* 15:13) states, *your children shall be strangers in a land that is not theirs, and they shall serve them and they shall oppress them for four hundred years.* From here we see that the exile was going to contain three stages: living in foreign land, servitude, and oppression. Each of these stages was harsher than the previous stage, but there was no amount of time specified for any specific stage of exile. From the time of Yitzchak's birth until the *shevatim* arrived in Mitzrayim, Klal Yisrael had always lived as people who were in foreign lands. But, not only was it necessary for Klal Yisrael to physically live in land that was not their own in order to fulfill this stage of their exile (see above, *Bris Bein HaBesarim*), they also had to *live* as people who were not in their own land. When Yosef made everyone in Mitzrayim feel as though they were living in a foreign land, he essentially created an environment similar to the one we have here in America — an environment where everybody felt equal, and where nobody felt less at home than anyone else. This resulted in Klal Yisrael also feeling more at home. After a while, they were no longer living as people who were in a foreign land, and as such, the next stage of the exile — the stage of servitude — had to begin.

Additionally, because Klal Yisrael was enjoying such unbelievable wealth and freedom in Mitzrayim, there was another catastrophic consequence of their success; the nation began to lose its connection with the *mesorah*. The *posuk* (*Bereishis* 47:27) states, *And [Bnei] Yisrael lived in the land of Mitzrayim, in the land of Goshen; and they grabbed hold of it, and were fruitful, and multiplied exceedingly.* This is the last *posuk* in *Parashas Vayigash*. Now, *Rashi* (*d"h vayeishev Yisrael*) explains that the *posuk* means to identify the location of Goshen. So, the *posuk* is to be understood as follows; *And [Klal] Yisrael settled in the land of Goshen.* Where was that? *In the land of Mitzrayim.* However, based upon several inferences that we have discussed (see above, *Lagur Sham*), I would like to humbly offer a different approach to understanding this *posuk*. As we noted there, it was Yosef's intention that Klal Yisrael settle exclusively in Goshen, while Pharaoh wanted them to settle in the main metropolis of Mitzrayim, so that they might intermingle with the Egyptians, become exposed to their culture, and become part of their society. When Pharaoh realized that the *shevatim* had chosen to live in Goshen, he ordered Yosef to give them alternate residences in Mitzrayim proper, so that they might assimilate into the Egyptian culture during their visits to these estates.

Here, we are taught that although Yosef had won the battle, Pharaoh had won the war. The Jewish people settled in the land of Mitzrayim, as

Pharaoh had hoped. And yes, they were situated in the land of Goshen also, but the damage was done. As the *posuk* continues; *vayei'achazu bah, and they grabbed hold of it.*

Klal Yisrael, in the absence of the check upon assimilation that rabid antisemitism born of nationalistic pride provides, simply took over the land. Economically speaking, the Jewish people were tremendously successful in Mitzrayim, and this only furthered their comfort there. In this manner, they fell into Pharaoh's trap, and began the process of assimilating into the culture around them, despite Yosef's best efforts. So, although Yaakov and his sons were still alive, the seeds of assimilation were sprouting. This marked the beginning of the exile in Mitzrayim; and as we explained there, also spurred the servitude that was to come after the passing of all of the *shevatim.*

Normally, when one passage in the Torah concludes, there is a space in the *Sefer Torah* before the next passage begins. An exception to this rule is *Parashas Vayechi,* which begins immediately after *Parashas Vayigash* concludes, with no extra spaces. This is known as a *parashah stumah, a closed passage. Rashi* (*d"h vayechi*) explains that this reflects the fact that upon Yaakov Avinu's passing, the eyes and hearts of Klal Yisrael were *nistatmu, closed,* because the Egyptians began to enslave them.

Now, the above is not factually accurate; the enslavement of the Jewish people began only after the death of Levi, who was the last of the brothers to die. And when Yaakov passed, not a single one of the brothers had died yet. Additionally, if, as *Rashi* indicates, the *parashah* is a *stumah* on account of Yaakov's death, why does the *parashah* not begin with the passing of Yaakov Avinu? Instead, in the beginning of *Parashas Vayechi,* Yaakov Avinu was still alive and well! He lived for seventeen more years, blessed Menasheh and Ephraim, and blessed all of his children. The Torah does not record Yaakov's death until over fifty *pesukim* — and ten passages — after the beginning of *Parashas Vayechi.* And if the reason that the Torah did not mention Yaakov's death in the very beginning of the *parashah* was in order not to start off a *parashah* on a bad note, it still could have placed the *parashah stumah* before the second *posuk* of the *parashah,* which opens with the words *Vayikrevu yemei Yisrael lamus, and the time for Yisrael to die approached, etc.* If the Torah had indeed done this, it might have at least served to connect the topic of Yaakov's passing — which, although still over fifty *pesukim* away, is at least alluded to in this *posuk* — with the fact that the eyes and hearts of the Jewish people were affected. Seemingly, it would have been even more appropriate to have the very last *parashah* break, before Yaakov Avinu's death is recorded, to be a *parashah stumah.* The placement of the *parashah stumah* where it actually appears, though, does not seem to establish any correlation between the attitude of Klal Yisrael and Yaakov's death.

I believe that the truth is that the *parashah stumah* is in the beginning of the *parashah* specifically because it was at this point that the battle to build and preserve a culture of Torah life in Mitzrayim was lost. As we explained above, the effort to send Yehudah to establish a Yeshiva was too little, too late; and the Jewish people began to get comfortable among the Egyptians and within their culture. At this point, instead of focusing completely on spiritual growth and toiling in Torah, the Jewish people found themselves fighting the temptation to take over the administration of the entire country. It was here and now that the true battle was lost — even with Yaakov and the *shevatim* alive — and this is hinted at by the fact that the *parashah* is a *parashah stumah*. [Parenthetically, to some degree, the battle we fight here in America is similar in nature to the battle they fought at that time. The freedoms that our society grants us are looked at as opportunities rather than *nisyonos*, and people are swept away from *ruchniyus* in their pursuit of those "opportunities."] Although the battle in Mitzrayim was already being lost, as indicated by the placement of the *parashah stumah*, the comment of *Rashi,* that Klal Yisrael felt disheartened upon Yaakov's passing, is still accurate. Why? Because at least when Yaakov was alive, he provided Klal Yisrael with the impetus they needed to stay the course, for the short time he was with them to guide them. They had the option to look to him, even though many of them actually did not. As soon as he died, however, Klal Yisrael became disheartened, for they now realized that the inevitable had arrived; the weakened *koach HaTorah* that existed in Mitzrayim was simply no match for the onslaught of Egyptian culture that had taken hold of them. And while those among Klal Yisrael who were wise enough to care about the future of the nation became disheartened, as *Rashi* tells us, the sad truth is that there were many, perhaps even most, who were not at all unhappy about it. This contributed greatly to the despair of the people who hoped for the *mesorah* to continue.

Thus, *Rashi's* comment can be understood as follows. The reason that this *parashah* — the subject of which is the years that Yaakov was yet alive in Mitzrayim — is a *parashah stumah*, is that even then, the downfall of Klal Yisrael was approaching with virtual certainty. Yes, it was true that Klal Yisrael did not realize the void in their spiritual lives until Yaakov actually passed, but even then, the void was actually opening up, and Yaakov could not stem it. The *shibud* to which *Rashi* alludes is not the *shibud* to the Egyptians — that was indeed many years away. Rather, it was the travails that the Jewish people created for themselves in the pursuit of wealth — the spiritual travails — which began to subjugate them when Yaakov passed away. Their guiding light was lost, and having sunk into the opportunities presented to them, they became swallowed up in the culture of capitalism, and into the culture of Mitzrayim.

גָּדוֹל עָצוּם. כְּמָה שֶׁנֶּאֱמַר, וּבְנֵי יִשְׂרָאֵל פָּרוּ וַיִּשְׁרְצוּ וַיִּרְבּוּ וַיַּעַצְמוּ בִּמְאֹד מְאֹד, וַתִּמָּלֵא הָאָרֶץ אֹתָם[1].

וָרָב. כְּמָה שֶׁנֶּאֱמַר, רְבָבָה כְּצֶמַח הַשָּׂדֶה נְתַתִּיךְ, וַתִּרְבִּי וַתִּגְדְּלִי וַתָּבֹאִי בַּעֲדִי עֲדָיִים, שָׁדַיִם נָכֹנוּ וּשְׂעָרֵךְ צִמֵּחַ, וְאַתְּ עֵרֹם וְעֶרְיָה; וָאֶעֱבֹר עָלַיִךְ וָאֶרְאֵךְ מִתְבּוֹסֶסֶת בְּדָמָיִךְ, וָאֹמַר לָךְ, בְּדָמַיִךְ חֲיִי, וָאֹמַר לָךְ, בְּדָמַיִךְ חֲיִי[2].

As always happens, the closer the Jewish people come to foreign cultures, the more strongly those cultures reject them. [As my wife, *Rebbetzin Shelia, a"h,* used to quip, "Non-Jewish people are able to tolerate doctors, lawyers, and bankers who are Jewish. But they cannot stomach a Jew on the football field." This quote expresses the idea that as long as the Jew is serving society, they can tolerate it. But for a Jew to be the *hero,* to be popular in society, the pinnacle of the dreams of a non-Jewish person's own goals; that is intolerable to them.] In the end, even though the scene was ripe for Jewish economic triumph, the fact that the Jewish people began to identify with Egyptian culture stoked the fires of hatred in the hearts of the Egyptians. Additionally, Yosef's strategy to prevent hatred of the Jewish people only worked when they were basically equal in economic status to their non-Jewish counterparts. But when the Jewish people became unbelievably successful, jealousy inevitably resulted. [Additionally, see below, *Hava Nischakmah Lo,* where we suggest that before enslaving the Jewish people, Pharaoh had ceased collecting the taxes Yosef had instituted from the Egyptians, making them feel less like slaves, and so they began to experience antisemitic and nationalistic feelings. These details set in motion the impetus for them to attempt to recoup "their" money from the Jewish people.]

— וָאֹמַר לָךְ בְּדָמַיִךְ חֲיִי, וָאֹמַר לָךְ בְּדָמַיִךְ חֲיִי

And I Said to You, "Through Your Blood Shall You Live!"
And I Said to You, "Through Your Blood Shall You Live!"

- ❒ **The *pesukim* in *Yechezkel* show us that Hashem made Klal Yisrael very numerous in their downtrodden state in Mitzrayim.**
- ❒ **Why is the phrase *Through your blood shall you live* repeated in the *posuk? HaRav HaGaon Reb Dovid, ztvk"l,* understood the double allusion to be to the redemption not only from exile in Mitzrayim, but also from future exiles.**

Great, mighty — As it is stated: "And Bnei Yisrael were fruitful, increased greatly, multiplied, and became very, very mighty; and the land was filled with them."[1]

Numerous — As it is stated: "I made you as numerous as the plants of the field; you grew and you developed, and became charming, beautiful of figure and your hair grown long; but you were naked and bare. And I passed over you and saw you downtrodden in your bloods, and I said to you, Through your blood shall you live! And I said to you, Through your blood shall you live!"[2]

(1) *Shemos* 1:7. (2) *Yechezkel* 16:7,6.

❒ **Another interpretation is that the first phrase alludes to the men of Klal Yisrael, who merited two *mitzvos* that they were obligated to fulfill; of which the women were obligated only in one. The second phrase alludes to the *mesiras nefesh* of the women, who ensure that Klal Yisrael performs the *mitzvos* which they must do.**

❒ **The *mitzvah* of *milah* is the beginning of the *chinuch* of a Jewish child, which enables that child to grow into a Torah Jew, despite the challenges of adolescence. Part and parcel of this *chinuch* is the attitude that Jewish parents must adopt toward carrying it out. The requirement that the *korban pesach* be roasted, which is the type of preparation that requires constant attention, alludes to the fact that *chinuch* must be constant. With early and constant *chinuch,* our children can and will grow successfully.**

The *Haggadah* explains that the meaning of *varav* in the *posuk* is that Klal Yisrael became numerous, and to do so it cites the *pesukim* in *Yechezkel.* There, Hashem recounts that he made Klal Yisrael numerous while they were in their downtrodden state, and this is seen as an allusion to our time in Mitzrayim. The message of the *pesukim,* however, is more than that; it suggests that Hashem saw that Klal Yisrael was "bare" of any merits, and gave them two *mitzvos* having to do with "blood" to perform, by which they would merit to be redeemed. These were *dam pesach* and *dam milah.*

See *Rashi* to *Shemos* 12:6 (*d"h vehayah*), where he notes that the plural wording of *misboseses bedamayich, downtrodden in your bloods,* alludes to the two *mitzvos* involving blood that Hashem gave to Klal Yisrael. In the *Anah Dodi Haggadah,* my brother, *HaRav HaGaon Reb Dovid, ztvk"l,* explains that the phrase, *And I said to you, "Through your blood shall you live!"* is repeated a second time because it alludes not only to Klal Yisrael being redeemed from Mitzrayim, but also to future

redemptions. I would humbly suggest another reason why the phrase is repeated.

It is noteworthy that in these *pesukim,* Hashem describes Klal Yisrael to Yechezkel as a young woman, and the *pesukim* are written in feminine form. And yet, one of the *mitzvos* which Hashem is referencing does not even apply to women! For not only is there no *milah* for a female to undergo, a female is also not obligated to circumcise her son in the absence of the baby's father. [It is true that *beis din* has an obligation to ensure that the *milah* takes place, and perhaps, as a part of that obligation, a mother would be seen as fulfilling a communal obligation if she carried out the circumcision. And it is also possible that a mother would accept upon herself the responsibility to see to it that her family enters into the *bris* of Avraham Avinu, even if she is not technically obligated to do so. But at the end of the day, she truly has no *obligation.*] So, if one of these *mitzvos* cannot apply to women, why does the *posuk* that hints to this merit speak in *lashon nekeivah?*

We know that Tzipporah circumcised her son Eliezer when Moshe was being attacked by the angel. Was she legally able to perform this circumcision? Clearly she was, because the angel released Moshe upon her action. Now, it might be suggested that since it was before *Matan Torah,* there was no requirement to be circumcised by another who is commanded to circumcise himself, but merely to ensure that the *orlah, foreskin,* is removed. Even so, we see that Tzipporah took responsibility, and made sure that the *mitzvah* was done — even though it was not her *mitzvah* — and the family survived.

The answer thus might be that there are two levels of *mitzvah* observance that Klal Yisrael adheres to which are going to serve as a merit on their behalf. The first is when they actually perform a *mitzvah,* such as *dam pesach,* that all of Klal Yisrael are obligated to do. In that same category is *dam milah* when carried out by a man, which is also obligatory. And then there is the additional merit of the *nashim tzidkaniyos* of Klal Yisrael, who *are not* obligated to perform *milah* on their children, who nevertheless step in to make sure that whether or not they are charged with carrying out the *mitzvah,* it *will* get done, and the children will receive their *milah.* This, then, might be a reason why there is a double expression here. For not only did Hashem grant Klal Yisrael's men the *zechus* of being obligated in the performance of the *mitzvah,* he also granted Klal Yisrael's women the *zechus,* despite not being obligated in the *mitzvah,* to be *moser nefesh* to make sure it happens.

As stated above, the phrase *"Through your blood shall you live!"* is seen as an assurance that the merit of *dam milah,* along with *dam pesach,* will allow Klal Yisrael to continue to exist. Let us explore the significance of *dam milah.* There was an interesting back-and-forth between Moshe and

Pharaoh after *Barad,* recounted in the beginning of *Parashas Bo.* Pharaoh, at the behest of his servants, called Moshe and Aharon back before him to hear their proposal, which was that all of Klal Yisrael, including the children, would be going to serve Hashem. Of course, as we know, Pharaoh rejected this idea. We are used to attributing Pharaoh's every argument to his selfishness and stubbornness, and therefore we assume that here, too, Pharaoh was simply not willing to take the risk of letting Klal Yisrael out with their children, lest they be tempted not to return. While it is certainly possible that Pharaoh indeed had this motivation, it is interesting that the words of the *posuk* (*Shemos* 10:10) tell us that Pharaoh was advancing an entirely different argument. Pharaoh said to Moshe, *Should I send you out with all of the children? Re'u, ki ra'a neged peneichem, See that "ra'a" faces you. Rashi* (*d"h re'u*) cites a Midrash, which explains that Pharaoh was telling Moshe that he was able to see with his astrological predictions that the star named Ra'a was going to influence Klal Yisrael in the Wilderness, and that he saw blood — a sure sign of their doom. So, it seems as though Pharaoh was trying to convince Moshe that his plan was folly because it would harm Klal Yisrael.

We must ask: Why would this argument of Pharaoh's only apply to Moshe's wish to bring out the entire nation, including the children? What Pharaoh was agreeing to, which was to allow the adults to go serve Hashem without the children, would certainly also be disastrous, if he believed that the influence of Ra'a was going to result in tragedy!

I therefore believe that the argument between Moshe and Pharaoh was as follows. Moshe had presented Pharaoh with the idea that he wished to take the nation out of Mitzrayim to serve Hashem. Certainly included in this was going to be the acceptance of Hashem's commandments, along with the consequences of failing to do so. Pharaoh argued to Moshe that children, until they reach adolescence, cannot be bound by religion and the "restrictive" lifestyle that accompanies it. Pharaoh argued that there are natural and hormonal changes that children and teens experience that necessitate a certain tolerance — if you try to force them to behave in a way that is not natural for them, they are doomed to failure, and will ultimately suffer punishments! This is what Pharaoh thought he foresaw.

Moshe, however, was not swayed by this argument. He did not budge from his insistence that the children be allowed to participate and serve Hashem as well. Moshe told Pharaoh that for Klal Yisrael, *chinuch* begins at birth; with the *dam milah,* a boy is entered into the fold of Klal Yisrael. A child is thus enveloped in an environment of service to, and love of, Hashem, and this is the life he will come to know and love. When it comes time to confront the challenges of adolescence, a Jewish boy is equipped with strong enough ideals to pull him through whatever confronts him. And if, *chas v'shalom,* a child falls prey to the inclinations of his *yetzer*

וַיָּרֵעוּ אֹתָנוּ הַמִּצְרִים, וַיְעַנּוּנוּ, וַיִּתְּנוּ עָלֵינוּ עֲבֹדָה קָשָׁה[1].

וַיָּרֵעוּ אֹתָנוּ הַמִּצְרִים. כְּמָה שֶׁנֶּאֱמַר, הָבָה נִתְחַכְּמָה לוֹ, פֶּן יִרְבֶּה, וְהָיָה כִּי תִקְרֶאנָה מִלְחָמָה, וְנוֹסַף גַּם הוּא עַל שֹׂנְאֵינוּ, וְנִלְחַם בָּנוּ, וְעָלָה מִן הָאָרֶץ[2].

---

hara, the strong bond formed in his childhood will, *b'ezras Hashem,* draw him back to Hashem's service.

In light of this understanding, it fits well that *Rashi* concludes that the blood that Pharaoh had foretold of ended up being the blood of *milah* — which is the very essence of the *chinuch* of Avraham Avinu, and it is carried out (when it can be) on infants. This speaks to the message that Moshe sought to explain to Pharaoh.

Now, it is certainly true that there is sometimes a struggle when teens reach their adolescent years, as they undergo physical and chemical changes. It can take some time to bring these new realities under the umbrella of *avodas Hashem,* and Hashem certainly takes this into account. I believe that this is why, even though we know that at the age of thirteen a young man becomes liable in *beis din*, it is not until the age of twenty that he is *chayav biy'dei Shamayaim,* liable in the Heavenly Court. We also know that any sin committed from the age of thirteen until the age of twenty that was not rectified before he reaches the age of twenty begins to count at that time. What is the reason for this gap? I believe that this is the window that Hashem gives adolescents to fix whatever they have not yet been able to bring under control, as they mature. They must always try their best — this goes without saying — but Hashem understands that they may need some time to adjust properly. Thus, if they will merit to do so by age twenty, and as long as they repent from any improper actions since the age of thirteen, they will have a fresh, clean slate in the eyes of Heaven.

The other *mitzvah* that is alluded to with the phrase *"Through your blood shall you live!"* is the *dam pesach*. There is a fundamental lesson which we learn from the *korban pesach,* which pertains to the *chinuch* of our youth. The Torah commands that the *korban pesach* must be roasted, as opposed to being raw or cooked. The preparation of the *korban pesach* is analogous to the *chinuch* of our children. This fits with not only the timing of the *mitzvah* in our history, but also with the theme of the night of Pesach, which is to teach our children about our special relationship with Hashem.

There are parents who take shortcuts in the raising of their children.

The Egyptians did evil to us and afflicted us; and imposed hard labor upon us.[1]

The Egyptians did evil to us — As it is stated: "Let us deal with them wisely lest they multiply and, if we happen to be at war, they may join our enemies and fight against us and uproot us from the country."[2]

(1) *Devarim* 26:6. (2) *Shemos* 1:10

They might feel that, in certain areas, no supervision at all is required over their kids; the children will "figure it out." This hands-off approach to *chinuch* is comparable to a raw *korban*. The Torah explicitly warns against eating the *korban pesach* raw, and this is a terrible method of *chinuch* as well.

A far more common occurrence is when parents utilize a system of supervision, but are not personally involved at all. [Parents who are not in contact with their children's *Rebbeim, Morahs*, and teachers might fall into this category.] These parents are raising their children by plugging them into a formula, and wiping their hands of the responsibility and privilege of *chinuch*. This can be compared to one who cooks his *korban pesach*. Cooking requires very little involvement — just put it in the water, and let it boil! This too is not the right way to eat the *korban*, and not the right way to raise children.

Roasting is a process that requires constant attention from the chef, otherwise the meat can be ruined. If there is too high a flame, the outside will sear while the inside will be very underdone, and placing it too close to the flame will ruin the meat. In order to have a perfect-tasting *korban pesach,* the Torah requires it to be roasted by someone who is going to pay constant attention to it, as constant adjustments will be required. This is the way true *chinuch* should be carried out. The true mission of parents is to constantly watch over their children's progression, always making the necessary adjustments to further help them, challenge them, and develop them; it is only through this attentive *chinuch* that parents can help them reach their full potential.

הָבָה נִּתְחַכְּמָה לוֹ — *Let Us Deal With Them Wisely*

❒ **To garner support from the Egyptian populace to quell the threat he felt from the Jewish people, Pharaoh stopped collecting taxes from them. This made the Egyptians feel more a part of Mitzrayim's society and less like Pharaoh's slaves, and so they, too, were wary of Klal Yisrael's success.**

In explanation of the *posuk* of *Vayarei'u* in *Devarim* 26:6, the *Haggadah* cites Shemos 1:10-11 and 13, all of which discuss the evils the Egyptians plotted against Klal Yisrael. It is important to note that the passage in *Shemos* begins with two introductory *pesukim,* 1:8-9, which read, *And there rose up a new king over Mitzrayim, who did not know Yosef. And he said to his nation, "Behold! This nation, Bnei Yisrael, is more numerous and stronger than we!"* This was followed with 1:10, cited here, wherein the evil plot of the Egyptians is detailed.

It is noteworthy that the prelude to Pharaoh's evil scheming was that he *did not know Yosef.* Surely, he knew of Yosef's saving the country — it was impossible for him not to know! *Rashi* (*Shemos* 1:8, *d"h asher*) comments that Pharaoh made himself as if he did not know Yosef. In other words, he acted with brazen disregard for the gratitude he owed Yosef. Interestingly, *Targum* renders this *posuk* as *vekam malka chad'ta al Mitzrayim, d'la mikayem gezeiras Yosef, and a new ruler arose upon Mitzrayim, who did not keep the decrees of Yosef.* Now, what decree had Yosef made that Pharaoh sought to do away with, and why?

The idea behind Pharaoh's plan to protect Mitzrayim from the Jewish people was to assimilate them, but to do so in a way that they would pose no threat to Egyptian society by diluting it with their foreign values, by becoming its highest-class citizens, or even by overwhelming it with sheer numbers. However, Pharaoh feared he might find few people who were interested in taking up his quest to preserve Egyptian elitism in Mitzrayim. After all, the whole of Mitzrayim was essentially the personal estate of Pharaoh — thanks to Yosef — and thus, there were precious few among the populace who had anything at stake in the struggle to maintain the "purity" of Egyptian society. Most Egyptians felt that whoever was going to be in power — whether it would be Pharaoh or the Jewish people — was going to treat them exactly the same; as slaves.

So, perhaps *Targum* understands that Pharaoh ended the policy enacted by Yosef of a 20% tax given to Pharaoh from each farmer's produce. In this way, although Pharaoh likely never moved all the Egyptians back to their previous locales, nor did he ever expressly tell them that they were free and no longer his servants, he still garnered tremendous goodwill through this. Additionally, it might have given them the feeling that they had a real stake in their success, and therefore, by extension, their financial standing and their place in Egyptian society. As this feeling of belonging to Mitzrayim would take root among the Egyptians, they would begin to feel the threat of "Jewish influence" upon their society, and to realize how their culture would begin to change if nothing were to be done to stem it. Pharaoh reasoned that at that point, the populace would back his every move to eliminate the influence of Klal Yisrael upon their society's culture.

וְנִלְחַם בָּנוּ וְעָלָה מִן הָאָרֶץ — *And Fight Against Us and Uproot Us From the Country*

❒ **Pharaoh falsely claimed that the Jewish people might eventually expel the Egyptians from Mitzrayim. Although this was *never* Klal Yisrael's desire, Hashem eventually punished Pharaoh by making him think that this was indeed Moshe Rabbeinu's plan.**

The literal translation of *Shemos* 1:10, cited here, is that the Egyptians feared that the Jewish people would become powerful and decide to leave Mitzrayim. [Indeed, many *Haggados* do translate it that way.] While it is true that the narrative between Moshe and Pharaoh throughout the *makkos* revolved around the issue of Klal Yisrael staying in Mitzrayim or leaving it, *Rashi* (*Shemos* 1:10, *d"h v'ala*) explains that *Chazal* understood this *posuk* differently. Pharaoh was saying something negative about himself, and because he did not want those words to emanate from his lips, he directed his words at others. So, while what he *said* was *and [Klal Yisrael] will ascend from the land,* what he actually *meant* was, *and "we" will ascend from the land,* as Klal Yisrael would take over the country.

As noted, in his negotiations with Moshe about potentially releasing Klal Yisrael, never once did Pharaoh broach the subject of the Egyptians original fear that they would lose their country. But, there was a moment, after *Makkas Bechoros* took place, where Pharaoh really did feel this fear. When he came running to Moshe in the middle of the night and essentially told him to just take everything and go, Moshe calmly declined to do so. In that moment, Pharaoh was surely petrified that Moshe had decided that he would be staying in Mitzrayim, and taking over the country. It was at this moment that the Egyptians actually came to fear what it was that they thought they might need to worry about all those years ago.

We see here an incredible *middah keneged middah*. The Egyptians were actually inspired to enslave the Jewish people by antisemitism and jealousy. They had never *actually* feared that the Jewish people would take over their country; this was just an excuse they had used to justify their actions. And as we know, even as the Jewish people unfortunately melded into Egyptians society, they surely never intended to uproot it and take over Mitzrayim. But, as Jew-haters are wont to do, they spread this untrue stereotype that "Jews are going to take over and chase us out." How just, then, that even as Klal Yisrael *never intended to do so,* Mitzrayim was gripped with the paralyzing fear that maybe, just maybe, their slander was indeed going to happen, and there was nothing they could do to stop it.

וַיְעַנּוּהוּ. כְּמָה שֶׁנֶּאֱמַר, וַיָּשִׂימוּ עָלָיו שָׂרֵי מִסִּים, לְמַעַן עַנֹּתוֹ בְּסִבְלֹתָם, וַיִּבֶן עָרֵי מִסְכְּנוֹת לְפַרְעֹה, אֶת פִּתֹם וְאֶת רַעַמְסֵס[1].

וַיָּשִׂימוּ עָלָיו שָׂרֵי מִסִּים לְמַעַן עַנֹּתוֹ בְּסִבְלֹתָם — *They Set Taskmasters Over Them, in Order to Oppress Them With Their Burdens*

❒ **The *shotrim*, Jewish overseers, were righteous people. They had, originally, been the ones to offer to their terrified brethren that they would give them their own extra bricks to fill their quotas, and there was no need to fear the beatings. The Egyptians were upset that their sport had been spoiled, and so they declared these kind-hearted Jews responsible for any shortfall of their brothers.**

During the Holocaust, there were those Jews who became "kapos." This meant that the Nazis, *ysh"v,* put them in charge of the Jewish prisoners. In Mitzrayim, too, the taskmasters of Pharaoh appointed *shotrim* over their Jewish slaves. However, there seems to be a discrepancy as to how we remember the legacies of these two groups. The kapos are absolutely vilified, while the *shotrim* were rewarded by the Torah, and eventually became the *Sanhedrin* (see *Shemos* 5:14, *Rashi d"h vayuku*). The difference, of course, was that the kapos, with a few exceptions, were sell-outs to the Nazis. [While I have heard that specific individual kapos might have had noble intentions, the majority were only out to save their own skins, whatever the cost.] They submitted completely to the Nazis, and acted as their surrogates with terrible malice, committing unspeakable atrocities against their brethren, the innocent Jewish population. The *shotrim* of Klal Yisrael were nothing like this. I believe that the *shotrim* were actually motivated by selflessness and the care they felt for their fellow Jewish slaves, not self-interest.

If we examine *Shemos* 5:14, which states, *And the shotrim of Bnei Yisrael, which Pharaoh's taskmasters had set over them, etc.*, we see that the *shotrim* were not volunteers, but were rather appointed by the taskmasters of Pharaoh. How did this come to be? Why had specifically these people been chosen to oversee the production of the entire population of slaves? I believe the answer is that even back before Pharaoh took away the straw the Jewish people needed for producing bricks, there had already been people who missed filling their quotas. These people were severely beaten by the Egyptians (see *Sefer HaYashar, Parashas Shemos, d"h Vayehi kishmoa Mitzrayim*), who most likely (not unlike the Nazis, *ysh"v*) delighted in carrying out these tortures. The system of Jewish overseers was at least partially instituted by the evil taskmasters, so that the Egyptians would have an excuse to beat us [see *Vayitnu,* as well as *V'es Lachatzeinu,* below.]

And they afflicted us — As it is stated: "They set taskmasters over them in order to oppress them with their burdens; and they built treasure cities for Pharaoh; Pisom and Raamseis."[1]

(1) *Shemos* 1:11.

Now, each person's quota was set according to his own maximum production pre-slavery, so it was not that the numbers — at that time — were impossible to reach. Rather, it was the fear of possibly suffering unspeakable torture at the hands of the Egyptian thugs at the end of the day that paralyzed (figuratively speaking) some Jews, causing them to work less effectively, and making them likely to miss their quotas again. It was then that other Jews stepped in. They encouraged the fearful slaves, and told them that they themselves were strong, and produced extra bricks anyway. They assured these poor, frightened slaves that there was no need to fear the beatings, because they would fill in any bricks missing at the end of the day from their own production. By removing this terrible cloud of fear from the slaves, these people actually helped the weaker slaves to achieve their quotas more often. This, in turn, disappointed Pharaoh's sadistic taskmasters, who enjoyed ending the day with the beating of Jewish slaves.

So, the taskmasters called these strong Jewish slaves in, and informed them that because they had been so good at ensuring that other people met their quotas, they would now be *responsible* for the brick production of everyone else — and would receive the beatings that accompanied the shortfall of any of their charges. The subject of this *posuk*, then, is the result of this arrangement under Pharaoh's new rule, where no raw material was provided to the slaves. Of course, the shortfalls — and the beatings of the *shotrim* — only increased. After all, the system of covering for the fearful slaves only worked as long as the *shotrim* could actually produce a surplus, and more importantly, when it was only mostly needed as a motivational device. As *Rashi* there points out, the *shotrim* never turned on their charges and demanded that they work harder or suffer whipping themselves; rather, they allowed the slaves to do whatever they could, and accepted the horrible beatings of the Egyptians upon themselves.

וַיִּבֶן עָרֵי מִסְכְּנוֹת לְפַרְעֹה אֶת פִּתֹם וְאֶת רַעַמְסֵס — *And They Built Treasure Cities for Pharaoh; Pisom and Raamseis*

- ❒ **According to some, Pisom and Raamseis were luxurious cities, and the idea of Pharaoh was to use the free labor, and perhaps Jewish ingenuity, to both improve Egyptian society and lower the Jew's place therein.**
- ❒ **Others explain that they were cities that always collapsed. Pharaoh made the Jewish people pay for all the construction materials, and since they were never able to deliver completely built cities, he never**

וַיִּתְּנוּ עָלֵינוּ עֲבֹדָה קָשָׁה. כְּמָה שֶׁנֶּאֱמַר, וַיַּעֲבִדוּ מִצְרַיִם אֶת בְּנֵי יִשְׂרָאֵל בְּפָרֶךְ[1].

---

paid them back. In this way, he siphoned the money of Klal Yisrael back into the Egyptian economy.

In order to address his fear that the Jewish people might eventually take the country from him, Pharaoh began the process of enslaving them. The *posuk* teaches that he ordered the Jewish people to build the cities of Pisom and Raamseis. What was the nature of these cities? The *posuk* refers to them as *arei miskenos. Rashi* (*Shemos* 1:11, *d"h* es *Pisom v'es Raamseis*) understands that Klal Yisrael made these once-unusable cities into fortified storehouses. There is an old *Yiddish* expression, used as a response to someone who is expecting a very high standard to be met. Loosely translated, it means, "What do you think this is, Pisom and Raamseis?!" This sentiment is consistent with the idea that Pisom and Raamseis were luxurious or otherwise superior cities. I presume that if Pharaoh was having fortified storehouses built, it was probably in order to contain his valuables and the treasures of the country. If they were entire cities, I imagine that they included many buildings for the upper class of Mitzrayim to dwell in. Let us realize that if Pharaoh was commissioning first-rate cities, to become treasury sites and elite neighborhoods, the details of the work were surely exacting. Just as one might find with a mansion being built for a modern-day billionaire, every detail of each structure was likely made to order, and every tiny detail had to be perfect, with no corners cut.

One might be tempted to suggest that today's contractors are far more detail-oriented than the workers of old. I therefore remind people that when Egypt was excavating the Temple of Ramses (the Abu Simbel temples) in Nubia to accommodate the construction of the Aswan Dam, they began raising the image of Ramses at the mouth of the structure. They discovered that the temple had been built so that the sun shone directly upon it only twice a year — the minute at which Ramses had been born, and the minute when he died. It took modern-day scientists — with the benefit of computers — half a year to replicate this effect. Thus, building such cities was probably far more difficult than we might have imagined. If this was the true nature of Pisom and Raamseis, it would seem that the goal of the Egyptians was to utilize the free labor of the Jewish people, whom they forced to do their bidding. By enslaving Klal Yisrael in this manner, Pharaoh exerted his authority and rule over the Jewish people, using them to make him ever richer, all the while placing them under his thumb and minimizing their influence. [The actual genius required for such feats of engineering was either already present due to the help of the Jewish slaves, or else such extraordinary knowledge was in the Egyptians' possession,

They imposed hard labor upon us — As it is stated: "The Egyptians subjugated Bnei Yisrael with crushing harshness."[1]

(1) *Shemos* 1:13.

and they were simply utilizing the free labor. It is no secret that often, throughout history, it was the Jewish people in a country who became its leading thinkers, discoverers, doctors, and scientists. For example, the influx of Russian scientists into Israel after the fall of communism is a demonstration of the tremendous effect that Jewish thinkers had upon Communist Russia. I personally had relatives who, because of their position in Russia as scientists, were not allowed to leave Russia for a long time.]

There is also another well-known description of Pisom and Raamseis, according to which these cities always crumbled, and the work of building them was never able to be completed (see further, *Shemos Rabbah* 1:10). We may ask: What was the point of having Klal Yisrael carry out this utterly pointless task? I believe that part of what bothered Pharaoh and the Egyptians about Klal Yisrael was the fact that they had much of the money in Mitzrayim's entire economy in their possession. This stemmed from the fact that Klal Yisrael had arrived in Mitzrayim after the Egyptians had already made themselves slaves to Pharaoh, just as the famine ended. Thus, the *shevatim* never gave up their liberty or their property to Pharaoh, and retained the ability to do business and amass wealth, and they did just that. Perhaps one way that Pharaoh sought to weaken the political and societal threat which he felt was presented by the wealth of the Jewish people was to find a way to cheat them out of their money. He therefore initiated a plan by which they were essentially spending money, but not making any money. As the money they were spending was pouring into Mitzrayim, it was stimulating their economy; but because the Jewish people accomplished nothing, they received no profit from their labor, and became progressively poorer. In other words, although Pharaoh was not yet ready to enslave Klal Yisrael or confiscate their property outright, he was perfectly willing to trick them. He ordered them to build beautiful cities for him, without paying them for things like materials and food in the meantime. Perhaps he told them that when they delivered the completed cities, they would be reimbursed for all expenses and paid handsomely. In the meantime, the Jewish people, who were well-off, spent their own money purchasing food and materials from the Egyptians, stimulating their economy. The finished cities never materialized, and so there was basically an unending flow of Jewish money into the economy of Mitzrayim, which made the Egyptians ever richer and Klal Yisrael ever poorer.

וַיִּתְּנוּ עָלֵינוּ עֲבֹדָה קָשָׁה — *They Imposed Hard Labor Upon Us*

❒ **Not only did the Egyptians impose harsh labor upon Klal Yisrael, but**

וַנִּצְעַק אֶל יהוה אֱלֹהֵי אֲבֹתֵינוּ, וַיִּשְׁמַע יהוה אֶת קֹלֵנוּ, וַיַּרְא אֶת עָנְיֵנוּ, וְאֶת עֲמָלֵנוּ, וְאֶת לַחֲצֵנוּ[1].

---

this *posuk* teaches us that they specifically designed the labor to be incredibly difficult, so that Klal Yisrael would suffer.

In explanation of the phrase, *They imposed hard labor upon us,* the *Haggadah* cites the *posuk* (*Shemos* 1:13), *The Egyptians subjugated Bnei Yisrael with crushing harshness.* We have already been taught in 1:11 (cited above in explanation of the phrase, *and they afflicted us*) that the Egyptians appointed taskmasters over Klal Yisrael, and that their intent in doing so was specifically to oppress the Jewish people. In the *posuk* following this one, 1:14 (which will be cited by Rabban Gamliel in explanation of *maror,* below) we are taught that *whatever service they made them perform was with crushing harshness.* So, what is meant by the expression in this *posuk,* 1:13, that the Egyptians made their slaves serve *befarech, with crushing harshness*? What idea is being taught to us here that is not included in the surrounding *pesukim*?

I believe that in this *posuk*, the word *befarech, crushing harshness*, describes not the labor itself, but rather the attitude with which the slave labor was designed. The Egyptians hated the Jewish people with a passion, and this led them to try their best to arrange that the tasks of Klal Yisrael would be as hard to accomplish as possible, so that they might inflict torturous punishments upon the slaves when they would fail. Accordingly, 1:13, cited here, is describing the attitude of the Egyptians in their arranging of the laborious tasks of Klal Yisrael, while 1:14 is discussing the harshness of the labor itself. This served to add a layer of servitude to the Egyptians' enslavement of Klal Yisrael, above and beyond the subjugation found in a "normal" slave-owner relationship. Normally, an owner is interested in production, and will punish his slave only when the expected results are not met. He might insensitively make the quotas higher than he should, with an eye toward his bottom line, and punish his slave if the quotas are not met, but the punishment would not be the goal of the task. Here, however, the Egyptians were trying their hardest to arrange for the Jewish people to fail, so that they could freely beat the objects of their ire.

Thus, this *posuk* describes the initiation of the *avodah kashah, the hard labor,* explaining that it was specifically designed with the aforementioned evil goals in mind. The next *posuk* describes when the crushing labor was actually put into effect, and that it *embittered the lives* of Klal Yisrael in Mitzrayim.

In light of the above, that the Egyptians were specifically arranging for the torturous beatings of the Jewish people, we can understand the

We cried out to HASHEM, the God of our fathers; and HASHEM heard our cry and saw our afflictions, our toil, and our oppression.[1]

(1) *Devarim* 26:7.

following *posuk*. *Shemos* 5:16 relates that the *shotrim* complained to Pharaoh that his new, harsh decree was causing his people to sin. Why did they not complain that Pharaoh *himself* was sinning? After all, it was Pharaoh's own decree that was the basis for their complaint!

The answer is that they knew that Klal Yisrael was going to be oppressed at the hands of a foreign nation, as had been foretold at the *Bris Bein HaBesarim*. As we know, the nations will not be taken to task by Hashem because the Jewish people suffered pain, for that was decreed by Hashem. Rather, their punishment will be for their choosing to be the agents who would inflict that pain, when it did not have to be specifically them who carried out the punishments, or even if it did have to be them, they will be punished for doing too much to the Jewish people, as well as for the enjoyment they took in doing so (see *Rambam, Hil. Teshuvah* 6:5 with *Raavad*). While Hashem had clearly decreed that Klal Yisrael would spend time suffering while in exile in Mitzrayim, it was theoretically possible for Pharaoh to decree that the Jewish people suffer only as much as he had to make them suffer in order to fulfill the prophecy. However, the punishment that was being wrought upon the *shotrim* due to this new decree was a product of the taskmasters of Pharaoh and their insatiable appetite for the "sport" of Jew-beating. This, then, was certainly "over the line," and constituted a sin committed by the people of Mitzrayim, even more so than Pharaoh himself.

וַנִּצְעַק אֶל ה׳ אֱלֹקֵי אֲבֹתֵינוּ — *We Cried Out to Hashem, the God of Our Fathers*

❒ **All of Klal Yisrael called out to Hashem, and He heard all of their cries. So, why were only a fraction of them redeemed?**

❒ **Every person's cry was heeded. Thus, those who wished for the cessation of the intense punishing labor received it, and those who wished to leave Mitzrayim received this as well.**

It was true that Klal Yisrael had become very numerous and very successful in Mitzrayim. And yet, we know that at *Yetzias Mitzrayim*, a large part of the nation — its vast majority, in fact — would not merit to be redeemed. [See further, *Melameid Shehayu,* above.] Despite the success of Klal Yisrael in Mitzrayim, and perhaps in part, even because of it, the

וַנִּצְעַק אֶל יהוה אֱלֹהֵי אֲבֹתֵינוּ. כְּמָה שֶׁנֶּאֱמַר, וַיְהִי בַיָּמִים הָרַבִּים הָהֵם, וַיָּמָת מֶלֶךְ מִצְרַיִם, וַיֵּאָנְחוּ בְנֵי יִשְׂרָאֵל מִן הָעֲבֹדָה, וַיִּזְעָקוּ, וַתַּעַל שַׁוְעָתָם אֶל הָאֱלֹהִים מִן הָעֲבֹדָה[1].

Egyptians decided to enslave Klal Yisrael, imposing upon them impossibly crushing labor. The relief from Mitzrayim came only from Hashem, and was a direct result of the *tze'akah, crying out,* that Klal Yisrael directed toward Hashem. He heard them, and remembered His promise to the *Avos,* and answered them, bringing the redemption. And again we may ask: Was only one-fifth of Klal Yisrael crying out? Of course not! Why were *all* of the prayers of Klal Yisrael not answered?

The key to understanding the answer to this question is to realize that while the entire nation of Klal Yisrael was crying out, their pleas did not all reflect the same desires. Most of them were praying fervently that the punishing physical labor and mental torture and the infanticide would cease, and their lives as God-fearing Jews in Mitzrayim could resume peacefully. But others among them longed for an escape from Mitzrayim and everything its society represented. They did not want freedom in Mitzrayim at all. They wished and begged that the exile would end, and they could fulfill the ideal of the *Avos* and return to Eretz Yisrael and serve Hashem on His terms, according to what they would be instructed to do by the Torah.

So, *everyone's* prayers were answered; meaning that all of Klal Yisrael ceased being subject to the slavery of Mitzrayim. Hashem provided everyone in the nation with relief, and four degrees of freedom [see *Kadeish,* above]. This was the pinnacle of freedom that a Jew in Mitzrayim could possibly hope to reach. Freedom from harsh labor, from any level of servitude at all, from being treated as a second-class citizen, all the way to being treated equally and fairly, with the opportunity to reach all the goals of Egyptian society even as an observant Jew. Hashem really did give them everything. But those who only yearned for this degree of freedom and no more could not go on to become Klal Yisrael, and so they perished during the *makkah* of *Choshech.*

It was only those who yearned for a greater degree of freedom — a fifth level — who left Mitzrayim. These people wanted the true and absolute freedom to live in a Torah society, where the morals of Hashem and His Torah would define everything in their lives; not merely to live according to the Torah, but to live *with* the Torah, in every sense of the word. This could only be accomplished with an exodus from Mitzrayim. They yearned to leave, to go *k'ish echad b'lev echad,* as one, with a singular purpose, and receive the Torah, and to establish a Land where Hashem's word reigned supreme, in the way that their forefathers, Avraham,

We cried out to HASHEM, the God of our fathers — As it is stated: "It happened in the course of those many days that the king of Mitzrayim died; and Bnei Yisrael groaned because of the servitude and cried; their cry because of the servitude rose up to God."[1]

(1) *Shemos* 2:23.

Yitzchak, and Yaakov, had dreamed that it would be. Their prayers were also answered, and they got to leave Mitzrayim and become Hashem's nation.

However, this does not mean that nobody from the first group who had prayed for salvation in Mitzrayim merited to leave. For Hashem attempted to convince the entirety of Klal Yisrael to want to leave. In His lowering Klal Yisrael into the crucible that was Mitzrayim, where they experienced untold suffering, and in His raising them out of it with the salvation of the *makkos,* Hashem sought to imbue Klal Yisrael with the feeling that they would want *nothing at all* to do with Egyptian society. He wished for them to reach the point where they would not envision life in Mitzrayim as the best-case scenario, but rather would shun anything to do with its culture [see further below, *Arbeh*]. And anyone who did reach this level before the *makkah* of *Choshech* was indeed redeemed, and merited to experience *Yetzias Mitzrayim.*

An example of this idea is the attitude that French Jews — and to a lesser degree, Jews all across Europe — are beginning to have in our time. Originally, France was seen as the birthplace of liberty, and Napoleon stood for an opportunity to experience religious freedom. For a long time, Jews who suffered in France longed for a time when they could experience French citizenry as Torah Jews without fear or consequence. But no longer is that the goal of a great many Jews. Now, whether they be Torah observant or not, many Jews are so disenchanted with the open antisemitism they experience in France that they want *nothing at all to do* with the country. They just want to leave, and to be dissociated from the country completely. Similarly, after World War II and even until today, many Jews will not buy a German-made vehicle or appliance, because they are simply repulsed by the association with Germany. Hashem will sometimes present circumstances which bring this attitude about a former host country to the fore, in order to reawaken Klal Yisrael's desire to serve Him optimally in Eretz Yisrael with no desire to be a part of their former society [see *Vehi She'amdah,* above]. Certainly, during *Yetzias Mitzrayim,* this idea was in play. But unfortunately, many people would not let go of what once was, and wished to return to being the elite class in Mitzrayim, as they had been before Pharaoh's enslavement of the Jews.

וַיִּשְׁמַע יהוה אֶת קֹלֵנוּ. כְּמָה שֶׁנֶּאֱמַר, וַיִּשְׁמַע אֱלֹהִים אֶת נַאֲקָתָם, וַיִּזְכֹּר אֱלֹהִים אֶת בְּרִיתוֹ אֶת אַבְרָהָם, אֶת יִצְחָק, וְאֶת יַעֲקֹב[1].

וַיַּרְא אֶת עָנְיֵנוּ. זוֹ פְּרִישׁוּת דֶּרֶךְ אֶרֶץ, כְּמָה שֶׁנֶּאֱמַר וַיַּרְא אֱלֹהִים אֶת בְּנֵי יִשְׂרָאֵל, וַיֵּדַע אֱלֹהִים[2].

— וַיִּזְכּוֹר אֱלֹהִים אֶת בְּרִיתוֹ אֶת אַבְרָהָם אֶת יִצְחָק וְאֶת יַעֲקֹב
And God Remembered His Covenant With Avraham, With Yitzchak, and With Yaakov

❒ **Even though Hashem heard the cries of the nation, they were only answered because they were the descendants of the *Avos*. Everything the *Avos* did was for the sake of Hashem, and this merit stands for us always.**

The *posuk* (*Shemos* 2:24) relates that Hashem heard the groans of Klal Yisrael, and He remembered the covenant he had made with the *Avos*. Clearly, the suffering that Klal Yisrael was enduring was not enough to secure their relief. Rather, it was only on account of the merits of Avraham, Yitzchak, and Yaakov that they were saved. [This is similar in concept to the reason we begin each *Shemoneh Esrei* by mentioning the merits of our forefathers.] However, people have a tendency to gloss over this fact, and to presume that the mention of the *Avos* here is merely a tangential detail of the story. They reason that since Hashem had promised the *Avos* that their descendants would inherit Eretz Yisrael, and the process of the fulfillment of that promise was about to begin, the covenant is mentioned here.

There is more we need to understand, and indeed internalize, about the merits of the service to Hashem that the *Avos* performed. Hashem tolerates our sins, accepting our repentance instead of abandoning us in favor of another nation, only on account of his love for the *Avos,* and the dedication they had for Him in their lifetimes. We are, in Hashem's eyes, the children of His beloved Avraham, Yitzchak, and Yaakov. While we constantly lose focus of living our lives *lesheim Shamayim* (see *Nishmas*), it was the sole focus of the *Avos* that their every action and decision should reflect the will of Hashem. Even when we are doing what we are supposed to do, we very often fall into the pattern of not imbuing our actions with meaning, something that the *Avos* always did; and that is even when we are acting our best. The *Avos* lived and breathed the *sheish mitzvos temidiyos,* and their every move reflected them. It was this commitment — this living with Hashem in real time, always — that stands as

HASHEM heard our cry — As it is stated: "God heard their groaning, and God remembered His covenant with Avraham, with Yitzchak, and with Yaakov."[1]

And He saw our afflictions — That is the disruption of married life, as it is stated: "God saw Bnei Yisrael and God knew."[2]

(1) *Shemos* 2:24. (2) 2:25.

---

an eternal merit for Klal Yisrael, and as an example for us of true dedication for Hashem. Every morning, during *Shacharis,* in the paragraph of *aval anachnu amcha* that we recite before *korbanos,* we make mention of the fact that we are different from the nations of the world because we are the children of Avraham, Yitzchak, and Yaakov, and the love Hashem had for them elevates us from the vanity and futility of mankind. The merit of our forefathers stood tall for us in Mitzrayim, and it continues to stand tall for us each and every day.

וַיַּרְא אֶת עָנְיֵנוּ — זוֹ פְּרִישׁוּת דֶּרֶךְ אֶרֶץ — *And He Saw Our Afflictions — That is the Disruption of Married Life*

- **As a result of their tortured existence, the men of Klal Yisrael had no will to procreate. In this way, the Egyptians interfered with their family life.**
- **The women of Klal Yisrael, also suffering terribly, were *moser nefesh* to encourage their husbands to continue to build Klal Yisroel.**
- **The mirrors that were used in this effort were so precious to Hashem that He instructed Moshe that specifically they be used in the construction of the *kiyor.***

How did the Egyptians disrupt the married lives of the Jewish people? On its most basic level, the unending torment for years on end literally robbed Klal Yisrael of their will to have children. When the men lay in the fields at night, physically exhausted and mentally broken from all the backbreaking labor of the day, they simply could not muster the will to join their wives. Why bother raising a family that would be doomed to this unbearable fate? There was no reason to try and raise children to suffer! Now, the *posuk* begs the question: If indeed the will of Klal Yisrael's men was broken, how was it that through their time in Mitzrayim, Klal Yisrael's population continued to increase?

The answer is that the women of Klal Yisrael were responsible for saving the nation. The *posuk* (*Shemos* 38:8) relates that the *kiyor* was made entirely of the copper mirrors of the Bnos Yisrael. *Rashi* there (*d"h b'maros hatzov'os*) explains that these very mirrors were used to ensure

וְאֶת עֲמָלֵנוּ. אֵלּוּ הַבָּנִים, כְּמָה שֶׁנֶּאֱמַר, כָּל הַבֵּן הַיִּלּוֹד הַיְאֹרָה תַּשְׁלִיכֻהוּ, וְכָל הַבַּת תְּחַיּוּן[1].

---

the continuity of Klal Yisrael in Mitzrayim. At first, Moshe Rabbeinu did not want to use the mirrors for the *Mishkan*, for they had been made for the *yetzer hara,* as a tool to enhance *taivah*. Hashem then told him that, on the contrary, these mirrors were *most precious to Him*, and were fit to be used, even more than anything else.

Rashi then explains how it was that these copper mirrors preserved the nation. When the husbands had given up for lack of strength and hope, their wives would dress themselves nicely, and come and feed them a good meal. Then they would show their husbands the reflection of both of them in the copper mirror and say, "See how I am so much prettier than you are!" This would awaken the husbands' desire to continue the nation together with their wives.

The question begs to be asked: Why would a woman telling her husband that she is better looking than he is bring him to want to build a family? Why, this type of insult would probably cause more fighting than anything else! The answer is that the women did a lot more than just make this statement. They went and dressed themselves up in all their finery and brought their husbands food in the field where they lay. The women came and told their spouses, "Look at me and look at you. I also work very hard, I also have *avodas perech* threatening my resolve. But I put myself together and got dressed up to come to you and feed you supper. Why? Because I want to build a family. It is my responsibility and my mission to ensure that this nation survives; I am not doing it for selfish reasons, but rather because it is the will of Hashem! And if I can do it, you can surely do it too! You, my dear husband, must also not be so negative!" The man was then empowered with the strength he needed to carry on under those trying circumstances. Only then could he muster up the strength and put himself in the right frame of mind to go and build a family.

Of course, there is indeed an element of *taivah* and of *yetzer hara* in this *mitzvah*, which is meant to involve physical desire; this was Moshe's original concern. Even the concept that we find by the loftiest of righteous men, the highest level of *megaleh tefach umechaseh tefachaim* (see *Nedarim* 20b and *Shulchan Aruch Orach Chaim* 240:8 with commentaries), does not mean to say that a man should not exhibit any *taivah*, but rather only the amount of *taivah* that is necessary. Since the *nashim tzidkaniyos* of Klal Yisrael acted purely for the sake of Heaven, what would normally have been seen as inciting *taivah* was actually considered pure and beautiful *kedushah* in Hashem's estimation; therefore, He bade Moshe to accept and use the mirrors.

Our toil — These are the children, as it is stated: "Every son that is born you shall cast into the river, but every daughter you shall let live."[1]

(1) *Shemos* 1:22.

וְאֶת עֲמָלֵנוּ — אֵלּוּ הַבָּנִים — *Our Toil — These Are the Children*

- **Pharaoh did not really *respect* Hashem, but was only afraid of consequences. Thus, when his plan to murder the Jewish boys without incurring a death sentence failed, he began to kill them openly, without regard for Hashem's will.**
- **A *rasha* will initially attempt to carry out his own agenda in accordance with what he is allowed to do. But when there is a conflict between his desire and the Torah, he will choose his own will and forsake the will of Hashem.**
- **It was already terribly difficult to raise a family in Mitzrayim; and as we mentioned above (*Vayar es Anyeinu*), it was difficult to even *want* to build a family. It was thus exceptionally torturous for the Jewish parents when the Egyptians would come and murder their babies.**

It is interesting to note that in the span of only a few *pesukim,* we find that Pharaoh's trepidation to anger Hashem simply vanished. Initially (see above, *Mah Bikeish Lavan*), Pharaoh initiated a system by which he could have Jewish baby boys exterminated without technically being guilty of murder. Why was he concerned with the halachic definition of murder? Clearly, his fear of Hashem's wrath was enough to keep him in check to some extent. Then, in short order, Pharaoh was willing to commit wholesale and outright infanticide by openly drowning the babies in the river! Clearly, he was no longer concerned with any legal definition of murder, including the Torah's. How can a person experience such a drastic change in so short a time frame?

The key to the answer to this question is that Pharaoh was never actually exhibiting fear of Hashem. True fear of Hashem would have entailed not killing, or even attempting to kill, anyone. What he was exhibiting, then, was nothing other than risk management. He wanted to eliminate Jewish boys, and had found a way to do it in which he avoided being charged in Heaven with a crime. But when that plan failed, Pharaoh had no qualms about outright murder, because that was the way to accomplish his goal. If a side effect was going to be guilt in Heaven, he was not all that concerned.

וְאֶת לַחֲצֵנוּ. זוֹ הַדְּחַק, כְּמָה שֶׁנֶּאֱמַר, וְגַם רָאִיתִי אֶת הַלַּחַץ אֲשֶׁר מִצְרַיִם לֹחֲצִים אֹתָם[1].

Through Pharaoh's actions here, we can clearly see the way the *yetzer hara* operates. Initially a person is drawn in by the *yetzer hara* and persuaded to transgress a less serious prohibition. Once he is "comfortable" with it, as *Chazal* teach us (*Kiddushin* 20a), *Keivan she'avar adam aveirah v'shanah bah, na'aseh lo k'heter, once a person transgresses a sin and repeats his transgression, it becomes as permitted to him* — the *yetzer hara* will draw the person in further, convincing him to commit a more serious sin. In this way, we see that Pharaoh's initial giving in to the temptation to murder "innocently" led to his ever-greater decline in morality, culminating in outright infanticide.

Essentially, Pharaoh's flawed attitude was that he made his own desire more primary than Hashem's desire. Once he had set a goal — stopping the ascension of the *moshian shel Yisrael* — he tried to "work around" Hashem, by committing "innocent murder." When that did not work, he stopped trying to fit Hashem's will into his agenda. This is the way of evildoers. They first establish goals that are inconsistent with those of the Torah, and then try to fit their observance around these goals. When their goals become increasingly incompatible with the Torah, they allow the Torah to fall by the wayside in favor of their established desires.

How does the *Haggadah* know that the *toil* alluded to in *Devarim* 2:27 is the fact that the children were being killed? There does not seem to be any reference to children in the wording of the *posuk*!

Perhaps the answer is that the *Haggadah* understood that the previous phrase in the *posuk, vayar es anyeinu, and He saw our suffering,* alluded to the separation of the husbands and wives, because that was something to which Hashem alone would have been privy. And, as we discussed above, the nation survived only due to incredible *mesiras nefesh* on the part of the Bnos Yisrael, who convinced the Bnei Yisrael to engage in building families. Imagine, then, the crushing blow it would have been to see that after such hopelessness, suffering, and selfless sacrifice, not to mention suffering through pregnancy while performing slave labor, the male babies were summarily rounded up and murdered in cold blood. What kind of an incredible torture must that have been for Klal Yisrael! Accordingly, the *Haggadah* understood that the following phrase of *v'es amaleinu, and our toil,* must have been alluding to the torturous effect of the loss of Klal Yisrael's children.

Our oppression — This refers to the pressure, as it is stated: "I have also seen how the Egyptians are oppressing them."[1]

(1) *Shemos* 3:9.

וְאֶת לַחֲצֵנוּ – זֶה הַדְּחַק — *Our Oppression — This Refers to the Pressure*

- **The Egyptians engaged in never-ending torture of their Jewish slaves. In doing so, they made them suffer a fate more painful than death.**
- **The hallmark of Mitzrayim was the cruelty of its people, and this is why an Egyptian convert must wait three generations before marrying into Klal Yisrael.**

The *Haggadah* has already noted that the Egyptians not only planned harsh work for the Jewish people, but also that they carried it out. What is the significance of the *lachatz, oppression,* which they forced upon Klal Yisrael, that warrants a special mention here?

We are accustomed to thinking about the evil Nazis, *ysh"v,* as being more wicked than the Egyptians. After all, the Nazis' main goal was the extermination of the Jews in many ways, gunning them down or gassing them in their death camps, whereas Pharaoh's goal was only the subjugation, and not necessarily the annihilation, of Klal Yisrael. Furthermore, aside from infanticide, we do not find the Torah or *Chazal* discussing the killings in Mitzrayim. If they indeed were not killing the Jewish people, can it not be said that the Nazis were worse?

[Note, of course, that we are comparing the foul to the rotten. I will cite something the Nazis, *ysh"v,* once did to help understand how terribly cruel the Egyptians were as a matter of course. I read in a Holocaust book that for sport, some Nazis took a man and placed him in a barrel of water and sat on the lid. When the man could literally no longer hold his breath, his adrenaline forced him to burst out of the barrel, popping the soldier off, whereupon the Nazis put him back in, to watch it all over again. This man suffered the pain of almost drowning multiple times.]

Routinely, the Nazis, *ysh"v,* systematically murdered our brethren, and many notable reports of their savage, inhuman cruelty are known to us. But the majority of their victims were simply murdered. When someone is murdered, they only have to die once. But when someone is tortured, they feel the pain of death anew each time.

The Egyptians were so cruel that they made it known to Klal Yisrael that they would always beat them within an inch of their life, and torture them, but that death would not be an escape. They would continue to live, and the torture would never end. In this way, they were far more cruel than the

וַיּוֹצִאֵנוּ יהוה מִמִּצְרַיִם בְּיָד חֲזָקָה, וּבִזְרֹעַ נְטוּיָה, וּבְמֹרָא גָּדֹל, וּבְאֹתוֹת וּבְמֹפְתִים[1].

וַיּוֹצִאֵנוּ יהוה מִמִּצְרַיִם. לֹא עַל יְדֵי מַלְאָךְ, וְלֹא עַל יְדֵי שָׂרָף, וְלֹא עַל יְדֵי שָׁלִיחַ, אֶלָּא הַקָּדוֹשׁ בָּרוּךְ הוּא בִּכְבוֹדוֹ וּבְעַצְמוֹ. שֶׁנֶּאֱמַר, וְעָבַרְתִּי בְאֶרֶץ מִצְרַיִם בַּלַּיְלָה הַזֶּה, וְהִכֵּיתִי כָל בְּכוֹר בְּאֶרֶץ מִצְרַיִם מֵאָדָם וְעַד בְּהֵמָה, וּבְכָל אֱלֹהֵי מִצְרַיִם אֶעֱשֶׂה שְׁפָטִים, אֲנִי יהוה[2].

וְעָבַרְתִּי בְאֶרֶץ מִצְרַיִם בַּלַּיְלָה הַזֶּה — אֲנִי וְלֹא מַלְאָךְ. וְהִכֵּיתִי כָל בְּכוֹר בְּאֶרֶץ מִצְרַיִם — אֲנִי וְלֹא שָׂרָף. וּבְכָל אֱלֹהֵי מִצְרַיִם אֶעֱשֶׂה שְׁפָטִים — אֲנִי וְלֹא הַשָּׁלִיחַ. אֲנִי יהוה — אֲנִי הוּא, וְלֹא אַחֵר.

בְּיָד חֲזָקָה. זוֹ הַדֶּבֶר, כְּמָה שֶׁנֶּאֱמַר, הִנֵּה יַד יהוה הוֹיָה בְּמִקְנְךָ אֲשֶׁר בַּשָּׂדֶה, בַּסּוּסִים בַּחֲמֹרִים בַּגְּמַלִּים בַּבָּקָר וּבַצֹּאן, דֶּבֶר כָּבֵד מְאֹד[3].

Nazis, who were themselves crueler than we can imagine. I believe that this is the *lachatz, oppression,* that receives special mention here. [See *Nahar Sholom, Devarim* 23:8, where we have explained that the attribute that an Egyptian convert carries is that of cruelty, and is the reason why, until three generations have passed, a descendant of an Egyptian convert may not marry into the congregation of Klal Yisrael.]

דֶּבֶר כָּבֵד מְאֹד — *A Very Severe Pestilence*

❒ ***Kaveid me'od* is a description of the *makkah* of *Dever.* The Torah is revealing to us that the nature of the *Dever* was far more severe than any we have ever seen.**

The expression of *kaveid me'od* is not describing *Dever* as an especially powerful *makkah* in comparison to the other *makkos;* it is rather describing the *Dever* itself. That is, as far as pestilences go, it was an extremely potent and deadly one.

What exactly might this mean? Generally, Hashem unleashes a sickness that makes a certain group of organisms sick, while others are not

HASHEM took us out of Mitzrayim with a mighty hand and with an outstretched arm, with great awe, with signs and with wonders.[1]

HASHEM took us out of Mitzrayim — Not through an angel, not through a seraph, not through a messenger, but the Holy One, blessed is He, in His glory, Himself, as it is stated: "I will pass through the land of Mitzrayim on that night; I will slay all the firstborn in the land of Mitzrayim from man to beast; and upon all the gods of Mitzrayim will I execute judgments; I, HASHEM."[2]

"I will pass through the land of Mitzrayim on that night" — I and no angel; "I will slay all the firstborn in the land of Mitzrayim" — I and no seraph; "and upon all the gods of Mitzrayim will I execute judgments" — I and no messenger; "I, HASHEM" — it is I and no other.

With a mighty hand — This refers to the *Dever*, Pestilence, as it is stated: "Behold, the hand of HASHEM shall strike your cattle which are in the field, the horses, the donkeys, the camels, the herds, and the flocks — a very severe pestilence."[3]

(1) *Devarim* 26:8. (2) *Shemos* 12:12. (3) 9:3.

---

affected by it, and cannot even transmit it. We have seen in recent history what can happen when a virus mutates from only sickening animals to infecting people. Swine flu, or the avian flu of 1918, and according to some researchers, even the Covid outbreak, are all examples of animal diseases that developed to infect humans, with devastating results.

A *Dever kaveid me'od,* then, might have either been a disease that was able to spread to and infect all different organisms and kill them with great speed, without being limited to a certain subset of species, or perhaps Hashem released many different strains of disease all at once, so that every species succumbed to a virus that was custom-tailored for it.

[In our own times, we can begin to appreciate such a deadly epidemic. But, the terrifying speed with which *Dever* arrived and killed everything in its wake immediately is unparalleled. And we can especially appreciate how great a miracle it was that as soon as Hashem wished to end the *makkah,* there were no more infections, symptoms, or deaths. The *Dever kaveid me'od* was simply *gone,* in a single moment!]

וּבִזְרֹעַ נְטוּיָה. זוֹ הַחֶרֶב, כְּמָה שֶׁנֶּאֱמַר, וְחַרְבּוֹ שְׁלוּפָה בְּיָדוֹ, נְטוּיָה עַל יְרוּשָׁלָיִם[1].

וּבְמֹרָא גָּדֹל. זוֹ גִלּוּי שְׁכִינָה, כְּמָה שֶׁנֶּאֱמַר, אוֹ הֲנִסָּה אֱלֹהִים לָבוֹא לָקַחַת לוֹ גוֹי מִקֶּרֶב גּוֹי, בְּמַסֹּת, בְּאֹתֹת, וּבְמוֹפְתִים, וּבְמִלְחָמָה, וּבְיָד חֲזָקָה, וּבִזְרוֹעַ נְטוּיָה, וּבְמוֹרָאִים גְּדֹלִים, כְּכֹל אֲשֶׁר עָשָׂה לָכֶם יהוה אֱלֹהֵיכֶם בְּמִצְרַיִם לְעֵינֶיךָ[2].

וּבְאֹתוֹת. זֶה הַמַּטֶּה, כְּמָה שֶׁנֶּאֱמַר, וְאֶת הַמַּטֶּה הַזֶּה תִּקַּח בְּיָדֶךָ, אֲשֶׁר תַּעֲשֶׂה בּוֹ אֶת הָאֹתֹת[3].

וּבִזְרֹעַ נְטוּיָה — זוֹ הַחֶרֶב — *With an Outstretched Arm — This Refers to the Sword*

❒ ***An outstretched arm,*** **which refers to a** ***sword,*** **alludes to which** ***makkah?*** **Presumably the reference is to** ***Makkas Bechoros.***

❒ **It can also be suggested that the Tanna is discussing a second detail about the aforementioned** ***makkah*** **of** ***Dever.***

The *Haggadah* understands the words *outstretched arm* as an allusion to death, similar to its meaning in the *posuk* in *Divrei HaYamim,* where David HaMelech saw the angel with his sword outstretched over Yerushalayim. Still, we may wonder: Which *makkah* is being alluded to with this reference?

It seems clear that the Tanna is referencing *Makkas Bechoros,* where Hashem killed all of the *bechorim* of Mitzrayim. [Some interpret this as referring to the war that took place between Pharaoh and the *bechorim* preceding *Makkas Bechoros.*] I wonder if it might be possible to suggest that the *Haggadah* is continuing to allude to *Dever,* which was referenced above with the words *yad chazakah.* Perhaps the *posuk* is pointing out two distinct qualities of the *Dever;* firstly, that it was a pestilence that affected all species of animals, and secondly, that it was deadly. [Perhaps the fact that the angel mentioned in *Divrei HaYamim* was holding a sword bolsters this understanding, for there, the people were indeed dying from a plague.]

וּבְמֹרָא גָּדֹל — זוֹ גִלּוּי שְׁכִינָה — *With Great Awe — This Alludes to the Revelation of the Shechinah*

❒ **We know that there must have been a direct revelation of the** ***Shechinah*** **when Hashem took us out of Mitzrayim. For removing a nation**

With an outstretched arm — This refers to the sword, as it is stated: "His drawn sword in His hand, outstretched over Yerushalayim."[1]

With great awe — This alludes to the revelation of the *Shechinah*, as it is stated: "Has God ever attempted to take unto Himself a nation from the midst of another nation by trials, miraculous signs, and wonders, by war and with a mighty hand and outstretched arm and by awesome revelations, as all that HASHEM, your God, did for you in Mitzrayim, before your eyes?"[2]

And with signs — This refers to the miracles performed with the staff as it is stated: "Take this staff in your hand, that you may perform the miraculous signs with it."[3]

(1) *I Divrei HaYamim* 21:16. (2) *Devarim* 4:34. (3) *Shemos* 4:17.

---

from the midst of another requires absolute precision, and angels are not granted that capability.

The *posuk* says that Hashem took us out of Mitzrayim with *great awe*, and the *Haggadah* explains that with these words, the Torah is alluding to the fact that there was *revelation of the Shechinah*. Where do we see evidence of any such revelation?

The answer is that in order to bring widespread destruction to an entire place, an angel could have been sent. But to delineate with pinpoint accuracy that one person should be affected and his neighbor not be affected at all, Hashem's own Presence is required. Thus, the idea expressed above in discussing the opening phrase of this *posuk, And Hashem took us out of Mitzrayim,* that it was Hashem Himself and no one else, applies here as well. There, we saw the pinpoint accuracy of *Makkas Bechoros,* which could only have been carried out by Hashem Himself. Here, we see that the very idea that Hashem could come and remove a nation from the midst of another was also only possible because of His doing so Himself. Klal Yisrael understood that Hashem must in fact be there with them in order for this to be taking place; this is why the *posuk* cited by the *Haggadah* here describes the revelation as *l'einecha, before your eyes*. There was thus a great revelation of the *Shechinah* not only through *Makkas Bechoros,* but also in the exodus of Klal Yisrael from among the Egyptians.

וּבְאֹתוֹת — זֶה הַמַּטֶּה – *And With Signs — This Refers to the Miracles Performed With the Staff*

❒ **Why does the *Haggadah* say that the expression *with signs* alludes to Moshe's staff? Why can it not simply allude to the *makkos* themselves?**

וּבְמֹפְתִים. זֶה הַדָּם, כְּמָה שֶׁנֶּאֱמַר, וְנָתַתִּי מוֹפְתִים בַּשָּׁמַיִם וּבָאָרֶץ:

As each of the words, *Dam* (Blood), *Eish* (Fire), and *Ashan* (Smoke), is recited, a bit of wine is removed from the cup, with a finger, or, if one is squeamish, by pouring.

דָּם וָאֵשׁ וְתִמְרוֹת עָשָׁן[1]**.**

❒ **How did Moshe know that Hashem would end the *makkah* of *Tzefardei'a* at the time that he would pray for it to cease?**

❒ **Hashem gave control to Moshe, symbolized by the command to take the staff and perform the *makkos,* to begin and end the *makkos* as His agent. This is the significance of the staff. As such, Moshe was confident that the *makkah* would end when he would pray, because Hashem had given him that ability.**

Which was of greater significance — the miraculous signs Moshe performed, or the staff with which he performed them? It would seem clear that the staff was only the means by which the signs were performed, and the signs themselves were more noteworthy. Why, then, does the *Haggadah* explain the expression *with signs* to allude to the staff? Would it not be easier to explain that the *signs* are a reference to the signs themselves?

We may ask another question as well. When Pharaoh asked Moshe Rabbeinu to pray that the *Tzefardei'a* would cease, Moshe said to Pharaoh, *hispa'er alai, glorify yourself through me* [by challenging me to do what you think I cannot do], wherein Moshe allowed Pharaoh to dictate the time frame of the end of the *makkah.* Pharaoh challenged Moshe, telling him that he wanted it to stop the next day. He had presumed that Moshe knew that the *makkah* was going to end immediately, and did not actually have any control over ending it. Moshe immediately prayed that the *Tzefardei'a* would cease the next day, and it did.

We do not doubt that Hashem has the capability to end a *makkah* whenever He wishes. But what gave Moshe Rabbeinu the idea that whenever he would ask that the *makkah* be stopped, it would be? When did Hashem tell Moshe that he would be given such great control? We can be sure that without such a declaration from Hashem, Moshe — the most humble man to ever live — would never have presumed himself to be in possession of such power.

I believe the answer to both of these questions is the same. In commanding Moshe Rabbeinu to perform the *maakos,* Hashem said, *Take this*

MINHAGIM

The *Rosh HaYeshiva, ztvk"l,* would use his pinky finger to remove the wine while reciting these words, which is the prevalent *minhag.*

And with wonders — This alludes to the blood, as it is stated: "I will show wonders in the Heavens and on the earth,

As each of the words, *Dam* (Blood), *Eish* (Fire), and *Ashan* (Smoke), is recited, a bit of wine is removed from the cup, with a finger, or, if one is squeamish, by pouring.

Blood, fire, and columns of smoke."[1]

(1) *Yoel* 3:3.

---

staff in your hand, that you may perform the miraculous signs with it. This was the moment that Hashem gave the agency of the *maakos* (aside from *Makkas Bechoros*) to Moshe. He empowered Moshe to decide the precise moment each *makkah* would begin, and, as we see in the context of *Tzefardei'a,* when each one would end as well.

Accordingly, *the signs* with which Hashem took Klal Yisrael out of Mitzrayim do not merely refer to the *makkos* themselves. They also allude to the staff of Moshe, which was the symbol through which we recognize that Hashem gave unbelievable power over Mitzrayim to Moshe Rabbeinu.

וּבְמֹפְתִים — זֶה הַדָּם — *And With Wonders — This Alludes to the Blood*

❒ **While the above-referenced *Dever* and *Makkos Bechoros* involved death, *Dam* did not. So why is the less severe *makkah* of *Dam* alluded to in this *posuk?***

❒ **The blood was symbolic of the retribution Hashem was going to exact on behalf of His people. Thus, the symbolism of *Dam* alluded to the death that would result from the other *makkos.***

It is interesting that, according to this Tanna, the *posuk* in *Devarim* alludes to three *makkos: Dever, Makkas Bechoros,* and *Dam.* Now, the severity of *Dever* and *Makkas Bechoros* might lie in the fact that they were *makkos* of death. Surely, many of the *makkos* presented mortal danger, and it makes sense to posit that many Egyptians and their animals did, in fact, die during *Arov* and *Barad.* But when it came to each of these two *makkos* of *Dever* and *Makkas Bechoros,* death was not a byproduct of the *makkah;* it *was* the *makkah. Dam*, though, was, relatively speaking, not nearly as severe. Why, then, is it also specifically referenced here?

The answer is that if Hashem wanted to ruin the water supply of Mitzrayim, he could have turned it to mud, or sewage, or simply dried it up. But Hashem specifically chose to carry out the plague of *Dam* as a very ominous foreboding. The blood was not simply a way to deny the Egyptians water for all of their needs. It was also an allusion to the Jewish blood that had been spilled in the river. Hashem was sending a message to Klal Yisrael and to the Egyptians that He was going to demand the

דָּבָר אַחֵר בְּיָד חֲזָקָה, שְׁתַּיִם. וּבִזְרֹעַ נְטוּיָה, שְׁתַּיִם. וּבְמֹרָא גָּדֹל, שְׁתַּיִם. וּבְאֹתוֹת, שְׁתַּיִם. וּבְמֹפְתִים, שְׁתַּיִם:
אֵלּוּ עֶשֶׂר מַכּוֹת שֶׁהֵבִיא הַקָּדוֹשׁ בָּרוּךְ הוּא עַל הַמִּצְרִים בְּמִצְרַיִם, וְאֵלּוּ הֵן:

As each of the *makkos* is mentioned, a bit of wine is removed from the cup, as above. The same is done when reciting each word of R' Yehudah's mnemonic.

דָּם. צְפַרְדֵּעַ. כִּנִּים. עָרוֹב. דֶּבֶר. שְׁחִין. בָּרָד. אַרְבֶּה. חֹשֶׁךְ. מַכַּת בְּכוֹרוֹת.

---

blood of Mitzrayim. Before *Yetzias Mitzrayim* was going to be complete, the Egyptians were going to pay for what they had done to Klal Yisrael for the last several generations — and the currency that Hashem was going to take from them would be their lives, symbolized by blood. So, even though the *makkah* itself was not one of death, the message it carried was that Hashem's vengeance, in the form of death, would be forthcoming.

דָּם / *Blood*

- ❒ **Hashem punished the deity of the Egyptians, by demonstrating it could not provide for them.**
- ❒ **Pharaoh's complete unconcern for his people was revealed through this *makkah.***

The Egyptians served the Nile River, because their water came from its banks. In keeping with *Chazal's* dictum that *when Hashem exacts retribution from a nation, He carries it out against their deities first* (*Midrash Tanchuma, Va'eira* §13; see also *Rashi* to *Shemos* 7:17, *d"h v'nehepchu*), Hashem struck the river. But why did He turn it into blood?

As we discussed above (see *Uvemofsim*), the *makkah* of *Dam* carried with it an ominous foreboding. Another byproduct of beginning the *makkos* with *Dam* was the revelation of Pharaoh's true character to all. The reaction Pharaoh was going to have to the *makkah* would be callous; he would not be terribly moved by the plight of his subjects, his own people, going for a week without water. The fact that Pharaoh was unwilling to bend his position in the face of such dire circumstances for his subjects did a lot to paint the picture of how evil a person he truly was. He was totally unconcerned about the plight of others.

Another explanation of the preceding verse: [Each phrase represents two plagues, hence]: **Mighty hand** — two; **outstretched arm** — two; **great awe** — two; **signs** — two; **wonders** — two. These are the Ten *Makkos* which the Holy One, blessed is He, brought upon the Egyptians in Mitzrayim, namely:

As each of the *makkos* is mentioned, a bit of wine is removed from the cup, as above. The same is done when reciting each word of R' Yehudah's mnemonic.

1. Blood 2. Frogs 3. Lice 4. Wild Beasts
5. Pestilence 6. Boils 7. Hail 8. Locusts
9. Darkness 10. Plague of the Firstborn.

❒ **Pharaoh's need to relieve himself in the Nile is a lesson for us — it is simpler to stick to the truth.**

There is another pertinent lesson here for us to impart to our children. *Rashi* (*d"h hinei yotzei hamai'mah*) tells us that Pharaoh had to schedule his early-morning swim in the Nile River to mask the fact that he needed to urinate. He needed to do this because he had claimed to be a god, and gods do not need to use the bathroom.

I would like to focus on the inconvenience of this pathetic situation. Going to the bathroom is a very basic need of all people, and Pharaoh was no exception. And many people need to use the bathroom very soon after they rise in the morning. Fortunately, we have indoor plumbing, and do not need to venture outside to do so. Pharaoh, however, had to schedule his morning swim right after he rose in the morning, so as to cover his lie to his people. The river was probably often frigid, and it did not matter — Pharaoh needed the bathroom. Some people have experienced, for one reason or another, needing the restroom but not having one accessible — Pharaoh essentially turned his days into one long strategy session of how he was going to go to the bathroom in hiding, time after time!

What was Pharaoh protecting? The false image that he had implanted into his people. And it made his life *so* much more difficult! I think the tremendous efforts that Pharaoh needed to undertake to protect his silly premise are a good lesson to remember, and to teach our children; life is a lot easier when you do not need to account for anything except reality. If you are living a lie, you must expend significant efforts in covering up that lie, and it is just not worth it. As my mother, *Rebbetzin Shima, a"h,* would often quip, *"De beste ligin iz de emes, The best lie is the truth."* This thought can help open the eyes of even people who are not yet mature enough to speak the truth simply because it is the right thing to do.

- ❐ ***Tzefardei'a*** **showed the Egyptians that not only could the Nile not help them, it was actually a source of harm to them. When the** ***makkah*** **ended, a** ***Tzefardei'a*** **maintained a presence in the Nile. Especially according to the opinion that crocodiles were included, this always reminded the Egyptians that their deity had been overtaken by dangerous predators.**
- ❐ **Pharaoh tested Moshe, telling him to end the** ***makkah*** **the next day. Moshe was confident that the** ***makkah*** **would end when he said it would, for Hashem had given him the power to pray and thereby stop a** ***makkah.***

The *Tzefardei'a* emanated from the Nile River. Why did Hashem choose to initiate this *makkah* from the Nile? Above, we mentioned that *Chazal* teach us that Hashem punishes a nation first by smiting its deities. The *makkah* of *Dam* had done a very effective job of showing the Egyptians that the object of their worship, the Nile River, to which they attributed their sustenance, was actually incapable of doing just that. This mockery served to prove a point to the Egyptians, by way of depriving them of the blessing of the river that Hashem had previously afforded them. But the blood was simply a way to arrange a lack of water — albeit in a very scary and foreboding way — so that the Egyptians would be forced to realize that the Nile could not provide for them. However, with the first *makkah*, the Nile was not shown to be actively aggressive against the Egyptians; rather, it was merely powerless to positively help them — useless without Hashem's influence.

Tzefardei'a, however, took the delegitimization of the Nile as a deity a step further. For not only was the Nile unable to contribute blessings to the people of Mitzrayim, it was shown to be the source of a great nuisance, and even danger. Here, the Nile was cast as the starting point for all of the frogs, and perhaps whatever other amphibious or reptilian creatures might have been included in the *makkah*. [See further below.]

According to the opinion cited by *Rashi* (to *Shemos* 8:2, *d"h vata'al haTzefardei'a*) that one large *Tzefardei'a* came out of the river, and as the Egyptians hit it, it spewed more and even more time *tzefarde'im,* the following question can be asked: The *makkah* lasted approximately a week. It takes longer than that for frogs to reproduce, and even more for frogs to reach maturity. So, any of the *tzefarde'im* that participated in the *makkah* were apparently first-generation frogs, spewed from the mouth of that giant frog. This means that even after hitting the frog many, many times, and seeing the resulting myriads of frogs pouring forth from it, the Egyptians continued to hit it, and hit it some more. This seems like self-destructive behavior! Why would they keep doing this?

I believe that the feeling they had here was probably similar to scratching an itch; we know it is bad, and that it can prevent healing or aggravate the affected site further, but we somehow all do it anyway. They were so bothered by seeing the giant frog, that the knowledge that they were causing themselves more pain simply could not stop them from beating it.

In any event, this *makkah* must have been unbelievably, impossibly annoying to the Egyptians. I say this because, even though Pharaoh's magicians were able to employ the use of procurement and delivery via *sheidim*, just as they had been able to do during the *makkah* of *Dam*, Pharaoh was still willing to negotiate the release of Klal Yisrael. Once Pharaoh's servants could replicate Aharon's signs, Pharaoh attributed Aharon's ability to simply being better than his magicians at some trick or spell. And yet here, he asked Moshe to pray that the *makkah* cease, and he agreed that he would let Klal Yisrael go!

And yet, despite the terrible cacophony and madness that the *Tzefardei'a* had wrought upon Pharaoh, when Moshe presented the choice of choosing the time to end the *makkah*, Pharaoh chose the next day, thinking that Moshe did not have to power to change the end-time of the *makkah*. To put this in perspective, to get rid of the nuisance of the *Tzefardei'a,* Pharaoh was willing to free millions of slaves (even if only for a few days) — losing tens of millions of work hours — to get rid of the plague. But, to prove Moshe and Aharon wrong, Pharaoh was willing to endure an extra twenty-four hours of this unbearable *makkah*! Why was he willing to do this?

The answer is that Pharaoh had now come to the realization that Hashem might indeed be behind these *makkos* after all; and so he devised another test to see if He was or not. By asking for an additional day of the *makkah* that he believed Moshe could not deliver, Pharaoh was betting an extra day of this craziness that Hashem was not behind the *makkos*. And that was when Moshe told him, *As you have spoken; so that you may know that there is no One like Hashem, our God.*

Had Hashem so desired, he could have done with the *Tzefardei'a* as he did with the *Arov* and the *Arbeh* later on, and have them completely disappear from the land of Mitzrayim at the conclusion of the *makkah*. Yet Hashem did not do so, on two counts. Firstly, Hashem arranged for a great multitude of the *Tzefardei'a* to die in Mitzrayim, and their carcasses made great piles, which was disgusting for the Egyptians. Secondly, the *Tzefardei'a* differed from the other *makkos* in that the *Tzefardei'a* maintained a presence in Mitzrayim after the *makkah* as well, as opposed to *Arov* and *Arbeh*, which Hashem removed from Mitzrayim completely after the *makkah* was concluded. Why was this so?

We know that the reason Hashem chose to have the first two *makkos* emanate from the Nile River itself was because the Egyptians served

the Nile, and ascribed power to it. The *Tzefardei'a* were symbolic of Hashem subduing the Nile because the Nile was reviled as the source of this plague (even though the water itself — although surely infested with frogs — was not changed, as it had been during the *makkah* of *Dam*). So, we can be sure that one of the reliefs that the Egyptains were hoping for in the aftermath of *Tzefardei'a* was the ability to once again believe in their deity, and to trust their river to care for them. Allowing the remnants of the *Tzefardei'a* to stay in the Nile River left a symbolic reminder in the minds of every Egyptian who accessed it. Every croak and every hop, every tadpole and every frog, would stand as an eternal reminder to the Egyptians who would come to the Nile that their river was powerless against the decree of Hashem. [And especially if the *Tzefardei'a* were (or included) giant reptiles such as the Nile crocodile, as some commentators maintain, the reminder of Hashem's Omniscience was all the more powerful! Now, instead of believing in sustenance from the River, the people needed to fear for their lives around these predators. This sign held true throughout, and there are still *Tzefardei'a* in and around the Nile River.]

See above, *U'Ve'osos,* where we explained that in the command that Moshe take the staff, Hashem empowered Moshe to begin and end each *makkah*. Thus, when he challenged Pharaoh, *hispa'eir alai, glorify yourself* [by challenging me to do what you think I cannot do], Moshe knew with certainty that his prayers would be answered. Here, perhaps the words *vaya'as Hashem kidvar Moshe, And Hashem did according to the word of Moshe,* allude to the fact that the power Moshe was given was not that he would begin or end the *makkah* on his own. He was rather the emissary of Hashem; he was empowered to follow Hashem's instructions and begin a *makkah,* and to pray for Hashem to end a *makkah*. But he was assured that his efforts would bear fruit. In other words, when Moshe or Aharon initiated a *makkah* (after Hashem commanded them to do so) with an action of stretching out a hand or striking with a staff, or even by just speaking (as he did at the beginning of *Arov*), Hashem had imbued them with the power to actually perform the *makkah*, just as He imbues us with the ability to eat and breathe. The same was true with praying for a *makkah* to end — the formula was that Moshe would pray, and Hashem gave his prayer the power to be effective.

Now, even when Hashem gives a *Navi* the power to carry out a certain mission, and also gives the reins to that *Navi,* so that he can appear to be exhibiting control, He wants the *Navi* to always remember that it is He Who is doing it all. [This was why the angels who were sent to save Lot and to destroy Sedom were punished for their phraseology when they used the words, "*We are destroying the city*" (*Bereishis* 19:13). They certainly knew Hashem was destroying the city, but their words made it seem as though

it was they who were going to do it.] Of course, Moshe would be praying that the *Tzefardei'a* would cease, but he knew Hashem would answer him. Hashem wanted Moshe to pray, so that it would be apparent to all that the result of the prayer was from Hashem.

Despite the impressive display of Moshe managing to end the *makkah* precisely when Pharaoh had requested that it should end, the *posuk* tells us that Pharaoh hardened his heart, and refused to honor his word. This, despite the fact that the Gemara (*Bava Basra* 3b) teaches us that a king is known to always honor his word! The explanation of Pharaoh's comfort in his deceit here is as follows: The circumstances themselves make it apparent that Pharaoh felt that he had been coerced into the agreement that he made. Moshe had demonstrated that he could control Pharaoh in the area of overrunning the country with frogs, and to save the sanity of his people, Pharaoh was forced into an agreement. To him, there was no right and wrong in this arrangement; rather, there was only powerful and weak. Because Moshe had proven more powerful than Pharaoh, Pharaoh had made a commitment. It is considered dishonorable when a person or king does not honor his word only when it seems as though the reneging occurred in the realm of right and wrong. But when a king is forced to make a commitment so he will not be killed, nobody expects that agreement to hold up as soon as the king has a choice in the matter. [This is the case with most peace treaties, which are routinely broken when the less powerful party no longer feels that they are in as poor a negotiating position as they were when the treaty was forced upon them.]

It emerges, then, that the reason Pharaoh was so easily able to go back on his word was because he agreed to Moshe's demand only tactically, but certainly not philosophically. He was thus perfectly comfortable reneging as soon as the opportunity presented itself. As far as why Pharaoh was unconcerned that Moshe might make the *makkah* return, perhaps the large frog that had been the source of the *makkah* to begin with had died, or perhaps the Egyptians had already observed that it had stopped reproducing. And as far as a future *makkah*, Pharaoh adopted a wait-and-see attitude; if he could survive this suffering, perhaps he could also survive the next, and the next, and so he was not about to give up so easily.

[An unintended consequence of the relief that the Egyptians had sought since the inception of the *makkah* was the new problem of the large mounds of dead and rotting frogs that were all over the land. This too was a part of the strike against the Egyptians, for although the *makkah* was over, it was still lingering in a very real sense.]

כִּנִּים / *Lice*

❒ ***Kinnim* came without warning, in response to Pharaoh's lie after *Tzefardei'a* that he would allow Klal Yisrael to go.**

- **The *makkah* also struck Goshen. Klal Yisrael might also have been exposed to it, either so they could appreciate the plight the Egyptians were in, or else because the lesson that Hashem controls the body of a person is pertinent to Klal Yisrael as well.**
- **Alternatively, although there were *kinnim* in Goshen, no Jews were infected with lice. This was a greater degree of Hashem's control than that which He demonstrated during *Arov*, for animals go only where they wish, but lice will infest anything they can reach.**

Unlike the first two *makkos*, the *makkah* of *Kinnim* came without any warning to Pharaoh at all. Why was this so? Perhaps it can be suggested that after *Dam,* Pharaoh had stubbornly refused to free Klal Yisrael. Thus, Hashem brought upon him the *makkah* of *Tzefardei'a.* But because Pharaoh had been upfront in his refusal to free them, Hashem was upfront with him about His plan to bring the second *makkah.* However, when Pharaoh was trying to get rid of the *Tzefardei'a,* he promised he would free Klal Yisrael if he was relieved from this nightmare. Of course, he did not keep this promise. So, Hashem punished Pharaoh by not issuing a warning as to the coming of the third *makkah.*

Aside from the fact that the magicians of Pharaoh were unable to manufacture *Kinnim,* it is also noteworthy that this *makkah* actually affected Goshen as well as the rest of Mitzrayim. We know this is so because one of the reasons that Yaakov Avinu did not want to be buried in Mitzrayim was because the dirt of Mitzrayim was destined to become *Kinnim.* Certainly Yaakov could have been buried in Goshen, in the Jewish community, if this would have solved the problem. Additionally, while we know from *Chazal* that the Jewish people were unaffected by *Dam,* and the *pesukim* surrounding *Tzefardei'a* do not say that that the *makkah* affected the entirety of the land of Mitzrayim, in regard to *Kinnim* the *posuk* does explicitly state that all of the land of Mitzrayim was affected; and we do not know with certainty that Goshen was unaffected by *Kinnim.*

Assuming, then, that this was indeed the case, we can perhaps explain that *Kinnim* was distinct from *Dam* and *Tzefarde'a* in that it was a lighter *makkah,* relative to the first two *makkos.* Hashem wanted to allow Klal Yisrael to experience the *makkah* firsthand so that they could better process what He was putting the Egyptians through.

Alternatively, perhaps there was a lesson to be learned from the *makkah* for Klal Yisrael as well. The previous *makkos* had attacked the notion that the Nile River was a deity of any kind, and showed that Hashem's power was beyond anything Pharaoh or any of the other idols of the Egyptians could withstand. This was a lesson for the Egyptians who believed in the Nile and in Pharaoh. Now, however, Hashem was moving the

demonstration of the *makkos* beyond the idols, and striking the bodies of the people themselves. The central idea of this shift was to demonstrate to the Egyptians that Hashem is to be feared, for He has control over everything, including the ability to punish each individual according to his deficiencies or sins. Klal Yisrael thus also had an opportunity to internalize the concept that Hashem is real, and that He should be served not only with love, but also with fear. This opportunity allowed them to strengthen their belief in Him as well. For although they had endured much greater suffering at the hands of the Egyptians, perhaps thousands of times greater than a case of lice, the suffering of *Kinnim* was clearly and obviously a direct and open message from Hashem. This can make much more of an impression upon a person than greater suffering that is less obviously coming from Hashem.

It is also very possible, and even likely, that although the ground of Goshen was turned into a bed of lice, no member of Klal Yisrael actually experienced any infestation, or itching of any kind. This alone was a tremendous lesson in the control Hashem has over His creations, for the Jewish people saw the multitudes of insects, and not one was attacking them. [Although the fact that the *Arov* did not enter Goshen offered a similar lesson, for it also showed the powerful reality that Hashem controls all of His creations, this lesson would have been even clearer. Large animals go where they feel like going, and so there would be room to claim that none of the animals were interested in coming to Goshen. Lice, however, live off the hosts they attack, and will infest anything wherever and whenever they have the opportunity. And still, no Jew was infested.]

While the fact that this *makkah* was on the "lighter side" may well have proven beneficial for Klal Yisrael, it also caused Pharaoh to take Hashem's threat less seriously. After all, compared to an entire country facing a hydration crisis, the whole populace coming down with terrible cases of lice infestation might have seemed trivial to him. Sure, it was terribly annoying, but by and large, it did not pose a threat to the lives of the citizens of Mitzrayim. So, despite the fact that his magicians could not themselves produce any *Kinnim*, Pharaoh mustered the confidence to wave off the potential for more *makkos*, because he saw that they were not as catastrophic as he could have imagined. [See, however, below, *D'tzach, Adash, B'Achav*.]

עָרוֹב / *Wild Beasts*

- **After *Arov*, Pharaoh began to actually negotiate with Moshe, showing he was serious.**
- **Seeing that Moshe did not push back on every counteroffer he made, Pharaoh fell into the trap of not taking Moshe seriously.**

After the *makkah* of *Tzefardei'a*, Pharaoh had lied about his intent to send Klal Yisrael out of Mitzrayim. After the devastation wreaked upon his people during *Arov*, though, Pharaoh began to change his tune. This is clear from the fact that the *pesukim* discuss the bargaining that seems to have taken place between Moshe Rabbeinu and Pharaoh at that time. If Pharaoh was bargaining, it would seem that he was at least planning at that time to uphold his end of the bargain. So, although his stubbornness was getting stronger, his negotiations were getting a little more truthful; in other words, he started saying what he actually felt, as opposed to simply making up a lie. This "honesty," or perhaps, realism, was an important step for Pharaoh.

As part of his position, Pharaoh would not allow the Jewish people to leave Mitzrayim for a journey to a distance of three days away. Rather, he insisted that they stay closer; he did not specify how close. And interestingly, Moshe did not counter that this would be unacceptable; he agreed to pray on Pharaoh's behalf, and warned Pharaoh not to back away from his pledge. Perhaps this was because Moshe saw that Pharaoh was making progress, in that He was beginning to take Moshe seriously. However, despite Pharaoh's interest in making a deal, this position proved only to be artificial, created out of fear when Pharaoh's feet were put to the fire. The second the danger had passed, Pharaoh proved to be as stubborn as ever. This defiance was not premeditated, as it had been during *Tzefardei'a*, but rather was a genuine shift in position; in other words, Pharaoh was dishonest, but not in a premeditated manner. This defiance would eventually grow to the level of *vayichazeik lev Pharaoh,* which we will discuss below; see *Shechin.*

Perhaps, because he saw that Moshe would not insist on every single detail of his proposal (such as the three-day travel distance — see *Ohr HaChaim*) Pharaoh became bolder, realizing that he was able to defy the requests made of him and get away with it! This served to boost his confidence in his position, and allowed him to think he was in a position to defy Moshe — and thus Hashem — completely. In his eyes, the fact that the *makkah* ended at all showed either that the *makkah* was limited, or that even if it was not, Pharaoh could demand more from Moshe, and he would not have to capitulate to all of Moshe Rabbeinu's demands.

דֶּבֶר / Pestilence

❒ **Because Pharaoh had not lied outright after *Arov,* but rather backed out of an actual intention to free the nation, Hashem gave him one more chance — *Dever* — before sending another *makkah* without warning.**

Above, when discussing *Kinnim*, we explained that Pharaoh deserved to receive the *makkah* of *Kinnim* without warning because he lied to Moshe

and did not follow through with his commitment. Here, the *makkah* of *Dever* marked the first *makkah* to occur after Pharaoh changed his mind yet again in the aftermath of *Arov*. So, it would seem logical that *Dever* would be the next plague to arrive without warning, rather than *Shechin*! Additionally, there seems to have been a leniency with the *makkah* of *Dever*, in that only the animals that were left in the fields perished, but the ones taken inside were safe. Why did Hashem grant this leniency, if the idea of this *makkah* ought to have been swift retribution against Pharaoh's stubbornness?

Perhaps we can explain this order based upon the understanding of the development of Pharaoh's position. During *Tzefardei'a*, Pharaoh was knowingly lying to Moshe, and this merited an immediate response. However, as we have pointed out above, when Pharaoh made his promise in the aftermath of *Arov*, he did so cautiously, trying to minimize the impact that freeing Klal Yisrael would have on his society. Although Pharaoh ended up not keeping his side of the bargain, it is apparent that during the negotiation process, he was being sincere and serious.

Accordingly, since we know Pharaoh was taking Hashem's position seriously, the issue that Pharaoh was displaying here was not disregard for Hashem's command, as much as it was a disrespect for Hashem's abilities. That is to say that in the aftermath of *Arov*, Pharaoh retracted because he felt that Hashem was not able to hurt him enough to make it worth his while to free Klal Yisrael. So, Hashem gave him a chance; He first brought the *makkah* of *Dever* upon Mitzrayim, which demonstrated Hashem's remarkable power in separating the animals belonging to the Egyptians from those that were owned by Klal Yisrael. When Pharaoh further ignored the consequences of the *makkah* of *Dever*, it was then time to smite Mitzrayim with *Shechin*, *boils,* without warning.

❒ **Perhaps the worship of the livestock in Mitzrayim was based on the fact that the animals provided for them — in the form of milk and wool.**

❒ **Why did *Dever* come now, and not in conjunction with the first two *makkos,* which smote the deity of the Egyptians? One reason Pharaoh did not keep his word after *Arov* was because he thought he was doing something good by "saving" his gods from being used as offerings by the Jewish people. Hashem sent the *Dever* to decimate those animals.**

Why would the Egyptians raise flocks of livestock if they considered them to be gods? Perhaps they believed that they could use the milk and the wool of the animals, but were not permitted to kill them. It can

even be that this was central to their belief in the livestock as deities. We find, for example, that the name of the idol of the Pelishtim was Dagan, which translates as *grain*. The Egyptians worshiped the Nile, presumably because their agriculture was so heavily dependent upon its ebb and flow. Perhaps the reason that the Egyptians worshiped their animals was because they provided sustenance for people without becoming diminished themselves, similar to the Nile.

It is interesting that only now, after the first four *makkos*, did Hashem see fit to strike the animals. We know that the Egyptians worshiped sheep and cattle, and so it might have been understandable if the livestock would have been struck in conjunction with the first two *makkos,* which were also intended to demonstrate the powerlessness of Mitzrayim's deities. Why, then, did the *makkah* of *Dever* take place only now?

Perhaps we can suggest that the message of *Dever* was not simply to show the futility of idolatry. It also served to deflate the hope of Pharaoh and the Egyptians. It is certainly possible that one of the factors driving Pharaoh to back out of his commitment after *Arov* was that he thought he was doing something righteous. In the society of Mitzrayim, allowing harm to befall cattle was frowned upon, and surely allowing Klal Yisrael the opportunity to slaughter cattle to their God would be tantamount to blasphemy! If he could get away with "saving the gods" by changing his mind again without incurring serious punishment, perhaps Pharaoh reasoned that he ought to do so.

To counter this thought, and indeed, to quash all hope that Pharaoh might have had that he might preserve his cattle from being used in the service of Hashem, Hashem brought the *Dever* at this point in time. *Dever* killed all of Pharaoh's livestock (that was outdoors, at any rate) showing that he and his gods were powerless to protect against Hashem's hand. [Similarly, before *Barad,* Moshe advised Pharaoh to tell those of his servants who feared Hashem to gather in their livestock. It is certainly ironic that these Egyptians were either going to have to listen to Hashem to save their deities, or else put faith in the animals themselves and watch them die.]

Additionally, Hashem made the *Dever* leave the animals of the Jewish people completely alone. This was to show Pharaoh that when Hashem wants something to be used for a purpose, it will be utilized for that purpose — end of discussion. Hashem had said that Klal Yisrael were going to offer *korbanos*, and so they were; Pharaoh had tried to stop them to save His gods, and all his gods perished, leaving only the ones that would be sacrificed by Klal Yisrael. This also showed Pharaoh that he would not win a war of attrition with Hashem; there would be no waiting Hashem out, because He can strike anything at any time.

Interestingly, the very factor that was supposed to aid Pharaoh in

understanding how unattainable his goal was — the fact that not a single animal among Klal Yisrael died in the *makkah* — actually served to strengthen his resolve that Hashem was not able to carry out complete and total annihilation of a species. It was not only the animals of Klal Yisrael which were saved. In fact, the Midrash (*Shemos Rabbah* 11:4) expounds from this *posuk* that any livestock that a Jew had a claim to, either through a lien or perhaps even a partnership, was saved from the *makkah* of *Dever*. Pharaoh took this as a sign that Moshe's prediction had not been accurate, for he had said that there would be no casualties among the Jewish livestock, and the implication was that there would be no survivors among the Egyptians' livestock. [In fact, *Shemos* 9:6 explicitly states that all of the livestock of Mitzrayim (that had been left in the fields) had died, so this inference was accurate.] However, Pharaoh saw that these specific animals that belonged, at least in part, to Egyptians had indeed survived, and therefore refused to honor his word.

Of course, the reason that this was actually not a contradiction at all was because such animals fell into the category of Jewish-owned animals, which Hashem had decreed would survive. But it gave Pharaoh the excuse he sought, by which he could express doubt that Hashem was as powerful as Moshe had proclaimed.

שְׁחִין / *Boils*

- ❒ **_Shechin_ came without warning, because Pharaoh had not freed Klal Yisrael after _Dever_. He was now punished for having changed his mind after _Arov_ (and not releasing the nation after _Dever_).**
- ❒ **Had Hashem not hardened Pharaoh's heart, the fact that his magicians were not able to stand before him would have caused him to give in.**
- ❒ **Alternatively, _Shechin_ was a torturous _makkah_ because of the insatiable itching that it caused. It was so terrible that had Hashem not hardened Pharaoh's heart, he would have sent Klal Yisrael free.**

The *posuk* states that after the *makkah* of *Shechin*, Hashem strengthened Pharaoh's heart, and as a result, he refused yet again to send Klal Yisrael out of Mitzrayim. [See below, *Lessons of the Makkos,* where we explain that this was a punishment that Pharaoh earned for denying Hashem's will after the first five *makkos*.] The clear indication is that had Hashem not intervened in this fashion, Pharaoh would have broken, and finally given in, freeing the Jewish people. What was so terrible about the *makkah* of *Shechin* that would have caused Pharaoh to capitulate had he had a choice? This was not one of the *makkos* that caused widespread death, and would seem to have perhaps been of the milder *makkos*!

Perhaps this had to do with how the *makkah* affected the magicians

of Pharaoh — this was the first *makkah* in which they were affected this way. With the magicians proven to be totally powerless in regard to this *makkah*, Pharaoh lost his excuse of blaming the *makkas* on magic, and was forced to realize that they were a punishment from Hashem. He therefore would have surrendered had Hashem not strengthened his heart.

Alternatively, the fact that the *makkah* caused insufferable itching might have simply proved too torturous for Pharaoh to bear. [Although the *makkah* of *Kinnim* was also a plague accompanied by itching, there was a big difference between the two. The lice of *Makkas Kinnim* were the source of the itching; remove a louse, and the itching in the affected area will cease. Here, the boils were in wounds on the bodies of the Egyptians, and there could not even be momentary escape from the itching. Still, it could be that after *Kinnim*, although Klal Yisrael was not freed, they were no longer forced to work — see further *D'tzach, A'dash B'Achav*.] After all, there are people that have very high thresholds for pain, or at least ways to cope with pain, even severe pain; but an extremely severe itch can truly drive a person mad. It is possible that aside from the pain the boils caused, the itching they caused was so bad that Hashem knew that if He would not strengthen Pharaoh, he would not have been able to withstand the terrible itching that the *Shechin* brought to bear.

בָּרָד / *Hail*

- **Barad caused Pharaoh to actually realize that he was wrong for holding the Jewish people prisoner. What may have made him realize this was the *middah keneged middah (measure for measure)* punishment he had received. He saw that hailstorms had come that were beyond the norm, and perhaps realized that his treatment of the Jewish people could be deemed the same.**
- **We must learn from here that *teshuvah* can ascend to Hashem in a moment!**
- **Because Pharaoh realized he was wrong, and yet *still* refused to free Klal Yisrael, Hashem sealed his fate; the last three *makkos* were going to come no matter what Pharaoh would say.**
- **Moshe's prayer was answered *immediately*. This shows us the efficacy of *tefillah*.**

Moshe warned Pharaoh that if he did not allow Klal Yisrael to leave, *Barad* would be arriving — in twenty-four-hours time. Pharaoh was thus faced with a choice of either backing down, or facing a devastating plague the very next day. Especially in an age before cell phones, cars, and supermarkets, one day is a very, very short amount of time to prepare for a national disaster.

The *makkah* of *Barad* was interesting in that although the hailstones were large enough to kill people and animals, and although they contained fire within them, they apparently did not cause structural damage to the houses of the Egyptians. Not only that, but Moshe had explicitly warned Pharaoh that the only safe place for people and livestock to ride out the *Barad* was going to be inside. This was really another clear message from Hashem, because according to "normal" scientific principles, there should have been many casualties due to falling or burning structures; but there were not.

Barad impacted Pharaoh in a way that none of the previous *makkos* had. Above, we explained that *Dam* did not move Pharaoh, *Tzefardei'a* caused him to lie, and *Arov* caused him to negotiate. Here, however, Pharaoh was genuine in his remorse when he agreed to free Klal Yisrael. He was ready to give up, and to allow them to go free completely. This is the meaning of the expression, *chatasi, I have sinned,* and the admission that *ani v'ami hareshaim, I and my nation are wicked*; Pharaoh came to realize that Hashem had been sending him message after message as to what he ought to be doing. He had been wrong to keep Klal Yisrael as slaves, and he had been wrong to defy Hashem's will. At this point, Pharaoh was ready to capitulate to Hashem not only tactically, but philosophically as well.

It was only after *Barad* that Pharaoh admitted that he had been wrong, and that Hashem was correct. What was it about the *makkah* of *Barad* that had such a profound impact upon Pharaoh, showing him that *ki ein Kamoni b'chol ha'aretz, there is none like Me (Hashem) in all the land,* and that he had been wrong this entire time?

Perhaps we can suggest that during the *Barad*, Pharaoh had occasion to witness something natural — stormy weather — take on unbelievably epic proportions, to the point that it turned into an incredibly deadly phenomenon. When a person is confronted with something that is normally fairly tame and has suddenly turned deadly, they might be inclined to entertain the thought, "Whoa! This is too much! This is not how this is supposed to work!"

There is something unique about the trait of *middah keneged middah* that Hashem uses to punish people. Aside from the fact that the punishments are absolutely fitting, they also include a similarity to the sin that brought them about. [This shows not only Hashem's absolute fairness, but also His kindness, because it allows people to realize, when reflecting upon the punishment they have received, just what they had done to deserve it.] When Pharaoh uttered these words to himself, in that instant, he may really have finally received Hashem's message. Just as his complaint against the onslaught of the *Barad* was likely, "It is not supposed to be this way!", he might have realized that he had changed slavery — a common

enough practice of the era — into something it was not supposed to be. The terrorization of Klal Yisrael in the name of economy had gone way, way too far under his rule. And when that realization hit home, Pharaoh might actually have received the message that he was absolutely wrong; if only for that second. That moment, that split second, was a moment of real *teshuvah* for Pharaoh. In his heart of hearts, he knew that he had been wrong, as evident from the fact that he admitted as much to Moshe.

A lesson we can take from here is that *teshuvah* can be attained in a moment. The Gemara (*Kiddushin* 49b) states that if an evil person marries a woman on condition that he is a righteous person, we suspect that the marriage could be valid; for perhaps the man had thoughts of *teshuvah*. Clearly, it is possible to achieve real *teshuvah* with a momentary thought.

How can we reconcile this reality with the famous statement of the *Rambam* (*Hil. Teshuvah* 2:2), that there are three things that are integral to *teshuvah*; *charatah* (*remorse*), *viduy* (*verbal confession*), and *kabbalah al ha'asid* (*acceptance not to sin in this manner again in the future*)? I believe that *Rambam* is explaining that if a person desires to do *teshuvah*, these three factors are necessary. However, when one is actually doing *teshuvah,* it can be accomplished even in a moment, as Pharaoh did here. A second of true remorse, although it does not formally include a verbal admission of guilt or the acceptance not to sin again, really does contain elements of both.

And still, somehow, even after his admission and his momentary *teshuvah,* Pharaoh managed to defy Hashem, and not allow Klal Yisrael to go free! This was a great demonstration of evil. To know with clarity that one is wrong, and that Hashem is commanding that Moshe be heeded, and still be able to defy Moshe and Hashem, was truly evil! Because Pharaoh was able to muster such evil in his heart, Hashem punished him by strengthening his heart after *Arbeh* and *Choshech*; essentially slamming him at this juncture with an inescapable sentence of the last three *makkos*. [See below, *Lessons From the Makkos*.]

Given the above, the fact that Hashem hardened Pharaoh's heart after *Arbeh* and *Choshech* was a far more significant punishment than it had been when He hardened his heart after *Shechin*. There is a concept of a sinner who has gone so far in his wicked ways that his repentance will simply not be accepted to save him from punishment; even if he feels he is wrong, and stops sinning, he will continue to be punished. This befell Pharaoh in two stages; after *Dever*, Pharaoh was punished with having his *bechirah* removed in the aftermath of *Shechin*. But he would still have a chance to make up for it, in that he would be able to free Klal Yisrael after *Barad*, if he would pass his *nisayon* then. However, after his decision in the aftermath of *Barad*, it was all over for Pharaoh — the decision was

no longer in his hands at all. Hashem decided that Pharaoh was, from this point on, going to be a vehicle for displaying miracles, and would play no part in the decision-making process. He had failed once and for all; no amount of punishment that Hashem would bring upon him would provide atonement for his sin. [Even now, however, the ability to show true remorse, *teshuvah mei'ahavah,* had not been removed, and if Pharaoh would have utilized it, it certainly would have helped him in the next world — see *Arbeh,* below.]

Practically speaking, how can we understand the notion that Pharaoh realized throughout the duration of the last three *makkos* that he and his nation had been wicked, while simultaneously having a hardened heart, pushing him to keep retracting his word? Perhaps Hashem planted the notion in Pharaoh's mind — against his will — that he simply could not afford to lose Klal Yisrael as slaves, and this caused Pharaoh not to try to repent, even though he knew he was in the wrong. This is no different from any sinner who knows that his habitual sins wreak havoc on his life, and endanger his *olam haba*, and yet he cannot muster the willpower to actually repent and change himself.

Pharaoh begged Moshe to pray for the *Barad* to cease, and Moshe did so. The *Rosh HaYeshiva, ztvk"l,* used to explain that from Moshe's prayer here we can see the potential power and effectiveness of our prayers. Moshe prayed that the *Barad* would stop, and it did so with such immediacy as to stop where it was, in midair, never reaching the ground. This was so, even though the rain and hail that had frozen in midair would not have made a terribly great difference. Given that the *makkah* had already lasted a week, another couple of seconds would not have changed things very much. Still, once Hashem has accepted a person's prayers, the decree that was in effect before has already become undone, and all consequences of that decree cease immediately from that point forward. Such is the great power of prayer!

אַרְבֶּה / *Locusts*

- **Pharaoh "flip-flopped" on the issue of freeing the Jewish people, and did so again — the other way around — after *Makkas Bechoros*. This is the fate of an unprincipled person.**
- **Real *teshuvah* is about repairing a relationship, not simply avoiding consequences. Thus, even though Pharaoh's fate was sealed, and his *bechirah* was removed, his *teshuvah mei'ahavah* would still have been accepted, and would have benefited him in the next world.**

A person who is motivated by his own principles acts the same way in any situation in which he is able to. Even when a person has his hand forced, and must depart from the tenets he holds dear, he will certainly do

so to as small a degree as possible. Here, we can observe how a person motivated by factors other than his adherence to something he believes to be right and correct will act if he comes under pressure.

Initially, Pharaoh was completely unmoved by the threat of the impending *Arbeh*. It was only after the urging of his servants that Pharaoh brought Moshe and Aharon back to the palace to reconsider his position. We can contrast this moment with the eventual Exodus, where Pharaoh allowed Klal Yisrael to go free. Clearly, at the time, he had no reservations about being rid of Klal Yisrael, despite the loss of his slaves. Yet the *posuk* (*Shemos* 14:5) mentions that Pharaoh and his servants soon regretted this action, and sought to chase after Klal Yisrael. This, of course, led to their destruction. We can contrast the wishy-washy nature of Pharaoh's actions with those of a principled individual. Whereas a person who is guided strictly by his morals will act in a consistent manner, Pharaoh, who bowed to social pressure, found himself on opposite sides of the issue of freeing Klal Yisrael on different occasions, which was only further exacerbated by his flip-flopping on both occasions.

When trying to extricate himself and his people from the *makkah* of *Arbeh,* Pharaoh did not bother with empty promises to release Klal Yisrael. Rather, his plea to Moshe contained an admission of guilt, and a clear recognition of Hashem and His supremacy, along with a desperate plea for salvation. He did not so much as mention Klal Yisrael. And yet, this was enough for Moshe to pray for the *makkah* to cease. Why?

The answer is, that from Pharaoh's perspective, he knew that he no longer needed to say he would release the Jewish people in order to be freed from a *makkah*. If Moshe did not ask for such a promise, Pharaoh was not going to offer it. After *Barad,* Pharaoh was going to be punished no matter what he *said*; the only way to stave off the final *makkos* from occurring would be to take the actual action of freeing Klal Yisrael.

Similarly, Moshe Rabbeinu did not need to hear any silly, false guarantees from Pharaoh. For Moshe knew that no matter what words emanated from Pharaoh's mouth, he was not in control of his stubbornness, and Hashem would harden his heart so he would retract his position. Accordingly, Moshe was simply waiting for a declaration from Pharaoh that showed his surrender to Hashem, for history to record that Pharaoh had recognized Hashem's power and bowed before it. For this purpose, Pharaoh's statement here was certainly appropriate, and so Moshe prayed for the *Arbeh* to leave.

As we have explained above, *Chazal* teach us that Pharaoh had reached the point where he no longer had a choice of whether or not to free Klal Yisrael, for Hashem had hardened his heart. Still, Hashem went through the charade of offering Pharaoh a chance to let Klal Yisrael go free, and hardened his heart each time. Why?

Perhaps it was so that people would not accuse Hashem of not giving Pharaoh a chance, because it looked like He did. Or, perhaps this was part and parcel of Pharaoh's punishment; he felt like he had the opportunity to give in, and Hashem pulled him back, not allowing him to, despite Pharaoh's own desire.

Often, people have a hard time reconciling this teaching with the principle that Hashem allows us to have free will to choose to act rightly or wrongly on our own. Does Hashem always accept *teshuvah*, at any point, or does He not?

In order to properly understand how these facts can coexist, it is important to put *teshuvah* in the proper perspective. What does *teshuvah* do? From the time we are young children, we are accustomed to viewing the purpose of *teshuvah* as a means of avoiding unwanted consequences, otherwise known as punishments. And when viewed from this angle, it is difficult to understand how Pharaoh could still have free will, in light of the fact that his consequences were "predetermined," based on his previous actions. How can we still posit that *teshuvah* even then would have helped him?

However, this is not the purpose of *teshuvah,* any more than the purpose of eating is to be satiated. Of course, the purpose of eating is so that we have strength and energy, and a byproduct of this is that we feel full. Similarly, the goal of *teshuvah* is to show remorse, and repair our relationship with Hashem. And we hope and pray that as a byproduct of our rekindled relationship with Him, He will shower us with mercy and change the circumstances we would have faced had we not come back to Him. But the real purpose is to come closer to Hashem.

So, although Pharaoh did not have a choice regarding the fate of Mitzrayim and whether or not he was going to free Klal Yisrael, because this was his deserved punishment, he certainly had a choice to appeal to Hashem and thereby mend his relationship with his Creator; that path is never sealed. And even if nothing would change in this world, the relationship in the next world would have been repaired.

There is a similar discussion pertaining to the story in the Gemara of R' Meir's Rebbi, Elisha ben Avuyah (or, as he was known, Acher). The Gemara (*Chagigah* 15a) relates that when R' Meir asked him why he would not do *teshuvah,* he answered that he had heard a Heavenly edict saying, *Shuvu vanim shovavim, chutz mei'Acher — Return, wayward children, except for Acher.* So, why should he do *teshuvah*? Many people can see this Gemara as a source that there is a point at which *teshuvah* does not help. Certainly, we must be aware that *teshuvah* is a gift, and we can all, God forbid, come to the point that our *teshuvah* will not be accepted to ward off punishment.

I believe, though, that if Acher had done *teshuvah despite* what he had

heard, it would have been accepted. But allowing Acher to hear what he did was intended as a *nisayon*. If Acher would treat *teshuvah* solely as a device by which to avoid punishment, there would be no need for him to do *teshuvah,* as Hashem had stated that in Acher's case, this would not happen. But, had he treated *teshuvah* more sincerely, as a way to express his remorse, and apologized to Hashem for the evil he had committed, even knowing that it would *not* save him from punishment — in other words, apologize because he had been wrong, not to save himself — he would have merited to, at the very least, come closer to Hashem. In this true light, *teshuvah* is never, ever too late.

An example of *teshuvah* that was ineffective when it came to warding off punishment, but was very effective in repairing a relationship with Hashem, was that of R' Elazar ben Durdaya. The Gemara (*Avodah Zarah* 17a) relates that Elazar was exceedingly attached to sins of forbidden relations. When a certain harlot told him that his repentance would not be accepted in Heaven, he went to ask the mountains, the heavens and earth, the sun and moon, and the stars and constellations, to beseech Heaven on his behalf; and none did. He then cried until his soul departed, and a *bas kol* proclaimed, "R' Elazar ben Durdaya has now been prepared for the World to Come!" Although his *teshuvah* did not prevent his death (see further there), the Gemara clearly states that it was accepted.

❒ **One of the goals of the *Arbeh* was to devalue Egyptian society in the eyes of Klal Yisrael, before the arrival of *Choshech,* when any Jews who wanted to stay in Mitzrayim perished.**

From *Arbeh* and on, Pharaoh no longer had a choice as to whether or not he would free Klal Yisrael. Hashem had decreed that the next three *makkos* were going to occur as a punishment.

The *posuk* (*Shemos* 10:2) tells us that one of the reasons Hashem sent Moshe to Pharaoh at this juncture was so that Klal Yisrael would know for all generations *eis asher hisalalti beMitzrayim, how I ridiculed Mitzrayim.* Did Hashem really need to show that He had the power to ridicule Mitzrayim?

I believe that one of the most important lessons that Klal Yisrael was supposed to take from the *makkah* of *Arbeh* was the absolute decimation of Mitzrayim. When there is no food, there is no grandeur to an upper class, no allure of the superior education and power of the aristocrats... just desperation and desolation everywhere one turns. The idea of *hisalalti* was to disperse every illusion about Egyptian culture that any Jew might have, so that they would abandon any notion of wanting to remain in Mitzrayim — and so they would not perish during the *makkah* of *Choshech.*

Hashem wanted it to be known for all time that *any* Jew could have seized this opportunity. While some did, unfortunately, many did not.

חֹשֶׁךְ / *Darkness*

- **❒ *Choshech* came without warning, and had an aspect of terrible itching, as did the other *makkos* which arrived without warning.**
- **❒ If millions of Jewish people perished during *Choshech*, how was this not noticed afterward by the Egyptians?**
- **❒ They missed the forest for the trees — they saw Jewish people as far as the eye could see, and were not able to tell if the number was three million or fifteen million.**

It is interesting to note that the three *makkos* that came without warning — *Kinnim, Shechin,* and *Choshech* — all involved terrible itching. For here, too, presumably the Egyptians would have been unable to scratch any itch that came upon them during the three days that they could not move. Although, as we noted above, these were *makkos* whose ultimate consequences were relatively lighter than other *makkos*, these contained a severity that other *makkos* did not have. This was because incessant itching can truly drive a person crazy. These three *makkos* came without warning, and they all involved similar itching, which can be torturous.

Hashem sent the *makkah* of *Choshech* without warning. At this point, seeing as the last three *makkos* were bound to occur, whether or not there was a warning is of little consequence. Perhaps the reason that there was no warning here was because although the *makkah* was terrible and torturous, it did not sound all that dire. Especially in light of the fact that the real reasons for the *makkah* were for the Jews who did not want to leave Mitzrayim to pass away, and for those who did, to seek out the treasures of the Egyptians, the *makkah* of *Choshech* was more about Klal Yisrael than it was about the Egyptians. [The fact that Klal Yisrael knew where all of these valuables were and not a single person took even a single item demonstrates the honesty of Klal Yisrael!]

Rashi (*Shemos* 10:22, *d"h vayehi*) teaches us that not all of Klal Yisrael made it out of Mitzrayim. Far from it. The Torah uses the word *chamushim* in *Shemos* 13:17 to describe the fraction of Klal Yisrael who went out. The simple translation of this word is that Klal Yisrael were armed, but the Midrash expounds an alternative understanding that they were one fifth of the original Jewish population in Mitzrayim. There are also Midrashim that record this fraction as far smaller (see further, *Mechilta to Parashas Beshalach, d"h vachamushim*).

Let us imagine the spectacle. There were six hundred thousand men between the ages of twenty and sixty who left Mitzrayim; thus, we can estimate that together with all the older men, the women, and the younger folk,

approximately three million people went out of Mitzrayim. If we conservatively estimate them to have been a fifth of the total original population, this means that approximately twelve million people did not leave Mitzrayim!

Accordingly, why did the Egyptians feel confident that the entire population of Jews had left? Most of them had not. And although we know that these twelve million people actually perished, from the perspective of the Egyptians, they were unaccounted for. The Egyptians ought to have assumed that those who remained were probably poised to take over the county! And similarly, why would the Egyptians not have noticed so many people missing after the *makkah* of *Choshech*, when these millions died?

The answer must be that the Egyptians missed the forest for the trees. Egypt is a flat land, and so when Klal Yisrael went to leave, the lines of people and belongings simply stretched long and wide, as far as the Egyptians could see. They thus made no calculation as to how many there were, and assumed that it was all of the Jewish people, and that they had all departed.

מַכַּת בְּכוֹרוֹת / *Plague of the Firstborn*

❒ **Pharaoh refused to allow the animals to leave Mitzrayim, either because he did not want to lose them, or because he felt that he was a deity, and did not want his slaves serving another God.**

After *Choshech,* one of the points of dispute between Moshe and Pharaoh regarding the proposed trip to the Wilderness to serve Hashem was whether or not Pharaoh would allow Klal Yisrael to bring along animals to offer as sacrifices in the service of Hashem. This was a clause of the deal that Pharaoh refused to accept.

We are accustomed to viewing this position as a product of Pharaoh's selfishness, in that he was not willing to allow any animals out of the country, for he felt they would eventually become his own; his plan was that as Klal Yisrael would become more and more destitute, they would have to part with their possessions. Alternatively, perhaps we can understand Pharaoh's concern as trying to prevent a mass escape. After all, animals would have provided food for those leaving Mitzrayim.

Perhaps, though, we can understand Pharaoh's objection in a different light. We must remember that Pharaoh fancied himself to be a deity. Perhaps he actually understood the concept of *korbanos,* which as we have discussed before, is the recognition that Hashem owns everything, and everything we have is but a gift from Him.

Pharaoh was not interested in the entire Jewish population coming back to Mitzrayim firm in the belief that someone other than Pharaoh was responsible for the gifts to humanity. This would tarnish history's view of the great Pharaoh, for whom the Nile rose, supplying the very life force of the entire empire of Mitzrayim. Pharaoh might therefore have been intent on

stopping the development and bolstering of a relationship between Klal Yisrael and Hashem that would have encouraged the belief that everything is from Hashem.

❒ **Moshe Rabbeinu was angry with Pharaoh because he refused to acknowledge the reality that he was not at all in control of what Hashem was going to do**

The *posuk* (*Shemos* 11:8) states that Moshe was angry with Pharaoh. Why? *Rashi* (*d"h veyordu*) explains that Moshe was angered by the brazen way Pharaoh had declared that he would no longer see Moshe's face. I believe that Moshe's anger can be attributed to the fact that Pharaoh was acting as though what would happen next was going to be up to Pharaoh. The level of inaccuracy in this representation was stupefying in its dismissal of Hashem, and this angered Moshe. In truth, it was never up to Pharaoh when he would be threatened by a *makkah*. But, there had always been an out for Pharaoh — all he had to do was acquiesce to Moshe. This would have accomplished removing the threat of the *makkos*. However, after *Arbeh*, Hashem had removed Pharaoh's *bechirah* to choose to free Klal Yisrael. So, now there was absolutely no way Pharaoh could stop Moshe from paying him a visit, because Hashem was not allowing him to free Klal Yisrael. Moshe was angered that Pharaoh, even in the midst of this incredible punishment, was still able to look him in the eye and say, "I am in control." Moshe's anger toward Pharaoh was as if to say, "No, you are not in control. Rather, you are putty in Hashem's hands, an example to show the world how Hashem deals with evildoers like yourself, and there is literally nothing you can do about it. The charade of negotiating with you is done. From now on, Hashem is openly and obviously in charge, and what you say is completely immaterial."

[The truth is that Pharaoh was not able to live up to his word, for after *Makkas Bechoros*, the *posuk* (*Shemos* 12:31) tells us that Pharaoh himself sought out Moshe and Aharon. Even though we know that once a king issues an edict, it is abnormal for him to go back on his word, the fear that gripped Pharaoh caused him to act differently than he normally would have. Perhaps, when Pharaoh finally located Moshe, he hid his face; after all, all Pharaoh had said was that he would not *see* Moshe. Either way, his brazen attitude was completely gone.]

❒ **The Torah mentions that *Makkas Bechoros* took place at night to highlight the fear Pharaoh experienced that night, even though we departed the next day. This is to highlight that the reason we left was not because Pharaoh chased us out, but rather because Hashem told us it was time to leave.**

❒ **Alternatively, the Torah highlights the fear Pharaoh experienced that whole night that perhaps Klal Yisrael was intent on taking over Mitzrayim.**

The Torah specifically mentions that *Makkas Bechoros* took place at midnight, that Pharaoh awoke to the cacophony of the *makkah* at night, and that the conversation he had with Moshe and Aharon telling them to leave happened at night. Why does the Torah keep stressing that these occurrences took place when it was yet night?

Of course, we know that Klal Yisrael did not actually leave Mitzrayim that night, but rather the next day. Firstly, this is clear from the fact that Moshe commanded Klal Yisrael to remain in their houses until daybreak. Secondly, the *posuk* clearly states (*Shemos* 12:41,51 with *Ramban*; see also *Bamidbar* 33:3, as well as *Rashi* to *Devarim* 16:1, *d"h miMitzrayim lailah*) that the actual Exodus took place on the day of the 15th of Nissan, not the night preceding it. So, what is the significance of all these happenings at night?

Certainly, up until the moment that Moshe Rabbeinu refused to listen to Pharaoh's demand that Klal Yisrael leave that night, Pharaoh was under the impression that it was up to him to send the Jewish people out — the moment he decided to free them, they would leave. What Moshe's ignoring Pharaoh here demonstrated to all — Egyptians and Jews alike — was that the reason Klal Yisrael was still in Mitzrayim was not because of Pharaoh's wishes; it was due only to the word of Hashem. The second Hashem said to go, they would go, and until then, they would wait, irrespective of Pharaoh's position on the matter. This also showed that up until this point it had also been this way — Pharaoh had never really been the reason that Klal Yisrael was not leaving Mitzrayim. It had been Hashem's will that they should stay.

An additional point to note here is that throughout his back and forth with Moshe and Aharon, Pharaoh had also always been under the (correct) impression that the ultimate goal of their campaign was to free Klal Yisrael to serve Hashem. He never imagined that their goal might be the conquest of his country. However, when he came to them in his frightened and vulnerable state and granted them permission to leave immediately, he was met with Moshe's reply of "No!" This most certainly threw Pharaoh into a frenzy of terror; realizing that if Moshe was of the mind, and he just might be, he could simply have the Jewish people overrun the entire country! Pharaoh surely thought in the hours between midnight and daybreak that Moshe had realized how easy it would be for him to depose Pharaoh and take over Mitzrayim, and was perhaps poised to do just that. [See above, *Vayarei'u*, where we have explained that this was *middah keneged middah*.]

- ❒ **Hashem orchestrated that the Egyptians would decide for their own well-being to treat the Jewish people with *chein*, and not be afraid that they would lose their valuables. These calculations were based on assumptions that did not materialize.**
- ❒ **Hashem makes people think and act in certain ways to achieve the results that He orchestrates — it is all part of His plan**

In the immediate aftermath of *Makkas Bechoros,* the *posuk* (*Shemos* 12:33) speaks of the pressure the Egyptians were trying to put on Klal Yisrael to leave. This indicates that the Egyptians were fearful of them, and were trying to be rid of them before even greater calamity might befall them. How can we reconcile this with the fact that three *pesukim* later, the Torah states that Hashem put the *chein* (*favor*) of the nation in the eyes of Mitzrayim, and that this resulted in their openly lending Klal Yisrael all of their valuables? Was their attitude toward Klal Yisrael one of fear, or one of graciousness?

As we pointed out above, Pharaoh wanted the Jewish people out of Mitzrayim immediately. When they declined, he realized with dread that they might not be interested in leaving, but rather in taking over Mitzrayim. The Egyptians surely felt a similar fear. They feared for their king and country to a degree, but more importantly, for their own safety, and their economy. The presence of Klal Yisrael in their land had, in recent months, brought nothing but desolation and death. From their perspective, if Klal Yisrael would just *leave*, they could begin the road to recovery from the *makkos*. This was why they pressured Klal Yisrael to depart; they were of the mind that this was the solution to the county's problems. When they saw that Klal Yisrael were not eagerly leaving, they did everything they could to encourage them to do so post-haste. The Egyptians held nothing back, giving Klal Yisrael even more than they asked to borrow. This was the attitude of *chein* described here. The Egyptians likely assumed that the Jewish people, who were trustworthy, would be returning the items, and so they did not fear Klal Yisrael were stealing their things. The Egyptians were not filled with animosity, but were rather doing their best to equip Klal Yisrael so they would be comfortable, and finally just leave.

As such, it emerges that the *chein* that the Egyptians felt toward the Jewish people was based on a presumption that never came to be. In short order, debilitating *makkos* would destroy the army of Mitzrayim at the *Yam Suf*, and the accompanying *makkos* would rain down on Mitzrayim itself at that time. Little did they know that most of them would end up dying in a short time. Thus, both the reason for the *chein* and the reason they were okay with it — the safety of the Egyptians, as well as the fact that they were assuming they were not losing their valuables — never played out.

This teaches us an important lesson. Although realities shift very quickly, and what is important one minute might be immaterial the next,

Hashem runs the world so exactly that each moment is imbued with His will. He wanted the Egyptians to treat Klal Yisrael well, and so he orchestrated a confluence of realities to bring this about. Just a short while later, though, Hashem ordained new realities, for new purposes.

- **To ensure that there would be firstborns dying in every Egyptian house, Hashem enacted a new type of *bechorah* at *Makkas Bechoros* — the firstborn to a mother, known as *bechor ha'eim.***
- **It is specifically this type of *bechorah* which is used in all the laws of *bechorah* that were given as a remembrance of the salvation from *Makkas Bechoros.***
- **Unlike *bechor ha'av, bechor ha'eim* is a transient *kedushah,* which is intended only as a remembrance.**

Up until *Makkas Bechoros*, the word *bechor* had always meant the firstborn of the father. This was defined as the first offspring of a father's seed to be born from the womb of a mother. [See *Nahar Sholom, Bereishis* 25:31, where the difference between *bechor ha'av* and *reishis oni* is discussed.] In fact, the only mention in the Torah of specifically a mother's firstborn before *Makkas Bechoros* is that of Tamar, who bore Peretz and Zerach. As Yehudah had already had Er, Onan, and Sheilah, neither of Tamar's children would have been Yehudah's *bechor*. Accordingly, the only difference it could have made if Peretz or Zerach was born first would be to know who *Tamar's* firstborn was! Now, was the midwife seeking to determine if one of them was a *bechor,* or just to know who was older? If we examine the words of the midwife when she tied the string around the hand of Zerach, whom she assumed was being born first, she says, *this one emerged first*; she did not say, "this one is the *bechor*." She was clearly seeking to determine only which of the boys would be older, and not who was Tamar's *bechor*. This serves to demonstrate that at that point in history, being a mother's firstborn had no significance.

Bechor ha'av, on the other hand, is the definition of *bechorah* that is used for the law of *pi shenayim,* the double portion allotted to a firstborn when brothers inherit together, and was used to determine who could do the *avodah* before *shevet Levi* received that honor after the sin of the *Eigel*. This was also the *bechorah* at the root of the deal between Yaakov and Eisav. [Yaakov was already Yitzchak's *reishis oni,* which actually superseded Eisav's having been born the *bechor ha'av* — we have discussed this further in the above-referenced comments to *Bereishis* 35:21.]

Why did the definition of *bechorah* change now? The answer is that Hashem had promised to kill all of the firstborns of the Egyptians. However, *Rashi* (to *Shemos* 12:30, *d"h ki ein bayis,* second interpretation) cites the Midrash, which states that the Egyptians were famously promiscuous.

The women of Egypt would commit adultery with unmarried Egyptian men. Thus, there was little chance that a married Egyptian woman's first child was the first her husband had ever fathered — if he was even the father at all. Moreover, there were likely many adulterous Egyptian women who had many children, each of whom was the firstborn of his respective father. If Hashem would have killed only the *bechorei ha'av,* there would have been many houses with no deaths at all, and some with many deaths! This would have resulted in the Egyptians claiming that Hashem had lied, for He had said He was going to kill all of the firstborns, while the plague had actually affected many in some houses, and none in other houses! To avoid this issue, Hashem broadened the definition of *bechorah* in the decree of *Makkas Bechoros* to include a new definition of *bechor* — the first child to leave the womb of a woman, no matter if he was the first child of his father or not. This child, a *bechor ha'eim*, would be killed in Mitzrayim by virtue of this new type of *bechorah,* because he was the first child to leave the womb of his mother, even though he was not the *bechor* of his father.

When Klal Yisrael left Mitzrayim the next day, Hashem commanded Moshe to commemorate *Makkas Bechoros,* and the fact that He spared the *bechoros* of Klal Yisrael, with the *mitzvos* of *pidyon haben*, *bechor beheimah*, and *peter chamor* (*Shemos* 13:11-13). The definition of *bechorah* for all of these *mitzvos* exclusively follows *bechor ha'eim,* the first to leave the womb of the mother, even to the exclusion of *bechor ha'av* — the "real" *bechor* — because these commandments specifically commemorate the fact that Hashem changed the definition of *bechorah* at *Makkas Bechoros* to include *bechor ha'eim.*

It is noteworthy that while *bechor ha'av* has a lasting effect on the recipient — in times of old, a *bechor ha'av* could perform the *avodah*, and the *bechor ha'av* takes a double potion of inheritance — while the holiness of a *bechor ha'eim* is only intended to be transient. The holiness must be transferred through redemption, or in the case of a firstborn kosher animal, offered as a sacrifice. This too is a reflection of the nature of the very classification of the firstborn of a woman as a *bechor* in the first place. Because it was added to the definition of *bechorah* for the purpose of *Makkas Bechoros,* its holiness extends only so far as to commemorate Hashem's salvation, through the process of redemption.

Rashi (ibid., first interpretation) mentions that during *Makkas Bechoros,* Hashem also killed the oldest son in the house if no firstborns were actually present. Presumably, this was to prevent the Egyptians from claiming that Hashem had "missed a house." Accordingly, the way that this first interpretation deals with the issue of the promiscuous Egyptian women and the cloudiness of who exactly was a *bechor,* was that it maintains that as part of the decree of the *gadol habayis* dying, no matter who was or

was not a real *bechor*, the oldest child in the house also died, along with any "hidden" firstborns. This raises the question: According to the second interpretation of *Rashi*, which we are explaining to mean that Hashem instituted *bechor ha'eim* at this point, what happened if the eldest child was a girl, and thus the boy born after that girl did not have the designation of either sort of *bechorah*? Did these boys die, or not? I presume that the second interpretation agrees that there was also a decree of the *gadol habayis* dying, and thus the boys who were born after their older sisters died as well.

Alternatively, perhaps if a girl was the oldest, she died as well. [We do find the concept of a woman fasting the fast of the *bechoros* on Erev Pesach, for in a case where her husband is a *bechor* and fasting for himself, some maintain that she must fast for her *bechor* until his *Bar Mitzvah*. Perhaps this is itself only on account of the fact that some women were included in the *makkah*; otherwise, it is hard to understand why a woman fasting on this day makes any sense at all.]

❒ **The reason the dogs are rewarded for not barking is because with such high tension emanating from all of the people of Mitzrayim, the normal nature of dogs is to work up a frenzy. They stayed calm, and are thus rewarded.**

The *posuk* tells us that on the night of *Makkas Bechoros*, no dog barked at Klal Yisrael. For this, the Torah rewards dogs for all time, by instructing Klal Yisrael to feed their *neveilos* to them. Why was it that the dogs did not bark that night? Some understand that the dogs would have been expected to bark even more than usual on the occasion of such widespread death, because, as the Gemara (*Bava Kamma* 60b) tells us, dogs are able to detect the Angel of Death, and when he is present in the city, they will howl.

However, on the night of *Makkas Bechoros*, the Angel of Death was not killing the firstborns! Rather, as the *Haggadah* states, *ani v'lo malach* — Hashem says that it was He alone who killed the Egyptians, without sending the Angel of Death. Accordingly, it seems strange that Hashem would reward the dogs for inaction when they would have had no inclination to act in the first place. Additionally, why would the *posuk* mention that the dogs did not bark at Klal Yisrael? They would seemingly not have had any reason to bark at Klal Yisrael specifically!

Rather, I think the simple understanding of the *posuk* is that dogs typically become excited and animated when things change, or are out of the ordinary in some way, and especially if there is a tenseness in the demeanor of their owners. With many tens of thousands of deaths happening at once, and many people mourning and panicking, the dogs

naturally ought to have been howling and barking across Mitzrayim; and yet, they stayed silent. Now, in the immediate aftermath of the *makkah*, even though Klal Yisrael could not leave their houses until morning, there was a great deal of communication with the Egyptians during that time. Firstly, there were Egyptians who had tried to avoid the *makkah* by moving into the houses of Jewish people. Secondly, the *pesukim* (*Shemos* 12:31, 33) relate that Pharaoh specifically, and the Egyptians in general, were trying during the entire second half of the night to spur Klal Yisrael to depart; clearly, this involved visiting them at their residences. Now, in all of those interactions, the Egyptians were surely very tense. They blamed the Jewish people for the deaths of their family members, and so when conversing with Klal Yisrael, were surely agitated, and their dogs would have picked up on this. Yet, because the dogs sensed that Hashem had carried out the *makkah,* they did not react as they normally would have in such a scenario, and instead were silent. It is ultimately the dogs, then, who bore witness — with their abnormal behavior — that Hashem had carried out the *makkah*. It is in return for this that they receive as reward all the *neveilos* of the animals of Klal Yisrael, for all time.

Lessons of the Makkos

- **The seven *makkos* that appear in *Parashas Va'eira* were initially intended to be enough to convince Pharaoh to release Klal Yisrael.**
- **When Pharaoh grew so wicked that he defied Hashem even after *Barad,* Hashem brought the last three *maakos* — the ones that appear in *Parashas Bo.* Rather than an impetus for him to release the nation, these were intended as a punishment for Pharaoh.**

There are seven *makkos* that appear in *Parashas Va'eira*, and three that appear in *Parashas Bo*. Why are they divided in this way?

I believe that the answer to this question is that the first seven *makkos* were part of a program that Hashem had enacted in order to cause Pharaoh to free Klal Yisrael. Hashem knew of the wickedness of Pharaoh, and that he would fail his test to release them initially. It was these seven *makkos* that were alluded to by Hashem when he told Moshe in *Parashas Shemos* that He would strike Mitzrayim *bechol nifle'osai, with all of My wonders* (*Shemos* 3:20). While certainly, at first glance, we would assume that *bechol nifle'osai* alludes to all of the *makkos*, I humbly maintain that this is not the case.

If we examine Hashem's statement to Moshe Rabbeinu in the prelude to the *makkah* of *Barad,* He tells Moshe, *this time I will send all of My plagues* (*kal mageifosai*), *etc.* (*Shemos* 9:14). The simplest meaning of the *posuk* would seem to be that *Barad* was the culmination of what Hashem

referred to as *kal mageifosai, all of My plagues.* This was perhaps due to the fact that the *makkah* of *Barad* contained many contradictions to natural law. There was the coexistence of fire and ice, the tremendous, never-before-seen hail, and the fact that the hailstones were suspended in midair as soon as Moshe prayed for the *makkah* to stop. And while of course all of the *makkos* defied the natural order, this was the one that most clearly defied what we know as natural laws. Physics, chemistry, and gravity were all, in one way or another, shown to be completely subjective to the supremacy of Hashem. If indeed the simplest understanding of the words *kal mageifosai* that appear in the prelude to *Barad* is as an allusion to all of the *makkos* up until, and including, *Barad,* it makes sense that the somewhat similar terminology of *kol nifle'osai* (of 3:20) can also be a reference to the very same set of seven *makkos.* [However, see *Rashi* to *Shemos* 9:14, *d"h es kal mageifosai,* who understands *kal mageifosai* to allude to *Makkas Bechoros.*]

Now, what does it mean that at the time that Hashem was discussing this sequence of events in *Shemos* 3:20, there should only have needed to be seven *makkos*? Let us explain. We know that Pharaoh was given a choice before the onset of the *makkos*; if he wished, he could have released Klal Yisrael at that time. It was only when he refused to do so that the *makkos* were guaranteed to come about. After each of the first five *makkos,* Pharaoh had this opportunity, and each time he refused to release them. Each of these times, he did so of his own volition, thinking for one reason or another that he could be dishonest, or else change his mind. These five opportunities that Pharaoh had to release Klal Yisrael were all under his own control, but Hashem told Moshe that Pharaoh would not be significantly impressed yet, and in his wickedness, would choose to refuse all of these opportunities. Pharaoh could have repented at any point, but his wickedness was such that barring repentance, he was going to fail each of these five tests.

However, in the aftermath of the fifth *makkah, Dever,* when Pharaoh had refused yet again to release the Jewish people, he earned a unique sort of punishment. Not only would the *makkah* of *Shechin* occur as a result of his refusal, but Hashem now removed his *bechirah* (free will); Pharaoh would be unable, under any circumstances, to free Klal Yisrael. There was nothing he could do to stop the *makkah* of *Barad* from occurring. [This is the intent of *Shemos* 9:12, which states, *And Hashem hardened Pharaoh's heart, etc.*]

However, by the time the seventh *makkah, Barad*, came about, Pharaoh was once again in full control of his decision making. In fact, in the aftermath of *Barad*, Pharaoh actually declared that Hashem was righteous, and that he and his people were the evildoers! This begs the question; if Pharaoh thought this, why did he keep Klal Yisrael slaves even after *Barad*?

He had his free will back! We will address this question in a moment.

So, in discussing the *seven makkos* of *Parashas Va'eira*, we find that Hashem told Moshe of a seven-step formula that would lead to redemption. Five times Hashem would strike Pharaoh and offer him the chance to repent, which Pharaoh, at his then current level of wickedness, would find ways to ignore. A sixth strike, *Shechin,* would follow, and Pharaoh would then experience the terror of not being able to use his own faculties to make the correct decision, and suffer the torment of a madman, unable to avoid self-destruction. Hashem was using *Shechin* to show Pharaoh how He did not need Pharaoh to decide to release Klal Yisrael at all, and could easily just torture him if He so desired. This was a wake-up call to Pharaoh, and in the aftermath of *Barad*, complete with his newly reacquired *bechirah*, and the realization that he had been wicked (*Shemos* 9:27), Pharaoh ought to have released Klal Yisrael! This, I believe, is the intent of the aforementioned *posuk, Shemos* 3:20. Hashem told Moshe that the program He had set forth in order to bring about the freedom of Klal Yisrael was *kal nifle'osai,* from *Dam* through *Barad.*

As we asked above, though, why did the program not work as prescribed? Why did Pharaoh refuse to let the Jewish people go after *Barad*, and why were there three more *makkos* before he finally relented? The answer is that Pharaoh actually grew in his wickedness as the months went by. As such, what had originally been prescribed for him — a wake-up call of *Shechin* — failed to cause him to relent; even after admitting that he was evil and Hashem was righteous, Pharaoh still found room in his own heart to deny Hashem's command. Hashem's response to this amazing brazenness was to punish Pharaoh by removing his *bechirah* during the *makkos* of *Arbeh* and *Choshech* (see *Shemos* 10:20 and 10:27, respectively), ensuring that the last three *makkos* were going to rain down upon Pharaoh and decimate Mitzrayim. The last three *makkos*, then, were dissimilar to the first seven. While the idea of the first seven was to cause Pharaoh to free Klal Yisrael, the last three *makkos* were brought upon Mitzrayim as a punishment for Pharaoh (and a message to the Jews who still did not want to leave). It is for this reason that I believe that they appear in a separate *Parashah, Parashas Bo*. [See also *D'tzach A'dash B'Acahav,* below.]

Thus, in the beginning of *Parashas Bo,* the *posuk* (*Shemos* 10:1) relates that Hashem commanded Moshe to come before Pharaoh, because He had hardened the hearts of Pharaoh and his servants. Seemingly, this should have been a reason for Moshe *not* to appear before Pharaoh. After all, why waste the time and energy trying to convince Pharaoh to do something, when Hashem had already guaranteed that it was not going to occur? The *posuk* itself answers the question — Moshe was to appear before Pharaoh as a vehicle for the remaining *makkos* to be carried out.

The last three *makkos* were a punishment for Pharaoh not freeing Klal Yisrael in the aftermath of *Barad*, when he finally experienced a moment of real remorse. I believe the expression, *Come to Pharaoh*, connotes this idea as well. Usually, the word "come" is used in conjunction with things familiar and known; most often, coming home. "Go," on the other hand, usually expresses venturing out past one's boundaries, and can connote the unknown. When Hashem told Moshe, *Come to Pharaoh*, this can be understood to mean that Hashem was saying, "Come to the place where we already know the outcome, which has been predetermined." Pharaoh had already earned his punishment, and Moshe already knew about it. This was all familiar territory, and so the expression of "come" was indeed appropriate.

In light of this explanation, it is curious that when Moshe was originally setting out with his family to Mitzrayim, Hashem made mention of *Makkas Bechoros*. In *Shemos* 4:23, Hashem tells Moshe that he should threaten Pharaoh that Klal Yisrael is His firstborn, and that if Pharaoh will not release Hashem's firstborn, He will kill Pharaoh's firstborn. This is very clearly a reference to *Makkas Bechoros*. And, if there was not yet any definite plan to unleash *Makkas Bechoros* on Mitzrayim, why would Hashem tell Moshe about it at that point?

The answer is that Hashem was not telling Pharaoh that there would *definitely* be a *Makkas Bechoros*. Rather, as *Rashi* (*d"h hinei Anochi horeig*) explains, Hashem bade Moshe to tell Pharaoh at the outset what might occur if he would be uncooperative. A person in this situation might be wary of revealing his "ultimate weapon," for fear of giving the enemy time to prepare for the attack. Hashem, however, knows the limits of men and is beyond them in every way. It is immaterial to Him whether the object of His ire knows what He might bring upon them, for there is nothing at all they can do to counter it. Accordingly, Hashem was not decreeing that there was definitely going to be a *Makkas Bechoros* at that time; rather, He was presenting Moshe with a threat that he should relate to Pharaoh, letting him know what might occur if he would not respect Hashem's request.

- **After *Tzefardei'a,* Pharaoh realized *ki ein kaShem Elokeinu, that there is none like Hashem, our God;* Hashem is greater than any magician.**
- **After *Arov,* he realized that *ki Ani Hashem b'kerev ha'aretz, that I am Hashem in the midst of the land,* that Hashem controls all of the creatures of the earth.**
- **In the beginning of *Barad,* he knew *ki ein Kamoni bechol ha'aretz, that there is no one like Me in all the land*; Hashem controls all**

elements of nature. And at the end of *Barad,* he knew *Ki LaShem ha'aretz, that the land is HASHEM's;* i.e., that Hashem controls all natural forces and laws as well.

- **At the *Yam Suf,* Pharaoh was made to know *ki Ani Hashem, that I am Hashem* — that Hashem is the One and Only God.**

The following discourse is a possible understanding of a very wide-ranging topic, and it is by no means exhaustive. It is merely one suggestion how to understand several similar expressions we find throughout the *pesukim,* and it is certainly worthwhile to think about the questions more. One's understanding of the lessons of *Yetzias Mitzrayim* can grow by gaining a proper insight into the stages of understanding of Hashem that Pharaoh was forced to realize as the *makkos* unfolded.

In *Shemos* 7:5, before the *makkos* began, Hashem told Moshe that after all was said and done, Mitzrayim would know *ki Ani Hashem, that I am Hashem.* In *Shemos* 8:6, at the end of *Tzefardei'a,* Moshe told Pharaoh that he would know *ki ein kaShem Elokeinu, that there is none like Hashem, our God.* Before *Arov* (*Shemos* 8:18), Hashem told Moshe to tell Pharaoh that he would know *ki Ani Hashem b'kerev ha'aretz, that I am Hashem in the midst of the land.* At the onset of *Barad* (*Shemos* 9:14) Moshe told Pharaoh that Hashem said he would know *ki ein Kamoni b'chol ha'aretz, that there is no one like Me in all the land,* and at the end of the *makkah* (*Shemos* 9:29), Moshe tells Pharaoh that he will know *ki laShem ha'aretz, that the land is Hashem's.* Finally, at the Splitting of the *Yam Suf,* Hashem told Moshe that Pharaoh would know *ki Ani Hashem, that I am Hashem,* as Hashem had predicted to Moshe before the *makkos* began. How can we explain the difference between these various stages of Pharaoh's recognition of Hashem?

The difference between these expressions might be as follows: At the end of *Tzefardei'a,* Pharaoh was taught that *ki ein kaShem Elokeinu, that there is none like Hashem, our God.* There, Pharaoh was shown that Hashem was greater than his best magicians. As *Rashi* (*Shemos* 8:6, *d"h Vayomer l'machar*) writes, Pharaoh challenged Moshe to pray on that day that the *makkah* would cease the next day. Apparently, this feat would have been too difficult to perform using magic with which Pharaoh was familiar. [Perhaps the next day, Pharaoh had someone watching Moshe to see that he did not utter any incantations at the time the *makkah* was going to stop, to be assured that the *makkah* had really stopped because of his prayer the day before.] Thus, in doing this, Moshe Rabbeinu demonstrated that Hashem possessed a level of power beyond Pharaoh's understanding, greater than anything he had ever known. This feat proved that Hashem was more powerful than any force that Pharaoh had ever encountered, and by demonstrating this, Moshe aimed to convince Pharaoh that Hashem

was Godly, and that the *makkos* were not due to magic or sorcery of any kind. However, there was no proof therein that Hashem was greater than any other god that Pharaoh might believe to exist; it was not Moshe's aim at the time to prove this. From Pharaoh's perspective, then, we might say that he was taught that *ein kaShem Elokeinu,* there is no known power as great as Hashem. However, because Pharaoh ascribed many powers to many deities, there was no proof offered that Hashem was supreme among these false gods. Rather, Pharaoh might have been left with the impression that Hashem was on a level with other deities he believed in, and that not one of them was necessarily the One Supreme God.

At the beginning of *Arov*, Moshe told Pharaoh that Hashem would control the wild animals so completely that although they would wreak havoc on Mitzrayim, Goshen would be left untouched. This demonstrated that Hashem's power was *b'kerev ha'aretz* — all beings in the land, small and great were completely under His control. Again, Hashem's exclusivity as a power was not demonstrated to Pharaoh, but he was shown a broader understanding of Hashem's power than he had seen after *Tzefardei'a.*

During *Barad,* Pharaoh was shown something new. Aside from the terrible punishment that would be inflicted upon Mitzrayim during *Barad*, Hashem's power was evident in the *Barad* itself. As we know, physical laws were suspended during the *makkah*; fire and ice acted in harmony. Those who had pagan beliefs, who could somehow entertain that different deities had different powers, could not believe that these powers could be combined. The gods of fire and water wage war, and do not ever work together. And so, when Hashem was able to suspend these principles, Pharaoh was astounded. This is perhaps the meaning of *ki ein Kamoni bechol ha'aretz, that there is no one like Me in all the land.* At that time, Pharaoh knew that Hashem could control natural forces, and was superior to any deity that there might be in the world — for Hashem Himself was able to control laws and forces that seemed to be the realm of numerous deities.

At the end of *Barad*, when Moshe prayed for the *makkah* to stop, the hailstones were withdrawn immediately — they did not even reach the ground. This amazing pinpoint control of the world was yet another level of realization of Hashem's power. *Ki laShem ha'aretz, that the land is Hashem's*, meant that Hashem demonstrated an unparalleled level of precise control over natural laws (such as gravity). It could not be clearer that Hashem could have His way with anything in the world, and no other deity, which Pharaoh still believed existed, had the power to stop Him.

Finally, at the Splitting of the *Yam Suf,* Hashem performed miracle upon miracle upon miracle — literally too many to count. From the myriad ways He was benevolent toward Klal Yisrael to the equally numerous ways He punished the Egyptians, Hashem's power was on awesome display.

Now, one of the ideas we, as believers in Hashem, espouse is that of a limitless, infinite God. One of the driving concepts of the belief in multiple deities is that each one has a limit to its power; this is itself a denial of Hashem. Part of true belief in Hashem is that His greatness is limitless, and thus completely beyond our comprehension. After contemplating (to the extent that it is humanly possible to capture in one's mind) His Omniscience, there can be no room to even entertain the thought that there is another power. This is the level of recognition that the Torah calls *ki Ani Hashem*. [It is similar, in a way, to the concept of *melo chol ha'aretz kevodo, His honor fills the entire world*.] There is no place in the world, physically or conceptually, that is not brimming with Hashem's influence and mastery. Recognition of this fact leaves no room for the entertainment of any other power — all imaginable power (and unimaginable power as well) is already attributed to Hashem. Thus, what Pharaoh realized when his mind was indeed completely overcome by Hashem's power, was that there was no room to believe in anything other than Hashem as the One True God.

This is the concept expressed in the declaration of *Shema,* and is also the focus of the first of the *Aseres HaDibros*. We can of course infer from the fact that Hashem is One that there is no second deity. In fact, the second of the *Aseres HaDibros* cautions against believing in anything other than, or together with, Hashem. But this prohibition against believing in a second power of any kind is not rooted in the evil of believing that another power can exist. It is rather rooted in the evil of believing that there is any power left over that Hashem does not already possess.

We are not capable of grasping the true power of Hashem. But, we know that it is infinite. For a person to believe that there is another deity with any power at all is akin to believing that Hashem's own capabilities are limited in some way — and that is *kefirah*. *Hashem echad* means that Hashem is the One Powerful One, Whose power knows no bounds, and thus there is no room to believe in the possibility of another power other than He.

Many pagans, such as Pharaoh, used to believe that there must be a God of good and another of evil. This was because they were unable to reconcile the evils they witnessed in the world with the good they perceived to be the will of God. But, in this way, they limited God in their minds. God is limitless and is not contained by human thought, emotion, or rationale. Of course, Hashem is the source of all good and all perceived bad; in fact, it is this knowledge that is the root of *bitachon*.

❒ **The *makkos* showed the world the truth of Hashem's power, and showed Klal Yisrael that we can rely on Him for all time.**

In Moshe's warning to Pharaoh regarding the *Barad,* the *posuk* (*Shemos* 9:16) states, *And only for this cause have I allowed you to endure, to show through you My power; and so that My Name may be proclaimed throughout.* These words express the thought that Hashem "propped Pharaoh up," so to speak, in order to maximize the potential sanctification of His Name that would result from the punishments that He was going to inflict upon Pharaoh. Now, if the point was to show Pharaoh the power of Hashem, it stands to reason that the last part of the *posuk* — which states that Hashem wished for His Name to be sanctified publicly — was going to result from the previous words, *to show you My power.* In other words, the power Hashem would show Pharaoh would then allow Pharaoh to realize the greatness of Hashem, and to retell His glory to the world. This is actually the source for the Midrash (*Yalkut Shimoni* §176) that states that Pharaoh became king of Nineveh. There, he led the people to repent, perhaps with personal stories of having seen Hashem's hand. However, according to the opinion that Pharaoh perished in the *Yam Suf* — which would seem to be the plain meaning of *Shemos* 14:28 — when did Pharaoh have this opportunity?

It would seem that the intent of the *posuk* was not that Pharaoh himself (who was busy attempting to keep Klal Yisrael from leaving) should do the publicizing of Hashem's Name, but rather that he should be the catalyst of that publicity; the object of the discussion of Hashem's power for time immemorial. [Accordingly, the fact that Hashem chose to show Pharaoh His strength was in order to make him a prime example of one who defied Hashem and was shown Hashem's might.] Who would be doing this publicizing the world over? Most likely the reference is to the Egyptians who suffered through the *makkos*, the Splitting of the *Yam Suf,* and the punishments that Mitzrayim received while their army was engaged at the *Yam Suf.* These survivors were well-equipped to relate the story to everyone. This did, of course, include Klal Yisrael relating the story of *Yetzias Mitzrayim,* which has remained an integral part of our *mesorah,* and is a large part of the *mitzvah* of *sippur Yetzias Mitzrayim,* which lives on at the *Seder* to this day. Still, the Torah is referring to the world at large finding out about this miracle, and that publicizing has been carried out, for the most part, by the nations of the world speaking of it to one another throughout history.

The story of Mitzrayim's punishment carries a stronger message of Hashem's greatness than, say, the destruction of Sedom. This is because a one-time event, no matter how awesome and spectacular, can be incorrectly attributed by people to nature or science. People can theorize, as we know some did with the *Mabul,* that every sixteen hundred and fifty-six years, this catastrophic event would take place. People might compare events like the *Mabul* and the destruction of Sedom to the way

people today view the eruption of Mt. Vesuvius, when the city of Pompei was obliterated in one fell swoop; as a scientific anomaly, but unrelated to Hashem's wrath. However, when Hashem displays so many varied strengths against one enemy in a single time period, the impression that He is the cause of everything that is happening is so much clearer. [See *Nahar Sholom, Bereishis* 19:24-25, where we explained that Hashem specifically destroyed Sedom in a supernatural way so that the world would realize that the beliefs that Sedom espoused were truly evil. This can be contrasted with known evildoers, such as the Nazis, *ysh"v*, whom Hashem defeated using the natural order of things. He did not destroy the Nazis as He did Sedom, because what they were doing was clearly heinous, whereas the evils of Sedom were masked by the pursuit of egregious equality and unfettered liberalism, which some feel is really correct. Here, we do not suggest that this message was inefficient; to the contrary, the destruction of Sedom was utter and complete. The decimation of Mitzrayim was simply an even greater demonstration of Hashem's greatness, because it was harder for non-believers who seek to dismiss Hashem's handiwork by blaming it on scientific phenomena to explain.]

The reason that Hashem had the opportunity to make a spectacle out of Pharaoh was because He had begun to punish Mitzrayim with the *makkos* a full year before the four-hundred-year exile was going to be completed. Accordingly, Hashem was telling Pharaoh that the time was going to be used to further Hashem's cause of imbuing Klal Yisrael with faith and trust in Him.

Hashem told Pharaoh that his stubbornness was going to be a vehicle for Klal Yisrael to become strong in their *bitachon* in Hashem, not only their *emunah*. Surely, after witnessing even one or two *makkos*, Klal Yisrael were able to absorb the belief that Hashem has unlimited ability. They had already believed it, and now were being shown it! However, Klal Yisrael had no guarantee that Hashem would continue to act in their best interests. How could they believe with certainty that Hashem was going to save them? How could they trust in His salvation, and go to sleep at night without worrying about it? Presumably, with each blow that Mitzrayim suffered, the plight of the Jewish people was incrementally changed for the positive — sometimes socially, sometimes financially, and sometimes physically. We know that there were four levels of redemption (see *Kadeish*), and perhaps in each of these, there were layers as well. Each time there was a miraculous occurrence where Egyptians suffered and Klal Yisrael were inexplicably saved, Hashem was telling them, "Do not worry! Trust Me! I will take care of you!" The *makkos* were thus a vehicle for Hashem to show Klal Yisrael His power, as well as how much He cared for them, increasing their *bitachon*.

רַבִּי יְהוּדָה הָיָה נוֹתֵן בָּהֶם סִמָּנִים:
דְּצַ״ךְ עֲדַ״שׁ בְּאַחַ״ב.

— רַבִּי יְהוּדָה הָיָה נוֹתֵן בָּהֶם סִמָּנִים
Rabbi Yehudah Gave Signs For Them

❒ **R' Yehudah gave us *simanim*. But, as everyone knows, these *simanim* were already on the staff of Moshe Rabbeinu!**

❒ **This is not problematic, because it was R' Yehudah who taught us both of these teachings: Firstly, that *D'tzach, A'dash, B'achav* is a *siman* for the *makkos*, and secondly, that it was also inscribed upon the staff of Moshe Rabbeinu.**

The *Haggadah* tells us that R' Yehudah gave us *simanim* by which to remember the *makkos,* wherein he gave us the *roshei teivos* of the *makkos* (that is, the first letter of the Hebrew name of each) and divided them into three groups. Interpretations abound as to the novelty of these *simanim,* and the lessons we learn from them (see further below for a possible explanation). One should not wonder, however, as to what novelty R' Yehudah was teaching us, being that it is well-known that the words *D'tzach, A'dash, B'achav* were inscribed on the staff of Moshe Rabbeinu. For if one examines the Midrash (*Shemos Rabbah* 8:3) which states that the staff of Moshe was inscribed with allusions to the ten *makkos* in the form of the abbreviations *D'tzach, A'dash B'achav,* the teacher of that statement is none other than R' Yehudah! So, it is not that the *Haggadah* is recounting to us that R' Yehudah taught us the *simanim* which we could have deduced on our own from Moshe's staff. Rather, at the same time that R' Yehudah taught us that these words, *D'tzach, A'dash B'achav,* symbolize the *makkos,* their order, and their groupings, he also taught us that they appeared on Moshe Rabbeinu's staff.

How did R' Yehudah deduce that there were *simanim* for the *makkos* on Moshe's staff? *Eitz Yosef* (to *Shemos Rabbah* 5:6) explains that when Hashem told Moshe (*Shemos* 4:21), *See all the miracles I have placed in your hand and perform them before Pharaoh,* He was alluding to the staff in Moshe's hand (see *Shemos* 4:17), which contained hints to all of the *makkos* that would be performed. Moshe was to "see" the *makkos* on the staff, which means he needed to look closely and decipher the meaning of the inscription. This is how R' Yehudah knew that there were only *simanim* to the *makkos* on the staff, not the names of the *makkos* themselves. Once he determined that the *siman* must have been *D'tzach, A'dash B'achav,* for the many reasons which are given, he knew both that this was a *siman* for the *makkos* that we should recall in the *Haggadah* to remind ourselves of

the *makkos* and their varied lessons at the *Seder,* and also that this must have been what Moshe saw on the staff.

See above, *Lessons From the Makkos.* According to what we have written there, we can perhaps lend some understanding to the groupings of *D'tzach, A'dash,* and *B'achav.* The first three *makkos* established a pattern. A *Makkah* was decreed (*Dam*), and Pharaoh refused to release Klal Yisrael. A second *Makkah* followed (*Tzefardei'a*), and Pharaoh said he would release Klal Yisrael, but did not do so. As a punishment for such insolence, Hashem sent a third *makkah* (*Kinnim*) with no warning. This might actually have had some effect; if the labor stopped the Rosh Hashanah prior to the Exodus, and the *makkos* were a month apart from one another, the *makkah* of *Kinnim* should have taken place shortly before Rosh Hashanah. Perhaps upon seeing that the *Kinnim* were "*etzba Elokim,*" the Egyptians ceased forcing Klal Yisrael to work.

A somewhat similar pattern repeated itself with the next three *makkos.* Hashem issued a *makkah* (*Arov*), and Pharaoh — after some attempted negotiations — failed to agree to release the nation. Hashem sent a second *makkah* (*Dever*), which Pharaoh did not heed. He was punished with a third *makkah* (*Shechin*) which arrived without warning. This *makkah* was so terrible that Pharaoh would have given in right then, and freed the nation outright.

Thus, there are a few commonalities between the first and second sets of *makkos.* In both sets, Pharaoh declined to send Klal Yisrael out, and thus his punishment was to receive another *makkah.* After the second *makkah* in each set, Pharaoh deserved a terrible punishment. [After *Tzefardei'a* because he lied, and after *Dever* because he was unmoved by it.] In both sets, the *makkah* that followed came without warning, and in both sets, that third *makkah* was powerful enough to be effective. [In the case of *Kinnim,* it led to the cessation of labor, and in the case of *Shechin,* it would actually have led to the total emancipation of Klal Yisrael, had Hashem not punished Pharaoh by hardening his heart.]

The third set of *makkos* would not have needed to be anything more than the *makkah* of *Barad,* which would have precipitated the Exodus. However, when Pharaoh changed his mind after *Barad,* he was punished with the final three *makkos.* Thus, the third set was distinct in that the *makkos* it contained were the *makkos* of *Geulah;* the *Barad* should have brought it, and the final three *makkos* actually did.

[In his alluding to the *makkos* as three groups of three, three, and four respectively, R' Yehudah presumably disagrees with the previous Tanna

רַבִּי יוֹסֵי הַגְּלִילִי אוֹמֵר: מִנַּיִן אַתָּה אוֹמֵר שֶׁלָּקוּ הַמִּצְרִים בְּמִצְרַיִם עֶשֶׂר מַכּוֹת, וְעַל הַיָּם לָקוּ חֲמִשִּׁים מַכּוֹת? בְּמִצְרַיִם מָה הוּא אוֹמֵר, וַיֹּאמְרוּ הַחַרְטֻמִּם אֶל פַּרְעֹה, אֶצְבַּע אֱלֹהִים הִוא[1]. וְעַל הַיָּם מָה הוּא אוֹמֵר, וַיַּרְא יִשְׂרָאֵל אֶת הַיָּד הַגְּדֹלָה אֲשֶׁר עָשָׂה יהוה בְּמִצְרַיִם, וַיִּירְאוּ הָעָם אֶת יהוה, וַיַּאֲמִינוּ בַּיהוה וּבְמֹשֶׁה עַבְדּוֹ[2]. כַּמָּה לָקוּ בְּאֶצְבַּע? עֶשֶׂר מַכּוֹת. אֱמוֹר מֵעַתָּה, בְּמִצְרַיִם לָקוּ עֶשֶׂר מַכּוֹת, וְעַל הַיָּם לָקוּ חֲמִשִּׁים מַכּוֹת.

---

cited in the *Haggadah,* who understood the *makkos* as five groups of two *makkos* each. The significance of that grouping requires further study.]

וְעַל הַיָּם לָקוּ חֲמִשִּׁים מַכּוֹת — *They Must Have Been Made to Suffer Fifty Makkos at the Sea [Where They Were Struck With a Whole Hand]*

❑ **R' Yose, who interprets the word *finger* in the context of the *makkos* and the word *hand* in the context of *Krias Yam Suf* to mean that there were more *makkos* at the *Yam Suf* by a factor of five, clearly disagrees with the Tanna who expounded *yad chazakah* to allude to *Dever.***

The exposition of R' Yose is based upon the fact that the expression describing Hashem's might at the splitting of the *Yam Suf* is His great "hand." A hand has five fingers, and in describing the *makkos* in Mitzrayim, the magicians recognized the "finger" of Hashem. So, by calculating ten *makkos* multiplied by the five fingers of a hand, R' Yose concludes that there must have been fifty *makkos* at the *Yam Suf.*

It would seem, in my humble opinion, that R' Yose must not agree with the exposition of the Tanna above, who expounded the words *yad chazakah* of *Devarim* 26:8 to allude to the *makkah* of *Dever.* For if he would understand the word *yad* (*hagedolah*) as a hint to something five times more numerous than the "finger" of the *makkos,* how can *yad* (*chazakah*) possibly refer to the single *makkah* of *Dever?*

Accordingly, we may ask: How indeed does that Tanna understand the words *yad hagedolah* in the context of *Krias Yam Suf?* Perhaps that Tanna will understand the phrase *yad hagedolah* to refer to *Krias Yam Suf,* and the reason why the word *yad* is used both in the context of *Dever* and *Krias Yam Suf* is that the *yad* of Hashem alludes to a punishment which includes

Rabbi Yose HaGlili said: How does one derive that the Egyptians were struck with ten *makkos* in Mitzrayim, and with fifty *makkos* at the Sea? Concerning the *makkos* in Mitzrayim, what does the Torah state? "The magicians said to Pharaoh, It is the finger of God."[1] However, of those at the Sea, the Torah states, "Yisrael saw the great 'hand' that HASHEM laid upon the Egyptians, the people feared HASHEM, and they believed in HASHEM and in His servant, Moshe."[2] How many *makkos* did they receive with the finger? Ten! Conclude from this that [if] they suffered ten *makkos* in Mitzrayim [where they were struck with a single finger], they must have been made to suffer fifty *makkos* at the Sea [where they were struck with a whole hand].

(1) *Shemos* 8:15. (2) 14:31.

death. Whether it be via a plague or through drowning, when the *hand* of Hashem is mentioned, the punishment is severe enough to kill. In reference to *Dever,* the expression the Torah uses is *yad chazakah,* meaning that the *Dever* was *chazak, strong.* In reference to *Krias Yam Suf,* the Torah uses the term *yad hagedolah, the great* — meaning, miraculous — *hand.* Accordingly, this Tanna does not hold that there is any allusion to a multiple of five in the *posuk's* usage of the word "hand."

וּבְמֹשֶׁה עַבְדּוֹ — *His Servant Moshe*

- ❒ **Why is Moshe virtually excluded from the *Haggadah's* text? And is it a coincidence that the one time he is mentioned, he is referred to as *Moshe avdo?***
- ❒ **In our pursuit of *parnassah,* the *mon* taught us that our success comes *only* from Hashem.**
- ❒ **In our pursuit of sanctifying Hashem's Name, the true meaning of *anavah* shows us that our success comes *only* from Hashem.**
- ❒ **Moshe, the greatest *anav* ever, understood that *Yetzias Mitzrayim* was completely carried out by Hashem, and that he was only fulfilling an opportunity that Hashem had bestowed upon him, by allowing him to play a part in it.**

When we read through the Torah's recounting of the entire episode of *Yetzias Mitzrayim,* Moshe Rabbeinu is, without question, one of the main protagonists. Would we even consider telling the story of *Yetzias Mitzrayim* without his name even being mentioned? Surely not! And yet, the *Haggadah* does just that — almost. There is only one mention of Moshe Rabbeinu

in the entirety of the text of the *Haggadah,* and that occurs right here.

Now, in the composition of the *Haggadah's* text, this mention of Moshe is almost an afterthought; he just happens to be mentioned in the latter segment of a *posuk* that is being cited because the beginning of that *posuk* uses the word *yad, hand,* in the context of *Krias Yam Suf.* Why is Moshe's role seemingly downplayed? And is it just a coincidence that Moshe is mentioned in the way that he is?

The answer begins as follows: Moshe Rabbeinu, the greatest man to ever live, is actually mentioned one *more* time than necessary. And, this lone mention actually holds the key as to why this is so, and also holds the key to Moshe Rabbeinu's greatness.

Earlier this year, during *Parashas Mikeitz,* I was, *lo aleinu,* hospitalized with a bout of pneumonia, and spent a short time in the hospital; *hodu laShem ki tov,* I was able to come home after a few days. In the hospital, I found myself reflecting upon the following ideas. I feel that they are worth reading, and those who internalize their message will have an easier time with some of life's more common *nisyonos.* Additionally, I think they shed some perspective on the war currently being waged in Eretz Yisrael.

In the context of Yosef's ascension to power, we see two extremes. At the very end of *Parashas Vayeishev,* Yosef did too much *hishtadlus* when he asked the *Sar HaMashkim* to intervene on his behalf. [We have discussed the details of why this was so in *Nahar Sholom, Bereishis* 40:14-15; see further there.] As a result, he was punished, and remained jailed for another two years.

In the beginning of *Parashas Mikeitz,* however, Yosef told Pharaoh that *biladai, Elokim ya'aneh es shlom Pharaoh, It is not from me; Elokim will answer with Pharaoh's welfare* (*Bereishis* 41:16). And in a matter of minutes, Yosef was the premier of the entire country! Clearly, when Yosef acknowledged that Hashem was in charge of everything, Hashem blessed him with instant success. So, the first step in understanding this vital lesson is realizing that a person's success is not based on his *hishtadlus,* but rather on Hashem.

This is certainly true when it comes to *parnassah* — a big *nisayon* for many people. In *Devarim* 8:16, the Torah describes the *mon* as an affliction to Klal Yisrael. For it states that Hashem fed *mon* to Klal Yisrael *in order to afflict them and in order to test them.* Was the *mon* a salvation (as indicated there by *Devarim* 8:3, where it says that they were afflicted with hunger, so Hashem gave them *mon*), or was it an affliction?

The truth is that there is no contradiction at all. Surely, the *mon* was, first and foremost, a wonderful blessing, which not only sustained Klal Yisrael, but also taught us so many valuable lessons. [If one studies the passage of the *mon* well, he can deduce several fundamental lessons about the actual relationship between *hishtadlus* and *parnsassah.* See further,

Nahar Sholom, Shemos 16:18, as well as to 16:4, 16:5, 16:20, 16:22, and *Devarim* 8:3,16.]

Now, by providing the *mon* in place of regular sustenance, Hashem obviously established that He can provide for anyone at any time, with or without their efforts. To those who have not had a chance to internalize this idea, it is at once incredible and also disheartening. It is amazing from the perspective of recognizing Hashem's greatness, His control over every aspect of the world at large and specifically the lives of Klal Yisrael, and the care He obviously demonstrates for every living thing. But, it is also disheartening in the respect that it can take the adrenaline away from a motivated person to learn that his success is actually not related to his efforts. When Hashem "pulled back the curtain," as it were, on the relationship between a person's efforts and his success, showing that they are not cause and effect, this might have robbed people of their motivation to be successful. In this light, the revelation served as an affliction. Hashem said, "I do not need help: The *mon,* the *Be'er Miriam,* the *Ananei HaKavod* provide for Klal Yisrael, and I do not need the efforts of people at all!"

What is the way to pass the *nisayon* presented by the realization that one's efforts do not result in his successes or failures in business? The answer is to understand that the true cause for one's success is Hashem's granting him that success, and that Hashem requires a person to perform *hishtadlus* before granting the *berachah* that is success. The two are not cause and effect, but rather Hashem does not release the *berachah* to one who has not performed the proper *hishtadlus.*

Hashem rejects the person who feels as though he is accomplishing something with his efforts. This lesson can be gleaned from the fact that after the conquest of the four kings, the king of Sedom offered Avram the spoils of war, but said he would keep the prisoners. Avram declined to take so much as a shoelace, out of concern that the king of Sedom would claim, "I made Avram rich!" But how could the king of Sedom make such an insane claim? He had been conquered by Kedorla'omer, who, in turn, was conquered by Avram. Everything belonging to the armies of Sedom and Kedarla'omer were now obviously Avram's. How could the king of Sedom take the position that he had made Avram rich, if nothing at all was his? Clearly, from the fact that he set forth to Avram such a proposal, the king of Sedom was delusional in feeling that he and his efforts mattered. When Avram saw this, he distanced himself completely, because there is no telling what such a person will attribute to himself. [This, as opposed to accepting gifts from Pharaoh, which Avram did, as part of his obligation to carry out *hishtadlus*. See *Nahar Sholom, Bereishis* 12:11-13, where we suggest that Avram actually did *hishtadlus* to *cause* Pharaoh to give him gifts.]

Thus far, we have explored the idea of Hashem controlling everything

and a person controlling nothing with respect to money and power. But in truth, the exact same principle is true regarding *avodas Hashem* as well.

The *Rosh HaYeshiva, ztvk"l,* would often speak about *anavah*. If we ask a child what *anavah* is, they will reply that it is humility. And what is humility? Is it feeling that we are less than we are? Not at all. The *Rosh HaYeshiva, ztvk"l,* would explain that *anavah* is knowing your abilities and strengths, and acknowledging that no credit is due to you because of your abilities. Everything you can accomplish is due to the gifts Hashem gave you. Whether they are genius, keen observation, good looks, riches, or any other conceivable benefit that sets you apart from another person, true *anavah* is to understand that, despite your advantage in one area or another over someone else, you are not a better person than they are. In some cases, your advantage may allow you to be greater than they, but you are not better.

Each of us is born with a mission to carry out in this world. And we are judged in Heaven based solely upon whether or not we achieved the goals that we were given the potential to achieve — nothing else. We will never be measured against other people, only against what we ourselves could have — and should have — accomplished. If, based on the gifts we were given and the situations in which He placed us, we accomplished whatever goals Hashem set for us, we will be rewarded greatly. But we must remember one thing clearly — the accomplishments are not ours. Everything we achieve is only because Hashem gave us the ability to do so.

The *Rosh HaYeshiva, ztvk"l,* would always reference the Gemara (*Pesachim* 50a), which relates that R' Yosef took ill, and when he awoke, he related to his father, R' Yehoshua ben Levi, that he had seen an upside-down world, for he had seen that the *elyonim* — the *superior ones* — were *lematah, on the bottom.* His father explained to him that, in fact, *olam barur ra'isa, you saw a correct world.* The *Rosh HaYeshiva, ztvk"l,* would ask: Everyone knows that it is possible to pretend in this world to be righteous. Is it any surprise that people who are *elyonim* in our eyes were really *lematah* in Heaven? And he explained that it must be that, actually, the *gedolei hador,* the truly righteous and great of the generation — true *elyonim* — were *lematah*. And R' Yosef's father explained the phenomenon to him by saying that actually, this was correct. For even though they were greater in Torah and *mitzvos* than others, they were still *lematah*. For they were not judged against the accomplishments of others, but rather against the accomplishments that they should have achieved. The *gadol* that finished *Shas* one hundred times, but could have done so two hundred times, will not reach the place of the person who could only recite *Tehillim* all day, but actually did so. The *elyonim* were bigger, but they were *lematah,* because the others were better.

Rashi (to *Shemos* 6:26, *d"h hu Aharon u'Moshe*) writes that there are places in the Torah where Aharon is listed before Moshe, and there are also places where Moshe is listed before Aharon. This comes to teach that Moshe and Aharon were equal. Can this statement possibly be taken at face value? The Torah itself states regarding Moshe that *v'lo kam Navi od b'Yisrael k'Moshe, never again has there arisen another Navi like Moshe.* Similarly, the Torah writes of Moshe that he was *anav mikal adam, humbler than any man.* Hashem told Aharon that Moshe experienced a different form of prophecy than other prophets; as the Torah states, *peh el peh Adaber bo, face to face I speak with him.* Moshe Rabbeinu was the redeemer of Klal Yisrael from Mitzrayim, and was also the one who transmitted the Torah to us on Har Sinai. How can it even be posited that Aharon was Moshe's equal?

The answer, of course, is that Aharon was equal to Moshe not in what he actually accomplished; for in this regard, Moshe remains unmatched in history. But when it came to what percentage of their respective potentials they accomplished, Aharon and Moshe were the same — both of them reached their potentials fully. This is the true barometer of how great a person is; how close he comes to completing the life's mission on which Hashem sent him. We cannot control how much money, strength, or smarts we will have throughout our lives. The only thing that we can control — the thing that defines the level of our service to Hashem – is if we are righteous, or God forbid, not so.

We can choose to try our hardest, and to do as much as it is possible for us to do. So yes, Moshe was truly "bigger" than Aharon, in the respect that he accomplished more, but not "better," meaning that they both fulfilled their potentials, which means that they were the same when it came to effort applied and righteousness of character. That is ultimately the only measurement that matters. [See further, *Nahar Sholom, Bereishis* 32:11.]

This mindset can help a person to truly be an *anav.* Everyone knows that their own potential is not yet reached. And when looking at anyone else, it is impossible to tell if they are reaching their potentials. So, while it might be possible to determine that a person is greater in Torah than his fellow, it is impossible to know which of them is closer to fulfilling his potential. And since that is really the measuring stick that Hashem uses, a person can truly feel that every single person with whom he interacts will be higher in the *Olam HaEmes* than he will be. As such, he can give them real honor, for he is able to perceive that they are quite possibly greater than he is. *Anavah* is thus the attribute of internalizing the concept that a person does not deserve anything for his accomplishments.

The point we are making here is that not only is a person not able to take credit for his accomplishments, but also that he is not even rewarded based simply on how much he accomplished. Rather, reward is

commensurate with how close a person came to fulfilling his potential.

Anavah opens for us the idea that what occurs in the world is not due to our efforts, or the efforts of other people. Rather, Hashem plans every occurrence and event precisely. As much as people may accomplish, this is only because they are taking an opportunity that Hashem carved out for them to be able to accomplish that they do so.

Another area where people sometimes struggle with this issue is pertaining to success in teaching, where they face a *nisayon* of feeling a lack of success in their efforts of *harbotzas haTorah*. The way Hashem controls the revelation of His Presence directly impacts how many people cling to the Torah. He can make His Name great if He wishes, and all will know Him instantly — and He chooses not to do so. But if He would, the success of the *harbotzas haTorah* would be His and His alone. As Hashem is the ultimate architect, it should be clear to us that just as He controls everything, He also controls how apparent His influence is in the world. Hashem does not need us for anything. He merely gives us the opportunity to spread His Name and His Torah; but the success of our efforts, much like the success of our monetary pursuits, is dependent on His will alone, and He needs no help.

In *Kaddish,* we say, *yisgadal veyiskadash Shmei Rabbah, be'alma di vera, May His Great Name be made great and holy, in the world that He created.* Now, the very next word in *Kaddish* means, *according to His will.* But there is a question about how this word should be pronounced. If it is pronounced *chi'rusei* (with a *chof*), it means *in the world that He created according to His will;* while if it is pronounced *kir'usei* (with a *kof),* it means *May His Great Name be made great and holy... according to His will.* The latter pronunciation and interpretation is preferred by the *Gra,* and it is how I personally received the tradition from the *Rosh HaYeshiva, ztvk"l,* to say it. [See further, *Nahar Sholom, Devarim* 33:19].

Accordingly, in *Kaddish* we are declaring that the measure of Hashem's greatness that the world recognizes at any given time is *precisely in accordance with the will of Hashem.* The second He wishes to reveal Himself in a more open fashion, the world will see and know Him. When a Rebbi works with *talmidim* and gets them to put on *tzitizis,* especially if they stick to this commitment, it is surely a great accomplishment. But when the war in Eretz Yisrael broke out, Hashem caused forty thousand *chilonim* to ask for *tzitizis* in a day or two! Hashem does not need help with anything, and certainly His Name will be *exactly* as recognized as He desires at any particular time.

We are taught that at *Matan Torah*, Hashem was *kafah aleihem har kegigis,* that Hashem suspended Har Sinai above the Jewish nation, and "forced" them to accept the Torah. While the *Rosh HaYeshiva, ztvk"l*, noted that this can indeed be literally what happened, we can also understand the words

of *Chazal* here differently. He explained that at Har Sinai, the knowledge of the presence of Hashem was so apparent that there was no *nisayon* to defy Him and to transgress the Torah. But, under such circumstances, to agree to observe the Torah is no big deal — anyone would do it. Hashem desires the *emunah* and *bitachon* of His people when His Presence is not as obvious. There exists a *nisayon* to study life, and determine that yes, Hashem is behind everything that happens, and He does what is best for a person. Hashem wants a person to be a *ma'amin* using his own *bechirah,* not to simply be compelled with overwhelming evidence that He is Omnipotent.

The *Rosh HaYeshiva, ztvk"l,* would make this point regarding the *posuk* (*Yirmiyah* 50:20), *ki eslach la'asher ashir,* where Hashem says that He will forgive Klal Yisrael's sins at the End of Days. He would ask: If Hashem wants to just forgive the sins of the people, why wait until then? Do it now! And he would explain that now, the *Middas HaDin* would have a complaint: The sins of the wicked destroy the world — how can this go unpunished? However, when it will be known to all that at the end of time, through all of the world's events, everything emerged precisely as Hashem had planned it, the *Middas HaDin* can have no complaint, and the sins of Klal Yisrael can be forgiven. Again, we see here that when Hashem's Name seems to be obscured and not apparent, this is precisely His plan. When He wishes to change that, He will. He guides the world exactly as He wishes, and He does not need help.

This idea is reminiscent of how the *Rosh HaYeshiva, ztvk"l,* understood the Midrash (*Eichah Rabbasi, Pesichta* §30) that details the difference between the ways that David, Asa, Yehoshafat, and Chizkiyahu prayed for Hashem to make them victorious in battle. The Midrash details that David asked Hashem to allow him to chase his enemies and defeat them, and Hashem granted this. Asa prayed that he chase his enemies, and asked that Hashem destroy them miraculously, and so Hashem did this. Yehoshafat's request of Hashem was that he would sing praise to Hashem, and Hashem should defeat his enemies completely for him, which Hashem did; and Chizkiyahu said that he would simply sleep and Hashem should wipe out his enemies, which He did.

The *Rosh HaYeshiva, ztvk"l* (see *Darash Moshe* to *Eikev* 8:17), explained that the progression was as follows. David knew that the people in his time were on a high level of *bitachon,* and so even if he would carry out the conquest, the people would not take the credit themselves for the victory Hashem had given them. Asa, however, knew that the people of his own generation would not be able to withstand this temptation if they were involved in actually defeating the enemy, so he prayed that Hashem should carry out that part. Yehoshafat knew that if he were to even give chase, his people would take credit for the victory, and so he simply sang Hashem's praises, and asked Hashem to carry out the conquest completely. Chizkiyahu,

רַבִּי אֱלִיעֶזֶר אוֹמֵר. מִנַּיִן שֶׁכָּל מַכָּה וּמַכָּה שֶׁהֵבִיא הַקָּדוֹשׁ בָּרוּךְ הוּא עַל הַמִּצְרִים בְּמִצְרַיִם הָיְתָה שֶׁל אַרְבַּע מַכּוֹת? שֶׁנֶּאֱמַר, יְשַׁלַּח בָּם חֲרוֹן אַפּוֹ – עֶבְרָה, וָזַעַם, וְצָרָה, מִשְׁלַחַת מַלְאֲכֵי רָעִים[1]. עֶבְרָה, אַחַת. וָזַעַם, שְׁתַּיִם. וְצָרָה, שָׁלֹשׁ. מִשְׁלַחַת מַלְאֲכֵי רָעִים, אַרְבַּע. אֱמוֹר מֵעַתָּה, בְּמִצְרַיִם לָקוּ אַרְבָּעִים מַכּוֹת, וְעַל הַיָּם לָקוּ מָאתַיִם מַכּוֹת.

רַבִּי עֲקִיבָא אוֹמֵר. מִנַּיִן שֶׁכָּל מַכָּה וּמַכָּה שֶׁהֵבִיא הַקָּדוֹשׁ בָּרוּךְ הוּא עַל הַמִּצְרִים בְּמִצְרַיִם הָיְתָה שֶׁל חָמֵשׁ מַכּוֹת? שֶׁנֶּאֱמַר, יְשַׁלַּח בָּם חֲרוֹן אַפּוֹ, עֶבְרָה, וָזַעַם, וְצָרָה, מִשְׁלַחַת מַלְאֲכֵי רָעִים[1].

---

though, knew that even if he were to sing to Hashem, his generation would attribute their victory to his prayers, and not to Hashem fighting for them, and so he asked that Hashem do everything while he slept! [See further there, where the *Rosh HaYeshiva, ztvk"l,* related this concept to the events of the Six-Day War. See also *Nahar Sholom* to *Shemos* 14:13-14.] The message here is clear; these kings were doing their very best to not take credit for what they were doing, and to remain focused on the fact that *everything* is from Hashem, and that He does not need anything from anyone.

Moshe was on the way to begin the most awesome and important journey the world has ever known. His immediate mission was to lead Klal Yisrael out of Mitzrayim, which was going to be followed by *Krias Yam Suf,* and ultimately *Kabbalas HaTorah* at Har Sinai. Moshe Rabbeinu is the one man who is most central to the narrative of the Torah, and who Hashem chose to transmit His Torah to us. If there was anyone in the history of the world who can be said to have been indispensable, it would have to be Moshe. And yet, we find that Hashem was willing to kill Moshe on account of his delaying his son's *bris milah* unnecessarily! Of course, had Moshe Rabbeinu been killed, Hashem would have brought the salvation of Klal Yisrael through another person. In fact, Hashem did "replace" Moshe Rabbeinu, when He brought Klal Yisrael into Eretz Yisrael with Yehoshua, after Moshe was not allowed to enter on account of his having hit the rock instead of speaking to it at the Mei Merivah. Similarly, we find Mordechai HaTzaddik expressing to Esther HaMalkah the very same idea, when he said (*Esther* 4:14), *revach vehatzalah ya'amod layehudim mimakom*

Rabbi Eliezer said: How does one derive that every *makkah* that the Holy One, blessed is He, inflicted upon the Egyptians in Mitzrayim was equal to four *makkos*? — for it is stated, "He sent upon them His fierce anger: wrath, fury, and trouble, a band of emissaries of evil."[1] [Since each *makkah* in Mitzrayim consisted of] (1) wrath, (2) fury, (3) trouble, and (4) a band of emissaries of evil, therefore conclude from this that in Mitzrayim they were struck by forty *makkos* and at the Sea by two hundred!

Rabbi Akiva said: How does one derive that each *makkah* that the Holy One, blessed is He, inflicted upon the Egyptians in Mitzrayim was equal to five *makkos*? — for it is stated: "He sent upon them His fierce anger, wrath, fury, trouble, and a band of emissaries of evil."[1] [Since each *makkah* in Mitzrayim consisted of]

(1) *Tehillim* 78:49.

---

acheir, ve'at u'veis avich toveidu, relief and salvation will arise for the Jewish people from another place, and you and your father's house will be lost. Hashem does not need any particular person in order to bring about the salvation of Klal Yisrael. The lesson here is stark. Even the holy Moshe Rabbeinu almost lost everything at this point, and Hashem would have chosen another person to lead Klal Yisrael forward. From this it is clear that Hashem *does not need any person for anything at all*; everyone is subject to His will, and nobody gets a free pass because of what they "are destined" to accomplish in the future. He gifted Moshe with tremendous, unparalleled, potential, and tremendous, unparalleled opportunity and responsibility. But make no mistake; Hashem did not need Moshe at all.

And there was never a person in the history of this earth who understood this lesson as clearly as Moshe Rabbeinu, the *anav mikal adam,* understood it. The cloudiness of *hishtadlus* makes people feel as though their achievements matter in Hashem's equation, and they really do not. The less a person interjects his own interests and his own self into the affairs of Hashem, the more directly he can understand the control of Hashem over the world. The greatness of his humility is thus directly related to his greatness as a servant of Hashem. And, the very reason that Moshe was the greatest *eved Hashem* to walk the planet is exactly the reason that his name need not appear in the *Haggadah* at all. Moshe knew, with more clarity than we ever will, that he had *nothing* to do with *Yetzias Mitzrayim,* and it was all Hashem's doing. And the *Haggadah* mentions the name of the great Moshe Rabbeinu only once, referencing him with the highest

חֲרוֹן אַפּוֹ, אַחַת. עֶבְרָה, שְׁתַּיִם. וָזַעַם, שָׁלֹשׁ. וְצָרָה, אַרְבַּע. מִשְׁלַחַת מַלְאֲכֵי רָעִים, חָמֵשׁ. אֱמוֹר מֵעַתָּה, בְּמִצְרַיִם לָקוּ חֲמִשִּׁים מַכּוֹת, וְעַל הַיָּם לָקוּ חֲמִשִּׁים וּמָאתַיִם מַכּוֹת.

כַּמָּה מַעֲלוֹת טוֹבוֹת לַמָּקוֹם עָלֵינוּ.

אִלּוּ הוֹצִיאָנוּ מִמִּצְרַיִם
וְלֹא עָשָׂה בָהֶם שְׁפָטִים — דַּיֵּנוּ.

---

honor of *Moshe avdo*, to show us that the reason for his lofty status was precisely because he knew that Hashem did everything, and not he.

דַּיֵּנוּ — *It Would Have Been Enough for Us.*

- ❒ ***Dayeinu*** **is not about declaring that we did not need Hashem to do these kindnesses for us. Of course, we needed them all!**
- ❒ **We are all obligated to find Hashem and believe in Him, the same way Avraham Avinu did. We thank Hashem that He made it so easy for us to do that, by affording us a history rich with His Providence.**
- ❒ **Thus,** ***Dayeinu*** **is really about declaring that even if Hashem had not continued to reveal Himself to us openly again and again, we would still have had sufficient evidence of His Providence to believe in Him forever; and it is also about thanking Him for relating with us so openly, so that we can more easily recognize Him and relate to Him!**

Here, we express to Hashem the unbelievable debt of gratitude we owe Him for all that He has bestowed upon us. Many people think that this means simply that we would have been lacking, and Hashem gave us what we needed in these fifteen instances between *Yetzias Mitzrayim* and the erection of the *Beis HaMikdash*. Famously, in this light, some of the lines of *Dayeinu* are difficult to understand. Take, for example, the line that states, *If You would have drowned our oppressors in the Yam Suf, and not provided for our needs for forty years in the Wilderness, it would have been enough*. Or the one that states, *If You would have brought us before Har Sinai, and not given us the Torah, it would have been enough*. On the surface, these lines do not really make any sense. How would it have been *enough?* What good would it have done for us to be saved from the Egyptian army, only to subsequently starve in the Wilderness? And what was the purpose of arriving at Har Sinai, if not expressly in order to accept the Torah? How, then, would it *have been enough* to be saved from our enemies at the Sea, or to be brought to Har Sinai?

(1) fierce anger, (2) wrath, (3) fury, (4) trouble, and (5) a band of emissaries of evil, therefore conclude from this that in Mitzrayim they were struck by fifty *makkos*, and at the Sea by two hundred and fifty *makkos*!

The Omnipresent has bestowed so many favors upon us!

Had He brought us out of Mitzrayim,
but not executed judgments against the Egyptians,
it would have been enough for us.

The answer is that we are not correctly interpreting the words *it would have been enough*. For *what,* exactly, would it have been enough? Alas, we are approaching *enough* from the perspective of *receiving* from Hashem. Clearly, in terms of accepting the Torah, arriving at Har Sinai would *not* have been enough. If we reframe our minds properly, and focus not on what we *receive,* but rather on what our *obligations* are, this praise becomes a lot clearer, and is a very powerful lesson.

In terms of the *obligation* that weighs upon every single person in the world to discover Hashem on his own, to know Him and relate with Him, similar to the way Avraham Avinu did, each of these fifteen favors Hashem did for Klal Yisrael made it progressively easier to recognize Him in the universe. These were all gifts that Klal Yisrael did not necessarily deserve or even need, but which Hashem performed for them anyway, and in the process, He revealed Himself more openly than He usually does. When *Dayeinu* is explained in that light, we can indeed see what it means that *it would have been enough* at each of the fifteen steps.

אִלּוּ הוֹצִיאָנוּ מִמִּצְרַיִם וְלֹא עָשָׂה בָהֶם שְׁפָטִים, דַּיֵּנוּ — *Had He brought us out of Mitzrayim, but not executed judgments against the Egyptians, it would have been enough for us.*

It would have been enough for us to experience *Yetzias Mitzrayim*. If Hashem would have redeemed Klal Yisrael from Mitzrayim, that occurrence alone would have served to demonstrate to us that there is a Hashem in the world, Who acts in our best interest. We are taught to recognize all the good that happens to us as Hashem's blessings, and we would certainly have done so when granted such an incredibly good turn of fortune. As the *posuk* (*Devarim* 4:34, cited below by the *Haggadah*) states, this is the only time Hashem took one nation out from among another nation, and this stands as a testament to His love for Klal Yisrael. This truly would have been enough for us to find Hashem.

אִלּוּ עָשָׂה בָהֶם שְׁפָטִים וְלֹא עָשָׂה בֵאלֹהֵיהֶם דַּיֵּנוּ.
אִלּוּ עָשָׂה בֵאלֹהֵיהֶם וְלֹא הָרַג אֶת בְּכוֹרֵיהֶם דַּיֵּנוּ.
אִלּוּ הָרַג אֶת בְּכוֹרֵיהֶם וְלֹא נָתַן לָנוּ אֶת מָמוֹנָם דַּיֵּנוּ.
אִלּוּ נָתַן לָנוּ אֶת מָמוֹנָם וְלֹא קָרַע לָנוּ אֶת הַיָּם דַּיֵּנוּ.
אִלּוּ קָרַע לָנוּ אֶת הַיָּם וְלֹא הֶעֱבִירָנוּ בְתוֹכוֹ בֶּחָרָבָה דַּיֵּנוּ.

אִלּוּ עָשָׂה בָהֶם שְׁפָטִים, וְלֹא עָשָׂה בֵאלֹהֵיהֶם, דַּיֵּנוּ — *Had He executed judgments against them, but not upon their gods, it would have been enough for us.*

But He did more than take us out of Mitzrayim; He also carried out judgments against the Egyptians. And Hashem's justice is like no other justice; it is *middah keneged middah,* and it is precise. When Klal Yisrael saw that the Egyptians were so obviously being punished for what they had done to the Jewish people, they got an incredible boost of *emunah.* Hashem was not only granting them a new lease on life by freeing them, but also exacting retribution on their behalf, demonstrating that He loves and protects His nation. Seeing this surely made Hashem more recognizable. It was not necessary for Hashem to do anything more; even had He not destroyed the gods of the Egyptians, Klal Yisrael would have sufficient reason to believe in Him.

אִלּוּ עָשָׂה בֵאלֹהֵיהֶם, וְלֹא הָרַג אֶת בְּכוֹרֵיהֶם, דַּיֵּנוּ — *Had He executed judgments against their gods, but not slain their firstborn, it would have been enough for us.*

Hashem made it even easier for Klal Yisrael to recognize His Presence in the world, by destroying the gods of the Egyptians. Now, this does not necessarily refer to idols, which are understandably and obviously powerless. It rather alludes to the Nile River, which the Egyptians served because it carried the waters that provided their sustenance. They also worshiped animals, which provide wool and milk even to those who do not eat their meat, and the animals were killed. Now, if a person is searching for a deity to whom to attribute power, there is an inclination to give credit to what is *apparently* bringing success, which was the motivation behind some of the idolatry practiced by Mitzrayim. By smiting the Nile and the animals, Hashem demonstrated that they are not the source of the goodness in the world that a person is supposed to find. This made it even easier for Klal Yisrael to be able to identify Him, and in truth, this would have been sufficient. He did not have to also kill the *bechorim* during *Makkas Bechoros.*

Had He executed judgments against them,
but not upon their gods, it would have been enough for us.
Had He executed judgments against their gods,
but not slain their firstborn, it would have been enough for us.
Had He slain their firstborn, but not given us their wealth,
it would have been enough for us.
Had He given us their wealth, but not split the Yam Suf for us,
it would have been enough for us.
Had He split the *Yam Suf* for us,
but not led us through it on dry land,
it would have been enough for us.

אִלּוּ הָרַג אֶת בְּכוֹרֵיהֶם וְלֹא נָתַן לָנוּ אֶת מָמוֹנָם, דַּיֵּנוּ — *Had He slain their firstborn, but not given us their wealth, it would have been enough for us.*

And yet, He chose to reveal Himself in this awesome way to Klal Yisrael as well. During *Makkas Bechoros,* Hashem showed that He is in absolute control of life and death, and also that He possesses the knowledge of who is and who is not a firstborn. This was even a greater degree of revelation, and certainly once they saw this miracle, Klal Yisrael would certainly have been able to find Hashem and believe in Him. Hashem would not have needed to also give us the spoils of Mitzrayim.

אִלּוּ נָתַן לָנוּ אֶת מָמוֹנָם וְלֹא קָרַע לָנוּ אֶת הַיָּם, דַּיֵּנוּ — *Had He given us their wealth, but not split the Yam Suf for us, it would have been enough for us.*

The fact that the Egyptians were tripping over themselves to load Klal Yisrael up with valuables and send them out was the total opposite of their previous attitude. They had always felt that the Jewish people should remain slaves, and that they should be destitute. And yet, Hashem demonstrated so clearly here that He could influence the minds of the Egyptians, to the point that they would completely alter their natural behavior. Upon seeing this degree of influence, Klal Yisrael surely would have had the ability to recognize Hashem. It would certainly not have been necessary to reveal Himself further by splitting the *Yam Suf.*

אִלּוּ קָרַע לָנוּ אֶת הַיָּם וְלֹא הֶעֱבִירָנוּ בְתוֹכוֹ בֶּחָרָבָה, דַּיֵּנוּ — *Had He split the Yam Suf for us, but not led us through it on dry land, it would have been enough for us.*

And yet, He did just that. At *Krias Yam Suf,* Hashem demonstrated complete and total mastery over Creation, performing many, many miracles

אִלּוּ הֶעֱבִירָנוּ בְתוֹכוֹ בֶּחָרָבָה
וְלֹא שִׁקַּע צָרֵינוּ בְּתוֹכוֹ דַּיֵּנוּ.
אִלּוּ שִׁקַּע צָרֵינוּ בְּתוֹכוֹ
וְלֹא סִפֵּק צָרְכֵּנוּ בַּמִּדְבָּר אַרְבָּעִים שָׁנָה דַּיֵּנוּ.

---

at once. The scope of this miraculous feat was so incredibly vast — see the discussion between the Tannaim above, who debate the number of miracles that occurred then. *Chazal* tell us that even a maidservant at the *Yam Suf* saw more Divine revelation than the *Navi*, Yechezkel ben Buzi. This means that if a person saw (and internalized) the miracles that occurred at the splitting of the *Yam Suf,* he would definitely be able to believe in Hashem. There was thus no reason for Hashem to take the additional step of drying out the ground of the *Yam Suf* so that Klal Yisrael would not be walking in mud.

אִלּוּ הֶעֱבִירָנוּ בְתוֹכוֹ בֶּחָרָבָה וְלֹא שִׁקַּע צָרֵנוּ בְּתוֹכוֹ, דַּיֵּנוּ — *Had He led us through it on dry land, but not drowned our oppressors in it, it would have been enough for us.*

And yet, this is exactly what Hashem did! Among the many miracles Hashem performed at the *Yam Suf* was a miracle — or rather, a series of miracles — that was intended to make it easier for Klal Yisrael to cross. In *Avos DeRabbi Nassan* (Ch. 33), we find that ten times, Klal Yisrael tried to proceed into the Sea, but they could not bring themselves to do so, until Hashem miraculously changed the Sea in one way or another to make it easier. Each time, Moshe Rabbeinu hit the water, and the next miracle they asked for occurred. Finally, after the tenth time, they were able to enter the *Yam Suf.* Even after all of these miraculous changes, it took the *bitachon* of Nachshon ben Aminadav to take the seemingly suicidal step of walking into the water. [Perhaps the miracles occurring in the water were there for them to see, but at a bit of a distance, so that they first needed to cross the seemingly impassable waters that were closer to them in order to reach the dry areas; and Nachshon alone was able to overcome his instincts and obey Moshe's command.] Now, if Klal Yisrael was satisfied with the final miraculous change, why did they not ask for it initially? Why did they first say they would go if a certain change would take place, only to retract their request a few moments later, on nine separate occasions? I would humbly suggest that it was because they truly wanted to pass the *nisayon,* and go into the water immediately. But their legs were frozen in place, paralyzed by their instinct to survive.

Had He led us through it on dry land,
but not drowned our oppressors in it,
it would have been enough for us.
Had He drowned our oppressors in it,
but not provided for our needs in the Wilderness for forty years,
it would have been enough for us.

They begged Moshe to ask Hashem to make a small change, so that they would still have a big *nisayon,* and receive reward for passing it. When they saw that they still could not move, they asked for another change, and another, until Nachshon was able to do the unthinkable, and others followed. [See further, *Nahar Sholom, Shemos* 14:15.] Here we see a marvelous thing; Hashem was willing to tailor the *nisayon* of our forefathers to make it as easy as it needed to be so they could pass, and yet as difficult as it could be to maximize their reward. Such attention to detail, and such caring for His people, would *never* be forgotten, and this would be enough for Klal Yisrael to know Hashem, and believe in Hashem forever. He did not need to further reveal Himself by decimating the Egyptian army. [One might ask: If Klal Yisrael wished for as little interference as possible to help them pass their *nisayon,* why are we thanking Hashem for revealing Himself to us again and again? Does this not diminish the reward we receive when we have *bitachon?* A parable can be given which will help us understand the distinction. A person can ace a test because he studied well, or because the teacher helps him with the answers when he takes the test. The person who studied well is analogous to one who reflects on Klal Yisrael's past experiences and derives his strong *bitachon* from them, so that when he is met with his own *nisayon,* he can pass with flying colors. However, the person who needs the teacher to help him with the answers is analogous to a person who needs Hashem's help to make the *nisayon* easier.]

אִלּוּ שִׁקַּע צָרֵינוּ בְּתוֹכוֹ וְלֹא סִפֵּק צָרְכֵּנוּ בַּמִּדְבָּר אַרְבָּעִים שָׁנָה, דַּיֵּנוּ — ***Had He drowned our oppressors in it, but not provided for our needs in the Wilderness for forty years, it would have been enough for us.***

And yet, Hashem used the splitting of the *Yam Suf* as a means to punish Mitzrayim. After so many decades of Mitzrayim's glory coming at the expense of Klal Yisrael, Hashem now reversed this dynamic; *Krias Yam Suf* brought about the salvation of Klal Yisrael, and at the same time,

אִלּוּ סִפֵּק צָרְכֵּנוּ בַּמִּדְבָּר אַרְבָּעִים שָׁנָה
וְלֹא הֶאֱכִילָנוּ אֶת הַמָּן דַּיֵּנוּ.
אִלּוּ הֶאֱכִילָנוּ אֶת הַמָּן וְלֹא נָתַן לָנוּ אֶת הַשַּׁבָּת דַּיֵּנוּ.
אִלּוּ נָתַן לָנוּ אֶת הַשַּׁבָּת וְלֹא קֵרְבָנוּ לִפְנֵי הַר סִינַי דַּיֵּנוּ.

---

the annihilation of the Egyptian army. This was another tremendous revelation of Hashem's Presence, and further aided Klal Yisrael's ability to understand Him. It would have thus been enough if Hashem had only done this — He did not also need to care for us in the Wilderness for forty years.

אִלּוּ סִפֵּק צָרְכֵּנוּ בַּמִּדְבָּר אַרְבָּעִים שָׁנָה וְלֹא הֶאֱכִילָנוּ אֶת הַמָּן, דַּיֵּנוּ ***— Had He provided for our needs in the Wilderness for forty years, but not fed us the mon, it would have been enough for us.***

Now, there is no question that we needed to be supported during the forty years in the Wilderness. But it could have happened the way other nomadic societies survive in harsh climates. Their dwellings are uncomfortable, and they live with barely enough water to drink, never mind bathing, or washing clothes. They experience rough terrain, and they must be wary of dangerous animals. Hashem showered the Jewish people with care while they were in the Wilderness. The *Ananei HaKavod* protected them from the heat and the sun's rays, and also kept their clothing fresh. The *Be'er Miriam* provided all the water they needed, and Hashem made their clothing grow with them, so that they never required new garments. These miracles practically announced Hashem's might and glory, and when Klal Yisrael witnessed them, their understanding of Hashem was certainly bolstered. This was a very great degree of help from Hashem, in a very open way, and would definitely have been enough for them to recognize Him. Hashem certainly did not need to provide Klal Yisrael with the *mon.*

אִלּוּ הֶאֱכִילָנוּ אֶת הַמָּן וְלֹא נָתַן לָנוּ אֶת הַשַּׁבָּת, דַּיֵּנוּ ***— Had He fed us the mon, but not given us the Shabbos, it would have been enough for us.***

And yet, Hashem did give the *mon* to Klal Yisrael. This was an even more open miracle than the aforementioned *Ananei HaKavod* and *Be'er Miriam* — clouds and water are earthly things, although in the Wilderness, Hashem provided them miraculously. *Mon,* on the other hand, is a completely Heavenly substance. The fact that Hashem sent *mon* was an even greater demonstration that He runs the world, and that He is constantly providing

Had He provided for our needs in the Wilderness for forty years,
but not fed us the *mon*, it would have been enough for us.
Had He fed us the *mon*,
but not given us the Shabbos,
it would have been enough for us.
Had He given us the Shabbos,
but not brought us before Har Sinai,
it would have been enough for us.

---

for everyone. The *mon* was a physical iteration of "bread from Heaven," and actually teaches us the relationship between our *hishtadlus* and our *parnassah*. The *mon* that a person received was always the right amount, and whether a person collected more or less, his total was always the same. The *mon* was a powerful reminder that Hashem exists, and controls the entire world. Thus, if the *mon* would have fallen, and Hashem had not given us the gift of Shabbos, we would still know Him and believe in Him.

אִלּוּ נָתַן לָנוּ אֶת הַשַּׁבָּת, וְלֹא קֵרְבָנוּ לִפְנֵי הַר סִינַי, דַּיֵּנוּ —
Had He given us the Shabbos, but not brought us before Har Sinai, it would have been enough for us.

But, give us the gift of Shabbos is precisely what Hashem did. The everlasting treaty between Klal Yisrael and Hashem to both sanctify and refrain from desecrating the Shabbos is rooted completely in our belief that Hashem created the world in six days, and rested on the seventh. While the giving of Shabbos is not a physical thing that can be examined and used to make a determination about Hashem, it is really the very foundation of the relationship between a person and his Creator. Keeping Shabbos is acting upon the recognition that Hashem created the world, and that He commanded abstinence from work on His day of rest. Moreover, the concept of resting on Shabbos is a "reflective rest" — a time to review the accomplishments of the previous six days, and to analyze if they were imbued with the right degree of spirituality, or spent pursuing merely physical goals. [This specific idea shifted for Klal Yisrael once we received the Torah, for the Torah reveals to us precisely what Hashem wants us to do at all times. Now, we are to utilize the aspect of "reflective rest" on Shabbos to analyze if we are adhering to the Torah optimally. See *Nahar Sholom, Bereishis* 2:3, where this topic is discussed at length.] So, with the gift of Shabbos, Hashem presented Klal Yisrael with a treaty by which to begin to know Him. This gift was enough to enable Klal Yisrael to know Hashem forever; it was not necessary for Him to bring us to Har Sinai.

אִלּוּ קֵרְבָנוּ לִפְנֵי הַר סִינַי וְלֹא נָתַן לָנוּ אֶת הַתּוֹרָה דַּיֵּנוּ.

אִלּוּ נָתַן לָנוּ אֶת הַתּוֹרָה
וְלֹא הִכְנִיסָנוּ לְאֶרֶץ יִשְׂרָאֵל דַּיֵּנוּ.

אִלּוּ הִכְנִיסָנוּ לְאֶרֶץ יִשְׂרָאֵל
וְלֹא בָנָה לָנוּ אֶת בֵּית הַבְּחִירָה דַּיֵּנוּ.

— אִלּוּ קֵרְבָנוּ לִפְנֵי הַר סִינַי, וְלֹא נָתַן לָנוּ אֶת הַתּוֹרָה, דַּיֵּנוּ
Had He brought us before Har Sinai, but not given us the Torah, it would have been enough for us.

But Hashem chose to reveal Himself even more, and brought Klal Yisrael to Har Sinai. At Har Sinai, Klal Yisrael experienced the greatest revelation in our history: Hashem *spoke to them!* The hearing of the lightning and the seeing of the thunder and the sound of the *shofar,* were experiences that would imprint a definitive knowledge of Hashem upon Klal Yisrael for all time. Additionally, Hashem was *kafa aleihem har kegigis, held the mountain over them like a barrel,* and "forced them" (according to the *Rosh HaYeshiva, ztvk"l,* by making Hashem's existence so incredibly real to them that His will could not be denied) to agree to adhere to the Torah with this incredible and undeniable revelation. This revelation was so convincing that nothing further was required in order to convince Klal Yisrael of Hashem's existence. The *Rosh HaYeshiva, ztvk"l,* explained that if Hashem would have done all of these miracles, but declined to actually reveal to us what the commandments of the Torah are, the inspiration from the revelation of Hashem at Har Sinai would have been the impetus to study all of Creation and deduce the six hundred and thirteen *mitzvos* on our own. [This is similar to the way the Avraham Avinu kept the Torah, even though he lived well before it was given at Har Sinai; see further, *Nahar Sholom, Devarim* 33:4.]

— אִלּוּ נָתַן לָנוּ אֶת הַתּוֹרָה וְלֹא הִכְנִיסָנוּ לְאֶרֶץ יִשְׂרָאֵל, דַּיֵּינוּ
Had He given us the Torah, but not brought us into Eretz Yisrael, it would have been enough for us.

But Hashem chose to develop our relationship with Him yet further. He gave us His Torah! He literally told us *exactly* what He wants us to do. We now have an eternal blueprint, and if we follow it, it will lead us to the ultimate relationship with Hashem. Surely, this would be enough for Klal Yisrael to believe in Hashem forever, and it would not be necessary for Hashem to bring us to Eretz Yisrael.

Had He brought us before *Har Sinai*,
but not given us the Torah, it would have been enough for us.
Had He given us the Torah,
but not brought us into Eretz Yisrael,
it would have been enough for us.
Had He brought us into Eretz Yisrael,
but not built the *Beis HaMikdash* for us,
it would have been enough for us.

אִלּוּ הִכְנִיסָנוּ לְאֶרֶץ יִשְׂרָאֵל וְלֹא בָנָה לָנוּ אֶת בֵּית הַבְּחִירָה, דַּיֵּנוּ — *Had He brought us into Eretz Yisrael, but not built the Beis HaMikdash for us, it would have been enough for us.*

And what did Hashem do? He brought us to Eretz Yisrael! [Much of the *Haggadah* actually centers around the benefits of living in Eretz Yisrael. See *Kadeish,* where we explained that it was only those Jewish people who wanted to leave Mitzrayim, and to serve Hashem in His land according to His Torah (which they had not yet received), who merited to experience *Yetzias Mitzrayim.*] Eretz Yisrael is the place where Klal Yisrael is given the opportunity to live optimally, according to the Torah, without the detracting influences of foreign societies or cultures. Surely, once this pinnacle had been achieved, it was enough! There would be nothing more that was needed for Klal Yisrael to know of Hashem and believe in Him forever.

And still, out of His love for Klal Yisrael, Hashem gave us the *Beis HaMikdash,* the place where His *Shechinah* rests on this earth, in the midst of His chosen people, and the place that was the physical and spiritual connection between Hashem and Klal Yisrael, where the relationship between Him and us was most actualized. The *Haggadah* alludes to the *Beis HaMikdash* as a vehicle by which we attain atonement for our sins. The essence of the connection between Hashem and Klal Yisrael is the observance of the Torah, which is His will; and sins that violate the Torah cloud that relationship. The *Beis HaMikdash* enabled Klal Yisrael to regain any lost closeness with Hashem. At this point, without a shadow of a doubt, Hashem had equipped Klal Yisrael to find Him, know Him, have *bitachon* in Him, commit to Him, remain loyal to Him in all circumstances, and relate with Him, for all time.

And what must our reaction be upon observing the levels upon levels of revelations Hashem has granted us? To thank Him profusely! For with each and every miracle discussed here, Hashem not only performed that kindness, but also demonstrated thereby another, deeper dimension of His relationship with us.

עַל אַחַת כַּמָּה וְכַמָּה טוֹבָה כְפוּלָה וּמְכֻפֶּלֶת לַמָּקוֹם עָלֵינוּ. שֶׁהוֹצִיאָנוּ מִמִּצְרַיִם, וְעָשָׂה בָהֶם שְׁפָטִים, וְעָשָׂה בֵאלֹהֵיהֶם, וְהָרַג אֶת בְּכוֹרֵיהֶם, וְנָתַן לָנוּ אֶת מָמוֹנָם, וְקָרַע לָנוּ אֶת הַיָּם, וְהֶעֱבִירָנוּ בְתוֹכוֹ בֶּחָרָבָה, וְשִׁקַּע צָרֵינוּ בְּתוֹכוֹ, וְסִפֵּק צָרְכֵּנוּ בַּמִּדְבָּר אַרְבָּעִים שָׁנָה, וְהֶאֱכִילָנוּ אֶת הַמָּן, וְנָתַן לָנוּ אֶת הַשַּׁבָּת, וְקֵרְבָנוּ לִפְנֵי הַר סִינַי, וְנָתַן לָנוּ אֶת הַתּוֹרָה, וְהִכְנִיסָנוּ לְאֶרֶץ יִשְׂרָאֵל, וּבָנָה לָנוּ אֶת בֵּית הַבְּחִירָה, לְכַפֵּר עַל כָּל עֲוֹנוֹתֵינוּ.

The cups are now refilled to the brim. The wine that was removed is not drunk.
If any of the *Seder's* participants have left the table for any reason, whether it be children who wandered off searching for *Afikomans,* or women who have been caring for babies or preparing the *seudah,* and were unable to recite the *Haggadah* as they should have, they must be called back to the *Seder* table to both recite and understand the section of the *Haggadah* of Rabban Gamliel's explanation of *Pesach, Matzah,* and *Maror.* The leader of the *Seder* should read and explain these paragraphs clearly, and translate them into whatever language necessary, so that everyone understands them. If a person does not say them and understand them on at least a basic level, he has not fulfilled his obligation.

רַבָּן גַּמְלִיאֵל הָיָה אוֹמֵר. כָּל שֶׁלֹּא אָמַר שְׁלֹשָׁה דְּבָרִים אֵלּוּ בַּפֶּסַח, לֹא יָצָא יְדֵי חוֹבָתוֹ, וְאֵלּוּ הֵן,

---

רַבָּן גַּמְלִיאֵל הָיָה אוֹמֵר — *Rabban Gamliel Would Say*

- **The Torah requires that we eat the *korban pesach* together with *matzah* and *maror.* As the *Haggadah* states here in the name of Rabban Gamliel, anyone who has not said and explained the *korban pesach, matzah, and maror* during his discussion on the *Seder* night has not fulfilled his obligation of retelling the story of *Yetzias Mitzrayim.***
- **Each of these foods holds a powerful and important lesson; lessons that were relevant when we first became a nation, and are still relevant today as we reaffirm our identity as Hashem's people.**

In *Shemos* 12:8, Klal Yisrael were commanded to eat the *korban pesach* together with *matzah* and *maror.* There is deep symbolism contained within this obligation, which we will discuss in the coming pages. But how did Rabban Gamliel arrive at the conclusion that if a person does not explain these three foods, he has not fulfilled his obligation of *sippur Yetzias Mitzrayim?* After all, one could theoretically spend the whole night discussing

Thus, how much more so should we be grateful to the Omnipresent for all of the numerous favors He showered upon us: He brought us out of Mitzrayim; executed judgments against the Egyptians; executed judgments against their gods; slew their firstborn; gave us their wealth; split the *Yam Suf* for us; led us through it on dry land; drowned our oppressors in it; provided for our needs in the Wilderness for forty years; fed us the *mon*; gave us the Shabbos; brought us before *Har Sinai*; gave us the Torah; brought us to Eretz Yisrael; and built us the *Beis HaMikdash*, to atone for all our sins.

The cups are now refilled to the brim. The wine that was removed is not drunk.

If any of the *Seder's* participants have left the table for any reason, whether it be children who wandered off searching for *Afikomans*, or women who have been caring for babies or preparing the *seudah*, and were unable to recite the *Haggadah* as they should have, they must be called back to the *Seder* table to both recite and understand the section of the *Haggadah* of Rabban Gamliel's explanation of *Pesach, Matzah*, and *Maror*. The leader of the *Seder* should read and explain these paragraphs clearly, and translate them into whatever language necessary, so that everyone understands them. If a person does not say them and understand them on at least a basic level, he has not fulfilled his obligation.

Rabban Gamliel would say, "Anyone who has not recited these explanations of these three things on Pesach has not fulfilled his obligation. And these are they:

---

with his children the evil of the Egyptians, the *makkos*, and *Krias Yam Suf*. Having done so, would he not have fulfilled his obligation? Rabban Gamliel holds that he would not have. [Indeed, in the original iteration of the *Mah Nishtanah*, three of the four questions revolved around the *korban pesach, matzah*, and *maror*.] How does Rabban Gamliel deduce this?

Perhaps Rabban Gamliel saw a hint to this idea in the *pesukim* that follow the command to eat these items. In 12:10, the Torah warns against leaving over the *korban pesach*. This necessarily means that there is an immediacy attached to its being eaten. It is not simply a ceremony that can be performed at any time; it needed to be done specifically on this night, with no wiggle room. This shows us that at the inception of Klal Yisrael as a nation, it was imperative for them to be cognizant of these vital lessons. And, in 12:14, the Torah commands that Klal Yisrael do the same every year, for all generations. That means that each year, on the night of the *Seder*, there is an immediacy attached to the ceremony of the *korban pesach*; it must take place annually, and cannot be pushed off or overlooked. This means that the *Seder* night is a time when we must

פֶּסַח. מַצָּה. וּמָרוֹר.

Gaze at the shankbone, but do not lift it,
as it is merely a remembrance of the *korban pesach*.

פֶּסַח שֶׁהָיוּ אֲבוֹתֵינוּ אוֹכְלִים בִּזְמַן שֶׁבֵּית הַמִּקְדָּשׁ הָיָה קַיָּם, עַל שׁוּם מָה? עַל שׁוּם שֶׁפָּסַח הַקָּדוֹשׁ בָּרוּךְ הוּא עַל בָּתֵּי אֲבוֹתֵינוּ בְּמִצְרַיִם. שֶׁנֶּאֱמַר, וַאֲמַרְתֶּם, זֶבַח פֶּסַח הוּא לַיהוה, אֲשֶׁר פָּסַח עַל בָּתֵּי בְנֵי יִשְׂרָאֵל בְּמִצְרַיִם בְּנָגְפּוֹ אֶת מִצְרַיִם, וְאֶת בָּתֵּינוּ הִצִּיל, וַיִּקֹּד הָעָם וַיִּשְׁתַּחֲווּ[1].

---

rededicate ourselves to the service of Hashem by truly internalizing the lessons of the *pesach, matzah,* and *maror.* While we are unable to eat the *korban,* perhaps Rabban Gamliel saw the call to hold the *Seder* annually as a directive to refresh the *hashkafos* embodied by the *korban pesach, matzah,* and *maror.* He saw in this command an obligation for each person, in every generation, to view himself as having left Mitzrayim, as the *Haggadah* says: *b'chol dor vador chayav adam lir'os es atzmo ke'ilu hu yatza miMitzrayim.* Thus, after having said the *Mah Nishtanah* and using it as a springboard to discuss *cheirus, freedom,* we discuss the core principles represented by the *pesach, matzah,* and the *maror.*

פֶּסַח שֶׁהָיוּ אֲבוֹתֵינוּ אוֹכְלִים בִּזְמַן שֶׁבֵּית הַמִּקְדָּשׁ הָיָה קַיָּם, עַל שׁוּם מָה — *The Korban Pesach That Our Forefathers Ate in the Time That the Beis HaMikdash Stood, on Account of What?*

- **The *korban pesach* commemorated the idea that Hashem passed over the houses of Klal Yisrael, even though they had no merits of their own, simply because they are the descendants of the *Avos*.**
- **This means that every single person in Klal Yisrael is precious in Hashem's eyes, and Hashem knows that he or she has the potential to be righteous, even if right now they are not.**
- **The *chinuch* we pass to our children must reflect this understanding. We never give up on anyone, and we thank Hashem for the opportunity to impart His Torah to the next generation, even if it is a challenge to do so.**

What is the message of the *korban pesach*? The *posuk* states that the reason we eat the *korban pesach* is in commemoration of the fact that

the *korban pesach*, *matzah*, and *maror*."

Gaze at the shankbone, but do not lift it,
as it is merely a remembrance of the *korban pesach*.

The *korban pesach* that our forefathers ate in the time that the *Beis HaMikdash* stood, on account of what? On account of the fact that the Holy One, blessed is He, passed over the houses of our forefathers in Mitzrayim, as it is stated: "And you shall say, It is a *pesach* offering to HASHEM, that He passed over the houses of Bnei Yisrael in Mitzrayim when he smote Mitzrayim, and our houses He saved. And the nation prostrated and bowed."[1]

(1) *Shemos* 12:27.

Hashem saved us by passing over our homes while He killed all of the firstborn Egyptians. Why did Hashem save Klal Yisrael? After all, *Chazal* teach us that at the *Yam Suf,* the angels cried out, "These are idolaters (the Egyptians) and these are idolaters (the Jewish people)!" It sounds like there was no specific merit that Klal Yisrael possessed by which to be saved; and yet we were saved. It was because Hashem saw in us the potential, as children of Avraham, Yitzchak, and Yaakov, to change for the better, and to serve Hashem in the proper way, as Klal Yisrael. Thus, the *korban pesach,* by commemorating this salvation, stands as a symbol of the eternal, undying potential of a Jew. No matter how far he has strayed, he can return, and Hashem will take him back. This is what it means to be a descendant of the *Avos*.

This idea is very clear when we examine where the Torah writes this *posuk*. As mentioned above (see above, *Rasha*), this is the *posuk* containing the words that the Torah instructs a father to say when his *ben rasha,* who is acting with cynicism, displays aloofness toward the *Seder*. And when Klal Yisrael heard this, what was their reaction? They bowed down to Hashem in thanks for the tidings that they would have children! Which children? Children who would act with this degree of disdain and disinterest... and Klal Yisrael were *thankful*. Why? Because even when children act this way, they are not too far gone. There is always hope that they will reach incredibly high levels, just as the generation who merited to leave Mitzrayim grew from people who had no merits, to become the nation that merited to receive the Torah.

The first *mitzvah* in the Torah that was given to Klal Yisrael as a nation is the commandment to declare Rosh Chodesh. The *Rosh HaYeshiva, ztvk"l,* used to say that there is a vitally important message for us in this *mitzvah*. We are commanded to declare the day of the new moon as the beginning of the month. However, simple observation is not enough; part of

The broken *matzah* is lifted and displayed while the following paragraph is recited.

מַצָּה זוֹ שֶׁאָנוּ אוֹכְלִים, עַל שׁוּם מָה? עַל שׁוּם שֶׁלֹּא הִסְפִּיק בְּצֵקָם שֶׁל אֲבוֹתֵינוּ לְהַחֲמִיץ, עַד שֶׁנִּגְלָה עֲלֵיהֶם מֶלֶךְ מַלְכֵי הַמְּלָכִים הַקָּדוֹשׁ בָּרוּךְ הוּא וּגְאָלָם. שֶׁנֶּאֱמַר, וַיֹּאפוּ אֶת הַבָּצֵק אֲשֶׁר הוֹצִיאוּ מִמִּצְרַיִם עֻגֹת מַצּוֹת כִּי לֹא חָמֵץ, כִּי גֹרְשׁוּ מִמִּצְרַיִם, וְלֹא יָכְלוּ לְהִתְמַהְמֵהַּ, וְגַם צֵדָה לֹא עָשׂוּ לָהֶם.[1]

---

the *mitzvah* is to be able to calculate the precise time for the new moon's astronomical appearance. Using *Chazal's* formula, one can calculate, virtually down to the second, when the appearance of this — or any — new moon will occur. Now, that moment — the *molad* — is a celestial event; it cannot be witnessed from earth. At the *molad,* mathematically speaking, the moon has begun a new phase, but at that moment of the *molad,* it is still too tiny to be observed with the naked eye.

This was a message for Klal Yisrael then, as it is to us now. Even when a Jew is so detached from Hashem and the Torah that one cannot observe even a shred of righteousness in him, still, his *pintele Yid,* his true desire to serve Hashem and to do what is right, retains the potential to bring him back to spiritual heights. We must never give up on anyone. Moreover, this is the goal of the *chinuch* we are charged with implanting in the next generation. We believe in them, as Hashem believes in them, and we will never give up on them.

So, just as the calculation of the new month speaks to potential that we do not see but we know is there, and how we need to focus on it, the *mitzvah* of the *korban pesach* speaks to the *chinuch* of our nation, and how we must never reject members of Klal Yisrael, even those who seem to have no potential. We must embrace them and teach them — and never, ever give up on them. This was the message of our first *mitzvah* as a nation, and of the *korban pesach,* and is the foundation for the building of Klal Yisrael as a nation of *avdei Hashem.* The first step in serving Hashem as a nation is to never give up on anyone in Klal Yisrael.

מַצָּה זוֹ שֶׁאָנוּ אוֹכְלִים, עַל שׁוּם מָה — *This Matzah That We Eat, on Account of What?*

❒ **The journey from Rameseis to Succos when Klal Yisrael departed from Mitzrayim took them less than eighteen minutes. This miraculously speedy journey teaches us two vital lessons:**

The broken *matzah* is lifted and displayed while the following paragraph is recited.

This *matzah* that we eat, on account of what? On account of the fact that the dough of our forefathers did not have a chance to rise before the King of kings, the Holy One, blessed is He, revealed Himself to them and redeemed them, as it is stated: "And they baked the dough that they had taken out of Mitzrayim as *matzos*, for it had not leavened; for they had been chased from Mitzrayim, and they had been unable to wait, and they did not bring provisions with them."[1]

(1) *Shemos* 12:39.

- **Once Hashem decides to do something, there is nothing that can stand in His way. When Klal Yisrael became His nation, He took us out of Mitzrayim, and the laws of nature folded before Him. With this speedy departure from Mitzrayim, Hashem symbolically showed Klal Yisrael His desire that they separate from foreign culture, and ready themselves to serve Him.**
- **We eat *matzah* the entire Pesach. *Matzah,* also known as *lechem oni,* poor man's bread, symbolizes satisfaction with the simplicities of life, and a willingness and an ability to separate from the extravagances of a materialistic existence, as they are part and parcel of foreign philosophy which Hashem wishes us to separate from.**

Why are we obligated by the Torah to eat *matzah* with the *korban pesach,* and what is the lesson of the *matzah*? The *Haggadah* cites the *posuk* that alludes to the *matzah* that was baked without being allowed to rise when Klal Yisrael left Mitzrayim. This was on account of the haste of the pace of Hashem's redemption. I understand this *posuk* to mean that Klal Yisrael took dough with them because they had no time to bake it, since the time of the redemption arrived too quickly, but that the bread did *not* bake while they were on the road. Rather, it was baked by Klal Yisrael upon their arrival in Succos. This is the approach followed by many *Rishonim;* see *Ibn Ezra* and *Chizkuni,* as well as *Ramban.* According to this approach, the reason why the dough was able to be baked as *matzah* in Succos was because the journey from Rameseis to Succos was incredibly fast. Not only was the redemption swift in its arrival, but the duration of their initial sojourn out of Mitzrayim was also incredibly fast. According to this, there is tremendous symbolism in the fact that the *matzah* was unleavened. For the fact that it had no chance to rise before their arrival in Succos means that the duration of that entire journey was less than eighteen minutes!

The lesson we are being shown by the *matzah,* then, is that Hashem can do anything at any time. He demonstrates to us that *yeshuas Hashem k'heref ayin, the salvation of Hashem can occur in the blink of an eye.* And He showed us, by not even allowing our dough to rise, that even after centuries of slavery, when the time came to go, we were *out,* faster than humanly possible. [To illustrate: It takes forty thousand people forty-five minutes to exit a stadium at the end of a ballgame, and yet it took three million people, with all of their belongings on donkeys, less than eighteen minutes to leave a country!] When Hashem is holding us in His hand, there are literally no rules to impede Him. This was, and is, important for us to realize in forming and maintaining our special relationship with Hashem. Bearing in mind the concept of *matzah* can imbue a person with the proper *bitachon,* strong enough that he can really believe that Hashem can help him in any situation that he faces. As the Gemara says (*Berachos* 10a), *afilu cherev chadah munachas al tzavaro shel adam, al yimna atzmo min harachamim; even if a sharp sword rests on the neck of a man, he should not despair of [Hashem's ability to have] mercy.*

The end of the *posuk* states, *v'gam tzeidah lo asu lahem, and also provisions they did not prepare for themselves.* This is an everlasting testament to the *bitachon* that Klal Yisrael possessed and acted upon at that time, going into the Wilderness with nothing, and relying completely on Hashem to provide for them. Hashem praised Klal Yisrael for this, as Yirmiyah said (*Yirmiyah* 2:2), *Zacharti lach chessed ne'urayich, ahavas kelulosayich, lechteich acharai bamidbar b'eretz lo zeru'ah, I remember for your sake the kindness of your youth, the love of your bridal days, when you went after Me into the Wilderness, into a land that could not be planted.* In this very *posuk,* where that amazing *bitachon* is expressed, we are taught an unbelievable lesson that empowers us to really feel and act upon our *bitachon* in Hashem. He can do anything, and He does do anything He wishes, and literally nothing at all can stand in His way. [See further below, *Ga'al Yisrael.*]

Additionally, we must note a second lesson that we are taught by the speed of the Exodus, which, as above, is encapsulated in the nature of the *matzah.* Hashem removed us from servitude and gave us freedom with alacrity. He did this to show us His eagerness that we experience a new level of freedom — the freedom to not be beholden to the ideas and goals of a foreign culture.

The *posuk* (*Devarim* 16:3) states, *You shall not eat [with] it leaven; seven days you shall eat matzos, lechem oni, for with haste you left Mitzrayim; so that you shall remember the day that you left Mitzrayim all the days of your life.*

The wording of the *posuk* indicates that the haste with which Klal Yisrael

left had something to do with the subject matter of its closing segment, *so that you shall remember the day that you left Mitzrayim.* Moreover, *Rashi* there (*d"h lema'an*) explains that by dint of eating the *matzah* and the *korban pesach,* we remember the day we left *Mitzrayim.* [Presumably, *Rashi* is explaining not only the expression of *chipazon, haste,* found here, but rather is also explaining *Shemos* 12:11, where *chipazon* is mentioned in the context of eating the *korban pesach.*] What is the significance of Klal Yisrael's *hasty* departure on that day, specifically?

As we know, the nation had been free from harsh labor since the previous Rosh Hashanah. There was a new, as of yet unreached, degree of freedom to serve Hashem that was to be achieved upon their departure from Mitzrayim. This was the *Yetzias Mitzrayim,* the departure of Mitzrayim from within Klal Yisrael's hearts and minds. Now, Klal Yisrael would not be tempted to always think and feel as an Egyptian might, and be beholden to the ideals and the morals of the society among whom they had dwelled for the previous two centuries. [Hashem made this transition easier for Klal Yisrael by utterly decimating the Egyptians in the prelude to the actual Exodus.] Hashem wants Klal Yisrael to remember that it was this "going out" that carried the greatest significance, and not the physical freedom experienced by Klal Yisrael.

What did Hashem choose to do to mark this transition? He placed a miraculous emphasis on the nation's physical departure, when they became free of the ideals of Egyptian society. Hashem performed wonders when they were leaving to stress to Klal Yisrael that He wanted them out of Mitzrayim, away from its culture, so they could continue growing on their path of *avodas Hashem.*

This lesson begins with the *shemurah matzah* of the *Seder* night, and continues with the *lechem oni* we are restricted to for the rest of Pesach. The *lechem oni,* which can be translated as *poor man's bread,* reminds us to realize that the simplicities of life are sufficient, allowing us to focus on *ruchniyus,* and they preclude many of the distractions of the *yetzer hara.* Such a lifestyle allows us not to run after material possessions, which is so very much a part of the ideals of other societies, from which Hashem dissociated us on Pesach night. A simpler, quieter life, void of needless competition and endless pleasure seeking, is the correct environment to be able to grow closer to Hashem. [See below, *Tzafun,* where we discuss another lesson that we learn from the *chipazon, haste,* with which we departed Mitzrayim.]

There are also several other important lessons gleaned from the *matzah,* not necessarily related to the *posuk* cited by the *Haggadah* here. We have discussed these other lessons in their proper places. See *Ha Lachma Anya,* above, as well as *Motzi Matzah* below.

The *maror* is lifted and displayed while the following paragraph is recited.

מָרוֹר זֶה שֶׁאָנוּ אוֹכְלִים, עַל שׁוּם מָה? עַל שׁוּם שֶׁמֵּרְרוּ הַמִּצְרִים אֶת חַיֵּי אֲבוֹתֵינוּ בְּמִצְרַיִם. שֶׁנֶּאֱמַר, וַיְמָרְרוּ אֶת חַיֵּיהֶם, בַּעֲבֹדָה קָשָׁה, בְּחֹמֶר וּבִלְבֵנִים, וּבְכָל עֲבֹדָה בַּשָּׂדֶה, אֵת כָּל עֲבֹדָתָם אֲשֶׁר עָבְדוּ בָהֶם בְּפָרֶךְ.[1]

מָרוֹר זֶה שֶׁאָנוּ אוֹכְלִים, עַל שׁוּם מָה — *This Maror That We Eat — On Account of What?*

- **The *maror* reminds us of the suffering we were subjected to in Mitzrayim at the hands of the Egyptians.**
- **The first fundamental lesson of *maror* is that the Torah commands us to eat it together with the *matzah* and the *korban pesach*. This alludes to the fact that Hashem does not ever do something that is truly "bad." There is always a greater good, and the *maror* we experience is to be viewed together with the goodness He provides for us. Because of the *maror,* Hashem ultimately brought a greater degree of goodness. In Mitzrayim, the *avodas perech* allowed us to leave 190 years early.**
- **The second lesson from the *maror* is that the Mishnah (*Pesachim* 39a) tells us that *chazeres* is the best type of *maror* — even though it is not so bitter. Why? To teach us that Hashem does not want us to suffer. If we get the messages He is sending us when the *maror* is "light," He will have no need to send stronger messages.**
- **A third lesson from *maror* is that experiencing hardship gives us the perspective of how good things normally are, which allows us to live with appreciation and purpose.**

The *posuk* (*Shemos* 12:8) tells us that we must eat the *korban pesach* and the *matzah* with *maror*. Rabban Gamliel points out that the *maror* is symbolic of the bitterness and affliction we suffered at the hands of the Egyptians. But why is it necessary to memorialize this suffering?

The answer lies in how the Torah requires the *maror* to be consumed — along with the *matzah* and the *korban pesach*. We all know that *bochurim* often pick up the Israeli term *"hakol b'seder,"* meaning, "everything is as it should be," while they are in Eretz Yisrael. I remember that Mr. Fruchter, a neighbor of mine on the Lower East Side, would often comment, when he heard someone using this expression, that, *"Gedenk az es iz du maror in der Seder oichet!" Remember that there is also maror in the Seder!* Although the comment was whimsical, it carries with it an important lesson. As part

The *maror* is lifted and displayed while the following paragraph is recited.

This *maror* that we eat, on account of what? On account of the fact that the Egyptians embittered the lives of our forefathers in Mitzrayim, as it is stated: "And they embittered their lives with harsh labor, with mortar and with bricks, and with all manner of labor in the field; all the work that they forced upon them was with hard labor."[1]

(1) *Shemos* 1:14.

---

of our birth as a nation (and by extension, as part of our living Torah lives) we experienced, and do experience, unpleasant occurrences. We must have enough *bitachon* in Hashem to know that *kol mah d'avid Rachmana l'tav avid, anything Hashem does is for the best.* There are many reasons why Hashem causes the *maror* in our lives to occur; but the principle that governs them all is the same — He does it because it is good for us, and allows us to flourish in the long run. An example of this is how the hardship of the intense labor in Mitzrayim paved the way for the Jewish people to be able to leave after only 210 years.

So, the lesson of the *maror* as an accompaniment to the *matzah* and the *korban pesach* is that we should not view the occurrence of *maror* on its own. Rather, together with the bountiful goodness Hashem bestows upon us, there is also sometimes a component of bitterness. And we must remember — it is all part of Hashem's *seder.* So, to answer the question: The reason we must remember the bitterness we experienced in Mitzrayim is in order to arm us with the proper perspective on suffering in this world. When we realize that even as extremely terrible an experience the *avodas perech* was, the salvation brought about through it made it well worth it, we can apply that measure of *bitachon* to all suffering that exists in the world, *lo aleinu.*

There is another vital lesson that we learn from the *maror.* There are two questions that the *Rosh HaYeshiva, ztvk"l,* would ask regarding *maror*: The first is that the Mishnah (*Pesachim* 39a) lists five types of herbs that one may use as *maror*, and the Gemara there clearly states that *chazeres*, the first herb on the Mishnah's list, is the preferred vegetable to use for *maror.* Seemingly, he asked, horseradish, which is very bitter, should be preferable, and yet it is listed after *chazeres*! Secondly, the Gemara there comments that when *chazeres* is young, it is not even bitter; it is only when it ages that it becomes bitter. The *Rosh HaYeshiva, ztvk"l,* asked: How can the *chazeres* be preferred, if it is not even bitter when it is young?

He answered that, sometimes, the reason Hashem puts *maror* in our lives is to let us know that we need to take corrective action of one sort

בְּכָל דּוֹר וָדוֹר חַיָּב אָדָם לִרְאוֹת אֶת עַצְמוֹ כְּאִלּוּ הוּא יָצָא מִמִּצְרָיִם. שֶׁנֶּאֱמַר, וְהִגַּדְתָּ לְבִנְךָ בַּיּוֹם הַהוּא לֵאמֹר, בַּעֲבוּר זֶה עָשָׂה יהוה לִי, בְּצֵאתִי מִמִּצְרָיִם[1]. לֹא

---

or another. Hashem prefers that we "get the message" with the tiniest amount of bitterness. Hashem loves us, and has no desire to see us suffer unnecessarily. If, unfortunately, the message is not received, then Hashem will have to send a stronger *maror.* What we learn from the *chazeres* of the *Seder* is that it is best if we get the message as early as we can.

This lesson has its roots in the story of *Yetzias Mitzrayim* as well. Unfortunately, Klal Yisrael had largely become assimilated into the culture of Mitzrayim, and Hashem was sending them a message: They needed to break away from it. Klal Yisrael got this message — that they needed to abandon Mitzrayim as a society and as a culture — only when the work became backbreakingly harsh. If it would not have been so urgent that we leave Mitzrayim because we had been able to remain apart from their culture, perhaps the slavery would not have needed to be so torturous, for so long. We must take this lesson with us, and realize that we are charged with remaining true to the Torah, and holding ourselves apart from the societies of the countries we visit in exile. *Maror* teaches us that *al tisya'esh min hapuraniyus,* do not be confident that no punishments shall come; and, if the message is gotten in time, the punishments do not need to be severe.

The *Rosh HaYeshiva, ztvk"l,* also noted that when they first descended to Mitzrayim, the Jewish people were treated well, and enjoyed freedom; and yet, in a short time, were enslaved and suffered greatly. If it happened there, it can happen anywhere; and we must pray for the coming of *Mashiach,* and the Final Redemption. In light of what we have explained above, we must also take care not to fall into the trap of acting in a way that would cause Hashem to send us such a message in exile, *lo aleinu.*

There is another lesson in the *maror* as well. Sometimes, the only way we can appreciate something is to know what the alternative is. There is an old joke that goes, "The purpose of Monday is to appreciate the other days of the week." In this one-liner there is a little bit of truth — we lose appreciation for what we have unless we also have the perspective of what it would be like not to have it.

Without the unpleasant experiences of life, we do not really know how good the pleasant experiences are. For example, if a couple has a fight, which is certainly unpleasant, and make up afterward, they can appreciate, in a new dimension, the love that they have. So, *maror* is part of life because it defines and highlights for us how good it is when we do not have the *maror.*

In every generation it is one's duty to regard himself as though he personally had gone out of Mitzrayim, as it is stated: "You shall tell your son on that day: It was because of this that HASHEM did for 'me' when I went out of Mitzrayim."[1] It was not only

(1) *Shemos* 13:8.

When building a nation, as Hashem did through our *Avos*, it is critical for there to be a *simchas hachaim, a joy in life*, that the nation will experience. This, in my humble opinion, is the reason why the Torah requires that *nischei hayayin, wine libations,* be offered with the *korbanos*. Wine is symbolic of the joys of life, and the person offering the *korban* expresses his desire that he will find and experience joy in the life of *avodas Hashem* that he is committing to live. Hashem desires this profound level, where a person seeks to enjoy his relationship with Hashem. [See further, *Nahar Sholom, Bamidbar* 15:5.]

How can a life of serving Hashem be considered exciting and joyous in the eyes of a regular person, who is not yet excited by Torah and *mitzvos*? If he or she knows that they came from being tortured slaves in Mitzrayim, and are now free to serve Hashem, they can appreciate it a lot more.

I saw this with my own eyes in witnessing the generation of Jews who escaped from Europe. Many of them saw the destruction firsthand. Even those who became non-observant knew of the fires from which they had escaped, and lived their lives with purpose, accomplishing great things. But the next generation of non-observant Jews, who knew of the Holocaust, but did not feel it as a part of their experience, are mostly assimilated, not having accomplished very much at all. Keeping the *maror* of our past fresh in our minds allows us to more easily live with purpose and appreciation.

בְּכָל דּוֹר וָדוֹר חַיָּב אָדָם לִרְאוֹת אֶת עַצְמוֹ כְּאִלּוּ הוּא יָצָא מִמִּצְרַיִם — *In Every Generation, It is One's Duty to Regard Himself as Though He Personally Had Gone Out of Mitzrayim*

❒ **We must feel as though we ourselves went out of Mitzrayim. This means that we must be ready and eager to leave all of the influences in our lives that are not from the Torah, but rather from the cultures which surround us, and cling only to the Torah.**

❒ **Additionally, we must feel the same *emunah* and *bitachon* that our forefathers did when they actually departed from Mitzrayim, as if all of Hashem's salvation happened to us.**

❒ **We must understand that true freedom is the unfettered ability to live with the ideal that is most important to us — the service of Hashem and the observance of His Torah.**

In every generation, we are obligated to see ourselves as experiencing *Yetzias Mitzrayim.* Most people understand this to mean that we must understand that the miracles and wonders Hashem performed thousands of years ago as our forefathers departed from Mitzrayim were literally performed on our behalf as well. The love and the care that Hashem expressed at that time, and thus, the degree of *emunah* and *bitachon* that Klal Yisrael had at that time, apply to us too. Hashem treated *us* in this manner, and so we can, and therefore must, have the same degree of *emunah* in His abilities and *bitachon* in His decisions as they did. And, surely, this is all true.

Additionally, we must understand what freedom actually is, in order to appreciate the freedom that our forefathers experienced, for we are charged with experiencing it as well. It is true that slaves are not able to take vacations when they wish, or eat what they want. Is that the freedom we are supposed to appreciate? Obviously not. A decision about how to spend our leisure time is, at the end of the day, a decision about something that is often of little or no import. Real freedom, then, is the ability to live with goals, and to accomplish those goals. Hashem took us out of Mitzrayim and freed us to carry out the goal of serving Him. This is the freedom we must feel today. One must be free to follow the directive of Hashem, no matter what befalls him, whether physically, emotionally, or psychologically. Perhaps a person might be tempted to ease up in his lifestyle, and not live with such fierce dedication to *yiras Shamayim*, Torah, and *mitzvos.* This is not expressing the freedom that we were granted when we left Mitzrayim. Freedom is the ability to ignore everything but one's relationship with Hashem, and to be absolutely faithful to that ideal. Many times, practicing our faith openly may lead to persecution; true freedom is the opportunity and the ability to withstand the pressures of society and stand up and choose to follow Hashem, no matter what stands in our way. Each person who left Mitzrayim had to reach this level — where they wanted to serve Hashem and focus on their relationship with Him, to the exclusion of other pursuits. It was these people whom Hashem redeemed from the lowest places, physically and spiritually, and made into His chosen nation. In this manner, we can experience the feeling of freedom that Klal Yisrael felt when they left Mitzrayim.

But there is much more to it than that. As we have mentioned several times, the day that the Torah bids us to commemorate with the *korban pesach* and the *Seder* is not the day on which we actually ceased to perform work in Mitzrayim, which was the second level of freedom we experienced. We are rather commanded to commemorate *the day we left Mitzrayim,* and it is this day that the *Haggadah* bids us to internalize in every generation. What was the level of freedom we experienced at that time? The separation from all things connected to the ways of Mitzrayim. The

things that were important in Egyptian lifestyle, and the ideas that they held in high esteem, and the goals they sought to accomplish, no longer held any place of importance in the hearts and minds of Klal Yisrael. All of the Jewish people who merited to leave Mitzrayim had one thing in common: They were looking forward to dedicating themselves totally to Hashem and His Torah. We call the Exodus *Yetzias Mitzrayim,* which literally translates as "The departure of Mitzrayim," because the association with Mitzrayim's culture departed from us when we left.

Here, in the *medinah shel chessed* of the United States, we have become wrapped up, to varying degrees, in the culture of our hosts. There is a place for us to play sports, in the pursuit of exercise and friendship. But competition that involves haughtiness, lying, and wishing for another person's downfall is a result of absorbed behaviors from our environment. There is a place for us to dress in a well-appointed, confident, and regal manner. But if we are dressing in a trendy way, we need to examine where the trends are coming from. And there is a place in the world for technology. But are we using it as Hashem desires, or as the people around us use it?

We are commanded to wake up, and realize that *we are also* mired in the society in which we live! Hashem demands from us now, as He demanded from Klal Yisrael then, to desire to depart from a culture that is foreign to Torah values, so that He will save us. Yes, we are charged with having the same *emunah* and *bitachon* as our forefathers did, and we are also obligated to appreciate the freedom to dedicate ourselves to Hashem, but it does not stop there. We are also commanded to assess our connection with the society in which we are living, and make the decision to reject its negative influences on us. In this way, when the time for *Mashiach* arrives, there will be no question that we will be saved; for we will be among those who wished to, and indeed, who saw ourselves, as *departing from Mitzrayim.*

And I want you to realize that this is not impossible; it is actually more doable than you may think. While the *galus* rages and both we and our brethren in Eretz Yisrael are all in *galus,* there are cultural challenges to our lifestyle that we face in the Diaspora that the *Chareidi* public in Eretz Yisrael does not have to deal with. And *baruch Hashem,* we often see young couples, who so enjoyed their time learning in Eretz Yisrael, decide to live there for a while. From the *shailos* I receive, I can tell you that more often than not, the reason they need to move back eventually is *parnassah*-related. But the desire to stay in Eretz Yisrael, living a Torah life, is there — and that desire needs to be kindled in every one of us. The ability to be ready to live our lives devoid of the influences of our environs, and to cling to the *Torah HaKedoshah,* to the path Hashem wants for us, is something that we can all strive to do, wherever we may be located.

אֶת אֲבוֹתֵינוּ בִּלְבָד גָּאַל הַקָּדוֹשׁ בָּרוּךְ הוּא, אֶלָּא אַף אוֹתָנוּ גָּאַל עִמָּהֶם. שֶׁנֶּאֱמַר, וְאוֹתָנוּ הוֹצִיא מִשָּׁם, לְמַעַן הָבִיא אֹתָנוּ לָתֶת לָנוּ אֶת הָאָרֶץ אֲשֶׁר נִשְׁבַּע לַאֲבוֹתֵינוּ.[1]

The *matzos* are covered, and the cup is lifted and held until it is to be drunk. If one finds it too difficult to hold the cup for this length of time, he may lift it after the first paragraph, and set it down momentarily between the subsequent paragraphs.

לְפִיכָךְ אֲנַחְנוּ חַיָּבִים לְהוֹדוֹת, לְהַלֵּל, לְשַׁבֵּחַ, לְפָאֵר, לְרוֹמֵם, לְהַדֵּר, לְבָרֵךְ, לְעַלֵּה, וּלְקַלֵּס, לְמִי שֶׁעָשָׂה לַאֲבוֹתֵינוּ וְלָנוּ אֶת כָּל הַנִּסִּים הָאֵלּוּ, הוֹצִיאָנוּ

וְאוֹתָנוּ הוֹצִיא מִשָּׁם — *He Brought "Us" Out From There*

❒ **The Torah specifically reiterates that Hashem took Klal Yisrael out of Mitzrayim, so it would be clear to us that He is responsible for all the good that occurs in our lives.**

There are two *pesukim, Shemos* 12:41 and 12:51, which seem to say the same thing. 12:41 states, *...and it was on that very day that all the legions of Hashem left the land of Mitzrayim.* Similarly, 12:51 states, *And it was on that very day; Hashem took Bnei Yisrael out of the land of Mitzrayim, in their legions.* However, if we look a bit closer, we can learn a lesson from the fact that both of these *pesukim* are written in the Torah.

Ask the average person if it was obvious to the Jewish people who were leaving that Hashem was taking them out of Mitzrayim. "Absolutely!" They would say, "Was there ever a time when Hashem showed Klal Yisrael more miracles than He did at *Yetzias Mitzrayim*?!" A fair point, to be sure. However, if we examine the wording of 12:41, it seems to say just that the legions of Hashem went out on that day. The point being made in that *posuk* is that despite all the Egyptians had done to hold Klal Yisrael back for the last two centuries, and despite all they had done in the last few hours to try to force them out, when the time came to leave, they left as if nothing had ever happened at all to try and hold them back, or to rush them out.

I believe that this is why the Torah reiterates the Exodus from Mitzrayim in 12:51. The Torah writes that on that very day, Hashem took Bnei Yisrael out of Mitzrayim. No matter what it looked like or felt like to walk out — it might have appeared effortless, like a stroll through a park — the Torah bids us to remember that Hashem was with us Himself, taking us out of Mitzrayim.

Similarly, when the *Haggadah* cites *Devarim* 6:23, stating that *He*

our fathers whom the Holy One, blessed is He, redeemed from slavery; we, too, were redeemed with them, as it is stated: "He brought 'us' out from there so that He might take us to the land which He had promised to our fathers."[1]

The *matzos* are covered, and the cup is lifted and held until it is to be drunk. If one finds it too difficult to hold the cup for this length of time, he may lift it after the first paragraph, and set it down momentarily between the subsequent paragraphs.

Therefore, it is our duty to thank, praise, pay tribute, glorify, exalt, honor, bless, extol, and acclaim the One Who performed all these miracles for our fathers and for us. He brought us forth

(1) *Devarim* 6:23.

---

brought "us" out from there, and instructs us that we must understand that we also left Mitzrayim, the message is the same. "We" left, the same way they did, because Hashem took us out. This is a lesson that always bears repeating — everything good that happens to us is only because Hashem is right alongside us, making it happen.

לְפִיכָךְ אֲנַחְנוּ חַיָּבִים לְהוֹדוֹת — *Therefore It Is Our Duty to Thank*

❒ **We thank Hashem because we recognize (as much as we are able) what He has done for us. For the uninitiated, it might seem as though Hashem's goal is to elicit praise from us. Is this true?**

❒ ***Pesukei DeZimrah* gives us a glimpse of what Hashem did, and does, for us. Once we are aware of that, how can we possibly not praise Him! Furthermore, after elaborating upon all that He does, we can properly ask Him to provide for our needs. The same formula is followed in the *Haggadah*.**

The truth is that the declaration of *lefichach* is self-evident, and it should not require any expounding upon. We owe Hashem all of these praises, and it is appropriate for us to declare them.

But, saying that to children who come from more modern homes, and especially from non-observant homes, will not go over well. Oftentimes, their minds are so swept up with science and its denial of a Creator that although they will never give voice to it, there is a doubt in their minds if Hashem is indeed the One and Only God Who created the universe. Because they have this doubt, when they are confronted with *lefichach,* it seems to them as though Hashem is demanding praise from them, and they resent it. "This is the culmination of the *Haggadah?!* To praise Hashem?! Do I really want to serve a God Who demands praise?! *Pesukei*

מֵעַבְדוּת לְחֵרוּת, מִיָּגוֹן לְשִׂמְחָה, וּמֵאֵבֶל לְיוֹם טוֹב, וּמֵאֲפֵלָה לְאוֹר גָּדוֹל, וּמִשִּׁעְבּוּד לִגְאֻלָּה. וְנֹאמַר לְפָנָיו שִׁירָה חֲדָשָׁה, הַלְלוּיָהּ.

הַלְלוּיָהּ הַלְלוּ עַבְדֵי יהוה, הַלְלוּ אֶת שֵׁם יהוה. יְהִי שֵׁם יהוה מְבֹרָךְ, מֵעַתָּה וְעַד עוֹלָם. מִמִּזְרַח שֶׁמֶשׁ עַד מְבוֹאוֹ, מְהֻלָּל שֵׁם יהוה. רָם עַל כָּל גּוֹיִם יהוה, עַל הַשָּׁמַיִם כְּבוֹדוֹ. מִי כַּיהוה אֱלֹהֵינוּ, הַמַּגְבִּיהִי לָשָׁבֶת. הַמַּשְׁפִּילִי לִרְאוֹת, בַּשָּׁמַיִם וּבָאָרֶץ. מְקִימִי מֵעָפָר דָּל, מֵאַשְׁפֹּת יָרִים אֶבְיוֹן. לְהוֹשִׁיבִי עִם נְדִיבִים, עִם נְדִיבֵי עַמּוֹ. מוֹשִׁיבִי עֲקֶרֶת הַבַּיִת, אֵם הַבָּנִים שְׂמֵחָה; הַלְלוּיָהּ[1].

DeZimrah, too, is replete with singing the praises of Hashem. Is this how He demands to be served?" We need to help our fellow Jews understand why we praise Hashem here, and also during our prayers.

In order to do so, we should first cite a *psak* that the *Rosh HaYeshiva, ztvk"l,* gave for women who are short on time for *davening Shacharis.* Conventional wisdom would be that *Krias Shema* and its accompanying blessings would take precedence over *Pesukei DeZimrah* (as they do in the case of a man who is late to *minyan* and needs to catch up to the congregation before *Shemoneh Esrei*). But, the *Rosh HaYeshiva, ztvk"l,* said that because women are not obligated in the *mitzvah* of reciting *Krias Shema,* actually, *Pesukei DeZimrah* takes precedence for a woman who has only a little time to *daven.* She should say *Pesukei DeZimrah,* and then *Shemoneh Esrei.* The reason for this, he said, is because in order to beg Hashem to give you everything you need, you first have to know that He is able to do so. Once you have iterated many of the marvels He did and does, you are confident in asking Hashem to care for you as well. Rather than a simple list of Hashem's accomplishments, as it were, *Chazal* composed *Pesukei DeZimrah* from David HaMelech's praises to Hashem (as well as other *pesukim*), which lend beauty and strength to the concept; but what is actually happening during *Pesukei DeZimrah* is that we are saying, "Hashem, what You have done, and what You do, is incredible!" And once we know of the unbelievable feats Hashem is responsible for, we proceed to pray for anything we wish from Him.

Once a person becomes cognizant of what Hashem does, how is it possible not to say thank you to Him? How is it possible not to praise Him?

from slavery to freedom, from grief to joy, from mourning to festivity, from darkness to great light, and from servitude to redemption. Let us, therefore, recite a new song before Him! Halleluyah!

Halleluyah! Praise, you servants of HASHEM, praise the Name of HASHEM. Blessed is the Name of HASHEM, from now and forever. From the rising of the sun to its setting, HASHEM's Name is praised. High above all nations is HASHEM, above the Heavens is His glory. Who is like HASHEM, our God, Who is enthroned on High, yet deigns to look upon Heaven and earth? He raises the destitute from the dust; from the trash heaps He lifts the needy — to seat them with nobles, with nobles of His people. He transforms the barren wife into a glad mother of children. Halleluyah![1]

(1) *Tehillim* 113.

Not because He demands it, but because you recognize so clearly what He has done for you and the world you live in. For a person of flesh and blood who would do such favors for us, we would surely be moved to offer thanks and praise; how much more so must we feel moved to thank and praise Hashem! And indeed, after we ask for our needs in *Shemoneh Esrei,* we conclude by thanking Hashem for everything He does for us.

So too in the *Haggadah*. The composition of the *Haggadah* is not relating Hashem's salvation in order to obligate us to give Him praise. It is rather educating us regarding the salvation He brought for us so we can better understand Who He is, and what He does for us. And when we have that knowledge, how is it possible *not* to want to thank Him, over and over!

מְקִימִי מֵעָפָר דָּל מֵאַשְׁפֹּת יָרִים אֶבְיוֹן — *He Raises the Destitute From the Dust; From the Trash Heaps He Lifts the Needy*

- **Hashem can grant even the greatest salvation to even the most downtrodden people. He is involved in every detail of everyone's lives.**
- **We should therefore be confident that He can provide for us as well, and ask Him for whatever we need.**

The opening *Hallelukah* of *Hallel* expresses the idea that Hashem is intimately involved in the world. There is no person who is too lowly to merit Hashem's attention, for nothing is beneath Him. At the same time, there is no feat that is too great for Him; there is nothing that Hashem cannot do

בְּצֵאת יִשְׂרָאֵל מִמִּצְרָיִם, בֵּית יַעֲקֹב מֵעַם לֹעֵז. הָיְתָה יְהוּדָה לְקָדְשׁוֹ, יִשְׂרָאֵל מַמְשְׁלוֹתָיו. הַיָּם רָאָה וַיָּנֹס, הַיַּרְדֵּן יִסֹּב לְאָחוֹר. הֶהָרִים רָקְדוּ כְאֵילִים, גְּבָעוֹת כִּבְנֵי צֹאן. מַה לְּךָ הַיָּם כִּי תָנוּס, הַיַּרְדֵּן תִּסֹּב לְאָחוֹר. הֶהָרִים תִּרְקְדוּ כְאֵילִים, גְּבָעוֹת כִּבְנֵי צֹאן. מִלִּפְנֵי אָדוֹן חוּלִי אָרֶץ, מִלִּפְנֵי אֱלוֹהַּ יַעֲקֹב. הַהֹפְכִי הַצּוּר אֲגַם מָיִם, חַלָּמִישׁ לְמַעְיְנוֹ מָיִם[1].

בָּרוּךְ אַתָּה יהוה אֱלֹהֵינוּ מֶלֶךְ הָעוֹלָם, אֲשֶׁר גְּאָלָנוּ וְגָאַל אֶת אֲבוֹתֵינוּ מִמִּצְרַיִם, וְהִגִּיעָנוּ הַלַּיְלָה הַזֶּה לֶאֱכָל בּוֹ מַצָּה וּמָרוֹר. כֵּן יהוה אֱלֹהֵינוּ וֵאלֹהֵי

---

for even such a downtrodden person. He is both totally involved with, and in control of, the world and all those who inhabit it.

As such, every person has the right to ask Hashem for anything he desires. Of course, mature people understand what they are asking Hashem for. An average person is not going to be asking Hashem for tickets to the Dodgers game, because he or she understands that such a thing is unimportant. But, if it really is important for a person, certainly it is in the purview of a legitimate request. And, even if it is trivial, a person can always ask Hashem for anything, even if it may be silly (though Hashem may decide that granting even a sincere request is not in a person's best interests).

How will you get what you ask for? That will be Hashem's decision. Whether through a gift, or making a person wealthy enough to make the purchase he desires, Hashem can do anything at all. But this paragraph assures us that Hashem is ready and waiting to listen to our *tefillos,* and provide for all of our needs.

בְּצֵאת יִשְׂרָאֵל — *When Yisrael Went Forth*

- **It is not only what we need that Hashem gives us. We see from how He treated us in the Wilderness that He also cares about us, and wants us to feel comfortable.**
- **Even more so than the *makkos,* the care He showed for Klal Yisroel in the Wilderness expresses His love for us.**

If we read the paragraph of *Betzeis Yisrael* carefully, we see that it demonstrates a higher degree of care for Klal Yisrael than did the *makkos* in

When Yisrael went forth from Mitzrayim, Yaakov's household from a people of alien tongue, Yehudah became His sanctuary, Yisrael His dominion. The *Yam Suf* saw and fled; the *Yarden* turned backward. The mountains skipped like rams, and the hills like young lambs. What ails you, O *Yam Suf*, that you flee? O *Yarden*, that you turn backward? O mountains, that you skip like rams? O hills, like young lambs? Before the Master's presence — tremble, O earth, before the presence of the God of Yaakov, Who turns the rock into a pond of water, the flint into a flowing fountain.[1]

Blessed are You, HASHEM, our God, King of the universe, Who redeemed us and redeemed our forefathers from Mitzrayim and enabled us to reach this night that we may eat on it *matzah* and *maror*. So, HASHEM, our God and God of

(1) *Tehillim* 114.

Mitzrayim. For the idea of the *makkos* was, primarily, the salvation of Klal Yisrael, and later, the decimation of Pharaoh and his country. But the ideas expressed here in *Betzeis Yisrael* are examples of miracles that Hashem performed for the comfort of Klal Yisrael.

He split the *Yam Suf* and the *Yarden* for us, and we were able to walk through on dry land. The mountains that moved from before the *Ananei HaKavod* cleared the terrain before us as we trekked through the Wilderness, which also allowed for more comfortable travel. And, of course, the *Be'er Miriam* provided water for us on our journey.

On the surface, it may seem as though these were "extras," when compared with the redemption from Mitzrayim. Were they really that important?

And the answer is a resounding "Yes!" Hashem made the experience comfortable and beautiful for us. This is the level of care He expresses for His beloved people, and we can ask Him not only to meet our basic needs, but to make it wonderful for us!

אֲשֶׁר גְּאָלָנוּ וְגָאַל אֶת אֲבוֹתֵינוּ מִמִּצְרַיִם — *Who Redeemed Us, and Redeemed Our Forefathers From Mitzrayim*

❒ **The reason that we left Mitzrayim in haste, without time to prepare for the journey, was because Hashem said the time to move was just then, and not because Pharaoh and his cohorts pressured us. Thus, the fact that we went out without provisions demonstrated our *bitachon* in Hashem.**

אֲבוֹתֵינוּ, יַגִּיעֵנוּ לְמוֹעֲדִים וְלִרְגָלִים אֲחֵרִים הַבָּאִים לִקְרָאתֵנוּ לְשָׁלוֹם, שְׂמֵחִים בְּבִנְיַן עִירֶךָ וְשָׂשִׂים בַּעֲבוֹדָתֶךָ, וְנֹאכַל שָׁם

On *Motza'ei Shabbos* the phrase in parentheses substitutes for the preceding phrase.

מִן הַזְּבָחִים וּמִן הַפְּסָחִים (מִן הַפְּסָחִים וּמִן הַזְּבָחִים) אֲשֶׁר יַגִּיעַ דָּמָם עַל קִיר מִזְבַּחֲךָ לְרָצוֹן. וְנוֹדֶה לְךָ שִׁיר חָדָשׁ עַל גְּאֻלָּתֵנוּ וְעַל פְּדוּת נַפְשֵׁנוּ. בָּרוּךְ אַתָּה יהוה, גָּאַל יִשְׂרָאֵל.

בָּרוּךְ אַתָּה יהוה אֱלֹהֵינוּ מֶלֶךְ הָעוֹלָם, בּוֹרֵא פְּרִי הַגָּפֶן.

The second cup is drunk while reclining on the left side; preferably the entire cup, but at least most of it. If this is too difficult, even when using the smallest cup that holds a *reviis*, one must, at the very least, drink a cheekful.

The *posuk* (*Shemos* 12:39, cited by Rabban Gamliel to explain why we eat *matzah*) seems to indicate that Klal Yisrael altered the way that they would have liked to prepare their bread because they were driven out of the country, in such a manner that they could not delay. Who was applying the pressure? Most people will tell you that it was the Egyptians. This impression is only bolstered by *Rashi's* comment (12:34, *d"h terem yechmatz*), that it was the Egyptians who did not allow the dough of Klal Yisrael to rise properly.

However, if this was the case, we can ask the following questions: Firstly, despite the enormous pressure that Pharaoh and the Egyptians were applying to Klal Yisrael, beginning at midnight, Moshe made it clear that they would be leaving on their own schedule, and, in fact, they did not depart until the next morning (see above, *Makkas Bechoros*). Clearly, then, they were doing just fine, and not yielding to this pressure. Secondly, Yirmiyah praises Klal Yisrael for faithfully coming out to the Wilderness without proper provisions (see *Yirmiyah* 2:2). How is this praiseworthy if the reason Klal Yisrael could not prepare properly — or even bake proper bread for themselves — was because the Egyptians had taken that option away from them by forcing them to leave?

Rather, I believe that the intent of the *posuk* is that Klal Yisrael were pressured not by the Egyptians, but rather by the instructions of Hashem through Moshe. When Moshe said to move, there was no time to do anything else; the time to move was now, because that was the will of Hashem! And this dedication, in the face of a bewildering Wilderness, is

our fathers, bring us also to future holidays and festivals in peace, gladdened in the rebuilding of Your city and joyful at Your service. There we shall eat of the

On *Motza'ei Shabbos* the phrase in parentheses substitutes for the preceding phrase.

offerings and *pesach*-sacrifices (*pesach*-sacrifices and offerings) whose blood will reach the sides of Your *Mizbei'ach* for gracious acceptance. We shall then sing a new song of praise to You for our redemption and for the liberation of our souls. Blessed are You, HASHEM, Who has redeemed Yisrael.

Blessed are You, HASHEM, our God, King of the universe, Who creates the fruit of the vine.

The second cup is drunk while reclining on the left side; preferably the entire cup, but at least most of it. If this is too difficult, even when using the smallest cup that holds a *reviis*, one must, at the very least, drink a cheekful.

---

truly a merit that will endure for Klal Yisrael until our Final Redemption, which we pray for here in the blessing of *Ga'al Yisrael.*

Now, the *posuk* clearly states that Klal Yisrael had bread, and also clearly states immediately afterward that they took no provisions for the journey. How are both possible? And, if they did have food with them — the dough they took, as well as the leftover *matzah* and *maror* from the previous night (see *Rashi* to *Shemos* 12:34, *d"h misharosam*) — how can we say that they left Mitzrayim without provisions?

The obvious answer is that the bread that they had prepared was really only a day's worth; or perhaps just a meal's worth. It had been prepared with the intention of eating it that day. When they took the dough, they were postponing their breakfasts, not preparing for the journey ahead. Anyone who has ever taken a camping trip knows that the last meal before getting into the car does not do much to assuage hunger a few hours later. Similarly, even if Klal Yisrael were expecting to arrive in Eretz Yisrael in a matter of days, considering the amount of preparation they had done, this was going to mean a few days without any food except some leftovers and a raw breakfast that they had not had a chance to eat before they left — nothing considered provisions by any stretch. Hashem performed a miracle, and these paltry supplies actually lasted for a full thirty days, until the *mon* began to descend. But Klal Yisrael trusted that Hashem would take care of them, and did not do any extra preparation of food once they heard He had decreed that they should leave. They simply took what they had — raw dough and leftovers — and marched, putting their full faith in Hashem.

רחצה

The hands are washed for *matzah* and the following blessing is recited. It is preferable to bring water for washing to the head of the household at the *Seder* table.

בָּרוּךְ אַתָּה יהוה אֱלֹהֵינוּ מֶלֶךְ הָעוֹלָם, אֲשֶׁר קִדְּשָׁנוּ בְּמִצְוֹתָיו, וְצִוָּנוּ עַל נְטִילַת יָדָיִם.

מוציא

The following two blessings are recited over the *matzos.* The first blessing is recited over the *matzah* as *lechem* (*bread*), and the second blessing is recited for the special *mitzvah* of eating *matzah* on the night of Pesach. [The latter blessing is to be made with the intention that it also applies to the *koreich* sandwich and the *Afikoman.*] Each person who has *matzos* set in front of him (see *Seder Preparations,* above, p. 37) raises his *matzos,* and recites the first blessing:

בָּרוּךְ אַתָּה יהוה אֱלֹהֵינוּ מֶלֶךְ הָעוֹלָם, הַמּוֹצִיא לֶחֶם מִן הָאָרֶץ.

מצה

If one is using two *matzos,* as the *Rosh HaYeshiva, shlit"a,* does, he continues with the next blessing while continuing to hold his broken *matzah* and his whole *matzah.* [If one is using three *matzos,* at this point, he puts down the bottom *matzah,* and, while still holding the top (unbroken) and middle (broken) *matzos,* recites the second blessing]:

בָּרוּךְ אַתָּה יהוה אֱלֹהֵינוּ מֶלֶךְ הָעוֹלָם, אֲשֶׁר קִדְּשָׁנוּ בְּמִצְוֹתָיו, וְצִוָּנוּ עַל אֲכִילַת מַצָּה.

The *matzos* should be eaten while reclining on the left side, and without delay. Each participant (including women) must eat a *kezayis* of *shemurah matzah* within three minutes. [The count of three minutes begins when one swallows the first bit of *matzah.*] At any point after the first swallow of *matzah,* one may drink water. [However, the time of drinking counts toward the three minutes during which one must finish their *matzah.*]

MINHAGIM

The *Rosh HaYeshiva, shlit"a,* does not have the *minhag* to dip his *matzah* in salt. Every man (or boy) at the *Seder* should have sufficient *matzah* to provide *kezeisim* for at least one woman (or girl) as well. This is true even for one who uses only two *matzos,* at least when using *matzah* of the thickness that the *Rosh HaYeshiva, shlit"a,* uses (see above, p. 37). [Regarding how much *matzah* one must eat, see above, *A Note From the Author Regarding Shiurim*, p. 41).]

In a situation where the women and girls are more numerous than the men and boys, and there simply is not enough *matzah* from the *matzos* upon which the blessings were recited for everyone to receive a *kezayis,* the

Rachtzah

The hands are washed for *matzah* and the following blessing is recited. It is preferable to bring water for washing to the head of the household at the *Seder* table.

Blessed are You, HASHEM, our God, King of the universe, Who has sanctified us with His commandments, and has commanded us concerning the washing of the hands.

Motzi

The following two blessings are recited over the *matzos*. The first blessing is recited over the *matzah* as *lechem* (*bread*), and the second blessing is recited for the special *mitzvah* of eating *matzah* on the night of Pesach. [The latter blessing is to be made with the intention that it also applies to the *koreich* sandwich and the *Afikoman*.] Each person who has *matzos* set in front of him (see *Seder Preparations*, above, p. 37) raises his *matzos*, and recites the first blessing:

Blessed are You, HASHEM, our God, King of the universe, Who brings forth bread from the earth.

Matzah

If one is using two *matzos*, as the *Rosh HaYeshiva, shlit"a*, does, he continues with the next blessing while continuing to hold his broken *matzah* and his whole *matzah*. [If one is using three *matzos*, at this point, he puts down the bottom *matzah*, and, while still holding the top (unbroken) and middle (broken) *matzos*, recites the second blessing]:

Blessed are You, HASHEM, our God, King of the universe, Who has sanctified us with His commandments, and has commanded us concerning the eating of the *matzah*.

The *matzos* should be eaten while reclining on the left side, and without delay. Each participant (including women) must eat a *kezayis* of *shemurah matzah* within three minutes. [The count of three minutes begins when one swallows the first bit of *matzah*.] At any point after the first swallow of *matzah*, one may drink water. [However, the time of drinking counts toward the three minutes during which one must finish their *matzah*.]

MINHAGIM

matzah may be supplemented with other *shemurah matzah*. However, each participant should receive at least a small piece from each of the two *matzos* upon which the blessings were recited, as part of their *kezayis*.

Although it is best not to interrupt from *Motzi Matzah* until after *Koreich*, interruptions for the purpose of the *Seder*, such as measuring *kezeisim* for people, asking or answering the question, "Have I eaten enough?", or asking someone to please pass the *matzah*, *maror*, or *charoses* (or even the water), are not interruptions. Saying the paragraph of *Zecher LeMikdash k'Hillel* prior to eating the *koreich* is also not an interruption.

מַצָּה — *Reciting the Blessing on the Matzah Eating a Kezayis of Matzah*

- **Why must we use *shemurah matzah* on the *Seder* night? After all, even if the *matzah* is not *shemurah,* it is still not *chametz*!**
- **We are required to actively prepare the *matzah* for the sake of the *mitzvah.* This alludes to the fact that when dedicating (or rededicating) themselves to Hashem's service, Klal Yisrael must actively and consciously dedicate themselves to Hashem; passive participation is not enough.**
- **The requirement on the rest of Pesach is simply not to eat *chametz,* and this is symbolic of the need to live while embracing the simplicity of the Torah's values, avoiding the allure of foreign cultures.**

The Torah (*Shemos* 12:17) bids us to guard the *matzos* that we eat on the first night of Pesach. This teaches us the requirement that the *matzah* we eat at the *Seder* during *Motzi Matzah* must be *shemurah matzah* (see below). This is in contrast to the very next *posuk,* which mentions the seven-day period of Pesach, and mandates simply that *matzah* be eaten during those days, rather than *chametz.* There is no obligation for us to guard those *matzos.* What are we to learn from this difference? As is clear from the *pesukim* that follow (*Shemos* 12:19-20), the prohibition to eat any *chametz* on Pesach is in full force for the entire holiday, and not only for the first night. Accordingly, we can deduce that the commandment to *guard the matzos* of the first night has no bearing on whether or not the *matzah* is going to contain any *chametz*; for if it did, surely we would then be mandated to "guard" the *matzah* we are going to eat during the entire Pesach!

Clearly, then, there must be a different reason for requiring "guarded *matzah*" only on the first night of Pesach. Perhaps we can explain the underlying ideas of these requirements — to make sure all our *matzah* remains unleavened for the entire Pesach, and to *guard* it for eating on the first night of Pesach — in the following way. The first day of the holiday of Pesach is the anniversary of the evening we ate the *korban pesach* in Mitzrayim, and the day we were redeemed and were taken out of Mitzrayim. This was the day of the actual *geulah*, and the commandment of this day reflects the attitude we needed to have at that time. What is the requirement to *guard the matzah*? The requirement of guarding the *matzos* is an added level; a positive process, by which we actively oversee the entire production of the *matzah,* beginning as early as the time that the wheat is cut, and carry out each and every step specifically for the sake of the *mitzvah* of eating *matzah*.

So, it emerges that the Torah is commanding us to eat *matzah* on the first day of Pesach that has been prepared completely for the sake of the

mitzvah. This is representative of the way we were obligated to actively calibrate our minds when we were on the precipice of leaving Mitzrayim. At the time we were being redeemed and becoming Hashem's people, He wanted (and still wants us, on our *Seder* nights) to focus our minds upon the fact that all that we do is *lesheim Shamayim.* It is not enough, during this critical time, merely that our actions are correct. We must be actively engaged with the thought that the actions we carry out are, in fact, being done for the service of Hashem. This focus is necessary at the time of redemption, because it is at this time that we dedicate ourselves to Hashem; and a dedication involving action without thought is simply not a true dedication.

The *matzah* we eat during the entire Pesach is symbolic of something else. *Chazal* teach us (see *Berachos* 17a) that *chametz* is analogous to the *yetzer hara. Matzah*, on the other hand, is symbolic of life without forbidden desires. The *shemurah matzah* is a level higher than this, and alludes to the dedication with which we carry out our life of service to Hashem. Once that is established, it is our job to follow up with lives that lock the *yetzer hara* out. The *matzah* of the rest of Pesach is thus symbolic of a commitment to live a life free of evil influences from the values of the cultures of the world. We are exposed all the time to things that can easily be on one side of this line or the other. Take, for example, sports. The concept of competitive sports is healthy, certainly from a physical standpoint, and when practiced properly, it can be mentally healthy as well. However, it can certainly be said that the world of sports crosses the line, and involves so many ways for the *yetzer hara* to creep in. Many athletes on advanced professional levels are *baalei gaavah,* and will preach that this is the attitude that one must have in order to perform their best. The desire to win can often lead to athletes being willing to do anything for a competitive advantage — whether that means to lie about a play, or to cheat in various ways — and these acts obviously run counter to Torah values. There are sports where it is considered appropriate to harm another person if they get in the way, and others where outright violence is part and parcel of the sport. These are pitfalls, and are the "*chametz*" in a potentially "clean" concept of sports, which is exercising the body and mind in healthy companionship. Pesach is a time to take stock and examine if our lifestyles have allowed things like this to "leaven," leaving us with more foreign influence than the Torah desires us to have in our lives. To clarify: Certainly, one should ideally have in mind while he plays sports correctly that he is doing so to keep himself healthy, so he can better serve Hashem. This is the ideal way to engage in sports, and everyone should aspire to this intent.

This, then, is the difference between the symbolism of *shemurah matzah* and that of regular *matzah. Shemurah matzah* reminds us that we must

מרור

Red grape juice or wine should be poured onto the *charoses* (which already has liquid mixed into it) to make it more liquid. It will now be thin enough to be able to dip the *maror* into it.

Each participant at the *Seder* (including women) receives a *kezayis* of *maror*. The *maror* is dipped into the *charoses*. If any solid pieces of *charoses* emerged from the dip on the *maror*, they are shaken off.

The following blessing is recited, with the intent that it should also apply to the *maror* in the *koreich* sandwich:

בָּרוּךְ אַתָּה יהוה אֱלֹהֵינוּ מֶלֶךְ הָעוֹלָם, אֲשֶׁר קִדְּשָׁנוּ בְּמִצְוֹתָיו, וְצִוָּנוּ עַל אֲכִילַת מָרוֹר.

After the blessing is recited, the *maror* is eaten without reclining, and must be finished within nine minutes. At any point after the first swallow of *maror*, one may drink water. [However, the time of drinking counts toward the nine minutes during which one must eat their *maror*.]

MINHAGIM

The *Rosh HaYeshiva, shlit"a,* explains that *mixing* the red liquid into the *charoses* will not make it more liquid, and could also potentially involve a Shabbos concern (of the *melachah* of *lash*) when the *Seder* is on Friday night. Thus, it should not be mixed in, but rather, simply be *poured* over the *charoses*. [If one has a very thick, dry *charoses* (like some packaged *charoses*), the wine should be added before Shabbos.]

Romaine lettuce is infested with more than a *miut hamatzui* of insects, and is considered to be *ischazeik issura;* thus, every leaf needs to be checked for insects. An *eitzah* that the *Rosh HaYeshiva, shlit"a,* would employ was to offer his young grandchildren a dollar for every insect that they found. And they did find bugs! He explained that without the motivation of the reward, the children will not necessarily look too hard. [It goes without saying that one who seeks to use this idea would need to educate the children as to what the insects look like, and how the leaves need to be checked. The children must be old enough to do an effective job.]

The *Rosh HaYeshiva, shlit"a,* when he was younger, would to eat a full *kezayis* of horseradish for *maror*. He explains that this was the *minhag* of the *Rosh HaYeshiva, ztvk"l,* as well. Even though the Mishnah (*Pesachim* 39a) lists *chazeres* as preferable to *tamcha,* and thus, it would seem that we should use romaine lettuce rather than horseradish, the locale that the *Rosh HaYeshiva, ztvk"l,* was from did not have romaine lettuce available, and so his *kabbalah* was to use horseradish. True, the *kabbalah* in Eretz Yisrael was that romaine lettuce is *chazeres,* but to adopt the *kabbalah* of other locales is not always so simple. [See also *Igros Moshe, Yoreh Deah* 1:34.] He felt that it was better to act on his own *kabbalah* that horseradish is *tamcha* rather than follow the *kabbalah* of others, that romaine is [the more preferable] *chazeres*. However, it should be noted that he accepted the *kabbalah* that

Maror

Red grape juice or wine should be poured onto the *charoses* (which already has liquid mixed into it) to make it more liquid. It will now be thin enough to be able to dip the *maror* into it.

Each participant at the *Seder* (including women) receives a *kezayis* of *maror.* The *maror* is dipped into the *charoses.* If any solid pieces of *charoses* emerged from the dip on the *maror,* they are shaken off.

The following blessing is recited, with the intent that it should also apply to the *maror* in the *koreich* sandwich:

Blessed are You, HASHEM, our God, King of the universe, Who has sanctified us with His commandments, and has commanded us concerning the eating of *maror.*

After the blessing is recited, the *maror* is eaten without reclining, and must be finished within nine minutes. At any point after the first swallow of *maror,* one may drink water. [However, the time of drinking counts toward the nine minutes during which one must eat their *maror.*]

---

dedicate all our actions to Hashem's service. This was, and is, necessary at a time of dedication or rededication — and this is why it is specific to the first day of Pesach. Regular *matzah* is symbolic of the need to live our lives free of evil influences, and therefore the necessity to examine what we do and make sure that we keep our lives free of those influences. The lesson of *matzah* here is that it represents a life free of the *yetzer hara.*

This goes hand-in-hand with another lesson of the *matzah* that we have mentioned in several places (see *Matzah* of Rabban Gamliel), which is that *matzah* teaches us to have *bitachon* in Hashem, because of the fact that He can, and does, provide salvation in the blink of an eye. The knowledge that we are capable of living a clean, Torah life, even if it comes with certain (apparent) sacrifices, is bolstered by the fact that we see that living the life of Hashem's service brings with it a powerful security — that Hashem can make everything better for us in an instant.

MINHAGIM

romaine lettuce is *chazeres;* in fact, when he was older, and not well enough to eat a *kezayis* of horseradish, he did indeed eat a *kezayis* of romaine lettuce. Still, because it was not his own *kabbalah,* he personally preferred the use of horseradish. The *Rosh HaYeshiva, shlit"a,* in the last few years, is no longer able to tolerate the full *kezayis* of horseradish, and therefore he also now uses a full *kezayis* of romaine lettuce without any horseradish.

The *Rosh HaYeshiva, shlit"a,* would use grated (not whole) horseradish, and would estimate the *shiur* of a *kezayis* of horseradish by packing the horseradish into a ball, and then eating it. The *minhag* of the *Rosh HaYeshiva, ztvk"l,* was to do this as well.

כורך

If one is using two *matzos*, as the *Rosh HaYeshiva, shlit"a,* does, the remnants of the lower *matzah* are now used to make the *koreich* sandwich. If three *matzos* are being used, the bottom, thus far unbroken, *matzah* is now used to make the *koreich* sandwich. Each participant receives a *kezayis* of *matzah* and a *kezayis* of *maror*. The *maror* is inserted between two pieces of *matzah*, forming a sandwich. The sandwich is then dipped in *charoses*. If any solid pieces of *charoses* emerged from the dip on the sandwich, they are shaken off.

The following paragraph is recited:

זֵכֶר לְמִקְדָּשׁ כְּהִלֵּל. כֵּן עָשָׂה הִלֵּל בִּזְמַן שֶׁבֵּית הַמִּקְדָּשׁ הָיָה קַיָּם. הָיָה כּוֹרֵךְ (פֶּסַח) מַצָּה וּמָרוֹר וְאוֹכֵל בְּיַחַד. לְקַיֵּם מַה שֶּׁנֶּאֱמַר, עַל מַצּוֹת וּמְרֹרִים יֹאכְלֻהוּ.[1]

The *koreich* sandwich is eaten while reclining on the left side, and must be finished within nine minutes.

הָיָה כּוֹרֵךְ (פֶּסַח) מַצָּה וּמָרוֹר וְאוֹכֵל בְּיַחַד — *He Would Combine (the Korban Pesach,) Matzah and Maror in a Sandwich and Eat Them Together*

❒ **The *halachah* is that one may not eat from a piece of bread (or *matzah*) held in his hand if it is the size of a *beitzah*, and if he does, he is considered gluttonous. How, then, was it appropriate for Hillel to eat his *korech*, which was at least that size?**

❒ **The prohibition applies only to foods where one generally eats the entire piece he is holding at once. But if a food is meant to be eaten *from*, one who does so is acting perfectly normally.**

There is a Baraisa in *Maseches Derech Eretz* (*Derech Eretz Rabbah* Ch. 6) which states that one who raises a piece of bread to his mouth that is the size of a *beitzah* or larger is a *gargeran, a glutton*. This dictum is codified

MINHAGIM

The prevalent *minhag*, as stated in *Shulchan Aruch* (*Orach Chaim* 475:1 with *Taz* there), is to use the bottom *matzah* for *Koreich*, as above. Nevertheless, the *Rosh HaYeshiva, shlit"a,* notes that there is no absolute *requirement* to eat from the third *matzah* at all. In fact, when there were guests at his *Sedarim* who used three *matzos,* he would often collect any bottom *matzos* that remained intact after *Koreich*, to use them as *sheleimim* for the other meals of Yom Tov; for in those days, every whole *matzah* was at a premium, to be used as *lechem mishneh* at a subsequent meal.

The *kezayis* of *matzah* required for *Koreich* is somewhat smaller than the one used for *Motzi Matzah*, as the requirement to eat *Koreich* is only Rabbinic.

Koreich

If one is using two *matzos,* as the *Rosh HaYeshiva, shlit"a,* does, the remnants of the lower *matzah* are now used to make the *koreich* sandwich. If three *matzos* are being used, the bottom, thus far unbroken, *matzah* is now used to make the *koreich* sandwich. Each participant receives a *kezayis* of *matzah* and a *kezayis* of *maror.* The *maror* is inserted between two pieces of *matzah,* forming a sandwich. The sandwich is then dipped in *charoses.* If any solid pieces of *charoses* emerged from the dip on the sandwich, they are shaken off.

The following paragraph is recited:

In remembrance of the *Beis HaMikdash*, we do as Hillel did. This is what Hillel would do when the *Beis HaMikdash* stood: He would combine (the *korban pesach,*) *matzah* and *maror* in a sandwich and eat them together, to fulfill what is written in the Torah: "They shall eat it with *matzos* and bitter herbs."[1]

The *koreich* sandwich is eaten while reclining on the left side, and must be finished within nine minutes.

(1) *Bamidbar* 9:11.

in *Shulchan Aruch, Orach Chaim* 170:7; and the *Shach* and *Taz* cite the *Beis Yosef's* ruling that even if a person is not stuffing the entire piece into his mouth, but rather raising it to his mouth and taking a bite, he is still considered a glutton if the piece in his hand is the size of a *beitzah*. The question is, then, can one take a bite out of an apple? Or a slice of pizza? What about a hamburger or a deli sandwich? What about a falafel or a shawarma in a laffa? What about a chicken finger or a drumstick?

What did Hillel do with his *korban pesach?* He was eating his *kezayis* of *matzah* (and it was a *mitzvah d'Oraisa,* so we can imagine he was not just eating the smallest possible *shiur kezayis* he could find). Together with that was a *kezayis* of his *korban,* with some *maror* as well. Without a doubt, then, he was eating a sandwich with a volume of more than two *kezeisim* (which equal one *beitzah*), and he was holding it in his hand, and taking bites out of it! Was Hillel a *gargeran?* Assuredly not!

In my humble opinion, the prohibition to eat a large piece, or even bite from it, applies when the item is such that it is meant to be eaten at one time, rather than to be eaten *from*. Let us explain. A piece of bread is meant to be taken into the hand, placed in the mouth and eaten. Depending on the size of the piece a person takes in his hand, we can judge whether or not he is gluttonous. If the piece in his hand is a normal, bite-sized piece, he is acting normally, and if he has a large piece in his hand — even if he has not stuffed the entire thing into his mouth — he appears to be a glutton. But if what he has in his hand is something that is intended to be eaten *from*, like a slice of pizza, there is no appearance of gluttony, even when he takes a bite directly from the slice. Why? Because he is eating the

Shulchan Oreich / שלחן עורך

It should be remembered that the *Afikoman* must be eaten while one still has some appetite for it. In fact, if one is so sated that he must literally force himself to eat it, he is not credited with the performance of the *mitzvah* of *Afikoman*. Therefore, it is unwise to eat more than a moderate amount during the meal.

On the second *Seder* night, during the meal is an appropriate time to remind all of the participants to count *Sefirah*, if they have not already done so in *Shul*.

Even though it is a *mitzvah* to speak about *Yetzias Mitzrayim*, care should be taken not to extend the meal too long, because the *Afikoman* needs to be eaten before *chatzos* (halachic midnight). Any further discussion of *Yetzias Mitzrayim* can take place after the *Afikoman* is eaten.

---

pizza exactly the way a regular, non-gluttonous person would eat it. So, to take a *challah* roll and bite into it appears gluttonous, because people usually eat the entire bite of *challah* that they have in their hand. But if he sliced open the roll and put cold cuts into it, it is now a deli sandwich, which is intended to be eaten *from*, not completely eaten in a single bite. This is certainly true of an apple, which a person did not even design. It is of a naturally occurring size, and the normal way to eat it is to bite from it.

MINHAGIM

There is a common *minhag* to eat an egg dipped in saltwater, which is served at the beginning of *Shulchan Oreich*. It is not the *Rosh HaYeshiva, shlit"a's minhag* to specifically use the egg from the *ke'arah,* although his opinion is that there would be no *prohibition* to do so (although it is roasted), as the prohibition to eat roasted food on the *Seder* night applies only to meat. The *Rosh HaYeshiva, shlit"a,* notes that this was the *minhag* at the *Sedarim* of the *Rosh HaYeshiva, ztvk"l,* as well, and that it was also the *minhag* of *Rebbetzin Shelia, a"h's* family.

What meat can be eaten at the *Seder?* The *Rosh HaYeshiva, shlit"a,* would commonly prepare beef chuck or breast of veal boiled together with potatoes, but boiled chicken, boiled hot dogs, or pickled meats such as tongue or corned beef are all permitted as well. These are all items that are not roasted, but rather cooked. [Obviously, it would be forbidden to eat these items if after cooking them, one then roasted them.] If one deep-fries schnitzel or the like (see next paragraph), this would also be permitted, as meat cooked in oil has the same status as meat cooked in water.

[In order for a food to be called cooked as opposed to roasted, the level of the water (or oil) in the pan must be deep enough so that more than fifty percent of the height of the meat is submerged at the start of the cooking process.]

Tzafun / צפון

The *Afikoman* should be eaten before *chatzos,* halachic midnight. There is a well-known *Avnei Nezer* who introduced a novel *"t'nai",* the idea of which was to allow for the meal and the *Afikoman* to be eaten past *chatzos.* The *Rosh HaYeshiva, ztvk"l,* was against this practice.

The *Rosh HaYeshiva, ztvk"l,* was of the opinion that *chatzos* is always the same time throughout the year; that is, it does not change from day to day. However, it is location-dependent. In New York, his reckoning of *chatzos* is 12:56 AM Daylight Savings Time (or 11:56 PM Eastern Standard Time), and he always made sure to finish eating the *Afikoman* by this time.

A *kezayis* of the *Afikoman* is given to each participant in the *Seder* (including women). If there is not enough *matzah* from the various *Afikomans* to give each person a *kezayis,* other *shemurah matzos* may be used to supplement what is missing; however, each person should receive at least a small piece from an *Afikoman.*

It is better to eat a large *kezayis* for *Afikoman,* because there is one opinion among the *Rishonim* that eating the *Afikoman* is the fulfillment of the obligation to eat *matzah.* Even according to the other opinions, although one could be lenient and use a smaller *kezayis,* it is still better to eat a large *kezayis,* because of the *inyan* to eat two *kezeisim* for *Afikoman* — one in remembrance of the *korban pesach,* and the other in remembrance of the *korban chagigah.*

However, in my humble opinion, the same reasoning can be applied to all the examples cited above; whether the food was designed by Hashem or by people to be eaten *from,* there is no prohibition to hold it and eat from it. This is why Hillel was able to eat his sandwich. The Torah prescribed that these foods be eaten together, and there is never a thought that one would stuff the entire sandwich in his mouth — it was not designed to be eaten that way. A person does usually eat the piece of bread that he is holding in his hand, however, and thus if he is biting from a large piece, he appears like a *gargeran,* who would stuff an entire piece of bread in his mouth.

MINHAGIM

The *Rosh HaYeshiva, shlit"a,* uses the calculation mentioned here to determine the time of *chatzos* for the *Afikoman,* and for all halachic matters (e.g., calculating halachic midday with respect to *zmanei tefillah,* or identifying the earliest time that one may *daven Minchah*). See Appendix B: Calculating the Time of *Chatzos,* for discussion of how to calculate the time of *chatzos* in any given location.

Before eating the *Afikoman*, the *Rosh HaYeshiva, ztvk"l,* would say a *Hineni Muchan U'mezuman* prayer, emphasizing that he was eating the *Afikoman* in remembrance of both the *korban pesach* and the *korban chagigah.*

הִנְנִי מוּכָן וּמְזוּמָן לְקַיֵּם מִצְוַת אֲכִילַת אֲפִיקוֹמָן זֵכֶר לְפֶסַח וְזֵכֶר לַחֲגִיגָה.

The *Afikoman* should be eaten while reclining, and finished within three minutes. Nothing may be eaten or drunk after the *Afikoman* (with the exception of water), except for the last two of the Four Cups of wine.

צָפוּן — *Eating the Afikoman*

❒ **The *Afikoman* is eaten in remembrance of the *korban pesach,* which was eaten with *chipazon, haste.* This, as well as the hasty departure from Mitzrayim which it recalls, teaches us that when we are faced with a decision to make, where both possibilities have pros and cons, we must not be frozen by indecision. The hastiness of Klal Yisrael's departure from Mitzrayim reminds us that sometimes, more than anything else, decisive action is needed.**

As the *Afikoman* is *matzah* that we eat in remembrance of the *korban pesach,* it is fitting to mention another lesson which pertains to both the *korban pesach* and the *matzah.* Above (see *Matzah* of Rabban Gamliel) we noted that the wording of the *posuk* in *Devarim* 16:3 indicates that the haste with which Klal Yisrael left Mitzrayim was related to the subject matter of its closing segment, *so that you shall remember the day you went out of Mitzrayim.* Moreover, *Rashi* there (*d"h lema'an*) explains that by dint of eating the *matzah* and the *korban pesach,* we remember the day we left Mitzrayim. [Presumably, *Rashi* is explaining not only the expression of *chipazon, haste,* found there, but rather he is also explaining *Shemos* 12:11, where *chipazon* is mentioned in the context of eating the *korban pesach.*] What is the significance of Klal Yisrael's hasty departure on that day? Above, we mentioned one important lesson we glean from this, and here we will present another.

The *chipazon* calls to our attention the perilous nature of indecision. I recall a meeting we once had in Yeshiva, where we had a question as to how to proceed on a certain issue. As we always did in those days when we were not sure what to do, we called the *Rosh HaYeshiva, ztvk"l,* for guidance. I presented the first possibility to him over the phone, and he advised that we choose that option. I proceeded to explain the second possibility to him, and he said to follow that option! So, I presented the first possibility once more to him. At that point, he told me, "Yes, of course there are two possibilities; otherwise, you would not have a question. Both

Before eating the *Afikoman,* the *Rosh HaYeshiva, ztvk"l,* would say a *Hineni Muchan U'mezuman* prayer, emphasizing that he was eating the *Afikoman* in remembrance of both the *korban pesach* and the *korban chagigah.*

Behold I am prepared and ready to fulfill the *mitzvah* of eating the *Afikoman* in remembrance of the *korban pesach* and in remembrance of the *korban chagigah.*

The *Afikoman* should be eaten while reclining, and finished within three minutes. Nothing may be eaten or drunk after the *Afikoman* (with the exception of water), except for the last two of the Four Cups of wine.

---

have benefits and both have detriments, and in this case, either one is correct — the important thing is that you make a decision, not necessarily what that decision is."

We find that Moshe made a choice when he was talking to Hashem at the *S'neh* (Burning Bush). He chose to turn away, exhibiting the wonderful qualities of humility and bashfulness; but he also, at the same instant, chose to decline a greater affiliation with Hashem. This decision came into play later on, when Hashem turned down Moshe's plea that he be able to see Hashem. Hashem answered him then by saying, "When I wanted (this closeness with you), you did not want it; now that you want it, I do not want it" (see *Yalkut Shimoni, Parashas Ki Sisa* §396, and *Berachos* 7a). [It is certainly true that Hashem also told Moshe that, as a mortal, he was simply incapable of seeing Hashem, as Hashem has no physical qualities. But, clearly, there was some level of appreciation of Hashem that Moshe would indeed have been able to attain, had he not made the choice he did at the *S'neh.*] I see in Moshe's quandary a powerful reality, and one that is quite prevalent — the perils of indecision. Let us analyze: Did Moshe choose correctly? On the one hand, he was rewarded for his bashfulness here with many wonderful things; as *Chazal* teach us, Moshe merited that his face shone, and that Klal Yisrael were fearful of approaching Moshe Rabbeinu when they saw the radiance of his face. Moshe also merited to gaze upon Hashem "from behind him," as it were; but on the other hand, he lost out on the opportunity to attain an even greater understanding of Hashem. There was no right or wrong — there were two paths, and it was Moshe's job at that moment to pick one of them.

[If one examines the Midrash and Gemara, there does actually appear to be a dispute as to whether or not Moshe made the "right" choice. My understanding of these two possibilities are that both opinions agree that Moshe had to choose between two possibilities, and that each had pros and cons. The dispute centers around what Moshe would have preferred to do had he had all of the facts in front of him. In other words, would

ברך

The third cup is rinsed inside and out, and then filled.
The Cup of Eliyahu is also poured at this point.

שִׁיר הַמַּעֲלוֹת בְּשׁוּב יהוה אֶת שִׁיבַת צִיּוֹן, הָיִינוּ כְּחֹלְמִים. אָז יִמָּלֵא שְׂחוֹק פִּינוּ, וּלְשׁוֹנֵנוּ רִנָּה; אָז יֹאמְרוּ בַגּוֹיִם: הִגְדִּיל יהוה לַעֲשׂוֹת עִם אֵלֶּה. הִגְדִּיל יהוה לַעֲשׂוֹת עִמָּנוּ, הָיִינוּ שְׂמֵחִים. שׁוּבָה יהוה אֶת שְׁבִיתֵנוּ, כַּאֲפִיקִים בַּנֶּגֶב. הַזֹּרְעִים בְּדִמְעָה, בְּרִנָּה יִקְצֹרוּ. הָלוֹךְ יֵלֵךְ וּבָכֹה נֹשֵׂא מֶשֶׁךְ הַזָּרַע; בֹּא יָבֹא בְרִנָּה, נֹשֵׂא אֲלֻמֹּתָיו.[1]

תְּהִלַּת יהוה יְדַבֶּר פִּי, וִיבָרֵךְ כָּל בָּשָׂר שֵׁם קָדְשׁוֹ לְעוֹלָם וָעֶד.[2] וַאֲנַחְנוּ נְבָרֵךְ יָהּ מֵעַתָּה וְעַד עוֹלָם; הַלְלוּיָהּ.[3] הוֹדוּ לַיהוה כִּי טוֹב, כִּי לְעוֹלָם חַסְדּוֹ.[4] מִי יְמַלֵּל גְּבוּרוֹת יהוה, יַשְׁמִיעַ כָּל תְּהִלָּתוֹ.[5]

Moshe Rabbeinu have willingly given up the opportunity to have an even closer relationship with, and greater understanding of, Hashem, if it came along with the need to employ a degree of brazenness to which Moshe was not accustomed? R' Yehoshua ben Levi maintains that Moshe would have wanted to forgo his attribute of bashfulness in this instance, and yet he could not bring himself to do so; in this way, Moshe made the "wrong" decision, because he would have loved to go against his nature on this occasion. R' Shmuel bar Nachmani in the name of R' Yonasan, however, maintains that Moshe knew that sticking with his attribute of bashfulness in this instance might one day, in the future, lead to a situation where Hashem could use it as a reason not to allow Moshe a better understanding of Hashem; and yet Moshe made the decision he did consciously, determining that it was not worth the departure from his normal way of bashfulness, even though there was a possibility that later on, he might suffer by not being able to attain that higher level in his understanding of Hashem.]

There are times in life where a commitment or some other decision needs to be made. When Hashem presents us with a true question as to what course of action we should take, where both sides of the issue

The third cup is rinsed inside and out, and then filled. The Cup of Eliyahu is also poured at this point.

A song of ascents: When HASHEM brings back the exiles to Tzion, we will have been like dreamers. Then our mouths will be filled with laughter, and our tongues with glad song. Then will it be said among the nations: HASHEM has done great things for them. HASHEM has done great things for us, and we rejoiced. Restore our captives, HASHEM, like streams in the dry land. Those who sow in tears shall reap in joy. Though the farmer bears the measure of seed to the field in tears, he shall come home with joy, bearing his sheaves.[1]

May my mouth declare the praise of HASHEM and may all flesh bless His Holy Name forever.[2] We shall bless HASHEM from now and forever, Halleluyah![3] Give thanks to HASHEM for He is good, His kindness endures forever![4] Who can express the mighty acts of HASHEM? Who can declare all His praise?[5]

(1) *Tehillim* 126. (2) 145:21. (3) 115:18. (4) 118:1. (5) 106:2.

---

have pros and cons, and even after seeking the council of our *Rabbeim,* the choice still seems impossible to make, what should we do? Hashem is telling us to choose the side with consequences that will be easier for us to live with. This is the will of Hashem, and how we must sometimes figure out the path He intends for us. [In such cases, people sometimes simply cannot figure out what they truly want. Often, my advice to them is to flip a coin. If they are happy with the result, fine. And if they are not, they have just uncovered what their true desire is; problem solved!] There are many people who, because they cannot make a decision, freeze up, and put their very lives on hold. Everyone needs to realize that there are *mitzvos* to do, lives to live, obligations to be met, and Torah to be learned! Life cannot be whittled away by indecision. The lesson of Klal Yisrael's incredibly hasty movement from being in Mitzrayim to being *avdei Hashem,* and the *chipazon* with which Klal Yisrael were instructed to eat the *korban pesach,* remind us that sometimes, the right thing to do is to decide quickly, without rehashing the benefits and drawbacks of each possibility ad infinitum.

If three or more males, aged thirteen or older, participated in the *Seder,* the head of the household formally invites the others *(zimun)* to join him in the recitation of *Bircas HaMazon*.

The cup should be held while reciting *Bircas HaMazon*.

The leader begins:

רַבּוֹתַי נְבָרֵךְ.

The group responds:

יְהִי שֵׁם יהוה מְבֹרָךְ מֵעַתָּה וְעַד עוֹלָם[1].

The leader continues:

יְהִי שֵׁם יהוה מְבֹרָךְ מֵעַתָּה וְעַד עוֹלָם[1].

If ten or more men are joining in the *zimun,* the words in brackets are added.

בִּרְשׁוּת מָרָנָן וְרַבָּנָן וְרַבּוֹתַי, נְבָרֵךְ [אֱלֹהֵינוּ] שֶׁאָכַלְנוּ מִשֶּׁלּוֹ.

The group responds:

בָּרוּךְ [אֱלֹהֵינוּ] שֶׁאָכַלְנוּ מִשֶּׁלּוֹ וּבְטוּבוֹ חָיִינוּ.

The leader continues:

בָּרוּךְ [אֱלֹהֵינוּ] שֶׁאָכַלְנוּ מִשֶּׁלּוֹ וּבְטוּבוֹ חָיִינוּ.

Some say אָמֵן, *"Amen"* at this point (this was the *minhag* of the *Rosh HaYeshiva, ztvk"l*); others hold that the end of the *Bircas HaZimun* is at הַזָּן אֶת הַכֹּל, and therefore no response is made here. Still others have the *minhag* to respond with בָּרוּךְ הוּא וּבָרוּךְ שְׁמוֹ.

אָמֵן.

אָמֵן, *"Amen"* is recited by the participants as the head of the household concludes each blessing. Otherwise, it is forbidden to interrupt *Bircas HaMazon* for any response other than those permitted during *Shema*.

בָּרוּךְ אַתָּה יהוה אֱלֹהֵינוּ מֶלֶךְ הָעוֹלָם, הַזָּן אֶת הָעוֹלָם כֻּלּוֹ, בְּטוּבוֹ, בְּחֵן בְּחֶסֶד וּבְרַחֲמִים, הוּא נֹתֵן לֶחֶם לְכָל בָּשָׂר, כִּי לְעוֹלָם חַסְדּוֹ. וּבְטוּבוֹ הַגָּדוֹל, תָּמִיד לֹא חָסַר לָנוּ, וְאַל יֶחְסַר לָנוּ מָזוֹן לְעוֹלָם וָעֶד. בַּעֲבוּר שְׁמוֹ הַגָּדוֹל, כִּי הוּא אֵל זָן וּמְפַרְנֵס לַכֹּל, וּמֵטִיב לַכֹּל, וּמֵכִין מָזוֹן לְכָל בְּרִיּוֹתָיו אֲשֶׁר בָּרָא. בָּרוּךְ אַתָּה יהוה, הַזָּן אֶת הַכֹּל. (Others — אָמֵן.)

If three or more males, aged thirteen or older, participated in the *Seder,* the head of the household formally invites the others *(zimun)* to join him in the recitation of *Bircas HaMazon.*

The cup should be held while reciting *Bircas HaMazon.*

The leader begins:

Gentlemen, let us bless.

The group responds:

Blessed is the Name of HASHEM from this moment and forever![1]

The leader continues:

Blessed is the Name of HASHEM from this moment and forever![1]

If ten or more men are joining in the *zimun,* the words in brackets are added.

With the permission of the distinguished people present, let us bless [our God] for we have eaten from what is His.

The group responds:

Blessed is He [our God] of Whose we have eaten and through Whose goodness we live.

The leader continues:

Blessed is He [our God] of Whose we have eaten and through Whose goodness we live.

Some say *"Amen"* at this point (this was the *minhag* of the *Rosh HaYeshiva, ztvk"l*); others hold that the end of the *Bircas HaZimun* is at *Who nourishes all,* and therefore no response is made here. Still others have the *minhag* to respond with *Blessed is He and blessed is His Name.*

Amen.

"Amen" is recited by the participants as the head of the household concludes each blessing. Otherwise, it is forbidden to interrupt *Bircas HaMazon* for any response other than those permitted during *Shema.*

Blessed are You, HASHEM, our God, King of the universe, Who nourishes the entire world; in His goodness, with grace, with kindness, and with mercy. He gives nourishment to all flesh, for His kindness is eternal. And through His great goodness, nourishment is never lacking to us, and may it never be lacking to us forever. For the sake of His Great Name, because He is God Who nourishes and sustains all, and benefits all, and He prepares food for all of His creatures which He has created. Blessed are You, HASHEM, Who nourishes all. (Others — Amen.)

(1) *Tehillim* 113:2.

נוֹדֶה לְּךָ יהוה אֱלֹהֵינוּ, עַל שֶׁהִנְחַלְתָּ לַאֲבוֹתֵינוּ אֶרֶץ חֶמְדָּה טוֹבָה וּרְחָבָה. וְעַל שֶׁהוֹצֵאתָנוּ יהוה אֱלֹהֵינוּ מֵאֶרֶץ מִצְרַיִם, וּפְדִיתָנוּ מִבֵּית עֲבָדִים, וְעַל בְּרִיתְךָ שֶׁחָתַמְתָּ בִּבְשָׂרֵנוּ, וְעַל תּוֹרָתְךָ שֶׁלִּמַּדְתָּנוּ, וְעַל חֻקֶּיךָ שֶׁהוֹדַעְתָּנוּ, וְעַל חַיִּים חֵן וָחֶסֶד שֶׁחוֹנַנְתָּנוּ, וְעַל אֲכִילַת מָזוֹן שָׁאַתָּה זָן וּמְפַרְנֵס אוֹתָנוּ תָּמִיד, בְּכָל יוֹם וּבְכָל עֵת וּבְכָל שָׁעָה.

וְעַל הַכֹּל יהוה אֱלֹהֵינוּ, אֲנַחְנוּ מוֹדִים לָךְ וּמְבָרְכִים אוֹתָךְ, יִתְבָּרַךְ שִׁמְךָ בְּפִי כָּל חַי תָּמִיד לְעוֹלָם וָעֶד. כַּכָּתוּב, וְאָכַלְתָּ וְשָׂבָעְתָּ, וּבֵרַכְתָּ אֶת יהוה אֱלֹהֶיךָ, עַל הָאָרֶץ הַטֹּבָה אֲשֶׁר נָתַן לָךְ[1]. בָּרוּךְ אַתָּה יהוה, עַל הָאָרֶץ וְעַל הַמָּזוֹן. (אָמֵן. – Others)

וְאָכַלְתָּ וְשָׂבָעְתָּ וּבֵרַכְתָּ — ***And You Shall Eat, and You Shall be Satisfied, and You Shall Bless***

- ❒ **Although the Biblical requirement to recite *Bircas HaMazon* applies only when we have eaten and are satiated, the Sages decreed that we recite it even if we have had a much smaller amount. Why is this not tantamount to requiring the recitation of an unnecessary blessing?**
- ❒ **Because it is not the amount of food per se that obligates us to recite *Bircas HaMazon,* but rather the gratitude we feel for what we have been given.**
- ❒ **Klal Yisrael, who express gratitude to Hashem even after having eaten only a little, have a unique relationship with Hashem. That relationship causes Hashem to shower Klal Yisrael with favor.**

In the first blessing of *Bircas HaMazon,* we recognize that Hashem feeds the entire world; He is the *Zan es hakol.* Then, in the beginning of the second blessing, we recognize that Hashem gave us, Klal Yisrael, our own land of Eretz Yisrael, and it is on this Land that He feeds us. We recognize that Hashem gave us the Land and the food that it produces, which is a little more personal than the general fact that Hashem cares for every living thing. We thank Hashem that He treats us, specifically, so well.

In the second part of the second blessing, *V'al HaKol,* we mention that

We thank You, HASHEM, our God, because You have given to our forefathers as a heritage a desirable, good, and spacious land; because You removed us, HASHEM, our God, from the land of Mitzrayim and You redeemed us from the house of bondage; for Your covenant which You sealed in our flesh; for Your Torah that You taught us and for Your statutes that You made known to us; for life, grace, and kindness which You granted us; and for the provision of food with which You nourish and You sustain us constantly, in every day, in every season, and in every hour.

For all, HASHEM, our God, we thank You and bless You. May Your Name be blessed by the mouth of all the living, continuously for all eternity, as it is written: "And you shall eat, and you shall be satisfied, and you shall bless HASHEM, your God, for the good land that He gave you."[1] Blessed are You, HASHEM, for the Land and for the food. (Others — Amen.)

(1) *Devarim* 8:10.

---

the *mitzvah d'Oraisa* of reciting *Bircas HaMazon* applies when we have eaten and are satiated. *Chazal,* however, instituted the requirement to recite *Bircas HaMazon* even if we have eaten less than this. The Gemara (*Berachos* 20b) notes that the ministering angels asked Hashem how He can possibly extend favor to Klal Yisrael (as indicated by the *Bircas Kohanim* in *Bamidbar* 6:24-26), if the Torah writes of Hashem that He displays no favoritism (*Devarim* 10:17)? Hashem replied to the ministering angels that He *must* show favoritism to Klal Yisrael, for the Biblical requirement to recite *Bircas HaMazon* applies only to one who achieved satiation with his meal; and yet Klal Yisrael recite *Bircas HaMazon* even after having eaten merely a *kezayis* or a *kebeitzah*! Just as Klal Yisrael shows "extra" favor to Hashem, He, in turn, showers them with extra favor.

The obvious question we must ask on this Gemara is that if there is no obligation to recite *Bircas HaMazon* after eating a small portion, then doing so ought to be considered nothing more than a *berachah levatalah,* a needless *berachah*. Why does Hashem find this act to be meritorious, and worthy of extra favor being showered upon Klal Yisrael? And if the answer is that *Chazal* instituted the practice of reciting *Bircas HaMazon* even after eating only a small portion, we must then explain why their decree is not tantamount to requiring people to make *berachos levatalah*!

The answer is that the Torah obligates a person who feels thankful for his food and drink to bless Hashem. Now, Hashem expects Klal Yisrael to have

רַחֵם (נָא) יהוה אֱלֹהֵינוּ עַל יִשְׂרָאֵל עַמֶּךָ, וְעַל יְרוּשָׁלַיִם עִירֶךָ, וְעַל צִיּוֹן מִשְׁכַּן כְּבוֹדֶךָ, וְעַל מַלְכוּת בֵּית דָּוִד מְשִׁיחֶךָ, וְעַל הַבַּיִת הַגָּדוֹל וְהַקָּדוֹשׁ שֶׁנִּקְרָא שִׁמְךָ עָלָיו. אֱלֹהֵינוּ אָבִינוּ, רְעֵנוּ זוּנֵנוּ פַּרְנְסֵנוּ וְכַלְכְּלֵנוּ וְהַרְוִיחֵנוּ, וְהַרְוַח לָנוּ יהוה אֱלֹהֵינוּ מְהֵרָה מִכָּל צָרוֹתֵינוּ. וְנָא אַל תַּצְרִיכֵנוּ, יהוה אֱלֹהֵינוּ, לֹא לִידֵי מַתְּנַת בָּשָׂר וָדָם, וְלֹא לִידֵי הַלְוָאָתָם, כִּי אִם לְיָדְךָ הַמְּלֵאָה הַפְּתוּחָה הַקְּדוֹשָׁה וְהָרְחָבָה, שֶׁלֹּא נֵבוֹשׁ וְלֹא נִכָּלֵם לְעוֹלָם וָעֶד.

---

gratitude when they experience satiation, and this is why the Torah obligates us to express that gratitude. [The *hashkafah* behind this idea is that we need to express gratitude to whoever benefits us; when Hashem gives us food, this means reciting *Bircas HaMazon,* but when people benefit us, we must express our thanks to them.] But, while we are only obligated to thank Hashem when we feel satiated, there is no prohibition against thanking Him when we are not; as long as we feel gratitude, we can thank Him. And what would the *halachah* be if a person truly felt gratitude to Hashem for a portion of food that did not bring him satiation at all? For example, if a person was, *Rachmana litzlan,* living through the Holocaust, and he came upon a tiny morsel of food that was able to keep him alive a little longer, he certainly would feel gratitude to Hashem. In such a scenario, would one be obligated to express that gratitude, despite the fact that the Torah does not expect him to feel gratitude after having eaten so little? I humbly maintain that the answer is yes; one who feels gratitude even when he is not satiated is obligated to express that gratitude to Hashem.

The obligation to recite *Bircas HaMazon* is thus, in my humble opinion, dependent upon a degree of satisfaction that has been reached, rather than a volume of food that has been consumed. Because it is the level of satiation that triggers the *mitzvah* of *Bircas HaMazon,* it can be that a person who ate only a *kezayis* would be satiated enough to have the obligation. What *Chazal* accomplished with their enactment that *Bircas HaMazon* be recited after a small measure of sustenance was, effectively, a training program. They wanted to instill in Klal Yisrael the feelings of gratitude that are expressed with the recitation of *Bircas HaMazon,* even if they have not eaten enough food to reach satiation, and so they decreed that the blessings *must* be recited after eating only a *kezayis* or a *kebeitzah.* After enough recitations of *Bircas HaMazon,* people would become trained in expressing, and eventually truly feeling, *hakaras hatov,* even

Have mercy (we beg You) HASHEM, our God, on Your people Yisrael, on Your city Yerushalayim, on Tzion the resting place of Your Glory, on the monarchy of the house of David, Your anointed, and on the great and holy House upon which Your Name is called. Our God, our Father — tend us, nourish us, sustain us, support us, relieve us; HASHEM, our God, grant us speedy relief from all our troubles. Please, HASHEM, our God, make us not needful of the gifts of human hands nor of their loans, but only of Your Hand that is full, open, holy, and generous, that we not feel inner shame nor be humiliated forever and ever.

---

for the smaller amount they had consumed — and when they did so, this would actually trigger an obligation. [The novelty that it is not the amount of food that creates the obligation to recite *Bircas HaMazon,* but rather the *hakaras hatov* that a person feels that triggers the obligation, is central to a *shiur* I wrote in *Maseches Berachos,* which, with Hashem's help, we will merit to publish one day soon.]

Accordingly, there is an element of Klal Yisrael showing "extra favor" to Hashem here. For the Torah requires the expression of gratitude of *Bircas HaMazon* to be recited only when a person has achieved satisfaction. There are righteous individuals who feel *hakaras hatov* for even a *kezayis*, and because of these people, *Chazal* instituted that Klal Yisrael train themselves to feel *hakaras hatov* after eating this small amount, and therefore incur the obligation to recite *Bircas HaMazon*. As such, Hashem explained to the ministering angels that Klal Yisrael shows extra favor to Him, and therefore He shows extra favor to Klal Yisrael. So, certainly, Hashem treats Klal Yisrael differently than He treats the other nations. But this is not "favoritism." It is a function of the relationship that they have voluntarily developed with Hashem. To illustrate: The *Mishloach Manos* a person gives to his employee, his neighbor, his son's Rebbi, his *chavrusa*, and his siblings might all look very different from one another. But this is not a display of favoritism; it is merely that each person's gift is a reflection of the relationship that the person enjoys with the recipient. Following this example, "favoritism" is when a person has two employees, and gives a larger gift to one than to the other, because even though their relationships are equivalent, one of the employees has curried favor with the boss. Here, however, Klal Yisrael have elevated their relationship with Hashem to the degree that the relationship itself calls for Hashem to grant favor to Klal Yisrael — not undeserved favor, but rather the degree of favor befitting the lofty relationship between Hashem and His nation, as we have described above.

On Shabbos, add the following. [If forgotten, see box below.]

רְצֵה וְהַחֲלִיצֵנוּ יהוה אֱלֹהֵינוּ בְּמִצְוֹתֶיךָ, וּבְמִצְוַת יוֹם הַשְּׁבִיעִי הַשַּׁבָּת הַגָּדוֹל וְהַקָּדוֹשׁ הַזֶּה, כִּי יוֹם זֶה גָּדוֹל וְקָדוֹשׁ הוּא לְפָנֶיךָ, לִשְׁבָּת בּוֹ וְלָנוּחַ בּוֹ בְּאַהֲבָה כְּמִצְוַת רְצוֹנֶךָ, וּבִרְצוֹנְךָ הָנִיחַ לָנוּ יהוה אֱלֹהֵינוּ, שֶׁלֹּא תְהֵא צָרָה וְיָגוֹן וַאֲנָחָה בְּיוֹם מְנוּחָתֵנוּ, וְהַרְאֵנוּ יהוה אֱלֹהֵינוּ בְּנֶחָמַת צִיּוֹן עִירֶךָ, וּבְבִנְיַן יְרוּשָׁלַיִם עִיר קָדְשֶׁךָ, כִּי אַתָּה הוּא בַּעַל הַיְשׁוּעוֹת וּבַעַל הַנֶּחָמוֹת.

אֱלֹהֵינוּ וֵאלֹהֵי אֲבוֹתֵינוּ, יַעֲלֶה, וְיָבֹא, וְיַגִּיעַ, וְיֵרָאֶה, וְיֵרָצֶה, וְיִשָּׁמַע, וְיִפָּקֵד, וְיִזָּכֵר זִכְרוֹנֵנוּ וּפִקְדוֹנֵנוּ, וְזִכְרוֹן אֲבוֹתֵינוּ, וְזִכְרוֹן מָשִׁיחַ בֶּן דָּוִד עַבְדֶּךָ, וְזִכְרוֹן יְרוּשָׁלַיִם עִיר קָדְשֶׁךָ, וְזִכְרוֹן כָּל עַמְּךָ בֵּית יִשְׂרָאֵל לְפָנֶיךָ, לִפְלֵיטָה לְטוֹבָה לְחֵן וּלְחֶסֶד וּלְרַחֲמִים, לְחַיִּים וּלְשָׁלוֹם, בְּיוֹם חַג הַמַּצּוֹת הַזֶּה. זָכְרֵנוּ יהוה אֱלֹהֵינוּ בּוֹ לְטוֹבָה, וּפָקְדֵנוּ בוֹ לִבְרָכָה, וְהוֹשִׁיעֵנוּ בוֹ לְחַיִּים (טוֹבִים). וּבִדְבַר יְשׁוּעָה וְרַחֲמִים, חוּס וְחָנֵּנוּ וְרַחֵם עָלֵינוּ וְהוֹשִׁיעֵנוּ, כִּי אֵלֶיךָ עֵינֵינוּ, כִּי אֵל (מֶלֶךְ) חַנּוּן וְרַחוּם אָתָּה.

וּבְנֵה יְרוּשָׁלַיִם עִיר הַקֹּדֶשׁ בִּמְהֵרָה בְיָמֵינוּ. בָּרוּךְ אַתָּה יהוה, בּוֹנֵה (בְרַחֲמָיו) יְרוּשָׁלָיִם. אָמֵן. (Others – אָמֵן.)

[When required, the appropriate Compensatory Blessing is recited (see page 370).]

If One Omitted רְצֵה or יַעֲלֶה וְיָבֹא

1. If he realizes his omission before reciting the Name "Hashem" in the blessing of בּוֹנֵה, he recites רְצֵה or יַעֲלֶה וְיָבֹא and continues with וּבְנֵה.
2. If he realizes his omission after the blessing of בּוֹנֵה, he recites the appropriate Compensatory Blessing (p. 370). (However, the blessing need not be recited after the third Shabbos meal if Bircas HaMazon is recited after sunset.)
3. If he realizes his omission after having recited the first six words of the fourth blessing, he may still switch immediately into the Compensatory Blessing since the words בָּרוּךְ אַתָּה ... הָעוֹלָם are identical in both blessings.

On Shabbos, add the following. [If forgotten, see box below.]

May it please You to strengthen us, HASHEM, our God — through Your commandments, and through the commandment of the seventh day, this great and holy Shabbos. For this day is great and holy before You to rest on it and be content on it in love, as ordained by Your will. May it be Your will, HASHEM, our God, to arrange that there be no distress, grief, or lament on this day of our contentment. And show us, HASHEM, our God, the consolation of Tzion, Your city, and the rebuilding of Yerushalayim, Your holy city, for You are the Master of salvations and Master of consolations.

Our God and God of our fathers, may there rise, come, reach, be noted, be favored, be heard, be considered, and be remembered before You — the remembrance and consideration of ourselves; the remembrance of our fathers; the remembrance of Mashiach, son of David, Your servant; the remembrance of Yerushalayim, Your holy city; and the remembrance of Your entire people, the House of Yisrael — for deliverance, for well-being, for grace, for kindness, and for mercy, for life and for peace on this day of the Festival of *Matzos*. Remember us on it, HASHEM, our God, for goodness; consider us on it for blessing; and help us on it for (good) life. In the matter of salvation and mercy, have pity, show grace, and be merciful upon us and help us, for our eyes are turned to You; for You are the Almighty (King), the gracious, and generous.

Rebuild Yerushalayim, the Holy City, soon in our days. Blessed are You, HASHEM, Who rebuilds Yerushalayim (in His mercy). Amen. (Others — Amen.)

[When required, the appropriate Compensatory Blessing is recited (see page 370).]

4. If the omission is discovered after having recited the word הָאֵל of the fourth blessing, it is too late for the Compensatory Blessing to be recited. In that case:
   (i) On Shabbos and on a Festival day, at the first two meals *Bircas HaMazon* must be repeated in its entirety; at the third Shabbos meal, nothing need be done.
   (ii) On Rosh Chodesh and on Chol HaMoed, nothing need be done except if the day fell on Shabbos and רְצֵה was omitted. In that case, at the first two meals *Bircas HaMazon* must be repeated. But if רְצֵה was recited and יַעֲלֶה וְיָבֹא was omitted, nothing need be done.

בָּרוּךְ אַתָּה יהוה אֱלֹהֵינוּ מֶלֶךְ הָעוֹלָם, הָאֵל אָבִינוּ מַלְכֵּנוּ אַדִּירֵנוּ בּוֹרְאֵנוּ גּוֹאֲלֵנוּ יוֹצְרֵנוּ קְדוֹשֵׁנוּ קְדוֹשׁ יַעֲקֹב, רוֹעֵנוּ רוֹעֵה יִשְׂרָאֵל, הַמֶּלֶךְ הַטּוֹב וְהַמֵּטִיב לַכֹּל, שֶׁבְּכָל יוֹם וָיוֹם הוּא הֵטִיב, הוּא מֵטִיב, הוּא יֵיטִיב לָנוּ. הוּא גְמָלָנוּ הוּא גוֹמְלֵנוּ הוּא יִגְמְלֵנוּ לָעַד, לְחֵן וּלְחֶסֶד וּלְרַחֲמִים וּלְרֶוַח הַצָּלָה וְהַצְלָחָה, בְּרָכָה וִישׁוּעָה נֶחָמָה פַּרְנָסָה וְכַלְכָּלָה וְרַחֲמִים וְחַיִּים וְשָׁלוֹם וְכָל טוֹב, וּמִכָּל טוּב לְעוֹלָם אַל יְחַסְּרֵנוּ. (Others — אָמֵן.)

הָרַחֲמָן הוּא יִמְלוֹךְ עָלֵינוּ לְעוֹלָם וָעֶד. הָרַחֲמָן הוּא יִתְבָּרַךְ בַּשָּׁמַיִם וּבָאָרֶץ. הָרַחֲמָן הוּא יִשְׁתַּבַּח לְדוֹר דּוֹרִים, וְיִתְפָּאַר בָּנוּ לָעַד וּלְנֵצַח נְצָחִים, וְיִתְהַדַּר בָּנוּ לָעַד וּלְעוֹלְמֵי עוֹלָמִים. הָרַחֲמָן הוּא יְפַרְנְסֵנוּ בְּכָבוֹד. הָרַחֲמָן הוּא יִשְׁבּוֹר עֻלֵּנוּ מֵעַל צַוָּארֵנוּ, וְהוּא יוֹלִיכֵנוּ קוֹמְמִיּוּת לְאַרְצֵנוּ. הָרַחֲמָן הוּא יִשְׁלַח לָנוּ בְּרָכָה מְרֻבָּה בַּבַּיִת הַזֶּה, וְעַל שֻׁלְחָן זֶה שֶׁאָכַלְנוּ עָלָיו. הָרַחֲמָן הוּא יִשְׁלַח לָנוּ אֶת אֵלִיָּהוּ הַנָּבִיא זָכוּר לַטּוֹב, וִיבַשֶּׂר לָנוּ בְּשׂוֹרוֹת טוֹבוֹת יְשׁוּעוֹת וְנֶחָמוֹת.

A guest recites the following blessing for his host (see *Berachos* 46a, and *Shulchan Aruch, Orach Chaim* 201:1):

יְהִי רָצוֹן שֶׁלֹּא יֵבוֹשׁ וְלֹא יִכָּלֵם בַּעַל הַבַּיִת הַזֶּה, לֹא בָעוֹלָם הַזֶּה, וְלֹא בָעוֹלָם הַבָּא, וְיַצְלִיחַ בְּכָל נְכָסָיו, וְיִהְיוּ נְכָסָיו (וּנְכָסֵינוּ) מוּצְלָחִים וּקְרוֹבִים לָעִיר, וְאַל יִשְׁלוֹט שָׂטָן לֹא בְּמַעֲשֵׂה יָדָיו (וְלֹא בְּמַעֲשֵׂה יָדֵינוּ), וְאַל יִזְדַּקֵּק לֹא לְפָנָיו (וְלֹא לְפָנֵינוּ) שׁוּם דְּבַר חֵטְא וְהִרְהוּר עָוֹן, מֵעַתָּה וְעַד עוֹלָם.

Blessed are You, HASHEM, our God, King of the universe, the Almighty, our Father, our King, our Sovereign, our Creator, our Redeemer, our Maker, our Holy One, Holy One of Yaakov, our Shepherd, the Shepherd of Yisrael, the King Who is good and beneficent to all. For every single day He did good, does good, and will do good to us. He was bountiful with us, is bountiful with us, and will forever be bountiful with us — with grace and with kindness and with mercy, with relief, salvation, success, blessing, help, consolation, sustenance, support, mercy, life, peace, and all good; and of all good things may He never deprive us. (Others – Amen.)

The Compassionate One! May He reign over us forever. The Compassionate One! May He be blessed in Heaven and on earth. The Compassionate One! May He be praised throughout all generations, may He be glorified through us forever and ever, and be honored through us forever and for all eternity. The Compassionate One! May He sustain us in honor. The Compassionate One! May He break the yoke of oppression from our necks and guide us erect to our Land. The Compassionate One! May He send us abundant blessing to this house and upon this table at which we have eaten. The Compassionate One! May He send us Eliyahu HaNavi — may he be remembered for good — to proclaim to us good tidings, salvations, and consolations.

A guest recites the following blessing for his host
(see *Berachos* 46a, and *Shulchan Aruch, Orach Chaim* 201:1):

May it be God's will that his host not be shamed nor humiliated in this world or in the World to Come. May he be successful in all his dealings. May his dealings (and our dealings) be successful and conveniently close at hand. May no evil impediment reign over his handiwork (nor over our handiwork), and may no semblance of sin or iniquitous thought attach itself to him (or to us) from this time and forever.

Those eating at their own table recite (including the words in parentheses that apply):

הָרַחֲמָן הוּא יְבָרֵךְ אוֹתִי (וְאֶת אִשְׁתִּי / וְאֶת בַּעְלִי. וְאֶת זַרְעִי) וְאֶת כָּל אֲשֶׁר לִי.

Guests recite the following (children at their parents' table include the words in parentheses):

הָרַחֲמָן הוּא יְבָרֵךְ אֶת (אָבִי מוֹרִי) בַּעַל הַבַּיִת הַזֶּה, וְאֶת (אִמִּי מוֹרָתִי) בַּעֲלַת הַבַּיִת הַזֶּה, אוֹתָם וְאֶת בֵּיתָם וְאֶת זַרְעָם וְאֶת כָּל אֲשֶׁר לָהֶם.

All continue here:

אוֹתָנוּ וְאֶת כָּל אֲשֶׁר לָנוּ, כְּמוֹ שֶׁנִּתְבָּרְכוּ אֲבוֹתֵינוּ אַבְרָהָם יִצְחָק וְיַעֲקֹב בַּכֹּל מִכֹּל כֹּל, כֵּן יְבָרֵךְ אוֹתָנוּ כֻּלָּנוּ יַחַד בִּבְרָכָה שְׁלֵמָה, וְנֹאמַר, אָמֵן.

בַּמָּרוֹם יְלַמְּדוּ עֲלֵיהֶם וְעָלֵינוּ זְכוּת, שֶׁתְּהֵא לְמִשְׁמֶרֶת שָׁלוֹם. וְנִשָּׂא בְרָכָה מֵאֵת יהוה, וּצְדָקָה מֵאֱלֹהֵי יִשְׁעֵנוּ, וְנִמְצָא חֵן וְשֵׂכֶל טוֹב בְּעֵינֵי אֱלֹהִים וְאָדָם.

(אָבִי מוֹרִי בַּעַל) הַבַּיִת הַזֶּה — ***(My Father, My Teacher,) Owner of This House***

❒ **Children should remember that their parents constantly extend kindness to them by caring for them. This will help them fulfill their obligations of honoring and respecting their parents, and also help them accept and adhere to the wishes of their parents.**

When I was growing up, I only remember mentioning in the *HaRachamans* that my *Avi Mori* and my *Imi Morasi* should be blessed; or, if I was a guest at someone else's house, that the *baal habayis* should be blessed. I never remember referring to my parents also as the owners of their own house, as the version found in many *bentchers* reads today. They state: *HaRachaman Hu yevareich es Avi Mori, baal habayis hazeh, v'es Imi Morasi, baalas habayis hazeh, The Merciful One, He should bless my father, my teacher, owner of this house, and my mother, my teacher, lady of this house.* Yet, I think this is a very appropriate phrasing for children to say and remember.

A lot of the trouble with children in this day and age is due to the fact that they do not realize that their parents own the house, and that the

Those eating at their own table recite (including the words in parentheses that apply):

The Compassionate One! May He bless me (my wife/husband and my children) and all that is mine.

Guests recite the following (children at their parents' table include the words in parentheses):

The Compassionate One! May He bless (my father, my teacher) the owner of this house, and (my mother, my teacher) the lady of this house, them, their house, their family, and all that is theirs.

All continue here:

we and all that is ours — just as our forefathers Avraham, Yitzchak, and Yaakov were blessed in everything, from everything, with everything. So may He bless all of us together, with a perfect blessing. And let us say: Amen!

On High, may merit be pleaded upon them and upon us, for a safeguard of peace. May we receive a blessing from HASHEM and just kindness from the God of our salvation, and find favor and good understanding in the eyes of God and man.

---

parents are doing their child a kindness by allowing them to stay there. Now, surely it is true that there is an obligation not to put one's children on the street; I am not debating that point. But the *chessed* that parents actually do for their children is absolutely taken for granted! And certainly if a child is older, and the parents could really ask them to leave, the child owes a very large debt of gratitude to his or her parents for this unparalleled kindness.

A child must realize that even though his or her parents are too nice and loving to make a point of it, the home does not belong to the children; it belongs to their parents. They may allow you to stay there, and clothe you and feed you, and take care of all your needs, but they do not have to do that. And just because they would never stop does not allow you to ignore or deny the *hakaras hatov* that you owe them for what they do.

If children would realize — at least once in a while, when they are *bentching* — that the house they live in belongs to their parents, it is my belief that they would be a lot quicker to accept their parents' *mussar,* and a lot slower to ignore their parents' wishes, and the hopes they have for them. More respect would be shown to parents (especially to mothers, whose eagerness to please and lovingly do everything for their children often erodes the respect that a child must have for a mother), and the sense of entitlement, as well as laziness, that affects some of our youth today would also be minimized.

On Shabbos add:

הָרַחֲמָן הוּא יַנְחִילֵנוּ יוֹם שֶׁכֻּלּוֹ שַׁבָּת וּמְנוּחָה לְחַיֵּי הָעוֹלָמִים.

Some add the words in parentheses on the two *Seder* nights.

הָרַחֲמָן הוּא יַנְחִילֵנוּ יוֹם שֶׁכֻּלּוֹ טוֹב (יוֹם שֶׁכֻּלּוֹ אָרוּךְ, יוֹם שֶׁצַּדִּיקִים יוֹשְׁבִים וְעַטְרוֹתֵיהֶם בְּרָאשֵׁיהֶם וְנֶהֱנִים מִזִּיו הַשְּׁכִינָה, וִיהִי חֶלְקֵנוּ עִמָּהֶם).

הָרַחֲמָן הוּא יְזַכֵּנוּ לִימוֹת הַמָּשִׁיחַ וּלְחַיֵּי הָעוֹלָם הַבָּא. מִגְדּוֹל יְשׁוּעוֹת מַלְכּוֹ וְעֹשֶׂה חֶסֶד לִמְשִׁיחוֹ לְדָוִד וּלְזַרְעוֹ עַד עוֹלָם[1]. עֹשֶׂה שָׁלוֹם בִּמְרוֹמָיו, הוּא יַעֲשֶׂה שָׁלוֹם עָלֵינוּ וְעַל כָּל יִשְׂרָאֵל. וְאִמְרוּ, אָמֵן.

יְראוּ אֶת יהוה קְדֹשָׁיו, כִּי אֵין מַחְסוֹר לִירֵאָיו. כְּפִירִים רָשׁוּ וְרָעֵבוּ, וְדֹרְשֵׁי יהוה לֹא יַחְסְרוּ כָל טוֹב[2]. הוֹדוּ לַיהוה כִּי טוֹב, כִּי לְעוֹלָם חַסְדּוֹ[3]. פּוֹתֵחַ אֶת יָדֶךָ, וּמַשְׂבִּיעַ לְכָל חַי רָצוֹן[4]. בָּרוּךְ הַגֶּבֶר אֲשֶׁר יִבְטַח בַּיהוה, וְהָיָה יהוה מִבְטַחוֹ[5]. נַעַר הָיִיתִי גַּם זָקַנְתִּי, וְלֹא רָאִיתִי צַדִּיק נֶעֱזָב, וְזַרְעוֹ מְבַקֶּשׁ לָחֶם[6]. יהוה עֹז לְעַמּוֹ יִתֵּן, יהוה יְבָרֵךְ אֶת עַמּוֹ בַשָּׁלוֹם[7].

Upon completion of *Bircas HaMazon*, the blessing over wine is recited and the third cup is drunk while reclining on the left side. It is preferable to drink the entire cup, but at the very least, most of the cup should be drunk. If this is too difficult, even when using the smallest cup that holds a *reviis*, one must, at the very least, drink a cheekful.

בָּרוּךְ אַתָּה יהוה אֱלֹהֵינוּ מֶלֶךְ הָעוֹלָם, בּוֹרֵא פְּרִי הַגָּפֶן.

On Shabbos add:

The Compassionate One! May He cause us to inherit the day which will be completely a Shabbos and rest day for eternal life.

Some add the words in parentheses on the two *Seder* nights.

The Compassionate One! May He cause us to inherit that day which is altogether good (that everlasting day, the day when the righteous will sit with crowns on their heads, enjoying the reflection of God's majesty — and may our portion be with them!)

The Compassionate One! May He make us worthy of the days of *Mashiach* and the life of the World to Come. He Who is a tower of salvations to His king and shows kindness for His anointed, to David and his descendants forever.[1] He Who makes peace in His Heavenly heights, may He make harmony for us and for all Yisrael. Say: Amen!

Fear HASHEM, His holy ones, for those who fear him feel no deprivation. Young lions may feel want and hunger, but those who seek HASHEM will not lack any good.[2] Give thanks to God for He is good; His kindness is eternal.[3] You open up Your hand and satisfy the desire of every living thing.[4] Blessed is the man who trusts in HASHEM, and HASHEM will be his trust.[5] I was a youth and also have aged, and I have not seen a righteous man forsaken, with his children begging for bread.[6] HASHEM will give might to His nation; HASHEM will bless His nation with peace.[7]

Upon completion of *Bircas HaMazon,* the blessing over wine is recited and the third cup is drunk while reclining on the left side. It is preferable to drink the entire cup, but at the very least, most of the cup should be drunk. If this is too difficult, even when using the smallest cup that holds a *reviis,* one must, at the very least, drink a cheekful.

Blessed are You, HASHEM, our God, King of the universe, Who creates the fruit of the vine.

---

(1) *II Shmuel* 22:51. (2) *Tehillim* 34:10-11. (3) 136:1. (4) 145:16.
(5) *Yirmiyahu* 17:7. (6) *Tehillim* 37:35. (7) 29:11.

While the Cup of Eliyahu remains on the table, symbolizing our belief that Eliyahu HaNavi will be sent soon to announce the Final Redemption, the door is opened, in accordance with the *posuk* (*Shemos* 12:42), *It is a guarded night* (*leil shimurim*), reflecting our *bitachon* that Hashem protects us.

Then the following paragraph is recited.

שְׁפֹךְ חֲמָתְךָ אֶל הַגּוֹיִם אֲשֶׁר לֹא יְדָעוּךָ וְעַל מַמְלָכוֹת אֲשֶׁר בְּשִׁמְךָ לֹא קָרָאוּ[1]. כִּי אָכַל אֶת יַעֲקֹב וְאֶת נָוֵהוּ הֵשַׁמּוּ. שְׁפָךְ עֲלֵיהֶם זַעְמֶךָ וַחֲרוֹן אַפְּךָ יַשִּׂיגֵם[2]. תִּרְדֹּף בְּאַף וְתַשְׁמִידֵם מִתַּחַת שְׁמֵי יהוה[3].

שְׁפֹךְ חֲמָתְךָ אֶל הַגּוֹיִם אֲשֶׁר לֹא יְדָעוּךָ — *Pour Your Wrath Upon The Nations That Do Not Know You*

- **We utter a prayer that those nations who *do not know* Hashem, and who have persecuted and who continue to persecute Klal Yisrael, will suffer His wrath.**
- **Which nations are these? Might they only be nations who do not recognize Hashem as God?**
- **Even though there are other religions which believe that our Hashem is the God of the world, their *understanding* of Hashem is very different from ours.**
- **David HaMelech, with the words *the nations that do not know You,* was alluding to even these nations, because even as they believe in Hashem's existence, they surely do not relate with Him the way we do and they do not understand Him the way we do.**

When David HaMelech composed the plea of *shfoch chamascha,* he was speaking of peoples who "do not know Hashem." Accordingly, no matter how desperately certain we may be that our enemies hate us, and no matter how they have persecuted us, we cannot presume that they are included in this prayer if they are not among those who "do not know Hashem."

Specifically, since the Holocaust, it is fair to say that the main enemies of the Jewish people have been the Arabs. Now, Arabs believe in the same Hashem as we do, and so it would certainly appear as though the request that Hashem pour out His anger not be directed at them. And according to those who maintain that *shituf* — the belief in Hashem as well as other powers — is not forbidden for a non-Jew, *shefoch chamascha* would not apply to Christians either. For they too believe that Hashem is God. For centuries, the main perpetrators of the persecution of the Jewish people were the Catholic Church. If the Arabs and the Christians are not included

While the Cup of Eliyahu remains on the table, symbolizing our belief that Eliyahu HaNavi will be sent soon to announce the Final Redemption, the door is opened, in accordance with the *posuk* (*Shemos* 12:42), *It is a guarded night* (*leil shimurim*), reflecting our *bitachon* that Hashem protects us.

Then the following paragraph is recited.

Pour Your wrath upon the nations that do not know You and upon the kingdoms that do not call out to Your Name. For they have devoured Yaakov and destroyed His dwelling.[1] Pour Your anger upon them and let Your fiery wrath overtake them.[2] Pursue them with wrath and annihilate them from beneath the heavens of HASHEM.[3]

(1) *Tehillim* 79:6-7. (2) 69:25. (3) *Eichah* 3:66.

---

in *shefoch chamascha,* who is? Presumably, *shefoch chamascha* would pertain to those among our enemies who worship idols, like much of the population of India, or those who do not practice religion at all, like many people in Russia and China.

Still, I humbly maintain that of course *shefoch chamascha* can be applied to all of our enemies, including the Arabs who hate us so very much. The prayer that Hashem visit His wrath upon these peoples appears in *Tehillim* 79:6-7. A few chapters later, in 83:7-10, David begs Hashem to take revenge upon several nations, and mentions them by name. Among them are Edom and Yishmael. So, it is logical to presume that David's plea of *shefoch chamascha* in Chapter 79 applied to the children of Yishmael in the same way his explicit plea in Chapter 83 did. [And although David's prayer predates the advent of Islam, I presume that Yishmael's descendants always did believe in Hashem as opposed to idols.] Accordingly, we must explain the phrase *asher lo yeda'ucha, who do not know You,* in a novel way; for after all, the Arabs and the Christians do indeed know Hashem.

Over Succos, an article in the *Mishpachah* magazine (Issue 979) about the Yom Kippur War caught my attention. The article noted that the War of Independence took place in the secular year of 1948, which was the Hebrew calendar year of 5708. Although the Gemara (*Kiddushin* 30a) is clear that we are not privy to exactly how many *pesukim* there are in the Torah — the breakup of words into *pesukim* which we have today is somewhat inexact — if one was to count 5,708 *pesukim* according to the breakup which appears in our *chumashim,* he would arrive at *Devarim* 30:5. There, the Torah states, *And Hashem shall bring you to the Land that your forefathers inherited, and you shall inherit it, and Hashem shall do good for you and increase for you more than your ancestors.* Similarly,

The door is closed, the fourth cup is poured, and the recitation of *Hallel* (by women as well as men) is continued. We remain seated while reciting it. It is appropriate to raise the cup during this recitation. [Some hold that *Hallel,* as well as the fourth cup of wine that follows it, must be completed before midnight. The *Rosh HaYeshiva, shlit"a,* does not have this *minhag.*]

---

the Six Day War took place in 1967, the Hebrew year for which was 5727. The 5,727th *posuk* in the Torah according to our reckoning is *Devarim* 31:4, which states, *And Hashem shall do to them as He did to Sichon and to Og, the kings of the Emori, and to their lands, that He destroyed them.* I did not count myself, but I found the tidbit to be interesting, as I'm sure anyone would. These two *pesukim* do clearly speak of Klal Yisrael's conquest of the Land, and there is no doubt that the War of Independence and the Six Day War were seminal moments in Hashem's still unfolding plan to give Eretz Yisrael back to Klal Yisrael.

A few days later, during *Shacharis* on Simchas Torah, through a *pikuach nefesh shailah* that was conveyed via Hatzolah, it became known to us that Hamas was committing a massacre against our people in Eretz Yisrael. We, like so many other communities, were faced with the question of how to balance acting in a way that would be a merit for our suffering brethren in Eretz Yisrael, and at the same time, celebrating Simchas Torah properly. We made some changes to the proceedings; the entire Yeshiva recited *Tehillim* for 30 minutes before *hakafos,* each *hakafah* was shortened to 15 minutes, the songs we sang reflected Hashem's mercy for Klal Yisrael, and we reset the *Beis HaMedrash* and learned for 45 minutes before *laining* at the conclusion of the *hakafos.* Additionally, we decided that a member of the *hanhalah* would speak after each *hakafah.* I spoke after the second *hakafah,* which corresponds to Yitzchak Avinu.

I related that on two occasions, I recall that the *Rosh HaYeshiva, ztvk"l,* spoke publicly about Yitzchak. Once, someone spoke improperly about Yitzchak Avinu. When the *Rosh HaYeshiva, ztvk"l,* got up to speak, he said, "Because Yitzchak was mentioned, I decided to speak about him." Similarly, on another occasion, he remarked to someone, "The way you are speaking about Yitzchak does not make me proud to be his descendant, and we are supposed to be beaming with pride that we are the children of Yitzchak!" He proceeded to retell the Gemara (*Shabbos* 89b), which states that of all the *Avos,* Yitzchak is the only one who is willing to be *meilitz yosher* on behalf of Klal Yisrael.

I then related the observation I had seen in the *Mishpachah* article, and noted that according to the formula there, the corresponding *posuk* to

Hallel

The door is closed, the fourth cup is poured, and the recitation of *Hallel* (by women as well as men) is continued. We remain seated while reciting it. It is appropriate to raise the cup during this recitation. [Some hold that *Hallel,* as well as the fourth cup of wine that follows it, must be completed before midnight. The *Rosh HaYeshiva, shlit"a,* does not have this *minhag.*]

---

the year 5784 — the current Hebrew year — is *Devarim* 32:31. Unlike the aforementioned *pesukim,* this *pasuk* is not an openly positive one. The *posuk* states, *For not like their creators is our Creator; and our enemies rule over us.* As *Rashi* explains, the *posuk* means that even though the enemies of Klal Yisrael have the upper hand, they must not make the mistake of equating their deities to Hashem. In doing so, they would suggest that (a) there are other powers, and (b) those other powers have strength over Hashem. But we know, and the Torah stresses, that neither of these presumptions is true. Hashem is One, and that means that He encompasses all power. It is He Who decrees successes, and it is also He Who decrees pitfalls. A Jew knows that no matter what happens — whether it looks good or it looks bad — Hashem's guiding hand is ultimately doing what He knows is best, and a Jew trusts in this with all his or her heart.

I explained that the attack of Hamas — the worst attack on world Jewry since the Holocaust — is an element of *ra* in the world, of that there is no question. But we *must* realize that it is not Hamas somehow doing this despite Hashem's will! For whatever reason, Hashem decided to bring this calamity upon us, and it is incumbent upon us to beg Him to have mercy on us. To that end, Yitzchak is the forefather who stands in defense of his children, and he should be *meilitz yosher* for us now, in our time of need, before Hashem.

The *posuk* calls to our attention that the gods of the nations are different than our God — meaning that the way we relate to Hashem and understand Him is distinct from the way the nations view their own deities — because when things "seem not to be going His way", we know that it is not at all an indication of our God's weakness. It is rather our steadfast belief — nay, our *knowledge* — that He has decreed that the evil must come. No power exists besides Him, and certainly there is nothing stronger than He — no matter what we observe in this world. This is the *true knowledge* of Hashem's Unity, and is encapsulated in the idea that Hashem is One.

So, while it is true that the Arabs serve the same God we do, our *understanding* of Hashem is completely different. It is only us who truly *understand* Him. And this, I believe, is what David HaMelech alluded to when he said, *Pour out Your anger upon the nations that do not know You.*

לֹא לָנוּ יהוה, לֹא לָנוּ; כִּי לְשִׁמְךָ תֵּן כָּבוֹד, עַל חַסְדְּךָ עַל אֲמִתֶּךָ. לָמָּה יֹאמְרוּ הַגּוֹיִם, אַיֵּה נָא אֱלֹהֵיהֶם. וֵאלֹהֵינוּ בַשָּׁמָיִם, כֹּל אֲשֶׁר חָפֵץ עָשָׂה. עֲצַבֵּיהֶם כֶּסֶף וְזָהָב, מַעֲשֵׂה יְדֵי אָדָם. פֶּה לָהֶם וְלֹא יְדַבֵּרוּ, עֵינַיִם לָהֶם וְלֹא יִרְאוּ. אָזְנַיִם לָהֶם וְלֹא יִשְׁמָעוּ, אַף לָהֶם וְלֹא יְרִיחוּן. יְדֵיהֶם וְלֹא יְמִישׁוּן, רַגְלֵיהֶם וְלֹא יְהַלֵּכוּ, לֹא יֶהְגּוּ בִּגְרוֹנָם. כְּמוֹהֶם יִהְיוּ עֹשֵׂיהֶם, כֹּל אֲשֶׁר בֹּטֵחַ בָּהֶם. יִשְׂרָאֵל בְּטַח בַּיהוה, עֶזְרָם וּמָגִנָּם הוּא. בֵּית אַהֲרֹן בִּטְחוּ בַיהוה, עֶזְרָם וּמָגִנָּם הוּא. יִרְאֵי יהוה בִּטְחוּ בַיהוה, עֶזְרָם וּמָגִנָּם הוּא.[1]

יהוה זְכָרָנוּ יְבָרֵךְ; יְבָרֵךְ אֶת בֵּית יִשְׂרָאֵל, יְבָרֵךְ אֶת בֵּית אַהֲרֹן. יְבָרֵךְ יִרְאֵי יהוה, הַקְּטַנִּים עִם הַגְּדֹלִים.

לֹא לָנוּ ה׳ לֹא לָנוּ — *Not For Our Sake, Hashem, Not For Our Sake*

- ❒ ***Lo Lanu*** **is a prayer that Hashem make His strength and His care for us known to the world by saving us from our enemies.**
- ❒ **The point is not that we be viewed as a force to be reckoned with because of our own might, but rather that Hashem should be feared, so nobody will disturb his people.**

Lo Lanu is a prayer for us, the Jewish people who exist today, and is a plea for Hashem's salvation from our enemies. We ask that Hashem save us, and thereby make His Name known to the nations of the world. The idea expressed here is that our travails are an opportunity for the nations to realize how powerful Hashem is through His protection of Klal Yisrael.

If I would have understood this idea as a young child, I would not have asked Hashem for what I asked him for then. In the days of my youth, growing up on the Lower East Side, there were often tensions between the Jewish community and the non-Jewish toughs from the neighborhood. What I noticed was that we were always afraid of them; even a single one of them could scare off several of us — but they were unafraid of us. This dynamic bothered me a lot. I felt as though the same way we look at them, they ought to look at us.

And so I prayed to Hashem that He increase the degree of fear that these gangs felt, so that they would be afraid to start up with us — not because

Not for our sake, HASHEM, not for our sake, but for Your Name's sake give glory, for the sake of Your kindness and Your truth! Why should the nations say, "Where is their God?" Our God is in the Heavens; whatever He pleases, He does! Their idols are silver and gold, the handiwork of man. They have a mouth, but cannot speak; they have eyes, but cannot see; they have ears, but cannot hear; they have a nose, but cannot smell; their hands — they cannot feel; their feet — they cannot walk; nor can they utter a sound with their throat. Those who make them should become like them, whoever trusts in them! O Yisrael! Trust in HASHEM; He is their help and their shield! House of Aharon! Trust in HASHEM! He is their help and their shield! You who fear HASHEM — trust in HASHEM, He is their help and their shield![1]

HASHEM Who has remembered us will bless — He will bless the House of Yisrael; He will bless the House of Aharon; He will bless those who fear HASHEM, the small as well as the great.

(1) *Tehillim* 115:1-11.

we have a powerful God Who cares for us, but because they would see that we were a force to be reckoned with; the same cautious respect that we have of them, I asked that they have of us.

From *Lo Lanu,* however, I learned that just the opposite is true. We should never ask that we be a feared opponent for our enemies. We should ask only that our salvation be a vehicle for *kevod Shamayim,* when the nations see how He cares for us and protects us from them. [Sadly, this is relevant again nowadays, when we see demonstrations and protests of those who bear hatred toward us. We must pray that Hashem shows the world that we are his precious and beloved people.]

ה' זְכָרָנוּ — *Hashem Who has Remembered Us*

- **In Heaven, the angels do everything the way Hashem desires; but on earth, people can choose to do His will, or to sin.**
- **Still, even as we may be undeserving, we ask for the chance to live, and continue to praise Hashem.**

The paragraph of *Hashem zecharanu,* the second part of *Tehillim* Ch. 115, continues with the same theme as the first, *Lo Lanu,* above. Namely, we ask Hashem to save us for His Own sake, because we do not necessarily deserve to be saved on our own merit. Here, the *pesukim* express this same idea.

יֹסֵף יהוה עֲלֵיכֶם, עֲלֵיכֶם וְעַל בְּנֵיכֶם. בְּרוּכִים אַתֶּם לַיהוה, עֹשֵׂה שָׁמַיִם וָאָרֶץ. הַשָּׁמַיִם שָׁמַיִם לַיהוה, וְהָאָרֶץ נָתַן לִבְנֵי אָדָם. לֹא הַמֵּתִים יְהַלְלוּ יָהּ, וְלֹא כָּל יֹרְדֵי דוּמָה. וַאֲנַחְנוּ נְבָרֵךְ יָהּ, מֵעַתָּה וְעַד עוֹלָם; הַלְלוּיָהּ[1].

אָהַבְתִּי כִּי יִשְׁמַע יהוה, אֶת קוֹלִי תַּחֲנוּנָי. כִּי הִטָּה אָזְנוֹ לִי, וּבְיָמַי אֶקְרָא. אֲפָפוּנִי חֶבְלֵי מָוֶת, וּמְצָרֵי שְׁאוֹל מְצָאוּנִי; צָרָה וְיָגוֹן אֶמְצָא. וּבְשֵׁם יהוה אֶקְרָא: אָנָּה יהוה מַלְּטָה נַפְשִׁי. חַנּוּן יהוה וְצַדִּיק, וֵאלֹהֵינוּ מְרַחֵם.

When we say that Heaven is Hashem's and He has given the earth to people, what we mean is that in Heaven, everything operates exactly the way it is supposed to. The angels do not disobey Hashem, and in that sense, before Him there is perfection — all actions taken there are exactly in accord with His desire. But Hashem has given the earth to people, and He gave those people the *bechirah, free will*, to disobey Him. In that sense, the land was "given over to people," meaning that the actions that occur here are reflective of *man's* decisions, not *Hashem's* decisions.

We acknowledge that we are not perfect, and, as we are living on this world, we err sometimes; and yet we pray for salvation. We say (*Tehillim* 115:17-18), *Neither the dead can praise God, nor any who descend into silence; but we will bless God henceforth and forever.* As the dead cannot praise Hashem, we beg of Him to spare us, and continue to allow us to praise Him, even as we may not deserve the opportunity to do so.

Another important lesson we learn from here (*Tehillim* 115:16), *The Heaven is Hashem's, but the earth He has given to mankind*, is found in the Gemara (*Berachos* 35a), which explains that the earth is given to mankind after they make a blessing; until then, it belongs to Hashem. We must realize that Hashem *wants* us to enjoy the bounty of this amazing world that He created — as long as we realize that it is a gift from Him, and express our thanks by making a *berachah*.

אָהַבְתִּי כִּי יִשְׁמַע ה׳ אֶת קוֹלִי, תַּחֲנוּנָי — *I Love Him, for Hashem Hears My Voice, My Supplications.*

- **We look back on the aid that Hashem has granted us in the past to fortify our belief that He is with us in the present as well and can save us from our current troubles.**

May HASHEM add upon you, upon you and your children! You are blessed of HASHEM, Maker of Heaven and earth. As for the Heaven — the Heaven is HASHEM's, but the earth He has given to mankind. Neither the dead can praise God, nor any who descend into silence; but we will bless God henceforth and forever. Halleluyah![1]

I love Him, for HASHEM hears my voice, my supplications. For He has inclined His ear to me, all my days I will call upon Him. The ropes of death encompassed me; the confines of the grave have found me; trouble and sorrow have I found. Then I called upon the Name of HASHEM: "Please, HASHEM, save my soul." Gracious is HASHEM and righteous, our God is merciful.

(1) *Tehillim* 115:12-18.

❒ **Therefore, we must not panic in situations of peril, but rather, we must recall Hashem's past kindnesses toward us, and believe in Him.**

The lens through which David HaMelech sees his past salvations, and therefore, continues to have *bitachon* in the future, is his victories over his enemies. Most of us are not fighting wars, and in that sense, may not relate to this. But we all see the salvation of Hashem daily. Especially as an older person who has difficulty with balance, I can tell you that there are many times that I see Hashem's salvation in the fact that I have, *bli ayin hara,* not fallen, or been harmed by a fall. [See *Nishmas,* below.]

David HaMelech says, *The ropes of death encompassed me; the confines of the grave have found me; trouble and sorrow have I found.* The implication of the *posuk* is that the troubles came upon him suddenly, without his realizing he was in a dangerous situation. And so it is with an elderly person who has, *lo aleinu,* fallen. One second they are going about their business, and the next, they are in a seriously perilous situation, where their very life is at risk. They are on the floor and cannot get up, and they manage to pull themselves up, or reach a phone and alert someone, or Hashem sends someone to check in on them at that time. But there are people who suffer the same travails, and Hashem does not send salvation to them, *Rachmana litzlan.*

Just as David HaMelech took Hashem's past salvation as a demonstration that Hashem is with him and will save him in the future, so too must we view the salvation Hashem grants to us. Thus, if, *chas v'shalom,* people

שֹׁמֵר פְּתָאיִם יהוה, דַּלּוֹתִי וְלִי יְהוֹשִׁיעַ. שׁוּבִי נַפְשִׁי לִמְנוּחָיְכִי, כִּי יהוה גָּמַל עָלָיְכִי. כִּי חִלַּצְתָּ נַפְשִׁי מִמָּוֶת; אֶת עֵינִי מִן דִּמְעָה, אֶת רַגְלִי מִדֶּחִי. אֶתְהַלֵּךְ לִפְנֵי יהוה, בְּאַרְצוֹת הַחַיִּים. הֶאֱמַנְתִּי כִּי אֲדַבֵּר, אֲנִי עָנִיתִי מְאֹד. אֲנִי אָמַרְתִּי בְחָפְזִי, כָּל הָאָדָם כֹּזֵב.[1]

---

find themselves in a perilous situation, they should not panic! They should calm themselves by recalling the myriad times that Hashem saved them in other circumstances, and hold strong to their *bitachon* in Him. [See also above, *Maror*.]

שֹׁמֵר פְּתָאיִם ה׳ — *Guardian of the Foolish Is Hashem*

- ❐ **Some behaviors are permitted because of *shomer pesa'im Hashem,* and others are forbidden because of the obligation of *venishmartem me'od lenafshoseichem.* Where is the line?**
- ❐ **If a person *needs* to do something, and does not have the choice to do it in another way, and he could not have avoided the situation in which he finds himself, the activity will generally be protected by the principle of *shomer pesa'im Hashem.***

In describing Hashem's mercy here, David HaMelech uses the phrase, *shomer pesa'im Hashem, Guardian of the fools is Hashem.* What does it mean that we are sometimes fools, and under what circumstances does Hashem nevertheless guard us?

Let us continue to discuss elderly people who would be in grave danger if they experienced a fall. Oftentimes, the elderly live in the same home they have lived in for decades, and when they moved in there was never a thought for fall prevention. Most of the time, the shower is in the bathtub, which means that to enter and exit it, they need to clear the bathtub wall. This can be very difficult for some, and indeed, many falls occur in just this scenario. In this case, one might argue that it is foolish for a person to continue to expose himself to this risk. It would be smarter to convert the existing bathtub into a walk-in shower, which is far safer. And everyone acknowledges that it would truly be safer. But, it is an expensive renovation that many people do not have money to do. And so, by and large, most people in our society, even though the regular tubs pose a risk, use their tubs anyway. In this case, Hashem is the *shomer pesa'im, Guardian of the foolish.* Is it technically a foolish decision, and Hashem can view the person as foolish? Yes; technically, just as one baby-proofs a house for toddlers to live there, an older person should "Zaidy-proof" a

Guardian of the foolish is HASHEM; I was brought low but He saved me. Return to your rest, my soul, for HASHEM has been kind to you. You delivered my soul from death, my eyes from tears, and my feet from stumbling. I shall walk before HASHEM in the lands of the living. I kept faith although I say: "I suffer exceedingly." I said in my haste: "All mankind is deceitful."[1]

(1) *Tehillim* 116:1-11.

---

house so it is safe for the elderly to live there! But since it is something that most people are not careful with, Hashem protects us.

[It would seem that such a situation is not considered a true *makom sakanah.* We know that a person is judged in Heaven when he enters into a truly dangerous situation, to determine whether he deserves to escape it or not. Even though Hashem often saves people even from very dangerous situations, if a person is found deserving of punishment, he may not be saved from a true *makom sakanah* (see *Rosh Hashanah* 16b and *Taanis* 20b).]

It is obvious that the dictum of *shomer pesa'im Hashem, Hashem is the Guardian of the foolish,* does not extend to all cases. For there is also a dictum of *venishmartem me'od lenafshoseichem, and you shall guard well your lives,* which tells us that it is forbidden to engage in dangerous activities. Obviously, there must be a separation between what falls under *shomer pesa'im Hashem* and what falls under *venishmartem me'od lenafshoseichem.* The line, in my humble opinion, between when *shomer pesa'im Hashem* applies and when it does not apply is this: Does a person *need* to do this action? If he or she is part of a society where everyone does the same "foolish" thing, then even if it is not the smartest choice, Hashem will afford them general protection. If, however, one is not part of a society that needs to rely on this particular "foolish" approach, it is forbidden for him to engage in it.

In the earlier years of plane travel, many people were afraid to fly. Not because they were afraid of heights, but rather because there was a much more significant crash rate in those years than there is today. It was considered somewhat risky to fly, and yet certain categories of people needed to do so. If their *parnassah* required them to fly, for example, they had a *heter;* because it was the way of businessmen who needed to travel to take planes, then *shomer pesa'im Hashem* applied.

But what happens if a person does not really belong to the society where they find themselves; for example, an American *bochur* learning in Yeshiva in Eretz Yisrael, or an Americal girl in seminary? They are

מָה אָשִׁיב לַיהוה, כָּל תַּגְמוּלוֹהִי עָלָי. כּוֹס יְשׁוּעוֹת אֶשָּׂא, וּבְשֵׁם יהוה אֶקְרָא. נְדָרַי לַיהוה אֲשַׁלֵּם, נֶגְדָה נָּא לְכָל עַמּוֹ. יָקָר בְּעֵינֵי יהוה, הַמָּֽוְתָה לַחֲסִידָיו. אָנָּה יהוה כִּי אֲנִי עַבְדֶּךָ; אֲנִי עַבְדְּךָ בֶּן אֲמָתֶךָ, פִּתַּחְתָּ לְמוֹסֵרָי. לְךָ אֶזְבַּח זֶבַח תּוֹדָה, וּבְשֵׁם יהוה אֶקְרָא. נְדָרַי לַיהוה אֲשַׁלֵּם, נֶגְדָה נָּא לְכָל עַמּוֹ. בְּחַצְרוֹת בֵּית יהוה, בְּתוֹכֵכִי יְרוּשָׁלָיִם; הַלְלוּיָהּ[1].

---

not a permanent part of Israeli society, but only temporary visitors; thus, they cannot take advantage of the *heter* of *shomer pesa'im Hashem* that the Israeli public always has. This is relevant with respect to riding public transit buses in Eretz Yisrael. Even though terrorists sometimes target these buses for their bombings, and thus one might argue that it is a "foolish" course of action to ride a bus, the Israeli public has no other choice. Many of them do not have cars, and the only way they get around is via the bus system — taking taxis everywhere would not be economically feasible. There is thus no question that they are permitted to use their public transit system, because *shomer pesa'im Hashem.* Americans, however, do not have this protection, for they are not permanent members of the society of Eretz Yisrael, and are there only temporarily. If so, when they wish to travel, they need to either use a (safe) taxi, an armored bus, or an unscheduled bus, which are not as likely to be targeted, and are thus not considered "foolish" actions. [Even if a couple lives in Eretz Yisrael for a few years after getting married, they still are not a permanent part of the society, and still have the adage of *venishmartem me'od lenafshoseichem* when it comes to riding the buses. If, however, they reach a point that they would plan to stay forever if they can, they are now considered Israeli. Not only do they now have the *heter* to ride buses, but they also keep only one day of *Yom Tov* (see above, *Lagur Ba'aretz*).]

מָה אָשִׁיב — *How Can I Repay*

- **For the many times we are saved, we owe a debt of gratitude to Hashem. Whenever danger is present, we must thank Him for sparing us.**
- **People who engage in dangerous behavior for fun have their senses dulled; how can they be thankful to Hashem for saving them from**

How can I repay HASHEM for all His kindness to me? I will raise the cup of salvations and invoke the Name of HASHEM. My vows to HASHEM I will pay in the presence of His entire people. Precious in the eyes of HASHEM is the death of His devout ones. Please, HASHEM — for I am Your servant, I am Your servant, son of Your handmaid — You have released my bonds. To You I sacrifice thanksgiving offerings, and the Name of HASHEM I will invoke. My vows to HASHEM I will pay in the presence of His entire people; in the Courtyards of the House of HASHEM, in your midst, O Yerushalayim, Halleluyah![1]

(1) *Tehillim* 116:12-19.

---

danger when they voluntarily engage in dangerous behavior for their own enjoyment?

Above, in the beginning of *Tehillim* Ch. 116, David HaMelech mentioned the salvation of Hashem when it occurred openly, and also the salvation of Hashem as He acted as the *Guardian of the foolish,* protecting us from the harm that, based upon our behavior, might have befallen us. Here, in *Mah Ashiv,* we give voice to the gratitude we must feel to Hashem for keeping us safe — not only from the dangers that we were aware of, but also for the many times that He protected us from our own "foolish" actions, in His role as the *Shomer pesa'im.* So, it emerges that a person who can recognize the many times he or she has been helped by Hashem should be able to feel a deeper debt of gratitude toward Him.

It should be noted that we can thank Hashem for saving us from so many dangerous circumstances with a straight face only if we are not actively seeking out danger. But there are people, mostly young people, who engage in "extreme" activities specifically designed to be dangerous, such as bungee-jumping and skydiving, in order to experience the thrill of cheating death. These activities are improper, for, obviously, they contain an element of danger. If we thank Hashem for saving us from such dangers, does it make any sense that we should be permitted to voluntarily bring those dangers upon ourselves? For people who engage in these types of activities, it would be difficult to properly appreciate the debt they have to Hashem for keeping them alive, because they do not look at danger as being dangerous. Everything short of actual injury or death is, to them, just a fun experience. This attitude is truly dangerous in its own right!

הַלְלוּ אֶת יהוה, כָּל גּוֹיִם; שַׁבְּחוּהוּ כָּל הָאֻמִּים. כִּי גָבַר עָלֵינוּ חַסְדּוֹ, וֶאֱמֶת יהוה לְעוֹלָם; הַלְלוּיָהּ.[1]

If there are at least three people at the *Seder,* the leader recites each of the following four lines, and the others respond by repeating the first line each time.

הוֹדוּ לַיהוה כִּי טוֹב, כִּי לְעוֹלָם חַסְדּוֹ.
יֹאמַר נָא יִשְׂרָאֵל, כִּי לְעוֹלָם חַסְדּוֹ.
יֹאמְרוּ נָא בֵית אַהֲרֹן, כִּי לְעוֹלָם חַסְדּוֹ.
יֹאמְרוּ נָא יִרְאֵי יהוה, כִּי לְעוֹלָם חַסְדּוֹ.[2]

מִן הַמֵּצַר קָרָאתִי יָּהּ, עָנָנִי בַמֶּרְחָב יָהּ. יהוה לִי לֹא אִירָא, מַה יַּעֲשֶׂה לִי אָדָם. יהוה לִי בְּעֹזְרָי, וַאֲנִי אֶרְאֶה בְשֹׂנְאָי. טוֹב לַחֲסוֹת בַּיהוה, מִבְּטֹחַ בָּאָדָם. טוֹב לַחֲסוֹת בַּיהוה, מִבְּטֹחַ בִּנְדִיבִים. כָּל גּוֹיִם סְבָבוּנִי,

---

הַלְלוּ אֶת ה׳ כָּל גּוֹיִם — *Praise Hashem, All You Nations*

❒ **We bid the nations to acknowledge the kindness of Hashem, as evidenced by our survival throughout history.**

Despite the never-ending campaign of our enemies among the nations to destroy us, we are still here. The story of our survival is truly exceptional, and it has occurred against all odds. It can only be attributed to Hashem's kindness with us, and it is so evident! Thus, we bid everyone, even the nations of the world, to praise Hashem. These nations, many of whom are themselves the enemies of Klal Yisrael, are not interested in witnessing the miraculous salvations we have experienced. And yet we bid them to praise Hashem, because the evidence of His kindness, both in their own lives and in what they see Hashem doing for us, is overwhelming!

In addition, although the nations would never admit it, the Jewish people have contributed greatly throughout history to world health, and benefited the economy of every nation that has "hosted" them throughout the long centuries in *galus.* Here, we ask them to acknowledge this as well.

כִּי לְעוֹלָם חַסְדּוֹ — *His Kindness Endures Forever!*

❒ **All of Klal Yisrael proclaim that Hashem's kindness is forever. What does that mean?**

❒ **Hashem has always helped us in the past, and we utter a prayer in the belief that He will surely continue to do so.**

Praise HASHEM, all you nations; praise Him all you peoples! For His kindness to us was overwhelming, and the truth of HASHEM is eternal, Halleluyah![1]

If there are at least three people at the *Seder,* the leader recites each of the following four lines, and the others respond by repeating the first line each time.

Give thanks to HASHEM, for He is good;
His kindness endures forever!
Let Yisrael say: His kindness endures forever!
Let the House of Aharon say: His kindness endures forever!
Let those who fear HASHEM say: His kindness endures forever![2]

From the straits did I call to God; God answered me with expansiveness. HASHEM is with me; I have no fear; how can man affect me? HASHEM is there for me through my helpers; therefore I can face my foes. It is better to take refuge in HASHEM than to rely on man. It is better to take refuge in HASHEM than to rely on princes. All the nations encompass me;

(1) *Tehillim* 117. (2) 118:1-4.

Here, all segments of Klal Yisrael are told to praise Hashem, declaring that His kindness endures forever. What does "forever" mean? Is the intent until the end of time, long past our own lifetimes? How does it make sense to thank Hashem for something that He has not yet done, or for things He will do but that we will not be alive to receive? Does the word "forever" in this context allude to only the past and the present, rather than the future?

We are a part of the chain of the *mesorah* of Klal Yisrael, and can therefore attest that since the beginning of that chain up until, and including, our own lifetimes, Hashem's kindness has always endured. For this, it is surely appropriate to thank Him. But, because He has done so much for us, we have *bitachon* that He will continue to do so. Thus, the knowledge of what has been gives rise to the ability to express the belief that it will also be so in the future. So we are thanking Hashem for everything that He has done to this point, which enables us to make the declaration with surety that even into the future, *His kindness endures forever!*

טוֹב לַחֲסוֹת בַּה׳ מִבְּטֹחַ בָּאָדָם. טוֹב לַחֲסוֹת בַּה׳ מִבְּטֹחַ בִּנְדִיבִים —
It Is Better to Take Refuge in Hashem Than to Rely on Man. It Is Better to Take Refuge in Hashem Than to Rely on Princes

❒ **We must always rely on Hashem. Aside from the fact that only He is actually capable of following through with anything, for everything is**

בְּשֵׁם יהוה כִּי אֲמִילַם. סַבּוּנִי גַם סְבָבוּנִי, בְּשֵׁם יהוה כִּי אֲמִילַם. סַבּוּנִי כִדְבֹרִים, דֹּעֲכוּ כְּאֵשׁ קוֹצִים; בְּשֵׁם יהוה כִּי אֲמִילַם. דָּחֹה דְחִיתַנִי לִנְפֹּל, וַיהוה עֲזָרָנִי. עָזִּי וְזִמְרָת יָהּ, וַיְהִי לִי לִישׁוּעָה. קוֹל רִנָּה וִישׁוּעָה בְּאָהֳלֵי צַדִּיקִים, יְמִין יהוה עֹשָׂה חָיִל. יְמִין יהוה רוֹמֵמָה, יְמִין יהוה עֹשָׂה חָיִל. לֹא אָמוּת כִּי אֶחְיֶה, וַאֲסַפֵּר מַעֲשֵׂי יָהּ. יַסֹּר יִסְּרַנִּי יָּהּ, וְלַמָּוֶת לֹא נְתָנָנִי. פִּתְחוּ לִי שַׁעֲרֵי צֶדֶק, אָבֹא בָם

---

in His control, He is also more trustworthy than regular people, and even princes, who will sometimes change their minds.

The main point of *Min HaMeitzar* is that Hashem is always with us and we can always trust in Him. This is expressed with the words of David HaMelech, when he says, *It is better to take refuge in Hashem than to rely on man. It is better to take refuge in Hashem than to rely on princes.* Obviously, the progression from *man* to *princes* is intended to demonstrate that it is better to rely upon Hashem than even on a very powerful person. So, why does it not say that we can rely on Hashem more so even than a king? Why stop at princes? Do we mean to say that a king is indeed reliable?

The answer lies in the proper understanding of what the *posuk* is telling us. If the *posuk* means to say that even a prince is a mortal, and there are factors beyond his control and so he is not able to be relied upon absolutely, this is obvious! There is nobody who can do anything with certainty, because Hashem is all-powerful, and Hashem can arrange for any person at any time to be unable to do anything, including kings. [For example, King Belshatzar, at the height of his power, lost everything in a single night.] This is obvious, and is known to everyone.

Rather, I believe that the intent of the *posuk* is that even as we accept as a given that there are factors beyond *everyone's* control, we cannot rely on people, and even princes, to keep their word even regarding things that *are* in their control. For people can be untrustworthy, depending on their agendas, and even princes can decide to grant their favors elsewhere. No one can be trusted absolutely not to change their mind and decide not to help a person. But in this regard, we generally do trust a king. For the Gemara (*Bava Basra* 3b) tells us that once a king makes a decision, he will not retract it. So, even though, of course, a king is also only a person, and is of course ultimately limited to his abilities, which are decided by Hashem, the point is that a king is trustworthy. A regular person and even

but in the Name of HASHEM I cut them down! They encompass me; they swarm around me; but in the Name of HASHEM I cut them down! They swarm around me like bees, but they are extinguished as a fire does thorns; in the Name of HASHEM I cut them down! You pushed me hard that I might fall, but HASHEM assisted me. My strength and song is God; He became my salvation. The sound of rejoicing and salvation is in the tents of the righteous: "The right hand of HASHEM does valiantly! The right hand of HASHEM is raised triumphantly! The right hand of HASHEM does valiantly!" I shall not die! I shall live and relate the deeds of God. God chastened me exceedingly, but He did not let me die. Open for me the gates of righteousness, I will enter them

---

a prince, on the other hand, are not trusted to keep their word even if they are able to do so.

יַסֹּר יִסְּרַנִּי יָּהּ, וְלַמָּוֶת לֹא נְתָנָנִי —
God Chastened Me Exceedingly

❒ **In punishing a person rather than killing him for his sins, Hashem preserves that person's potential to recover from his past, and draw close to Hashem.**

David HaMelech praises Hashem for the fact that He caused him to suffer, but did not kill him. What is the explanation of this? Why does he not have a complaint against Hashem for the fact that He caused him to suffer in the first place? Obviously, David understood that his suffering was because Hashem had a reason to punish him; perhaps to help him atone for something he did, or another reason. But, if that is the case, then even if Hashem *would* have killed him, it would have been understood in the same vein, as an atonement, or for some other purpose that only Hashem knows. So, what is the specific praise, *He chastened me exceedingly, but did not let me die,* supposed to mean?

It would seem that the intent of the *posuk* must be that Hashem was going to punish a person for a sin by killing him, and instead, mercifully waived the death penalty in favor of lesser punishments. Either punishment would have been an atonement, and Hashem chose to punish the person rather than kill him, allowing for the potential for future *mitzvos* to be carried out; for death is final, and it does not allow for the possibility of rehabilitation. In other words, Hashem metes out punishment in a merciful manner, which allows the penitent a chance to regain his closeness to Hashem in this world. More than anything else, Hashem demonstrates in

אוֹדְךָ כִּי עֲנִיתָנִי, וַתְּהִי לִי לִישׁוּעָה. אוֹדְךָ כִּי עֲנִיתָנִי, וַתְּהִי לִי לִישׁוּעָה. אֶבֶן מָאֲסוּ הַבּוֹנִים, הָיְתָה לְרֹאשׁ פִּנָּה. אֶבֶן מָאֲסוּ הַבּוֹנִים, הָיְתָה לְרֹאשׁ פִּנָּה. מֵאֵת יהוה הָיְתָה זֹּאת, הִיא נִפְלָאת בְּעֵינֵינוּ. מֵאֵת יהוה הָיְתָה זֹּאת, הִיא נִפְלָאת בְּעֵינֵינוּ. זֶה הַיּוֹם עָשָׂה יהוה, נָגִילָה וְנִשְׂמְחָה בוֹ. זֶה הַיּוֹם עָשָׂה יהוה, נָגִילָה וְנִשְׂמְחָה בוֹ.

If there are at least three people at the *Seder,*
the following is recited responsively.

אָנָּא יהוה, הוֹשִׁיעָה נָּא.
אָנָּא יהוה, הוֹשִׁיעָה נָּא.

---

this act a love for the person He punishes in that He desires his *mitzvos;* Hashem still wants such a person to draw close to Him, because He loves him, despite his past sins!

אָנָּא ה׳ הוֹשִׁיעָה נָּא — *Please, Hashem, Save Now!*

❒ ***Please, Hashem, save now,* connotes that someone other than He is responsible for our plight, which is of course untrue! What is the meaning, then, of the prayer?**

❒ **We are asking to be saved from the thought that our troubles are caused by anyone but Hashem.**

The *posuk* (*Devarim* 32:39) states that Hashem is the One Who gives life and the One Who removes it. This really drives home the central point of *Parashas Haazinu,* which is that there are no two powers, no conflicting agendas of good and evil. There is only Hashem, and His judgment, His plan, and His mercy. This is the most fundamental principle of *bitachon,* and is part of the very foundation of our relationship with Hashem.

Accordingly, it would seem that the prayer, *Please, Hashem, save now!,* that we recite during *Hallel* does not paint the full picture. For who is it that is causing the pain to begin with? It is also Hashem! So, it would seem more appropriate for a person to beg Hashem, "Please, stop making me suffer!", rather than, "Please, save me from the suffering I have to endure!" To acknowledge that it was Hashem Who put the person in his predicament to begin with reflects a more complete understanding of Hashem and His power over the world and His relationship with it. So, how are we

and thank God. This is the gate of HASHEM; the righteous shall enter through it. I thank You for You answered me and became my salvation! I thank You for You answered me and became my salvation! The stone which the builders despised has become the cornerstone! The stone which the builders despised has become the cornerstone! This has emanated from HASHEM; it is wondrous in our eyes! This has emanated from HASHEM; it is wondrous in our eyes! This is the day HASHEM has made; we will rejoice and be glad in it! This is the day HASHEM has made; we will rejoice and be glad in it!

If there are at least three people at the *Seder,*
the following is recited responsively.

Please, HASHEM, save now!
Please, HASHEM, save now!

---

to explain these words? Should we not recognize that the issue itself was caused by Hashem too?

I believe that the answer is that we are asking Hashem to save us *from ourselves;* from mistakenly thinking that our pitfalls and our tribulations are somehow caused by foreign forces other than Hashem, and thus not turning to Hashem in sincere and total repentance. [See also *Heights of Hallel,* authored by my grandson, *R' Avrohom Meir Weiss, n"y,* whose *peirush* on *Hallel* deals extensively with the theme of recognizing that everything that happens in our lives — not only the salvations, but also the tribulations — all come from Hashem.]

This is really the critical realization which Klal Yisrael needs so badly to internalize, and to see with crystal clarity. Why do we need to endlessly relive the cycle of *vayishman yeshurun,* where Klal Yisrael are blessed with Hashem's bounty, followed by *vayiv'at,* their rebellion, followed by Hashem's punishments, followed by Klal Yisrael's repentance, followed by a blessing from Hashem, followed once more by sinful behavior? This pattern of "up and down" has repeated itself for millennia. Why must it continue? Because we do not recognize that Hashem, Who brings us "up" with His blessings, is the same Hashem Who brings us "down" with his rebuke. We must realize that Hashem is both the *Shomei'a Tefillah, the One Who hears prayers,* and the One Who issues punishments (as in *Shefoch Chamascha*). [It is noteworthy that none of the other major religions embrace the concept of both good and bad emanating from a single source.]

There should really never be a lapse in Klal Yisrael's consciousness of

אָנָּא יהוה, הַצְלִיחָה נָּא.
אָנָּא יהוה, הַצְלִיחָה נָּא.

בָּרוּךְ הַבָּא בְּשֵׁם יהוה, בֵּרַכְנוּכֶם מִבֵּית יהוה. בָּרוּךְ הַבָּא בְּשֵׁם יהוה, בֵּרַכְנוּכֶם מִבֵּית יהוה. אֵל יהוה וַיָּאֶר לָנוּ, אִסְרוּ חַג בַּעֲבֹתִים עַד קַרְנוֹת הַמִּזְבֵּחַ. אֵל יהוה וַיָּאֶר לָנוּ, אִסְרוּ חַג בַּעֲבֹתִים עַד קַרְנוֹת הַמִּזְבֵּחַ. אֵלִי אַתָּה וְאוֹדֶךָּ, אֱלֹהַי אֲרוֹמְמֶךָּ. אֵלִי אַתָּה וְאוֹדֶךָּ, אֱלֹהַי אֲרוֹמְמֶךָּ. הוֹדוּ לַיהוה כִּי טוֹב, כִּי לְעוֹלָם חַסְדּוֹ. הוֹדוּ לַיהוה כִּי טוֹב, כִּי לְעוֹלָם חַסְדּוֹ.[1]

---

their relationship with Hashem, allowing them to forget that Hashem gives them the blessing, and that in response to their lapses, He rebukes them with punishments, so they will repent. We must work to internalize the idea that everything in our lives is from Hashem, and this will help us not to attribute our successes to ourselves. If we would know with absolute certainty that Hashem is behind everything, we would never take credit for ourselves, causing us to stray from His word; and then there would never be any reason for us to be brought down!

אָנָּא ה׳ הַצְלִיחָה נָּא — *Please, Hashem, Bring Success Now!*

❒ **We pray that Hashem bless our endeavors with *hatzlachah*. Sometimes, the reward that Hashem gives us for the good deeds that we do is that He blesses our efforts with success.**

We pray that Hashem grant us *hatzlachah, success*. It is important that we realize how great success in our endeavors truly is, in order for us to ask for it with the proper fervor. In *Shemos* 1:17, the Torah tells us that Yocheved and Miriam selflessly risked their lives, and defied Pharaoh's orders to kill all the Jewish baby boys. *Rashi* (*Shemos* 1:20, *d"h vayeitev*) comments that the following *posuk*, 1:21, is the Torah's description of the benevolence that Hashem showered upon Yocheved and Miriam; they merited that the houses of *kehunah, leviyah*, and *malchus* would emanate from them. Clearly, *Rashi* understands the *pesukim* to be relating that a) Hashem rewarded the midwives; b) their actions resulted in the furtherance of Klal Yisrael; and c) the detailing of their reward. This seems puzzling, for if this was the intent of the *posuk*, would not the appropriate

Please, HASHEM, bring success now!
Please, HASHEM, bring success now!

Blessed be he who comes in the Name of HASHEM; we bless you from the House of HASHEM. Blessed be he who comes in the Name of HASHEM; we bless you from the House of HASHEM. HASHEM is God and He illuminated for us; bind the festival offering with cords to the corners of the *Mizbei'ach*. HASHEM is God and He illuminated for us; bind the festival offering with cords to the corners of the *Mizbei'ach*. You are my God and I shall thank You; my God and I shall exalt You. You are my God, and I shall thank You; my God and I shall exalt You. Give thanks to HASHEM, for He is good; His kindness endures forever! Give thanks to HASHEM, for He is good; His kindness endures forever![1]

(1) *Tehillim* 118:5-25.

---

sequence have been to first explain that the actions of the midwives (a) had great results; and only afterward, recount that (b) they merited reward; which was (c) the emanating of the houses of *kehunah, leviyah,* and *malchus* from them?

I believe that the *pesukim* are describing two distinct rewards that the midwives merited. The second was, as *Rashi* details, the honor of those great houses that issued from them. But the first was, as the *posuk* states, that the people multiplied, and became very mighty. This was not simply the result of their actions, but part and parcel of their reward. One of the greatest rewards it is possible to give a person for their efforts is that those efforts be met with success.

If we were to approach any *talmid chacham* with the choice of being the generation's greatest Rosh Yeshiva, but it would come along with great poverty, any *talmid chacham* would happily sign up for this. Why? Because seeing the fruits of one's labor — in this example, in the form of Torah influence on the entire generation — is so satisfying as to be its own reward, and it will outweigh virtually any inconvenience that comes along with it.

[This lofty idea is found not only among those of Klal Yisrael; there have been non-Jews, as well, who sacrificed everything for the satisfaction of the success of what they identified as their noble causes. Mother Teresa was famous for living among lepers in order to help them; she surely

יְהַלְלוּךָ יהוה אֱלֹהֵינוּ כָּל מַעֲשֶׂיךָ, וַחֲסִידֶיךָ צַדִּיקִים עוֹשֵׂי רְצוֹנֶךָ, וְכָל עַמְּךָ בֵּית יִשְׂרָאֵל בְּרִנָּה יוֹדוּ וִיבָרְכוּ וִישַׁבְּחוּ וִיפָאֲרוּ וִירוֹמְמוּ וְיַעֲרִיצוּ וְיַקְדִּישׁוּ וְיַמְלִיכוּ אֶת שִׁמְךָ מַלְכֵּנוּ. כִּי לְךָ טוֹב לְהוֹדוֹת וּלְשִׁמְךָ נָאֶה לְזַמֵּר, כִּי מֵעוֹלָם וְעַד עוֹלָם אַתָּה אֵל.

הוֹדוּ לַיהוה כִּי טוֹב, כִּי לְעוֹלָם חַסְדּוֹ.
הוֹדוּ לֵאלֹהֵי הָאֱלֹהִים, כִּי לְעוֹלָם חַסְדּוֹ.
הוֹדוּ לַאֲדֹנֵי הָאֲדֹנִים, כִּי לְעוֹלָם חַסְדּוֹ.
לְעֹשֵׂה נִפְלָאוֹת גְּדֹלוֹת לְבַדּוֹ, כִּי לְעוֹלָם חַסְדּוֹ.
לְעֹשֵׂה הַשָּׁמַיִם בִּתְבוּנָה, כִּי לְעוֹלָם חַסְדּוֹ.
לְרֹקַע הָאָרֶץ עַל הַמָּיִם, כִּי לְעוֹלָם חַסְדּוֹ.
לְעֹשֵׂה אוֹרִים גְּדֹלִים, כִּי לְעוֹלָם חַסְדּוֹ.
אֶת הַשֶּׁמֶשׁ לְמֶמְשֶׁלֶת בַּיּוֹם, כִּי לְעוֹלָם חַסְדּוֹ.
אֶת הַיָּרֵחַ וְכוֹכָבִים לְמֶמְשְׁלוֹת בַּלָּיְלָה, כִּי לְעוֹלָם חַסְדּוֹ.
לְמַכֵּה מִצְרַיִם בִּבְכוֹרֵיהֶם, כִּי לְעוֹלָם חַסְדּוֹ.
וַיּוֹצֵא יִשְׂרָאֵל מִתּוֹכָם, כִּי לְעוֹלָם חַסְדּוֹ.
בְּיָד חֲזָקָה וּבִזְרוֹעַ נְטוּיָה, כִּי לְעוֹלָם חַסְדּוֹ.
לְגֹזֵר יַם סוּף לִגְזָרִים, כִּי לְעוֹלָם חַסְדּוֹ.
וְהֶעֱבִיר יִשְׂרָאֵל בְּתוֹכוֹ, כִּי לְעוֹלָם חַסְדּוֹ.
וְנִעֵר פַּרְעֹה וְחֵילוֹ בְיַם סוּף, כִּי לְעוֹלָם חַסְדּוֹ.

---

gained satisfaction from knowing how much she was able to change their lives. Similarly, in my own youth, there was a man named Dr. Shweitzer who famously lived among the diseased in order to care for them.]

So, when we beg Hashem to grant us success in our efforts, we are asking that He give us this ultimate realization of our goals, which is so great that it is sometimes the very reward for the good deeds we perform!

They shall praise You, HASHEM our God, for all Your works, along with Your pious followers, the righteous, who do Your will, and Your entire people, the House of Yisrael, with joy will thank, bless, praise, glorify, exalt, revere, sanctify, and coronate Your Name, our King! For to You it is fitting to give thanks, and unto Your Name it is proper to sing praises, for from eternity to eternity You are God.

Give thanks to HASHEM, for He is good;
His kindness endures forever!
Give thanks to the God of gods; His kindness endures forever!
Give thanks to the Master of masters;
His kindness endures forever!
To Him Who alone does great wonders;
His kindness endures forever!
To Him Who makes the heaven with understanding;
His kindness endures forever!
To Him Who stretched out the earth over the waters;
His kindness endures forever!
To Him Who makes great luminaries;
His kindness endures forever!
The sun for the reign of the day; His kindness endures forever!
The moon and the stars for the reign of the night;
His kindness endures forever!
To Him Who struck the Egyptians through their firstborn;
His kindness endures forever!
And took Yisrael out from their midst;
His kindness endures forever!
With strong hand and outstretched arm;
His kindness endures forever!
To Him Who divided the *Yam Suf* into parts;
His kindness endures forever!
And caused Yisrael to pass through it;
His kindness endures forever!
And threw Pharaoh and his army into the *Yam Suf*;
His kindness endures forever!

לְמוֹלִיךְ עַמּוֹ בַּמִּדְבָּר,	כִּי לְעוֹלָם חַסְדּוֹ.
לְמַכֵּה מְלָכִים גְּדֹלִים,	כִּי לְעוֹלָם חַסְדּוֹ.
וַיַּהֲרֹג מְלָכִים אַדִּירִים,	כִּי לְעוֹלָם חַסְדּוֹ.
לְסִיחוֹן מֶלֶךְ הָאֱמֹרִי,	כִּי לְעוֹלָם חַסְדּוֹ.
וּלְעוֹג מֶלֶךְ הַבָּשָׁן,	כִּי לְעוֹלָם חַסְדּוֹ.
וְנָתַן אַרְצָם לְנַחֲלָה,	כִּי לְעוֹלָם חַסְדּוֹ.
נַחֲלָה לְיִשְׂרָאֵל עַבְדּוֹ,	כִּי לְעוֹלָם חַסְדּוֹ.
שֶׁבְּשִׁפְלֵנוּ זָכַר לָנוּ,	כִּי לְעוֹלָם חַסְדּוֹ.
וַיִּפְרְקֵנוּ מִצָּרֵינוּ,	כִּי לְעוֹלָם חַסְדּוֹ.
נֹתֵן לֶחֶם לְכָל בָּשָׂר,	כִּי לְעוֹלָם חַסְדּוֹ.
הוֹדוּ לְאֵל הַשָּׁמָיִם,	כִּי לְעוֹלָם חַסְדּוֹ[1].

וְנָתַן אַרְצָם לְנַחֲלָה כִּי לְעוֹלָם חַסְדּוֹ — נַחֲלָה לְיִשְׂרָאֵל עַבְדּוֹ כִּי לְעוֹלָם חַסְדּוֹ

And gave their land as an inheritance;
His kindness endures forever!
An inheritance to Yisrael His servant;
His kindness endures forever!

- ❐ **Why are the fact that Hashem gave the land of Sichon as an inheritance and the fact that the inheritance was for Klal Yisrael mentioned as two separate acts of kindness?**
- ❐ **One was that He gave us the land of Sichon, and another was that first, He had Sichon conquer parts of Ammon and Moav, so we received those portions as well.**

It is curious that when describing the conquest of the lands of Sichon and Og, we thank Hashem for what seems like one thing over two *pesukim,* and treat it like two different things about which we need to thank Hashem for doing for us. We say, *And He gave their land as an inheritance, for His kindness endures forever; An inheritance for Yisrael, His servant, for His kindness endures forever.* Why are the *pesukim* written this way?

Someone once told me the following explanation in the name of the *Rosh HaYeshiva, ztvk"l.* In the conquest of Sichon's land, there was indeed another favor that Hashem did for us. Klal Yisrael had been forbidden from conquering Ammon and Moav, and thus, any land that belonged to them

To Him Who led His people through the Wilderness;
His kindness endures forever!
To Him Who smote great kings; His kindness endures forever!
And slew mighty kings; His kindness endures forever!
Sichon, king of the Emorites; His kindness endures forever!
And Og, king of Bashan; His kindness endures forever!
And gave their land as an inheritance;
His kindness endures forever!
An inheritance to Yisrael His servant;
His kindness endures forever!
Who remembered us in our lowliness;
His kindness endures forever!
And released us from our foes; His kindness endures forever!
He gives food to all living creatures;
His kindness endures forever!
Give thanks to God of Heaven; His kindness endures forever![1]

(1) *Tehillim* 136.

was off-limits to Klal Yisrael (at least until *le'asid lavo*). However, the Torah tells us (*Bamidbar* 21:26) that Sichon had waged war with Moav (and, as is clear from *Shoftim* Ch.11, Ammon as well), and conquered portions of their lands. This was very significant, because when Klal Yisrael, in turn, defeated Sichon, all of his lands became theirs. The Gemara (*Chullin* 60b) cites R' Pappa, who coined the term, *Ammon and Moav were purified by Sichon*. This means that the fact that Sichon initially conquered these portions rendered them halachically no longer part of the territory of Ammon and Moav, and thus, permissible for Klal Yisrael to conquer.

So, the *Rosh HaYeshiva, ztvk"l,* explained that Hashem actually did two distinct acts of *chessed* for us here. The first was that *He gave* the portions of *their land* that had been conquered from Ammon and Moav *as an inheritance* — meaning, that He arranged for it to be a permissible inheritance, *for His kindness endures forever.* Subsequently, Hashem did a second *chessed* for us by delivering the lands of Sichon, which were now all permitted to Klal Yisrael, as *An inheritance for Yisrael, His servant — for His kindness endures forever.*

After we know that the lands of Ammon and Moav ended up being divided into two segments, and Klal Yisrael therefore ended up conquering plots which they had owned, the following very interesting fact emerges: As we discussed above (*Mitchilah*), *Rashi* (*Bereishis* 15:19, *d"h es*

נִשְׁמַת כָּל חַי תְּבָרֵךְ אֶת שִׁמְךָ יהוה אֱלֹהֵינוּ, וְרוּחַ כָּל בָּשָׂר תְּפָאֵר וּתְרוֹמֵם זִכְרְךָ מַלְכֵּנוּ תָּמִיד. מִן הָעוֹלָם וְעַד הָעוֹלָם אַתָּה אֵל, וּמִבַּלְעָדֶיךָ אֵין לָנוּ מֶלֶךְ גּוֹאֵל וּמוֹשִׁיעַ. פּוֹדֶה וּמַצִּיל וּמְפַרְנֵס וּמְרַחֵם, בְּכָל עֵת צָרָה וְצוּקָה, אֵין לָנוּ מֶלֶךְ אֶלָּא אָתָּה. אֱלֹהֵי הָרִאשׁוֹנִים

---

haKeini) explains that even though, at the *Bris Bein HaBesarim,* Avram was promised the territories of ten nations, including the Keini, Kezini, and Kadmoni, those three were only going to be given to Klal Yisrael *le'asid lavo, in the Future to Come.* And yet, what actually happened was that Eisav ceded the portion of the Chivi that was inside Eretz Yisrael to Yaakov Avinu (as we discussed there), and parts of the territories of Ammon and Moav were initially conquered by Sichon, as discussed here, and so Klal Yisrael got portions of these nations' lands as well.

At the *Bris Bein HaBesarim*, Hashem promised the lands of ten nations to Avram. When Hashem made this pledge, the portions of the Kenizi and the Kadmoni were inhabited by the Rephaim; the Keini, Kenizi, and Kadmoni nations did not yet exist at that time. Essentially, Hashem used ten names to describe the territory that was inhabited at that time by a total of only eight nations. What He intended with this, however, was to give the rights to part of the land of the Rephaim to the Kenizi (another name for Ammon) and the Kadmoni (another name for Moav). The *pesukim* in *Parashas Devarim* (2:9-11) go to great length to explain that the territory of Moav (who were also known as the Kadmoni) had been previously inhabited by the Eimim; and the Torah explains that the name Eimim was the moniker that the people of Moav had given the Rephaim who had lived there before them. *Rashi* (2:10 *d"h haEimim*) adds that the Torah means to tell us that although the territory of the Rephaim is promised to Klal Yisrael, this section of the land of the Rephaim — the part inhabited by those that the Moavim called "Eimim" — was reserved for Moav, who had indeed taken and settled that land. Similarly, the *pesukim* there in *Devarim* 2:19-21 go to great length to explain that the territory of Ammon (also known as the Kenizi) had been previously inhabited by the Zamzumim; and the Torah explains that the name Zamzumim was the moniker that the people of Ammon had given the Rephaim who had lived there before them. *Rashi* (*Devarim* 2:20 *d"h eretz Rephaim*) adds that the Torah means to tell us that although the territory of the Rephaim is promised to Klal Yisrael, this section of the land of the Rephaim — the ones the Ammonim called "Zamzumim" — was reserved for Ammon, who had indeed taken

The soul of every living being shall bless Your Name, HASHEM, our God; the spirit of all flesh shall always glorify and exalt Your remembrance, our King. From eternity to eternity, You are God, and except for You we have no king, redeemer, or helper. O Rescuer, and Redeemer, Sustainer, and Merciful One in every time of trouble and distress. We have no king but You — God of the first

---

and settled that land. [See *Nahar Sholom, Bamidbar* 21:21, as well as *Devarim* 2:5,9,19.]

The territory of Edom (also known as the Keini) has a slightly different history to it. While the Kenizi and Kadmoni areas had been inhabited by the Eimim and the Zamzumim, the area of the Keini had been occupied by the Chivi nation. The Chivi's territory was partially in Eretz Yisrael, presumably including the area approximate to Shechem, and partially in Har Se'ir.

We can prove that the land that was to belong to the Keini (Edom) mentioned at the *Bris Bein HaBesarim* was none other than the land that was inhabited by the Chivi, as follows: When Hashem promised the Land of Eretz Yisrael to Avraham Avinu at the *Bris Bein HaBesarim*, He mentioned six of the seven Canaanite nations. They are, the Chiti, Perizi, Emori, Canaani, Girgashi, and Yevusi. No mention at all is made of the Chivi. Hashem also mentioned four other territories: Rephaim, Keini, Kenizi, and Kadmoni. The Torah explicitly states that the territory of the Rephaim that is referenced separately from the Keini, Kenizi, and Kadmoni, is the land inhabited by Og — see *Devarim* 3:13. [*Rashi* there, *d"h hahu,* writes that *this* is the land of the Rephaim that Hashem promised Avram.] This must mean that the territories of the Keini, Kenizi, and Kadmoni are those that were inhabited by the Eimim, the Zamzumim... and the seventh Canaanite nation, the Chivi. [See further, *Nahar Sholom, Bereishis* 26:34, where we explain that the Chivi are also sometimes called the Chori.]

It emerges, then, that we may divide the physical parcels of land that Hashem mentioned to Avraham Avinu at the *Bris Bein HaBesarim* into thirteen sections of land. The lands of six Canaanite nations went to Klal Yisrael right away, as did the territory of Og. The portions of Ammon and Moav that were conquered by Sichon and subsequently, by Klal Yisrael, were also given to them right away, and the territory of Edom that was part of Eretz Yisrael was forfeited by Eisav to Klal Yisrael. Thus, these ten parcels of land were given to Klal Yisrael immediately. The lands that were retained by Ammon, Moav, and Edom, however, will be given to Klal Yisrael *le'asid lavo.*

וְהָאַחֲרוֹנִים, אֱלוֹהַּ כָּל בְּרִיּוֹת, אֲדוֹן כָּל תּוֹלָדוֹת, הַמְּהֻלָּל בְּרֹב הַתִּשְׁבָּחוֹת, הַמְּנַהֵג עוֹלָמוֹ בְּחֶסֶד וּבְרִיּוֹתָיו בְּרַחֲמִים. וַיהוה לֹא יָנוּם וְלֹא יִישָׁן. הַמְּעוֹרֵר יְשֵׁנִים, וְהַמֵּקִיץ נִרְדָּמִים, וְהַמֵּשִׂיחַ אִלְּמִים, וְהַמַּתִּיר אֲסוּרִים, וְהַסּוֹמֵךְ נוֹפְלִים, וְהַזּוֹקֵף כְּפוּפִים. לְךָ לְבַדְּךָ אֲנַחְנוּ מוֹדִים. אִלּוּ פִינוּ מָלֵא שִׁירָה כַּיָּם, וּלְשׁוֹנֵנוּ רִנָּה כַּהֲמוֹן

הַמְּעוֹרֵר יְשֵׁנִים, וְהַמֵּקִיץ נִרְדָּמִים — *He Rouses the Sleepers and Awakens the Slumberers*

❒ **We say that Hashem rouses the sleeping and wakens the slumbering; this means that Hashem sends us reminders that we need Him, which cause us to focus on Him and what He wants from us, rather than on the emptiness of the physical world.**

In *Nishmas,* one of the many praises we say about Hashem is that *He rouses the sleepers and awakens the slumberers.* What does this mean? Surely, the simple meaning of the words is that He returns our souls to us when we awake each morning. And yet, I believe that there is a deeper and more profound meaning in these words.

The *Rambam* (*Hil. Teshuvah* 3:4) famously writes: *Even though the tekios of Rosh Hashanah are mandated by Scriptural decree, there is a hint in their fulfillment: [That is], Rouse, sleepers, from your sleep, and wake up slumberers from your slumber, and examine your actions, and repent, and remember your Creator, these who forget the truth with the futility of [the world which occurs over] time, and they fritter away their year with futility and emptiness that is of no help and no salvation — look to your souls, and look at your ways and plans, and each one shall abandon his evil path and thought that is not good.*

Rambam bids us to tune in to what is really important — what we have forgotten between last Rosh Hashanah and now. The rigors and pressures of our daily lives are, at the very least, distracting us from our goals in *avodas Hashem,* and more than likely, actively preventing us from achieving them. He explains that the *shofar* serves as our alarm clock, so to speak, and that when we hear it, we ought to remember the important goals we have lost track of, and recalibrate.

Rambam is discussing what we must to as we approach the *Yom HaDin,* the day when Hashem judges us, when we are all commanded to actively inspect ourselves. But should this exercise go neglected throughout the

and of the last, God of all creatures, Master of all generations, Who is extolled through a multitude of praises, Who guides His world with kindness and His creatures with mercy. HASHEM neither slumbers nor sleeps; He rouses the sleepers and awakens the slumberers; He makes the mute speak and releases the bound; He supports the falling and raises erect the bowed down. To You alone we give thanks. Were our mouths as full of song as the sea, and our tongue as full of jubilation as its multitude

---

whole year? Certainly not! A thinking person should definitely not wait until right before Rosh Hashanah in order to analyze his or her path in life. But, as *Rambam* writes, living our regular lives is often incongruent with how we really want to live our lives, the way we wish we would have when we are standing before Hashem on the *Yamim Noraim*. How can we retain our focus throughout the year on our *real* goals, so that the fake goals that grab our attention do not distract us so completely? How can we keep our eye on what is really important, so that next year, we are not coming back before Hashem on the same *madreigah* we were on last year, having fallen into the same traps?

One answer is that a person should keep his (or her) eye on how it is that Hashem interacts with him. Hashem is the One Who *rouses the sleepers,* and *awakens the slumberers;* as we begin to fall into the rote of daily life, Hashem comes to our aid with a wake-up call, but He does so with mercy. He awakens us to show us that we need Him. If a person is paying attention to Hashem's messages, he will have a much easier time zeroing in on what is important to Hashem, and paying a little less attention to the silly demands of society.

We must remember that Hashem is not necessarily punishing us when He shows us that we need Him. He is rather sometimes just giving us a tap on the shoulder, as it were, to remind us to wake up and focus on Him. [See *Darash Moshe, Rosh Hashanah,* where the *Rosh HaYeshiva, ztvk"l,* explains that the *posuk* that says that Klal Yisrael are *yod'ei seru'ah* means that we *love* the wakeup calls of the *shofar*. Otherwise, we would be unreceptive to them. (See further there, where he also explains the difference between *sleepers* and *slumberers*.)] He wants to be asked for help; He is a King Who wants to help everybody, He is a Father Who wants to help His children. But we need to approach and ask Him for that help! And by waking us up, Hashem keeps us out of trouble.

This is truly a great praise, for Hashem helps us correct the way we think and act, should we be wise enough to take advantage of the reminders, by rousing us to remember Him and how much we need Him.

גַּלָּיו, וְשִׂפְתוֹתֵינוּ שֶׁבַח כְּמֶרְחֲבֵי רָקִיעַ, וְעֵינֵינוּ מְאִירוֹת כַּשֶּׁמֶשׁ וְכַיָּרֵחַ, וְיָדֵינוּ פְרוּשׂוֹת כְּנִשְׁרֵי שָׁמָיִם, וְרַגְלֵינוּ קַלּוֹת כָּאַיָּלוֹת, אֵין אֲנַחְנוּ מַסְפִּיקִים לְהוֹדוֹת לְךָ, יהוה אֱלֹהֵינוּ וֵאלֹהֵי אֲבוֹתֵינוּ, וּלְבָרֵךְ אֶת שְׁמֶךָ עַל אַחַת מֵאָלֶף אֶלֶף אַלְפֵי אֲלָפִים וְרִבֵּי רְבָבוֹת פְּעָמִים הַטּוֹבוֹת שֶׁעָשִׂיתָ עִם אֲבוֹתֵינוּ וְעִמָּנוּ. מִמִּצְרַיִם גְּאַלְתָּנוּ יהוה אֱלֹהֵינוּ, וּמִבֵּית עֲבָדִים פְּדִיתָנוּ. בְּרָעָב זַנְתָּנוּ, וּבְשָׂבָע כִּלְכַּלְתָּנוּ, מֵחֶרֶב הִצַּלְתָּנוּ, וּמִדֶּבֶר מִלַּטְתָּנוּ, וּמֵחֳלָיִם רָעִים וְנֶאֱמָנִים דִּלִּיתָנוּ. עַד הֵנָּה עֲזָרוּנוּ רַחֲמֶיךָ, וְלֹא עֲזָבוּנוּ חֲסָדֶיךָ. וְאַל תִּטְּשֵׁנוּ יהוה אֱלֹהֵינוּ לָנֶצַח. עַל כֵּן אֵבָרִים שֶׁפִּלַּגְתָּ בָּנוּ, וְרוּחַ וּנְשָׁמָה שֶׁנָּפַחְתָּ בְּאַפֵּינוּ, וְלָשׁוֹן אֲשֶׁר שַׂמְתָּ בְּפִינוּ,

---

עַל אַחַת מֵאָלֶף אֶלֶף אַלְפֵי אֲלָפִים וְרִבֵּי רְבָבוֹת פְּעָמִים הַטּוֹבוֹת שֶׁעָשִׂיתָ — *For Even One of the Thousand Thousand, Thousands of Thousands, and Myriad Myriads of Favors That You Performed*

- ❒ **If Hashem is performing billions of miracles for us all the time, why are we not aware of them?**
- ❒ **If we pay attention, we will see that Hashem is with us every second, helping us. And for every miracle we recognize, there are tens of thousands we have not even thought of that are happening all the time.**

We proclaim to Hashem that even if we had all of the capabilities this world has to offer, we could not even properly thank Him for a single one of the *many* miracles He has performed for us and our forefathers. How many? *Alef elef alfei alafim* is a thousand thousands (one million) multiplied by a thousand (one billion), and again by a thousand, which totals one trillion. And *ribei revavos* means ten thousand times ten thousand, which equals a hundred million. So, we are saying that Hashem performs an astronomical number of miracles for us. I would challenge the reader to recall the last miracle they witnessed. If there are billions of miracles happening, you should be able to mention *one,* right? And even though Klal Yisrael's existence and survival through the ages has been nothing short

of waves, and our lips as full of praise as the breadth of the heavens, and our eyes as brilliant as the sun and the moon, and our hands as outspread [in prayer] as eagles of the sky and our feet as swift as deer, we still could not sufficiently thank You, HASHEM our God and the God of our forefathers, and bless Your Name for even one of the thousand thousand, thousands of thousands, and myriad myriads of favors, that You performed for our ancestors and for us. You redeemed us from Mitzrayim, HASHEM our God, and liberated us from the house of bondage. In famine You nourished us and in plenty You supported us. From the sword You saved us; from plague You let us escape; and You spared us from severe and enduring diseases. Until now Your mercy has helped us and Your kindness has not forsaken us; do not abandon us, HASHEM, our God, for eternity. Therefore, the limbs that You have set within us, and the spirit and soul that You breathed into our nostrils, and the tongue that You have placed in our mouth,

---

of miraculous, how many miracles is that? It is surely a lot, but a million is a big number; and a billion is a very big number, never mind a trillion. So, what does it mean when we say that there are so many miracles occurring all the time?

But this I can tell you with clarity; every single day, I see miracles that Hashem does for me, personally. It happens all the time that I will be walking and I will catch my foot on something, perhaps a rise in the carpet, or because I could not lift my foot high enough as I walked, or I might slip on something. In any one of these cases, I could have, Heaven forbid, fallen and hit my head on something hard or pointy. Zaidy-proofing a house is not as simple as baby-proofing it! But there is something to be said for Zaidy-proofing a house too. And as excellent as the care my family surrounds me with is, it cannot be foolproof. So, I see Hashem's *hashgachah* dozens of times a day, and sometimes hundreds of times, because it is difficult and sometimes precarious for me to walk around. And with each step, Hashem is holding my hand, in one way or another.

When we train ourselves to look at our lives in this way, every breath, every step we take, every word we speak, and every time we use the bathroom, many, many miracles are occurring; and indeed, it would take all of time to thank Hashem for even a single one of them.

הֵן הֵם יוֹדוּ וִיבָרְכוּ וִישַׁבְּחוּ וִיפָאֲרוּ וִירוֹמְמוּ וְיַעֲרִיצוּ וְיַקְדִּישׁוּ וְיַמְלִיכוּ אֶת שִׁמְךָ מַלְכֵּנוּ. כִּי כָל פֶּה לְךָ יוֹדֶה, וְכָל לָשׁוֹן לְךָ תִשָּׁבַע, וְכָל בֶּרֶךְ לְךָ תִכְרַע, וְכָל קוֹמָה לְפָנֶיךָ תִשְׁתַּחֲוֶה, וְכָל לְבָבוֹת יִירָאוּךָ, וְכָל קֶרֶב וּכְלָיוֹת יְזַמְּרוּ לִשְׁמֶךָ, כַּדָּבָר שֶׁכָּתוּב: כָּל עַצְמֹתַי תֹּאמַרְנָה, יהוה מִי כָמוֹךָ, מַצִּיל עָנִי מֵחָזָק מִמֶּנּוּ, וְעָנִי וְאֶבְיוֹן מִגֹּזְלוֹ[1]. מִי יִדְמֶה לָּךְ, וּמִי יִשְׁוֶה לָּךְ, וּמִי יַעֲרָךְ לָךְ. הָאֵל הַגָּדוֹל הַגִּבּוֹר וְהַנּוֹרָא, אֵל עֶלְיוֹן, קֹנֵה שָׁמַיִם וָאָרֶץ. נְהַלֶּלְךָ וּנְשַׁבֵּחֲךָ וּנְפָאֶרְךָ וּנְבָרֵךְ אֶת שֵׁם קָדְשֶׁךָ, כָּאָמוּר: לְדָוִד, בָּרְכִי נַפְשִׁי אֶת יהוה, וְכָל קְרָבַי אֶת שֵׁם קָדְשׁוֹ[2].

הָאֵל בְּתַעֲצֻמוֹת עֻזֶּךָ, הַגָּדוֹל בִּכְבוֹד שְׁמֶךָ, הַגִּבּוֹר לָנֶצַח וְהַנּוֹרָא בְּנוֹרְאוֹתֶיךָ. הַמֶּלֶךְ הַיּוֹשֵׁב עַל כִּסֵּא רָם וְנִשָּׂא.

שׁוֹכֵן עַד מָרוֹם וְקָדוֹשׁ שְׁמוֹ. וְכָתוּב: רַנְּנוּ צַדִּיקִים בַּיהוה לַיְשָׁרִים נָאוָה תְהִלָּה[3]. בְּפִי יְשָׁרִים תִּתְהַלָּל. וּבְדִבְרֵי צַדִּיקִים תִּתְבָּרַךְ. וּבִלְשׁוֹן חֲסִידִים תִּתְרוֹמָם. וּבְקֶרֶב קְדוֹשִׁים תִּתְקַדָּשׁ.

וּבְמַקְהֲלוֹת רִבְבוֹת עַמְּךָ בֵּית יִשְׂרָאֵל, בְּרִנָּה יִתְפָּאַר שִׁמְךָ מַלְכֵּנוּ בְּכָל דּוֹר וָדוֹר. שֶׁכֵּן חוֹבַת כָּל הַיְצוּרִים, לְפָנֶיךָ יהוה אֱלֹהֵינוּ וֵאלֹהֵי אֲבוֹתֵינוּ, לְהוֹדוֹת לְהַלֵּל לְשַׁבֵּחַ לְפָאֵר לְרוֹמֵם לְהַדֵּר לְבָרֵךְ לְעַלֵּה וּלְקַלֵּס, עַל כָּל דִּבְרֵי שִׁירוֹת וְתִשְׁבְּחוֹת דָּוִד בֶּן יִשַׁי עַבְדְּךָ מְשִׁיחֶךָ.

---

(1) *Tehillim* 35:10. (2) 103:1. (3) 33:1.

they shall thank and bless, praise and glorify, exalt, be devoted to, sanctify, and do homage to Your Name, our King forever. For every mouth shall offer thanks to You; every tongue shall vow allegiance to You; every knee shall bend to You; all who stand erect shall bow before You; all hearts shall fear You; and all men's innermost feelings and thoughts shall sing praises to Your Name, as it is written: "All my bones declare: HASHEM, who is like You? You save the poor man from one stronger than him, the poor and needy from one who would rob him."[1] Who may be likened to You? Who is equal to You? Who can be compared to You? O great, mighty, and awesome God, supreme God, Maker of Heaven and earth. We shall praise, acclaim, and glorify You and bless Your holy Name, as it is said, "To David: Bless HASHEM, O my soul, and let my whole inner being bless His holy Name!"[2]

O God, in the omnipotence of Your strength, great in the honor of Your Name, powerful forever and awesome through Your awesome deeds, O King enthroned upon a high and lofty throne!

He Who abides forever, exalted and holy is His Name. And it is written: "Rejoice in HASHEM, you righteous; for the upright, His praise is pleasant."[3] By the mouth of the upright You shall be praised; by the words of the righteous You shall be blessed; by the tongue of the pious You shall be exalted; and amid the holy You shall be sanctified.

And in the assemblies of the myriads of Your people, the House of Yisrael, with jubilation shall Your Name, our King, be glorified in every generation. For such is the duty of all creatures — before You, HASHEM, our God, and the God of our fathers, to thank, praise, laud, glorify, exalt, adore, bless, raise high, and sing praises — even beyond all expressions of the songs and praises of David, the son of Yishai, Your servant, Your anointed.

יִשְׁתַּבַּח שִׁמְךָ לָעַד, מַלְכֵּנוּ, הָאֵל הַמֶּלֶךְ הַגָּדוֹל וְהַקָּדוֹשׁ, בַּשָּׁמַיִם וּבָאָרֶץ. כִּי לְךָ נָאֶה, יהוה אֱלֹהֵינוּ וֵאלֹהֵי אֲבוֹתֵינוּ, שִׁיר וּשְׁבָחָה, הַלֵּל וְזִמְרָה, עֹז וּמֶמְשָׁלָה, נֶצַח גְּדֻלָּה וּגְבוּרָה, תְּהִלָּה וְתִפְאֶרֶת, קְדֻשָּׁה וּמַלְכוּת, בְּרָכוֹת וְהוֹדָאוֹת מֵעַתָּה וְעַד עוֹלָם. בָּרוּךְ אַתָּה יהוה, אֵל מֶלֶךְ גָּדוֹל בַּתִּשְׁבָּחוֹת, אֵל הַהוֹדָאוֹת, אֲדוֹן הַנִּפְלָאוֹת, הַבּוֹחֵר בְּשִׁירֵי זִמְרָה, מֶלֶךְ אֵל חֵי הָעוֹלָמִים.

The blessing over wine is recited, and the fourth cup is drunk while reclining on the left side. It is preferable to drink the entire cup, but at the very least, most of the cup should be drunk. If this is too difficult, even when using the smallest cup that holds a *reviis*, one must at the very least drink a cheekful.

בָּרוּךְ אַתָּה יהוה אֱלֹהֵינוּ מֶלֶךְ הָעוֹלָם, בּוֹרֵא פְּרִי הַגָּפֶן.

After drinking the fourth cup, the concluding blessing is recited, provided one drank a *reviis* from either the third or the fourth cup. On Shabbos, include the passage in brackets.

בָּרוּךְ אַתָּה יהוה אֱלֹהֵינוּ מֶלֶךְ הָעוֹלָם, עַל הַגֶּפֶן וְעַל פְּרִי הַגֶּפֶן, וְעַל תְּנוּבַת הַשָּׂדֶה, וְעַל אֶרֶץ חֶמְדָּה טוֹבָה וּרְחָבָה, שֶׁרָצִיתָ וְהִנְחַלְתָּ לַאֲבוֹתֵינוּ, לֶאֱכוֹל מִפִּרְיָהּ וְלִשְׂבּוֹעַ מִטּוּבָהּ. רַחֵם (נָא) יהוה אֱלֹהֵינוּ עַל יִשְׂרָאֵל עַמֶּךָ, וְעַל יְרוּשָׁלַיִם עִירֶךָ, וְעַל צִיּוֹן מִשְׁכַּן כְּבוֹדֶךָ, וְעַל מִזְבְּחֶךָ וְעַל הֵיכָלֶךָ. וּבְנֵה יְרוּשָׁלַיִם עִיר הַקֹּדֶשׁ בִּמְהֵרָה בְיָמֵינוּ, וְהַעֲלֵנוּ לְתוֹכָהּ, וְשַׂמְּחֵנוּ בְּבִנְיָנָהּ, וְנֹאכַל מִפִּרְיָהּ, וְנִשְׂבַּע מִטּוּבָהּ, וּנְבָרֶכְךָ עָלֶיהָ בִּקְדֻשָּׁה וּבְטָהֳרָה [וּרְצֵה וְהַחֲלִיצֵנוּ בְּיוֹם הַשַּׁבָּת הַזֶּה]. וְשַׂמְּחֵנוּ בְּיוֹם חַג הַמַּצּוֹת הַזֶּה. כִּי אַתָּה יהוה טוֹב וּמֵטִיב לַכֹּל, וְנוֹדֶה לְּךָ עַל הָאָרֶץ וְעַל פְּרִי הַגָּפֶן. בָּרוּךְ אַתָּה יהוה, עַל הָאָרֶץ וְעַל פְּרִי הַגָּפֶן.

MINHAGIM

Often, there are people at the *Seder* who are not sure if they drank a full *reviis*. The *minhag* at the *Rosh HaYeshiva, shlit"a's Sedarim* is therefore

Praised be Your Name forever, our King, the God, and King Who is great and holy in Heaven and on earth; for to You, HASHEM, our God, and the God of our fathers, it is fitting to render song and praise, *Hallel* and hymns, power and dominion, victory, greatness and might, praise and glory, holiness and sovereignty, blessings and thanksgivings, from now and forever. Blessed are You, HASHEM, God, King, great in praises, God of thanksgivings, Master of wonders, Who favors songs of praise — King, God, Life of all worlds.

The blessing over wine is recited, and the fourth cup is drunk while reclining on the left side. It is preferable to drink the entire cup, but at the very least, most of the cup should be drunk. If this is too difficult, even when using the smallest cup that holds a *reviis*, one must at the very least drink a cheekful.

Blessed are You, HASHEM, our God, King of the universe, Who creates the fruit of the vine.

After drinking the fourth cup, the concluding blessing is recited, provided one drank a *reviis* from either the third or the fourth cup. On Shabbos, include the passage in brackets.

Blessed are You, HASHEM, our God, King of the universe, for the vine and the fruit of the vine, and for the produce of the field. For the desirable, good, and spacious Land that You were pleased to give our forefathers as a heritage, to eat of its fruit and to be satisfied with its goodness. Have mercy, (we beg You,) HASHEM, our God, on Yisrael, Your people; on Yerushalayim, Your city; on Tzion, resting place of Your glory; Your *Mizbei'ach*, and Your *Beis HaMikdash*. Rebuild Yerushalayim the city of holiness, speedily in our days. Bring us up into it and gladden us in its rebuilding, and let us eat from its fruit and be satisfied with its goodness and bless You upon it in holiness and purity. [Favor us and strengthen us on this Shabbos day] and grant us happiness on this Festival of Matzos; for You, HASHEM, are good and do good to all, and we thank You for the land and for the fruit of the vine. Blessed are You, HASHEM, for the Land and for the fruit of the vine.

MINHAGIM

that either he or someone else who definitely drank a *reviis* recites *Al Hagefen* at this point for all the participants who want to be *yotzei* with him.

נרצה

חֲסַל סִדּוּר פֶּסַח כְּהִלְכָתוֹ, כְּכָל מִשְׁפָּטוֹ וְחֻקָּתוֹ. כַּאֲשֶׁר זָכִינוּ לְסַדֵּר אוֹתוֹ, כֵּן נִזְכֶּה לַעֲשׂוֹתוֹ. זָךְ שׁוֹכֵן מְעוֹנָה, קוֹמֵם קְהַל עֲדַת מִי מָנָה. בְּקָרוֹב נַהֵל נִטְעֵי כַנָּה, פְּדוּיִם לְצִיּוֹן בְּרִנָּה.

לְשָׁנָה הַבָּאָה בִּירוּשָׁלָיִם.

It was the *minhag* of the Rosh HaYeshiva, *ztvk"l,* to recite both of the following *piyutim* on both *Seder* nights.

וּבְכֵן וַיְהִי בַּחֲצִי הַלַּיְלָה.

אָז רוֹב נִסִּים הִפְלֵאתָ בַּלַּיְלָה,
בְּרֹאשׁ אַשְׁמוֹרֶת זֶה הַלַּיְלָה,
גֵּר צֶדֶק נִצַּחְתּוֹ כְּנֶחֱלַק לוֹ לַיְלָה,
וַיְהִי בַּחֲצִי הַלַּיְלָה.

דַּנְתָּ מֶלֶךְ גְּרָר בַּחֲלוֹם הַלַּיְלָה,
הִפְחַדְתָּ אֲרַמִּי בְּאֶמֶשׁ לַיְלָה,
וַיָּשַׂר יִשְׂרָאֵל לְמַלְאָךְ וַיּוּכַל לוֹ לַיְלָה,
וַיְהִי בַּחֲצִי הַלַּיְלָה.

לְשָׁנָה הַבָּאָה בִּירוּשָׁלָיִם — ***Next Year in Yerushalayim***

❐ **This prayer should also be a declaration that we are ready to have a *Yetziah* from our current exile.**

The prayer for *Leshanah Haba'ah* expresses the timeless prayer of Klal Yisrael. But tonight, it is so much more than that. See above, *Ha Lachma Anya*. There, we explained that we begin the *Seder* expressing our realization that we, just like the generation who experienced the Exodus, are also awaiting our own exodus from exile. We stressed this idea in *Bechol Dor VaDor,* explaining that we too must be ready to disengage from the cultures we are among in our exile. At the conclusion of the *Seder,* with the declaration of *Leshanah Haba'ah BiYerushalayim,* we proclaim, "We

Nirtzah

The *Seder* is now concluded in accordance with its laws, with all its ordinances and statutes. Just as we were privileged to arrange it, so may we merit to perform it. O Pure One, Who dwells on High, raise up the countless congregation, soon — guide the offshoots of Your plants, redeemed to Tziyon with glad song.

Next Year In Yerushalayim

It was the *minhag* of the *Rosh HaYeshiva, ztvk"l,* to recite both of the following *piyutim* on both *Seder* nights.

It came to pass at midnight.

You have, of old, performed many wonders by night.
At the head of the watches of this night,
To the righteous convert (Avraham)
You gave triumph by dividing for him the night.
It came to pass at midnight.

You judged the king of Gerar (Avimelech),
in a dream by night.
You frightened the Aramean (Lavan), in the dark of night.
Yisrael (Yaakov) fought with an angel
and overcame him by night.
It came to pass at midnight.

---

are ready to be redeemed, just as Hashem wants us to be! May we merit to see *Mashiach* soon!

וַיְהִי בַּחֲצִי הַלַּיְלָה ... וַאֲמַרְתֶּם זֶבַח פֶּסַח — *It Came to Pass at Midnight ... And You Shall Say: This Is the Feast of Pesach*

- **These *piyutim* discuss many occurrences that are unrelated to *Yetzias Mitzrayim*. Why is it appropriate to discuss these now?**
- **At the Burning Bush, Hashem had assured Moshe Rabbeinu that He would be with Klal Yisrael always, in all the travails they would face. Moshe asked Hashem not to reveal this to the nation then, so they would not be overwhelmed by the specter of future *nisyonos*.**
- **But now, in hindsight, we recognize Hashem's help through all of those difficulties, and thank Him for it!**

זֶרַע בְּכוֹרֵי פַּתְרוֹס מָחַצְתָּ בַּחֲצִי הַלַּיְלָה,
חֵילָם לֹא מָצְאוּ בְּקוּמָם בַּלַּיְלָה,
טִישַׁת נְגִיד חֲרוֹשֶׁת סִלִּיתָ בְּכוֹכְבֵי לַיְלָה,
וַיְהִי בַּחֲצִי הַלַּיְלָה.

יָעַץ מְחָרֵף לְנוֹפֵף אִוּוּי הוֹבַשְׁתָּ פְגָרָיו בַּלַּיְלָה,
כָּרַע בֵּל וּמַצָּבוֹ בְּאִישׁוֹן לַיְלָה,
לְאִישׁ חֲמוּדוֹת נִגְלָה רָז חֲזוֹת לַיְלָה,
וַיְהִי בַּחֲצִי הַלַּיְלָה.

מִשְׁתַּכֵּר בִּכְלֵי קֹדֶשׁ נֶהֱרַג בּוֹ בַּלַּיְלָה,
נוֹשַׁע מִבּוֹר אֲרָיוֹת פּוֹתֵר בִּעֲתוּתֵי לַיְלָה,
שִׂנְאָה נָטַר אֲגָגִי וְכָתַב סְפָרִים בַּלַּיְלָה,
וַיְהִי בַּחֲצִי הַלַּיְלָה.

The *piyutim* cited here in the *Haggadah* are not limited to discussion of the slavery of Klal Yisrael in Mitzrayim. They also discuss events that occurred later on in our history, such as the salvation from such enemies as Sisera, Sancheirev, and Haman; we mention the downfall of Belshatzar, and the impending arrival of *Mashiach*. Why are we mentioning these other salvations now?

When Hashem was instructing Moshe Rabbeinu at the *S'neh* (Burning Bush) to go and emancipate Klal Yisrael, Moshe asked Hashem what he should tell them. Hashem replied (*Shemos* 3:14), *Eheyeh asher Eheyeh. And He said, So shall you say to Bnei Yisrael, Eheyeh has sent me to you.* This *posuk* is hard to understand. At first glance, it appears as though Hashem told Moshe to relate to Klal Yisrael that he had been sent by *Eheyeh asher Eheyeh*. Then, immediately, Hashem seemingly issued a second directive, which was to tell them that he had been sent by *Eheyeh*! *Rashi* (ibid, *d"h Eheyeh asher Eheyeh*) explains the two different descriptions of Hashem as follows: *Eheyeh asher Eheyeh* (literally, *I Am that I Am*) alludes to the fact that Hashem is constantly with us, i.e., *I Am* with you in this travail and *I Am* also with you in all future travails. The expression *Eheyeh* (literally, *I Am*), on the other hand, connotes only that Hashem is with us in the current difficult situation. *Rashi* further elaborates that, in between the two directives Hashem gave, Moshe Rabbeinu had exclaimed, "Master of the world! Why must I mention other travails to the Bnei Yisrael

Mitzrayim's firstborn You crushed at midnight.
Their host they found not upon arising at night.
The army of the prince of Charoshes (Sisera)
You swept away with stars of the night.
It came to pass at midnight.

The blasphemer (Sancheiriv) planned to raise
his hand [against Yerushalayim] —
but You withered his corpses by night.
Bel was overturned with its pedestal, in the darkness of night.
To the man of Your delights (Daniel)
was revealed the mystery of the visions of night.
It came to pass at midnight.

He (Belshatzar) who caroused with the holy vessels
was killed that very night.
From the lions' den was rescued he (Daniel)
who interpreted the "terrors" of the night.
The Agagite (Haman) nursed hatred
and wrote decrees at night.
It came to pass at midnight.

— it is enough for them that they are going through this current difficulty!" Thereupon, Hashem replied to Moshe, "What you are saying is proper! [Rather,] so shall you say, etc." Hashem then issued the second directive, to only mention *Eheyeh,* referencing only the exile in Mitzrayim.

We see, then, that there was a discussion between Hashem and Moshe regarding precisely how Moshe should identify Hashem to Klal Yisrael. It is clear from *Rashi* that the idea of this identification was not only to describe Hashem as being the God of the forefathers of the Jewish people who was sending Moshe, but that there was also a message of hope that was to be delivered to them as well. Initially, Hashem told Moshe to use one expression, but Moshe protested that using that expression would cause Klal Yisrael to actually lose hope rather than instill hope in them, and so Hashem changed His command, telling Moshe to instead use a different expression.

This understanding begs the following questions: Firstly, why did Hashem initially choose an expression that was, in fact, not the most superior one? And secondly, does the fact that Hashem will be with us in the future not give us more encouragement, rather than hopelessness?

עוֹרַרְתָּ נִצְחֲךָ עָלָיו בְּנֶדֶד שְׁנַת לַיְלָה,
פּוּרָה תִדְרוֹךְ לְשׁוֹמֵר מַה מִלַּיְלָה,
צָרַח כַּשּׁוֹמֵר וְשָׂח אָתָא בֹקֶר וְגַם לַיְלָה,
וַיְהִי בַּחֲצִי הַלַּיְלָה.

קָרֵב יוֹם אֲשֶׁר הוּא לֹא יוֹם וְלֹא לַיְלָה,
רָם הוֹדַע כִּי לְךָ הַיּוֹם אַף לְךָ הַלַּיְלָה,
שׁוֹמְרִים הַפְקֵד לְעִירְךָ כָּל הַיּוֹם וְכָל הַלַּיְלָה,
תָּאִיר כְּאוֹר יוֹם חֶשְׁכַת לַיְלָה,
וַיְהִי בַּחֲצִי הַלַּיְלָה.

Did Moshe presume that Klal Yisrael were under the impression that this would be the very last *galus* they would ever face?

It seems to me that the truth is that of course *Eheyeh asher Eheyeh* is a greater comfort to those who have the openness of mind to think globally. In other words, someone who has already lived through both a difficult situation and Hashem's salvation from it will be comforted by the thought that Hashem will always be there in every future difficulty he will ever face, and it will enable him to be secure in the knowledge that He will always provide salvation. However, in a scenario where someone is born into a situation of slavery and has never yet experienced Hashem's salvation from that situation, he can often be afflicted with tunnel vision. He cannot see past his pain and desperation, and therefore cannot picture in his mind's eye the salvation that Hashem is yet going to bring him. In that situation, mentioning that Hashem is the One Who will save him from future travails only serves to weigh down his heart. Instead of taking the message as it is intended — to mean that Hashem will always save him — he might well take it to mean that even the long-awaited salvation he yearns for will only be temporary. This can be a crushing blow to his psyche and can cause him to give up hope.

Accordingly, we may explain as follows: Hashem had actually directed Moshe to use the expression that would offer the most comfort — the formula which most accurately reflected the relationship that Hashem has with Klal Yisrael — that He will be with us always. Hashem also knew that it would be hard for Klal Yisrael to swallow this message, due to their tunnel vision, but once they would, the comfort would be more real. Moshe Rabbeinu, though, begged Hashem for mercy; that He allow Moshe to

You began Your triumph over him
  when You disturbed (Achashveirosh's) sleep at night.
Trample the winepress to help those who ask
  the watchman, "What of the long night?"
He will shout, like a watchman, and say:
  "Morning shall come after night."
It came to pass at midnight.

Hasten the day (of *Mashiach*), that is neither day nor night.
Most High — make known that Yours are day and night.
Appoint guards for Your city, all the day and all the night.
Brighten like the light of day the darkness of night.
It came to pass at midnight.

---

carry a lighter message, which would be more palatable for Klal Yisrael in their current situation — even though it would be a more temporary comfort, and less reflective of Hashem's true nature.

Of course, even people who are in the throes of pain brought about by a sorry situation also realize that this problem will likely not be their very last. But if they hear that Hashem will save them from this travail and future travails, they are apt to worry that perhaps they will never merit Hashem's salvation, and even if this difficulty does not totally overwhelm them, the next one might. It was in response to this concern that Hashem told Moshe to relate to Klal Yisrael that He is *Eheyeh*, and is with them. As the next *posuk* continues, Hashem also told Moshe to relate that He is Hashem, the God of their forefathers — the God of Avraham, the God of Yitzchak, and the God of Yaakov. By doing so, Hashem sent a reassuring message to Klal Yisrael. He was telling them that they would be saved in the merits of their forefathers. This would not stir worry in their hearts, because they would not be confronted with the fear of lack of merits — they would always remain their forefathers' descendants. Again, even this was not as crystal-clear a message as *Eheyeh asher Eheyeh* would have been, for that would have referenced concrete future tribulations and salvations, whereas this gentler message referenced salvation from this travail and also eternal merits, but not definitive future difficulties and salvations.

Looking back over the millennia, Hashem has been with us the entire time, through every step of the way, and every *nisayon* our nation has faced. So, while Moshe was cautious that in Mitzrayim we would be afraid to hear that Hashem will be with us through our future travails, we can now, in hindsight, definitively praise Hashem for the salvations that we were too fragile to hear about before they occurred.

וּבְכֵן וַאֲמַרְתֶּם זֶבַח פֶּסַח:

אֹמֶץ גְּבוּרוֹתֶיךָ הִפְלֵאתָ בַּפֶּסַח.
בְּרֹאשׁ כָּל מוֹעֲדוֹת נִשֵּׂאתָ פֶּסַח.
גִּלִּיתָ לְאֶזְרָחִי חֲצוֹת לֵיל פֶּסַח.
וַאֲמַרְתֶּם זֶבַח פֶּסַח.

דְּלָתָיו דָּפַקְתָּ כְּחֹם הַיּוֹם בַּפֶּסַח.
הִסְעִיד נוֹצְצִים עֻגוֹת מַצּוֹת בַּפֶּסַח.
וְאֶל הַבָּקָר רָץ זֵכֶר לְשׁוֹר עֵרֶךְ פֶּסַח.
וַאֲמַרְתֶּם זֶבַח פֶּסַח.

זוֹעֲמוּ סְדוֹמִים וְלוֹהֲטוּ בָּאֵשׁ בַּפֶּסַח.
חֻלַּץ לוֹט מֵהֶם וּמַצּוֹת אָפָה בְּקֵץ פֶּסַח.
טִאטֵאתָ אַדְמַת מוֹף וְנוֹף בְּעָבְרְךָ בַּפֶּסַח.
וַאֲמַרְתֶּם זֶבַח פֶּסַח.

יָהּ רֹאשׁ כָּל אוֹן מָחַצְתָּ בְּלֵיל שִׁמּוּר פֶּסַח.
כַּבִּיר עַל בֵּן בְּכוֹר פָּסַחְתָּ בְּדַם פֶּסַח.
לְבִלְתִּי תֵּת מַשְׁחִית לָבֹא בִּפְתָחַי בַּפֶּסַח.
וַאֲמַרְתֶּם זֶבַח פֶּסַח.

מְסֻגֶּרֶת סֻגָּרָה בְּעִתּוֹתֵי פֶּסַח.
נִשְׁמְדָה מִדְיָן בִּצְלִיל שְׂעוֹרֵי עֹמֶר פֶּסַח.
שׂוֹרְפוּ מִשְׁמַנֵּי פּוּל וְלוּד בִּיקַד יְקוֹד פֶּסַח.
וַאֲמַרְתֶּם זֶבַח פֶּסַח.

עוֹד הַיּוֹם בְּנֹב לַעֲמוֹד עַד גָּעָה עוֹנַת פֶּסַח.
פַּס יַד כָּתְבָה לְקַעֲקֵעַ צוּל בַּפֶּסַח.
צָפֹה הַצָּפִית עָרוֹךְ הַשֻּׁלְחָן בַּפֶּסַח.
וַאֲמַרְתֶּם זֶבַח פֶּסַח.

And you shall say: This is the feast of Pesach.

You displayed wondrously Your mighty powers on Pesach.
Above all festivals You elevated Pesach.
To the Oriental (Avraham) You revealed
the future midnight of Pesach.
And you shall say: This is the feast of Pesach.

At his door You knocked in the heat of the day on Pesach;
He satiated the angels with *matzah*-cakes on Pesach.
And he ran to the herd —
symbolic of the sacrificial feast of Pesach.
And you shall say: This is the feast of Pesach.

The Sedomites provoked (God)
and were devoured by fire on Pesach;
Lot was withdrawn from them —
he had baked *matzos* at the time of Pesach.
You swept clean the soil of Mof and Nof (in Mitzrayim)
when You passed through on Pesach.
And you shall say: This is the feast of Pesach.

God, You crushed every firstborn of On (in Mitzrayim)
on the watchful night of Pesach.
But Master — Your own firstborn,
You skipped by merit of the blood of Pesach,
Not to allow the Destroyer to enter my doors on Pesach.
And you shall say: This is the feast of Pesach.

The beleaguered (Yericho) was besieged on Pesach.
Midyan was destroyed with a barley cake,
from the *Omer* of Pesach.
The mighty nobles of Pul and Lud (Ashur) were
consumed in a great conflagration on Pesach.
And you shall say: This is the feast of Pesach.

He (Sancheiriv) would have stood that day at Nov,
but for the advent of Pesach.
A hand inscribed the destruction of Zul (Bavel) on Pesach.
As the watch was set, and the royal table decked on Pesach.
And you shall say: This is the feast of Pesach.

קָהָל כִּנְּסָה הֲדַסָּה צוֹם לְשַׁלֵּשׁ בַּפֶּסַח.
רֹאשׁ מִבֵּית רָשָׁע מָחַצְתָּ בְּעֵץ חֲמִשִּׁים בַּפֶּסַח.
שְׁתֵּי אֵלֶּה רֶגַע תָּבִיא לְעוּצִית בַּפֶּסַח.
תָּעֹז יָדְךָ וְתָרוּם יְמִינְךָ כְּלֵיל הִתְקַדֵּשׁ חַג פֶּסַח.
וַאֲמַרְתֶּם זֶבַח פֶּסַח.

כִּי לוֹ נָאֶה, כִּי לוֹ יָאֶה:

אַדִּיר בִּמְלוּכָה, **בָּ**חוּר כַּהֲלָכָה, **גְּ**דוּדָיו יֹאמְרוּ לוֹ, לְךָ וּלְךָ, לְךָ כִּי לְךָ, לְךָ אַף לְךָ, לְךָ יהוה הַמַּמְלָכָה, כִּי לוֹ נָאֶה, כִּי לוֹ יָאֶה.

דָּגוּל בִּמְלוּכָה, **הָ**דוּר כַּהֲלָכָה, **וָ**תִיקָיו יֹאמְרוּ לוֹ, לְךָ וּלְךָ, לְךָ כִּי לְךָ, לְךָ אַף לְךָ, לְךָ יהוה הַמַּמְלָכָה, כִּי לוֹ נָאֶה, כִּי לוֹ יָאֶה.

זַכַּאי בִּמְלוּכָה, **חָ**סִין כַּהֲלָכָה, **טַ**פְסְרָיו יֹאמְרוּ לוֹ, לְךָ וּלְךָ, לְךָ כִּי לְךָ, לְךָ אַף לְךָ, לְךָ יהוה הַמַּמְלָכָה, כִּי לוֹ נָאֶה, כִּי לוֹ יָאֶה.

יָחִיד בִּמְלוּכָה, **כַּ**בִּיר כַּהֲלָכָה, **לִ**מּוּדָיו יֹאמְרוּ לוֹ, לְךָ וּלְךָ, לְךָ כִּי לְךָ, לְךָ אַף לְךָ, לְךָ יהוה הַמַּמְלָכָה, כִּי לוֹ נָאֶה, כִּי לוֹ יָאֶה.

מוֹשֵׁל בִּמְלוּכָה, **נ**וֹרָא כַּהֲלָכָה, **סְ**בִיבָיו יֹאמְרוּ לוֹ, לְךָ וּלְךָ, לְךָ כִּי לְךָ, לְךָ אַף לְךָ, לְךָ יהוה הַמַּמְלָכָה, כִּי לוֹ נָאֶה, כִּי לוֹ יָאֶה.

עָנָיו בִּמְלוּכָה, **פּ**וֹדֶה כַּהֲלָכָה, **צַ**דִּיקָיו יֹאמְרוּ לוֹ, לְךָ וּלְךָ, לְךָ כִּי לְךָ, לְךָ אַף לְךָ, לְךָ יהוה הַמַּמְלָכָה, כִּי לוֹ נָאֶה, כִּי לוֹ יָאֶה.

קָדוֹשׁ בִּמְלוּכָה, **רַ**חוּם כַּהֲלָכָה, **שִׁ**נְאַנָּיו יֹאמְרוּ לוֹ,

Hadassah (Esther) gathered a congregation
for a three-day fast on Pesach.
You caused the head of the evil clan (Haman)
to be hanged on a fifty-cubit gallows on Pesach.
Doubly, will You bring in an instant upon Utzis (Edom) on Pesach.
Let Your hand be strong, and Your right arm exalted,
as on that night when You hallowed the Festival of Pesach.
And you shall say: This is the feast of Pesach.

To Him praise is due! To Him praise is fitting!

Mighty in majesty, perfectly distinguished, His companies of angels say to Him: Yours and only Yours; Yours, yes Yours; Yours, surely Yours; Yours, HASHEM, is the sovereignty. To Him praise is due! To Him praise is fitting!

Supreme in kingship, perfectly glorious, His faithful say to Him: Yours and only Yours; Yours, yes Yours; Yours, surely Yours; Yours, HASHEM, is the sovereignty. To Him praise is due! To Him praise is fitting!

Pure in kingship, perfectly mighty, His angels say to Him: Yours and only Yours; Yours, yes Yours; Yours, surely Yours; Yours, HASHEM, is the sovereignty. To Him praise is due! To Him praise is fitting!

Alone in kingship, perfectly Omnipotent, His wise ones say to Him: Yours and only Yours; Yours, yes Yours; Yours, surely Yours; Yours, HASHEM, is the sovereignty. To Him praise is due! To Him praise is fitting!

Commanding in kingship, perfectly wondrous, His surrounding (angels) say to Him: Yours and only Yours; Yours, yes Yours; Yours, surely Yours; Yours, HASHEM, is the sovereignty. To Him praise is due! To Him praise is fitting!

Humble in kingship, perfectly the Redeemer, His righteous say to Him: Yours and only Yours; Yours, yes Yours; Yours, surely Yours; Yours, HASHEM, is the sovereignty. To Him praise is due! To Him praise is fitting!

Holy in kingship, perfectly merciful, His troops of angels say

לְךָ וּלְךָ, לְךָ כִּי לְךָ, לְךָ אַף לְךָ, לְךָ יהוה הַמַּמְלָכָה, כִּי לוֹ נָאֶה, כִּי לוֹ יָאֶה.

תַּקִּיף בִּמְלוּכָה, **תּוֹ**מֵךְ כַּהֲלָכָה, **תְּ**מִימָיו יֹאמְרוּ לוֹ, לְךָ וּלְךָ, לְךָ כִּי לְךָ, לְךָ אַף לְךָ, לְךָ יהוה הַמַּמְלָכָה, כִּי לוֹ נָאֶה, כִּי לוֹ יָאֶה.

אַדִּיר הוּא יִבְנֶה בֵיתוֹ בְּקָרוֹב, בִּמְהֵרָה, בִּמְהֵרָה, בְּיָמֵינוּ בְּקָרוֹב. אֵל בְּנֵה, אֵל בְּנֵה, בְּנֵה בֵיתְךָ בְּקָרוֹב.

בָּחוּר הוּא. **גָּ**דוֹל הוּא. **דָּ**גוּל הוּא. יִבְנֶה בֵיתוֹ בְּקָרוֹב, בִּמְהֵרָה, בִּמְהֵרָה, בְּיָמֵינוּ בְּקָרוֹב. אֵל בְּנֵה, אֵל בְּנֵה, בְּנֵה בֵיתְךָ בְּקָרוֹב.

הָדוּר הוּא. **וָ**תִיק הוּא. **זַ**כַּאי הוּא. **חָ**סִיד הוּא. יִבְנֶה בֵיתוֹ בְּקָרוֹב, בִּמְהֵרָה, בִּמְהֵרָה, בְּיָמֵינוּ בְּקָרוֹב. אֵל בְּנֵה, אֵל בְּנֵה, בְּנֵה בֵיתְךָ בְּקָרוֹב.

טָהוֹר הוּא. **יָ**חִיד הוּא. **כַּ**בִּיר הוּא. **לָ**מוּד הוּא. **מֶ**לֶךְ הוּא. **נוֹ**רָא הוּא. **סַ**גִּיב הוּא. **עִ**זּוּז הוּא. **פּוֹ**דֶה הוּא. **צַ**דִּיק הוּא. יִבְנֶה בֵיתוֹ בְּקָרוֹב, בִּמְהֵרָה, בִּמְהֵרָה, בְּיָמֵינוּ בְּקָרוֹב. אֵל בְּנֵה, אֵל בְּנֵה, בְּנֵה בֵיתְךָ בְּקָרוֹב.

קָדוֹשׁ הוּא. **רַ**חוּם הוּא. **שַׁ**דַּי הוּא. **תַּ**קִּיף הוּא. יִבְנֶה בֵיתוֹ בְּקָרוֹב, בִּמְהֵרָה, בִּמְהֵרָה, בְּיָמֵינוּ בְּקָרוֹב. אֵל בְּנֵה, אֵל בְּנֵה, בְּנֵה בֵיתְךָ בְּקָרוֹב.

אֶחָד מִי יוֹדֵעַ? אֶחָד אֲנִי יוֹדֵעַ. אֶחָד אֱלֹהֵינוּ שֶׁבַּשָּׁמַיִם וּבָאָרֶץ.

שְׁנַיִם מִי יוֹדֵעַ? שְׁנַיִם אֲנִי יוֹדֵעַ. שְׁנֵי לֻחוֹת הַבְּרִית, אֶחָד אֱלֹהֵינוּ שֶׁבַּשָּׁמַיִם וּבָאָרֶץ.

שְׁלֹשָׁה מִי יוֹדֵעַ? שְׁלֹשָׁה אֲנִי יוֹדֵעַ. שְׁלֹשָׁה אָבוֹת, שְׁנֵי לֻחוֹת הַבְּרִית, אֶחָד אֱלֹהֵינוּ שֶׁבַּשָּׁמַיִם וּבָאָרֶץ.

to Him: Yours and only Yours; Yours, yes Yours; Yours, surely Yours; Yours, HASHEM, is the sovereignty. To Him praise is due! To Him praise is fitting.

Almighty in kingship, perfectly sustaining, His perfect ones say to Him: Yours and only Yours; Yours, yes Yours; Yours, surely Yours; Yours, HASHEM, is the sovereignty. To Him praise is due! To Him praise is fitting!

He is most mighty. May He soon rebuild His House, speedily, yes speedily, in our days, soon. God, rebuild, God, rebuild, rebuild Your House soon!

He is distinguished, He is great, He is exalted. May He soon rebuild His House, speedily, yes speedily, in our days, soon. God, rebuild, God, rebuild, rebuild Your House soon!

He is all glorious, He is faithful, He is faultless, He is pious. May He soon rebuild His House, speedily, yes speedily, in our days, soon. God, rebuild, God, rebuild, rebuild Your House soon!

He is pure, He is unique, He is powerful, He is all-wise, He is King, He is awesome, He is sublime, He is all-powerful, He is the Redeemer, He is the all-righteous. May He soon rebuild His House, speedily, yes speedily, in our days, soon. God, rebuild, God, rebuild, rebuild Your House soon!

He is holy, He is meciful, He is Almighty, He is omnipotent. May He soon rebuild His House, speedily, yes speedily, in our days, soon. God, rebuild, God, rebuild, rebuild Your House soon!

Who knows one? I know one: One is our God, in the Heavens and on the earth.

Who knows two? I know two: two are the *Luchos* of the Covenant; One is our God, in the Heavens and on the earth.

Who knows three? I know three: three are the Patriarchs; two are the *Luchos* of the Covenant; One is our God, in the Heavens and on the earth.

אַרְבַּע מִי יוֹדֵעַ? אַרְבַּע אֲנִי יוֹדֵעַ. אַרְבַּע אִמָּהוֹת, שְׁלֹשָׁה אָבוֹת, שְׁנֵי לֻחוֹת הַבְּרִית, אֶחָד אֱלֹהֵינוּ שֶׁבַּשָּׁמַיִם וּבָאָרֶץ.

חֲמִשָּׁה מִי יוֹדֵעַ? חֲמִשָּׁה אֲנִי יוֹדֵעַ. חֲמִשָּׁה חֻמְשֵׁי תוֹרָה, אַרְבַּע אִמָּהוֹת, שְׁלֹשָׁה אָבוֹת, שְׁנֵי לֻחוֹת הַבְּרִית, אֶחָד אֱלֹהֵינוּ שֶׁבַּשָּׁמַיִם וּבָאָרֶץ.

שִׁשָּׁה מִי יוֹדֵעַ? שִׁשָּׁה אֲנִי יוֹדֵעַ. שִׁשָּׁה סִדְרֵי מִשְׁנָה, חֲמִשָּׁה חֻמְשֵׁי תוֹרָה, אַרְבַּע אִמָּהוֹת, שְׁלֹשָׁה אָבוֹת, שְׁנֵי לֻחוֹת הַבְּרִית, אֶחָד אֱלֹהֵינוּ שֶׁבַּשָּׁמַיִם וּבָאָרֶץ.

שִׁבְעָה מִי יוֹדֵעַ? שִׁבְעָה אֲנִי יוֹדֵעַ. שִׁבְעָה יְמֵי שַׁבַּתָּא, שִׁשָּׁה סִדְרֵי מִשְׁנָה, חֲמִשָּׁה חֻמְשֵׁי תוֹרָה, אַרְבַּע אִמָּהוֹת, שְׁלֹשָׁה אָבוֹת, שְׁנֵי לֻחוֹת הַבְּרִית, אֶחָד אֱלֹהֵינוּ שֶׁבַּשָּׁמַיִם וּבָאָרֶץ.

שְׁמוֹנָה מִי יוֹדֵעַ? שְׁמוֹנָה אֲנִי יוֹדֵעַ. שְׁמוֹנָה יְמֵי מִילָה, שִׁבְעָה יְמֵי שַׁבַּתָּא, שִׁשָּׁה סִדְרֵי מִשְׁנָה, חֲמִשָּׁה חֻמְשֵׁי תוֹרָה, אַרְבַּע אִמָּהוֹת, שְׁלֹשָׁה אָבוֹת, שְׁנֵי לֻחוֹת הַבְּרִית, אֶחָד אֱלֹהֵינוּ שֶׁבַּשָּׁמַיִם וּבָאָרֶץ.

תִּשְׁעָה מִי יוֹדֵעַ? תִּשְׁעָה אֲנִי יוֹדֵעַ. תִּשְׁעָה יַרְחֵי לֵדָה, שְׁמוֹנָה יְמֵי מִילָה, שִׁבְעָה יְמֵי שַׁבַּתָּא, שִׁשָּׁה סִדְרֵי מִשְׁנָה, חֲמִשָּׁה חֻמְשֵׁי תוֹרָה, אַרְבַּע אִמָּהוֹת, שְׁלֹשָׁה אָבוֹת, שְׁנֵי לֻחוֹת הַבְּרִית, אֶחָד אֱלֹהֵינוּ שֶׁבַּשָּׁמַיִם וּבָאָרֶץ.

עֲשָׂרָה מִי יוֹדֵעַ? עֲשָׂרָה אֲנִי יוֹדֵעַ. עֲשָׂרָה דִבְּרַיָּא, תִּשְׁעָה יַרְחֵי לֵדָה, שְׁמוֹנָה יְמֵי מִילָה, שִׁבְעָה יְמֵי שַׁבַּתָּא, שִׁשָּׁה סִדְרֵי מִשְׁנָה, חֲמִשָּׁה חֻמְשֵׁי תוֹרָה, אַרְבַּע אִמָּהוֹת, שְׁלֹשָׁה אָבוֹת, שְׁנֵי לֻחוֹת הַבְּרִית, אֶחָד אֱלֹהֵינוּ שֶׁבַּשָּׁמַיִם וּבָאָרֶץ.

Who knows four? I know four: four are the Matriarchs; three are the Patriarchs; two are the *Luchos* of the Covenant; One is our God, in the Heavens and on the earth.

Who knows five? I know five: five are the Books of the Torah; four are the Matriarchs; three are the Patriarchs; two are the *Luchos* of the Covenant; One is our God, in the Heavens and on the earth.

Who knows six? I know six: six are the Orders of the Mishnah; five are the Books of the Torah; four are the Matriarchs; three are the Patriarchs; two are the *Luchos* of the Covenant; One is our God, in the Heavens and on the earth.

Who knows seven? I know seven: seven are the days of the week; six are the Orders of the Mishnah; five are the Books of the Torah; four are the Matriarchs; three are the Patriarchs; two are the *Luchos* of the Covenant; One is our God, in the Heavens and on the earth.

Who knows eight? I know eight: eight are the days of circumcision; seven are the days of the week; six are the Orders of the Mishnah; five are the Books of the Torah; four are the Matriarchs; three are the Patriarchs; two are the *Luchos* of the Covenant; One is our God, in the Heavens and on the earth.

Who knows nine? I know nine: nine are the months of pregnancy; eight are the days of circumcision; seven are the days of the week; six are the Orders of the Mishnah; five are the Books of the Torah; four are the Matriarchs; three are the Patriarchs; two are the *Luchos* of the Covenant; One is our God, in the Heavens and on the earth.

Who knows ten? I know ten: ten are the Ten Commandments; nine are the months of pregnancy; eight are the days of circumcision; seven are the days of the week; six are the Orders of the Mishnah; five are the Books of the Torah; four are the Matriarchs; three are the Patriarchs; two are the *Luchos* of the Covenant; One is our God, in the Heavens and on the earth.

אַחַד עָשָׂר מִי יוֹדֵעַ? אַחַד עָשָׂר אֲנִי יוֹדֵעַ. אַחַד עָשָׂר כּוֹכְבַיָּא, עֲשָׂרָה דִּבְּרַיָּא, תִּשְׁעָה יַרְחֵי לֵדָה, שְׁמוֹנָה יְמֵי מִילָה, שִׁבְעָה יְמֵי שַׁבַּתָּא, שִׁשָּׁה סִדְרֵי מִשְׁנָה, חֲמִשָּׁה חֻמְשֵׁי תוֹרָה, אַרְבַּע אִמָּהוֹת, שְׁלֹשָׁה אָבוֹת, שְׁנֵי לֻחוֹת הַבְּרִית, אֶחָד אֱלֹהֵינוּ שֶׁבַּשָּׁמַיִם וּבָאָרֶץ.

שְׁנֵים עָשָׂר מִי יוֹדֵעַ? שְׁנֵים עָשָׂר אֲנִי יוֹדֵעַ. שְׁנֵים עָשָׂר שִׁבְטַיָּא, אַחַד עָשָׂר כּוֹכְבַיָּא, עֲשָׂרָה דִבְּרַיָּא, תִּשְׁעָה יַרְחֵי לֵדָה, שְׁמוֹנָה יְמֵי מִילָה, שִׁבְעָה יְמֵי שַׁבַּתָּא, שִׁשָּׁה סִדְרֵי מִשְׁנָה, חֲמִשָּׁה חֻמְשֵׁי תוֹרָה, אַרְבַּע אִמָּהוֹת, שְׁלֹשָׁה אָבוֹת, שְׁנֵי לֻחוֹת הַבְּרִית, אֶחָד אֱלֹהֵינוּ שֶׁבַּשָּׁמַיִם וּבָאָרֶץ.

שְׁלֹשָׁה עָשָׂר מִי יוֹדֵעַ? שְׁלֹשָׁה עָשָׂר אֲנִי יוֹדֵעַ. שְׁלֹשָׁה עָשָׂר מִדַּיָּא, שְׁנֵים עָשָׂר שִׁבְטַיָּא, אַחַד עָשָׂר כּוֹכְבַיָּא, עֲשָׂרָה דִבְּרַיָּא, תִּשְׁעָה יַרְחֵי לֵדָה, שְׁמוֹנָה יְמֵי מִילָה, שִׁבְעָה יְמֵי שַׁבַּתָּא, שִׁשָּׁה סִדְרֵי מִשְׁנָה, חֲמִשָּׁה חֻמְשֵׁי תוֹרָה, אַרְבַּע אִמָּהוֹת, שְׁלֹשָׁה אָבוֹת, שְׁנֵי לֻחוֹת הַבְּרִית, אֶחָד אֱלֹהֵינוּ שֶׁבַּשָּׁמַיִם וּבָאָרֶץ.

חַד גַּדְיָא, חַד גַּדְיָא, דְּזַבִּין אַבָּא בִּתְרֵי זוּזֵי, חַד גַּדְיָא חַד גַּדְיָא.

וְאָתָא שׁוּנְרָא וְאָכְלָה לְגַדְיָא, דְּזַבִּין אַבָּא בִּתְרֵי זוּזֵי, חַד גַּדְיָא חַד גַּדְיָא.

וְאָתָא כַלְבָּא וְנָשַׁךְ לְשׁוּנְרָא, דְּאָכְלָא לְגַדְיָא, דְּזַבִּין אַבָּא בִּתְרֵי זוּזֵי, חַד גַּדְיָא חַד גַּדְיָא.

וְאָתָא חוּטְרָא וְהִכָּה לְכַלְבָּא, דְּנָשַׁךְ לְשׁוּנְרָא, דְּאָכְלָה לְגַדְיָא, דְּזַבִּין אַבָּא בִּתְרֵי זוּזֵי, חַד גַּדְיָא חַד גַּדְיָא.

וְאָתָא נוּרָא וְשָׂרַף לְחוּטְרָא, דְּהִכָּה לְכַלְבָּא, דְּנָשַׁךְ

Who knows eleven? I know eleven: eleven are the stars (in Yosef's dream); ten are the Ten Commandments; nine are the months of pregnancy; eight are the days of circumcision; seven are the days of the week; six are the Orders of the Mishnah; five are the Books of the Torah; four are the Matriarchs; three are the Patriarchs; two are the *Luchos* of the Covenant; One is our God, in the Heavens and on the earth.

Who knows twelve? I know twelve: twelve are the tribes; eleven are the stars (in Yosef's dream); ten are the Ten Commandments; nine are the months of pregnancy; eight are the days of circumcision; seven are the days of the week; six are the Orders of the Mishnah; five are the Books of the Torah; four are the Matriarchs; three are the Patriarchs; two are the *Luchos* of the Covenant; One is our God, in the Heavens and on the earth.

Who knows thirteen? I know thirteen: thirteen are the attributes of Hashem; twelve are the tribes; eleven are the stars (in Yosef's dream); ten are the Ten Commandments; nine are the months of pregnancy; eight are the days of circumcision; seven are the days of the week; six are the Orders of the Mishnah; five are the Books of the Torah; four are the Matriarchs; three are the Patriarchs; two are the *Luchos* of the Covenant; One is our God, in the Heavens and on the earth.

A kid, a kid, that father bought for two *zuzim*,
a kid, a kid.

A cat then came and devoured the kid that father bought for two *zuzim*, a kid, a kid.

A dog then came and bit the cat, that devoured the kid that father bought for two *zuzim*, a kid, a kid.

A stick then came and beat the dog, that bit the cat, that devoured the kid that father bought for two *zuzim*, a kid, a kid.

A fire then came and burnt the stick, that beat the dog, that bit

לְשׁוּנְרָא, דְּאָכְלָה לְגַדְיָא, דְּזַבִּין אַבָּא בִּתְרֵי זוּזֵי, חַד גַּדְיָא חַד גַּדְיָא.

וְאָתָא מַיָּא וְכָבָה לְנוּרָא, דְּשָׂרַף לְחוּטְרָא, דְּהִכָּה לְכַלְבָּא, דְּנָשַׁךְ לְשׁוּנְרָא, דְּאָכְלָה לְגַדְיָא, דְּזַבִּין אַבָּא בִּתְרֵי זוּזֵי, חַד גַּדְיָא חַד גַּדְיָא.

וְאָתָא תוֹרָא וְשָׁתָה לְמַיָּא, דְּכָבָה לְנוּרָא, דְּשָׂרַף לְחוּטְרָא, דְּהִכָּה לְכַלְבָּא, דְּנָשַׁךְ לְשׁוּנְרָא, דְּאָכְלָה לְגַדְיָא, דְּזַבִּין אַבָּא בִּתְרֵי זוּזֵי, חַד גַּדְיָא חַד גַּדְיָא.

וְאָתָא הַשּׁוֹחֵט וְשָׁחַט לְתוֹרָא, דְּשָׁתָא לְמַיָּא, דְּכָבָה לְנוּרָא, דְּשָׂרַף לְחוּטְרָא, דְּהִכָּה לְכַלְבָּא, דְּנָשַׁךְ לְשׁוּנְרָא, דְּאָכְלָה לְגַדְיָא, דְּזַבִּין אַבָּא בִּתְרֵי זוּזֵי, חַד גַּדְיָא חַד גַּדְיָא.

וְאָתָא מַלְאַךְ הַמָּוֶת וְשָׁחַט לְשׁוֹחֵט, דְּשָׁחַט לְתוֹרָא, דְּשָׁתָה לְמַיָּא, דְּכָבָה לְנוּרָא, דְּשָׂרַף לְחוּטְרָא, דְּהִכָּה לְכַלְבָּא, דְּנָשַׁךְ לְשׁוּנְרָא, דְּאָכְלָה לְגַדְיָא, דְּזַבִּין אַבָּא בִּתְרֵי זוּזֵי, חַד גַּדְיָא חַד גַּדְיָא.

וְאָתָא הַקָּדוֹשׁ בָּרוּךְ הוּא וְשָׁחַט לְמַלְאַךְ הַמָּוֶת, דְּשָׁחַט לְשׁוֹחֵט, דְּשָׁחַט לְתוֹרָא, דְּשָׁתָה לְמַיָּא, דְּכָבָה לְנוּרָא, דְּשָׂרַף לְחוּטְרָא, דְּהִכָּה לְכַלְבָּא, דְּנָשַׁךְ לְשׁוּנְרָא, דְּאָכְלָה לְגַדְיָא, דְּזַבִּין אַבָּא בִּתְרֵי זוּזֵי, חַד גַּדְיָא חַד גַּדְיָא.

the cat, that devoured the kid that father bought for two *zuzim*, a kid, a kid.

Water then came and extinguished the fire, that burnt the stick, that beat the dog, that bit the cat, that devoured the kid that father bought for two *zuzim*, a kid, a kid.

An ox then came and drank the water, that extinguished the fire, that burnt the stick, that beat the dog, that bit the cat, that devoured the kid that father bought for two *zuzim*, a kid, a kid.

A slaughterer then came and slaughtered the ox, that drank the water, that extinguished the fire, that burnt the stick, that beat the dog, that bit the cat, that devoured the kid that father bought for two *zuzim*, a kid, a kid.

The Angel of Death then came and killed the slaughterer, who slaughtered the ox, that drank the water, that extinguished the fire, that burnt the stick, that beat the dog, that bit the cat, that devoured the kid that father bought for two *zuzim*, a kid, a kid.

The Holy One, blessed is He, then came and slew the Angel of Death, who killed the slaughterer, who slaughtered the ox, that drank the water, that extinguished the fire, that burnt the stick, that beat the dog, that bit the cat, that devoured the kid that father bought for two *zuzim*, a kid, a kid.

שיר השירים
Shir HaShirim

Shir HaShirim / שיר השירים

The *minhag* of the *Rosh HaYeshiva, ztvk"l,* was to recite *Shir HaShirim* after the *Seder.*

פרק א

א שִׁיר הַשִּׁירִים אֲשֶׁר לִשְׁלֹמֹה׃ ב יִשָּׁקֵנִי מִנְּשִׁיקוֹת פִּיהוּ
כִּי־טוֹבִים דֹּדֶיךָ מִיָּיִן׃ ג לְרֵיחַ שְׁמָנֶיךָ טוֹבִים שֶׁמֶן תּוּרַק
שְׁמֶךָ עַל־כֵּן עֲלָמוֹת אֲהֵבוּךָ׃ ד מָשְׁכֵנִי אַחֲרֶיךָ נָּרוּצָה
הֱבִיאַנִי הַמֶּלֶךְ חֲדָרָיו נָגִילָה וְנִשְׂמְחָה בָּךְ נַזְכִּירָה
דֹדֶיךָ מִיַּיִן מֵישָׁרִים אֲהֵבוּךָ׃ ה שְׁחוֹרָה אֲנִי וְנָאוָה בְּנוֹת
יְרוּשָׁלָם כְּאָהֳלֵי קֵדָר כִּירִיעוֹת שְׁלֹמֹה׃ ו אַל־תִּרְאֻנִי
שֶׁאֲנִי שְׁחַרְחֹרֶת שֶׁשְּׁזָפַתְנִי הַשָּׁמֶשׁ בְּנֵי אִמִּי נִחֲרוּ־בִי
שָׂמֻנִי נֹטֵרָה אֶת־הַכְּרָמִים כַּרְמִי שֶׁלִּי לֹא נָטָרְתִּי׃ ז הַגִּידָה
לִּי שֶׁאָהֲבָה נַפְשִׁי אֵיכָה תִרְעֶה אֵיכָה תַּרְבִּיץ בַּצָּהֳרָיִם

(The translation presented here is allegorical, based on *Rashi's* Commentary.)

CHAPTER ONE

1 The song that excels all songs dedicated to God, Him to Whom peace belongs. 2 Communicate Your innermost wisdom to me again in loving closeness, for Your friendship is dearer than all earthly delights. 3 Like the scent of goodly oils is the spreading fame of Your great deeds; Your very name is Flowing Oil, therefore have nations loved You.

[KLAL YISRAEL IN EXILE TO HASHEM:] 4 Upon perceiving a mere hint that You wished to draw me, we rushed with perfect faith after You into the Wilderness. The King brought me into His cloud-pillared chamber; whatever our travail we shall always be glad and rejoice in Your Torah. We recall Your love more than earthly delights, unrestrainedly do we love You.

[KLAL YISRAEL TO THE NATIONS:] 5 Though I am black with sin, I am comely with virtue, O nations who are destined to ascend to Yerushalayim; though sullied as the tents of Kedar, I will be immaculate as the draperies of Him to Whom peace belongs. 6 Do not view me with contempt despite my swarthiness, for it is but the sun that has glared upon me. The alien children of my mother were incensed with me and made me a keeper of the vineyards of idols, but the vineyard of my own true God I did not keep.

[KLAL YISRAEL TO HASHEM:] 7 Tell me, You Whom my soul loves: Where will You graze Your flock? Where will You rest them under the fiercest sun of harshest Exile?

שַׁלָּמָה אֶהְיֶה כְּעֹטְיָה עַל עֶדְרֵי חֲבֵרֶיךָ: ח אִם־לֹא תֵדְעִי
לָךְ הַיָּפָה בַּנָּשִׁים צְאִי־לָךְ בְּעִקְבֵי הַצֹּאן וּרְעִי אֶת־גְּדִיֹּתַיִךְ
עַל מִשְׁכְּנוֹת הָרֹעִים: ט לְסֻסָתִי בְּרִכְבֵי פַרְעֹה דִּמִּיתִיךְ
רַעְיָתִי: י נָאווּ לְחָיַיִךְ בַּתֹּרִים צַוָּארֵךְ בַּחֲרוּזִים: יא תּוֹרֵי זָהָב
נַעֲשֶׂה־לָּךְ עִם נְקֻדּוֹת הַכָּסֶף: יב עַד־שֶׁהַמֶּלֶךְ בִּמְסִבּוֹ נִרְדִּי
נָתַן רֵיחוֹ: יג צְרוֹר הַמֹּר | דּוֹדִי לִי בֵּין שָׁדַי יָלִין: יד אֶשְׁכֹּל
הַכֹּפֶר דּוֹדִי לִי בְּכַרְמֵי עֵין גֶּדִי: טו הִנָּךְ יָפָה רַעְיָתִי הִנָּךְ
יָפָה עֵינַיִךְ יוֹנִים: טז הִנְּךָ יָפֶה דוֹדִי אַף נָעִים אַף־עַרְשֵׂנוּ
רַעֲנָנָה: יז קֹרוֹת בָּתֵּינוּ אֲרָזִים רַחִיטֵנוּ בְּרוֹתִים:

פרק ב

א אֲנִי חֲבַצֶּלֶת הַשָּׁרוֹן שׁוֹשַׁנַּת הָעֲמָקִים: ב כְּשׁוֹשַׁנָּה

Why shall I be like one veiled in mourning among the flocks of Your fellow shepherds?

[HASHEM RESPONDS TO KLAL YISRAEL:] 8 If you know not where to graze, O fairest of nations, follow the footsteps of the sheep — your forefathers who traced a straight, unswerving path after My Torah. Then you can graze your tender kids even among the dwellings of foreign shepherds. 9 With My mighty steeds who battled Pharaoh's riders I revealed that you are My beloved. 10 Your cheeks are lovely with rows of gems, your neck with necklaces — My gifts to you from the splitting Sea, 11 by inducing Pharaoh to engage in pursuit, to add circlets of gold to your spangles of silver.

[KLAL YISRAEL ABOUT HASHEM:] 12 While the King was yet at Sinai my malodorous deed gave forth its scent, as my Golden Calf defiled the covenant. 13 But my Beloved responded with a bundle of myrrh — the fragrant atonement of erecting a Mishkan where His Presence would dwell amid the Holy *Aron's* staves. 14 Like a cluster of henna in Ein-gedi vineyards has my Beloved multiplied His forgiveness to me. 15 He said, "I forgive you, My friend, for you are lovely in deed and lovely in resolve. The righteous among you are loyal as a dove."

[KLAL YISRAEL TO HASHEM:] 16 It is You Who are lovely, my Beloved, so pleasant that You pardoned my sin, enabling our Mikdash to make me ever fresh. 17 The beams of our House are cedar, our panels are cypress.

CHAPTER TWO

1 I am but a rose of Sharon, even an ever-fresh rose of the valleys.

בֵּין הַחוֹחִים כֵּן רַעְיָתִי בֵּין הַבָּנוֹת: ג כְּתַפּוּחַ בַּעֲצֵי
הַיַּעַר כֵּן דּוֹדִי בֵּין הַבָּנִים בְּצִלּוֹ חִמַּדְתִּי וְיָשַׁבְתִּי וּפִרְיוֹ
מָתוֹק לְחִכִּי: ד הֱבִיאַנִי אֶל־בֵּית הַיָּיִן וְדִגְלוֹ עָלַי אַהֲבָה:
ה סַמְּכוּנִי בָּאֲשִׁישׁוֹת רַפְּדוּנִי בַּתַּפּוּחִים כִּי־חוֹלַת אַהֲבָה
אָנִי: ו שְׂמֹאלוֹ תַּחַת לְרֹאשִׁי וִימִינוֹ תְּחַבְּקֵנִי: ז הִשְׁבַּעְתִּי
אֶתְכֶם בְּנוֹת יְרוּשָׁלַם בִּצְבָאוֹת אוֹ בְּאַיְלוֹת הַשָּׂדֶה אִם־
תָּעִירוּ | וְאִם־תְּעוֹרְרוּ אֶת־הָאַהֲבָה עַד שֶׁתֶּחְפָּץ: ח קוֹל
דּוֹדִי הִנֵּה־זֶה בָּא מְדַלֵּג עַל־הֶהָרִים מְקַפֵּץ עַל־הַגְּבָעוֹת:
ט דּוֹמֶה דוֹדִי לִצְבִי אוֹ לְעֹפֶר הָאַיָּלִים הִנֵּה־זֶה עוֹמֵד אַחַר
כָּתְלֵנוּ מַשְׁגִּיחַ מִן־הַחַלֹּנוֹת מֵצִיץ מִן־הַחֲרַכִּים: י עָנָה דוֹדִי
וְאָמַר לִי קוּמִי לָךְ רַעְיָתִי יָפָתִי וּלְכִי־לָךְ: יא כִּי־הִנֵּה הַסְּתָו

[HASHEM TO KLAL YISRAEL:] [2] Like the rose maintaining its beauty among the thorns, so is My faithful beloved among the nations.

[KLAL YISRAEL REMINISCES ...:] [3] Like the fruitful, fragrant apple tree among the barren trees of the forest, so is my Beloved among the gods.

In His shade I delighted and there I sat, and the fruit of His Torah was sweet to my palate. [4] He brought me to the chamber of Torah delights and clustered my encampments about Him in love. [5] I say to Him, "Sustain me in exile with dainty cakes, spread fragrant apples about me to comfort my dispersion — for, bereft of Your Presence, I am sick with love." [6] With memories of His loving support in the desert, of His left hand under my head, of His right hand enveloping me.

[TURNS TO THE NATIONS:] [7] I adjure you, O nations who are destined to ascend to Yerushalayim — for if you violate your oath you will become as defenseless as gazelles or hinds of the field — if you dare provoke God to hate me or disturb His love for me while He still desires it.

[THEN REMINISCES FURTHER:] [8] The voice of my Beloved! Behold — it came suddenly to redeem me, as if leaping over mountains, skipping over hills. [9] In His swiftness to redeem me, my Beloved is like a gazelle or a young hart. I thought I would be forever alone, but behold! He was standing behind our wall, observing through the windows, peering through the lattices.

[10] When He redeemed me from Mitzrayim, my Beloved called out and said to me, "Arise My love, My fair one, and go forth. [11] For the winter of bondage

עָבָר הַגֶּשֶׁם חָלַף הָלַךְ לוֹ: יב הַנִּצָּנִים נִרְאוּ בָאָרֶץ עֵת
הַזָּמִיר הִגִּיעַ וְקוֹל הַתּוֹר נִשְׁמַע בְּאַרְצֵנוּ: יג הַתְּאֵנָה חָנְטָה
פַגֶּיהָ וְהַגְּפָנִים סְמָדַר נָתְנוּ רֵיחַ קוּמִי לָךְ רַעְיָתִי יָפָתִי
וּלְכִי־לָךְ: יד יוֹנָתִי בְּחַגְוֵי הַסֶּלַע בְּסֵתֶר הַמַּדְרֵגָה הַרְאִינִי
אֶת־מַרְאַיִךְ הַשְׁמִיעִנִי אֶת־קוֹלֵךְ כִּי־קוֹלֵךְ עָרֵב וּמַרְאֵיךְ
נָאוֶה: טו אֶחֱזוּ־לָנוּ שֻׁעָלִים שֻׁעָלִים קְטַנִּים מְחַבְּלִים כְּרָמִים
וּכְרָמֵינוּ סְמָדַר: טז דּוֹדִי לִי וַאֲנִי לוֹ הָרֹעֶה בַּשּׁוֹשַׁנִּים: יז עַד
שֶׁיָּפוּחַ הַיּוֹם וְנָסוּ הַצְּלָלִים סֹב דְּמֵה־לְךָ דוֹדִי לִצְבִי אוֹ
לְעֹפֶר הָאַיָּלִים עַל־הָרֵי בָתֶר:

פרק ג

א עַל־מִשְׁכָּבִי בַּלֵּילוֹת בִּקַּשְׁתִּי אֵת שֶׁאָהֲבָה נַפְשִׁי
בִּקַּשְׁתִּיו וְלֹא מְצָאתִיו: ב אָקוּמָה נָּא וַאֲסוֹבְבָה בָעִיר

---

has passed, the deluge of suffering is over and gone. [12]The righteous blossoms are seen in the land, the time of your song has arrived, and the voice of your guide is heard in the land. [13]The fig tree has formed its first small figs, ready for ascent to the Mikdash. The vines are in blossom, their fragrance declaring they are ready for libation. Arise, My love, My fair one, and go forth!"

[14]At the *Yam Suf*, He said to me, "O My dove, trapped at the sea as if in the clefts of the rock, the concealment of the terrace. Show Me your prayerful gaze, let Me hear your supplicating voice, for your voice is sweet and your countenance comely." [15]Then He told the *Yam Suf*, "Seize for us the Egyptian foxes, even the small foxes who spoiled Klal Yisrael's vineyards while our vineyards had just begun to blossom."

[16]My Beloved is mine, He fills all my needs and I seek from Him and none other. He grazes me in roselike bounty. [17]Until my sin blows His friendship away and sears me like the midday sun and His protection departs, my sin caused Him to turn away.

I say to him, 'My Beloved, You became like a gazelle or a young hart on the distant mountains.'

CHAPTER THREE

[KLAL YISRAEL TO THE NATIONS:] [1]As I lay on my bed in the night of my desert travail, I sought Him Whom my soul loves. I sought Him but I found Him not, for He maintained His aloofness. [2]I resolved to arise then, and roam through

בַּשְּׁוָקִים֙ וּבָ֣רְחֹב֔וֹת אֲבַקְשָׁ֕ה אֵ֥ת שֶׁאָהֲבָ֖ה נַפְשִׁ֑י בִּקַּשְׁתִּ֖יו
וְלֹ֥א מְצָאתִֽיו׃ ג מְצָא֙וּנִי֙ הַשֹּׁ֣מְרִ֔ים הַסֹּבְבִ֖ים בָּעִ֑יר אֵ֛ת
שֶׁאָהֲבָ֥ה נַפְשִׁ֖י רְאִיתֶֽם׃ ד כִּמְעַט֙ שֶׁעָבַ֣רְתִּי מֵהֶ֔ם עַ֥ד
שֶׁמָּצָ֕אתִי אֵ֥ת שֶׁאָהֲבָ֖ה נַפְשִׁ֑י אֲחַזְתִּיו֙ וְלֹ֣א אַרְפֶּ֔נּוּ עַד־
שֶׁהֲבֵיאתִיו֙ אֶל־בֵּ֣ית אִמִּ֔י וְאֶל־חֶ֖דֶר הוֹרָתִֽי׃ ה הִשְׁבַּ֨עְתִּי
אֶתְכֶ֜ם בְּנ֤וֹת יְרֽוּשָׁלִַ֙ם֙ בִּצְבָא֔וֹת א֖וֹ בְּאַיְל֣וֹת הַשָּׂדֶ֑ה אִם־
תָּעִ֧ירוּ ׀ וְאִם־תְּעֽוֹרְר֛וּ אֶת־הָאַהֲבָ֖ה עַ֥ד שֶׁתֶּחְפָּֽץ׃ ו מִ֣י זֹ֗את
עֹלָה֙ מִן־הַמִּדְבָּ֔ר כְּתִֽימֲר֖וֹת עָשָׁ֑ן מְקֻטֶּ֤רֶת מֹר֙ וּלְבוֹנָ֔ה מִכֹּ֖ל
אַבְקַ֥ת רוֹכֵֽל׃ ז הִנֵּ֗ה מִטָּתוֹ֙ שֶׁלִּשְׁלֹמֹ֔ה שִׁשִּׁ֥ים גִּבֹּרִ֖ים סָבִ֣יב
לָ֑הּ מִגִּבֹּרֵ֖י יִשְׂרָאֵֽל׃ ח כֻּלָּם֙ אֲחֻ֣זֵי חֶ֔רֶב מְלֻמְּדֵ֖י מִלְחָמָ֑ה
אִ֤ישׁ חַרְבּוֹ֙ עַל־יְרֵכ֔וֹ מִפַּ֖חַד בַּלֵּילֽוֹת׃ ט אַפִּרְי֗וֹן עָ֤שָׂה לוֹ֙
הַמֶּ֣לֶךְ שְׁלֹמֹ֔ה מֵעֲצֵ֖י הַלְּבָנֽוֹן׃ י עַמּוּדָיו֙ עָ֣שָׂה כֶ֔סֶף רְפִידָת֣וֹ
זָהָ֔ב מֶרְכָּב֖וֹ אַרְגָּמָ֑ן תּוֹכוֹ֙ רָצ֣וּף אַהֲבָ֔ה מִבְּנ֖וֹת יְרוּשָׁלִָֽם׃

---

the city, in the streets and squares; that through Moshe I would seek Him
Whom my soul loved. I sought Him, but I found Him not. 3 They found me,
Moshe and Aharon, the watchmen patrolling the city. 'You have seen Him
Whom my soul loves — what has He said?' 4 Scarcely had I departed from
them when, in the days of Yehoshua, I found Him Whom my soul loves. I
grasped Him, determined that my deeds would never again cause me to
lose hold of Him, until I brought His Presence to the Mishkan of my mother
and to the chamber of the one who conceived me. 5 I adjure you, O nations
who are destined to ascend to Yerushalayim — for if you violate your oath
you will become as defenseless as gazelles or hinds of the field — if you dare
provoke God to hate me or disturb His love for me while He still desires it.
6 You nations have asked, "Who is this ascending from the desert, its way
secured and smoothed by palmlike pillars of smoke, burning fragrant myrrh
and frankincense, of all the perfumer's powders?" 7 Behold the resting place
of Him to Whom peace belongs, with sixty myriads of Klal Yisrael's mighty
encircling it. 8 All of them gripping the sword of tradition, skilled in the battle of Torah, each with his sword ready at his side, lest he succumb in the
nights of exile. 9 A Mikdash for His presence has the King to Whom peace
belongs made of the wood of Levanon. 10 Its pillars He made of silver, His
resting place was gold, its suspended curtain was purple wool, its midst was
decked with implements bespeaking love by the daughters of Yerushalayim.

יא צְאֶינָה וּרְאֶינָה בְּנוֹת צִיּוֹן בַּמֶּלֶךְ שְׁלֹמֹה בָּעֲטָרָה
שֶׁעִטְּרָה־לּוֹ אִמּוֹ בְּיוֹם חֲתֻנָּתוֹ וּבְיוֹם שִׂמְחַת לִבּוֹ׃

פרק ד

א הִנָּךְ יָפָה רַעְיָתִי הִנָּךְ יָפָה עֵינַיִךְ יוֹנִים מִבַּעַד לְצַמָּתֵךְ
שַׂעְרֵךְ כְּעֵדֶר הָעִזִּים שֶׁגָּלְשׁוּ מֵהַר גִּלְעָד׃ ב שִׁנַּיִךְ כְּעֵדֶר
הַקְּצוּבוֹת שֶׁעָלוּ מִן־הָרַחְצָה שֶׁכֻּלָּם מַתְאִימוֹת וְשַׁכֻּלָה
אֵין בָּהֶם׃ ג כְּחוּט הַשָּׁנִי שִׂפְתוֹתַיִךְ וּמִדְבָּרֵךְ נָאוֶה כְּפֶלַח
הָרִמּוֹן רַקָּתֵךְ מִבַּעַד לְצַמָּתֵךְ׃ ד כְּמִגְדַּל דָּוִיד צַוָּארֵךְ בָּנוּי
לְתַלְפִּיּוֹת אֶלֶף הַמָּגֵן תָּלוּי עָלָיו כֹּל שִׁלְטֵי הַגִּבֹּרִים׃ ה שְׁנֵי
שָׁדַיִךְ כִּשְׁנֵי עֳפָרִים תְּאוֹמֵי צְבִיָּה הָרוֹעִים בַּשּׁוֹשַׁנִּים׃ ו עַד
שֶׁיָּפוּחַ הַיּוֹם וְנָסוּ הַצְּלָלִים אֵלֶךְ לִי אֶל־הַר הַמּוֹר וְאֶל־

---

11 Go forth and gaze, O daughters distinguished by loyalty to God, upon the King to Whom peace belongs adorned with the crown His nation made for Him, on the day His Law was given and He became one with Israel, and on the day His heart was gladdened by His Mishkan's consecration.

CHAPTER FOUR

[HASHEM TO KLAL YISRAEL:] 1 Behold, you are lovely, My friend, behold you are lovely, your very appearance radiates dovelike constancy. The most common sons within your encampments are as dearly beloved as the children of Yaakov in the goatlike procession descending the slopes of Mount Gilad. 2 Accountable in deed are your fiercest warriors like a well-numbered flock come up from the washing, all of them unblemished with no miscarriage of action in them.

3 Like the scarlet thread, guarantor of Rachav's safety, is the sincerity of your lips, and your word is unfeigned. As many as a pomegranate's seeds are the merits of your unworthiest within your modest veil. 4 As stately as the Tower of David is the site of your Sanhedrin, built as a model to emulate, with a thousand shields of Torah armor hung upon it, all the disciple-filled quivers of the mighty. 5 Moshe and Aharon, your two sustainers, are like two fawns, twins of the gazelle, who graze their sheep in roselike bounty.

6 Until My sunny benevolence was withdrawn from Shiloh and the protective shadows were dispersed by your sin. I will go to Mount Moriah and

גִּבְעַ֖ת הַלְּבוֹנָֽה׃ ז כֻּלָּ֤ךְ יָפָה֙ רַעְיָתִ֔י וּמ֖וּם אֵ֥ין בָּֽךְ׃ ח אִתִּ֤י
מִלְּבָנוֹן֙ כַּלָּ֔ה אִתִּ֖י מִלְּבָנ֣וֹן תָּב֑וֹאִי תָּשׁ֣וּרִי ׀ מֵרֹ֣אשׁ אֲמָנָ֗ה
מֵרֹ֤אשׁ שְׂנִיר֙ וְחֶרְמ֔וֹן מִמְּעֹנ֣וֹת אֲרָי֔וֹת מֵהַרְרֵ֖י נְמֵרִֽים׃
ט לִבַּבְתִּ֖נִי אֲחֹתִ֣י כַלָּ֑ה לִבַּבְתִּ֙נִי֙ בְּאַחַ֣ת מֵעֵינַ֔יִךְ בְּאַחַ֥ד עֲנָ֖ק
מִצַּוְּרֹנָֽיִךְ׃ י מַה־יָּפ֥וּ דֹדַ֖יִךְ אֲחֹתִ֣י כַלָּ֑ה מַה־טֹּ֤בוּ דֹדַ֙יִךְ֙ מִיַּ֔יִן
וְרֵ֥יחַ שְׁמָנַ֖יִךְ מִכָּל־בְּשָׂמִֽים׃ יא נֹ֛פֶת תִּטֹּ֥פְנָה שִׂפְתוֹתַ֖יִךְ
כַּלָּ֑ה דְּבַ֤שׁ וְחָלָב֙ תַּ֣חַת לְשׁוֹנֵ֔ךְ וְרֵ֥יחַ שַׂלְמֹתַ֖יִךְ כְּרֵ֥יחַ
לְבָנֽוֹן׃ יב גַּ֥ן ׀ נָע֖וּל אֲחֹתִ֣י כַלָּ֑ה גַּ֥ל ׀ נָע֖וּל מַעְיָ֥ן חָתֽוּם׃
יג שְׁלָחַ֙יִךְ֙ פַּרְדֵּ֣ס רִמּוֹנִ֔ים עִ֖ם פְּרִ֣י מְגָדִ֑ים כְּפָרִ֖ים עִם־
נְרָדִֽים׃ יד נֵ֣רְדְּ ׀ וְכַרְכֹּ֗ם קָנֶה֙ וְקִנָּמ֔וֹן עִ֖ם כָּל־עֲצֵ֣י לְבוֹנָ֑ה
מֹ֚ר וַאֲהָל֔וֹת עִ֖ם כָּל־רָאשֵׁ֥י בְשָׂמִֽים׃ טו מַעְיַ֣ן גַּנִּ֔ים בְּאֵ֖ר
מַ֣יִם חַיִּ֑ים וְנֹזְלִ֖ים מִן־לְבָנֽוֹן׃ טז ע֤וּרִי צָפוֹן֙ וּב֣וֹאִי תֵימָ֔ן

---

the hill of frankincense — [7] where you will be completely fair, My beloved, and no blemish will be in you.

[8] With Me will you be exiled from the Mikdash, O bride, with Me from the Mikdash until you return; then to contemplate the fruits of your faith from its earliest beginnings from your first arrival at the summits of Senir and of Chermon, the lands of mighty Sichon and Og, as impregnable as dens of lions, and as mountains of leopards.

[9] You captured My heart, My sister, O bride; you captured My heart with but one of your virtues, with but one of the precepts that adorn you like beads of a necklace resplendent. [10] How fair was your love in so many settings, My sister, O bride; so superior is your love to wine and your spreading fame to all perfumes.

[11] The sweetness of Torah drops from your lips, like honey and milk it lies under your tongue; your very garments are scented with precepts like the scent of Levanon. [12] As chaste as a garden locked, My sister, O bride; a spring locked up, a fountain sealed. [13] Your least gifted ones are a pomegranate orchard with luscious fruit; henna with nard; [14] nard and saffron, calamus and cinnamon, with all trees of frankincense, myrrh and aloes with all the chief spices; [15] purified in a garden spring, a well of waters alive and flowing clean from Levanon.

[16] Awake from the north and come from the south! Like the winds

הָפִיחִי גַנִּי יִזְּלוּ בְשָׂמָיו יָבֹא דוֹדִי לְגַנּוֹ וְיֹאכַל פְּרִי מְגָדָיו׃

פרק ה

א בָּאתִי לְגַנִּי אֲחֹתִי כַלָּה אָרִיתִי מוֹרִי עִם־בְּשָׂמִי אָכַלְתִּי
יַעְרִי עִם־דִּבְשִׁי שָׁתִיתִי יֵינִי עִם־חֲלָבִי אִכְלוּ רֵעִים שְׁתוּ
וְשִׁכְרוּ דּוֹדִים׃ ב אֲנִי יְשֵׁנָה וְלִבִּי עֵר קוֹל | דּוֹדִי דוֹפֵק
פִּתְחִי־לִי אֲחֹתִי רַעְיָתִי יוֹנָתִי תַמָּתִי שֶׁרֹּאשִׁי נִמְלָא־
טָל קְוֻצּוֹתַי רְסִיסֵי לָיְלָה׃ ג פָּשַׁטְתִּי אֶת־כֻּתָּנְתִּי אֵיכָכָה
אֶלְבָּשֶׁנָּה רָחַצְתִּי אֶת־רַגְלַי אֵיכָכָה אֲטַנְּפֵם׃ ד דּוֹדִי
שָׁלַח יָדוֹ מִן־הַחוֹר וּמֵעַי הָמוּ עָלָיו׃ ה קַמְתִּי אֲנִי לִפְתֹּחַ
לְדוֹדִי וְיָדַי נָטְפוּ־מוֹר וְאֶצְבְּעֹתַי מוֹר עֹבֵר עַל כַּפּוֹת
הַמַּנְעוּל׃ ו פָּתַחְתִּי אֲנִי לְדוֹדִי וְדוֹדִי חָמַק עָבָר נַפְשִׁי

---

let My exiles return to My garden, let their fragrant goodness flow in Yerushalayim.

[KLAL YISRAEL RESPONDS:] Let but my Beloved come to His garden and enjoy His precious people.

CHAPTER FIVE

[HASHEM REPLIES:] 1To your Mishkan Dedication, My sister, O bride, I came as if to My garden. I gathered My myrrh with My spice from your princely incense; I accepted your unbidden as well as your bidden offerings to Me; I drank your libations pure as milk. Eat, My beloved priests! Drink and become God-intoxicated, O friends!

[KLAL YISRAEL REMINISCES REGRETFULLY:] 2I let my devotion slumber, but the God of my heart was awake! A sound! My Beloved knocks!

He said, "Open your heart to Me, My sister, My love, My dove, My perfection; admit Me and My head is filled with dewlike memories of Avraham; spurn Me and I bear collections of punishing rains in exile-nights."

3And I responded, "I have doffed my robe of devotion; how can I don it? I have washed my feet that trod Your path; how can I soil them?"

4In anger at my recalcitrance, my Beloved sent forth His hand from the portal in wrath, and my intestines churned with longing for Him. 5I arose to open for my Beloved and my hands dripped myrrh of repentant devotion to Torah and Hashem, and my fingers flowing with myrrh to remove the traces of my foolish rebuke from the handles of the lock. 6I opened for my Beloved; but, alas, my Beloved had turned His back on my plea and was gone. My soul

יָֽצְאָה בְדַבְּרוֹ בִּקַּשְׁתִּיהוּ וְלֹא מְצָאתִיהוּ קְרָאתִיו וְלֹא עָנָנִי׃
ז מְצָאֻנִי הַשֹּׁמְרִים הַסֹּבְבִים בָּעִיר הִכּוּנִי פְצָעוּנִי נָשְׂאוּ
אֶת־רְדִידִי מֵעָלַי שֹׁמְרֵי הַחֹמוֹת׃ ח הִשְׁבַּעְתִּי אֶתְכֶם בְּנוֹת
יְרוּשָׁלָם אִם־תִּמְצְאוּ אֶת־דּוֹדִי מַה־תַּגִּידוּ לוֹ שֶׁחוֹלַת
אַהֲבָה אָנִי׃ ט מַה־ דּוֹדֵךְ מִדּוֹד הַיָּפָה בַּנָּשִׁים מַה־דּוֹדֵךְ
מִדּוֹד שֶׁכָּכָה הִשְׁבַּעְתָּנוּ׃ י דּוֹדִי צַח וְאָדוֹם דָּגוּל מֵרְבָבָה׃
יא רֹאשׁוֹ כֶּתֶם פָּז קְוֻצּוֹתָיו תַּלְתַּלִּים שְׁחֹרוֹת כָּעוֹרֵב׃
יב עֵינָיו כְּיוֹנִים עַל־אֲפִיקֵי מָיִם רֹחֲצוֹת בֶּחָלָב יֹשְׁבוֹת
עַל־מִלֵּאת׃ יג לְחָיָו כַּעֲרוּגַת הַבֹּשֶׂם מִגְדְּלוֹת מֶרְקָחִים
שִׂפְתוֹתָיו שׁוֹשַׁנִּים נֹטְפוֹת מוֹר עֹבֵר׃ יד יָדָיו גְּלִילֵי זָהָב
מְמֻלָּאִים בַּתַּרְשִׁישׁ מֵעָיו עֶשֶׁת שֵׁן מְעֻלֶּפֶת סַפִּירִים׃

---

departed at His decree! I sought His closeness but could not find it; I beseeched Him but He would not answer.

7 They found me, the enemy watchmen patrolling the city; they struck me, they bloodied me, wreaking God's revenge on me. They stripped my mantle of holiness from me, the angelic watchmen of the wall.

[KLAL YISRAEL TO THE NATIONS:] 8 I adjure you, O nations who are destined to ascend to Yerushalayim, when you see my Beloved on the future Day of Judgment, won't you tell Him that I bore all travails for love of Him?

[THE NATIONS ASK KLAL YISRAEL:] 9 With what does your beloved God excel all others that you suffer for His Name, O fairest of nations? With what does your beloved God excel all others that you dare to adjure us?

[KLAL YISRAEL RESPONDS:] 10 My Beloved is pure and purifies sin, and ruddy with vengeance to punish betrayers, surrounded with myriad angels. 11 His opening words were finest gold, His crowns hold mounds of statutes written in raven-black flame.

12 Like the gaze of doves toward their cotes, His eyes are fixed on the waters of Torah, bathing all things in clarity, established upon creation's fullness. 13 Like a bed of spices are His words at Sinai, like towers of perfume. His comforting words from the Mishkan are roses dripping flowing myrrh. 14 The *Luchos*, His handiwork, are desirable above even rolls of gold; they are studded with commandments precious as gems, the Torah's innards are sparkling as ivory intricately overlaid with precious stone.

טו שׁוֹקָיו עַמּוּדֵי שֵׁשׁ מְיֻסָּדִים עַל־אַדְנֵי־פָז מַרְאֵהוּ כַּלְּבָנוֹן
בָּחוּר כָּאֲרָזִים׃ טז חִכּוֹ מַמְתַקִּים וְכֻלּוֹ מַחֲמַדִּים זֶה דוֹדִי
וְזֶה רֵעִי בְּנוֹת יְרוּשָׁלִָם׃

פרק ו

א אָנָה הָלַךְ דּוֹדֵךְ הַיָּפָה בַּנָּשִׁים אָנָה פָּנָה דוֹדֵךְ וּנְבַקְשֶׁנּוּ
עִמָּךְ׃ ב דּוֹדִי יָרַד לְגַנּוֹ לַעֲרֻגוֹת הַבֹּשֶׂם לִרְעוֹת בַּגַּנִּים
וְלִלְקֹט שׁוֹשַׁנִּים׃ ג אֲנִי לְדוֹדִי וְדוֹדִי לִי הָרוֹעֶה בַּשּׁוֹשַׁנִּים׃
ד יָפָה אַתְּ רַעְיָתִי כְּתִרְצָה נָאוָה כִּירוּשָׁלִָם אֲיֻמָּה
כַּנִּדְגָּלוֹת׃ ה הָסֵבִּי עֵינַיִךְ מִנֶּגְדִּי שֶׁהֵם הִרְהִיבֻנִי שַׂעְרֵךְ
כְּעֵדֶר הָעִזִּים שֶׁגָּלְשׁוּ מִן־הַגִּלְעָד׃ ו שִׁנַּיִךְ כְּעֵדֶר הָרְחֵלִים
שֶׁעָלוּ מִן־הָרַחְצָה שֶׁכֻּלָּם מַתְאִימוֹת וְשַׁכֻּלָה אֵין בָּהֶם׃

---

[15]The Torah's columns are marble set in contexts of finest gold, its contemplation flowers like Levanon, it is sturdy as cedars. [16]The words of His palate are sweet and He is all delight.

This is my Beloved and this is my Friend, O nations who are destined to ascend to Yerushalayim.

CHAPTER SIX

[THE NATIONS DERISIVELY, TO KLAL YISRAEL:] [1]Where has your Beloved gone, O forsaken fairest among women? Where has your Beloved turned to rejoin you? Let us seek Him with you and build His Mikdash with you.

[KLAL YISRAEL RESPONDS:] [2]My Beloved has descended to His Mikdash garden, to His incense altar, yet still He grazes my brethren remaining in gardens of exile to gather the roseate fragrance of their words of Torah. [3]I alone am my Beloved's and my Beloved is mine, He Who grazes His sheep in roselike pastures.

[HASHEM TO KLAL YISRAEL:] [4]You are beautiful, My love, when your deeds are pleasing, as comely now as once you were in Yerushalayim of old, hosts of angels stand in awe of you. [5]Turn your pleading eyes from Me lest I be tempted to bestow upon you holiness more than you can bear. But with all your flaws, your most common sons are as dearly beloved as the children of Yaakov in the goatlike procession descending the slopes of Mount Gilad. [6]Your mighty leaders are perfect, as a flock of ewes come up from the washing, all of them unblemished with no miscarriage of action in them.

ז כְּפֶלַח הָרִמּוֹן רַקָּתֵךְ מִבַּעַד לְצַמָּתֵךְ׃ ח שִׁשִּׁים הֵמָּה
מְלָכוֹת וּשְׁמֹנִים פִּילַגְשִׁים וַעֲלָמוֹת אֵין מִסְפָּר׃ ט אַחַת
הִיא יוֹנָתִי תַמָּתִי אַחַת הִיא לְאִמָּהּ בָּרָה הִיא לְיוֹלַדְתָּהּ
רָאוּהָ בָנוֹת וַיְאַשְּׁרוּהָ מְלָכוֹת וּפִילַגְשִׁים וַיְהַלְלוּהָ׃ י מִי־
זֹאת הַנִּשְׁקָפָה כְּמוֹ־שָׁחַר יָפָה כַלְּבָנָה בָּרָה כַּחַמָּה אֲיֻמָּה
כַּנִּדְגָּלוֹת׃ יא אֶל־גִּנַּת אֱגוֹז יָרַדְתִּי לִרְאוֹת בְּאִבֵּי הַנָּחַל
לִרְאוֹת הֲפָרְחָה הַגֶּפֶן הֵנֵצוּ הָרִמֹּנִים׃ יב לֹא יָדַעְתִּי נַפְשִׁי
שָׂמַתְנִי מַרְכְּבוֹת עַמִּי נָדִיב׃

פרק ז

א שׁוּבִי שׁוּבִי הַשּׁוּלַמִּית שׁוּבִי שׁוּבִי וְנֶחֱזֶה־בָּךְ מַה־
תֶּחֱזוּ בַּשּׁוּלַמִּית כִּמְחֹלַת הַמַּחֲנָיִם׃ ב מַה־יָּפוּ פְעָמַיִךְ

---

7 As many as a pomegranate's seeds are the merits of your unworthiest within your modest veil. 8 The queenly offspring of Avraham are sixty, compared to whom the eighty Noahides and all their countless nations are like mere concubines.

9 Unique is she, My constant dove, My perfect one. Unique is she, this nation striving for the truth; pure is she to Yaakov who begot her. Nations saw her and acclaimed her; queens and concubines, and they praised her: 10 "Who is this that gazes down from atop the Har HaBayis, brightening like the dawn, beautiful as the moon, brilliant as the sun, awesome as the bannered hosts of kings?"

11 I descended upon the deceptively simple holiness of the Second Mikdash to see your moisture-laden deeds in valleys. Had your Torah scholars budded on the vine, had your merit-laden righteous flowered like the pomegranates filled with seeds?

[KLAL YISRAEL RESPONDS:] 12 Alas, I knew not how to guard myself from sin! My own devices harnessed me, like chariots subject to a foreign nation's mercies.

CHAPTER SEVEN

1 The nations have said to me, "Turn away, turn away from God, O nation whose faith in Him is perfect, turn away, turn away, and we shall choose nobility from you."

But I replied to them, "What can you bestow upon a nation whole in faith to Him commensurate even with the desert camps encircling?"

[THE NATIONS TO KLAL YISRAEL:] 2 But your footsteps were so lovely when shod

בַּנְּעָלִים בַּת־נָדִיב חַמּוּקֵי יְרֵכַיִךְ כְּמוֹ חֲלָאִים מַעֲשֵׂה יְדֵי
אָמָּן׃ ג שָׁרְרֵךְ אַגַּן הַסַּהַר אַל־יֶחְסַר הַמָּזֶג בִּטְנֵךְ עֲרֵמַת
חִטִּים סוּגָה בַּשּׁוֹשַׁנִּים׃ ד שְׁנֵי שָׁדַיִךְ כִּשְׁנֵי עֳפָרִים תָּאֳמֵי
צְבִיָּה׃ ה צַוָּארֵךְ כְּמִגְדַּל הַשֵּׁן עֵינַיִךְ בְּרֵכוֹת בְּחֶשְׁבּוֹן עַל־
שַׁעַר בַּת־רַבִּים אַפֵּךְ כְּמִגְדַּל הַלְּבָנוֹן צוֹפֶה פְּנֵי דַמָּשֶׂק׃
ו רֹאשֵׁךְ עָלַיִךְ כַּכַּרְמֶל וְדַלַּת רֹאשֵׁךְ כָּאַרְגָּמָן מֶלֶךְ אָסוּר
בָּרְהָטִים׃ ז מַה־יָּפִית וּמַה־נָּעַמְתְּ אַהֲבָה בַּתַּעֲנוּגִים׃ ח זֹאת
קוֹמָתֵךְ דָּמְתָה לְתָמָר וְשָׁדַיִךְ לְאַשְׁכֹּלוֹת׃ ט אָמַרְתִּי אֶעֱלֶה
בְתָמָר אֹחֲזָה בְּסַנְסִנָּיו וְיִהְיוּ־נָא שָׁדַיִךְ כְּאֶשְׁכְּלוֹת הַגֶּפֶן
וְרֵיחַ אַפֵּךְ כַּתַּפּוּחִים׃ י וְחִכֵּךְ כְּיֵין הַטּוֹב הוֹלֵךְ לְדוֹדִי
לְמֵישָׁרִים דּוֹבֵב שִׂפְתֵי יְשֵׁנִים׃ יא אֲנִי לְדוֹדִי וְעָלַי תְּשׁוּקָתוֹ׃

---

in pilgrim's sandals, O daughter of nobles. The rounded shafts for your libations' abysslike trenches, handiwork of the Master Craftsman. 3 At earth's very center your Sanhedrin site is an ivory basin of ceaseless, flowing teaching; your national center an indispensable heap of nourishing knowledge hedged about with roses. 4 Your twin sustainers, the *Luchos* of the Law, are like two fawns, twins of the gazelle. 5 Your *Mizbei'ach* and Mikdash, erect and stately as an ivory tower; your wise men aflow with springs of complex wisdom at the gate of the many-peopled city; your face, like a Lebanese tower, looks to your future boundary as far as Damascus.

6 The Godly name on your head is as mighty as Carmel; your crowning braid is royal purple, your King is bound in nazaritic tresses. 7 How beautiful and pleasant are you, befitting the pleasures of spiritual love. 8 Such is your stature, likened to a towering palm tree, from your teachers flow sustenance like wine-filled clusters.

[HASHEM TO KLAL YISRAEL:] 9 I boast on High that your deeds cause Me to ascend on your palm tree, I grasp onto your branches. I beg now your teachers that they may remain like clusters of grapes from which flow strength to your weakest ones, and the fragrance of your face like apples. [KLAL YISRAEL INTERJECTS:] 10 and may Your utterance be like finest wine.

I shall heed Your plea to uphold my faith before my Beloved in love so upright and honest that my slumbering fathers will move their lips in approval.

11 I say to the nations, "I am my Beloved's and He longs for my perfection."

יב לְכָ֤ה דוֹדִי֙ נֵצֵ֣א הַשָּׂדֶ֔ה נָלִ֖ינָה בַּכְּפָרִֽים׃ יג נַשְׁכִּ֙ימָה֙
לַכְּרָמִ֔ים נִרְאֶ֞ה אִם־פָּֽרְחָ֤ה הַגֶּ֙פֶן֙ פִּתַּ֣ח הַסְּמָדַ֔ר הֵנֵ֖צוּ
הָרִמּוֹנִ֑ים שָׁ֛ם אֶתֵּ֥ן אֶת־דֹּדַ֖י לָֽךְ׃ יד הַֽדּוּדָאִ֣ים נָֽתְנוּ־רֵ֗יחַ
וְעַל־פְּתָחֵ֙ינוּ֙ כָּל־מְגָדִ֔ים חֲדָשִׁ֖ים גַּם־יְשָׁנִ֑ים דּוֹדִ֖י צָפַ֥נְתִּי לָֽךְ׃

פרק ח

א מִ֤י יִתֶּנְךָ֙ כְּאָ֣ח לִ֔י יוֹנֵ֖ק שְׁדֵ֣י אִמִּ֑י אֶמְצָֽאֲךָ֤ בַחוּץ֙
אֶשָּׁ֣קְךָ֔ גַּ֖ם לֹא־יָב֥וּזוּ לִֽי׃ ב אֶנְהָֽגְךָ֗ אֲבִֽיאֲךָ֛ אֶל־בֵּ֥ית אִמִּ֖י
תְּלַמְּדֵ֑נִי אַשְׁקְךָ֙ מִיַּ֣יִן הָרֶ֔קַח מֵעֲסִ֖יס רִמֹּנִֽי׃ ג שְׂמֹאלוֹ֙
תַּ֣חַת רֹאשִׁ֔י וִימִינ֖וֹ תְּחַבְּקֵֽנִי׃ ד הִשְׁבַּ֥עְתִּי אֶתְכֶ֖ם בְּנ֣וֹת
יְרוּשָׁלִָ֑ם מַה־תָּעִ֣ירוּ ׀ וּמַה־תְּעֹֽרְר֥וּ אֶת־הָאַהֲבָ֖ה עַ֥ד
שֶׁתֶּחְפָּֽץ׃ ה מִ֣י זֹ֗את עֹלָה֙ מִן־הַמִּדְבָּ֔ר מִתְרַפֶּ֖קֶת עַל־דּוֹדָ֑הּ

---

[12] Come, my Beloved, let us go to the fields where Your children serve You in want, there let us lodge with Eisav's children who are blessed with plenty yet still deny.

[13] Let us wake at dawn in vineyards of prayer and study. Let us see if students of the Written Torah have budded, if students of Oral Law have blossomed, if ripened scholars have bloomed — there I will display my finest products to You.

[14] All my baskets, good and bad, emit a fragrance, all at our doors have the precious fruits of comely deeds — those the Scribes have newly ordained and Your Torah's timeless wisdom, for You, Beloved, has my heart stored them.

CHAPTER EIGHT

If only, despite my wrongs, You could comfort me as Yosef did, like a brother nurtured at the bosom of my mother, if in the streets I found Your prophets I would kiss You and embrace You through them, nor could anyone despise me for it. [2] I would lead You, I would bring You to my mother's Mikdash for You to teach me as You did in Moshe's Tent; to drink I'd give You spiced libations, wines like pomegranate nectar.

[KLAL YISRAEL TO THE NATIONS:] [3] Despite my laments in Exile, His left hand supports my head and His right hand embraces me in support. [4] I adjure you, O nations destined to ascend to Yerushalayim — for if you violate your oath you will become defenseless — if you dare provoke God to hate me or disturb His love for me while He still desires it.

[HASHEM AND THE HEAVENLY TRIBUNAL:] [5] How worthy she is who rises from the desert bearing Torah and His Presence, clinging to her Beloved!

תַּ֤חַת הַתַּפּ֙וּחַ֙ עֽוֹרַרְתִּ֔יךָ שָׁ֚מָּה חִבְּלַ֣תְךָ אִמֶּ֔ךָ שָׁ֖מָּה חִבְּלָ֥ה
יְלָדַֽתְךָ׃ ו שִׂימֵ֨נִי כַֽחוֹתָ֜ם עַל־לִבֶּ֗ךָ כַּֽחוֹתָם֙ עַל־זְרוֹעֶ֔ךָ כִּֽי־
עַזָּ֤ה כַמָּ֙וֶת֙ אַהֲבָ֔ה קָשָׁ֥ה כִשְׁא֖וֹל קִנְאָ֑ה רְשָׁפֶ֕יהָ רִשְׁפֵּ֕י
אֵ֖שׁ שַׁלְהֶ֥בֶתְיָֽה׃ ז מַ֣יִם רַבִּ֗ים לֹ֤א יֽוּכְלוּ֙ לְכַבּ֣וֹת אֶת־
הָֽאַהֲבָ֔ה וּנְהָר֖וֹת לֹ֣א יִשְׁטְפ֑וּהָ אִם־יִתֵּ֨ן אִ֜ישׁ אֶת־כָּל־ה֤וֹן
בֵּיתוֹ֙ בָּאַ֣הֲבָ֔ה בּ֖וֹז יָב֥וּזוּ לֽוֹ׃ ח אָח֤וֹת לָ֙נוּ֙ קְטַנָּ֔ה וְשָׁדַ֖יִם
אֵ֣ין לָ֑הּ מַֽה־נַּעֲשֶׂה֙ לַאֲחוֹתֵ֔נוּ בַּיּ֖וֹם שֶׁיְּדֻבַּר־בָּֽהּ׃ ט אִם־
חוֹמָ֣ה הִ֔יא נִבְנֶ֥ה עָלֶ֖יהָ טִ֣ירַת כָּ֑סֶף וְאִם־דֶּ֣לֶת הִ֔יא נָצ֥וּר
עָלֶ֖יהָ ל֥וּחַ אָֽרֶז׃ י אֲנִ֣י חוֹמָ֔ה וְשָׁדַ֖י כַּמִּגְדָּל֑וֹת אָ֛ז הָיִ֥יתִי
בְעֵינָ֖יו כְּמוֹצְאֵ֥ת שָׁלֽוֹם׃ יא כֶּ֣רֶם הָיָ֤ה לִשְׁלֹמֹה֙ בְּבַ֣עַל
הָמ֔וֹן נָתַ֥ן אֶת־הַכֶּ֖רֶם לַנֹּטְרִ֑ים אִ֚ישׁ יָבִ֣א בְּפִרְי֔וֹ אֶ֖לֶף כָּֽסֶף׃

[KLAL YISRAEL INTERJECTS:] Under Sinai suspended above me, there I roused Your love, there was Your people born; a mother to other nations, there she endured the travail of her birth. 6 For the sake of my love, place me like a seal on Your heart, like a seal to dedicate Your strength for me, for strong till the death is my love; though their zeal for vengeance is hard as the grave, its flashes are flashes of fire from the flame of God. 7 Many waters of heathen tribulation cannot extinguish the fire of this love, nor rivers of royal seduction or torture wash it away.

[HASHEM REPLIES TO KLAL YISRAEL:] Were any man to offer all the treasure of his home to entice you away from your love, they would scorn him to extreme.

[THE HEAVENLY TRIBUNAL REFLECTS:] 8 Klal Yisrael desires to cleave to us, the small and humble one, but her time of spiritual maturity has not come. What shall we do for our cleaving one on the day the nations plot against her?

9 If her faith and belief are strong as a wall withstanding incursions from without, we shall become her fortress and beauty; building her City and Mikdash; but if she wavers like a door, succumbing to every alien knock, with fragile cedar panels shall we then enclose her.

[KLAL YISRAEL REPLIES PROUDLY:] 10 My faith is firm as a wall, and my nourishing synagogues and study halls are strong as towers! Then, having said so, I become in His eyes like a bride found perfect.

[... AND REMINISCES:] 11 Israel was the vineyard of Him to Whom peace belongs in populous Yerushalayim. He gave His vineyard to harsh, cruel guardians; each one came to extort his fruit, even a thousand silver pieces.

יב כַּרְמִי שֶׁלִּי לְפָנָי הָאֶלֶף לְךָ שְׁלֹמֹה וּמָאתַיִם לְנֹטְרִים
אֶת־פִּרְיוֹ׃ יג הַיּוֹשֶׁבֶת בַּגַּנִּים חֲבֵרִים מַקְשִׁיבִים לְקוֹלֵךְ
הַשְׁמִיעִנִי׃ יד בְּרַח | דּוֹדִי וּדְמֵה־לְךָ לִצְבִי אוֹ לְעֹפֶר
הָאַיָּלִים עַל הָרֵי בְשָׂמִים׃

[HASHEM TO NATIONS ON THE DAY OF JUDGMENT:] 12 The vineyard is Mine! Your iniquities are before Me!

[THE NATIONS WILL REPLY:] The thousand silver pieces are Yours, You to Whom peace belongs, and two hundred more to the Sages who guarded the fruit of Torah from our designs.

[HASHEM TO KLAL YISRAEL:] 13 O My beloved, dwelling in far-flung gardens, your fellows, the angels, hearken to your voice of Torah and prayer. Let Me hear it that they may then sanctify Me.

[KLAL YISRAEL TO HASHEM:] 14 Flee, my Beloved, from our common Exile and be like a gazelle or a young hart in Your swiftness to redeem and rest your Presence among us on the fragrant Mount Moriah, site of Your Beis HaMikdash.

Appendices

Appendix A: Laws of Bedikah and Biur for Those Who Will Not Be Home for Pesach

If one is going away for Pesach to a hotel that is owned by a Torah-observant Jew (as was often the case with hotels that were located in the Catskills years ago), it can be presumed that the owner was *bodeik* the rooms he is renting out for Pesach. This is because the premises were his at the time of *bedikah,* and the obligation to perform the *bedikah* rested with him. But the way most Pesach programs are run today is that the hotels are rented from non-observant Jews or non-Jews, and the organizers may only take possession of the rented rooms on Erev Pesach. Accordingly, there is no *chazakah* that a *bedikah* was performed before the renter arrives. Therefore, when one arrives at his hotel (or a house that he is renting from a non-Jew), he is obligated to perform *bedikah.* One cannot rely on a cleaning crew that was supposed to ready the room for guests, because such a crew will not necessarily check corners and crevices in the manner required for *bedikah*; furthermore, since they have no concept of the laws of Pesach, they can often leave packaged items that are *chametz* (such as packaged snacks included in guest hospitality packages, or even liquors in hotel room minibars) in place.

At the same time, exactly what each person must do depends on his travel plans. If one is leaving his home a few days before Pesach, and arriving at a hotel in time to make a *bedikah* there on the night of *bedikah,* he makes a *bedikah* in his home without a *berachah* on the last night before leaving, and *bedikah* with a *berachah* at the hotel on the night before Erev Pesach. On the other hand, if he will still be home to make *bedikah* with a *berachah* on *bedikah* night, and he will then leave and arrive at his destination later that night, or on Erev Pesach morning in time to burn the *chametz* at his destination, he should take any *chametz*

found during his *bedikah* at home along with him to the hotel, make a *bedikah* at the hotel without a *berachah* upon arrival, and then burn the *chametz* at the hotel. If one is afraid that he will not have time to burn the *chametz* at the hotel, he should make someone a *shliach* (agent) to burn his *chametz,* and give the *chametz* to him before he leaves.

If one is not arriving at his hotel until the afternoon of Erev Pesach, and the time for *biur chametz* will have already passed, he must burn his *chametz* before he leaves home (or entrust it to a *shliach,* as above). He still must make a *bedikah* (without a *berachah*) upon his arrival at the hotel, and he must burn or destroy any *chametz* that he finds. If one arrived at his hotel and forgot to make a *bedikah,* and only remembers to do so after Yom Tov has begun, he should make a *bedikah* on Yom Tov (again, without a *berachah*). Any *chametz* that is found should be covered up, and it must be burned on Chol HaMoed.

Often, a person knows that he will surely not be returning to his home at all over Pesach (for example, if he is traveling to Eretz Yisrael and staying there for all of Yom Tov). In such a case, people may want to sell their entire house to a non-Jew, so they do not have to clean for Pesach. This is permitted, but there is still an obligation to perform *bedikah.* Therefore, *bedikah* should be performed on one room (one may pick the easiest room to be *bodeik,* such as a spare bedroom), and then the rest of the house may be sold. If a person intends to come back to his house on Pesach, but he will be there only for a short time and he will not be using most of the house (for example, if a person is spending half of Pesach with his parents and half with his in-laws, and there are a few hours in between that he will come by to repack and drop off things that he does not need to bring along), he must be *bodeik* a path from the door he will use to enter the house to the room(s) he will use, and all of the rooms. The parts of the house that he will not enter (for example, the basement, the upstairs, etc., according to the particular situation) may be sold, and need not be cleaned.

Appendix B: How to Calculate the Time of Chatzos

The calculation to determine when *chatzos* is according to the *Rosh HaYeshiva, ztvk"l,* can be made as follows.

First, some necessary background information: The globe is divided into three hundred and sixty degrees of longitude, and into twenty-four time zones. Each time zone comprises fifteen degrees, or lines, of longitude. For purposes of this discussion, we will refer to the line of longitude at the beginning (that is, the eastern side) of each time zone as that time zone's "base meridian."

Local standardized time — the time it says on our clocks — is the local time at the base meridian to one's east. The premise of the *Rosh HaYeshiva, ztvk"l,* is that *chatzos hayom* is 12 pm at the base meridian of each time zone, and *chatzos halailah* is 12 am at the base meridian. [When Daylight Savings Time is being observed, as it generally is nowadays at Pesach time, we refer to these times as 1 pm and 1 am respectively.] Every sixty minutes, the sun reaches the next base meridian, and at that local time zone, at the same time *chatzos* arrives, the clock resets to 12 pm (1 am DST) local time.

However, even though it takes the sun sixty minutes to transverse the full time zone, and, thus, the farther west into a time zone a particular location is, the later *chatzos* will be, everyone in that time zone has the same time on their clocks. This obviously means that while at the base meridian itself, *chatzos* will be at 12, at five degrees of longitude to the west of the base meridian, it will be at 12:20, and at ten degrees to the west of the base meridian, it will be at 12:40. [As there are fifteen degrees in each one-hour time zone, every degree equals four minutes.] At the next base meridian, *chatzos halailah* would be at 1 am, except for the fact that because a new time zone has been entered, the clock resets to 12 am.

Accordingly, to provide some examples, in Cherry Hill, New Jersey, which sits at 75.0246° W, which is almost directly on the base meridian of the Eastern time zone, *chatzos* is 12 am (1 am DST). In South Bend, Indiana, which sits at 86.2520° W, which is approximately 11.25 degrees west of the base meridian of the Eastern time zone, *chatzos* will be approximately 12:45 am (1:45 am DST).

In Yerushalayim, which sits at 35.2137° E, and is thus approximately 9.8 degrees of longitude west of the base meridian of its time zone (Israel Standard Time), *chatzos halailah* will be approximately 12:39 am (1:39 am DST). [East of the Prime Meridian, the lines of longitude are counted upward to the east and downward to the west. Thus, the time zones, which move from their base meridians to the west, actually go *down* in number. The base meridian for Israel Standard Time is 45° E, and extends westward to 30° E. Thus, Yerushalayim, at 35.2137° E, is approximately 9.8 degrees of longitude west of the base meridian of 45° E.]

There are certain cities, however, which keep the same time as the time zone to their *west*. New York, Chicago, and Los Angeles are examples of this phenomenon. Even though New York City, and thus it lies at 74.0060° W, is just about one degree east of the 75th meridian, and thus it is technically within the area of the Atlantic time zone, it sets its clocks as part of the Eastern time zone, which runs from 75° W-90° W, keeping the same time as cities such as Washington D.C. and Detroit, MI. Similarly, Chicago, which lies at 87.6298° W, should use the same time as those cities, as it too lies between 75° W-90° W. Yet, Chicago keeps Central time (the time used by the cities that lie between 90°W and 105°W), rather than Eastern time. Similarly, Los Angeles, which lies at 118.2426° W, should use Mountain time, like Phoenix, Arizona, because it, like Phoenix, lies between 105° W-120° W. Yet, Los Angeles keeps Pacific time (the time used by the locations that lie between 120°W and 135°W), rather than Mountain time. In all these cities, after we make the calculation for *chatzos,* we have to subtract an hour, because these cities keep time in concert with the time zone to their *west*.

Thus, because New York City is located approximately 14 degrees west of the Atlantic time zone's base meridian, *chatzos halailah* should really be at 12:56 am (1:56 am DST). However, in New York, they refer to what should be 12:56 am (1:56 am DST) as 11:56 pm (12:56 am DST), because they keep Eastern time. Similarly, Chicago is located approximately 12.6 degrees west of the base meridian of the Eastern time zone, and so *chatzos halailah* in Chicago should be at 12:50 am (1:50 am DST). However, in Chicago, they refer to what should be 12:50 am

(1:50 am DST) as 11:50 pm (12:50 am DST), because they keep Central time. And Los Angeles, California, which sits at 118.2426° W, is approximately 13.25 degrees west of the base meridian of the Mountain time zone, and so *chatzos halailah* in Los Angeles should be approximately 12:53 am (1:53 am DST). However, in Los Angeles, they refer to what should be 12:53 am (1:53 am DST) as 11:53 pm (12:53 am DST), because they keep Pacific time.

Thus, to determine *chatzos* according to the *Rosh HaYeshiva, ztvk"l,* in one's location, the following formula can be used:

1) Determine the longitude of your location.
2) Determine how many degrees to the west of the base meridian of your time zone (which is to your east) you are located. [This number will be between 0 and 15.]
3) For every degree west of that base meridian, add four minutes past 12 am.
4) Be aware that some cities that are within a few degrees of the base meridian to their west sometimes keep the same time as the time zone that is to their west, and so an hour needs to be subtracted after the calculation is made in these cases.

ברכות למי ששכח

When this blessing is recited at the first or second Shabbos or Festival meal, one concludes with ... בָּרוּךְ אַתָּה ה׳ מְקַדֵּשׁ. At the third meal this closing blessing is not recited. After the appropriate blessing, continue with the fourth blessing (p. 288).

If one forgot רְצֵה on Shabbos:

בָּרוּךְ אַתָּה יהוה אֱלֹהֵינוּ מֶלֶךְ הָעוֹלָם, אֲשֶׁר נָתַן שַׁבָּתוֹת לִמְנוּחָה לְעַמּוֹ יִשְׂרָאֵל בְּאַהֲבָה, לְאוֹת וְלִבְרִית. בָּרוּךְ אַתָּה יהוה, מְקַדֵּשׁ הַשַּׁבָּת.

If one forgot יַעֲלֶה וְיָבֹא on a Festival:

בָּרוּךְ אַתָּה יהוה אֱלֹהֵינוּ מֶלֶךְ הָעוֹלָם, אֲשֶׁר נָתַן יָמִים טוֹבִים לְעַמּוֹ יִשְׂרָאֵל לְשָׂשׂוֹן וּלְשִׂמְחָה, אֶת יוֹם חַג הַמַּצּוֹת הַזֶּה. בָּרוּךְ אַתָּה יהוה, מְקַדֵּשׁ יִשְׂרָאֵל וְהַזְּמַנִּים.

If one forgot רְצֵה and יַעֲלֶה וְיָבֹא on a Festival that falls on Shabbos:

בָּרוּךְ אַתָּה יהוה אֱלֹהֵינוּ מֶלֶךְ הָעוֹלָם, אֲשֶׁר נָתַן שַׁבָּתוֹת לִמְנוּחָה לְעַמּוֹ יִשְׂרָאֵל בְּאַהֲבָה, לְאוֹת וְלִבְרִית, וְיָמִים טוֹבִים לְשָׂשׂוֹן וּלְשִׂמְחָה, אֶת יוֹם חַג הַמַּצּוֹת הַזֶּה. בָּרוּךְ אַתָּה יהוה, מְקַדֵּשׁ הַשַּׁבָּת וְיִשְׂרָאֵל וְהַזְּמַנִּים.

If one forgot יַעֲלֶה וְיָבֹא on Chol HaMoed:

בָּרוּךְ אַתָּה יהוה אֱלֹהֵינוּ מֶלֶךְ הָעוֹלָם, אֲשֶׁר נָתַן מוֹעֲדִים לְעַמּוֹ יִשְׂרָאֵל לְשָׂשׂוֹן וּלְשִׂמְחָה, אֶת יוֹם חַג הַמַּצּוֹת הַזֶּה.

If one forgot רְצֵה and יַעֲלֶה וְיָבֹא on Chol HaMoed that falls on Shabbos:

בָּרוּךְ אַתָּה יהוה אֱלֹהֵינוּ מֶלֶךְ הָעוֹלָם, אֲשֶׁר נָתַן שַׁבָּתוֹת לִמְנוּחָה לְעַמּוֹ יִשְׂרָאֵל בְּאַהֲבָה, לְאוֹת וְלִבְרִית, וּמוֹעֲדִים לְשָׂשׂוֹן וּלְשִׂמְחָה, אֶת יוֹם חַג הַמַּצּוֹת הַזֶּה. בָּרוּךְ אַתָּה יהוה, מְקַדֵּשׁ הַשַּׁבָּת וְיִשְׂרָאֵל וְהַזְּמַנִּים.

Compensatory Blessings

When this blessing is recited at the first or second Shabbos or Festival meal, one concludes with *Blessed are You, Hashem, Who sanctifies the Shabbos* .... At the third meal this closing blessing is not recited. After the appropriate blessing, continue with the fourth blessing (p. 288).

If one forgot *Retzei* on Shabbos:

Blessed are You, HASHEM, our God, King of the universe, Who gave Shabbosos for contentment to His people Yisrael with love, as a sign and a covenant. Blessed are You, HASHEM, Who sanctifies the Shabbos.

If one forgot *Yaaleh VeYavo* on a Festival:

Blessed are You, HASHEM, our God, King of the universe, Who gave Festivals to His people Yisrael for happiness and gladness, this Festival day of *Matzos*. Blessed are You, HASHEM, Who sanctifies Yisrael and the seasons.

If one forgot *Retzei* and *Yaaleh VeYavo* on a Festival that falls on Shabbos:

Blessed are You, HASHEM, our God, King of the universe, Who gave Sabbaths for contentment to His people Israel with love, as a sign and a covenant, and Festivals for happiness and gladness, this Festival day of *Matzos*. Blessed are You, HASHEM, Who sanctifies the Shabbos, Yisrael, and the seasons.

If one forgot *Yaaleh VeYavo* on Chol HaMoed:

Blessed are You, HASHEM, our God, King of the universe, Who gave appointed festivals to His people Israel for happiness and gladness, this Festival day of *Matzos*.

If one forgot *Retzei* and *Yaaleh Veyavo* on Chol HaMoed that falls on Shabbos:

Blessed are You, HASHEM, our God, King of the universe, Who gave Shabbosos for contentment to His people Yisrael with love, as a sign and a covenant, and appointed festivals for happiness and gladness, this Festival day of *Matzos*. Blessed are You, HASHEM, Who sanctifies the Shabbos, Yisrael, and the seasons.

Darchei Sholom Associates

(in formation)

The Rosh HaYeshiva, shlit"a, would like to thank the following individuals for supporting the publishing of his works

Eliyahu and Rebeccah Berger
Mr. and Mrs. Mayer Berkovits
R' Zvi and Mrs. Faygie Bokow
Pinky and Miri Friedman
Rabbi Shmuel Lipa and Mrs. Chevi Friedman
Mr. and Mrs. Goldman
Rabbi Nochum and Mrs. Sarah Tamar Greenberg
Ms. Shoshana Greenberg
Mr. Dovid Hirsch
Nisson and Gitty Hirsch
Mr. Dovid and Mrs. Shayna Hertzka
Mr. And Mrs. Avromi Kaluszyner
Mr. Eli and Mrs. Sirki Lax
The Reisman Family
Mr. Chesky and Mrs. Miriam Rosenberg
Rabbi David and Mrs. Mimi Samuels
R' Naftali and Mrs. Leah Solomon
Mr. Yank and Mrs. Avigail Stoll
Rabbi Nechemia and Mrs. Rivkie Weiss
Dr. Shloimy and Mrs. Rivky Weissman
R' Yehudah and Mrs. Mindy Zachter

לז"נ אסתר מלכה בת ר' ישראל שלמה ולז"נ חנה בת ר' ברוך בענדיט
לזכות רפו"ש בעד עלקא דבורה בת מרים רבקה חנה

For more information, visit darcheisholom.com

This volume is part of
THE ARTSCROLL® SERIES
an ongoing project of
translations, commentaries and expositions on
Scripture, Mishnah, Talmud, Midrash, Halachah,
liturgy, history, the classic Rabbinic writings,
biographies and thought.

For a brochure of current publications
visit your local Hebrew bookseller
or contact the publisher:

Mesorah Publications, ltd

313 Regina Avenue
Rahway, New Jersey 07065
(718) 921-9000
www.artscroll.com

MW01633855